Virginia Public Library

Virginia, Minnesota

THE
JACK
VANCE
TREASURY

Edited by
Terry Dowling
and
Jonathan Strahan

SUBTERRANEAN PRESS 2006

ACKNOWLEDGEMENTS

The Editors extend sincere thanks to Ralph Vicinanza, George R.R. Martin, Tom Kidd, and Gardner Dozois, and would also like to thank Charles N. Brown, A.E. Cunningham, Nick Gevers, Jerry Hewett, Russell Letson, Daniel J.H. Levack, Daryl F. Mallett, Charles F. Miller, Charles Platt, Jesse C. Polhemus, Tim Underwood, Paul Rhoads, John Schwab and the members of the Vance Integral Edition team. Special thanks to Jack Vance, Norma Vance and John Vance for their enthusiastic support and assistance.

DEDICATION

In loving memory of Tammy Vance

CONTENTS

Preface, *Jack Vance* 11

Jack Vance: An Appreciation, *George R.R. Martin* . . 13

Introduction: Fruit from the Tree of Life,
  Terry Dowling and Jonathan Strahan 17

1. The Dragon Masters 25

2. Liane the Wayfarer 107

3. Sail 25 119

4. The Gift of Gab 149

5. The Miracle Workers 201

6. Guyal of Sfere 267

7. Noise 311

8. The Kokod Warriors 325

9. The Overworld 359

10. The Men Return 385

11. The Sorcerer Pharesm 395

12. The New Prime 419

13. The Secret 443

14. The Moon Moth 453

15. The Bagful of Dreams 489

16. The Mitr 517

17. Morreion 525

18. The Last Castle 567

Biographical Sketch & Other Facts, *Jack Vance* . . . 623

Editor Bios 632

PREFACE

When I look down over the table of contents in this collection, I think back over many years, to times when I had attitudes far different from the day I wrote the end to *Lurulu* which—as of some of you will be aware—was my final book. At one time I tried to be a million-words-a-year writer, and over one weekend I produced, first draft, the first two Magnus Ridolph stories: low-quality efforts of which I am not proud. However, I sold one of these to Twentieth Century Fox for enough money to take us on our first trip to Europe, where we stayed thirteen months. At Positano, on the Amalfi coast below Sorrento, I wrote a boys' book, *Vandals of the Void,* for the Winston series.

In general, most of the stories here collected were produced under different, often unique, circumstances. *The Dying Earth* sequence was produced while I was an able seaman in the merchant marine. I wrote *The Last Castle* for Fred Pohl at *Galaxy* for free, because of some disaster in connection with *The Dragon Masters. The Miracle Workers* was aimed for *Astounding* because John Campbell, the editor, had a predilection for unusual ideas.

Some of the stories here included I am pleased with; others less so. Still, I am happy to have them in print. Thanks go to Terry Dowling, Jonathan Strahan, and all who worked to create the Vance Integral Edition. (I have known Terry since the days when the world was young, and we have had many adventures together, including a visit to a haunted house and a sojourn at the Hydro Majestic Hotel in the Blue Mountains where Graeme Bell was playing the piano. For non-jazz types, Graeme Bell once managed a world-famous jazz band).

There is much more that I could say about the included stories and past years, but this will have to do. I hope everyone gets half the pleasure reading the stories as I did writing them.

> —Jack Vance
> Oakland, California, June 16, 2006

JACK VANCE: AN APPRECIATION

George R. R. Martin

There is only one Jack Vance.

I am sometimes asked which writers have most influenced my own work. That's a tricky question, since the writers who have the most profound impact on you are the ones you read when you are young, and hardly aware of whatever influences it was you were absorbing.

I will confess, however, that Jack Vance is one of only two writers that I have ever set out consciously to imitate (the other one was H.P. Lovecraft, for what it's worth). Along about the mid 70s, I was a young writer with a couple dozen short story sales under my belt, still struggling to improve my craft. I would pore over every book and magazine that I could get my hands on, and try to dissect the stories that impressed me, looking for techniques that I could incorporate into my own repertoire…and there was no one who impressed me as much as Vance. So one day I decided to try my hand at a Vance story, and wrote a novelette called "A Beast for Norn," introducing Haviland Tuf, whose ancestry owed more than a little to Vance's Magnus Ridolph. The story sold and Tuf went on to have a long and successful run, but the experiment convinced me that no one but Jack Vance could write like Jack Vance.

You could say that Jack Vance is the Fred Astaire of letters. Astaire brought such grace and style to his dancing that he made it seem almost easy, just as Vance does when he writes. Nothing could be less true. Vance has often been hailed, justifiably, as SF's preeminent stylist, and it is certainly true that he has a wonderful gift for language, for words and names and colorful turns of phrase. His talents go well beyond that, however. For inventive plots, wry humor, knowing and ironic dialogue, and imaginative panache, he has no equal in or outside of our genre.

These days, more and more, the publishers seem determined to split fantasy and science fiction into two entirely separate categories, but that was certainly not the case when I was growing up. Science fiction was the more popular genre then, fantasy less so, but most of the major writers did both...and none more successfully than Jack Vance.

As an SF writer, he has given us the Gaean Reach and the Oikumene and the Alastor Cluster, Emphyrio and the Faceless Man, the showboats of the Big Planet and the hoodwinks of the Blue World, such a myriad of unforgettable settings peopled by a cast of delightfully perverse and wonderfully named characters. In a field where all too many galactic empires still share a suspicious resemblance to the Roman Empire of Augustus or the British Empire of Queen Victoria, Jack Vance's worlds are true originals. The worlds he creates are sometimes bizarre, but always colorful, usually fascinating, and always rendered in gorgeous detail.

And they have *depth*. Jack Vance knows how to tell a story, and his tales move along at such a cracking good pace that it is easy to regard them as no more than fun reads, and overlook all the things going on beneath the surface.

Consider, for example, the sport of hussade, a popular pastime in the Alastor Cluster novels. Unlike quidditch or moopsball or some of the other made-up sports found in SF and fantasy, hussade actually convinces. It sounds as if it would fun to play and fun to watch. It makes sense as a sport. Go a little deeper, though, and you'll soon realize that this game reveals all sorts of interesting things about the culture it derives from. The ritual denuding of the *shierl*, for instance, which tells us something about the position of women in the Alastor Cluster, and the sexual mores of the people of Trullion. Or the fact that the game is played over a tank of water, on a planet whose early history included a bloody struggle with a race of aquatic aliens. Vance's game has roots as well as rules, and functions as a commentary on his society as well as plot device and a spectacle.

Perhaps more than any other SF writer past or present, Vance seems to understand that if man does indeed spread across ten thousand stars, ten thousand different societies will spring up, as different from each other as from the world of the reader. The exotic human cultures of the

Gaean Reach are ten times stranger and a hundred times more interesting than the alien cultures of many less imaginative SF writers, and when Vance goes beyond humanity and creates an actual alien...well, visit the *Planet of Adventure* with Adam Reith and make the acquaintance of the Pnume, the Dirdir, the Chasch, and the unfortunately named Wankh (if Jove can nod from time to time, so can Jack), and you'll see just how alien an alien can actually be.

Even when Vance chooses to write of well-worn ideas, he seems to work his peculiar alchemy on them, taking them to places previously undreamed of. The notion of alternate worlds, for instance, is a familiar SF trope, but no one has ever used it the way that Vance does in "Chateau d'If." Dozens of other SF writers have made use of genetic engineering as a plot device and hundreds of fantasists have given us variations on dragons, but only Vance could ever put the two together to create something like "The Dragon Masters." The effects that a multiple star system might have on human civilization were most famously explored by Isaac Asimov in his classic "Nightfall"—but in *Marune: Alastor 933* Vance gives us a planet and a society where every aspect of human life is governed by which sun is in the sky. Revenge stories are as old as the Count of Monte Cristo and its SF counterpart, Alfred Bester's classic *The Stars My Destination*, but Kirth Gersen goes Gully Foyle four better when he sets out after Attel Malagate (the Woe), Kokor Hekkus, Lens Larque, Viole Falushe, and Howard Alan Treesong...and yet Vance manages to ring a note on the futility of vengeance in the final sentence of the final book of his Demon Princes sequence.

His contributions to fantasy, while less numerous, have been even more profound. Vance's Lyonesse trilogy remains one of the best fantasy epics since Tolkien, and his Cugel the Clever surely deserves a place in the fantasy hall of fame alongside such worthies as Conan the Cimmerian, Aragorn son of Arathorn, Fafhrd and the Grey Mouser, and Elric of Melniboné. Get them all together in the same place and Cugel would doubtless attempt to cozen and swindle the others out of their swords, cloaks, and jewels (though somehow it would turn out badly for him in the end).

Even more memorable than Cugel himself is the world through which he moves, the Dying Earth that Vance first imagined in *The Dying Earth,* a collection of short stories first published in 1950 by the obscure paperback house Hillman. This is Earth at the end of its days when the sun hangs red and swollen in the sky, an Earth where ten thousand civilizations have risen and fallen, and sorcery and superstition have returned to the world even as science has waned. The setting owes perhaps a little to Clark Ashton Smith and his Zothique stories, but as usual Vance made it very much his own, and the Hillman collection includes some of his most gorgeous and evocative writing, along with a host of wonderful characters. Though I first read the book in high school, the characters still haunt me now even in my dotage...T'sain and T'sais...Guyal of Sfere in the Museum of Man...Liane the Wayfarer, oh, and Chun...Chun the Unavoidable, who is also Chun the Unforgettable...

(It was also in *The Dying Earth* that Vance first put forth the basics of a unique and original magical system. If that system now seems old and overly familiar to readers coming to the book for the first time, it is only because the creators of the original *Dungeons & Dragons* game appropriated it and used it as the foundation for magic in *D&D*.)

SF or fantasy, it makes no matter. Jack Vance is a master. The truth is, his gifts have little to do with genre, as he has proved with his forays into mystery, writing both as John Holbrook Vance and (from time to time) as Ellery Queen. He is one of the few writers who can boast of winning an Edgar Award from the Mystery Writers of America to place beside his Hugos and his Nebulas. He won for his novel *The Man in the Cage*, oddly enough not even his best mystery. That distinction has to go to *Bad Ronald*, a marvelously macabre and disturbing little tale that lingers in the memories of everyone who reads it, a mystery without a mystery that works equally well as a horror story. I have no doubt that Vance could also have won awards for westerns, gothics, thrillers, and nurse novels, if he had ever tried his hand at those genres.

I am grateful he did not, however. SF and fantasy would both be a good deal poorer if Vance had not chosen to grace us with his talents. He is our finest stylist and a master storyteller, and it is more than apt that the volume you hold is your hands is called a *treasury* rather than a compendium, collection, or retrospective.

Jack Vance is a treasure, and we will not soon see his like again.

—George R.R. Martin
July, 2006

INTRODUCTION:
FRUIT FROM THE TREE OF LIFE

In a scrapbook Jack Vance kept as a young man, a tiny black and white picture, clipped from some old book or magazine, shows a kilted winged figure, eagle-headed, human-bodied, picking fruit from a stylized tree. Beneath it is the legend: *Winged Being, Plucking Fruit From The Tree Of Life.* The creature, wings spread, one leg set against the trunk to assist in its task, is an Assyro-Babylonian guardian figure, a genie, probably a *shedu* or a *lamassu,* possibly a less benign *utukku,* and the tree is probably sacred to Enlil, but such details hardly matter here. It's the mystery, the force, the ineffable power of the image that no doubt appealed to the younger Vance, the Romance of it, the Eternal Yes if you like. It's a fitting image for a book like this and the contents within.

John Holbrook Vance—Jack Vance as we know him—is not only one of the 20th century's truly distinctive voices in telling stories of romantic adventure (in the true meaning of the word Romance) and one of its major writers of fantasy and science fiction, but he is also that rare and precious thing—a writer's writer, perhaps more correctly a maker's maker, someone who has become a seminal influence on what so many others have gone on to accomplish. It's not for nothing that Harlan Ellison wrote "The Wine Has Been Left Open Too Long and the Memory Has Gone Flat" for editor Terry Carr in a deliberately Vancean style, or that Dan Simmons dedicated his final Hyperion novel to Vance and admits that the whole series is a grateful homage, or that Gene Wolfe happily acknowledges the influence of the same Grand Master with regards to his own awarded and much-acclaimed *The Book of the New Sun,* or that Robert Silverberg says how Vance's writing has never failed to give him "a very special sort of pleasure." Jack Vance is a writer who attracts this sort of professional admiration, just as he does the admiration of his countless readers.

Vance, himself formed (as much as an author ever can be) by the works of others—among them writers as diverse as Lord Dunsany, Edgar Rice Burroughs, P.G. Wodehouse and L. Frank Baum, Robert W. Chambers, C.L. Moore, Clark Ashton Smith and Jeffrey Farnol—synthesized for himself a style, a voice, a way of storytelling that displays a lucky blend of swashbuckling derring-do, a sparkling sense of mischief, a fine eye for detail, a wonderful ear for cadence and—essential to the man's signature style—an exquisite awareness of the moment, of "the sweet fugacity of existence" celebrated so fulsomely by Benruth Droad and his kin in Vance's 1976 novel *Maske: Thaery.*

In making use of this distinctive blend, Vance has structured nearly all of his stories as mysteries. Whether we consider the conventional crime novels like the award-winning *The Man in the Cage,* the much underrated *The Fox Valley Murders* and his work-for-hire Ellery Queen titles, or his many fantasy tales and planetary adventures, in fact almost everything he wrote—from his first published story, "The World-Thinker," in 1945 to what is probably his last, *Lurulu,* in 2004—they are, without exception, xenographical mysteries of one sort or another (ie: read 'regional' writ large). Just count the sleuths, effectuators and resolutely questing protagonists sometime: Magnus Ridolph, Miro Hetzel and Glawen Clattuc by profession, Kirth Gersen, Adam Reith, Glinnes Hulden, Sklar Hast and Gastel Etzwane, so many others, by circumstance, Cugel the Clever almost by default, the list goes on.

But in presenting such marvelous worlds as Aerlith, Tschai and Big Planet, Durdane, Koryphon and Halma, Blue World, Sirene, Lyonesse and the Dying Earth, and introducing us to unforgettable characters like Cugel, Madouc and Adam Reith, the indomitable Kirth Gersen, the mad poet Navarth and the Demon Princes themselves, Vance does more. Among his many keen, irreverent and wryly fond observations on the human condition, he serves up moments of exquisite seeing: Ghyl Tarvoke's reverie at the fading light in Undle Square or as he gazes across the mudflats of ancient Ambroy, Glinnes Hulden's meditations as avness—"that melancholy dying-time of day"—settles over the Welgen Fens, or Kirth Gersen's wonderful, madcap lapse of discipline when he chooses to carry out Lens Larque's grand scheme himself. In there, too, is the finely rendered bittersweetness of childhood and youth, the rapture of first love, the wisdoms and quirks of age and custom, the bathos and irony of schemes gone awry, the expansiveness of spirit that causes glasses to be lifted in the celebration of a shared moment.

These are exotic mysteries, yes, but—as one would expect from a seasoned world traveler like Vance—they are also ways of taking us on journeys, of putting us into situations where our humanity becomes the thing in focus, measured against alien overlords, exotic worlds and different cultures, defined and tested by what we have become among the stars, in faerie realms or at the end of time. As Ursula Le Guin puts it so well in *The Left Hand of Darkness:* "It is good to have an end to journey towards; but it is the journey that matters, in the end." This is so true of what Vance achieves repeatedly in his *oeuvre.* Here is an author who savours the journey, the encounter, the mystery, and returns to such things again and again in his storytelling.

Given how loved Vance's work is, for a career retrospective like this we might have sought out appreciations and testimonials to help commemorate the occasion, over and above George Martin's kind and generous foreword. They would have been readily forthcoming. So, too, we might have included some appropriately positive critical appraisals of the man's career. Again, these would have been heartfelt and in no short supply; Vance's work remains fertile territory in that regard and is sure to reward patient study.

And while the author himself has never liked to discuss his work or have it analyzed too closely, the clues are there. Think, for instance, of what some would make of the title similarity between Vance's 1950 *Dying Earth* story "Guyal of Sfere" and the 1928 Jeffrey Farnol novel *Guyfford of Weare* that sits on his bookshelf, or how just the title "Liane the Wayfarer" from the same Vance book invites all sorts of expeditions among other Farnol novels on the same shelf like *John O' the Green: A Romance* and *Beltane the Smith: A Romance of the Greenwood.* But it's the Romantic spirit that is the main thing here, some likeness of seeing and sensibility that made the young Vance *respond* to someone like Farnol. As for artists and storytellers everywhere, everything is grist to the mill.

Nor would a new interview have been out of place or much made of existing interview data, such as when Vance says that "Sail 25", "Dodkin's Job" and "Ulward's Retreat" are among his favorite stories, or that, in giving advice on technique, he urges writers to take out as many adjectives and adverbs as possible on any rewrite (interestingly, very close to the same advice offered by his equally acclaimed contemporary, mystery writer Tony Hillerman). It would have even been appropriate to mention the roads not taken, projects planned and abandoned, the tantalizing might-have-beens, since, where fans and favorite writers are concerned, how can anything ever be enough? Many will feel a definite pang to learn that Vance planned further Maske novels to succeed *Maske: Thaery* and that *Pharism: Alastor 458* sits in tantalizing miniature as a few scrawled notes in one of his multi-colored journals. So too Miro Hetzel had further outings planned, and for a time even Milton Hack, the man from Zodiac, waited in the interstellar wings for the worlds to beat a path to his door. The list goes on.

Suffice to say that there is ample material for such ongoing appraisal: whether it's fathoming the significance of something like the VLON symbol for Vance as for his cherished creation, Howard Alan Treesong, or considering the impact on the author of that small Mesopotamian relief, or reckoning the significance of quotes in the scrapbook, much loved by Vance, such as this from Robert Louis Stevenson—

On we rode, the others and I,
Over the mountains blue, and by
The Silver River, the sounding sea,
And the robber woods of Tartary.

—or this uncredited piece on the same page, often quoted at dinner:

I can not stand where once I stood. It takes a
life to learn
That none may steer his course to shear the trail
of light astern.

What an evocative leitmotif these things make where the Vance *oeuvre* is concerned, especially when taken alongside the words given to family stalwart Vaidro Droad at the end of *Maske: Thaery:*

"While we are alive we should sit among colored lights and taste good wines, and discuss our adventures in far places; when we are dead, the opportunity is past."

But it is our intention that this be a book for the stranger as much as for the aficionado, and so we stand properly cautioned by Vance's dictum given to Baron Bodissey in *The Killing Machine* that "when erudition comes in, poetry departs." So, too, his closing envoi to *The Dogtown Tourist Agency* regarding process that: "The master chef slaughters no chickens in the dining room" cautions us to step back and let the featured stories speak for themselves.

With this and the good Baron's aphorism in mind, that is what we have done: brought together a selection of stories that celebrate and commemorate the work of this particular romantic spirit, who as a boy dug underground tunnels and secret chambers, who lay in a field and watched his kite idling overhead, who as a "somewhat taciturn merchant seaman" sat at the bow of a freighter playing his cornet, who, in time, went on to become the writer of the rather special stories presented here. This time we will let them give us the man.

"The Miracle Workers," "The Moon Moth," "The Dragon Masters" and "The Last Castle" are works of a piece from a time when Jack produced polished and mature mid-length planetary adventures for a thriving magazine market. All four stories are essential Vance and highlight themes the author returned to again and again in the novel-length planetary romances and which culminated in the Tschai, Durdane, Alastor and Cadwal books among others, and, arguably, Jack's finest single novel, *Emphyrio*.

"The Miracle Workers" was the lead story for the July 1958 issue of *Astounding Science Fiction*. It featured an apt and evocative cover by the late Kelly Freas and was nominated for a Hugo Award for Best Novelette the following year. "The Moon Moth," published in *Galaxy Magazine* in August 1961, remains one of Jack's most admired and reprinted stories, turning as it does on a truly classic xenological conundrum—how to catch a criminal in a society where everyone goes masked. Rather than simply focusing on the determination and ingenuity of its protagonist in classic space opera fashion, Vance reminds us how important it may be to have a sense of irony among the stars.

"The Dragon Masters" appeared in *Galaxy Magazine* in August 1962, accompanied by a striking cover and what, for many, became definitive text illustrations by the late Jack Gaughan. It won the Hugo Award for Best Short Fiction in 1963. "The Last Castle" appeared in *Galaxy Science Fiction* in April 1966, again with an evocative cover and interior art by Gaughan, and won both the 1967 Hugo for Best Novelette and the 1967 Nebula Award for Best Novella.

The Dying Earth stories are also quintessential Vance and are generously represented here. From the original 1950 linked collection *The Dying Earth* we have "Liane the Wayfarer" and "Guyal of Sfere." From its more formally structured sequel *The Eyes of the Overworld* (1966) comes "The Overworld", our first introduction to Cugel the Clever, possibly Jack's single most loved character and certainly his own favorite. This opening tale originally appeared in *The Magazine of Fantasy & Science Fiction* for December 1965. From the same engaging story suite is "The Sorcerer Pharesm", originally published in that magazine's April 1966 issue. From *Cugel's Saga*, the 1983 linked collection that brought Cugel's adventures to a welcome if (knowing our wayward hero) probably temporary happy ending, there is "The Bagful of Dreams", which first appeared in *Flashing Swords* in 1977. From the final Dying Earth collection *Rhialto the Marvelous* comes "Morreion", which originally appeared in *Flashing Swords* in 1973.

Between July 1948 and February 1958, Jack published ten stories in various magazines featuring the fortunes of his earliest and most urbane interstellar effectuator, Magnus Ridolph. "The Kokod Warriors", one of the best in the series, appeared in *Thrilling Wonder Stories* for October 1952 and in key aspects anticipates *The Dogtown Tourist Agency* from 1975. There is an intriguing alien species under scrutiny, an exotic planetary dilemma to be faced, and a biter-bit conclusion that ensures Ridolph continues to enjoy the perquisites of his chosen profession.

"Sail 25" first appeared as "Gateway to Strangeness" in *Amazing Fact and Science Fiction* for August 1962. Arthur C. Clarke's solar sail story "The Wind from the Sun" appeared in 1963, and Cordwainer Smith's Instrumentality sailships were already plying the starways around that time. Given completion as opposed to publication dates, it's hard to say who got there first, but Vance's story is certainly among the contenders for the title.

"The Gift of Gab" was published in *Astounding Science Fiction* in September 1955 and features another intriguing xenological mystery. Like other stories from this period, it might as easily have been given to Magnus Ridolph to solve, but its success as a standalone highlights the fact that Vance's professional effectuators, whether Ridolph, Milton Hack or Miro Hetzel, were very much the means to an end: a way of presenting encounters with alien species and alien mind-sets in exotic otherworldly settings.

"Noise", from *Startling Stories* for August 1952, is a haunting, bittersweet tale that shows in miniature the sort of evocative *mise-en-scène* used to such memorable effect in the novels. For the modern reader there may be a few dated touches, but Howard Charles Evans' experiences on that forlorn multi-sunned world will quite likely stay with the reader no less than they do for the beleaguered star-traveler himself.

"The Men Return" first appeared in *Infinity Science Fiction* in July 1957 and in many ways is one of Jack's most ambitious stories. How to render a pocket of non-causality? Vance's answer, of course, was to throw language at it and leave it to our readily seconded imaginations to do the rest. "The New Prime" first saw print as "Brain of the Galaxy" in *Worlds Beyond* for February 1951 and reminds us of the importance of humility—and, yet again, irony—in human affairs. "The Mitr", published in the debut issue of *Vortex Science Fiction* in 1953, is a subtle, understated story of loss and reflection that grows more touching on every reading and stands in striking, even shocking, contrast to the more elaborate, action-oriented stories presented here.

"The Secret" has an interesting publishing history. Originally intended for Damon Knight's *Worlds Beyond*, the manuscript was lost with that magazine's demise. A subsequent version, written five years later and mailed off to another prospective market, failed to arrive. The story finally turned up in the UK publication *Impulse* for March 1966 without Jack's knowledge.

Eighteen stories then, giving a representative and worthy cross-section. Not for everyone, certainly, not every reader's mug of Blue Ruin, Saskadoodle or Pink-eye Punch. But for those eager to experience one of the most effective, cherished and influential voices in all science fiction and fantasy for the first time, this will be an ideal place to start. For those who already treasure this voice, who know full well how this particular druithine, like his own creation, Sessily Veder, in *Araminta Station*, has been "impelled to pluck the highest fruit from the Tree of Life," why, no doubt you're nodding and smiling already, eager to set off for the wilds of Old Caraz once more or the robber woods of Tartary or wherever else the journey takes us.

—Terry Dowling and Jonathan Strahan
Sydney and Perth, August 1 2006

THE DRAGON MASTERS

CHAPTER I

The apartments of Joaz Banbeck, carved deep from the heart of a limestone crag, consisted of five principal chambers, on five different levels. At the top were the reliquarium and a formal council chamber: the first a room of somber magnificence housing the various archives, trophies and mementos of the Banbecks; the second a long narrow hall, with dark wainscoting chest-high and a white plaster vault above, extending the entire width of the crag, so that balconies overlooked Banbeck Vale at one end and Kergan's Way at the other.

Below were Joaz Banbeck's private quarters: a parlor and bedchamber, then next his study and finally, at the bottom, a workroom where Joaz permitted none but himself.

Entry to the apartments was through the study, a large L-shaped room with an elaborate groined ceiling, from which depended four garnet-encrusted chandeliers. These were now dark; into the room came only a watery gray light from four honed-glass plates on which, in the manner of a camera obscura, were focused views across Banbeck Vale. The walls were paneled with lignified reed; a rug patterned in angles, squares and circles of maroon, brown and black covered the floor.

In the middle of the study stood a naked man, his only covering the long fine brown hair which flowed down his back, the golden torc which clasped his neck. His features were sharp and angular, his body thin; he appeared to be listening, or perhaps meditating. Occasionally he glanced at a yellow marble globe on a nearby shelf, whereupon his lips would move, as if he were committing to memory some phrase or sequence of ideas.

At the far end of the study a heavy door eased open. A flower-faced young woman peered through, her expression mischievous, arch. At the sight of the naked man, she clapped her hands to her mouth, stifling a gasp. The naked man turned—but the heavy door had already swung shut.

For a moment he stood deep in frowning reflection, then slowly went to the wall on the inside leg of the L. He swung out a section of the bookcase, passed through the opening. Behind him the bookcase thudded shut. Descending a spiral staircase he came out into a chamber rough-hewn from the rock: Joaz Banbeck's private workroom. A bench supported tools, metal shapes and fragments, a bank of electromotive cells, oddments of circuitry: the current objects of Joaz Banbeck's curiosity.

The naked man glanced at the bench, picked up one of the devices, inspected it with something like condescension, though his gaze was as clear and wondering as that of a child.

Muffled voices from the study penetrated to the workroom. The naked man raised his head to listen, then stooped under the bench. He lifted a block of stone, slipped through the gap into a dark void. Replacing the stone, he took up a luminous wand, and set off down a narrow tunnel, which presently dipped to join a natural cavern. At irregular intervals luminous tubes exuded a wan light, barely enough to pierce the murk. The naked man jogged forward swiftly, the silken hair flowing like a nimbus behind him.

Back in the study the minstrel-maiden Phade and an elderly seneschal were at odds. "Indeed I saw him!" Phade insisted. "With these two eyes of mine, one of the sacerdotes, standing thus and so, as I have described." She tugged angrily at his elbow. "Do you think me bereft of my wits, or hysterical?"

Rife the seneschal shrugged, committing himself neither one way nor the other. "I do not see him now." He climbed the staircase, peered into the sleeping parlor. "Empty. The doors above are bolted." He peered owlishly at Phade. "And I sat at my post in the entry."

"You sat sleeping. Even when I came past you snored!"

"You are mistaken; I did but cough."

"With your eyes closed, your head lolling back?"

Rife shrugged once more. "Asleep or awake, it is all the same. Admitting that the creature gained access, how did he leave? I was wakeful after you summoned me, as you must agree."

"Then remain on guard, while I find Joaz Banbeck." Phade ran down the passage which presently joined Bird Walk, so called for the series of fabulous birds of lapis, gold, cinnabar, malachite and marcasite inlaid into the marble. Through an arcade of green and gray jade in spiral columns she passed out into Kergan's Way, a natural defile which formed the main thoroughfare of Banbeck Village. Reaching the portal, she summoned a pair of lads from the fields. "Run to the brooder, find Joaz Banbeck! Hasten, bring him here; I must speak with him."

The boys ran off toward a low cylinder of black brick a mile to the north.

Phade waited. With the sun Skene at its nooning, the air was warm; the fields of vetch, bellegarde, spharganum, gave off a pleasant odor. Phade went to lean against a fence. Now she began to wonder about the urgency of her news, even its basic reality. "No!" she told herself fiercely. "I saw! I saw!"

At either side tall white cliffs rose to Banbeck Verge, with mountains and crags beyond, and spanning all the dark sky flecked with feathers of cirrus. Skene glittered dazzling bright, a minuscule flake of brilliance.

Phade sighed, half-convinced of her own mistake. Once more, less vehemently, she reassured herself. Never before had she seen a sacerdote; why should she imagine one now?

The boys, reaching the brooder, had disappeared into the dust of the exercise pens. Scales gleamed and winked; grooms, dragon masters, armorers in black leather moved about their work.

After a moment Joaz Banbeck came into view. He mounted a tall thin-legged Spider, urged it to the full extent of its head-jerking lope, pounded down the track toward Banbeck Village.

Phade's uncertainty grew. Might Joaz become exasperated, would he dismiss her news with an unbelieving stare? Uneasily she watched his approach. Coming to Banbeck Vale only a month before she still felt unsure of her status. Her preceptors had trained her diligently in the barren little valley to the south where she had been born, but the disparity between teaching and practical reality at times bewildered her. She had learned that all men obeyed a small and identical group of behaviors; Joaz Banbeck, however, observed no such limits, and Phade found him completely unpredictable.

She knew him to be a relatively young man, though his appearance provided no guide to his age. He had a pale austere face in which gray eyes shone like crystals, a long thin mouth which suggested flexibility, yet never curved far from a straight line. He moved languidly; his voice carried no vehemence; he made no pretense of skill with either saber or pistol. He seemed deliberately to shun any gesture which might win the admiration or affection of his subjects. Yet he had both.

Phade originally had thought him cold, but presently changed her mind. He was, so she decided, a man bored and lonely, with a quiet humor which at times seemed rather grim. But he treated her without discourtesy, and Phade, testing him with all her hundred and one coquetries, not infrequently thought to detect a spark of response.

Joaz Banbeck dismounted from the Spider, ordered it back to its quarters. Phade came diffidently forward, and Joaz turned her a quizzical look. "What requires so urgent a summons? Have you remembered the nineteenth location?"

Phade flushed in confusion. Artlessly she had described the painstaking rigors of her training; Joaz now referred to an item in one of the classifications which had slipped her mind.

Phade spoke rapidly, excited once more. "I opened the door into your study, softly, gently. And what did I see? A sacerdote, naked in his hair! He did not hear me. I shut the door, I ran to fetch Rife. When we returned—the chamber was empty!"

Joaz's eyebrows contracted a trifle; he looked up the valley. "Odd." After a moment he asked, "You are sure that he saw nothing of you?"

"No. I think not. Yet, when I returned with stupid old Rife he had disappeared! Is it true that they know magic?"

"As to that, I cannot say," replied Joaz.

They returned up Kergan's Way, traversed tunnels and rock-walled corridors, finally came to the entry chamber.

Rife once more dozed at his desk. Joaz signaled Phade back, and going quietly forward, thrust aside the door to his study. He glanced here and there, nostrils twitching. The room was empty.

He climbed the stairs, investigated the sleeping-parlor, returned to the study. Unless magic were indeed involved, the sacerdote had provided himself a secret entrance. With this thought in mind, he swung back the bookcase door, descended to the workshop, and again tested the air for the sour-sweet odor of the sacerdotes. A trace? Possibly.

Joaz examined the room inch by inch, peering from every angle. At last, along the wall below the bench, he discovered a barely perceptible crack, marking out an oblong.

Joaz nodded with dour satisfaction. He rose to his feet, returned to his study. He considered his shelves: what was here to interest a sacerdote? Books, folios, pamphlets? Had they even mastered the art of reading? When next I meet a sacerdote I must inquire, thought Joaz vaguely; at least he will tell me the truth. On second thought, he knew the question to be ludicrous; the sacerdotes, for all their nakedness, were by no means barbarians, and in fact had provided him his four vision-panes—a technical engineering feat of no small skill.

He inspected the yellowed marble globe which he considered his most valued possession: a representation of mythical Eden. Apparently it had not been disturbed. Another shelf displayed models of the Banbeck dragons: the rust-red Termagant; the Long-horned Murderer and its cousin the Striding Murderer; the Blue Horror; the Fiend, low to the ground, immensely strong, tail tipped with a steel barbel; the ponderous Jugger, skull-cap polished and white as an egg. A little apart stood the progenitor of the entire group—a pearl-pallid creature upright on two legs, with two versatile central members, a pair of multi-articulated brachs at the neck. Beautifully detailed though these models might be, why should they pique the curiosity of a sacerdote? No reason whatever, when the originals could be studied daily without hindrance.

What of the workshop, then? Joaz rubbed his long pale chin. He had no illusions about the value of his work. Idle tinkering, no more. Joaz put aside conjecture. Most likely the sacerdote had come upon no specific mission, the visit perhaps being part of a continued inspection. But why?

A pounding at the door: old Rife's irreverent fist. Joaz opened to him.

"Joaz Banbeck, a notice from Ervis Carcolo of Happy Valley. He wishes to confer with you, and at this moment awaits your response on Banbeck Verge."

"Very well," said Joaz. "I will confer with Ervis Carcolo."

"Here? Or on Banbeck Verge?"

"On the Verge, in half an hour."

CHAPTER II

Ten miles from Banbeck Vale, across a wind-scoured wilderness of ridges, crags, spines of stone, amazing crevasses, barren fells and fields of tumbled boulders lay Happy Valley. As wide as Banbeck Vale but only half as long and half as deep, its bed of wind-deposited soil was only half as thick and correspondingly less productive.

The Chief Councilor of Happy Valley was Ervis Carcolo, a thick-bodied short-legged man with a vehement face, a heavy mouth, a disposition by turns jocose and wrathful. Unlike Joaz Banbeck, Carcolo enjoyed nothing more than his visits to the dragon barracks, where he treated dragon masters, grooms and dragons alike to a spate of bawled criticism, exhortation, invective.

Ervis Carcolo was an energetic man, intent upon restoring Happy Valley to the ascendancy it had enjoyed some twelve generations before. During those harsh times, before the advent of the dragons, men fought their own battles, and the men of Happy Valley had been notably daring, deft and ruthless. Banbeck Vale, the Great Northern Rift, Clewhaven, Sadro Valley, Phosphor Gulch: all acknowledged the authority of the Carcolos.

Then down from space came a ship of the Basics, or grephs, as they were known at that time. The ship killed or took prisoner the entire population of Clewhaven; attempted as much in the Great Northern Rift, but only partially succeeded; then bombarded the remaining settlements with explosive pellets.

When the survivors crept back to their devastated valleys, the dominance of Happy Valley was a fiction. A generation later, during the Age of Wet Iron, even the fiction collapsed. In a climactic battle Goss Carcolo was captured by Kergan Banbeck and forced to emasculate himself with his own knife.

Five years of peace elapsed, and then the Basics returned. After depopulating Sadro Valley, the great black ship landed in Banbeck Vale, but the inhabitants had taken warning and had fled into the mountains. Toward nightfall twenty-three of the Basics sallied forth behind their precisely trained warriors: several platoons of Heavy Troops, a squad of Weaponeers—these hardly distinguishable from the men of Aerlith—and a squad of Trackers: these emphatically different. The sunset storm broke over the Vale, rendering the flyers from the ship useless, which allowed Kergan Banbeck to perform the amazing feat which made his name a legend on Aerlith. Rather than joining the terrified flight of his people to the High Jambles, he assembled sixty warriors, shamed them to courage with jeers and taunts.

It was a suicidal venture—fitting the circumstances.

Leaping from ambush they hacked to pieces one platoon of the Heavy Troops, routed the others, captured the twenty-three Basics almost before they realized that anything was amiss. The Weaponeers stood back frantic with frustration, unable to use their weapons for fear of destroying their masters. The Heavy Troopers blundered forward to attack, halting only when Kergan Banbeck performed an unmistakable pantomime to make it clear that the Basics would be the first to die. Confused, the Heavy Troopers drew back; Kergan Banbeck, his men and the twenty-three captives escaped into the darkness.

The long Aerlith night passed; the dawn storm swept out of the east, thundered overhead, retreated majestically into the west; Skene rose like a blazing storm. Three men emerged from the Basic ship: a Weaponeer and a pair of Trackers. They climbed the cliffs to Banbeck Verge, while above flitted a small Basic flyer, no more than a buoyant platform, diving and veering in the wind like a poorly-balanced kite. The three men trudged south toward the High Jambles, a region of chaotic shadows and lights, splintered rock and fallen crags, boulders heaped on boulders. It was the traditional refuge of hunted men.

Halting in front of the Jambles the Weaponeer called out for Kergan Banbeck, asking him to parley.

Kergan Banbeck came forth, and now ensued the strangest colloquy in the history of Aerlith. The Weaponeer spoke the language of men with difficulty, his lips, tongue and glottal passages more adapted to the language of the Basics.

"You are restraining twenty-three of our Revered. It is necessary that you usher them forth, in all humility." He spoke soberly, with an air of gentle melancholy, neither asserting, commanding, nor urging. As his linguistic habits had been shaped to Basic patterns, so with his mental processes.

Kergan Banbeck, a tall spare man with varnished black eyebrows, black hair shaped and varnished into a crest of five tall spikes, gave a bark of humorless laughter. "What of the Aerlith folk killed, what of the folk seized aboard your ship?"

The Weaponeer bent forward earnestly, himself an impressive man with a noble aquiline head. He was hairless except for small rolls of wispy yellow fleece. His skin shone as if burnished; his ears, where he differed most noticeably from the unadapted men of Aerlith, were small fragile flaps. He wore a simple garment of dark blue and white, carried no weapons save a small multi-purpose ejector. With complete poise and quiet reasonableness he responded to Kergan Banbeck's question: "The Aerlith folk who have been killed are dead. Those aboard the ship will be merged into the understratum, where the infusion of fresh outside blood is of value."

Kergan Banbeck inspected the Weaponeer with contemptuous deliberation. In some respects, thought Kergan Banbeck, this modified and carefully inbred man resembled the sacerdotes of his own planet, notably in the clear fair skin, the strongly modeled features, the long legs and arms. Perhaps telepathy was at work, or perhaps a trace of the characteristic sour-sweet odor had been carried to him: turning his head he noticed a sacerdote standing among the rocks not fifty feet away—a man naked except for his golden torc and long brown hair blowing behind him like a pennant. By the ancient etiquette, Kergan Banbeck looked through him, pretended that he had no existence. The Weaponeer after a swift glance did likewise.

"I demand that you release the folk of Aerlith from your ship," said Kergan Banbeck in a flat voice.

The Weaponeer smilingly shook his head, bent his best efforts to the task of making himself intelligible. "These persons are not under discussion; their—" he paused, seeking words "—their destiny is…parceled, quantum-type, ordained. Established. Nothing can be said more."

Kergan Banbeck's smile became a cynical grimace. He stood aloof and silent while the Weaponeer croaked on. The sacerdote came slowly forward, a few steps at a time. "You will understand," said the Weaponeer, "that a pattern for events exists. It is the function of such as myself to shape events so that they will fit the pattern." He bent, and with a graceful sweep of arm seized a small jagged pebble. "Just as I can grind this bit of rock to fit a round aperture."

Kergan Banbeck reached forward, took the pebble, tossed it high over the tumbled boulders. "That bit of rock you shall never shape to fit a round hole."

The Weaponeer shook his head in mild deprecation. "There is always more rock."

"And there are always more holes," declared Kergan Banbeck.

"To business then," said the Weaponeer. "I propose to shape this situation to its correct arrangement."

"What do you offer in exchange for the twenty-three grephs?"

The Weaponeer gave his shoulder an uneasy shake. The ideas of this man were as wild, barbaric and arbitrary as the varnished spikes of his hair-dress. "If you desire I will give you instruction and advice, so that—"

Kergan Banbeck made a sudden gesture. "I make three conditions." The sacerdote now stood only ten feet away, face blind, gaze vague. "First," said Kergan Banbeck, "a guarantee against future attacks upon the men of Aerlith. Five grephs must always remain in our custody as hostages. Second—further to secure the perpetual validity of the guarantee—you must deliver me a spaceship, equipped, energized, armed, and you must instruct me in its use."

The Weaponeer threw back his head, made a series of bleating sounds through his nose.

"Third," continued Kergan Banbeck, "you must release all the men and women presently aboard your ship."

The Weaponeer blinked, spoke rapid hoarse words of amazement to the Trackers. They stirred, uneasy and impatient, watching Kergan Banbeck sidelong as if he were not only savage, but mad. Overhead hovered the flyer; the Weaponeer looked up and seemed to derive encouragement from the sight. Turning back to Kergan Banbeck with a firm fresh attitude, he spoke as if the previous interchange had never occurred. "I have come to instruct you that the twenty-three Revered must be instantly released."

Kergan Banbeck repeated his own demands. "You must furnish me a spaceship, you must raid no more, you must release the captives. Do you agree, yes or no?"

The Weaponeer seemed confused. "This is a peculiar situation—indefinite, unquantizable."

"Can you not understand me?" barked Kergan Banbeck in exasperation. He glanced at the sacerdote, an act of questionable decorum, then performed in a manner completely unconventional: "Sacerdote, how can I deal with this blockhead? He does not seem to hear me."

The sacerdote moved a step nearer, his face as bland and blank as before. Living by a doctrine which proscribed active or intentional interference in the affairs of other men, he could make to any question only a specific and limited answer. "He hears you, but there is no meeting of ideas between you. His thought-structure is derived from that of his masters. It is incommensurable with yours. As to how you must deal with him, I cannot say."

Kergan Banbeck looked back to the Weaponeer. "Have you heard what I asked of you? Did you understand my conditions for the release of the grephs?"

"I heard you distinctly," replied the Weaponeer. "Your words have no meaning, they are absurdities, paradoxes. Listen to me carefully. It is ordained, complete, a quantum of destiny, that you deliver to us the Revered. It is irregular, it is not ordainment that you should have a ship, or that your other demands be met."

Kergan Banbeck's face became red; he half-turned toward his men but restraining his anger, spoke slowly and with careful clarity. "I have something you want. You have something I want. Let us trade."

For twenty seconds the two men stared eye to eye. Then the Weaponeer drew a deep breath. "I will explain in your words, so that you will comprehend. Certainties—no, not certainties: definites…Definites exist. These are units of certainty, quanta of necessity and order. Existence is the steady succession of these units, one after the other. The activity of the universe can be expressed by reference to these units. Irregularity, absurdity—these are like half a man, with half a brain, half a heart, half of all his vital organs. Neither are allowed to exist. That you hold twenty-three Revered as captives is such an absurdity: an outrage to the rational flow of the universe."

Kergan Banbeck threw up his hands, turned once more to the sacerdote. "How can I halt his nonsense? How can I make him see reason?"

The sacerdote reflected. "He speaks not nonsense, but rather a language you fail to understand. You can make him understand your language by erasing all knowledge and training from his mind, and replacing it with patterns of your own."

Kergan Banbeck fought back an unsettling sense of frustration and unreality. In order to elicit exact answers from a sacerdote, an exact question was required; indeed it was remarkable that this sacerdote stayed to be questioned. Thinking carefully, he asked, "How do you suggest that I deal with this man?"

"Release the twenty-three grephs." The sacerdote touched the twin knobs at the front of his golden torc: a ritual gesture indicating that, no matter how reluctantly, he had performed an act which conceivably might alter the course of the future. Again he tapped his torc, and intoned, "Release the grephs; he will then depart."

Kergan Banbeck cried out in unrestrained anger. "Who then do you serve? Man or greph? Let us have the truth! Speak!"

"By my faith, by my creed, by the truth of my tand I serve no one but myself." The sacerdote turned his face toward the great crag of Mount Gethron and moved slowly off; the wind blew his long fine hair to the side.

Kergan Banbeck watched him go, then with cold decisiveness turned back to the Weaponeer. "Your discussion of certainties and absurdities is interesting. I feel that you have confused the two. Here is certainty from my viewpoint! I will not release the twenty-three grephs unless you meet my terms. If you attack us further, I will cut them in half, to illustrate and realize your figure of speech, and perhaps convince you that absurdities are possible. I say no more."

The Weaponeer shook his head slowly, pityingly. "Listen, I will explain. Certain conditions are unthinkable, they are unquantized, undestined—"

"Go," thundered Kergan Banbeck. "Otherwise you will join your twenty-three revered grephs, and I will teach you how real the unthinkable can become!"

The Weaponeer and the two Trackers, croaking and muttering, turned, retreated from the Jambles to Banbeck Verge, descended into the valley. Over them the flyer darted, veered, fluttered, settled like a falling leaf.

Watching from their retreat among the crags, the men of Banbeck Vale presently witnessed a remarkable scene. Half an hour after the Weaponeer had returned to the ship, he came leaping forth once again, dancing, cavorting. Others followed him—Weaponeers, Trackers, Heavy Troopers and eight more grephs—all jerking, jumping, running back and forth in distracted steps. The ports of the ship flashed lights of various colors, and there came a slow rising sound of tortured machinery.

"They have gone mad!" muttered Kergan Banbeck. He hesitated an instant, then gave an order. "Assemble every man; we attack while they are helpless!"

Down from the High Jambles rushed the men of Banbeck Vale. As they descended the cliffs, a few of the captured men and women from Sadro Valley came timidly forth from the ship and meeting no restraint fled to freedom across Banbeck Vale. Others followed—and now the Banbeck warriors reached the valley floor.

Beside the ship the insanity had quieted; the out-worlders huddled quietly beside the hull. There came a sudden mind-shattering explosion: a blankness of yellow and white fire. The ship disintegrated. A great crater marred the valley floor; fragments of metal began to fall among the attacking Banbeck warriors.

Kergan Banbeck stared at the scene of destruction. Slowly, his shoulders sagging, he summoned his people and led them back to their ruined valley. At the rear, marching single-file, tied together with ropes, came the twenty-three grephs, dull-eyed, pliant, already remote from their previous existence. The texture of Destiny was inevitable: the present circumstances could not apply to twenty-three of the Revered. The mechanism must therefore adjust to insure the halcyon progression of events. The twenty-three, hence, were something other than the Revered: a different order of creature entirely. If this were true, what were they? Asking each other the question in sad croaking undertones, they marched down the cliff into Banbeck Vale.

CHAPTER III

Across the long Aerlith years the fortunes of Happy Valley and Banbeck Vale fluctuated with the capabilities of the opposing Carcolos and Banbecks. Golden Banbeck, Joaz's grandfather, was forced to release Happy Valley from clientship when Uttern Carcolo, an accomplished dragon-breeder, produced the first Fiends. Golden Banbeck, in his turn, developed the Juggers, but allowed an uneasy truce to continue.

Further years passed; Ilden Banbeck, the son of Golden, a frail ineffectual man, was killed in a fall from a mutinous Spider. With Joaz yet an ailing child, Grode Carcolo decided to try his chances against Banbeck Vale. He failed to reckon with old Hendel Banbeck, granduncle to Joaz and Chief Dragon Master. The Happy Valley forces were routed on Starbreak Fell; Grode Carcolo was killed and young Ervis gored by a Murderer. For various reasons, including Hendel's age and Joaz's youth, the Banbeck army failed to press to a decisive advantage. Ervis Carcolo, though exhausted by loss of blood and pain, withdrew in some degree of order, and for further years a suspicious truce held between the neighboring valleys.

Joaz matured into a saturnine young man who, if he excited no enthusiastic affection from his people, at least aroused no violent dislike. He and Ervis Carcolo were united in a mutual contempt. At the mention of Joaz's study, with its books, scrolls, models and plans, its complicated viewing-system across Banbeck Vale (the optics furnished, it was rumored, by the sacerdotes), Carcolo would throw up his hands in disgust. "Learning? Pah! What avails all this rolling in bygone vomit? Where does it lead? He should have been born a sacerdote; he is the same sort of sour-mouthed cloud-minded weakling!"

An itinerant, one Dae Alvonso, who combined the trades of minstrel, child-buyer, psychiatrist and chiropractor, reported Carcolo's obloquies to Joaz, who shrugged. "Ervis Carcolo should breed himself to one of his own Juggers," said Joaz. "He would thereby produce an impregnable creature with the Jugger's armor and his own unflinching stupidity."

The remark in due course returned to Ervis Carcolo, and by coincidence, touched him in a particularly sore spot. Secretly he had been attempting an innovation at his brooders: a dragon almost as massive as the Jugger with the savage intelligence and agility of the Blue Horror. But Ervis Carcolo worked with an intuitive and over-optimistic approach, ignoring the advice of Bast Givven, his Chief Dragon Master.

The eggs hatched; a dozen spratlings survived. Ervis Carcolo nurtured them with alternate tenderness and objurgation. Eventually the dragons matured. Carcolo's hoped-for combination of fury and impregnability was realized in four sluggish irritable creatures, with bloated torsos, spindly legs, insatiable appetites. ("As if one can breed a dragon by commanding it: 'Exist!'" sneered Bast Givven to his helpers, and advised them: "Be wary of the beasts; they are competent only at luring you within reach of their brachs.")

The time, effort, facilities and provender wasted upon the useless hybrid had weakened Carcolo's army. Of the fecund Termagants he had no lack; there was a sufficiency of Long-horned Murderers and Striding Murderers, but the heavier and more specialized types, especially Juggers, were far from adequate to his plans. The memory of Happy Valley's ancient glory haunted his dreams; first he would subdue Banbeck Vale, and often he planned the ceremony whereby he would reduce Joaz Banbeck to the office of apprentice barracks-boy.

Ervis Carcolo's ambitions were complicated by a set of basic difficulties. Happy Valley's population had doubled but rather than extending the city by breaching new pinnacles or driving tunnels, Carcolo constructed three new dragon-brooders, a dozen barracks and an enormous training compound. The folk of the valley could choose either to cram the fetid existing tunnels or build ramshackle dwellings along the base of the cliff. Brooders, barracks, training compounds and huts encroached on Happy Valley's already inadequate fields. Water was diverted from the pond to maintain the brooders; enormous quantities of produce went to feed dragons. The folk of Happy Valley, undernourished, sickly, miserable, shared none of Carcolo's aspirations, and their lack of enthusiasm infuriated him.

In any event, when the itinerant Dae Alvonso repeated Joaz Banbeck's recommendation that Ervis Carcolo breed himself to a Jugger, Carcolo seethed with choler. "Bah! What does Joaz Banbeck know about dragon-breeding? I doubt if he understands his own dragon-talk." He referred to the means by which orders and instructions were transmitted to the dragons: a secret jargon distinctive to every army. To learn an opponent's dragon-talk was the prime goal of every Dragon Master, for he thereby gained a certain degree of control over his enemies' forces. "I am a practical man, worth two of him," Carcolo went on. "Can he design, nurture, rear and teach dragons? Can he impose discipline, teach ferocity? No. He leaves all this to his dragon masters, while he lolls on a couch eating sweetmeats, campaigning only against the patience of his minstrel-maidens. They say that by astrological divination he predicts the return of the Basics, that he walks with his neck cocked, watching the sky. Is such a man deserving of power and a prosperous life? I say no! Is Ervis Carcolo of Happy Valley such a man? I say yes, and this I will demonstrate!"

Dae Alvonso judiciously held up his hand. "Not so fast. He is more alert than you think. His dragons are in prime condition; he visits them often. And as for the Basics—"

"Do not speak to me of Basics," stormed Carcolo. "I am no child to be frightened by bugbears!"

Again Dae Alvonso held up his hand. "Listen. I am serious, and you can profit by my news. Joaz Banbeck took me into his private study—"

"The famous study, indeed!"

"From a cabinet he brought out a ball of crystal mounted on a black box."

"Aha!" jeered Carcolo. "A crystal ball!"

Dae Alvonso went on placidly, ignoring the interruption. "I examined this globe, and indeed it seemed to hold all of space; within it floated stars and planets, all the bodies of the cluster. 'Look well,' said Joaz Banbeck, 'you will never see the like of this anywhere. It was built by the olden men and brought to Aerlith when our people first arrived.'

"'Indeed,' I said. 'And what is this object?'

"'It is a celestial armamentarium,' said Joaz. 'It depicts all the nearby stars, and their positions at any time I choose to specify. Now—' here he pointed '—see this white dot? This is our sun. See this red star? In the old almanacs it is named Coralyne. It swings near us at irregular intervals, for such is the flow of stars in this cluster. These intervals have always coincided with the attacks of the Basics.'

"Here I expressed astonishment; Joaz assured me regarding the matter. 'The history of men on Aerlith records six attacks by the Basics, or grephs as they were originally known. Apparently as Coralyne swings through space the Basics scour nearby worlds for hidden dens of humanity. The last of these was long ago during the time of Kergan Banbeck, with the results you know about. At that time Coralyne passed close in the heavens. For the first time since, Coralyne is once more close at hand.' This," Alvonso told Carcolo, "is what Joaz Banbeck told me, and this is what I saw."

Carcolo was impressed in spite of himself. "Do you mean to tell me," demanded Carcolo, "that within this globe swim all the stars of space?"

"As to that, I cannot vouch," replied Dae Alvonso. "The globe is set in a black box, and I suspect that an inner mechanism projects images or perhaps controls luminous spots which simulate the stars. Either way it is a marvelous device, one which I would be proud to own. I offered Joaz several precious objects in exchange, but he would have none of them."

Carcolo curled his lip in disgust. "You and your stolen children. Have you no shame?"

"No more than my customers," said Dae Alvonso stoutly. "As I recall, I have dealt profitably with you on several occasions."

Ervis Carcolo turned away, pretended to watch a pair of Termagants exercising with wooden scimitars. The two men stood by a stone fence behind which scores of dragons practiced evolutions, dueled with spears and swords, strengthened their muscles. Scales flashed, dust rose up under splayed stamping feet; the acrid odor of dragon-sweat permeated the air.

Carcolo muttered, "He is crafty, that Joaz. He knew you would report to me in detail."

Dae Alvonso nodded. "Precisely. His words were—but perhaps I should be discreet." He glanced slyly toward Carcolo from under shaggy white eyebrows.

"Speak," said Ervis Carcolo gruffly.

"Very well. Mind you, I quote Joaz Banbeck. 'Tell blundering old Carcolo that he is in great danger. If the Basics return to Aerlith, as well they may, Happy Valley is absolutely vulnerable and will be ruined. Where can his people hide? They will be herded into the black ship, transported to a cold new planet. If Carcolo is not completely heartless he will drive new tunnels, prepare hidden avenues. Otherwise—'"

"Otherwise what?" demanded Carcolo.

"'Otherwise there will be no more Happy Valley, no more Ervis Carcolo.'"

"Bah," said Carcolo in a subdued voice. "The young jackanapes barks in shrill tones."

"Perhaps he extends an honest warning. His further words—but I fear to offend your dignity."

"Continue! Speak!"

"These are his words—but no, I dare not repeat them. Essentially he considers your efforts to create an army ludicrous; he contrasts your intelligence unfavorably to his own; he predicts—"

"Enough!" roared Ervis Carcolo, waving his fists. "He is a subtle adversary, but why do you lend yourself to his tricks?"

Dae Alvonso shook his frosty old head. "I merely repeat, with reluctance, that which you demand to hear. Now then, since you have wrung me dry, do me some profit. Will you buy drugs, elixirs, wambles or potions? I have here a salve of eternal youth which I stole from the Demie Sacerdote's personal coffer. In my train are both boy and girl children, obsequious and handsome, at a fair price. I will listen to your woes, cure your lisp, guarantee a placidity of disposition—or perhaps you would buy dragon eggs?"

"I need none of those," grunted Carcolo. "Especially dragon's eggs which hatch to lizards. As for children, Happy Valley seethes with them. Bring me a dozen sound Juggers and you may depart with a hundred children of your choice."

Dae Alvonso shook his head sadly, lurched away. Carcolo slumped against the fence, staring across the dragon pens.

The sun hung low over the crags of Mount Despoire; evening was close at hand. This was the most pleasant time of the Aerlith day, when the winds ceased, leaving a vast velvet quiet. Skene's blaze softened to a smoky yellow, with a bronze aureole; the clouds of the approaching evening storm gathered, rose, fell, shifted, swirled; glowing and changing in every tone of gold, orange-brown, gold-brown and dusty violet.

Skene sank; the golds and oranges became oak-brown and purple; lightning threaded the clouds and the rain fell in a black curtain. In the barracks men moved with vigilance, for now the dragons became unpredictable: by turns watchful, torpid, quarrelsome. With the passing of the rain, evening became night, and a cool quiet breeze drifted through the valleys. The dark sky began to burn and dazzle with the stars of the cluster. One of the most effulgent twinkled red, green, white, red, green.

Ervis Carcolo studied this star thoughtfully. One idea led to another, and presently to a course of action which seemed to dissolve the entire tangle of uncertainties and dissatisfactions which marred his life. Carcolo twisted his mouth to a sour grimace; he must make overtures to that popinjay Joaz Banbeck—but if this were unavoidable: so be it!

Hence, the following morning, shortly after Phade the minstrel-maiden discovered the sacerdote in Joaz's study, a messenger appeared in the Vale, inviting Joaz Banbeck up to Banbeck Verge for a conference with Ervis Carcolo.

CHAPTER IV

Ervis Carcolo waited on Banbeck Verge with Chief Dragon Master Bast Givven and a pair of young fuglemen. Behind, in a row, stood their mounts: four glistening Spiders, brachs folded, legs splayed at exactly identical angles. These were of Carcolo's newest breed and he was immoderately proud of them. The barbs surrounding the horny visages were clasped with cinnabar cabochons; a round target enameled black and studded with a central spike covered each chest. The men wore the traditional black leather breeches, with short maroon cloaks, black leather helmets with long flaps slanting back across the ears and down to the shoulders.

The four men waited, patient or restless as their natures dictated, surveying the well-tended length of Banbeck Vale. To the south stretched fields of various food-stuffs: vetch, bellegarde, moss-cake, a loquat grove. Directly opposite, near the mouth of Clybourne Crevasse, the shape of the crater created by the explosion of the Basic ship could still be seen. North lay more fields, then the dragon compounds, consisting of black-brick barracks, a brooder, an exercise field. Beyond lay Banbeck Jambles—an area of wasteland where ages previously a section of the cliff had fallen, creating a wilderness of tumbled rock similar to the High Jambles under Mount Gethron, but smaller in compass.

One of the young fuglemen rather tactlessly commented upon the evident prosperity of Banbeck Vale, to the implicit deprecation of Happy Valley. Ervis Carcolo listened glumly a moment or two, then turned a haughty stare toward the offender.

"Notice the dam," said the fugleman. "We waste half our water in seepage."

"True," said the other. "That rock facing is a good idea. I wonder why we don't do something similar."

Carcolo started to speak, thought better of it. With a growling sound in his throat, he turned away. Bast Givven made a sign; the fuglemen hastily fell silent.

A few moments later Givven announced: "Joaz Banbeck has set forth."

Carcolo peered down toward Kergan's Way. "Where is his company? Does he ride alone?"

"So it seems."

A few minutes later Joaz Banbeck appeared on Banbeck Verge riding a Spider caparisoned in gray and red velvet. Joaz wore a loose lounge cloak of soft brown cloth over a gray shirt and gray trousers, with a long-billed hat of blue velvet. He held up his hand in casual greeting; brusquely Ervis Carcolo returned the salute, and with a jerk of his head sent Givven and the fuglemen off out of earshot.

Carcolo said gruffly, "You sent me a message by old Alvonso."

Joaz nodded. "I trust he rendered my remarks accurately?"

Carcolo grinned wolfishly. "At times he felt obliged to paraphrase."

"Tactful old Dae Alvonso."

"I am given to understand," said Carcolo, "that you consider me rash, ineffectual, callous to the best interests of Happy Valley. Alvonso admitted that you used the word 'blunderer' in reference to me."

Joaz smiled politely. "Sentiments of this sort are best transmitted through intermediaries."

Carcolo made a great show of dignified forbearance. "Apparently you feel that another Basic attack is imminent."

"Just so," agreed Joaz, "if my theory, which puts their home by the star Coralyne, is correct. In which case, as I pointed out to Alvonso, Happy Valley is seriously vulnerable."

"And why not Banbeck Vale as well?" barked Carcolo.

Joaz stared at him in surprise. "Is it not obvious? I have taken precautions. My people are housed in tunnels, rather than huts. We have several escape routes, should this prove necessary, both to the High Jambles and to Banbeck Jambles."

"Very interesting." Carcolo made an effort to soften his voice. "If your theory is accurate—and I pass no immediate judgment—then perhaps I would be wise to take similar measures. But I think in different terms. I prefer attack, activity, to passive defense."

"Admirable," said Joaz Banbeck. "Important deeds are done by men such as you."

Carcolo became a trifle pink in the face. "This is neither here nor there," he said. "I have come to propose a joint project. It is entirely novel, but carefully thought out. I have considered various aspects of this matter for several years."

"I attend you with great interest," said Joaz.

Carcolo blew out his cheeks. "You know the legends as well as I, perhaps better. Our people came to Aerlith as exiles during the War of the Ten Stars. The Nightmare Coalition apparently had defeated the Old Rule, but how the war ended—" he threw up his hands "—who can say?"

"There is a significant indication," said Joaz. "The Basics revisit Aerlith and ravage us at their pleasure. We have seen no men visiting except those who serve the Basics."

"'Men'?" Carcolo demanded scornfully. "I call them something else. Nevertheless, this is no more than a deduction, and we are ignorant as to the course of history. Perhaps Basics rule the cluster; perhaps they plague us only because we are weak and weaponless. Perhaps we are the last men; perhaps the Old Rule is resurgent. And never forget that many years have elapsed since the Basics last appeared on Aerlith."

"Many years have elapsed since Aerlith and Coralyne were in such convenient apposition."

Carcolo made an impatient gesture. "A supposition, which may or may not be relevant. Let me explain the basic axiom of my proposal. It is simple enough. I feel that Banbeck Vale and Happy Valley are too small a compass for men such as ourselves. We deserve larger scope."

Joaz agreed. "I wish it were possible to ignore the practical difficulties involved."

"I am able to suggest a method to counter these difficulties," asserted Carcolo.

"In that case," said Joaz, "power, glory and wealth are as good as ours."

Carcolo glanced at him sharply, slapped his breeches with the gold-beaded tassel to his scabbard. "Reflect," he said. "The sacerdotes inhabited Aerlith before us. How long no one can say. It is a mystery. In fact, what do we know of the sacerdotes? Next to nothing. They trade their metal and glass for our food, they live in deep caverns, their creed is disassociation, reverie, detachment, whatever one may wish to call it— totally incomprehensible to one such as myself." He challenged Joaz with a look; Joaz merely fingered his long chin. "They put themselves forward as simple metaphysical cultists; actually they are a very mysterious people. Has anyone yet seen a sacerdote woman? What of the blue lights, what of the lightning towers, what of the sacerdote magic? What of weird comings and goings by night, what of strange shapes moving across the sky, perhaps to other planets?"

"The tales exist, certainly," said Joaz. "As to the degree of credence to be placed in them—"

"Now we reach the meat of my proposal!" declared Ervis Carcolo. "The creed of the sacerdotes apparently forbids shame, inhibition, fear, regard for consequence. Hence, they are forced to answer any question put to them. Nevertheless, creed or no creed, they completely befog any information an assiduous man is able to wheedle from them."

Joaz inspected him curiously. "Evidently you have made the attempt."

Ervis Carcolo nodded. "Yes. Why should I deny it? I have questioned three sacerdotes with determination and persistence. They answered all my questions with gravity and calm reflection, but told me nothing." He shook his head in vexation. "Therefore, I suggest that we apply coercion."

"You are a brave man."

Carcolo shook his head modestly. "I would dare no direct measures: But they must eat. If Banbeck Vale and Happy Valley co-operate, we can apply a very cogent persuasion: hunger. Presently their words may be more to the point."

Joaz considered a moment or two. Ervis Carcolo twitched his scabbard tassel. "Your plan," said Joaz at last, "is not a frivolous one, and is ingenious—at least at first glance. What sort of information do you hope to secure? In short, what are your ultimate aims?"

Carcolo sidled close, prodded Joaz with his forefinger. "We know nothing of the outer worlds. We are marooned on this miserable world of stone and wind while life passes us by. You assume that Basics rule the cluster, but suppose you are wrong? Suppose the Old Rule has returned? Think of the rich cities, the gay resorts, the palaces, the pleasure-islands! Look up into the night sky, ponder the bounties which might be ours! You ask how can we implement these desires? I respond, the process may be so simple that the sacerdotes will reveal it without reluctance."

"You mean—"

"Communication with the worlds of men! Deliverance from this lonely little world at the edge of the universe!"

Joaz Banbeck nodded dubiously. "A fine vision, but the evidence suggests a situation far different, namely the destruction of man, and the Human Empire."

Carcolo held out his hands in a gesture of open-minded tolerance. "Perhaps you are right. But why should we not make inquiries of the sacerdotes? Concretely I propose as follows: that you and I agree to the mutual cause I have outlined. Next, we request an audience with the Demie Sacerdote. We put our questions. If he responds freely, well and good. If he evades, then we act in mutuality. No more food to the sacerdotes until they tell us plainly what we want to hear."

"Other valleys, vales, and gulches exist," said Joaz thoughtfully.

Carcolo made a brisk gesture. "We can deter any such trade by persuasion or by the power of our dragons."

"The essence of your idea appeals to me," said Joaz, "but I fear that all is not so simple."

Carcolo rapped his thigh smartly with the tassel. "And why not?"

"In the first place, Coralyne shines bright in the sky. This is our first concern. Should Coralyne pass, should the Basics not attack—then is the time to pursue this matter. Again—and perhaps more to the point—

I doubt that we can starve the sacerdotes into submission. In fact, I think it highly unlikely. I will go farther. I consider it impossible."

Carcolo blinked. "In what wise?"

"They walk naked through sleet and storm; do you think they fear hunger? And there is wild lichen to be gathered. How could we forbid this? You might dare some sort of coercion, but not I. The tales told of the sacerdotes may be no more than superstition—or they may be understatement."

Ervis Carcolo heaved a deep disgusted sigh. "Joaz Banbeck, I took you for a man of decision. But you merely pick flaws."

"These are not flaws, they are major errors which would lead to disaster."

"Well then. Do you have any suggestions of your own?"

Joaz fingered his chin. "If Coralyne recedes and we are still on Aerlith—rather than in the hold of the Basic ship—then let us plan to plunder the secrets of the sacerdotes. In the meantime I strongly recommend that you prepare Happy Valley against a new raid. You are overextended, with your new brooders and barracks. Let them rest, while you dig yourself secure tunnels!"

Ervis Carcolo stared straight across Banbeck Vale. "I am not a man to defend. I attack!"

"You will attack heat-beams and ion-rays with your dragons?"

Ervis Carcolo turned his gaze back to Joaz Banbeck. "Can I consider us allies in the plan I have proposed?"

"In its broadest principles, certainly. However I don't care to cooperate in starving or otherwise coercing the sacerdotes. It might be dangerous, as well as futile."

For an instant Carcolo could not control his detestation of Joaz Banbeck; his lip curled, his hands clenched. "Danger? Pah! What danger from a handful of naked pacifists?"

"We do not know that they are pacifists. We do know that they are men."

Carcolo once more became brightly cordial. "Perhaps you are right. But—essentially at least—we are allies."

"To a degree."

"Good. I suggest that in the case of the attack you fear, we act together, with a common strategy."

Joaz nodded distantly. "This might be effective."

"Let us coordinate our plans. Let us assume that the Basics drop down into Banbeck Vale. I suggest that your folk take refuge in Happy Valley, while the Happy Valley army joins with yours to cover their retreat. And likewise, should they attack Happy Valley, my people will take refuge in Banbeck Vale."

Joaz laughed in sheer amusement. "Ervis Carcolo, what sort of lunatic do you take me for? Return to your valley, put aside your foolish grandiosities, dig yourself protection. And fast! Coralyne is bright!"

Carcolo stood stiffly. "Do I understand that you reject my offer of alliance?"

"Not at all. But I cannot undertake to protect you and your people if you will not help yourselves. Meet my requirements, satisfy me that you are a fit ally—then we shall speak further of alliance."

Ervis Carcolo whirled on his heel, signaled to Bast Givven and the two young fuglemen. With no further word or glance he mounted his splendid Spider, goaded him into a sudden leaping run across the Verge, and up the slope toward Starbreak Fell. His men followed, somewhat less precipitously.

Joaz watched them go, shaking his head in sad wonder. Then, mounting his own Spider, he returned down the trail to the floor of Banbeck Vale.

CHAPTER V

The long Aerlith day, equivalent to six of the old Diurnal Units, passed. In Happy Valley there was grim activity, a sense of purpose and impending decision. The dragons exercised in tighter formation, the fuglemen and cornets called orders with harsher voices. In the armory bullets were cast, powder mixed, swords ground and honed.

Ervis Carcolo drove himself with dramatic bravado, wearing out Spider after Spider as he sent his dragons through various evolutions. In the case of the Happy Valley forces, these were for the most part Termagants—small active dragons with rust-red scales, narrow darting heads, chisel-sharp fangs. Their brachs were strong and well-developed: they used lance, cutlass or mace with equal skill. A man pitted against a Termagant stood no chance, for the scales warded off bullets as well as any blow the man might have strength enough to deal. On the other hand a single slash of fang, the rip of a scythe-like claw, meant death to the man.

The Termagants were fecund and hardy and throve even under the conditions which existed in the Happy Valley brooders; hence their predominance in Carcolo's army. This was a situation not to the liking of Bast Givven, Chief Dragon Master, a spare wiry man with a flat crooked-nosed face, eyes black and blank as drops of ink on a plate. Habitually terse and tight-lipped, he waxed almost eloquent in opposition to the attack upon Banbeck Vale. "Look you, Ervis Carcolo, we are able to deploy a horde of Termagants, with sufficient Striding Murderers and Long-horned Murderers. But Blue Horrors, Fiends and Juggers—no! We are lost if they trap us on the fells!"

"I do not plan to fight on the fells," said Carcolo. "I will force battle upon Joaz Banbeck. His Juggers and Fiends are useless on the cliffs. And in the matter of Blue Horrors we are almost his equal."

"You overlook a single difficulty," said Bast Givven.

"And what is this?"

"The improbability that Joaz Banbeck plans to permit all this. I allow him greater intelligence."

"Show me evidence!" charged Carcolo. "What I know of him suggests vacillation and stupidity! So we will strike—hard!" Carcolo smacked fist into palm. "Thus we will finish the haughty Banbecks!"

Bast Givven turned to go; Carcolo wrathfully called him back. "You show no enthusiasm for this campaign!"

"I know what our army can do and what it cannot do," said Givven bluntly. "If Joaz Banbeck is the man you think he is, we might succeed. If he has even the sagacity of a pair of grooms I listened to ten minutes ago, we face disaster."

In a voice thick with rage, Carcolo said, "Return to your Fiends and Juggers. I want them quick as Termagants."

Bast Givven went his way. Carcolo jumped on a nearby Spider, kicked it with his heels. The creature sprang forward, halted sharply, twisted its long neck about to look Carcolo in the face. Carcolo cried, "Hust, hust! Forward at speed, smartly now! Show these louts what snap and spirit mean!" The Spider jumped ahead with such vehemence that Carcolo tumbled over backward, landing on his neck, where he lay groaning. Grooms came running, assisted him to a bench where he sat cursing in a steady low voice. A surgeon examined, pressed, prodded, recommended that Carcolo take to his couch, and administered a sedative potion.

Carcolo was carried to his apartments beneath the west wall of Happy Valley, placed under the care of his wives, and so slept for twenty hours. When he awoke the day was half gone. He wished to arise, but found himself too stiff to move, and groaning, lay back. Presently he called for Bast Givven, who appeared and listened without comment to Carcolo's adjurations.

Evening arrived; the dragons returned to the barracks. There was nothing to do now but wait for daybreak.

During the long night Carcolo underwent a variety of treatments: massage, hot baths, infusions, poultices. He exercised with diligence, and as the night reached its end, he declared himself fit. Overhead the star Coralyne vibrated poisonous colors: red, green, white, by far the brightest star of the cluster. Carcolo refused to look up at the star, but its radiance struck through the corners of his eyes whenever he walked on the valley floor.

Dawn approached. Carcolo planned to march at the earliest moment the dragons were manageable. A flickering to the east told of the oncoming dawn storm, still invisible across the horizon. With great caution the dragons were mustered from their barracks and ordered into a marching column. There were almost three hundred Termagants; eighty-five Striding Murderers; as many Long-horned Murderers; a hundred Blue Horrors; fifty-two squat, immensely powerful Fiends, their tails tipped with spiked steel balls; eighteen Juggers. They growled and muttered evilly among themselves, watching an opportunity to kick each other or to snip a leg from an unwary groom. Darkness stimulated their latent hatred for humanity, though they had been taught nothing of their past, nor the circumstances by which they had become enslaved.

The dawn lightning blazed and crackled, outlining the vertical steeples, the astonishing peaks of the Malheur Mountains. Overhead passed the storm, with wailing gusts of wind and thrashing banks of rain moving on toward Banbeck Vale. The east glowed with a gray-green pallor, and Carcolo gave the signal to march. Still stiff and sore he hobbled to his Spider, mounted, ordered the creature into a special and dramatic curvet. Carcolo had miscalculated; malice of the night still gripped the mind of the dragon. It ended its curvet with a lash of the neck which once again dashed Carcolo to the ground, where he lay half-mad with pain and frustration.

He tried to rise, collapsed; tried again, fainted. Five minutes he lay unconscious, then seemed to rouse himself by sheer force of will. "Lift me," he whispered huskily. "Tie me into the saddle. We must march." This being manifestly impossible, no one made a move. Carcolo raged, finally called hoarsely for Bast Givven. "Proceed; we cannot stop now. You must lead the troops."

Givven nodded glumly. This was an honor for which he had no stomach.

"You know the battle-plan," wheezed Carcolo. "Circle north of the Fang, cross the Skanse with all speed, swing north around Blue Crevasse, then south along Banbeck Verge. There Joaz Banbeck may be expected to discover you. You must deploy so that when he brings up his Juggers you can topple them back with Fiends. Avoid committing our Juggers, harry him with Termagants; reserve the Murderers to strike wherever he reaches the edge. Do you understand me?"

"As you explain it, victory is certain," muttered Bast Givven.

"And so it is, unless you blunder grievously. Ah, my back! I can't move. While the great battle rages I must sit by the brooder and watch eggs hatch! Now go! Strike hard for Happy Valley!"

Givven gave an order; the troops set forth. Termagants darted into the lead, followed by silken Striding Murderers and the heavier Long-horned Murderers, their fantastic chest-spikes tipped with steel. Behind came the ponderous Juggers, grunting, gurgling, teeth clashing together with the vibration of their steps. Flanking the Juggers marched the Fiends, carrying heavy cutlasses, flourishing their terminal steel balls as a scorpion carries his sting; then at the rear came the Blue Horrors, who were both massive and quick, good climbers, no less intelligent than the Termagants. To the flanks rode a hundred men: dragon masters, knights, fuglemen and cornets. They were armed with swords, pistols and large-bore blunderbusses.

Carcolo, on a stretcher, watched till the last of his forces had passed from view, then commanded himself carried back to the portal which led into the Happy Valley caves. Never before had the caves seemed so dingy and shallow. Sourly he eyed the straggle of huts along the cliff, built of rock, slabs of resin-impregnated lichen, canes bound with tar. With the Banbeck campaign at an end, he would set about cutting new chambers and halls into the cliff. The splendid decorations of Banbeck Village were well-known; Happy Valley would be even more magnificent. The halls would glow with opal and nacre, silver and gold...and yet, to what end? If events went as planned, there was his great dream in prospect. And then, what consequence a few paltry decorations in the tunnels of Happy Valley?

Groaning, he allowed himself to be laid on his couch and entertained himself picturing the progress of his troops. By now they should be working down from Dangle Ridge, circling the mile-high Fang. He tentatively stretched his arms, worked his legs. His muscles protested, pain shot back and forth along his body—but it seemed as if the injuries were less than before. By now the army would be mounting the ramparts which rimmed that wide area of upland fell known as the Skanse. The surgeon brought Carcolo a potion; he drank and slept, to awake with a start. What was the time? His troops might well have joined battle!

He ordered himself carried to the outer portal; then, still dissatisfied, commanded his servants to transport him across the valley to the new dragon brooder, the walkway of which commanded a view up and down the valley. Despite the protests of his wives, here he was conveyed, and made as comfortable as bruises and sprains permitted.

He settled himself for an indeterminate wait, but news was not long in coming.

Down the North Trail came a cornet on a foam-bearded Spider. Carcolo sent a groom to intercept him, and heedless of aches and pains raised himself from his couch. The cornet threw himself off his mount, staggered up the ramp, sagged exhausted against the rail.

"Ambush!" he panted. "Bloody disaster!"

"Ambush?" groaned Carcolo in a hollow voice. "Where?"

"As we mounted the Skanse Ramparts. They waited till our Termagants and Murderers were over, then charged with Horrors, Fiends and Juggers. They cut us apart, drove us back, then rolled boulders on our Juggers! Our army is broken!"

Carcolo sank back on the couch, lay staring at the sky. "How many are lost?"

"I do not know. Givven called the retreat; we withdrew in the best style possible."

Carcolo lay as if comatose; the cornet flung himself down on a bench.

A column of dust appeared to the north, which presently dissolved and separated to reveal a number of Happy Valley dragons. All were wounded; they marched, hopped, limped, dragged themselves at random, croaking, glaring, bugling. First came a group of Termagants, darting ugly heads from side to side; then a pair of Blue Horrors, brachs twisting and clasping almost like human arms; then a Jugger, massive, toad-like, legs splayed out in weariness. Even as it neared the barracks it toppled, fell with a thud to lie still, legs and talons jutting into the air.

Down from the North Trail rode Bast Givven, dust-stained and haggard. He dismounted from his drooping Spider, mounted the ramp. With a wrenching effort, Carcolo once more raised himself on the couch.

Givven reported in a voice so even and light as to seem careless, but even the insensitive Carcolo was not deceived. He asked in puzzlement: "Exactly where did the ambush occur?"

"We mounted the Ramparts by way of Chloris Ravine. Where the Skanse falls off into the ravine a porphyry outcrop juts up and over. Here they awaited us."

Carcolo hissed through his teeth. "Amazing."

Bast Givven gave the faintest of nods.

Carcolo said, "Assume that Joaz Banbeck set forth during the dawnstorm, an hour earlier than I would think possible; assume that he forced his troops at a run. How could he reach the Skanse Ramparts before us even so?"

"By my reckoning," said Givven, "ambush was no threat until we had crossed the Skanse. I had planned to patrol Barchback, all the way down Blue Fell, and across Blue Crevasse."

Carcolo gave somber agreement. "How then did Joaz Banbeck bring his troops to the Ramparts so soon?"

Givven turned, looked up the valley, where wounded dragons and men still straggled down the North Trail. "I have no idea."

"A drug?" puzzled Carcolo. "A potion to pacify the dragons? Could he have made bivouac on the Skanse the whole night long?"

"The last is possible," admitted Givven grudgingly. "Under Barch Spike are empty caves. If he quartered his troops there during the night, then he had only to march across the Skanse to waylay us."

Carcolo grunted. "Perhaps we have underestimated Joaz Banbeck." He sank back on his couch with a groan. "Well then, what are our losses?"

The reckoning made dreary news. Of the already inadequate squad of Juggers, only six remained. From a force of fifty-two Fiends, forty survived and of these five were sorely wounded. Termagants, Blue Horrors and Murderers had suffered greatly. A large number had been torn apart in the first onslaught, many others had been toppled down the Ramparts to strew their armored husks through the detritus. Of the hundred men, twelve had been killed by bullets, another fourteen by dragon attack; a score more were wounded in various degree.

Carcolo lay back, his eyes closed, his mouth working feebly.

"The terrain alone saved us," said Givven. "Joaz Banbeck refused to commit his troops to the ravine. If there were any tactical error on either side, it was his. He brought an insufficiency of Termagants and Blue Horrors."

"Small comfort," growled Carcolo. "Where is the balance of the army?"

"We have good position on Dangle Ridge. We have seen none of Banbeck's scouts, either man or Termagant. He may conceivably believe we have retreated to the valley. In any event his main forces were still collected on the Skanse."

Carcolo, by an enormous effort raised himself to his feet. He tottered across the walkway to look down into the dispensary. Five Fiends crouched in vats of balsam, muttering, sighing. A Blue Horror hung in a sling, whining as surgeons cut broken fragments of armor from its gray flesh. As Carcolo watched, one of the Fiends raised itself high on its anterior legs, foam gushing from its gills. It cried out in a peculiar poignant tone, fell back dead into the balsam.

Carcolo turned back to Givven. "This is what you must do. Joaz Banbeck surely has sent forth patrols. Retire along Dangle Ridge, then taking all concealment from the patrols, swing up into one of the Despoire Cols—Tourmaline Col will serve. This is my reasoning. Banbeck will assume that you are retiring to Happy Valley, so he will hurry south behind the Fang, to attack as you come down off Dangle Ridge. As he passes below Tourmaline Col, you have the advantage and may well destroy Joaz Banbeck there with all his troops."

Bast Givven shook his head decisively. "What if his patrols locate us in spite of our precautions? He need only follow our tracks to bottle us into Tourmaline Col, with no escape except over Mount Despoire or out on Starbreak Fell. And if we venture out on Starbreak Fell his Juggers will destroy us in minutes."

Ervis Carcolo sagged back down upon the couch. "Bring the troops back to Happy Valley. We will await another occasion."

CHAPTER VI

Cut into the cliff south of the crag which housed Joaz's apartments was a large chamber known as Kergan's Hall. The proportions of the room, the simplicity and lack of ornament, the massive antique furniture contributed to the sense of lingering personality, as well as an odor unique to the room. This odor exhaled from naked stone walls, the petrified moss parquetry, old wood—a rough ripe redolence which Joaz had always disliked, together with every other aspect of the room. The dimensions seemed arrogant in their extent, the lack of ornament impressed him as rude, if not brutal. One day it occurred to Joaz that he disliked not the room but Kergan Banbeck himself, together with the entire system of overblown legends which surrounded him.

The room nevertheless in many respects was pleasant. Three tall groined windows overlooked the vale. The casements were set with small square panes of green-blue glass in muntins of black ironwood. The ceiling likewise was paneled in wood, and here a certain amount of the typical Banbeck intricacy had been permitted. There were mock pilaster capitals with gargoyle heads, a frieze carved with conventionalized fern-fronds. The furniture consisted of three pieces: two tall carved chairs and a massive table, all polished dark wood, all of enormous antiquity.

Joaz had found a use for the room. The table supported a carefully detailed relief map of the district, on a scale of three inches to the mile. At the center was Banbeck Vale, on the right hand Happy Valley, separated by a turmoil of crags and chasms, cliffs, spikes, walls and five titanic peaks: Mount Gethron to the south, Mount Despoire in the center, Barch Spike, the Fang and Mount Halcyon to the north.

At the front of Mount Gethron lay the High Jambles, then Starbreak Fell extended to Mount Despoire and Barch Spike. Beyond Mount Despoire, between the Skanse Ramparts and Barchback, the Skanse reached all the way to the tormented basalt ravines and bluffs at the foot of Mount Halcyon.

As Joaz stood studying the map, into the room came Phade, mischievously quiet. But Joaz sensed her nearness by the scent of incense, in the smoke of which she had steeped herself before seeking out Joaz. She wore a traditional holiday costume of Banbeck maidens: a tight-fitting sheath of dragon intestine, with muffs of brown fur at neck, elbows and knees. A tall cylindrical hat, notched around the upper edge, perched on her rich brown curls, and from the top of this hat soared a red plume.

Joaz feigned unconsciousness of her presence; she came up behind him to tickle his neck with the fur of her neckpiece. Joaz pretended stolid indifference; Phade, not at all deceived, put on a face of woeful concern. "Must we all be slain? How goes the war?"

"For Banbeck Vale the war goes well. For poor Ervis Carcolo and Happy Valley the war goes ill indeed."

"You plan his destruction," Phade intoned in a voice of hushed accusation. "You will kill him! Poor Ervis Carcolo!"

"He deserves no better."

"But what will befall Happy Valley?"

Joaz Banbeck shrugged idly. "Changes for the better."

"Will you seek to rule?"

"Not I."

"Think!" whispered Phade. "Joaz Banbeck, Tyrant of Banbeck Vale, Happy Valley, Phosphor Gulch, Glore, the Tarn, Clewhaven and the Great Northern Rift."

"Not I," said Joaz. "Perhaps you would rule in my stead?"

"Oh! Indeed! What changes there would be! I'd dress the sacerdotes in red and yellow ribbons. I'd order them to sing and dance and drink May wine; the dragons I'd send south to Arcady, except for a few gentle Termagants to nursemaid the children. And no more of these furious battles. I'd burn the armor and break the swords, I'd—"

"My dear little flutterbug," said Joaz with a laugh. "What a swift reign you'd have indeed!"

"Why swift? Why not forever? If men had no means to fight—"

"And when the Basics came down, you'd throw garlands around their necks?"

"Pah. They shall never be seen again. What do they gain by molesting a few remote valleys?"

"Who knows what they gain? We are free men—perhaps the last free men in the universe. Who knows? And will they be back? Coralyne is bright in the sky!"

Phade became suddenly interested in the relief map. "And your current war—dreadful! Will you attack, will you defend?"

"This depends on Ervis Carcolo," said Joaz. "I need only wait till he exposes himself." Looking down at the map he added thoughtfully, "He is clever enough to do me damage, unless I move with care."

"And what if the Basics come while you bicker with Carcolo?"

Joaz smiled. "Perhaps we shall all flee to the Jambles. Perhaps we shall all fight."

"I will fight beside you," declared Phade, striking a brave attitude. "We will attack the great Basic spaceship, braving the heat-rays, fending off the power-bolts. We will storm to the very portal, we will pull the nose of the first marauder who shows himself!"

"At one point your otherwise sage strategy falls short," said Joaz. "How does one find the nose of a Basic?"

"In that case," said Phade, "we shall seize their—" She turned her head at a sound in the hall. Joaz strode across the room, flung back the door. Old Rife the porter sidled forward. "You told me to call when the bottle either overturned or broke. Well, it's done both and irreparably, not five minutes ago."

Joaz pushed past Rife, ran down the corridor. "What means this?" demanded Phade. "Rife, what have you said to disturb him?"

Rife shook his head fretfully. "I am as perplexed as you. A bottle is pointed out to me. 'Watch this bottle day and night'—so I am commanded. And also, 'When the bottle breaks or tips, call me at once.' I tell myself that here in all truth is a sinecure. And I wonder, does Joaz consider me so senile that I will rest content with a make-work task such as watching a bottle? I am old, my jaws tremble, but I am not witless. To my surprise the bottle breaks! The explanation admittedly is workaday: a fall to the floor. Nevertheless, without knowledge of what it all means, I obey orders and notify Joaz Banbeck."

Phade had been squirming impatiently. "Where then is this bottle?"

"In the studio of Joaz Banbeck."

Phade ran off as swiftly as the tight sheath about her thighs permitted: through a transverse tunnel, across Kergan's Way by a covered bridge, then up at a slant toward Joaz's apartments.

Down the long hall ran Phade, through the anteroom where a bottle lay shattered on the floor, into the studio, where she halted in astonishment. No one was to be seen. She noticed a section of shelving which stood at an angle. Quietly, timorously, she stole across the room, peered down into the workshop.

The scene was an odd one. Joaz stood negligently, smiling a cool smile, as across the room a naked sacerdote gravely sought to shift a barrier which had sprung down across an area of the wall. But the gate was cunningly locked in place, and the sacerdote's efforts were to no avail. He turned, glanced briefly at Joaz, then started for the exit into the studio.

Phade sucked in her breath, backed away.

The sacerdote came out into the studio, started for the door.

"Just a moment," said Joaz. "I wish to speak to you."

The sacerdote paused, turned his head in mild inquiry. He was a young man, his face bland, blank, almost beautiful. Fine transparent skin stretched over his pale bones. His eyes—wide, blue, innocent—seemed to stare without focus. He was delicate of frame, sparsely fleshed; his hands were thin, with fingers trembling in some kind of nervous imbalance. Down his back, almost to his waist, hung the mane of long light-brown hair.

Joaz seated himself with ostentatious deliberation, never taking his eyes from the sacerdote. Presently he spoke in a voice pitched at an ominous level. "I find your conduct far from ingratiating." This was a declaration requiring no response, and the sacerdote made none.

"Please sit," said Joaz. He indicated a bench. "You have a great deal of explaining to do."

Was it Phade's imagination? Or did a spark of something like wild amusement flicker and die almost instantaneously in the sacerdote's eyes? But again he made no response. Joaz, adapting to the peculiar rules by which communication with the sacerdotes must be conducted, asked, "Do you care to sit?"

"It is immaterial," said the sacerdote. "Since I am standing now, I will stand."

Joaz rose to his feet and performed an act without precedent. He pushed the bench behind the sacerdote, rapped the back of the knobby knees, thrust the sacerdote firmly down upon the bench. "Since you are sitting now," said Joaz, "you might as well sit."

With gentle dignity the sacerdote regained his feet. "I shall stand."

Joaz shrugged. "As you wish. I intend to ask you some questions. I hope that you will cooperate and answer with precision."

The sacerdote blinked owlishly.

"Will you do so?"

"Certainly. I prefer, however, to return the way I came."

Joaz ignored the remark. "First," he asked, "why do you come to my study?"

The sacerdote spoke carefully, in the voice of one talking to a child. "Your language is vague; I am confused and must not respond, since I am vowed to give only truth to anyone who requires it."

Joaz settled himself in his chair. "There is no hurry. I am ready for a long discussion. Let me ask you then: did you have impulses which you can explain to me, which persuaded or impelled you to come to my studio?"

"Yes."

"How many of these impulses did you recognize?"

"I don't know."

"More than one?"

"Perhaps."

"Less than ten?"

"I don't know."

"Hmm...Why are you uncertain?"

"I am not uncertain."

"Then why can't you specify the number as I requested?"

"There is no such number."

"I see…You mean, possibly, that there are several elements of a single motive which directed your brain to signal your muscles in order that they might carry you here?"

"Possibly."

Joaz's thin lips twisted in a faint smile of triumph. "Can you describe an element of the eventual motive?"

"Yes."

"Do so, then."

There was an imperative, against which the sacerdote was proof. Any form of coercion known to Joaz—fire, sword, thirst, mutilation— these to a sacerdote were no more than inconveniences; he ignored them as if they did not exist. His personal inner world was the single world of reality; either acting upon or reacting against the affairs of the Utter Men demeaned him; absolute passivity, absolute candor were his necessary courses of action. Understanding something of this, Joaz rephrased his command: "Can you think of an element of the motive which impelled you to come here?"

"Yes."

"What is it?"

"A desire to wander about."

"Can you think of another?"

"Yes."

"What is it?"

"A desire to exercise myself by walking."

"I see…Incidentally, are you trying to evade answering my questions?"

"I answer such questions as you put to me. So long as I do so, so long as I open my mind to all who seek knowledge—for this is our creed—there can be no question of evasion."

"So you say. However, you have not provided me an answer that I find satisfactory."

The sacerdote's reply to the comment was an almost imperceptible widening of the pupils.

"Very well then," said Joaz Banbeck. "Can you think of another element to this complex motive we have been discussing?"

"Yes."

"What is it?"

"I am interested in antiques. I came to your study to admire your relicts of the old worlds."

"Indeed?" Joaz raised his eyebrows. "I am lucky to possess such fascinating treasures. Which of my antiques interests you particularly?"

"Your books. Your maps. Your great globe of the Arch-world."

"The Arch-world? Eden?"

"This is one of its names."

Joaz pursed his lips. "So you come here to study my antiques. Well then, what other elements to this motive exist?"

The sacerdote hesitated an instant. "It was suggested to me that I come here."

"By whom?"

"By the Demie."

"Why did he so suggest?"

"I am uncertain."

"Can you conjecture?"

"Yes."

"What are these conjectures?"

The sacerdote made a small bland gesture with the fingers of one hand. "The Demie might wish to become an Utter Man, and so seeks to learn the principles of your existence. Or the Demie might wish to change the trade articles. The Demie might be fascinated by my descriptions of your antiques. Or the Demie might be curious regarding the focus of your vision-panels. Or—"

"Enough. Which of these conjectures, and of other conjectures you have not yet divulged, do you consider most probable?"

"None."

Joaz raised his eyebrows once more. "How do you justify this?"

"Since any desired number of conjectures can be formed, the denominator of any probability-ratio is variable and the entire concept becomes arithmetically meaningless."

Joaz grinned wearily. "Of the conjectures which to this moment have occurred to you, which do you regard as the most likely?"

"I suspect that the Demie might think it desirable that I come here to stand."

"What do you achieve by standing?"

"Nothing."

"Then the Demie does not send you here to stand."

To Joaz's assertion, the sacerdote made no comment.

Joaz framed a question with great care. "What do you believe that the Demie hopes you will achieve by coming here to stand?"

"I believe that he wishes me to learn how Utter Men think."

"And you learn how I think by coming here?"

"I am learning a great deal."

"How does it help you?"

"I don't know."

"How many times have you visited my study?"

"Seven times."

"Why were you chosen specially to come?"

"The synod has approved my tand. I may well be the next Demie."

Joaz spoke over his shoulder to Phade. "Brew tea." He turned back to the sacerdote. "What is a tand?"

The sacerdote took a deep breath. "My tand is the representation of my soul."

"Hmm. What does it look like?"

The sacerdote's expression was unfathomable. "It cannot be described."

"Do I have one?"

"No."

Joaz shrugged. "Then you can read my thoughts."

Silence.

"Can you read my thoughts?"

"Not well."

"Why should you wish to read my thoughts?"

"We are alive in the universe together. Since we are not permitted to act, we are obliged to know."

Joaz smiled skeptically. "How does knowledge help you, if you will not act upon it?"

"Events follow the Rationale, as water drains into a hollow and forms a pool."

"Bah!" said Joaz, in sudden irritation. "Your doctrine commits you to non-interference in our affairs, nevertheless you allow your 'Rationale' to create conditions by which events are influenced. Is this correct?"

"I am not sure. We are a passive people."

"Still, your Demie must have had a plan in mind when he sent you here. Is this not correct?"

"I cannot say."

Joaz veered to a new line of questioning. "Where does the tunnel behind my workshop lead?"

"Into a cavern."

Phade set a silver pot before Joaz. He poured, sipped reflectively. Of contests there were numberless varieties; he and the sacerdote were engaged in a hide-and-seek game of words and ideas. The sacerdote was schooled in patience and supple evasions, to counter which Joaz could bring pride and determination. The sacerdote was handicapped by an innate necessity to speak truth; Joaz, on the other hand, must grope like a man blindfolded, unacquainted with the goal he sought, ignorant of the prize to be won. Very well, thought Joaz, let us continue. We shall see whose nerves fray first. He offered tea to the sacerdote, who refused with a shake of the head so quick and of such small compass as to seem a shudder.

Joaz made a gesture signifying it was all the same to him. "Should you desire sustenance or drink," he said, "please let it be known. I enjoy our conversation so inordinately that I fear I may prolong it to the limits of your patience. Surely you would prefer to sit?"

"No."

"As you wish. Well then, back to our discussion. This cavern you mentioned—is it inhabited by sacerdotes?"

"I fail to understand your question."

"Do sacerdotes use the cavern?"

"Yes."

Eventually, fragment by fragment, Joaz extracted the information that the cavern connected with a series of chambers, in which the sacerdotes smelted metal, boiled glass, ate, slept, performed their rituals. At one time there had been an opening into Banbeck Vale, but long ago this had been blocked. Why? There were wars throughout the cluster; bands of defeated men were taking refuge upon Aerlith, settling in rifts and valleys. The sacerdotes preferred a detached existence and had shut their caverns away from sight. Where was this opening? The sacerdote seemed vague, indefinite. Somewhere to the north end of the valley. Behind Banbeck Jambles? Possibly. But trading between men and sacerdotes was conducted at a cave entrance below Mount Gethron. Why? A matter of usage, declared the sacerdote. In addition this location was more readily accessible to Happy Valley and Phosphor Gulch. How many sacerdotes lived in these caves? Uncertainty. Some might have died, others might have been born. Approximately how many this morning? Perhaps five hundred.

At this juncture the sacerdote was swaying and Joaz was hoarse. "Back to your motive—or the elements of your motives—for coming to my studio. Are they connected in any manner with the star Coralyne, and a possible new coming of the Basics, or the grephs, as they were formerly called?"

Again the sacerdote seemed to hesitate. Then: "Yes."

"Will the sacerdotes help us against the Basics, should they come?"

"No." This answer was terse and definite.

"But I assume that the sacerdotes wish the Basics driven off?"

No answer.

Joaz rephrased his words. "Do the sacerdotes wish the Basics repelled from Aerlith?"

"The Rationale bids us stand aloof from affairs of men and non-men alike."

Joaz curled his lip. "Suppose the Basics invaded your caves, dragged you off to the Coralyne planet. Then what?"

The sacerdote almost seemed to laugh. "The question cannot be answered."

"Would you resist the Basics if they made the attempt?"

"I cannot answer your question."

Joaz laughed. "But the answer is not no?"

The sacerdote assented.

"Do you have weapons, then?"

The sacerdote's mild blue eyes seemed to droop. Secrecy? Fatigue? Joaz repeated the question.

"Yes," said the sacerdote. His knees sagged, but he snapped them tight.

"What kind of weapons?"

"Numberless varieties. Projectiles, such as rocks. Piercing weapons, such as broken sticks. Cutting and slashing weapons such as cooking utensils." His voice began to fade as if he were moving away. "Poisons: arsenic, sulfur, triventidum, acid, black-spore. Burning weapons, such as torches and lenses to focus the sunlight. Weapons to suffocate: ropes, nooses, slings, cords. Cisterns, to drown the enemy…"

"Sit down, rest," Joaz urged him. "Your inventory interests me, but its total effect seems inadequate. Have you other weapons which might decisively repel the Basics should they attack you?"

The question, by design or chance, was never answered. The sacerdote sank to his knees, slowly, as if praying. He fell forward on his face, then sprawled to the side. Joaz sprang forward, yanked up the drooping head by its hair. The eyes, half-open, revealed a hideous white expanse. "Speak!" croaked Joaz. "Answer my last question! Do you have weapons—or a weapon—to repel a Basic attack?"

The pallid lips moved. "I don't know."

Joaz frowned, peered into the waxen face, drew back in bewilderment. "The man is dead."

CHAPTER VII

Phade looked up from drowsing on a couch, face pink, hair tossed. "You have killed him!" she cried in a voice of hushed horror.

"No. He has died—or caused himself to die."

Phade staggered blinking across the room, sidled close to Joaz, who pushed her absently away. Phade scowled, shrugged and then, as Joaz paid her no heed, marched from the room.

Joaz sat back, staring at the limp body. "He did not tire," muttered Joaz, "until I verged upon secrets."

Presently he jumped to his feet, went to the entry hall, sent Rife to fetch a barber. An hour later the corpse, stripped of hair, lay on a wooden pallet covered by a sheet, and Joaz held in his hands a rude wig fashioned from the long hair.

The barber departed; servants carried away the corpse. Joaz stood alone in his studio, tense and light-headed. He removed his garments, to stand naked as the sacerdote. Gingerly he drew the wig across his scalp and examined himself in the mirror. To a casual eye, where the difference? Something was lacking: the torc. Joaz fitted it about his neck, once more examined his reflection, with dubious satisfaction.

He entered the workshop, hesitated, disengaged the trap, cautiously pulled away the stone slab. On hands and knees he peered into the tunnel and since it was dark, held forward a glass vial of luminescent algae. In the faint light the tunnel seemed empty. Irrevocably putting down his fears, Joaz clambered through the opening. The tunnel was narrow and low; Joaz moved forward tentatively, nerves thrilling with wariness. He stopped often to listen, but heard nothing but the whisper of his own pulse.

After perhaps a hundred yards the tunnel broke out into a natural cavern. Joaz stopped, stood indecisively, straining his ears through the gloom. Luminescent vials fixed to the walls at irregular intervals provided a measure of light, enough to delineate the direction of the cavern, which seemed to be north, parallel to the length of the valley. Joaz set forth once again, halting to listen every few yards. To the best of his knowledge the sacerdotes were a mild unaggressive folk, but they were also intensely secretive. How would they respond to the presence of an interloper? Joaz could not be sure, and proceeded with great caution.

The cavern rose, fell, widened, narrowed. Joaz presently came upon evidences of use: small cubicles, hollowed into the walls, lit by candelabra holding tall vials of luminous stuff. In two of the cubicles Joaz came upon sacerdotes, the first asleep on a reed rug, the second sitting cross-legged, gazing fixedly at a contrivance of twisted metal rods. They gave Joaz no attention; he continued with a more confident step.

The cave sloped downward, widened like a cornucopia, suddenly broke into a cavern so enormous that Joaz thought for a startled instant that he had stepped out into the night. The ceiling reached beyond the flicker of the myriad of lamps, fires and glowing vials. Ahead and to the left smelters and forges were in operation; then a twist in the cavern wall obscured something of the view. Joaz glimpsed a tiered tubular construction which seemed to be some sort of workshop, for a large number of sacerdotes were occupied at complicated tasks. To the right was a stack of bales, a row of bins containing goods of unknown nature.

Joaz for the first time saw sacerdote women: neither the nymphs nor the half-human witches of popular legend. Like the men they seemed pallid and frail, with sharply defined features; like the men they moved with care and deliberation; like the men they wore only their waist-long hair. There was little conversation and no laughter: rather an atmosphere of not unhappy placidity and concentration. The cavern exuded a sense of time, use and custom. The stone floor was polished by endless padding of bare feet; the exhalations of many generations had stained the walls.

No one heeded Joaz. He moved slowly forward, keeping to the shadows, and paused under the stack of bales. To the right the cavern dwindled by irregular proportions into a vast horizontal funnel, receding, twisting, telescoping, losing all reality in the dim light.

Joaz searched the entire sweep of vast cavern. Where would be the armory, with the weapons of whose existence the sacerdote, by the very act of dying, had assured him? Joaz turned his attention once more to the left, straining to see detail in the odd tiered workshop which rose fifty feet from the stone floor. A strange edifice, thought Joaz, craning his neck; one whose nature he could not entirely comprehend. But every aspect of the great cavern—so close beside Banbeck Vale and so remote—was strange and marvelous. Weapons? They might be any-where; certainly he dared seek no further for them.

There was nothing more he could learn without risk of discovery. He turned back the way he had come: up the dim passage, past the occasional side cubicles, where the two sacerdotes remained as he had found them before: the one asleep, the other intent on the contrivance of twisted metal. He plodded on and on. Had he come so far? Where was the fissure which led to his own apartments? Had he passed it by, must he search? Panic rose in his throat, but he continued, watching carefully. There, he had not gone wrong! There it opened to his right, a fissure almost dear and familiar. He plunged into it, walked with long loping strides, like a man under water, holding his luminous tube ahead.

An apparition rose before him, a tall white shape. Joaz stood rigid. The gaunt figure bore down upon him. Joaz pressed against the wall. The figure stalked forward, and suddenly shrank to human scale. It was the young sacerdote whom Joaz had shorn and left for dead. He confronted Joaz, mild blue eyes bright with reproach and contempt. "Give me my torc."

With numb fingers Joaz removed the golden collar. The sacerdote took it, but made no move to clasp it upon himself. He looked at the hair which weighted heavy upon Joaz's scalp. With a foolish grimace Joaz doffed the disheveled wig, proffered it. The sacerdote sprang back as if Joaz had become a cave-goblin. Sidling past, as far from Joaz as the wall of the passage allowed, he paced swiftly off down the tunnel. Joaz dropped the wig to the floor, stared down at the unkempt pile of hair. He turned, looked after the sacerdote, a pallid figure which soon became one with the murk. Slowly Joaz continued up the tunnel. There—an oblong blank of light, the opening to his workshop. He crawled through, back to the real world. Savagely, with all his strength, he thrust the slab back in the hole, slammed down the gate which originally had trapped the sacerdote.

Joaz's garments lay where he had tossed them. Wrapping himself in a cloak he went to the outer door, looked forth into the anteroom where Rife sat dozing. Joaz snapped his fingers. "Fetch masons, with mortar, steel and stone."

Joaz bathed with diligence, rubbing himself time after time with emulsion, rinsing and re-rinsing himself. Emerging from the bath he took the waiting masons into his workshop, ordered the sealing of the hole.

Then he took himself to his couch. Sipping a cup of wine, he let his mind rove and wander. Recollection became reverie, reverie became dream. Joaz once again traversed the tunnel, on feet light as thistledown, down the long cavern, and the sacerdotes in their cubicles now raised their heads to look after him. At last he stood in the entrance to the great underground void, and once more looked right and left in awe. Now he drifted across the floor, past sacerdotes laboring earnestly over fires and anvils. Sparks rose from retorts, blue gas flickered above melting metal.

Joaz moved beyond to a small chamber cut into the stone. Here sat an old man, thin as a pole, his waist-long mane of hair snow-white. The man examined Joaz with fathomless blue eyes, and spoke, but his voice was muffled, inaudible. He spoke again; the words rang loud in Joaz's mind.

"I bring you here to caution you, lest you do us harm, and with no profit to yourself. The weapon you seek is both non-existent and beyond your imagination. Put it outside your ambition."

By great effort Joaz managed to stammer, "The young sacerdote made no denial; this weapon must exist!"

"Only within the narrow limits of special interpretation. The lad can speak no more than the literal truth, nor can he act with other than grace. How can you wonder why we hold ourselves apart? You Utter folk find purity incomprehensible; you thought to advantage yourself, but achieved nothing but an exercise in rat-like stealth. Lest you try again with greater boldness I must abase myself to set matters correct. I assure you, this so-called weapon is absolutely beyond your control."

First shame, then indignation came over Joaz; he cried out, "You do not understand my urgencies! Why should I act differently? Coralyne is close; the Basics are at hand. Are you not men? Why will you not help us defend the planet?"

The Demie shook his head, and the white hair rippled with hypnotic slowness. "I quote you the Rationale: passivity, complete and absolute. This implies solitude, sanctity, quiescence, peace. Can you imagine the anguish I risk in speaking to you? I intervene, I interfere, at vast pain of the spirit. Let there be an end to it. We have made free with your studio, doing you no harm, offering you no indignity. You have paid a visit to our hall, demeaning a noble young man in the process. Let us be quits, let there be no further spying on either side. Do you agree?"

Joaz heard his voice respond, quite without his conscious prompting; it sounded more nasal and shrill than he liked. "You offer this agreement now when you have learned your fill of my secrets, but I know none of yours."

The Demie's face seemed to recede and quiver. Joaz read contempt, and in his sleep he tossed and twitched. He made an effort to speak in a voice of calm reason: "Come, we are men together; why should we be at odds? Let us share our secrets, let each help the other. Examine my archives, my cases, my relics at your leisure, and then allow me to study this existent but nonexistent weapon. I swear it shall be used only against the Basics, for the protection of both of us."

The Demie's eyes sparkled. "No."

"Why not?" argued Joaz. "Surely you wish us no harm?"

"We are detached and passionless. We await your extinction. You are the Utter Men, the last of humanity. And when you are gone, your dark thoughts and grim plots will be gone; murder and pain and malice will be gone."

"I cannot believe this," said Joaz. "There may be no men in the cluster, but what of the universe? The Old Rule reached far! Sooner or later men will return to Aerlith."

The Demie's voice became plangent. "Do you think we speak only from faith? Do you doubt our knowledge?"

"The universe is large. The Old Rule reached far."

"The last men dwell on Aerlith," said the Demie. "The Utter men and the sacerdotes. You shall pass; we will carry forth the Rationale like a banner of glory, through all the worlds of the sky."

"And how will you transport yourselves on this mission?" Joaz asked cunningly. "Can you fly to the stars as naked as you walk the fells?"

"There will be a means. Time is long."

"For your purposes, time needs to be long. Even on the Coralyne planets there are men. Enslaved, reshaped in body and mind, but men. What of them? It seems that you are wrong, that you are guided by faith indeed."

The Demie fell silent. His face seemed to stiffen.

"Are these not facts?" asked Joaz. "How do you reconcile them with your faith?"

The Demie said mildly, "Facts can never be reconciled with faith. By our faith, these men, if they exist, will also pass. Time is long. Oh, the worlds of brightness: they await us!"

"It is clear," said Joaz, "that you ally yourselves with the Basics and that you hope for our destruction. This can only change our attitudes toward you. I fear that Ervis Carcolo was right and I wrong."

"We remain passive," said the Demie. His face wavered, seemed to swim with mottled colors. "Without emotion, we will stand witness to the passing of the Utter men, neither helping nor hindering."

Joaz spoke in fury, "Your faith, your Rationale—whatever you call it—misleads you. I make this threat: if you fail to help us, you will suffer as we suffer."

"We are passive, we are indifferent."

"What of your children? The Basics make no difference between us. They will herd you to their pens as readily as they do us. Why should we fight to protect you?"

The Demie's face faded, became splotched with fog, transparent mist; his eyes glowed like rotten meat. "We need no protection," he howled. "We are secure."

"You will suffer our fate," cried Joaz, "I promise you this!"

The Demie collapsed suddenly into a small dry husk, like a dead mosquito; with incredible speed, Joaz fled back through the caves, the tunnels, up through his workroom, his studio, into his bed chamber where now he jerked upright, eyes starting, throat distended, mouth dry.

The door opened; Rife's head appeared. "Did you call, sir?"

Joaz raised himself on his elbows, looked around the room. "No. I did not call."

Rife withdrew. Joaz settled back on the couch, lay staring at the ceiling. He had dreamed a most peculiar dream. Dream? A synthesis of his own imaginings? Or, in all verity, a confrontation and exchange between two minds? Impossible to decide, and perhaps irrelevant; the event carried its own conviction.

Joaz swung his legs over the side of the couch, blinked at the floor. Dream or colloquy, it was all the same. He rose to his feet, donned sandals and a robe of yellow fur, limped morosely up to the Council Room and stepped out on a sunny balcony.

The day was two-thirds over. Shadows hung dense along the western cliffs. Right and left stretched Banbeck Vale. Never had it seemed more prosperous or more fruitful, and never before unreal: as if he were a stranger to the planet. He looked north along the great bulwark of stone which rose sheer to Banbeck Verge. This too was unreal, a façade behind which lived the sacerdotes. He gauged the rock face, superimposing a mental projection of the great cavern. The cliff toward the north end of the vale must be scarcely more than a shell!

Joaz turned his attention to the exercise field, where Juggers were thudding briskly through defensive evolutions. How strange was the quality of life, which had produced Basic and Jugger, sacerdote and himself. He thought of Ervis Carcolo, and wrestled with sudden exasperation. Carcolo was a distraction most unwelcome at the present time. There would be no tolerance when Carcolo was finally brought to account. A light step behind him, the pressure of fur, the touch of gay hands, the scent of incense. Joaz's tensions melted. If there were no such creatures as minstrel-maidens, it would be necessary to invent them.

Deep under Banbeck Scarp, in a cubicle lit by a twelve-vial candelabra, a naked white-haired man sat quietly. On a pedestal at the level of his eyes rested his *tand*, an intricate construction of gold rods and silver wire, woven and bent seemingly at random. The fortuitousness of the design, however, was only apparent. Each curve symbolized an aspect of Final Sentience; the shadow cast upon the wall represented the Rationale, ever-shifting, always the same. The object was sacred to the sacerdotes, and served as a source of revelation.

There was never an end to the study of the *tand*: new intuitions were continually derived from some heretofore overlooked relationship of angle and curve. The nomenclature was elaborate: each part, juncture, sweep and twist had its name; each aspect of the relationships between the various parts was likewise categorized. Such was the cult of the *tand*: abstruse, exacting, without compromise. At his puberty rites the young sacerdote might study the original *tand* for as long as he chose; each must construct a duplicate *tand*, relying upon memory alone. Then occurred the most significant event of his lifetime: the viewing of his *tand* by a synod of elders. In awesome stillness, for hours at a time they would ponder his creation, weigh the infinitesimal variations of proportion, radius, sweep and angle. So they would infer the initiate's quality, judge his personal attributes, determine his understanding of Final Sentience, the Rationale and the Basis.

Occasionally the testimony of the *tand* revealed a character so tainted as to be reckoned intolerable; the vile tand would be cast into a furnace, the molten metal consigned to a latrine, the unlucky initiate expelled to the face of the planet, to live on his own terms.

The naked white-haired Demie, contemplating his own beautiful *tand*, sighed, moved restlessly. He had been visited by an influence so ardent, so passionate, so simultaneously cruel and tender, that his mind was oppressed. Unbidden, into his mind, came a dark seep of doubt. Can it be, he asked himself, that we have insensibly wandered from the true Rationale? Do we study our *tands* with blinded eyes?...How to know, oh how to know! All is relative ease and facility in orthodoxy, yet how can it be denied that good is in itself undeniable? Absolutes are the most uncertain of all formulations, while the uncertainties are the most real...

Twenty miles over the mountains, in the long pale light of the Aerlith afternoon, Ervis Carcolo planned his own plans. "By daring, by striking hard, by cutting deep can I defeat him! In resolve, in courage, in endurance, I am more than his equal. Not again will he trick me, to slaughter my dragons and kill my men! Oh, Joaz Banbeck, how I will pay you for your deceit!" He raised his arms in wrath. "Oh Joaz Banbeck, you whey-faced sheep!" Carcolo smote the air with his fist. "I will crush you like a clod of dry moss!" He frowned, rubbed his round red chin. "But how? Where? He has every advantage!"

Carcolo pondered his possible stratagems. "He will expect me to strike, so much is certain. Doubtless he will again wait in ambush. So I will patrol every inch, but this too he will expect and so be wary lest I thunder upon him from above. Will he hide behind Despoire, or along Northguard, to catch me as I cross the Skanse? If so, I must approach by another route—through Maudlin Pass and under Mount Gethron? Then, if he is tardy in his march, I will meet him on Banbeck Verge. And if he is early, I stalk him through the peaks and chasms..."

CHAPTER VIII

With the cold rain of dawn pelting down upon them, with the trail illuminated only by lightning-glare, Ervis Carcolo, his dragons and his men set forth. When the first sparkle of sunlight struck Mount Despoire, they had already traversed Maudlin Pass.

So far, so good, exulted Ervis Carcolo. He stood high in his stirrups to scan Starbreak Fell. No sign of the Banbeck forces. He waited, scanning the far edge of Northguard Ridge, black against the sky. A minute passed. Two minutes. The men beat their hands together, the dragons rumbled and muttered fretfully.

Impatience began to prickle along Carcolo's ribs; he fidgeted and cursed. Could not the simplest of plans be carried through without mistake? But now the flicker of a heliograph from Barch Spike, and another to the southeast from the slopes of Mount Gethron. Carcolo waved forward his army; the way lay clear across Starbreak Fell. Down from Maudlin Pass surged the Happy Valley army: first the Long-horned Murderers, steel-spiked and crested with steel prongs; then the rolling red seethe of the Termagants, darting their heads as they ran; and behind came the balance of the forces.

Starbreak Fell spread wide before them, a rolling slope strewn with flinty meteoric fragments which glinted like flowers on the gray-green moss. To all sides rose majestic peaks, snow blazing white in the clear morning light: Mount Gethron, Mount Despoire, Barch Spike and far to the south, Clew Taw.

The scouts converged from left and right. They brought identical reports: there was no sign of Joaz Banbeck or his troops. Carcolo began to toy with a new possibility. Perhaps Joaz Banbeck had not deigned to take the field. The idea enraged him and filled him with a great joy; if so, Joaz would pay dearly for his neglect.

Halfway across Starbreak Fell they came upon a pen occupied by two hundred of Joaz Banbeck's spratling Fiends. Two old men and a boy tended the pen, and watched the Happy Valley horde advance with manifest terror.

But Carcolo rode past leaving the pen unmolested. If he won the day, it would become part of his spoils; if he lost, the spratling Fiends could do him no harm.

The old men and the boy stood on the roof of their turf hut, watching Carcolo and his troops pass: the men in black uniforms and black peaked caps with back-slanting ear-flaps; the dragons bounding, crawling, loping, plodding, according to their kind, scales glinting: the dull red and maroon of Termagants; the poisonous shine of the Blue Horrors; the black-green Fiends; the gray and brown Juggers and Murderers. Ervis Carcolo rode on the right flank, Bast Givven rode to the rear. And now Carcolo hastened the pace, haunted by the anxiety that Joaz Banbeck might bring his Fiends and Juggers up Banbeck Scarp before he arrived to thrust him back—assuming that Joaz Banbeck in all actuality had been caught napping.

But Carcolo reached Banbeck Verge without challenge. He shouted out in triumph, waved his cap high. "Joaz Banbeck the sluggard! Let him try now the ascent of Banbeck Scarp!" And Ervis Carcolo surveyed Banbeck Vale with the eye of a conqueror.

Bast Givven seemed to share none of Carcolo's triumph, and kept an uneasy watch to north and south and to the rear.

Carcolo observed him peevishly from the corner of his eye and presently called out, "Ho, ho, then! What's amiss?"

"Perhaps much, perhaps nothing," said Bast Givven, searching the landscape.

Carcolo blew out his mustaches. Givven went on, in the cool voice which so completely irritated Carcolo. "Joaz Banbeck seems to be tricking us as before."

"Why do you say this?"

"Judge for yourself. Would he allow us advantage without claiming a miser's price?"

"Nonsense!" muttered Carcolo. "The sluggard is fat with his last victory." But he rubbed his chin and peered uneasily down into Banbeck Vale. From here it seemed curiously quiet. There was a strange inactivity in the fields and barracks. A chill began to grip Carcolo's heart—then he cried out. "Look at the brooder: there are the Banbeck dragons!"

Givven squinted down into the vale, glanced sidewise at Carcolo. "Three Termagants, in egg." He straightened, abandoned all interest in the vale and scrutinized the peaks and ridges to the north and east. "Assume that Joaz Banbeck set out before dawn, came up to the Verge, by the Slickenslides, crossed Blue Fell in strength—"

"What of Blue Crevasse?"

"He avoids Blue Crevasse to the north, comes over Barchback, steals across the Skanse and around Barch Spike..."

Carcolo studied Northguard Ridge with new and startled awareness. A quiver of movement, the glint of scales?

"Retreat!" roared Carcolo. "Make for Barch Spike! They're behind us!"

Startled, his army broke ranks, fled across Banbeck Verge, up into the harsh spurs of Barch Spike. Joaz, his strategy discovered, launched squads of Murderers to intercept the Happy Valley army, to engage and delay and, if possible, deny them the broken slopes of Barch Spike.

Carcolo calculated swiftly. His own Murderers he considered his finest troops, and held them in great pride. Purposely now he delayed, hoping to engage the Banbeck skirmishers, quickly destroy them and still gain the protection of the Barch declivities.

The Banbeck Murderers, however, refused to close, and scrambled for height up Barch Spike. Carcolo sent forward his Termagants and Blue Horrors; with a horrid snarling the two lines met. The Banbeck Termagants rushed up, to be met by Carcolo's Striding Murderers and forced into humping pounding flight.

The main body of Carcolo's troops, excited at the sight of retreating foes, could not be restrained. They veered off from Barch Spike, plunged down upon Starbreak Fell. The Striding Murderers overtook the Banbeck Termagants, climbed up their backs, toppled them over squealing and kicking, then knifed open the exposed pink bellies.

Banbeck's Long-horned Murderers came circling, struck from the flank into Carcolo's Striding Murderers, goring with steel-tipped horns, impaling on lances. Somehow they overlooked Carcolo's Blue Horrors who sprang down upon them. With axes and maces they laid the Murderers low, performing the rather grisly entertainment of clambering on a subdued Murderer, seizing the horn, stripping back horn, skin and scales, from head to tail. So Joaz Banbeck lost thirty Termagants and perhaps two dozen Murderers. Nevertheless, the attack served its purpose, allowing him to bring his knights, Fiends and Juggers down from Northguard before Carcolo could gain the heights of Barch Spike.

Carcolo retreated in a slantwise line up the pocked slopes, and meanwhile sent six men across the fell to the pen where the spratling Fiends milled in fear at the battle. The men broke the gates, struck down the two old men, herded the young Fiends across the fell toward the Banbeck troops. The hysterical spratlings obeyed their instincts, clasped themselves to the neck of whatever dragon they first encountered; which thereupon became sorely hampered, for its own instincts prevented it from detaching the spratling by force.

This ruse, a brilliant improvisation, created enormous disorder among the Banbeck troops. Ervis Carcolo now charged with all his power directly into the Banbeck center. Two squads of Termagants fanned out to harass the men; his Murderers—the only category in which he outnumbered Joaz Banbeck—were sent to engage Fiends, while Carcolo's own Fiends, pampered, strong, glistening with oily strength, snaked in toward the Banbeck Juggers. Under the great brown hulks they darted, lashing the fifty-pound steel ball at the tip of their tails against the inner side of the Jugger's legs.

A roaring mêlée ensued. Battle lines were uncertain; both men and dragons were crushed, torn apart, hacked to bits. The air sang with bullets, whistled with steel, reverberated to trumpeting, whistles, shouts, screams and bellows.

The reckless abandon of Carcolo's tactics achieved results out of proportion to his numbers. His Fiends burrowed ever deeper into the crazed and almost helpless Banbeck Juggers, while the Carcolo Murderers and Blue Horrors held back the Banbeck Fiends. Joaz Banbeck himself, assailed by Termagants, escaped with his life only by fleeing around behind the battle, where he picked up the support of a squad of Blue Horrors. In a fury he blew a withdrawal signal, and his army backed off down the slopes, leaving the ground littered with struggling and kicking bodies.

Carcolo, throwing aside all restraint, rose in his saddle, signaled to commit his own Juggers, which so far he had treasured like his own children. Shrilling, hiccuping, they lumbered down into the seethe, tearing away great mouthfuls of flesh to right and left, ripping apart lesser dragons with their brachs, treading on Termagants, seizing Blue Horrors and Murderers, flinging them wailing and clawing through the air. Six Banbeck knights sought to stem the charge, firing their muskets point-blank into the demoniac faces; they went down and were seen no more.

Down on Starbreak Fell tumbled the battle. The nucleus of the fighting became less concentrated, the Happy Valley advantage dissipated. Carcolo hesitated, a long heady instant. He and his troops alike were afire; the intoxication of unexpected success tingled in their brains— but here on Starbreak Fell, could they counter the odds posed by the greater Banbeck forces? Caution dictated that Carcolo withdraw up Barch Spike, to make the most of his limited victory. Already a strong platoon of Fiends had grouped and were maneuvering to charge his meager force of Juggers. Bast Givven approached, clearly expecting the word to retreat. But Carcolo still waited, reveling in the havoc being wrought by his paltry six Juggers.

Bast Givven's saturnine face was stern. "Withdraw, withdraw! It's annihilation when their flanks bear in on us!"

Carcolo seized his elbow. "Look! See where those Fiends gather, see where Joaz Banbeck rides! As soon as they charge, send six Striding Murderers from either side; close in on him, kill him!"

Givven opened his mouth to protest, looked where Carcolo pointed, rode to obey the orders.

Here came the Banbeck Fiends, moving with stealthy certainty toward the Happy Valley Juggers. Joaz, raising in his saddle, watched their progress. Suddenly from either side the Striding Murderers were on him. Four of his knights and six young cornets, screaming alarm, dashed back to protect him; there was clanging of steel on steel and steel on scale. The Murderers fought with sword and mace; the knights, their muskets useless, countered with cutlasses, one by one going under. Rearing on hind legs the Murderer corporal hacked down at Joaz, who desperately fended off the blow. The Murderer raised sword and mace together—and from fifty yards a musket pellet smashed into its ear. Crazy with pain, it dropped its weapons, fell forward upon Joaz, writhing and kicking. Banbeck Blue Horrors came to attack; the Murderers darted back and forth over the thrashing corporal, stabbing down at Joaz, kicking at him, finally fleeing the Blue Horrors.

Ervis Carcolo groaned in disappointment; by a half-second only had he fallen short of victory. Joaz Banbeck, bruised, mauled, perhaps wounded, had escaped with his life.

Over the crest of the hill came a rider: an unarmed youth whipping a staggering Spider. Bast Givven pointed him out to Carcolo. "A messenger from the Valley, in urgency."

The lad careened down the fell toward Carcolo, shouting ahead, but his message was lost in the din of battle. At last he drew close. "The Basics, the Basics!"

Carcolo slumped like a half-empty bladder. "Where?"

"A great black ship, half the valley wide. I was up on the heath, I managed to escape." He pointed, whimpered.

"Speak, boy!" husked Carcolo. "What do they do?"

"I did not see; I ran to you."

Carcolo gazed across the battle field; the Banbeck Fiends had almost reached his Juggers, who were backing slowly, with heads lowered, fangs fully extended.

Carcolo threw up his hands in despair; he ordered Givven, "Blow a retreat, break clear!"

Waving a white kerchief he rode around the battle to where Joaz Banbeck still lay on the ground, the quivering Murderer only just now being lifted from his legs. Joaz stared up, his face white as Carcolo's kerchief. At the sight of Carcolo his eyes grew wide and dark, his mouth became still.

Carcolo blurted, "The Basics have come once more; they have dropped into Happy Valley, they are destroying my people."

Joaz Banbeck, assisted by his knights, gained his feet. He stood swaying, arms limp, looking silently into Carcolo's face.

Carcolo spoke once more. "We must call truce; this battle is waste! With all our forces let us march to Happy Valley and attack the monsters before they destroy all of us! Ah, think what we could have achieved with the weapons of the sacerdotes!"

Joaz stood silent. Another ten seconds passed. Carcolo cried angrily, "Come now, what do you say?"

In a hoarse voice Joaz spoke, "I say no truce. You rejected my warning, you thought to loot Banbeck Vale. I will show you no mercy."

Carcolo gaped, his mouth a red hole under the sweep of his mustaches. "But the Basics—"

"Return to your troops. You as well as the Basics are my enemy; why should I choose between you? Prepare to fight for your life; I give you no truce."

Carcolo drew back, face as pale as Joaz's own. "Never shall you rest! Even though you win this battle here on Starbreak Fell, yet you shall never know victory. I will persecute you until you cry for relief."

Banbeck motioned to his knights. "Whip this dog back to his own."

Carcolo backed his Spider from the threatening flails, turned, loped away.

The tide of battle had turned. The Banbeck Fiends now had broken past his Blue Horrors; one of his Juggers was gone; another, facing three sidling Fiends, snapped its great jaws, waved its monstrous sword. The Fiends flicked and feinted with their steel balls, scuttled forward. The Jugger chopped, shattered its sword on the rockhard armor of the Fiends; they were underneath, slamming their steel balls into the monstrous legs. It tried to hop clear, toppled majestically. The Fiends slit its belly, and now Carcolo had only five Juggers left.

"Back!" he cried. "Disengage!"

Up Barch Spike toiled his troops, the battle-front a roaring seethe of scales, armor, flickering metal. Luckily for Carcolo his rear was to the high ground, and after ten horrible minutes he was able to establish an orderly retreat. Two more Juggers had fallen; the three remaining scrambled free. Seizing boulders, they hurled them down into the attackers, who, after a series of sallies and lunges, were well content to break clear. In any event, Joaz, after hearing Carcolo's news, was of no disposition to spend further troops.

Carcolo, waving his sword in desperate defiance, led his troops back around Barch Spike, presently down across the dreary Skanse. Joaz turned back to Banbeck Vale. The news of the Basic raid had spread to all ears. The men rode sober and quiet, looking behind and overhead. Even the dragons seemed infected, and muttered restlessly among themselves.

As they crossed Blue Fell the almost omnipresent wind died; the stillness added to the oppression. Termagants, like the men, began to watch the sky. Joaz wondered, how could they know, how could they sense the Basics? He himself searched the sky, and as his army passed down over the scarp he thought to see, high over Mount Gethron, a flitting little black rectangle, which presently disappeared behind a crag.

CHAPTER IX

Ervis Carcolo and the remnants of his army raced pell-mell down from the Skanse, through the wilderness of ravines and gulches at the base of Mount Despoire, out on the barrens to the west of Happy Valley. All pretense of military precision had been abandoned. Carcolo led the way, his Spider sobbing with fatigue. Behind in disarray pounded first Murderers and Blue Horrors, with Termagants hurrying along behind, then the Fiends, racing low to the ground, steel balls grinding on rocks, sending up sparks. Far in the rear lumbered the Juggers and their attendants.

Down to the verge of Happy Valley plunged the army and pulled up short, stamping and squealing. Carcolo jumped from his Spider, ran to the brink, stood looking down into the valley.

He had expected to see the ship, yet the actuality of the thing was so immediate and intense as to shock him. It was a tapered cylinder, glossy and black, resting in a field of legumes not far from ramshackle Happy Town. Polished metal disks at either end shimmered and glistened with fleeting films of color. There were three entrance ports: forward, central and aft, and from the central port a ramp had been extended to the ground.

The Basics had worked with ferocious efficiency. From the town straggled a line of people, herded by Heavy Troopers. Approaching the ship they passed through an inspection apparatus controlled by a pair of Basics. A series of instruments and the eyes of the Basics appraised each man, woman and child, classified them by some system not instantly obvious, whereupon the captives were either hustled up the ramp into the ship or prodded into a nearby booth. Peculiarly, no matter how many persons entered, the booth never seemed to fill.

Carcolo rubbed his forehead with trembling fingers, turned his eyes to the ground. When once more he looked up, Bast Givven stood beside him, and together they stared down into the valley.

From behind came a cry of alarm. Starting around, Carcolo saw a black rectangular flyer sliding silently down from above Mount Gethron. Waving his arms Carcolo ran for the rocks, bellowing orders to take cover. Dragons and men scuttled up the gulch. Overhead slid the flyer. A hatch opened, releasing a load of explosive pellets. They struck with a great rattling volley, and up into the air flew pebbles, rock splinters, fragments of bone, scales, skin and flesh. All who failed to reach cover were shredded. The Termagants fared relatively well. The Fiends, though battered and scraped, had all survived. Two of the Juggers had been blinded, and could fight no more till they had grown new eyes.

The flyer slid back once more. Several of the men fired their muskets—an act of apparently futile defiance—but the flyer was struck and damaged. It twisted, veered, soared up in a roaring curve, swooped over on its back, plunged toward the mountainside, crashed in a brilliant orange gush of fire. Carcolo shouted in maniac glee, jumped up and down, ran to the verge of the cliff, shook his fist at the ship below. He quickly quieted, to stand glum and shivering. Then, turning to the ragged cluster of men and dragons who once more had crept down from the gulch, Carcolo cried hoarsely, "What do you say? Shall we fight? Shall we charge down upon them?"

There was silence; Bast Givven replied in a colorless voice, "We are helpless. We can accomplish nothing. Why commit suicide?"

Carcolo turned away, heart too full for words. Givven spoke the obvious truth. They would either be killed or dragged aboard the ship; and then, on a world too strange for imagining, be put to uses too dismal to be borne. Carcolo clenched his fists, looked westward with bitter hatred. "Joaz Banbeck, you brought me to this! When I might yet have fought for my people you detained me!"

"The Basics were here already," said Givven with unwelcome rationality. "We could have done nothing since we had nothing to do with."

"We could have fought!" bellowed Carcolo. "We might have swept down the Crotch, come upon them with all force! A hundred warriors and four hundred dragons—are these to be despised?"

Bast Givven judged further argument to be pointless. He pointed. "They now examine our brooders."

Carcolo turned to look, gave a wild laugh. "They are astonished! They are awed! And well have they a right to be."

Givven agreed. "I imagine the sight of a Fiend or a Blue Horror—not to mention a Jugger—gives them pause for reflection."

Down in the valley the grim business had ended. The Heavy Troopers marched back into the ship; a pair of enormous men twelve feet high came forth, lifted the booth, carried it up the ramp into the ship. Carcolo and his men watched with protruding eyes. "Giants!"

Bast Givven chuckled dryly. "The Basics stare at our Juggers; we ponder their Giants."

The Basics presently returned to the ship. The ramp was drawn up, the ports closed. From a turret in the bow came a shaft of energy, touching each of the three brooders in succession, and each exploded with great eruption of black bricks.

Carcolo moaned softly under his breath, but said nothing.

The ship trembled, floated; Carcolo bellowed an order; men and dragons rushed for cover. Flattened behind boulders they watched the black cylinder rise from the valley, drift to the west. "They make for Banbeck Vale," said Bast Givven.

Carcolo laughed, a cackle of mirthless glee. Bast Givven looked at him sidelong. Had Ervis Carcolo become addled? He turned away. A matter of no great moment.

Carcolo came to a sudden resolve. He stalked to one of the Spiders, mounted, swung around to face his men. "I ride to Banbeck Vale. Joaz Banbeck has done his best to despoil me; I shall do my best against him. I give no orders: come or stay as you wish. Only remember! Joaz Banbeck would not allow us to fight the Basics!"

He rode off. The men stared into the plundered valley, turned to look after Carcolo. The black ship was just now slipping over Mount Despoire. There was nothing for them in the valley. Grumbling and muttering they summoned the bone-tired dragons, set off up the dreary mountainside.

❋

Ervis Carcolo rode his Spider at a plunging run across the Skanse. Tremendous crags soared to either side, the blazing sun hung halfway up the black sky. Behind, the Skanse Ramparts; ahead, Barchback, Barch Spike and Northguard Ridge. Oblivious to the fatigue of his Spider,

Carcolo whipped it on; gray-green moss pounded back from its wild feet, the narrow head hung low, foam trailed from its gill-vents. Carcolo cared nothing; his mind was empty of all but hate—for the Basics, for Joaz Banbeck, for Aerlith, for man, for human history.

Approaching Northguard the Spider staggered and fell. It lay moaning, neck outstretched, legs trailing back. Carcolo dismounted in disgust, looked back down the long rolling slope of the Skanse to see how many of his troops had followed him. A man riding a Spider at a modest lope turned out to be Bast Givven, who presently came up beside him, inspected the fallen Spider. "Loosen the surcingle; he will recover the sooner."

Carcolo glared, thinking to hear a new note in Givven's voice. Nevertheless he bent over the foundered dragon, slipped loose the broad bronze buckle. Givven dismounted, stretched his arms, massaged his thin legs. He pointed. "The Basic ship descends into Banbeck Vale."

Carcolo nodded grimly. "I would be an audience to the landing." He kicked the Spider. "Come, get up, have you not rested enough? Do you wish me to walk?"

The Spider whimpered its fatigue, but nevertheless struggled to its feet. Carcolo started to mount, but Bast Givven laid a restraining hand on his shoulder. Carcolo looked back in outrage; here was impertinence! Givven said calmly, "Tighten the surcingle, otherwise you will fall on the rocks, and once more break your bones."

Uttering a spiteful phrase under his breath, Carcolo clasped the buckle back into position, the Spider crying out in despair. Paying no heed, Carcolo mounted, and the Spider moved off with trembling steps.

Barch Spike rose ahead like the prow of a white ship, dividing Northguard Ridge from Barchback. Carcolo paused to consider the landscape, tugging his mustaches.

Givven was tactfully silent. Carcolo looked back down the Skanse to the listless straggle of his army, set off to the left.

Passing close under Mount Gethron, skirting the High Jambles, they descended an ancient watercourse to Banbeck Verge. Though perforce they had come without great speed, the Basic ship had moved no faster and had only started to settle into the vale, the disks at bow and stern swirling with furious colors.

Carcolo grunted bitterly. "Trust Joaz Banbeck to scratch his own itch. Not a soul in sight! He's taken to his tunnels, dragons and all." Pursing his mouth he rendered a mincing parody of Joaz's voice: "'Ervis Carcolo, my dear friend, there is but one answer to attack: dig tunnels!'

And I replied to him, 'Am I a sacerdote to live underground? Burrow and delve, Joaz Banbeck, do as you will, I am but an old-time man; I go under the cliffs only when I must.'"

Givven gave the faintest of shrugs.

Carcolo went on, "Tunnels or not, they'll winkle him out. If need be they'll blast open the entire valley. They've no lack of tricks."

Givven grinned sardonically. "Joaz Banbeck knows a trick or two— as we know to our sorrow."

"Let him capture two dozen Basics today," snapped Carcolo. "Then I'll concede him a clever man." He stalked away to the very brink of the cliff, standing in full view of the Basic ship. Givven watched without expression.

Carcolo pointed. "Aha! Look there!"

"Not I," said Givven. "I respect the Basic weapons too greatly."

"Pah!" spat Carcolo. Nevertheless he moved a trifle back from the brink. "There are dragons in Kergan's Way. For all Joaz Banbeck's talk of tunnels." He gazed north along the valley a moment or two, then threw up his hands in frustration. "Joaz Banbeck will not come up here to me; there is nothing I can do. Unless I walk down into the village, seek him out and strike him down, he will escape me."

"Unless the Basics captured the two of you and confined you in the same pen," said Givven.

"Bah!" muttered Carcolo, and moved off to one side.

CHAPTER X

The vision-plates which allowed Joaz Banbeck to observe the length and breadth of Banbeck Vale for the first time were being put to practical use. He had evolved the scheme while playing with a set of old lenses, and dismissed it as quickly. Then one day, while trading with the sacerdotes in the cavern under Mount Gethron, he had proposed that they design and supply the optics for such a system.

The blind old sacerdote who conducted the trading gave an ambiguous reply: the possibility of such a project, under certain circumstances, might well deserve consideration. Three months passed; the scheme receded to the back of Joaz Banbeck's mind. Then the sacerdote in the trading-cave inquired if Joaz still planned to install the viewing system; if so he might take immediate delivery of the optics. Joaz agreed to the barter price, returned to Banbeck Vale with four heavy crates. He ordered the necessary tunnels driven, installed the lenses, and found that with the study darkened he could command all quarters of Banbeck Vale.

Now, with the Basic ship darkening the sky, Joaz Banbeck stood in his study, watching the descent of the great black hulk.

At the back of the chamber maroon portieres parted. Clutching the cloth with taut fingers stood the minstrel-maiden Phade. Her face was pale, her eyes bright as opals. In a husky voice she called, "The ship of death; it has come to gather souls!"

Joaz turned her a stony glance, turned back to the honed-glass screen. "The ship is clearly visible."

Phade ran forward, clasped Joaz's arm, swung around to look into his face. "Let us try to escape! Into the mountains, the High Jambles; don't let them take us so soon!"

"No one deters you," said Joaz indifferently. "Escape in any direction you choose."

Phade stared at him blankly, then turned her head and watched the screen. The great black ship sank with sinister deliberation, the disks at bow and stern now shimmering mother-of-pearl. Phade looked back to Joaz, licked her lips. "Are you not afraid?"

Joaz smiled thinly. "What good to run? Their Trackers are swifter than Murderers, more vicious than Termagants. They can smell you a mile away, take you from the very center of the Jambles."

Phade shivered with superstitious horror. She whispered, "Let them take me dead, then; I can't go with them alive."

Joaz suddenly cursed. "Look where they land! In our best field of bellegarde!"

"What is the difference?"

"'Difference'? Must we stop eating because they pay their visit?"

Phade looked at him in a daze, beyond comprehension. She sank slowly to her knees and began to perform the ritual gestures of the Theurgic cult: hands palm down to either side, slowly up till the back of the hand touched the ears, and the simultaneous protrusion of the tongue; over and over again, eyes staring with hypnotic intensity into emptiness.

Joaz ignored the gesticulations, until Phade, her face screwed up into a fantastic mask, began to sigh and whimper; then he swung the flaps of his jacket into her face. "Give over your folly!"

Phade collapsed moaning to the floor; Joaz's lips twitched in annoyance. Impatiently he hoisted her erect. "Look you, these Basics are neither ghouls nor angels of death; they are no more than pallid Termagants, the basic stock of our dragons. So now, give over your idiocy, or I'll have Rife take you away."

"Why do you not make ready? You watch and do nothing."

"There is nothing more that I can do."

Phade drew a deep shuddering sigh, stared dully at the screen. "Will you fight them?"

"Naturally."

"How can you hope to counter such miraculous power?"

"We will do what we can. They have not yet met our dragons."

The ship came to rest in a purple and green vine-field across the valley, near the mouth of Clybourne Crevasse. The port slid back, a ramp rolled forth. "Look," said Joaz, "there you see them."

Phade stared at the queer pale shapes who had come tentatively out on the ramp. "They seem strange and twisted, like silver puzzles for children."

"They are the Basics. From their eggs came our dragons. They have done as well with men: look, here are their Heavy Troops."

Down the ramp, four abreast, in exact cadence, marched the Heavy Troops, to halt fifty yards in front of the ship. There were three squads of twenty: short men with massive shoulders, thick necks, stern down-drawn faces. They wore armor fashioned from overlapping scales of black and blue metal, a wide belt slung with pistol and sword. Black epaulettes extending past their shoulders supported a short ceremonial flap of black cloth ranging down their backs; their helmets bore a crest of sharp spikes, their knee-high boots were armed with kick-knives.

A number of Basics now rode forth. Their mounts, creatures only remotely resembling men, ran on hands and feet, backs high off the ground. Their heads were long and hairless, with quivering loose lips. The Basics controlled them with negligent touches of a quirt, and once on the ground set them cantering smartly through the bellegarde. Meanwhile a team of Heavy Troopers rolled a three-wheeled mechanism down the ramp, directed its complex snout toward the village.

"Never before have they prepared so carefully," muttered Joaz. "Here come the Trackers." He counted. "Only two dozen? Perhaps they are hard to breed. Generations pass slowly with men; dragons lay a clutch of eggs every year..."

The Trackers moved to the side and stood in a loose restless group: gaunt creatures seven feet tall, with bulging black eyes, beaked noses, small undershot mouths pursed as if for kissing. From narrow shoulders long arms dangled and swung like ropes. As they waited they flexed their knees, staring sharply up and down the valley, in constant restless motion. After them came a group of Weaponeers—unmodified men wearing loose cloth smocks and cloth hats of green and yellow. They brought with them two more three-wheeled contrivances which they at once began to adjust and test.

The entire group became still and tense. The Heavy Troopers stepped forward with a stumping, heavy-legged gait, hands ready at pistols and swords. "Here they come," said Joaz. Phade made a quiet desperate sound, knelt, once more began to perform Theurgic gesticulations. Joaz in disgust ordered her from the study, went to a panel equipped with a bank of six direct-wire communications, the construction of which he had personally supervised. He spoke into three of the telephones, assuring himself that his defenses were alert, then returned to the honed-glass screens.

Across the field of bellegarde came the Heavy Troopers, faces heavy, hard, marked with down-veering creases. Upon either flank the Weaponeers trundled their three-wheeled mechanisms, but the Trackers waited beside the ship. About a dozen Basics rode behind the Heavy Troopers, carrying bulbous weapons on their backs.

A hundred yards from the portal into Kergan's Way, beyond the range of the Banbeck muskets, the invaders halted. A Heavy Trooper ran to one of the Weaponeers' carts, thrust his shoulders under a harness, stood erect. He now carried a gray machine, from which extended a pair of black globes. The Trooper scuttled toward the village like an enormous rat, while from the black globes streamed a flux, intended to interfere with the neural currents of the Banbeck defenders, and so immobilize them.

Explosions sounded, puffs of smoke appeared from nooks and vantages through the crags. Bullets spat into the ground beside the Trooper, several caromed off his armor. At once heat-beams from the ship stabbed against the cliff walls. In his study Joaz Banbeck smiled. The smoke puffs were decoys, the actual shots came from other areas. The Trooper, dodging and jerking, avoided a rain of bullets, ran under the portal, above which two men waited. Affected by the flux, they tottered, stiffened, but nevertheless, they dropped a great stone which struck the

Trooper where the neck joined his shoulders, hurled him to the ground. He thrashed his arms and legs up and down, rolled over and over; then bouncing to his feet, he raced back into the valley, soaring and bounding, finally to stumble, plunge headlong to the ground and lay kicking and quivering.

The Basic army watched with no apparent concern or interest.

There was a moment of inactivity. Then from the ship came an invisible field of vibration, traveling across the face of the cliff. Where the focus struck, puffs of dust arose and loose rock became dislodged. A man, lying on a ledge, sprang to his feet, dancing and twisting, plunged two hundred feet to his death. Passing across one of Joaz Banbeck's spy-holes, the vibration was carried into the study where it set up a nerve-grinding howl. The vibration passed along the cliff; Joaz rubbed his aching head.

Meanwhile the Weaponeers discharged one of their instruments: first there came a muffled explosion, then through the air curved a wobbling gray sphere. Inaccurately aimed, it struck the cliff and burst in a great gush of yellow-white gas. The mechanism exploded once more, and this time lobbed the bomb accurately into Kergan's Way— which was now deserted. The bomb produced no effect.

In his study Joaz waited grimly. To now the Basics had taken only tentative, almost playful, steps; more serious efforts would surely follow.

Wind dispersed the gas; the situation remained as before. The casualties so far had been one Heavy Trooper and one Banbeck rifleman.

From the ship now came a stab of red flame, harsh, decisive. The rock at the portal shattered; slivers sang and spun; the Heavy Troopers jogged forward. Joaz spoke into his telephone, bidding his captains caution, lest counter-attacking against a feint, they expose themselves to a new gas bomb.

But the Heavy Troopers stormed into Kergan's Way—in Joaz's mind an act of contemptuous recklessness. He gave a curt order; out from passages and areas swarmed his dragons: Blue Horrors, Fiends, Termagants.

The squat Troopers stared with sagging jaws. Here were unexpected antagonists! Kergan's Way resounded with their calls and orders. First they fell back, then, with the courage of desperation, fought furiously. Up and down Kergan's Way raged the battle. Certain relationships quickly became evident. In the narrow defile neither the Trooper pistols nor the steel-weighted tails of the Fiends could be used effectively. Cutlasses were useless against dragon-scale, but the pincers of the Blue Horrors, the

Termagant daggers, the axes, swords, fangs and claws of the Fiends, did bloody work against the Heavy Troopers. A single Trooper and a single Termagant were approximately a match; though the Trooper, gripping the dragon with massive arms, tearing away its brachs, breaking back its neck, won more often than the Termagant. But if two or three Termagants confronted a single Trooper, he was doomed. As soon as he committed himself to one, another would crush his legs, blind him or hack open his throat.

So the Troopers fell back to the valley floor, leaving twenty of their fellows dead in Kergan's Way. The Banbeck men once more opened fire, but once more with minor effect.

Joaz watched from his study, wondering as to the next Basic tactic. Enlightenment was not long in coming. The Heavy Troopers regrouped, stood panting, while the Basics rode back and forth receiving information, admonishing, advising, chiding.

From the black ship came a gush of energy, to strike the cliff above Kergan's Way; the study rocked with the concussion.

Joaz backed away from the vision-plates. What if a ray struck one of his collecting lenses? Might not the energy be guided and reflected directly toward him? He departed his study as it shook to a new explosion.

He ran through a passage, descended a staircase, emerged into one of the central galleries, to find apparent confusion. White-faced women and children, retiring deeper into the mountain, pushed past dragons and men in battle-gear entering one of the new tunnels. Joaz watched for a moment or two to satisfy himself that the confusion held nothing of panic, then joined his warriors in the tunnel leading north.

In some past era an entire section of the cliff at the head of the valley had sloughed off, creating a jungle of piled rock and boulders: the Banbeck Jambles. Here, through a fissure, the new tunnel opened; and here Joaz went with his warriors. Behind them, down the valley, sounded the rumble of explosions as the black ship began to demolish Banbeck Village.

Joaz, peering around a boulder, watched in a fury, as great slabs of rock began to scale away from the cliff. Then he stared in astonishment, for to the Basic troops had come an extraordinary reinforcement: eight Giants twice an ordinary man's stature—barrel-chested monsters, gnarled of arm and leg, with pale eyes, shocks of tawny hair. They wore brown and red armor with black epaulettes, and carried swords, maces and blast-cannon slung over their backs.

Joaz considered. The presence of the Giants gave him no reason to alter his central strategy, which in any event was vague and intuitive. He must be prepared to suffer losses, and could only hope to inflict greater losses on the Basics. But what did they care for the lives of their troops? Less than he cared for his dragons. And if they destroyed Banbeck Village, ruined the Vale, how could he do corresponding damage to them?

He looked over his shoulder at the tall white cliffs, wondering how closely he had estimated the position of the sacerdotes' hall. And now he must act; the time had come. He signaled to a small boy, one of his own sons, who took a deep breath, hurled himself blindly away from the shelter of the rocks, ran helter-skelter out to the valley floor. A moment later his mother ran forth to snatch him up and dash back into the Jambles.

"Done well," Joaz commended them. "Done well indeed." Cautiously he again looked forth through the rocks. The Basics were gazing intently in his direction.

For a long moment, while Joaz tingled with suspense, it seemed that they had ignored his ploy. They conferred, came to a decision, flicked the leathery buttocks of their mounts with their quirts. The creatures pranced sidewise, then loped north up the valley. The Trackers fell in behind, then came the Heavy Troopers moving at a humping quick-step. The Weaponeers followed with their three-wheeled mechanisms, and ponderously at the rear came the eight Giants. Across the fields of bellegarde and vetch, over vines, hedges, beds of berries and stands of oil-pod tramped the raiders, destroying with a certain morose satisfaction.

The Basics prudently halted before the Banbeck Jambles while the Trackers ran ahead like dogs, clambering over the first boulders, rearing high to test the air for odor, peering, listening, pointing, twittering doubtfully to each other. The Heavy Troopers moved in carefully, and their near presence spurred on the Trackers. Abandoning caution they bounded into the heart of the Jambles, emitting squeals of horrified consternation when a dozen Blue Horrors dropped among them. They clawed out heat-guns, in their excitement burning friend and foe alike. With silken ferocity the Blue Horrors ripped them apart. Screaming for aid, kicking, flailing, thrashing, those who were able fled as precipitously as they had come. Only twelve from the original twenty-four regained the valley floor; and even as they did so, even as they cried out in relief at winning free from death, a squad of Long-horned Murderers burst out upon them, and these surviving Trackers were knocked down, gored, hacked.

The Heavy Troopers charged forward with hoarse calls of rage, aiming pistols, swinging swords; but the Murderers retreated to the shelter of the boulders.

Within the Jambles the Banbeck men had appropriated the heat-guns dropped by the Trackers, and warily coming forward, tried to burn the Basics. But, unfamiliar with the weapons, the men neglected either to focus or condense the flame and the Basics, no more than mildly singed, hastily whipped their mounts back out of range. The Heavy Troopers, halting not a hundred feet in front of the Jambles, sent in a volley of explosive pellets, which killed two of the Banbeck knights and forced the others back.

At a discreet distance the Basics appraised the situation. The Weaponeers came up and while awaiting instructions, conferred in low tones with the mounts. One of these Weaponeers was now summoned and given orders. He divested himself of all his weapons and holding his empty hands in the air marched forward to the edge of the Jambles. Choosing a gap between a pair of ten-foot boulders, he resolutely entered the rock-maze.

A Banbeck knight escorted him to Joaz. Here, by chance, were also half a dozen Termagants. The Weaponeer paused uncertainly, made a mental readjustment, approached the Termagants. Bowing respectfully he started to speak. The Termagants listened without interest, and presently one of the knights directed him to Joaz.

"Dragons do not rule men on Aerlith," said Joaz dryly. "What is your message?"

The Weaponeer looked dubiously toward the Termagants, then somberly back to Joaz. "You are authorized to act for the entire warren?" He spoke slowly in a dry bland voice, selecting his words with conscientious care.

Joaz repeated shortly, "What is your message?"

"I bring an integration from my masters."

"'Integration'? I do not understand you."

"An integration of the instantaneous vectors of destiny. An interpretation of the future. They wish the sense conveyed to you in the following terms: 'Do not waste lives, both ours and your own. You are valuable to us and will be given treatment in accordance with this value. Surrender to the Rule. Cease the wasteful destruction of enterprise.'"

Joaz frowned. "'Destruction of enterprise'?"

"The reference is to the content of your genes. The message is at its end. I advise you to accede. Why waste your blood, why destroy yourselves? Come forth now with me; all will be for the best."

Joaz gave a brittle laugh. "You are a slave. How can you judge what is best for us?"

The Weaponeer blinked. "What choice is there for you? All residual pockets of disorganized life are to be expunged. The way of facility is best." He inclined his head respectfully toward the Termagants. "If you doubt me, consult your own Revered Ones. They will advise you."

"There are no Revered Ones here," said Joaz. "The dragons fight with us and for us; they are our fellow-warriors. But I have an alternate proposal. Why do not you and your fellows join us? Throw off your slavery, become free men! We will take the ship and go searching for the old worlds of men."

The Weaponeer exhibited only polite interest. "'Worlds of men'? There are none of them. A few residuals such as yourself remain in the desolate regions. All are to be expunged. Would you not prefer to serve the Rule?"

"Would you not prefer to be a free man?"

The Weaponeer's face showed mild bewilderment. "You do not understand me. If you choose—"

"Listen carefully," said Joaz. "You and your fellows can be your own masters, live among other men."

The Weaponeer frowned. "Who would wish to be a wild savage? To whom would we look for law, control, direction, order?"

Joaz threw up his hands in disgust, but made one last attempt. "I will provide all these; I will undertake such a responsibility. Go back, kill all the Basics—the Revered Ones, as you call them. These are my first orders."

"Kill them?" The Weaponeer's voice was soft with horror.

"Kill them." Joaz spoke as if to a child. "Then we men will possess the ship. We will go to find the worlds where men are powerful—"

"There are no such worlds."

"Ah, but there must be! At one time men roamed every star in the sky."

"No longer."

"What of Eden?"

"I know nothing of it."

Joaz threw up his hands. "Will you join us?"

"What would be the meaning of such an act?" said the Weaponeer gently. "Come then, lay down your arms, submit to the Rule." He glanced doubtfully toward the Termagants. "Your own Revered Ones will receive fitting treatment, have no fear on this account."

"You fool! These 'Revered Ones' are slaves, just as you are a slave to the Basics! We breed them to serve us, just as you are bred! Have at least the grace to recognize your own degradation!"

The Weaponeer blinked. "You speak in terms I do not completely understand. You will not surrender then?"

"No. We will kill all of you, if our strength holds out."

The Weaponeer bowed, turned, departed through the rocks. Joaz followed, peered out over the valley floor.

The Weaponeer made his report to the Basics, who listened with characteristic detachment. They gave an order, and the Heavy Troopers, spreading out in a skirmish line, moved slowly in toward the rocks. Behind lumbered the Giants, blasters slung forward at the ready, and about twenty Trackers, survivors of the first foray. The Heavy Troopers reached the rocks, peered in. The Trackers clambered above, searching for ambushes, and finding none, signaled back. With great caution the Heavy Troopers entered the Jambles, necessarily breaking formation. Twenty feet they advanced, fifty feet, a hundred feet. Emboldened, the vengeful Trackers sprang forward over the rocks and up surged the Termagants.

Screaming and cursing, the Trackers scrambled back pursued by the dragons. The Heavy Troopers recoiled, then swung up their weapons, fired. Two Termagants were struck under the lower armpits, their most vulnerable spot. Floundering, they tumbled down among the rocks. Others, maddened, jumped squarely down upon the Troopers. There was roaring, squealing, cries of shock and pain. The Giants lumbered up, and grinning vastly plucked away the Termagants, wrenched off their heads, flung them high over the rocks. Those Termagants who were able scuttled back, leaving half a dozen Heavy Troopers wounded, two with their throats torn open.

Again the Heavy Troopers moved forward, with the Trackers reconnoitering above, but more warily. The Trackers froze, yelled a warning. The Heavy Troopers stopped short, calling to each other, swinging their guns nervously. Overhead the Trackers scrambled back, and through the rocks, over the rocks, came dozens of Fiends and Blue Horrors. The Heavy Troopers, grimacing dourly, fired their pistols; and the air reeked with the stench of burning scale, exploded viscera. The dragons surged in upon the men, and now began a terrible battle among the rocks, with the pistols, the maces, even the swords useless for lack of room. The Giants lumbered forward and in turn were attacked by Fiends. Astonished, the idiotic grins faded from their faces; they hopped awkwardly back from the steel-weighted tails, but among the rocks the Fiends were also at a disadvantage, their steel balls clattering and jarring away from rock more often than flesh.

The Giants, recovering, discharged their chest-projectors into the mêlée; Fiends were torn apart as well as Blue Horrors and Heavy Troopers, the Giants making no distinction.

Over the rocks came another wave of dragons: Blue Horrors. They slid down on the heads of the Giants, clawing, stabbing, tearing. In a frenzy the Giants tore at the creatures, flung them to the ground, stamped on them, and the Heavy Troopers burnt them with their pistols.

From nowhere, for no reason, there came a lull. Ten seconds, fifteen seconds passed, with no sound but whimpering and moaning from wounded dragons and men. A sense of imminence weighted the air, and here came the Juggers, looming through the passages. For a brief period Giants and Juggers looked each other face to face. Then Giants groped for their blast-projectors, while Blue Horrors sprang down once more, grappling the Giant arms. The Juggers stumped quickly forward. Dragon brachs grappled Giant arms; bludgeons and maces swung, dragon armor and man armor crushed and ground apart. Man and dragon tumbled over and over, ignoring pain, shock, mutilation.

The struggle became quiet; sobbing and wheezing replaced the roars, and presently eight Juggers, superior in mass and natural armament, staggered away from eight destroyed Giants.

The Troopers meanwhile had drawn together, standing back to back in clots. Step by step, burning with heat-beams the screaming Horrors, Termagants and Fiends who lunged after them, they retreated toward the valley floor, and finally won free of the rocks. The pursuing Fiends, anxious to fight in the open, sprang into their midst, while from the flanks came Long-horned Murderers and Striding Murderers. In a spirit of reckless jubilation, a dozen men riding Spiders, carrying blast-cannon taken from the fallen Giants, charged the Basics and

Weaponeers, who waited beside the rather casual emplacement of three-wheeled weapons. The Basics, without shame, jerked their man-mounts around and fled toward the black ship. The Weaponeers swiveled their mechanisms, aimed, discharged bursts of energy. One man fell, two men, three men—then the others were among the Weaponeers, who were soon hacked to pieces...including the one who had served as envoy.

Several of the men, whooping and hooting, set out in chase of the Basics, but the human mounts, springing along like monstrous rabbits, carried the Basics as fast as the Spiders carried the men. From the Jambles came a horn signal; the mounted men halted, wheeled back; the entire Banbeck force turned and retreated full speed into the Jambles.

The Troopers stumbled a few defiant steps in pursuit, then halted in sheer fatigue. Of the original three squads, not enough men to make up a single squad survived. The eight Giants had perished, all Weaponeers and almost the entire group of Trackers.

The Banbeck forces gained the Jambles with seconds only to spare. From the black ship came a volley of explosive pellets, to shatter the rocks at the spot where they had disappeared.

CHAPTER XI

On a wind-polished cape of rock above Banbeck Vale Ervis Carcolo and Bast Givven had watched the battle. The rocks hid the greater part of the fighting; the cries and clangor rose faint and tinny, like insect noise. There would be the glint of dragon scale, glimpses of running men, the shadow and flicker of movement, but not until the mangled forces of the Basics staggered forth did the outcome of the battle reveal itself. Carcolo shook his head in sour bewilderment. "The crafty devil, Joaz Banbeck! He's turned them back, he's slaughtered their best!"

"It would appear," said Bast Givven, "that dragons armed with fangs, swords and steel balls are more effective than men with guns and heat-beams—at least in close quarters."

Carcolo grunted. "I might have done as well myself, under like circumstances." He turned Bast Givven a waspish glance. "Do you not agree?"

"Certainly. Beyond all question."

"Of course," Carcolo went on, "I had not the advantage of preparation. The Basics surprised me, but Joaz Banbeck labored under no such handicap." He looked back down into Banbeck Vale, where the Basic ship was bombarding the Jambles, shattering rocks into splinters. "Do they plan to blast the Jambles out of the valley? In which case, of course, Joaz Banbeck would have no further refuge. Their strategy is clear. And as I suspected: reserve forces!"

Another thirty Troopers had marched down the ramp to stand immobile in the trampled field before the ship.

Carcolo pounded his fist into his palm. "Bast Givven, listen now, listen carefully! For it is in our power to do a great deed, to reverse our fortunes! Notice Clybourne Crevasse, how it opens into the Vale, directly behind the Basic ship."

"Your ambition will yet cost us our lives."

Carcolo laughed. "Come, Givven, how many times does a man die? What better way to lose a life than in the pursuit of glory?"

Bast Givven turned, surveyed the meager remnants of the Happy Valley army. "We could win glory by trouncing a dozen sacerdotes. Flinging ourselves upon a Basic ship is hardly needful."

"Nevertheless," said Ervis Carcolo, "that is how it must be. I ride ahead, you marshal the forces and follow. We meet at the head of Clybourne Crevasse, on the west edge of the Vale!"

CHAPTER XII

Stamping his feet, muttering nervous curses, Ervis Carcolo waited at the head of Clybourne Crevasse. Unlucky chance after chance paraded before his imagination. The Basics might surrender to the difficulties of Banbeck Vale and depart. Joaz Banbeck might attack across the open fields to save Banbeck Village from destruction and so destroy himself. Bast Givven might be unable to control the disheartened men and mutinous dragons of Happy Valley. Any of these situations might occur; any would expunge Carcolo's dreams of glory and leave him a broken man. Back and forth he paced the scarred granite; every few seconds he peered down into Banbeck Vale; every few seconds he turned to scan the bleak skylines for the dark shapes of his dragons, the taller silhouettes of his men.

Beside the Basic ship waited a scanty two squads of Heavy Troopers: those who had survived the original attack and the reserves. They squatted in silent groups, watching the leisurely destruction of

Banbeck Village. Fragment by fragment, the spires, towers and cliffs which had housed the Banbeck folk cracked off, slumped down into an ever-growing mound of rubble. An even heavier barrage poured against the Jambles. Boulders broke like eggs; rock splinters drifted down the valley.

A half hour passed. Ervis Carcolo seated himself glumly on a rock.

A jingle, the pad of feet. Carcolo bounded to his feet. Winding across the skyline came the sorry remnants of his forces, the men dispirited, the Termagants surly and petulant, a mere handful each of Fiends, Blue Horrors and Murderers.

Carcolo's shoulders sagged. What could be accomplished with a force so futile as this? He took a deep breath. Show a brave front! Never say die! He assumed his bluffest mien. Stepping forward, he cried out, "Men, dragons! Today we have known defeat, but the day is not over. The time of redemption is at hand; we shall revenge ourselves on both the Basics and Joaz Banbeck!"

He searched the faces of his men, hoping for enthusiasm. They looked back at him without interest. The dragons, their understanding less complete, snorted softly, hissed and whispered. "Men and dragons!" bawled Carcolo. "You ask me, how shall we achieve these glories? I answer, follow where I lead! Fight where I fight! What is death to us, with our valley despoiled?"

Again he inspected his troops, once more finding only listlessness and apathy. Carcolo stifled the roar of frustration which rose into his throat, and turned away. "Advance!" he called gruffly over his shoulder. Mounting his drooping Spider, he set off down Clybourne Crevasse.

The Basic ship pounded the Jambles and Banbeck Village with equal vehemence. From a vantage on the west rim of the valley Joaz Banbeck watched the blasting of corridor after familiar corridor. Apartments and halls hewn earnestly from the rock, carved, tooled, polished across the generations—all opened, destroyed, pulverized. Now the target became that spire which contained Joaz Banbeck's private apartments, with his study, his workroom, the Banbeck reliquarium.

Joaz clenched and unclenched his fists, furious at his own helplessness. The goal of the Basics was clear. They intended to destroy Banbeck Vale, to exterminate as completely as possible the men of Aerlith—and what could prevent them? Joaz studied the Jambles. The old talus had been splintered away almost to the sheer face of the cliff. Where was the opening into the Great Hall of the sacerdotes? His farfetched hypotheses were diminishing to futility. Another hour would see the utter devastation of Banbeck Village.

Joaz tried to control a sickening sense of frustration. How to stop the destruction? He forced himself to calculate. Clearly, an attack across the valley floor was equivalent to suicide. But behind the black ship opened a ravine similar to that in which Joaz stood concealed: Clybourne Crevasse. The ship's entry gaped wide, Heavy Troopers squatted listlessly to the side. Joaz shook his head with a sour grimace. Inconceivable that the Basics could neglect so obvious a threat.

Still—in their arrogance might they not overlook the possibility of so insolent an act?

Indecision tugged Joaz forward and backward. And now a barrage of explosive pellets split open the spire which housed his apartments. The reliquarium, the ancient trove of the Banbecks, was about to be destroyed. Joaz made a blind gesture, jumped to his feet, called the closest of his dragon masters. "Assemble the Murderers, three squads of Termagants, two dozen Blue Horrors, ten Fiends, all the riders. We climb to Banbeck Verge, we descend Clybourne Crevasse, we attack the ship!"

The dragon master departed; Joaz gave himself to gloomy contemplation. If the Basics intended to draw him into a trap, they were about to succeed.

The dragon master returned. "The force is assembled."

"We ride."

Up the ravine surged men and dragons, emerging upon Banbeck Verge. Swinging south, they came to the head of Clybourne Crevasse.

A knight at the head of the column suddenly signaled a halt. When Joaz approached he pointed out marks on the floor of the crevasse. "Dragons and men have passed here recently."

Joaz studied the tracks. "Heading down the crevasse."

"Yes."

Joaz dispatched a party of scouts who presently came galloping wildly back. "Ervis Carcolo, with men and dragons, is attacking the ship!"

Joaz wheeled his Spider, plunged headlong down the dim passage, followed by his army.

Outcries and screams of battle reached their ears as they approached the mouth of the crevasse. Bursting out on the valley floor Joaz came upon a scene of desperate carnage, with dragon and Heavy Trooper hacking, stabbing, burning, blasting. Where was Ervis Carcolo? Joaz recklessly rode to look into the entry port which hung wide. Ervis Carcolo then had forced his way into the ship! A trap? Or had he effectuated Joaz's own plan of seizing the ship? What of the Heavy Troopers? Would the Basics sacrifice forty warriors to capture a handful of men? Unreasonable—but now the Heavy Troopers were holding their own. They had formed a phalanx, they now concentrated the energy of their weapons on those dragons who yet opposed them. A trap? If so, it was sprung—unless Ervis Carcolo already had captured the ship. Joaz rose in his saddle, signaled his company. "Attack!"

The Heavy Troopers were doomed. Striding Murderers hewed from above, Long-horned Murderers thrust from below, Blue Horrors pinched, clipped, dismembered. The battle was done, but Joaz, with men and Termagants, had already charged up the ramp. From within came the hum and throb of power, and also human sounds—cries, shouts of fury.

The sheer ponderous bulk struck at Joaz; he stopped short, peered uncertainly into the ship. Behind him his men waited, muttering under their breath. Joaz asked himself, "Am I as brave as Ervis Carcolo? What is bravery, in any case? I am completely afraid: I dare not enter, I dare not stay outside." He put aside all caution, rushed forward, followed by his men and a horde of scuttling Termagants.

Even as Joaz entered the ship he knew Ervis Carcolo had not succeeded; above him the guns still sang and hissed. Joaz's apartments splintered apart. Another tremendous volley struck into the Jambles, laying bare the naked stone of the cliff, and what was hitherto hidden: the edge of a tall opening.

Joaz, inside the ship, found himself in an antechamber. The inner port was closed. He sidled forward, peered through a rectangular pane into what seemed a lobby or staging chamber. Ervis Carcolo and his knights crouched against the far wall, casually guarded by about twenty Weaponeers. A group of Basics rested in an alcove to the side, relaxed, quiet, their attitude one of contemplation.

Carcolo and his men were not completely subdued; as Joaz watched Carcolo lunged furiously forward. A purple crackle of energy punished him, hurled him back against the wall.

From the alcove one of the Basics, staring across the inner chamber, took note of Joaz Banbeck; he flicked out with his brach, touched a rod. An alarm whistle sounded, the outer port slid shut. A trap? An emergency process? The result was the same. Joaz motioned to four men, heavily burdened. They came forward, kneeled, placed on the deck four of the blast cannon which the Giants had carried into the Jambles.

Joaz swung his arm. Cannon belched; metal creaked, melted; acrid odors permeated the room. The hole was still too small. "Again!" The cannon flamed; the inner port vanished. Into the gap sprang Weaponeers, firing their energy guns. Purple fire cut into the Banbeck ranks. Men curled, twisted, wilted, fell with clenched fingers and contorted faces. Before the cannon could respond, red-scaled shapes scuttled forward: Termagants. Hissing and wailing they swarmed over the Weaponeers, on into the staging chamber. In front of the alcove occupied by the Basics they stopped short, as if in astonishment. The men crowding after fell silent: even Carcolo watched in fascination. Basic stock confronted its derivative, each seeing in the other its caricature. The Termagants crept forward with sinister deliberation; the Basics waved their brachs, whistled, fluted. The Termagants scuttled forward, sprang into the alcove. There was a horrid tumbling and croaking; Joaz, sickened at some elementary level, was forced to look away. The struggle was soon over; there was silence in the alcove. Joaz turned to examine Ervis Carcolo, who stared back, rendered inarticulate by anger, humiliation, pain and fright.

Finally finding his voice Carcolo made an awkward gesture of menace and fury. "Be off with you," he croaked. "I claim this ship. Unless you would lie in your own blood, leave me to my conquest!"

Joaz snorted contemptuously, turned his back on Carcolo, who sucked in his breath, and with a whispered curse, lurched forward. Bast Givven seized him, drew him back. Carcolo struggled, Givven talked earnestly into his ear, and Carcolo at last relaxed, half-weeping.

Joaz meanwhile examined the chamber. The walls were blank, gray; the deck was covered with resilient black foam. There was no obvious illumination, but light was everywhere, exuding from the walls. The air chilled the skin, and smelled unpleasantly acrid: an odor which Joaz had not previously noticed. He coughed, his eardrums rang. A frightening suspicion became certainty; on heavy legs he lunged for the port, beckoning to his troops. "Outside, they poison us!" He stumbled out on the ramp, gulped fresh air; his men and Termagants followed, and then in a stumbling rush came Ervis Carcolo and his men. Under the hulk of the great ship the group stood gasping, tottering on limp legs, eyes dim and swimming.

Above them, oblivious or careless of their presence, the ship's guns sent forth another barrage. The spire housing Joaz's apartments tottered, collapsed; the Jambles were no more than a heap of rock splinters drifting into a high arched opening. Inside the opening Joaz glimpsed a dark shape, a glint, a shine, a structure—then he was distracted by an ominous sound at his back. From a port at the other end of the ship, a new force of Heavy Troopers had alighted—three new squads of twenty men each, accompanied by a dozen Weaponeers with four of the rolling projectors.

Joaz sagged back in dismay. He glanced along his troops; they were in no condition either to attack or defend. A single alternative remained: flight. "Make for Clybourne Crevasse," he called thickly.

Stumbling, lurching, the remnants of the two armies fled under the brow of the great black ship. Behind them Heavy Troopers swung smartly forward, but without haste.

Rounding the ship, Joaz stopped short. In the mouth of Clybourne Crevasse waited a fourth squad of Heavy Troopers, with another Weaponeer and his weapon.

Joaz looked to right and left, up and down the valley. Which way to run, where to turn? The Jambles? They were nonexistent. Motion, slow and ponderous in the opening, previously concealed by tumbled rock, caught his attention. A dark object moved forth; a shutter drew back, a bright disk glittered. Almost instantly a pencil of milky-blue radiance lanced at, into, through the end disk of the Basic ship.

Within, tortured machinery whined, simultaneously up and down the scale, to inaudibility at either end. The luster of the end disks vanished; they became gray, dull; the whisper of power and life previously pervading the ship gave way to dead quiet; the ship itself was dead, and its mass, suddenly unsupported, crushed groaning into the ground.

The Heavy Troopers gazed up in consternation at the hulk which had brought them to Aerlith. Joaz, taking advantage of their indecision, called, "Retreat! North—up the valley!"

The Heavy Troopers doggedly followed; the Weaponeers however cried out an order to halt. They emplaced their weapons, brought them to bear on the cavern behind the Jambles. Within the opening naked shapes moved with frantic haste; there was slow shifting of massive machinery, a change of lights and shadows, and the milky-blue shaft of radiance struck forth once more. It flicked down; Weaponeers, weapons, two-thirds of the Heavy Troopers vanished like moths in a furnace. The surviving Heavy Troopers halted, retreated uncertainly toward the ship.

In the mouth of Clybourne Crevasse waited the remaining squad of Heavy Troopers. The single Weaponeer crouched over his three-wheeled mechanism. With fateful care he made his adjustments; within the dark opening the naked sacerdotes worked furiously, thrusting, wedging, the strain of their sinews and hearts and minds communicating itself to every man in the valley. The shaft of milky-blue light sprang forth, but too soon: it melted the rock a hundred yards south of Clybourne Crevasse, and now from the Weaponeer's gun came a splash of orange and green flame. Seconds later the mouth of the sacerdotes' cavern erupted. Rocks, bodies, fragments of metal, glass, rubber arched through the air.

The sound of the explosion reverberated through the valley. And the dark object in the cavern was destroyed, was no more than tatters and shreds of metal.

Joaz took three deep breaths, throwing off the effects of the narcotic gas by sheer power of will. He signaled to his Murderers. "Charge! Kill!"

The Murderers loped forward; the Heavy Troopers threw themselves flat, aimed their weapons, but soon died. In the mouth of Clybourne Crevasse the final squad of Troopers charged wildly forth, to be instantly attacked by Termagants and Blue Horrors who had sidled along the face of the cliff. The Weaponeer was gored by a Murderer; there was no further resistance in the valley, and the ship lay open to attack.

Joaz led the way back up the ramp, through the entry into the now dim staging-chamber. The blast-cannon captured from the Giants lay where his men had dropped them.

Three portals led from the chamber, and these were swiftly burned down. The first revealed a spiral ramp; the second, a long empty hall lined with tiers of bunks; the third, a similar hall in which the bunks were occupied. Pale faces peered from the tiers, pallid hands flickered. Up and down the central corridor marched squat matrons in gray gowns. Ervis Carcolo rushed forward, buffeting the matrons to the deck, peering into the bunks. "Outside," he bellowed. "You are rescued, you are saved. Outside quickly, while there is opportunity."

But there was only meager resistance to overcome from a half-dozen Weaponeers and Trackers, none whatever from twenty

Mechanics—these, short thin men with sharp features and dark hair—and none from the sixteen remaining Basics. All were marched off the ship as prisoners.

CHAPTER XIII

Quiet filled the valley floor, the silence of exhaustion. Men and dragons sprawled in the trampled fields; the captives stood in a dejected huddle beside the ship. Occasionally an isolated sound came to emphasize the silence: the creak of cooling metal within the ship, the fall of a loose rock from the shattered cliffs; an occasional murmur from the liberated Happy Valley folk, who sat in a group apart from the surviving warriors.

Ervis Carcolo alone seemed restless. For a space he stood with his back to Joaz, slapping his thigh with his scabbard tassel. He contemplated the sky where Skene, a dazzling atom, hung close over the western cliffs, then turned, studied the shattered gap at the north of the valley, filled with the twisted remains of the sacerdotes' construction. He gave his thigh a final slap, looked toward Joaz Banbeck, turned to stalk through the huddle of Happy Valley folk, making brusque motions of no particular significance, pausing here and there to harangue or cajole, apparently attempting to instill spirit and purpose into his defeated people.

In this purpose he was unsuccessful. Presently he swung sharply about, marched across the field to where Joaz Banbeck lay outstretched. Carcolo stared down. "Well then," he said bluffly, "the battle is over, the ship is won."

Joaz raised himself up on one elbow. "True."

"Let us have no misunderstanding on one point," said Carcolo. "Ship and contents are mine. An ancient rule defines the rights of him who is first to attack. On this rule I base my claim."

Joaz looked up in surprise, and seemed almost amused. "By a rule even more ancient, I have already assumed possession."

"I dispute this assertion," said Carcolo hotly. "Who—"

Joaz held up his hand wearily. "Silence, Carcolo! You are alive now only because I am sick of blood and violence. Do not test my patience!"

Carcolo turned away, twitching his scabbard tassel with restrained fury. He looked up the valley, turned back to Joaz. "Here come the sacerdotes, who in fact demolished the ship. I remind you of my proposal, by which we might have prevented this destruction and slaughter."

Joaz smiled. "You made your proposal only two days ago. Further, the sacerdotes possess no weapons."

Carcolo stared as if Joaz had taken leave of his wits. "How then did they destroy the ship?"

Joaz shrugged. "I can only make conjectures."

Carcolo asked sarcastically, "And what direction do these conjectures lead?"

"I wonder if they had constructed the frame of a spaceship. I wonder if they turned the propulsion beam against the Basic ship."

Carcolo pursed his mouth dubiously. "Why should the sacerdotes build themselves a spaceship?"

"The Demie approaches. Why do you not put your question to him?"

"I will do so," said Carcolo with dignity.

But the Demie, followed by four younger sacerdotes and walking with the air of a man in a dream, passed without speaking.

Joaz rose to his knees, watched after him. The Demie apparently planned to mount the ramp and enter the ship. Joaz jumped to his feet, followed, barred the way to the ramp. Politely he asked, "What do you seek, Demie?"

"I seek to board the ship."

"To what end? I ask, of course, from sheer curiosity."

The Demie inspected him a moment without reply. His face was haggard and tight; his eyes gleamed like frost-stars. Finally he replied, in a voice hoarse with emotion. "I wish to determine if the ship can be repaired."

Joaz considered a moment, then spoke in a gentle rational voice. "The information can be of little interest to you. Would the sacerdotes place themselves so completely under my command?"

"We obey no one."

"In that case, I can hardly take you with me when I leave."

The Demie swung around, and for a moment seemed as if he would walk away. His eyes fell on the shattered opening at the end of the vale, and he turned back. He spoke, not in the measured voice of a sacerdote, but in a burst of grief and fury. "This is your doing! You preen yourself, you count yourself resourceful and clever; you forced us to act, and thereby violate ourselves and our dedication!"

Joaz nodded, with a faint grim smile. "I knew the opening must lie behind the Jambles; I wondered if you might be building a spaceship; I hoped that you might protect yourselves against the Basics, and so serve my purposes. I admit your charges. I used you and your construction as a weapon, to save myself and my people. Did I do wrong?"

"Right or wrong—who can weigh? You wasted our effort across more than eight hundred Aerlith years! You destroyed more than you can ever replace."

"I destroyed nothing, Demie. The Basics destroyed your ship. If you had cooperated with us in the defense of Banbeck Vale this disaster would have never occurred. You chose neutrality, you thought yourselves immune from our grief and pain. As you see, such is not the case."

"And meanwhile our labor of eight hundred and twelve years goes for naught."

Joaz asked with feigned innocence, "Why did you need a spaceship? Where do you plan to travel?"

The Demie's eyes burst with flames as intense as those of Skene. "When the race of men is gone, then we go abroad. We move across the galaxy, we repopulate the terrible old worlds, and the new universal history starts from that day, with the past wiped clean as if it never existed. If the grephs destroy you, what is it to us? We await only the death of the last man in the universe."

"Do you not consider yourselves men?"

"We are as you know us—Above Men."

At Joaz's shoulder someone laughed coarsely. Joaz turned his head to see Ervis Carcolo. "'Above Men'?" mocked Carcolo. "Poor naked waifs of the caves! What can you display to prove your superiority?"

The Demie's mouth drooped, the lines of his face deepened. "We have our tands. We have our knowledge. We have our strength."

Carcolo turned away with another coarse laugh. Joaz said in a subdued voice, "I feel more pity for you than you ever felt for us."

Carcolo returned. "And where did you learn to build a spaceship? From your own efforts? Or from the work of men before you, men of the old times?"

"We are the ultimate men," said the Demie. "We know all that men have ever thought, spoken or devised. We are the last and the first. And when the under-folk are gone, we shall renew the cosmos as innocent and fresh as rain."

"But men have never gone and will never go," said Joaz. "A setback yes, but is not the universe wide? Somewhere are the worlds of men. With the help of the Basics and their Mechanics, I will repair the ship and go forth to find these worlds."

"You will seek in vain," said the Demie.

"These worlds do not exist?"

"The Human Empire is dissolved; men exist only in feeble groups."

"What of Eden, old Eden?"

"A myth, no more."

"My marble globe, what of that?"

"A toy, an imaginative fabrication."

"How can you be sure?" asked Joaz, troubled in spite of himself.

"Have I not said that we know all of history? We can look into our tands and see deep into the past, until the recollections are dim and misty, and never do we remember planet Eden."

Joaz shook his head stubbornly. "There must be an original world from which men came. Call it Earth or Tempe or Eden—somewhere it exists."

The Demie started to speak, then in a rare show of irresolution held his tongue. Joaz said, "Perhaps you are right, perhaps we are the last men. But I shall go forth to look."

"I shall come with you," said Ervis Carcolo.

"You will be fortunate to find yourself alive tomorrow," said Joaz.

Carcolo drew himself up. "Do not dismiss my claim to the ship so carelessly!"

Joaz struggled for words, but could find none. What to do with the unruly Carcolo? He could not find in himself enough harshness to do what he knew should be done. He temporized, turned his back on Carcolo. "Now you know my plans," he told the Demie. "If you do not interfere with me, I shall not interfere with you."

The Demie moved slowly back. "Go then. We are a passive race; we despise ourselves for our activity of today. Perhaps it was our greatest mistake...But go, seek your forgotten world. You will only perish somewhere among the stars. We will wait, as already we have waited." He turned and walked away, followed by the four younger sacerdotes, who had all the time stood gravely to the side.

Joaz called after him. "And if the Basics come again? Will you fight with us? Or against us?"

The Demie made no response, but walked to the north, the long white hair swinging down his thin shoulder blades.

Joaz watched him a moment, gazed up and down the ruined valley, shook his head in wonder and puzzlement, turned back to study the great black ship.

Skene touched the western cliffs; there was an instant dimming of light, a sudden chill. Carcolo approached him. "Tonight I shall hold my folk here in Banbeck Vale, and send them home on the morrow. Meanwhile, I suggest that you board the ship with me and make a preliminary survey."

Joaz took a deep breath. Why could it not come easier for him? Carcolo had twice sought his life, and, had positions been reversed, would have shown him no mercy. He forced himself to act. His duty to himself, to his people, to his ultimate goal was clear.

He called to those of his knights who carried the captured heat-guns. They approached.

Joaz said, "Take Carcolo into Clybourne Crevasse. Execute him. Do this at once."

Protesting, bellowing, Carcolo was dragged off. Joaz turned away with a heavy heart, and sought Bast Givven. "I take you for a sensible man."

"I regard myself so."

"I set you in charge of Happy Valley. Take your folk home, before darkness falls."

Bast Givven silently went to his people. They stirred, and presently departed Banbeck Vale.

Joaz crossed the valley floor to the tumble of rubble which choked Kergan's Way. He choked with fury as he looked upon the destruction, and for a moment almost wavered in his resolve. Might it not be fit to fly the black ship to Coralyne and take revenge on the Basics? He walked around to stand under the spire which had housed his apartments, and by some strange freak of chance came upon a rounded fragment of yellow marble.

Weighing this in his palm he looked up into the sky where Coralyne already twinkled red, and tried to bring order to his mind.

The Banbeck folk had emerged from the deep tunnels. Phade the minstrel-maiden came to find him. "What a terrible day," she murmured. "What awful events; what a great victory."

Joaz tossed the bit of yellow marble back into the rubble. "I feel much the same way. And where it all ends, no one knows less than I."

AFTERWORD TO "THE DRAGON MASTERS"

On certain occasions, where it has been necessary, I have completely reasoned out an environment. When you specify a world or planet of some kind, you can usually justify it if you want to take the trouble. You can assume a dense core, or, as in the case of Big Planet, you can assume a very light core—made of very light materials, with a world of a large diameter. In general, it's possible to justify almost any kind of world you might like.

Although on the other hand, there are certainly instances where, if you take too much for granted, you might wind up with a fiasco...which happened to me with the worlds of Rigel in the Demon Princes series. I know and knew then that Rigel is a relatively young star; therefore any set of Rigellian planets would not have had time to cool. This idea simply slipped from my mind. I thought: here's a very radiant sun that has potential for a great number of inhabitable worlds; it could have what is called a large Habitable Zone. So I ignored the other consideration. Poul Anderson called it to my attention and I justified it, after a lame fashion, in the next books. In general, I take it for granted that about any world is possible, or at least that no one will sue for any contradictions.

—Jack Vance 1977

LIANE THE WAYFARER

Through the dim forest came Liane the Wayfarer, passing along the shadowed glades with a prancing light-footed gait. He whistled, he caroled, he was plainly in high spirits. Around his finger he twirled a bit of wrought bronze—a circlet graved with angular crabbed characters, now stained black.

By excellent chance he had found it, banded around the root of an ancient yew. Hacking it free, he had seen the characters on the inner surface—rude forceful symbols, doubtless the cast of a powerful antique rune...Best take it to a magician and have it tested for sorcery.

Liane made a wry mouth. There were objections to the course. Sometimes it seemed as if all living creatures conspired to exasperate him. Only this morning, the spice merchant—what a tumult he had made dying! How carelessly he had spewed blood on Liane's cock comb sandals! Still, thought Liane, every unpleasantness carried with it compensation. While digging the grave he had found the bronze ring.

And Liane's spirits soared; he laughed in pure joy. He bounded, he leapt. His green cape flapped behind him, the red feather in his cap winked and blinked...But still—Liane slowed his step—he was no whit closer to the mystery of the magic, if magic the ring possessed.

Experiment, that was the word!

He stopped where the ruby sunlight slanted down without hindrance from the high foliage, examined the ring, traced the glyphs with his fingernail. He peered through. A faint film, a flicker? He held it at arm's length. It was clearly a coronet. He whipped off his cap, set the band on his brow, rolled his great golden eyes, preened himself...Odd. It slipped down on his ears. It tipped across his eyes. Darkness. Frantically Liane clawed it off...A bronze ring, a hand's-breadth in diameter. Queer.

He tried again. It slipped down over his head, his shoulders. His head was in the darkness of a strange separate space. Looking down, he saw the level of the outside light dropping as he dropped the ring.

Slowly down...Now it was around his ankles—and in sudden panic, Liane snatched the ring up over his body, emerged blinking into the maroon light of the forest.

He saw a blue-white, green-white flicker against the foliage. It was a Twk-man, mounted on a dragon-fly, and light glinted from the dragon-fly's wings.

Liane called sharply, "Here, sir! Here, sir!"

The Twk-man perched his mount on a twig. "Well, Liane, what do you wish?"

"Watch now, and remember what you see." Liane pulled the ring over his head, dropped it to his feet, lifted it back. He looked up to the Twk-man, who was chewing a leaf. "And what did you see?"

"I saw Liane vanish from mortal sight—except for the red curled toes of his sandals. All else was as air."

"Ha!" cried Liane. "Think of it! Have you ever seen the like?"

The Twk-man asked carelessly, "Do you have salt? I would have salt."

Liane cut his exultations short, eyed the Twk-man closely.

"What news do you bring me?"

"Three erbs killed Florejin the Dream-builder, and burst all his bubbles. The air above the manse was colored for many minutes with the flitting fragments."

"A gram."

"Lord Kandive the Golden has built a barge of carven mo-wood ten lengths high, and it floats on the River Scaum for the Regatta, full of treasure."

"Two grams."

"A golden witch named Lith has come to live on Thamber Meadow. She is quiet and very beautiful."

"Three grams."

"Enough," said the Twk-man, and leaned forward to watch while Liane weighed out the salt in a tiny balance. He packed it in small panniers hanging on each side of the ribbed thorax, then twitched the insect into the air and flicked off through the forest vaults.

Once more Liane tried his bronze ring, and this time brought it entirely past his feet, stepped out of it and brought the ring up into the darkness beside him. What a wonderful sanctuary! A hole whose opening could be hidden inside the hole itself! Down with the ring to his feet, step through, bring it up his slender frame and over his shoulders, out into the forest with a small bronze ring in his hand.

Ho! and off to Thamber Meadow to see the beautiful golden witch.

Her hut was a simple affair of woven reeds—a low dome with two round windows and a low door. He saw Lith at the pond bare-legged among the water shoots, catching frogs for her supper. A white kirtle was gathered up tight around her thighs; stock-still she stood and the dark water rippled rings away from her slender knees.

She was more beautiful than Liane could have imagined, as if one of Florejin's wasted bubbles had burst here on the water. Her skin was pale creamed stirred gold, her hair a denser, wetter gold. Her eyes were like Liane's own, great golden orbs, and hers were wide apart, tilted slightly.

Liane strode forward and planted himself on the bank. She looked up startled, her ripe mouth half-open.

"Behold, golden witch, here is Liane. He has come to welcome you to Thamber; and he offers you his friendship, his love…"

Lith bent, scooped a handful of slime from the bank and flung it into his face.

Shouting the most violent curses, Liane wiped his eyes free, but the door to the hut had slammed shut.

Liane strode to the door and pounded it with his fist.

"Open and show your witch's face, or I burn the hut!"

The door opened, and the girl looked forth, smiling. "What now?"

Liane entered the hut and lunged for the girl, but twenty thin shafts darted out, twenty points pricking his chest. He halted, eyebrows raised, mouth twitching.

"Down, steel," said Lith. The blades snapped from view. "So easily could I seek your vitality," said Lith, "had I willed."

Liane frowned and rubbed his chin as if pondering. "You understand," he said earnestly, "what a witless thing you do. Liane is feared by those who fear fear, loved by those who love love. And you—" his eyes swam the golden glory of her body "—you are ripe as a sweet fruit, you are eager, you glisten and tremble with love. You please Liane, and he will spend much warmness on you."

"No, no," said Lith, with a slow smile. "You are too hasty."

Liane looked at her in surprise. "Indeed?"

"I am Lith," said she. "I am what you say I am. I ferment, I burn, I seethe. Yet I may have no lover but him who has served me. He must be brave, swift, cunning."

"I am he," said Liane. He chewed at his lip. "It is not usually thus. I detest this indecision." He took a step forward. "Come, let us—"

She backed away. "No, no. You forget. How have you served me, how have you gained the right to my love?"

"Absurdity!" stormed Liane. "Look at me! Note my perfect grace, the beauty of my form and feature, my great eyes, as golden as your own, my manifest will and power...It is you who should serve me. That is how I will have it." He sank upon a low divan. "Woman, give me wine."

She shook her head. "In my small domed hut I cannot be forced. Perhaps outside on Thamber Meadow—but in here, among my blue and red tassels, with twenty blades of steel at my call, you must obey me...So choose. Either arise and go, never to return, or else agree to serve me on one small mission, and then have me and all my ardor."

Liane sat straight and stiff. An odd creature, the golden witch. But, indeed, she was worth some exertion, and he would make her pay for her impudence.

"Very well then," he said blandly. "I will serve you. What do you wish? Jewels? I can suffocate you in pearls, blind you with diamonds. I have two emeralds the size of your fist, and they are green oceans, where the gaze is trapped and wanders forever among vertical green prisms..."

"No, no jewels—"

"An enemy, perhaps. Ah, so simple. Liane will kill you ten men. Two steps forward, thrust—thus!" He lunged. "And souls go thrilling up like bubbles in a beaker of mead."

"No. I want no killing."

He sat back, frowning. "What then?"

She stepped to the back of the room and pulled at a drape. It swung aside, displaying a golden tapestry. The scene was a valley bounded by two steep mountains, a broad valley where a placid river ran, past a quiet village and so into a grove of trees. Golden was the river, golden the mountains, golden the trees—golds so various, so rich, so subtle that the effect was like a many-colored landscape. But the tapestry had been rudely hacked in half.

Liane was entranced. "Exquisite, exquisite..."

Lith said, "It is the Magic Valley of Ariventa so depicted. The other half has been stolen from me, and its recovery is the service I wish of you."

"Where is the other half?" demanded Liane. "Who is the dastard?"

Now she watched him closely. "Have you ever heard of Chun? Chun the Unavoidable?"

Liane considered. "No."

"He stole the half to my tapestry, and hung it in a marble hall, and this hall is in the ruins to the north of Kaiin."

"Ha!" muttered Liane.

"The hall is by the Place of Whispers, and is marked by a leaning column with a black medallion of a phoenix and a two-headed lizard."

"I go," said Liane. He rose. "One day to Kaiin, one day to steal, one day to return. Three days."

Lith followed him to the door. "Beware of Chun the Unavoidable," she whispered.

And Liane strode away whistling, the red feather bobbing in his green cap. Lith watched him, then turned and slowly approached the golden tapestry. "Golden Ariventa," she whispered, "my heart cries and hurts with longing for you..."

The Derna is a swifter, thinner river than the Scaum, its bosomy sister to the south. And where the Scaum wallows through a broad dale, purple with horse-blossom, pocked white and gray with crumbling castles, the Derna has sheered a steep canyon, overhung by forested bluffs.

An ancient flint road long ago followed the course of the Derna, but now the exaggeration of the meandering has cut into the pavement, so that Liane, treading the road to Kaiin, was occasionally forced to leave the road and make a detour through banks of thorn and tubegrass which whistled in the breeze.

The red sun, drifting across the universe like an old man creeping to his death-bed, hung low to the horizon when Liane breasted Porphiron Scar, looked across white-walled Kaiin and the blue bay of Sanreale beyond.

Directly below was the market-place, a medley of stalls selling fruit, slabs of pale meat, molluscs from the slime banks, dull flagons of wine. And the quiet people of Kaiin moved among the stalls, buying their sustenance, carrying it loosely to their stone chambers.

Beyond the market-place rose a bank of ruined columns, like broken teeth—legs to the arena built two hundred feet from the ground by Mad King Shin; beyond, in a grove of bay trees, the glossy dome of the palace was visible, where Kandive the Golden ruled Kaiin and as much of Ascolais as one could see from a vantage on Porphiron Scar.

The Derna, no longer a flow of clear water, poured through a network of dank canals and subterranean tubes, and finally seeped past rotting wharves into the Bay of Sanreale.

A bed for the night, thought Liane; then to his business in the morning.

He leapt down the zig-zag steps—back, forth, back, forth—and came out into the market-place. And now he put on a grave demeanor. Liane the Wayfarer was not unknown in Kaiin, and many were ill-minded enough to work him harm.

He moved sedately in the shade of the Pannone Wall, turned through a narrow cobbled street, bordered by old wooden houses glowing the rich brown of old stump-water in the rays of the setting sun, and so came to a small square and the high stone face of the Magician's Inn.

The host, a small fat man, sad of eye, with a small fat nose the identical shape of his body, was scraping ashes from the hearth. He straightened his back and hurried behind the counter of his little alcove.

Liane said, "A chamber, well-aired, and a supper of mushrooms, wine and oysters."

The innkeeper bowed humbly.

"Indeed, sir—and how will you pay?"

Liane flung down a leather sack, taken this very morning. The innkeeper raised his eyebrows in pleasure at the fragrance.

"The ground buds of the spase-bush, brought from a far land," said Liane.

"Excellent, excellent...Your chamber sir, and your supper at once."

As Liane ate, several other guests of the house appeared and sat before the fire with wine, and the talk grew large, and dwelt on wizards of the past and the great days of magic.

"Great Phandaal knew a lore now forgot," said one old man with hair dyed orange. "He tied white and black strings to the legs of sparrows and sent them veering to his direction. And where they wove their magic woof, great trees appeared, laden with flowers, fruits, nuts, or bulbs of rare liqueurs. It is said that thus he wove Great Da Forest on the shores of Sanra Water."

"Ha," said a dour man in a garment of dark blue, brown and black, "this I can do." He brought forth a bit of string, flicked it, whirled it, spoke a quiet word, and the vitality of the pattern fused the string into a tongue of red and yellow fire, which danced, curled, darted back and forth along the table till the dour man killed it with a gesture.

"And this I can do," said a hooded figure in a black cape sprinkled with silver circles. He brought forth a small tray, laid it on the table and sprinkled therein a pinch of ashes from the hearth. He brought forth a whistle and blew a clear tone, and up from the tray came glittering motes, flashing the prismatic colors red, blue, green, yellow. They floated up a foot and burst in coruscations of brilliant colors, each a beautiful star-shaped pattern, and each burst sounded a tiny repetition of the original tone—the clearest, purest sound in the world. The motes became fewer, the magician blew a different tone, and again the motes floated up to burst in glorious ornamental spangles. Another time—another swarm of motes. At last the magician replaced his whistle, wiped off the tray, tucked it inside his cloak and lapsed back to silence.

Now the other wizards surged forward, and soon the air above the table swarmed with visions, quivered with spells. One showed the group nine new colors of ineffable charm and radiance; another caused a mouth to form on the landlord's forehead and revile the crowd, much to the landlord's discomfiture, since it was his own voice. Another displayed a green glass bottle from which the face of a demon peered and grimaced; another a ball of pure crystal which rolled back and forward to the command of the sorcerer who owned it, and who claimed it to be an earring of the fabled master Sankaferrin.

Liane had attentively watched all, crowing in delight at the bottled imp, and trying to cozen the obedient crystal from its owner, without success.

And Liane became pettish, complaining that the world was full of rock-hearted men, but the sorcerer with the crystal earring remained indifferent, and even when Liane spread out twelve packets of rare spice he refused to part with his toy.

Liane pleaded, "I wish only to please the witch Lith."

"Please her with the spice, then."

Liane said ingenuously, "Indeed, she has but one wish, a bit of tap-estry which I must steal from Chun the Unavoidable."

And he looked from face to suddenly silent face.

"What causes such immediate sobriety? Ho, Landlord, more wine!"

The sorcerer with the earring said, "If the floor swam ankle-deep with wine—the rich red wine of Tanvilkat—the leaden print of that name would still ride the air."

"Ha," laughed Liane, "let only a taste of that wine pass your lips, and the fumes would erase all memory."

"See his eyes," came a whisper. "Great and golden."

"And quick to see," spoke Liane. "And these legs—quick to run, fleet as starlight on the waves. And this arm—quick to stab with steel. And my magic—which will set me to a refuge that is out of all cog-nizance." He gulped wine from a beaker. "Now behold. This is magic from antique days." He set the bronze band over his head, stepped through, brought it up inside the darkness. When he deemed that suf-ficient time had elapsed, he stepped through once more.

The fire glowed, the landlord stood in his alcove, Liane's wine was at hand. But of the assembled magicians, there was no trace.

Liane looked about in puzzlement. "And where are my wizardly friends?"

The landlord turned his head. "They took to their chambers; the name you spoke weighed on their souls."

And Liane drank his wine in frowning silence.

Next morning he left the inn and picked a roundabout way to the Old Town—a gray wilderness of tumbled pillars, weathered blocks of sandstone, slumped pediments with crumbled inscriptions, flagged ter-races overgrown with rusty moss. Lizards, snakes, insects crawled the ruins; no other life did he see.

Threading a way through the rubble, he almost stumbled on a corpse—the body of a youth, one who stared at the sky with empty eye-sockets.

Liane felt a presence. He leapt back, rapier half-bared. A stooped old man stood watching him. He spoke in a feeble, quavering voice: "And what will you have in the Old Town?"

Liane replaced his rapier. "I seek the Place of Whispers. Perhaps you will direct me."

The old man made a croaking sound at the back of his throat. "Another? Another? When will it cease..." He motioned to the corpse. "This one came yesterday seeking the Place of Whispers. He would steal from Chun the Unavoidable. See him now." He turned away. "Come with me." He disappeared over a tumble of rock.

Liane followed. The old man stood by another corpse with eye-sockets bereft and bloody. "This one came four days ago, and he met Chun the Unavoidable...And over there behind the arch is another still, a great warrior in cloison armor. And there—and there—" he pointed, pointed. "And there—and there—like crushed flies."

He turned his watery blue gaze back to Liane. "Return, young man, return—lest your body lie here in its green cloak to rot on the flagstones."

Liane drew his rapier and flourished it. "I am Liane the Wayfarer; let them who offend me have fear. And where is the Place of Whispers?"

"If you must know," said the old man, "it is beyond that broken obelisk. But you go to your peril."

"I am Liane the Wayfarer. Peril goes with me."

The old man stood like a piece of weathered statuary as Liane strode off.

And Liane asked himself, suppose this old man were an agent of Chun, and at this minute were on his way to warn him?...Best to take all precautions. He leapt up on a high entablature and ran crouching back to where he had left the ancient.

Here he came, muttering to himself, leaning on his staff. Liane dropped a block of granite as large as his head. A thud, a croak, a gasp—and Liane went his way.

He strode past the broken obelisk into a wide court—the Place of Whispers. Directly opposite was a long wide hall, marked by a leaning column with a big black medallion, the sign of a phoenix and a two-headed lizard.

Liane merged himself with the shadow of a wall, and stood watching like a wolf, alert for any flicker of motion.

All was quiet. The sunlight invested the ruins with dreary splendor. To all sides, as far as the eye could reach, was broken stone, a wasteland leached by a thousand rains, until now the sense of man had departed and the stone was one with the natural earth.

The sun moved across the dark-blue sky. Liane presently stole from his vantage-point and circled the hall. No sight nor sign did he see.

He approached the building from the rear and pressed his ear to the stone. It was dead, without vibration. Around the side—watching up, down, to all sides; a breach in the wall. Liane peered inside. At the back hung half a golden tapestry. Otherwise the hall was empty.

Liane looked up, down, this side, that. There was nothing in sight. He continued around the hall.

He came to another broken place. He looked within. To the rear hung the golden tapestry. Nothing else, to right or left, no sight or sound.

Liane continued to the front of the hall and sought into the eaves; dead as dust.

He had a clear view of the room. Bare, barren, except for the bit of golden tapestry.

Liane entered, striding with long soft steps. He halted in the middle of the floor. Light came to him from all sides except the rear wall. There were a dozen openings from which to flee and no sound except the dull thudding of his heart.

He took two steps forward. The tapestry was almost at his fingertips.

He stepped forward and swiftly jerked the tapestry down from the wall. And behind was Chun the Unavoidable.

Liane screamed. He turned on paralyzed legs and they were leaden, like legs in a dream which refused to run.

Chun dropped out of the wall and advanced. Over his shiny black back he wore a robe of eyeballs threaded on silk.

Liane was running, fleetly now. He sprang, he soared. The tips of his toes scarcely touched the ground. Out the hall, across the square, into the wilderness of broken statues and fallen columns. And behind came Chun, running like a dog.

Liane sped along the crest of a wall and sprang a great gap to a shattered fountain. Behind came Chun.

Liane darted up a narrow alley, climbed over a pile of refuse, over a roof, down into a court. Behind came Chun.

Liane sped down a wide avenue lined with a few stunted old cypress trees, and he heard Chun close at his heels. He turned into an archway, pulled his bronze ring over his head, down to his feet. He stepped through, brought the ring up inside the darkness. Sanctuary. He was alone in a dark magic space, vanished from earthly gaze and knowledge. Brooding silence, dead space...

He felt a stir behind him, a breath of air. At his elbow a voice said, "I am Chun the Unavoidable."

Lith sat on her couch near the candles, weaving a cap from frogskins. The door to her hut was barred, the windows shuttered. Outside, Thamber Meadow dwelled in darkness.

A scrape at her door, a creak as the lock was tested. Lith became rigid and stared at the door.

A voice said, "Tonight, O Lith, tonight it is two long bright threads for you. Two because the eyes were so great, so large, so golden..."

Lith sat quiet. She waited an hour; then, creeping to the door, she listened. The sense of presence was absent. A frog croaked nearby.

She eased the door ajar, found the threads and closed the door. She ran to her golden tapestry and fitted the threads into the ravelled warp.

And she stared at the golden valley, sick with longing for Ariventa, and tears blurred out the peaceful river, the quiet golden forest. "The cloth slowly grows wider...One day it will be done, and I will come home..."

AFTERWORD TO "LIANE THE WAYFARER"

I am aware of using no inflexible or predetermined style. Each story generates its own style, so to speak. In theory, I feel that the only good style is the style which no one notices, but I suppose that in practice this may not be altogether or at all times possible. In actuality the subject of style is much too large to be covered in a sentence or two and no doubt every writer has his own ideas on the subject.

—Jack Vance 1976

SAIL 25

I

Henry Belt came limping into the conference room, mounted the dais, settled himself at the desk. He looked once around the room: a swift bright glance which, focusing nowhere, treated the eight young men who faced him to an almost insulting disinterest. He reached in his pocket, brought forth a pencil and a flat red book, which he placed on the desk. The eight young men watched in absolute silence. They were much alike: healthy, clean, smart, their expressions identically alert and wary. Each had heard legends of Henry Belt, each had formed his private plans and private determinations.

Henry Belt seemed a man of a different species. His face was broad, flat, roped with cartilage and muscle, with skin the color and texture of bacon rind. Coarse white grizzle covered his scalp, his eyes were crafty slits, his nose a misshapen lump. His shoulders were massive, his legs short and gnarled: as he sat before the eight young men he seemed like a horned toad among a group of dapper young frogs.

"First of all," said Henry Belt, with a gap-toothed grin, "I'll make it clear that I don't expect you to like me. If you do I'll be surprised and displeased. It will mean that I haven't pushed you hard enough."

He leaned back in his chair, surveyed the silent group. "You've heard stories about me. Why haven't they kicked me out of the service? Incorrigible, arrogant, dangerous Henry Belt. Drunken Henry Belt. (This last of course is slander. Henry Belt has never been drunk in his life.) Why do they tolerate me? For one simple reason: out of necessity. No one wants to take on this kind of job. Only a man like Henry Belt can stand up to it: year after year in space, with nothing to look at but a half-dozen round-faced young scrubs. He takes them out, he brings them back. Not all of them, and not all of those who come back are space-men today. But they'll all cross the street when they see him coming. Henry Belt? you say. They'll turn pale or go red. None of them will smile. Some of them are high-placed now. They could kick me loose if they chose. Ask them why they don't. Henry Belt is a terror, they'll tell you. He's wicked, he's a tyrant. Cruel as an axe, fickle as a woman. But a voyage with Henry Belt blows the foam off the beer. He's ruined many a man, he's killed a few, but those that come out of it are proud to say, I trained with Henry Belt!

"Another thing you may hear: Henry Belt has luck. But don't pay any heed. Luck runs out. You'll be my thirteenth class, and that's unlucky. I've taken out seventy-two young sprats no different from yourselves; I've come back twelve times: which is partly Henry Belt and partly luck. The voyages average about two years long: how can a man stand it? There's only one who could: Henry Belt. I've got more space-time than any man alive, and now I'll tell you a secret: this is my last time out. I'm starting to wake up at night to strange visions. After this class I'll quit. I hope you lads aren't superstitious. A white-eyed woman told me that I'd die in space. She told me other things and they've all come true. Who knows? If I survive this last trip I figure to buy a cottage in the country and grow roses." Henry Belt pushed himself back in the chair and surveyed the group with sardonic placidity. The man sitting closest to him caught a whiff of alcohol; he peered more closely at Henry Belt. Was it possible that even now the man was drunk?

Henry Belt continued. "We'll get to know each other well. And you'll be wondering on what basis I make my recommendations. Am I objective and fair? Do I put aside personal animosity? Naturally there won't be any friendship. Well, here's my system. I keep a red book. Here it is. I'll put your names down right now. You, sir?"

"I'm Cadet Lewis Lynch, sir."

"You?"

"Edward Culpepper, sir."

"Marcus Verona, sir."

"Vidal Weske, sir."

"Marvin McGrath, sir."

"Barry Ostrander, sir."

"Clyde von Gluck, sir."

"Joseph Sutton, sir."

Henry Belt wrote the names in the red book. "This is the system. When you do something to annoy me, I mark you down demerits. At the end of the voyage I total these demerits, add a few here and there for luck, and am so guided. I'm sure nothing could be clearer than this. What annoys me? Ah, that's a question which is hard to answer. If you talk too much: demerits. If you're surly and taciturn: demerits. If you slouch and laze and dog the dirty work: demerits. If you're over-zealous and forever scuttling about: demerits. Obsequiousness: demerits. Truculence: demerits. If you sing and whistle: demerits. If you're a stolid bloody bore: demerits. You can see that the line is hard to draw. There's a hint which can save you many marks: no gossip. I've seen ships where the backbiting ran so thick it could have been jetted astern for thrust. I'm an eavesdropper. I hear everything. I don't like gossip, especially when it concerns myself. I'm a sensitive man, and I open my red book fast when I think I'm being insulted." Henry Belt once more leaned back in his chair. "Any questions?"

No one spoke.

Henry Belt nodded. "Wise. Best not to flaunt your ignorance so early in the game. Here's some miscellaneous information. First, wear what you like. Personally I dislike uniforms. I never wear a uniform. I never have worn a uniform. Secondly, if you have a religion, keep it to yourself. I dislike religions. I have always disliked religions. In response to the thought passing through each of your skulls, I do not think of myself as God. But you may do so, if you choose. And this—" he held up the red book "—you may regard as the Syncretic Compendium. Very well. Any questions?"

"Yes sir," said Culpepper.

"Speak, sir."

"Any objection to alcoholic beverages aboard ship, sir?"

"For the cadets, yes indeed. I concede that the water must be carried in any event, that the organic compounds present may be reconstituted, but unluckily the bottles weigh far too much."

"I understand, sir."

Henry Belt rose to his feet. "One last word. Have I mentioned that I run a tight ship? When I say jump, you must jump. When I say hop, you must hop. When I say stand on your head, I hope instantly to see twelve feet. Perhaps you will think me arbitrary—others have done so. After my tenth voyage several of the cadets urged that I had been unreasonable. I don't know where you'd go to question them; all were discharged from the hospital long ago. But now we understand each other. Rather, you understand me, because it is unnecessary that I understand you. This is dangerous work, of course. I don't guarantee your safety. Far from it, especially since we are assigned to old 25, which should have been broken up long ago. There are eight of you present. Only six cadets will make the voyage. Before the week is over I will make the appropriate notifications. Any more questions?…Very well, then. Cheerio." He stepped down from the dais, swaying just a trifle, and Culpepper once again caught the odor of alcohol. Limping on his thin legs as if his feet hurt Henry Belt departed into the back passage.

For a moment or two there was silence. Then von Gluck said in a soft voice, "My gracious."

"He's a tyrannical lunatic," grumbled Weske. "I've never heard anything like it! Megalomania!"

"Easy," said Culpepper. "Remember, no gossiping."

"Bah!" muttered McGrath. "This is a free country. I'll damn well say what I like."

"Mr. Belt admits it's a free country," said Culpepper. "He'll grade you as he likes, too."

Weske rose to his feet. "A wonder somebody hasn't killed him."

"I wouldn't want to try it," said Culpepper. "He looks tough." He made a gesture, stood up, brow furrowed in thought. Then he went to look along the passageway into which Henry Belt had made his departure. There, pressed to the wall, stood Henry Belt. "Yes, sir," said Culpepper suavely. "I forgot to inquire when you wanted us to convene again."

Henry Belt returned to the rostrum. "Now is as good a time as any." He took his seat, opened his red book. "You, Mr. von Gluck, made the remark, 'My gracious' in an offensive tone of voice. One demerit. You, Mr. Weske, employed the terms 'tyrannical lunatic' and 'megalomania', in reference to myself. Three demerits. Mr. McGrath, you observed that freedom of speech is the official doctrine of this country. It is a theory which presently we have no time to explore, but I believe that the statement in its present context carries an overtone of insubordination. One demerit. Mr. Culpepper, your imperturbable complacence irritates me. I prefer that you display more uncertainty, or even uneasiness."

"Sorry, sir."

"However, you took occasion to remind your colleagues of my rule, and so I will not mark you down."

"Thank you, sir."

Henry Belt leaned back in the chair, stared at the ceiling. "Listen closely, as I do not care to repeat myself. Take notes if you wish. Topic: Solar Sails, Theory and Practice thereof. Material with which you should already be familiar, but which I will repeat in order to avoid ambiguity.

"First, why bother with the sail, when nuclear jet-ships are faster, more dependable, more direct, safer and easier to navigate? The answer is three-fold. First, a sail is not a bad way to move heavy cargo slowly but cheaply through space. Secondly, the range of the sail is unlimited, since we employ the mechanical pressure of light for thrust, and therefore need carry neither propulsive machinery, material to be ejected, nor energy source. The solar sail is much lighter than its nuclear-powered counterpart, and may carry a larger complement of men in a larger hull. Thirdly, to train a man for space there is no better instrument than the handling of a sail. The computer naturally calculates sail cant and plots the course; in fact, without the computer we'd be dead ducks. Nevertheless the control of a sail provides working familiarity with the cosmic elementals: light, gravity, mass, space.

"There are two types of sail: pure and composite. The first relies on solar energy exclusively, the second carries a secondary power source. We have been assigned Number 25, which is the first sort. It consists of a hull, a large parabolic reflector which serves as radar and radio antenna as well as reflector for the power generator, and the sail itself. The pressure of radiation, of course, is extremely slight—on the order of an ounce per acre at this distance from the sun. Necessarily the sail must be extremely large and extremely light. We use a fluoro-siliconic film a tenth of a mil in gauge, fogged with lithium to the state of opacity. I believe the layer of lithium is about a thousand two hundred molecules thick. Such a foil weighs about four tons to the square mile. It is fitted to a hoop of thin-walled tubing, from which mono-crystalline iron cords lead to the hull.

"We try to achieve a weight factor of six tons to the square mile, which produces an acceleration of between g/100 and g/1000 depending on proximity to the sun, angle of cant, circumsolar orbital speed, reflectivity of surface. These accelerations seem minute, but calculation shows them to be cumulatively enormous. g/100 yields a velocity increment of 800 miles per hour every hour, 18,000 miles per hour each day, or five miles per second each day. At this rate interplanetary distances are readily negotiable—with proper manipulation of the sail, I need hardly say.

"The virtues of the sail I've mentioned. It is cheap to build and cheap to operate. It requires neither fuel nor ejectant. As it travels through space, the great area captures various ions, which may be expelled in the plasma jet powered by the parabolic reflector, which adds another increment to the acceleration.

"The disadvantages of the sail are those of the glider or sailing ship, in that we must use natural forces with great precision and delicacy.

"There is no particular limit to the size of the sail. On 25 we use about four square miles of sail. For the present voyage we will install a new sail, as the old is well-worn and eroded.

"That will be all for today." Once more Henry Belt limped down from the dais and out into the passage. On this occasion there were no comments after his departure.

II

The eight cadets shared a dormitory, attended classes together, ate at the same table in the mess-hall. "You think you know each other well," said Henry Belt. "Wait till we are alone in space. The similarities, the areas of agreement become invisible, only the distinctions and differences remain."

In various shops and laboratories the cadets assembled, disassembled and reassembled computers, pumps, generators, gyro-platforms, star-trackers, communication gear. "It's not enough to be clever with your hands," said Henry Belt. "Dexterity is not enough. Resourcefulness, creativity, the ability to make successful improvisations—these are more important. We'll test you out." And presently each of the cadets was introduced into a room on the floor of which lay a great heap of mingled housings, wires, flexes, gears, components of a dozen varieties of mechanism. "This is a twenty-six hour test," said Henry Belt. "Each of you has an identical set of components and supplies. There shall be no exchange of parts or information between you. Those whom I suspect of this fault will be dropped from the class, without recommendation. What I want you to build is, first, one standard Aminex Mark 9 Computer. Second, a servo-mechanism to orient a mass of ten kilograms toward Mu Hercules. Why do I specify Mu Hercules?"

"Because, sir, the solar system moves in the direction of Mu Hercules, and we thereby avoid parallax error. Negligible though it may be, sir."

"The final comment smacks of frivolity, Mr. McGrath, which serves only to distract the attention of those who are trying to take careful note of my instructions. One demerit."

"Sorry, sir. I merely intended to express my awareness that for many practical purposes such a degree of accuracy is unnecessary."

"That idea, cadet, is sufficiently elemental that it need not be labored. I appreciate brevity and precision."

"Yes, sir."

"Thirdly, from these materials, assemble a communication system, operating on one hundred watts, which will permit two-way conversation between Tycho Base and Phobos, at whatever frequency you deem suitable."

The cadets started in identical fashion, by sorting the material into various piles, then calibrating and checking the test instruments. Achievement thereafter was disparate. Culpepper and von Gluck, diagnosing the test as partly one of mechanical ingenuity and partly ordeal by frustration, failed to become excited when several indispensable components proved either to be missing or inoperative, and carried each project as far as immediately feasible. McGrath and Weske, beginning with the computer, were reduced to rage and random action. Lynch and Sutton worked doggedly at the computer, Verona at the communication system.

Culpepper alone managed to complete one of the instruments, by the process of sawing, polishing and cementing together sections of two broken crystals into a crude, inefficient but operative maser unit.

The day after this test McGrath and Weske disappeared from the dormitory, whether by their own volition or notification from Henry Belt, no one ever knew.

The test was followed by weekend leave. Cadet Lynch, attending a cocktail party, found himself in conversation with a Lieutenant-Colonel Trenchard, who shook his head pityingly to hear that Lynch was training with Henry Belt.

"I was up with Old Horrors myself. I tell you it's a miracle we ever got back. Belt was drunk two-thirds of the voyage."

"How does he escape court-martial?" asked Lynch with an involuntary glance over his shoulder, for fear that Henry Belt might be standing near by with his red book.

"Very simple. All the top men seem to have trained under Henry Belt. Naturally they hate his guts but they all take a perverse pride in the fact. And maybe they hope that someday a cadet will take him apart."

"Have any ever tried?"

"Oh yes. I took a swing at Henry once. I was lucky to escape with a broken collarbone and two sprained ankles. And he wasn't even angry. Good old Henry, the son of a bitch. If you come back alive—and that's no idle remark—you'll stand a good chance of reaching the top."

Lynch winced. "Is it worth two years with Henry Belt?"

"I don't regret it. Not now," said Trenchard. "What's your ship?"

"Old 25."

Trenchard shook his head. "An antique. It's tied together with bits of string."

"So I've heard," said Lynch glumly. "If I didn't have so much vanity I'd quit tomorrow. Learn to sell insurance, or work in an office…"

●

The next evening Henry Belt passed the word. "Next Tuesday morning we go up. Have your gear packed; take a last look at the scenes of your childhood. We'll be gone several months."

On Tuesday morning the cadets took their places in the angel-wagon. Henry Belt presently appeared. "Last chance to play it safe. Anyone decide they're really not space people after all?"

The pilot of the angel-wagon was disposed to be facetious. "Now, Henry, behave yourself. You're not scaring anybody but yourself."

Henry Belt swung his flat dark face around. "Is that the case, mister? I'll pay you ten thousand dollars to make the trip in the place of one of the cads."

The pilot shook his head. "Not for a hundred thousand, Henry. One of these days your luck is going to run out, and there'll be a sad quiet hulk drifting in orbit forever."

"I expect it, mister. If I wanted to die of fatbelly I'd take your job."

"If you'd stay sober, Henry, there might be an opening for you."

Henry Belt gave him his wolfish smile. "I'm a better man drunk than you are sober, except for mouth. Any way you can think of, from dancing the fandango to Calcutta roughhouse."

"I'd be ashamed to thrash an old man, Henry. You're safe."

"Thank you, mister. If you are quite ready, we are."

"Hold your hats. On the count..." The projectile thrust against the earth, strained, rose, went streaking up into the sky. An hour later the pilot pointed. "There's your boat. Old 25. And 39 right beside it, just in from space."

Henry Belt stared aghast from the port. "What's been done to the ship? The decoration? The red? the white? the yellow? The checkerboard."

"Thank some idiot of a landlubber," said the pilot. "The word came to pretty the old boats for a junket of congressmen. This is what transpired."

Henry Belt turned to the cadets. "Observe this foolishness. It is the result of vanity and ignorance. We will be occupied several days removing the paint."

They drifted close below the two sails: No. 39 just down from space, spare and polished beside the bedizened structure of No. 25. In 39's exit port a group of men waited, their gear floating at the end of cords.

"Observe those men," said Henry Belt. "They are jaunty. They have been on a pleasant outing around the planet Mars. They are poorly trained. When you gentlemen return you will be haggard and desperate. You will be well trained."

"If you live," said the pilot.

"That is something which cannot be foretold," said Henry Belt. "Now, gentlemen, clamp your helmets, and we will proceed."

The helmets were secured. Henry Belt's voice came by radio. "Lynch, Ostrander, will remain here to discharge cargo. Verona, Culpepper, von Gluck, Sutton, leap with cords to the ship; ferry across the cargo, stow it in the proper hatches."

Henry Belt took charge of his personal cargo, which consisted of several large cases. He eased them out into space, clipped on lines, thrust them toward 25, leapt after. Pulling himself and the cases to the entrance port he disappeared within.

Discharge of cargo was effected. The crew from 39 transferred to the carrier, which thereupon swung down and away, thrust itself dwindling back toward earth.

When the cargo had been stowed, the cadets gathered in the wardroom. Henry Belt appeared from the master's cubicle. He wore a black T shirt which was ridged and lumped to the configuration of his chest, black shorts from which his thin legs extended, and sandals with magnetic filaments in the soles.

"Gentlemen," said Henry Belt in a soft voice. "At last we are alone. How do you like the surroundings? Eh, Mr. Culpepper?"

"The hull is commodious, sir. The view is superb."

Henry Belt nodded. "Mr. Lynch? Your impressions?"

"I'm afraid I haven't sorted them out yet, sir."

"I see. You, Mr. Sutton?"

"Space is larger than I imagined it, sir."

"True. Space is unimaginable. A good space-man must either be larger than space, or he must ignore it. Both difficult. Well, gentlemen, I will make a few comments, then I will retire and enjoy the voyage. Since this is my last time out, I intend to do nothing whatever. The operation of the ship will be completely in your hands. I will merely appear from time to time to beam benevolently about or alas! to make marks in my red book. Nominally I shall be in command, but you six will enjoy complete control over the ship. If you return us safely to Earth I will make an approving entry in my red book. If you wreck us or fling us into the sun, you will be more unhappy than I, since it is my destiny to die in space. Mr. von Gluck, do I perceive a smirk on your face?"

"No, sir, it is a thoughtful half-smile."

"What is humorous in the concept of my demise, may I ask?"

"It will be a great tragedy, sir. I merely was reflecting upon the contemporary persistence of, well, not exactly superstition, but, let us say, the conviction of a subjective cosmos."

Henry Belt made a notation in the red book. "Whatever is meant by this barbaric jargon I'm sure I don't know, Mr. von Gluck. It is clear that you fancy yourself a philosopher and dialectician. I will not fault this, so long as your remarks conceal no overtones of malice and insolence, to which I am extremely sensitive. Now as to the persistence of superstition, only an impoverished mind considers itself the repository of absolute knowledge. Hamlet spoke on this subject to Horatio, as I recall, in the well-known work by William Shakespeare. I myself have seen strange and terrifying sights. Were they hallucinations? Were they the manipulation of the cosmos by my mind or the mind of someone—or something—other than myself? I do not know. I therefore counsel a flexible attitude toward matters where the truth is still unknown. For this reason: the impact of an inexplicable experience may well destroy a mind which is too brittle. Do I make myself clear?"

"Perfectly, sir."

"Very good. To return, then. We shall set a system of watches whereby each man works in turn with each of the other five. I thereby hope to discourage the formation of special friendships, or cliques. Such arrangements irritate me, and I shall mark accordingly.

"You have inspected the ship. The hull is a sandwich of lithium—beryllium, insulating foam, fiber and an interior skin. Very light, held rigid by air pressure rather than by any innate strength of the material. We can therefore afford enough space to stretch our legs and provide all of us with privacy.

"The master's cubicle is to the left; under no circumstances is anyone permitted in my quarters. If you wish to speak to me, knock on my door. If I appear, good. If I do not appear, go away. To the right are six cubicles which you may now distribute among yourselves by lot. Each of you has the right to demand the same privacy I do myself. Keep your personal belongings in your cubicles. I have been known to cast into space articles which I persistently find strewn about the wardroom.

"Your schedule will be two hours study, four hours on watch, six hours off. I will require no specific rate of study progress, but I recommend that you make good use of your time.

"Our destination is Mars. We will presently construct a new sail, then while orbital velocity builds up, you will carefully test and check all equipment aboard. Each of you will compute sail cant and course and work out among yourselves any discrepancies which may appear. I shall take no hand in navigation. I prefer that you involve me in no disaster. If any such occur I shall severely mark down the persons responsible.

"Singing, whistling, humming, are forbidden, as are sniffing, nose-picking, smacking the lips, and cracking knuckles. I disapprove of fear and hysteria, and mark accordingly. No one dies more than once; we are well aware of the risks of this, our chosen occupation. There will be no practical jokes. You may fight, so long as you do not disturb me or break any instruments; however I counsel against it, as it leads to resentment, and I have known cadets to kill each other. I suggest coolness and detachment in your personal relations. Use of the micro-film projector is of course at your own option. You may not use the radio either to dispatch or receive messages. In fact I have put the radio out of commission, as is my practice. I do this to emphasize the fact that, sink or swim, we must make do with our own resources. Are there any questions?...Very good. You will find that if you all behave with scrupulous correctness and accuracy, we shall in due course return safe and sound, with a minimum of demerits and no casualties. I am bound to say, however, that in twelve previous voyages this has failed to occur."

"Perhaps this will be the time, sir," offered Culpepper suavely.

"We shall see. Now you may select your cubicles, stow your gear, generally make the place shipshape. The carrier will bring up the new sail tomorrow, and you will go to work."

III

The carrier discharged a great bundle of three-inch tubing: paper-thin lithium hardened with beryllium, reinforced with filaments of mono-crystalline iron—a total length of eight miles. The cadets fitted the tubes end to end, cementing the joints. When the tube extended a quarter-mile it was bent bow-shaped by a cord stretched between two ends, and further sections added. As the process continued the free end curved far out and around, and presently began to veer back in toward the hull. When the last tube was in place the loose end was hauled down, socketed home, to form a great hoop two miles and a half in diameter.

Henry Belt came out occasionally in his space-suit to look on, and occasionally spoke a few words of sardonic comment, to which the cadets paid little heed. Their mood had changed; this was exhilaration, to be weightlessly afloat above the bright cloud-marked globe, with continent and ocean wheeling massively below. Anything seemed possible, even the training voyage with Henry Belt! When he came out to inspect their work, they grinned at each other with indulgent amusement. Henry Belt suddenly seemed a rather pitiful creature, a poor vagabond suited only for drunken bluster. Fortunate indeed that they were less naïve than Henry Belt's previous classes! They had taken Belt seriously; he had cowed them, reduced them to nervous pulp. Not this crew, not by a long shot! They saw through Henry Belt! Just keep your nose clean, do your work, keep cheerful. The training voyage won't last but a few months, and then real life begins. Gut it out, ignore Henry Belt as much as possible.

Already the group had made a composite assessment of its members, arriving at a set of convenient labels. Culpepper: smooth, suave, easy-going. Lynch: excitable, argumentative, hot-tempered. Von Gluck: the artistic temperament, delicate with his hands and sensibilities. Ostrander: prissy, finicky, over-tidy. Sutton: moody, suspicious, competitive. Verona: the plugger, rough at the edges, but persistent and reliable.

Around the hull swung the gleaming hoop, and now the carrier brought up the sail, a great roll of darkly shining stuff. When unfolded and unrolled, and unfolded many times more, it became a tough gleaming film, flimsy as gold leaf. Unfolded to its fullest extent it was a shimmering disk, already rippling and bulging to the light of the sun. The cadets fitted the film to the hoop, stretched it taut as a drum-head, cemented it in place. Now the sail must carefully be held edge on to the sun, or it would quickly move away, under a thrust of about a hundred pounds.

From the rim braided-iron threads were led to a ring at the back of the parabolic reflector, dwarfing this as the reflector dwarfed the hull, and now the sail was ready to move.

The carrier brought up a final cargo: water, food, spare parts, a new magazine for the microfilm viewer, mail. Then Henry Belt said, "Make sail."

This was the process of turning the sail to catch the sunlight while the hull moved around Earth away from the sun, canting it parallel to the sun-rays when the ship moved on the sunward leg of its orbit: in short, building up an orbital velocity which in due course would stretch loose the bonds of terrestrial gravity and send Sail 25 kiting out toward Mars.

During this period the cadets checked every item of equipment aboard the vessel. They grimaced with disgust and dismay at some of the instruments: 25 was an old ship, with antiquated gear. Henry Belt seemed to enjoy their grumbling. "This is a training voyage, not a pleasure cruise. If you wanted your noses wiped, you should have taken a post on the ground. I warn you, gentlemen, I have no sympathy for fault-finders. If you wish a model by which to form your own conduct, observe me. I accept every vicissitude placidly. You will never hear me curse or flap my arms in astonishment at the turns of fortune."

The moody introspective Sutton, usually the most diffident and laconic of individuals, ventured an ill-advised witticism. "If we modeled ourselves after you, sir, there'd be no room to move for the whiskey."

Out came the red book. "Extraordinary impudence, Mr. Sutton. How can you yield so easily to malice? You must control the razor edge of your wit; you will make yourself unpopular aboard this ship."

Sutton flushed pink; his eyes glistened, he opened his mouth to speak, then closed it firmly. Henry Belt, waiting politely expectant, turned away. "You gentlemen will perceive that I rigorously obey my own rules of conduct. I am regular as a clock. There is no better, more genial shipmate than Henry Belt. There is not a fairer man alive. Mr. Culpepper, you have a remark to make?"

"Nothing of consequence, sir. I am merely grateful not to be making a voyage with a man less regular, less genial, and less fair than yourself."

Henry Belt considered. "I suppose I can take no exception to the remark. There is indeed a hint of tartness and glancing obloquy—but, well, I will grant you the benefit of the doubt, and accept your statement at its face value."

"Thank you, sir."

"But I must warn you, Mr. Culpepper, that there is a certain ease to your behavior that gives me cause for distress. I counsel you to a greater show of earnest sincerity, which will minimize the risk of misunderstanding. A man less indulgent than myself might well have read impertinence into your remark and charged you one demerit."

"I understand, sir, and shall cultivate the qualities you mention."

Henry Belt found nothing more to say. He went to the port, glared out at the sail. He swung around instantly. "Who is on watch?"

"Sutton and Ostrander, sir."

"Gentlemen, have you noticed the sail? It has swung about and is canting to show its back to the sun. In another ten minutes we shall be tangled in a hundred miles of guy-wires."

Sutton and Ostrander sprang to repair the situation. Henry Belt shook his head disparagingly. "This is precisely what is meant by the words 'negligence' and 'inattentiveness'. You two have committed a serious error. This is poor spacemanship. The sail must always be in such a position as to hold the wires taut."

"There seems to be something wrong with the sensor, sir," Sutton blurted. "It should notify us when the sail swings behind us."

"I fear I must charge you an additional demerit for making excuses, Mr. Sutton. It is your duty to assure yourself that all the warning devices are functioning properly, at all times. Machinery must never be used as a substitute for vigilance."

Ostrander looked up from the control console. "Someone has turned off the switch, sir. I do not offer this as an excuse, but as an explanation."

"The line of distinction is often hard to define, Mr. Ostrander. Please bear in mind my remarks on the subject of vigilance."

"Yes, sir, but—who turned off the switch?"

"Both you and Mr. Sutton are theoretically hard at work watching for any such accident or occurrence. Did you not observe it?"

"No, sir."

"I might almost accuse you of further inattention and neglect, in this case."

Ostrander gave Henry Belt a long dubious side-glance. "The only person I recall going near the console is yourself, sir. I'm sure you wouldn't do such a thing."

Henry Belt shook his head sadly. "In space you must never rely on anyone for rational conduct. A few moments ago Mr. Sutton unfairly imputed to me an unusual thirst for whiskey. Suppose this were the case? Suppose, as an example of pure irony, that I had indeed been drinking whiskey, that I was in fact drunk?"

"I will agree, sir, that anything is possible."

Henry Belt shook his head again. "That is the type of remark, Mr. Ostrander, that I have come to associate with Mr. Culpepper. A better response would have been, 'In the future, I will try to be ready for any conceivable contingency.' Mr. Sutton, did you make a hissing sound between your teeth?"

"I was breathing, sir."

"Please breathe with less vehemence. A more suspicious man than myself might mark you for sulking and harboring black thoughts."

"Sorry, sir, I will breathe to myself."

"Very well, Mr. Sutton." Henry Belt turned away and wandered back and forth about the wardroom, scrutinizing cases, frowning at smudges on polished metal. Ostrander muttered something to Sutton, and both watched Henry Belt closely as he moved here and there. Presently Henry Belt lurched toward them. "You show great interest in my movements, gentlemen."

"We were on the watch for another unlikely contingency, sir."

"Very good, Mr. Ostrander. Stick with it. In space nothing is impossible. I'll vouch for this personally."

IV

Henry Belt sent all hands out to remove the paint from the surface of the parabolic reflector. When this had been accomplished, incident sunlight was now focused upon an expanse of photo-electric cells. The power so generated was used to operate plasma jets, expelling ions collected by the vast expanse of sail, further accelerating the ship, thrusting it ever out into an orbit of escape. And finally one day, at an exact instant dictated by the computer, the ship departed from Earth and floated tangentially out into space, off at an angle for the orbit of Mars. At an acceleration of g/100 velocity built up rapidly. Earth dwindled behind; the ship was isolated in space. The cadets' exhilaration vanished, to be replaced by an almost funereal solemnity. The vision of Earth dwindling and retreating is an awesome symbol, equivalent to eternal loss, to the act of dying itself. The more impressionable cadets— Sutton, von Gluck, Ostrander—could not look astern without finding their eyes swimming with tears. Even the suave Culpepper was awed by the magnificence of the spectacle, the sun an aching pit not to be tolerated, Earth a plump pearl rolling on black velvet among a myriad glittering diamonds. And away from Earth, away from the sun, opened an exalted magnificence of another order entirely. For the first time the cadets became dimly aware that Henry Belt had spoken truly of strange visions. Here was death, here was peace, solitude, star-blazing beauty which promised not oblivion in death, but eternity…Streams and spatters of stars…The familiar constellations, the stars with their prideful names presenting themselves like heroes: Achernar, Fomalhaut, Sadal Suud, Canopus…

Sutton could not bear to look into the sky. "It's not that I feel fear," he told von Gluck, "or yes, perhaps it is fear. It sucks at me, draws me out there…I suppose in due course I'll become accustomed to it."

"I'm not so sure," said von Gluck. "I wouldn't be surprised if space could become a psychological addiction, a need—so that whenever you walked on Earth you felt hot and breathless."

Life settled into a routine. Henry Belt no longer seemed a man, but a capricious aspect of nature, like storm or lightning; and like some natural cataclysm, Henry Belt showed no favoritism, nor forgave one jot or tittle of offense. Apart from the private cubicles no place on the ship escaped his attention. Always he reeked of whiskey, and it became a matter of covert speculation as to exactly how much whiskey he had brought aboard. But no matter how he reeked or how he swayed on his feet, his eyes remained clever and steady, and he spoke without slurring in his paradoxically clear sweet voice.

One day he seemed slightly drunker than usual, and ordered all hands into space-suits and out to inspect the sail for meteoric puncture. The order seemed sufficiently odd that the cadets stared at him in disbelief. "Gentlemen, you hesitate, you fail to exert yourselves, you luxuriate in sloth. Do you fancy yourselves at the Riviera? Into the space-suits, on the double, and a demerit to the last man dressed!"

The last man proved to be Culpepper. "Well, sir?" demanded Henry Belt. "You have earned yourself a mark. Is it below your dignity to compete?"

Culpepper considered. "Well, sir, that might be the case. Somebody had to get the demerit, and I figured it might as well be me."

"I deplore your attitude, Mr. Culpepper. I interpret it as an act of deliberate defiance."

"Sorry, sir. I don't mean it that way."

"You feel then that I am mistaken?" Henry Belt studied Culpepper carefully.

"Yes, sir," said Culpepper with engaging simplicity. "You are absolutely wrong. My attitude is not one of defiance. I think I would call it fatalism. I look at it this way. If it turns out that I accumulate so many demerits that you hold back my commission, then perhaps I wasn't cut out for the job in the first place."

For a moment Henry Belt had nothing to say. Then he grinned wolfishly. "We shall see, Mr. Culpepper. I assure you that at the present moment I am far from being confident of your abilities. Now, everybody into space. Check hoop, sail, reflector, struts and sensor. You will be adrift for two hours. When you return I want a comprehensive report. Mr. Lynch, I believe you are in charge of this watch. You will present the report."

"Yes, sir."

"One more matter. You will notice that the sail is slightly bellied by the continual radiation pressure. It therefore acts as a focusing device, the focal point presumably occurring behind the cab. But this is not a matter to be taken for granted. I have seen a man burnt to death in such a freak accident. Bear this in mind."

For two hours the cadets drifted through space, propelled by tanks of gas and thrust tubes. All enjoyed the experience except Sutton, who found himself appalled by the immensity of his emotions. Probably least affected was the practical Verona, who inspected the sail with a care exacting enough even to satisfy Henry Belt.

The next day the computer went wrong. Ostrander was in charge of the watch and knocked on Henry Belt's door to make the report.

Henry Belt appeared in the doorway. He apparently had been asleep. "What is the difficulty, Mr. Ostrander?"

"We're in trouble, sir. The computer has gone out."

Henry Belt rubbed his grizzled pate. "This is not an unusual circumstance. We prepare for this contingency by schooling all cadets thoroughly in computer design and repair. Have you identified the difficulty?"

"The bearings which suspend the data separation disks have broken. The shaft has several millimeters play and as a result there is total confusion in the data presented to the analyzer."

"An interesting problem. Why do you present it to me?"

"I thought you should be notified, sir. I don't believe we carry spares for this particular bearing."

Henry Belt shook his head sadly. "Mr. Ostrander, do you recall my statement at the beginning of this voyage, that you six gentlemen are totally responsible for the navigation of the ship?"

"Yes, sir. But——"

"This is an applicable situation. You must either repair the computer, or perform the calculations yourself."

"Very well, sir. I will do my best."

V

Lynch, Verona, Ostrander and Sutton disassembled the mechanism, removed the worn bearing. "Confounded antique!" said Lynch. "Why can't they give us decent equipment? Or if they want to kill us, why not shoot us and save us all trouble?"

"We're not dead yet," said Verona. "You've looked for a spare?"

"Naturally. There's nothing remotely like this."

Verona looked at the bearing dubiously. "I suppose we could cast a babbitt sleeve and machine it to fit. That's what we'll have to do—unless you fellows are awfully fast with your math."

Sutton glanced out the port, quickly turned away his eyes. "I wonder if we should cut sail."

"Why?" asked Ostrander.

"We don't want to build up too much velocity. We're already going 30 miles a second."

"Mars is a long way off."

"And if we miss, we go shooting past. Then where are we?"

"Sutton, you're a pessimist. A shame to find morbid tendencies in one so young." This from von Gluck, speaking from the console across the room.

"I'd rather be a live pessimist than a dead comedian."

The new sleeve was duly cast, machined and fitted. Anxiously the alignment of the data disks was checked. "Well," said Verona dubiously, "there's wobble. How much that affects the functioning remains to be seen. We can take some of it out by shimming the mount..."

Shims of tissue paper were inserted and the wobble seemed to be reduced. "Now—feed in the data," said Sutton. "Let's see how we stand."

Coordinates were fed into the system; the indicator swung. "Enlarge sail cant four degrees," said von Gluck, "we're making too much left concentric. Projected course..." he tapped buttons, watched the bright line extend across the screen, swing around a dot representing the center of gravity of Mars. "I make it an elliptical pass, about twenty thousand miles out. That's at present acceleration, and it should toss us right back at Earth."

"Great. Simply great. Let's go, 25!" This was Lynch. "I've heard of guys dropping flat on their faces and kissing Earth when they put down. Me, I'm going to live in a cave the rest of my life."

Sutton went to look at the data disks. The wobble was slight but perceptible. "Good Lord," he said huskily. "The other end of the shaft is loose too."

Lynch started to spit curses; Verona's shoulders slumped. "Let's get to work and fix it."

Another bearing was cast, machined, polished, mounted. The disks wobbled, scraped. Mars, an ocher disk, shouldered ever closer in from the side. With the computer unreliable the cadets calculated and plotted the course manually. The results were at slight but significant variance with those of the computer. The cadets looked dourly at each other. "Well," growled Ostrander, "there's error. Is it the instruments? The calculation? The plotting? Or the computer?"

Culpepper said in a subdued voice, "Well, we're not about to crash head-on, at any rate."

Verona went back to study the computer. "I can't imagine why the bearings don't work better...The mounting brackets—could they have shifted?" He removed the side housing, studied the frame, then went to the case for tools.

"What are you going to do?" demanded Sutton.

"Try to ease the mounting brackets around. I think that's our trouble."

"Leave them alone! You'll bugger the machine so it'll never work."

Verona paused, looked questioningly around the group. "Well? What's the verdict?"

"Maybe we'd better check with the old man," said Ostrander nervously.

"All well and good—but you know what he'll say."

"Let's deal cards. Ace of spades goes to ask him."

Culpepper received the ace. He knocked on Henry Belt's door. There was no response. He started to knock again, but restrained himself.

He returned to the group. "Wait till he shows himself. I'd rather crash into Mars than bring forth Henry Belt and his red book."

The ship crossed the orbit of Mars well ahead of the looming red planet. It came toppling at them with a peculiar clumsy grandeur, a mass obviously bulky and globular, but so fine and clear was the detail, so absent the perspective, that the distance and size might have been anything. Instead of swinging in a sharp elliptical curve back toward Earth, the ship swerved aside in a blunt hyperbola and proceeded outward, now at a velocity of close to fifty miles a second. Mars receded astern and to the side. A new part of space lay ahead. The sun was noticeably smaller. Earth could no longer be differentiated from the stars. Mars departed quickly and politely, and space seemed lonely and forlorn.

Henry Belt had not appeared for two days. At last Culpepper went to knock on the door—once, twice, three times: a strange face looked out. It was Henry Belt, face haggard, skin like pulled taffy. His eyes were red and glared, his hair seemed matted and more unkempt than hair a quarter-inch long should be.

But he spoke in his quiet clear voice. "Mr. Culpepper, your merciless din has disturbed me. I am quite put out with you."

"Sorry, sir. We feared that you were ill."

Henry Belt made no response. He looked past Culpepper, around the circle of faces. "You gentlemen are unwontedly serious. Has this presumptive illness of mine caused you all distress?"

Sutton spoke in a rush, "The computer is out of order."

"Why then, you must repair it."

"It's a matter of altering the housing. If we do it incorrectly—"

"Mr. Sutton, please do not harass me with the hour-by-hour minutiae of running the ship."

"But, sir, the matter has become serious; we need your advice. We missed the Mars turn-around—"

"Well, I suppose there's always Jupiter. Must I explain the basic elements of astrogation to you?"

"But the computer's out of order—definitely."

"Then, if you wish to return to Earth, you must perform the calculations with pencil and paper. Why is it necessary to explain the obvious?"

"Jupiter is a long way out," said Sutton in a shrill voice. "Why can't we just turn around and go home?" This last was almost a whisper.

"I see I've been too easy on you cads," said Henry Belt. "You stand around idly; you chatter nonsense while the machinery goes to pieces and the ship flies at random. Everybody into space-suits for sail inspection. Come now. Let's have some snap. What are you all? Walking corpses? You, Mr. Culpepper, why the delay?"

"It occurred to me, sir, that we are approaching the asteroid belt. As chief of the watch I consider it my duty to cant sail to swing us around the area."

"You may do this; then join the rest in hull and sail inspection."

"Yes, sir."

The cadets donned space-suits, Sutton with the utmost reluctance. Out into the dark void they went, and now here was loneliness indeed.

When they returned, Henry Belt had returned to his compartment.

"As Mr. Belt points out, we have no great choice," said Ostrander. "We missed Mars, so let's hit Jupiter. Luckily it's in good position—otherwise we'd have to swing out to Saturn or Uranus—"

"They're off behind the sun," said Lynch. "Jupiter's our last chance."

"Let's do it right then. I say, let's make one last attempt to set those confounded bearings..."

But now it seemed as if the wobble and twist had been eliminated. The disks tracked perfectly, the accuracy monitor glowed green.

"Great!" yelled Lynch. "Feed it the dope. Let's get going! All sail for Jupiter. Good Lord, but we're having a trip!"

"Wait till it's over," said Sutton. Since his return from sail inspection, he had stood to one side, cheeks pinched, eyes staring. "It's not over yet. And maybe it's not meant to be."

The other five pretended not to have heard him. The computer spat out figures and angles. There was a billion miles to travel. Acceleration was less, due to the diminution in the intensity of sunlight. At least a month must pass before Jupiter came close.

VI

The ship, great sail spread to the fading sunlight, fled like a ghost—out, always out. Each of the cadets had quietly performed the same calculation, and arrived at the same result. If the swing around Jupiter were not performed with exactitude, if the ship were not slung back like a stone on a string, there was nothing beyond. Saturn, Uranus, Neptune, Pluto were far around the sun; the ship, speeding at a hundred miles a second, could not be halted by the waning gravity of the sun, nor yet sufficiently accelerated in a concentric direction by sail and jet into a true orbit. The very nature of the sail made it useless as a brake, always the thrust was outward.

Within the hull seven men lived and thought, and the psychic relationship worked and stirred like yeast in a vat of decaying fruit. The fundamental similarity, the human identity of the seven men, was utterly canceled; apparent only were the disparities. Each cadet appeared to others only as a walking characteristic, and Henry Belt was an incomprehensible Thing, who appeared from his compartment at unpredictable times, to move quietly here and there with the blind blank grin of an archaic Attic hero.

Jupiter loomed and bulked. The ship, at last within reach of the Jovian gravity, sidled over to meet it. The cadets gave ever more careful attention to the computer, checking and counterchecking the instructions. Verona was the most assiduous at this, Sutton the most harassed and ineffectual. Lynch growled and cursed and sweated; Ostrander complained in a thin peevish voice. Von Gluck worked with the calm of pessimistic fatalism; Culpepper seemed unconcerned, almost debonair, a blandness which bewildered Ostrander, infuriated Lynch, awoke a malignant hate in Sutton. Verona and von Gluck on the other hand seemed to derive strength and refreshment from Culpepper's placid acceptance of the situation. Henry Belt said nothing. Occasionally he emerged from his compartment, to survey the wardroom and the cadets with the detached interest of a visitor to an asylum.

It was Lynch who made the discovery. He signaled it with an odd growl of sheer dismay, which brought a resonant questioning sound from Sutton. "My God, my God," muttered Lynch.

Verona was at his side. "What's the trouble?"

"Look. This gear. When we replaced the disks we de-phased the whole apparatus one notch. This white dot and this other white dot should synchronize. They're one sprocket apart. All the results would check and be consistent because they'd all be off by the same factor."

Verona sprang into action. Off came the housing, off came various components. Gently he lifted the gear, set it back into correct alignment. The other cadets leaned over him as he worked, except Culpepper who was chief of the watch.

Henry Belt appeared. "You gentlemen are certainly diligent in your navigation," he said presently. "Perfectionists, almost."

"We do our best," grated Lynch between set teeth. "It's a damn shame sending us out with a machine like this."

The red book appeared. "Mr. Lynch, I mark you down not for your private sentiments, which are of course yours to entertain, but for voicing them and thereby contributing to an unhealthy atmosphere of despairing and hysterical pessimism."

A tide of red crept up from Lynch's neck. He bent over the computer, made no comment. But Sutton suddenly cried out, "What else do you expect from us? Do you think we're fish or insects? We came out here to learn, not to suffer, or to fly on forever!" He gave a ghastly laugh. Henry Belt listened patiently. "Think of it!" cried Sutton. "The seven of us. In this capsule, forever!"

"All of us must die in due course, Mr. Sutton. I expect to die in space."

"I'm not afraid of death." But Sutton's voice trailed off as he glanced toward the port.

"I am afraid that I must charge you two demerits for your outburst, Mr. Sutton. A good space-man maintains his dignity at all costs, and values it more than his life."

Lynch looked up from the computer. "Well, now we've got a corrected reading. Do you know what it says?"

Henry Belt turned him a look of polite inquiry.

"We're going to miss," said Lynch. "We're going to pass by just as we passed Mars. Jupiter is pulling us around and sending us out toward Gemini."

The silence was thick in the room. Sutton seemed to whisper something, soundlessly. Henry Belt turned to look at Culpepper, who was standing by the porthole, photographing Jupiter with his personal camera.

"Mr. Culpepper?"

"Yes, sir."

"You seem unconcerned by the prospect which Mr. Sutton has set forth."

"I hope it's not imminent, sir."

"How do you propose to avoid it?"

"I imagine that we will radio for help, sir."

"You forget that I have destroyed the radio."

"I remember noting a crate marked 'Radio Parts' stored in the starboard jet-pod."

"I am sorry to disillusion you, Mr. Culpepper. That case is mislabeled."

Ostrander jumped to his feet, left the wardroom. There was the sound of moving crates. A moment of silence. Then he returned. He glared at Henry Belt. "Whiskey. Bottles of whiskey."

Henry Belt nodded. "I told you as much."

"But now we have no radio," said Lynch in an ugly voice.

"We never have had a radio, Mr. Lynch. You were warned that you would have to depend on your own resources to bring us home. You have failed, and in the process doomed me as well as yourself. Incidentally, I must mark you all down ten demerits for a faulty cargo check."

"Demerits," said Ostrander in a bleak voice.

"Now, Mr. Culpepper," said Henry Belt. "What is your next proposal?"

"I don't know, sir."

Verona spoke in a placatory voice. "What would you do, sir, if you were in our position?"

Henry Belt shook his head. "I am an imaginative man, Mr. Verona, but there are certain leaps of the mind which are beyond my powers." He returned to his compartment.

Von Gluck looked curiously at Culpepper. "It is a fact. You're not at all concerned."

"Oh, I'm concerned. But I believe that Mr. Belt wants to get home too. He's too good a space-man not to know exactly what he's doing."

The door from Henry Belt's compartment slid back. Henry Belt stood in the opening. "Mr. Culpepper, I chanced to overhear your remark, and I now note down ten demerits against you. This attitude expresses a complacence as dangerous as Mr. Sutton's utter funk. You rely on my capabilities; Mr. Sutton is afraid to rely on his own. This is not the first time I have cautioned you against this easy vice."

"Very sorry, sir."

Henry Belt looked about the room. "Pay no heed to Mr. Culpepper. He is wrong. Even if I could repair this disaster, I would not raise a hand. For I expect to die in space."

VII

The sail was canted vectorless, edgewise to the sun. Jupiter was a smudge astern. There were five cadets in the wardroom. Culpepper, Verona, and von Gluck sat talking in low voices. Ostrander and Lynch lay crouched, arms to knees, faces to the wall. Sutton had gone two days before. Quietly donning his space-suit, he had stepped into the exit chamber and thrust himself headlong into space. A propulsion unit gave him added speed, and before any of the cadets could intervene he was gone.

He had left a short note: "I fear the void because of the terrible attraction of its glory. I briefly felt the exaltation when we went out on sail inspection, and I fought it back. Now, since we must die, I will die this way, by embracing this black radiance, by giving myself wholly. Do not be sorry for me. I will die mad, but the madness will be ecstasy."

Henry Belt, when shown the note, merely shrugged. "Mr. Sutton was perhaps too imaginative and emotional to make a sound space-man. He could not have been relied upon in any emergency." And his sardonic glance seemed to include the rest of them.

Shortly thereafter Lynch and Ostrander succumbed to inanition, a kind of despondent helplessness: manic-depression in its most stupefying phase. Culpepper the suave, Verona the pragmatic and von Gluck the sensitive remained.

They spoke quietly to themselves, out of earshot of Henry Belt's room. "I still believe," said Culpepper, "that somehow there is a means to get ourselves out of this mess, and that Henry Belt knows it."

Verona said, "I wish I could think so...We've been over it a hundred times. If we set sail for Saturn or Neptune or Uranus, the outward vector of thrust plus the outward vector of our momentum will take us far beyond Pluto before we're anywhere near. The plasma jets could stop us if we had enough energy, but the shield can't supply it and we don't have another power source…"

Von Gluck hit his fist into his hand. "Gentlemen," he said in a soft delighted voice.

Culpepper and Verona stared at him, absorbing warmth from the light in his face.

"Gentlemen," said von Gluck, "I believe we have sufficient energy at hand. We will use the sail. Remember? It is bellied. It can function as a mirror. It spreads five square miles of surface. Sunlight out here is thin—but so long as we collect enough of it—"

"I understand!" said Culpepper. "We back off the hull till the reactor is at the focus of the sail and turn on the jets!"

Verona said dubiously, "We'll still be receiving radiation pressure. And what's worse, the jets will impinge back on the sail. Effect—cancellation. We'll be nowhere."

"If we cut the center out of the sail—just enough to allow the plasma through—we'd beat that objection. And as for the radiation pressure—we'll surely do better with the plasma drive."

"What do we use to make plasma? We don't have the stock."

"Anything that can be ionized. The radio, the computer, your shoes, my shirt, Culpepper's camera, Henry Belt's whiskey…"

VIII

The angel-wagon came up to meet Sail 25, in orbit beside Sail 40, which was just making ready to take out a new crew.

Henry Belt said, "Gentlemen, I beg that you leave no trash, rubbish, old clothing aboard. There is nothing more troublesome than coming aboard an untidy ship. While we wait for the lighter to discharge, I suggest that you give the ship a final thorough policing."

The cargo carrier drifted near, eased into position. Three men sprang across space to Sail 40, a few hundred yards behind 25, tossed lines back to the carrier, pulled bales of cargo and equipment across the gap.

The five cadets and Henry Belt, clad in space-suits, stepped out into the sunlight. Earth spread below, green and blue, white and brown, the contours so precious and dear to bring tears to the eyes. The cadets transferring cargo to Sail 40 gazed at them curiously as they worked. At last they were finished, and the six men of Sail 25 boarded the carrier.

"Back safe and sound, eh, Henry?" said the pilot. "Well, I'm always surprised."

Henry Belt made no answer. The cadets stowed their cargo, and standing by the port, took a final look at Sail 25. The carrier retro-jetted; the two sails seemed to rise above them.

The lighter nosed in and out of the atmosphere, braking, extended its wings, glided to an easy landing on the Mojave Desert.

The cadets, their legs suddenly loose and weak to the unaccustomed gravity, limped after Henry Belt to the carry-all, seated themselves and were conveyed to the administration complex. They alighted from the carry-all, and now Henry Belt motioned the five to the side.

"Here, gentlemen, is where I leave you. I go my way, you go yours. Tonight I will check my red book, and after various adjustments I will prepare my official report. But I believe I can present you an unofficial resumé of my impressions.

"First of all, this is neither my best nor my worst class. Mr. Lynch and Mr. Ostrander, I feel that you are ill-suited either for command or for any situation which might inflict prolonged emotional pressure upon you. I cannot recommend you for space-duty.

"Mr. von Gluck, Mr. Culpepper and Mr. Verona, all of you meet my minimum requirements for a recommendation, although I shall write the words 'Especially Recommended' only beside the names 'Clyde von Gluck' and 'Marcus Verona'. You brought the sail back to Earth by essentially faultless navigation. It means that if I am to fulfill my destiny I must make at least one more voyage into space.

"So now our association ends. I trust you have profited by it." Henry Belt nodded briefly to each of the five and limped off around the building.

The cadets looked after him. Culpepper reached in his pocket and brought forth a pair of small metal objects which he displayed in his palm. "Recognize these?"

"Hmf," said Lynch in a flat voice. "Bearings for the computer disks. The original ones."

"I found them in the little spare-parts tray. They weren't there before."

Von Gluck nodded. "The machinery always seemed to fail immediately after sail check, as I recall."

Lynch drew in his breath with a sharp hiss. He turned, strode away. Ostrander followed him. Culpepper shrugged. To Verona he gave one of the bearings, to von Gluck the other. "For souvenirs—or medals. You fellows deserve them."

"Thanks, Ed," said von Gluck.

"Thanks," muttered Verona. "I'll make a stick-pin of this thing."

The three, not able to look at each other, glanced up into the sky where the first stars of twilight were appearing, then continued on into the building where family and friends and sweethearts awaited them.

AFTERWORD TO "SAIL 25"

Several years ago, Cele Goldsmith edited *Amazing Stories*. One evening at the home of Poul Anderson she produced a set of cover illustrations which she had bought by the dozen for reasons of economy, and asked those present to formulate stories based upon them. Poul rather gingerly accepted a cover whose subject I forget. Frank Herbert was assigned the representation of a human head, with a cutaway revealing an inferno of hellfire, scurrying half-human creatures, and the paraphernalia of a nuclear power plant. I was rather more fortunate and received a picture purporting to display a fleet of spaceships driven by sun-sails. Theoretically the idea is sound, and space scientists have long included this concept among their speculations for future planetary voyages. Astrogation, of course, becomes immensely complex, but by carefully canting the sail and using planetary and/or solar gravities, any region of the solar system may be visited—not always by the most direct route, but neither did the clipper ships sail great-circle routes.

The disadvantages are the complication of the gear and the tremendous expanse of sail—to be measured in square miles—necessary to accelerate any mass of ship to any appreciable velocity within a reasonable time-span.

Which brings me back to my cover picture. The artist, no doubt for purposes of artistry, had depicted the ships with sails about the size of spinnakers for a twelve-meter, which at Earth radius from the sun would possibly produce as much as one fly-power of thrust. Additionally the sails were painted in gaudy colors, in defiance of the conventional wisdom which specifies that sun-sails shall be flimsy membranes of plastic, coated with a film of reflective metal a few molecules thick. Still, no matter how illogical the illustration, I felt that I must justify each detail by one means or another. After considerable toil I succeeded, with enormous gratitude that I had not been selected to write about the cutaway head which had been the lot of Frank Herbert.

—Jack Vance 1976

THE GIFT OF GAB

Middle afternoon had come to the Shallows; the wind had died; the sea was listless and spread with silken gloss. In the south a black broom of rain hung under the clouds; elsewhere the air was thick with pink murk. Thick crusts of seaweed floated over the Shallows; one of these supported the Bio-Minerals raft, a metal rectangle two hundred feet long, a hundred feet wide.

At four o'clock an air horn high on the mast announced the change of shift. Sam Fletcher, assistant superintendent, came out of the mess hall, crossed the deck to the office, slid back the door, looked in. Where Carl Raight usually sat, filling out his production report, the chair was empty. Fletcher looked over his shoulder, down the deck toward the processing house, but Raight was nowhere in sight. Strange. Fletcher crossed the office, checked the day's tonnage:

Rhodium trichloride...................4.01
Tantalum sulfide........................0.87
Tripyridyl rhenichloride............0.43

The gross tonnage, by Fletcher's calculations, came to 5.31—an average shift. He still led Raight in the Pinch-bottle Sweepstakes. Tomorrow was the end of the month; Fletcher could hardly fail to make off with Raight's Haig & Haig. Anticipating Raight's protests and complaints,

Fletcher smiled and whistled through his teeth. He felt cheerful and confident. Another month would bring to an end his six-months contract; then it was back to Starholme with six months' pay to his credit.

Where in thunder was Raight? Fletcher looked out the window. In his range of vision was the helicopter—guyed to the deck against the Sabrian line-squalls—the mast, the black hump of the generator, the water tank, and at the far end of the raft, the pulverizers, the leaching vats, the Tswett columns, and the storage bins.

A dark shape filled the door. Fletcher turned, but it was Agostino, the day-shift operator, who had just now been relieved by Blue Murphy, Fletcher's operator.

"Where's Raight?" asked Fletcher.

Agostino looked around the office. "I thought he was in here."

"I thought he was over in the works."

"No, I just came from there."

Fletcher crossed the room, looked into the washroom. "Wrong again."

Agostino turned away. "I'm going up for a shower." He looked back from the door. "We're low on barnacles."

"I'll send out the barge." Fletcher followed Agostino out on deck, headed for the processing house.

He passed the dock where the barges were tied up, entered the pulverizing room. The No. 1 Rotary was grinding barnacles for tantalum; the No. 2 was pulverizing rhenium-rich sea-slugs. The ball mill waited for a load of coral, orange-pink with nodules of rhodium salts.

Blue Murphy, who had a red face and a meager fringe of red hair, was making a routine check of bearings, shafts, chains, journals, valves and gauges. Fletcher called in his ear to be heard over the noise of the crushers, "Has Raight come through?"

Murphy shook his head.

Fletcher went on, into the leaching chamber where the first separation of salts from pulp was effected, through the forest of Tswett tubes, and once more out upon the deck. No Raight. He must have gone on ahead to the office.

But the office was empty.

Fletcher continued around to the mess hall. Agostino was busy with a bowl of chili. Dave Jones, the hatchet-faced steward, stood in the doorway to the galley.

"Raight been here?" asked Fletcher.

Jones, who never used two words when one would do, gave his head a morose shake. Agostino looked around. "Did you check the barnacle barge? He might have gone out to the shelves."

Fletcher looked puzzled. "What's wrong with Mahlberg?"

"He's putting new teeth on the drag-line bucket."

Fletcher tried to recall the line-up of barges along the dock. If Mahlberg, the barge-tender, had been busy with repairs, Raight might well have gone out himself. Fletcher drew himself a cup of coffee. "That's where he must be." He sat down. "It's not like Raight to put in free overtime."

Mahlberg came into the mess hall. "Where's Carl? I want to order some more teeth for the bucket."

"He's gone fishing," said Agostino.

Mahlberg laughed at the joke. "Catch himself a nice wire eel maybe. Or a dekabrach."

Dave Jones grunted. "He'll cook it himself."

"Seems like a dekabrach should make good eatin'," said Mahlberg, "close as they are to a seal."

"Who likes seal?" growled Jones.

"I'd say they're more like mermaids," Agostino remarked, "with ten-armed starfish for heads."

Fletcher put down his cup. "I wonder what time Raight left?"

Mahlberg shrugged; Agostino looked blank.

"It's only an hour out to the shelves. He ought to be back by now."

"He might have had a breakdown," said Mahlberg. "Although the barge has been running good."

Fletcher rose to his feet. "I'll give him a call." He left the mess hall, returned to the office, where he dialled T3 on the intercom screen—the signal for the barnacle barge.

The screen remained blank.

Fletcher waited. The neon bulb pulsed off and on, indicating the call of the alarm on the barge.

No reply.

Fletcher felt a vague disturbance. He left the office, went to the mast, rode up the man-lift to the cupola. From here he could overlook the half-acre of raft, the five-acre crust of seaweed and a great circle of ocean.

In the far northeast distance, up near the edge of the Shallows, the new Pelagic Recoveries raft showed as a small dark spot, almost smeared from sight by the haze. To the south, where the Equatorial

Current raced through a gap in the Shallows, the barnacle shelves were strung out in a long loose line. To the north, where the Macpherson Ridge, rising from the Deeps, came within thirty feet of breaking the surface, aluminum piles supported the sea-slug traps. Here and there floated masses of seaweed, sometimes anchored to the bottom, sometimes maintained in place by action of the currents.

Fletcher turned his binoculars along the line of barnacle shelves, spotted the barge immediately. He steadied his arms, screwed up the magnification, focused on the control cabin. He saw no one, although he could not hold the binoculars steady enough to make sure.

Fletcher scrutinized the rest of the barge.

Where was Carl Raight? Possibly in the control cabin, out of sight.

Fletcher descended to the deck, went around to the processing house, looked in. "Hey, Blue!"

Murphy appeared, wiping his big red hands on a rag.

"I'm taking the launch out to the shelves," said Fletcher. "The barge is out there, but Raight doesn't answer the screen."

Murphy shook his big bald head in puzzlement. He accompanied Fletcher to the dock, where the launch floated at moorings. Fletcher heaved at the painter, swung in the stern of the launch, jumped down on the deck.

Murphy called down to him, "Want me to come along? I'll get Hans to watch the works." Hans Heinz was the engineer—mechanic.

Fletcher hesitated. "I don't think so. If anything's happened to Raight—well, I can manage. Just keep an eye on the screen. I might call back in."

He stepped into the cockpit, seated himself, closed the dome over his head, started the pump.

The launch rolled and bounced, picked up speed, shoved its blunt nose under the surface, submerged till only the dome was clear.

Fletcher disengaged the pump; water rammed in through the nose, converted to steam, spat aft.

Bio-Minerals became a gray blot in the pink haze, while the outlines of the barge and the shelves became hard and distinct, and gradually grew large. Fletcher de-staged the power; the launch surfaced, coasted up to the dark hull, grappled with magnetic balls that allowed barge and launch to surge independently on the slow swells.

Fletcher slid back the dome, jumped up to the deck.

"Raight! Hey, Carl!"

There was no answer.

Fletcher looked up and down the deck. Raight was a big man, strong and active—but there might have been an accident. Fletcher walked down the deck toward the control cabin. He passed the No. 1 hold, heaped with black-green barnacles. At the No. 2 hold the boom was winged out, with the grab engaged on a shelf, ready to hoist it clear of the water.

The No. 3 hold was still unladen. The control cabin was empty.

Carl Raight was nowhere aboard the barge.

He might have been taken off by helicopter or launch, or he might have fallen over the side. Fletcher made a slow check of the dark water in all directions. He suddenly leaned over the side, trying to see through the surface reflections. But the pale shape under the water was a dekabrach, long as a man, sleek as satin, moving quietly about its business.

Fletcher looked thoughtfully to the northeast, where the Pelagic Recoveries raft floated behind a curtain of pink murk. It was a new venture, only three months old, owned and operated by Ted Chrystal, former biochemist on the Bio-Minerals raft. The Sabrian Ocean was inexhaustible; the market for metal was insatiable; the two rafts were in no sense competitors. By no stretch of imagination could Fletcher conceive Chrystal or his men attacking Carl Raight.

He must have fallen overboard.

Fletcher returned to the control cabin, climbed the ladder to the flying bridge on top. He made a last check of the water around the barge, although he knew it to be a useless gesture—the current, moving through the gap at a steady two knots, would have swept Raight's body out over the Deeps. Fletcher scanned the horizon. The line of shelves dwindled away into the pink gloom. The mast on the Bio-Minerals raft marked the sky to the northwest. The Pelagic Recoveries raft could not be seen. There was no living creature in sight.

The screen signal sounded from the cabin. Fletcher went inside. Blue Murphy was calling from the raft. "What's the news?"

"None whatever," said Fletcher.

"What do you mean?"

"Raight's not out here."

The big red face creased. "Just who is out there?"

"Nobody. It looks like Raight fell over the side."

Murphy whistled. There seemed nothing to say. Finally he asked, "Any idea how it happened?"

Fletcher shook his head. "I can't figure it out."

Murphy licked his lips. "Maybe we ought to close down."

"Why?" asked Fletcher.

"Well—reverence to the dead, you might say."

Fletcher grinned crookedly. "We might as well keep running."

"Just as you like. But we're low on the barnacles."

"Carl loaded a hold and a half—" Fletcher hesitated, heaved a deep sigh. "I might as well shake in a few more shelves."

Murphy winced. "It's a squeamish business, Sam. You haven't a nerve in your body."

"It doesn't make any difference to Carl now," said Fletcher. "We've got to scrape barnacles sometime. There's nothing to be gained by moping."

"I suppose you're right," said Murphy dubiously.

"I'll be back in a couple hours."

"Don't go overboard like Raight now."

The screen went blank. Fletcher reflected that he was in charge, superintendent of the raft, until the arrival of the new crew, a month away. Responsibility, which he did not particularly want, was his.

He went slowly back out on deck, climbed into the winch pulpit. For an hour he pulled sections of shelves from the sea, suspended them over the hold while scraper arms wiped off the black-green clusters, then slid the shelves back into the ocean. Here was where Raight had been working just before his disappearance. How could he have fallen overboard from the winch pulpit?

Uneasiness inched along Fletcher's nerves, up into his brain. He shut down the winch, climbed down from the pulpit. He stopped short, staring at the rope on the deck.

It was a strange rope—glistening, translucent, an inch thick. It lay in a loose loop on the deck, and one end led over the side. Fletcher started down, then hesitated. Rope? Certainly none of the barge's equipment.

Careful, thought Fletcher.

A hand-scraper hung on the king-post, a tool like a small adze. It was used for manual scraping of the shelves, if for some reason the automatic scrapers failed. It was two steps distant, across the rope. Fletcher stepped down to the deck. The rope quivered; the loop contracted, snapped around Fletcher's ankles.

Fletcher lunged, caught hold of the scraper. The rope gave a cruel jerk; Fletcher sprawled flat on his face, and the scraper jarred out of his hands. He kicked, struggled, but the rope drew him easily toward the gunwale. Fletcher made a convulsive grab for the scraper, barely reached it. The rope was lifting his ankles, to pull him over the rail. Fletcher strained forward, hacked, again and again. The rope sagged, fell apart, snaked over the side.

Fletcher gained his feet, staggered to the rail. Down into the water slid the rope, out of sight among the oily reflections of the sky. Then, for half a second, a wave-front held itself perpendicular to Fletcher's line of vision. Three feet under the surface swam a dekabrach. Fletcher saw the pink-golden cluster of arms, radiating like the arms of a starfish, the black patch at their core which might be an eye.

Fletcher drew back from the gunwale, puzzled, frightened, oppressed by the nearness of death. He cursed his stupidity, his reckless carelessness; how could he have been so undiscerning as to remain out here loading the barge? It was clear from the first that Raight had never died by accident. Something had killed Raight, and Fletcher had invited it to kill him too. He limped to the control cabin, started the pumps. Water sucked in through the bow orifice, thrust out through the vents. The barge moved out away from the shelves; Fletcher set the course to northwest, toward Bio-Minerals, then went out on deck.

Day was almost at an end; the sky was darkening to maroon; the gloom grew thick as bloody water. Geideon, a dull red giant, largest of Sabria's two suns, dropped out of the sky. For a few minutes only the light from blue-green Atreus played on the clouds. The gloom changed its quality to pale green, which by some illusion seemed brighter than the previous pink. Atreus sank and the sky went dark.

Ahead shone the Bio-Minerals mast-head light, climbing into the sky as the barge approached. Fletcher saw the black shapes of men outlined against the glow. The entire crew was waiting for him: the two operators, Agostino and Murphy, Mahlberg the barge-tender, Damon the biochemist, Dave Jones the steward, Manners the technician, Hans Heinz the engineer.

Fletcher docked the barge, climbed the soft stairs hacked from the wadded seaweed, stopped in front of the silent men. He looked from face to face. Waiting on the raft they had felt the strangeness of Raight's death more vividly than he had; so much showed in their expressions.

Fletcher, answering the unspoken question, said, "It wasn't an accident. I know what happened."

"What?" someone asked.

"There's a thing like a white rope," said Fletcher. "It slides up out of the sea. If a man comes near it, it snaps around his leg and pulls him overboard."

Murphy asked in a hushed voice, "You're sure?"

"It just about got me."

Damon the biochemist asked in a skeptical voice, "A live rope?"

"I suppose it might have been alive."

"What else could it have been?"

Fletcher hesitated. "I looked over the side. I saw dekabrachs. One for sure, maybe two or three others."

There was silence. The men looked out over the water. Murphy asked in a wondering voice, "Then the dekabrachs are the ones?"

"I don't know," said Fletcher in a strained sharp voice. "A white rope, or fiber, nearly snared me. I cut it apart. When I looked over the side I saw dekabrachs."

The men made hushed noises of wonder and awe.

Fletcher turned away, started toward the mess hall. The men lingered on the dock, examining the ocean, talking in subdued voices. The lights of the raft shone past them, out into the darkness. There was nothing to be seen.

❀

Later in the evening Fletcher climbed the stairs to the laboratory over the office, to find Eugene Damon busy at the micro-film viewer.

Damon had a thin, long-jawed face, lank blond hair, a fanatic's eyes. He was industrious and thorough, but he worked in the shadow of Ted Chrystal, who had quit Bio-Minerals to bring his own raft to Sabria. Chrystal was a man of great ability. He had adapted the vanadium-sequestering sea-slug of Earth to Sabrian waters; he had developed the tantalum-barnacle from a rare and sickly species into the hardy high-yield producer that it was. Damon worked twice the hours that Chrystal had put in, and while he performed his routine duties efficiently, he lacked the flair and imaginative resource which Chrystal used to leap from problem to solution without apparent steps in between.

He looked up when Fletcher came into the lab, then applied himself once more to the micro-screen.

Fletcher watched a moment. "What are you looking for?" he asked presently.

Damon responded in the ponderous, slightly pedantic manner that sometimes amused, sometimes irritated Fletcher. "I've been searching the index to identify the long white 'rope' which attacked you."

Fletcher made a noncommittal sound, went to look at the settings on the micro-file throw-out. Damon had coded for 'long', 'thin', dimensional classification 'E, F, G'. On these instructions, the selector, scanning the entire roster of Sabrian life forms, had pulled the cards of seven organisms.

"Find anything?" Fletcher asked.

"Not so far." Damon slid another card into the viewer. 'Sabrian Annelid, RRS-4924', read the title, and on the screen appeared a schematic outline of a long segmented worm. The scale showed it to be about two and a half meters long.

Fletcher shook his head. "The thing that got me was four or five times that long. And I don't think it was segmented."

"That's the most likely of the lot so far," said Damon. He turned a quizzical glance up at Fletcher. "I imagine you're pretty sure about this...long white marine 'rope'?"

Fletcher ignored him, scooped up the seven cards, dropped them back into the file, looked in the code book, reset the selector.

Damon had the codes memorized and was able to read directly off the dials. "'Appendages'—'long'—'dimensions D, E, F, G'."

The selector kicked three cards into the viewer.

The first was a pale saucer which swam like a skate, trailing four long whiskers. "That's not it," said Fletcher.

The second was a black, bullet-shaped water-beetle, with a posterior flagellum.

"Not that one."

The third was a kind of mollusk, with a plasm based on selenium, silicon, fluorine and carbon. The shell was a hemisphere of silicon carbide, with a hump from which protruded a thin prehensile tendril.

The creature bore the name 'Stryzkal's Monitor', after Esteban Stryzkal, the famous pioneer taxonomist of Sabria.

"That might be the guilty party," said Fletcher.

"It's not mobile," objected Damon. "Stryzkal finds it anchored to the North Shallows pegmatite dikes, in conjunction with the dekabrach colonies."

Fletcher was reading the descriptive material. "'The feeler is elastic without observable limit, and apparently functions as a food-gathering, spore-disseminating, exploratory organ. The monitor typically is found near the dekabrach colonies. Symbiosis between the two life forms is not impossible.'"

Damon looked at him questioningly. "Well?"

"I saw some dekabrachs out along the shelves."

"You can't be sure you were attacked by a monitor," Damon said dubiously. "After all, they don't swim."

"So they don't," said Fletcher, "according to Stryzkal."

Damon started to speak, then noticing Fletcher's expression, said in a subdued voice, "Of course there's room for error. Not even Stryzkal could work out much more than a summary of planetary life."

Fletcher had been reading the screen. "Here's Chrystal's analysis of the one he brought up."

They studied the elements and primary compounds of a Stryzkal Monitor's constitution.

"Nothing of commercial interest," said Fletcher.

Damon was absorbed in a personal chain of thought. "Did Chrystal actually go down and trap a monitor?"

"That's right. In the water-bug. He spent lots of time underwater."

"Everybody to their own methods," said Damon shortly.

Fletcher dropped the cards back in the file. "Whether you like him or not, he's a good field man. Give the devil his due."

"It seems to me that the field phase is over and done with," muttered Damon. "We've got the production line set up; it's a full-time job trying to increase the yield. Of course I may be wrong."

Fletcher laughed, slapped Damon on the skinny shoulder. "I'm not finding fault, Gene. The plain fact is that there's too many avenues for one man to explore. We could keep four men busy."

"Four men?" said Damon. "A dozen is more like it. Three different protoplasmic phases on Sabria, to the single carbon group on Earth! Even Stryzkal only scratched the surface!"

He watched Fletcher for a while, then asked curiously: "What are you after now?"

Fletcher was once more running through the index. "What I came in here to check. The dekabrachs."

Damon leaned back in his chair. "Dekabrachs? Why?"

"There's lots of things about Sabria we don't know," said Fletcher mildly. "Have you ever been down to look at a dekabrach colony?"

Damon compressed his mouth. "No. I certainly haven't."

Fletcher dialled for the dekabrach card.

It snapped out of the file into the viewer. The screen showed Stryzkal's original photo-drawing, which in many ways conveyed more information than the color stereos. The specimen depicted was something over six feet long, with a pale seal-like body terminating in three propulsive vanes. At the head radiated the ten arms from which the creature derived its name—flexible members eighteen inches long, surrounding the black disk which Stryzkal assumed to be an eye.

Fletcher skimmed through the rather sketchy account of the creature's habitat, diet, reproductive methods, and protoplasmic classification. He frowned in dissatisfaction. "There's not much information here—considering that they're one of the more important species. Let's look at the anatomy."

The dekabrach's skeleton was based on an anterior dome of bone with three flexible cartilaginous vertebrae, each terminating in a propulsive vane.

The information on the card came to an end. "I thought you said Chrystal made observations on the dekabrachs," growled Damon.

"So he did."

"If he's such a howling good field man, where's his data?"

Fletcher grinned. "Don't blame me, I just work here." He put the card through the screen again.

Under 'General Comments', Stryzkal had noted, *Dekabrachs appear to belong in the Sabrian Class A group, the silico-carbo-nitride phase, although they deviate in important respects.* He had added a few lines of speculation regarding dekabrach relationships to other Sabrian species.

Chrystal merely made the comment, "Checked for commercial application; no specific recommendation."

Fletcher made no comment.

"How closely did he check?" asked Damon.

"In his usual spectacular way. He went down in the water-bug, harpooned one of them, dragged it to the laboratory. Spent three days dissecting it."

"Precious little he's noted here," grumbled Damon. "If I worked three days on a new species like the dekabrachs, I could write a book."

They watched the information repeat itself.

Damon stabbed out with his long bony finger. "Look! That's been blanked over. See those black triangles in the margin? Cancellation marks!"

Fletcher rubbed his chin. "Stranger and stranger."

"It's downright mischievous," Damon cried indignantly, "erasing material without indicating motive or correction."

Fletcher nodded slowly. "It looks like somebody's going to have to consult Chrystal." He considered. "Well—why not now?" He descended to the office, where he called the Pelagic Recoveries raft.

✺

Chrystal himself appeared on the screen. He was a large blond man with a blooming pink skin and an affable innocence that camouflaged the directness of his mind; his plumpness similarly disguised a powerful musculature. He greeted Fletcher with cautious heartiness. "How's it going on Bio-Minerals? Sometimes I wish I was back with you fellows—this working on your own isn't all it's cracked up to be."

"We've had an accident over here," said Fletcher. "I thought I'd better pass on a warning."

"Accident?" Chrystal looked anxious. "What's happened?"

"Carl Raight took the barge out—and never came back."

Chrystal was shocked. "That's terrible! How…why—"

"Apparently something pulled him in. I think it was a monitor mollusk—Stryzkal's Monitor."

Chrystal's pink face wrinkled in puzzlement. "A monitor? Was the barge over shallow water? But there wouldn't be water that shallow. I don't get it."

"I don't either."

Chrystal twisted a cube of white metal between his fingers. "That's certainly strange. Raight must be—dead?"

Fletcher nodded somberly. "That's the presumption. I've warned everybody here not to go out alone; I thought I'd better do the same for you."

"That's decent of you, Sam." Chrystal frowned, looked at the cube of metal, put it down. "There's never been trouble on Sabria before."

"I saw dekabrachs under the barge. They might be involved somehow."

Chrystal looked blank. "Dekabrachs? They're harmless enough."

Fletcher nodded noncommittally. "Incidentally, I tried to check on dekabrachs in the micro-library. There wasn't much information. Quite a bit of material has been cancelled out."

Chrystal raised his pale eyebrows. "Why tell me?"

"Because you might have done the cancelling."

Chrystal looked aggrieved. "Now why should I do something like that? I worked hard for Bio-Minerals, Sam—you know that as well as I do. Now I'm trying to make money for myself. It's no bed of roses, I'll tell you." He touched the cube of white metal, then noticing Fletcher's eyes on it, pushed it to the side of his desk, against Cosey's *Universal Handbook of Constants and Physical Relationships*.

After a pause Fletcher asked, "Well, did you or didn't you blank out part of the dekabrach story?"

Chrystal frowned in deep thought. "I might have cancelled one or two ideas that turned out bad—nothing very important. I have a hazy idea that I pulled them out of the bank."

"Just what were those ideas?" Fletcher asked in a sardonic voice.

"I don't remember offhand. Something about feeding habits, probably. I suspected that the deks ingested plankton, but that doesn't seem to be the case."

"No?"

"They browse on underwater fungus that grows on the coral banks. That's my best guess."

"Is that all you cut out?"

"I can't think of anything more."

Fletcher's eyes went back to the cube of metal. He noticed that it covered the Handbook title from the angle of the V in 'Universal' to the center of the O in 'of'. "What's that you've got on your desk, Chrystal? Interesting yourself in metallurgy?"

"No, no," said Chrystal. He picked up the cube, looked at it critically. "Just a bit of alloy. I'm checking it for resistance to reagents. Well, thanks for calling, Sam."

"You don't have any personal ideas on how Raight got it?"

Chrystal looked surprised. "Why on earth do you ask me?"

"You know more about the dekabrachs than anyone else on Sabria."

"I'm afraid I can't help you, Sam."

Fletcher nodded. "Good night."

"Good night, Sam."

Fletcher sat looking at the blank screen. Monitor mollusks—dekabrachs—the blanked micro-film. There was a drift here whose direction he could not identify. The dekabrachs seemed to be involved, and by association, Chrystal. Fletcher put no credence in Chrystal's protestations; he suspected that Chrystal lied as a matter of policy, on almost any subject. Fletcher's mind went to the cube of metal. Chrystal had seemed rather too casual, too quick to brush the matter aside. Fletcher brought out his own Handbook. He measured the distance between the fork of the V and the center of the O: 4.9 centimeters. Now,

161

if the block represented a kilogram mass, as was likely with such sample blocks—Fletcher calculated. In a cube, 4.9 centimeters on a side, were 119 cc. Hypothesizing a mass of 1000 grams, the density worked out to 8.4 grams per cc.

Fletcher looked at the figure. In itself it was not particularly suggestive. It might be one of a hundred alloys. There was no point in going too far on a string of hypotheses—still, he looked in the Handbook. Nickel, 8.6 grams per cc. Cobalt, 8.7 grams per cc. Niobium, 8.4 grams per cc.

Fletcher sat back and considered. Niobium? An element costly and tedious to synthesize, with limited natural sources and an unsatisfied market. The idea was stimulating. Had Chrystal developed a biological source of niobium? If so, his fortune was made.

Fletcher relaxed in his chair. He felt done in—mentally and physically. His mind went to Carl Raight. He pictured the body drifting loose and haphazard through the night, sinking through miles of water into places where light would never reach. Why had Carl Raight been pillaged of life?

Fletcher began to ache with anger and frustration, at the futility, the indignity of Raight's passing. Carl Raight was too good a man to be dragged to his death into the dark ocean of Sabria.

Fletcher jerked himself upright, marched out of the office, up the steps to the laboratory.

Damon was still busy with his routine work. He had three projects under way: two involving the sequestering of platinum by species of Sabrian algae; the third an attempt to increase the rhenium absorption of an Alphard-Alpha flat-sponge. In each case his basic technique was the same: subjecting succeeding generations to an increasing concentration of metallic salt, under conditions favoring mutation. Certain of the organisms would presently begin to make functional use of the metal; they would be isolated and transferred to Sabrian brine. A few might survive the shock; some might adapt to the new conditions and begin to absorb the now necessary element.

By selective breeding the desirable qualities of these latter organisms would be intensified; they would then be cultivated on a large-scale basis and the inexhaustible Sabrian waters would presently be made to yield another product.

Coming into the lab, Fletcher found Damon arranging trays of algae cultures in geometrically exact lines. He looked rather sourly over his shoulder at Fletcher.

"I talked to Chrystal," said Fletcher.

Damon became interested. "What did he say?"

"He says he might have wiped a few bad guesses off the film."

"Ridiculous," snapped Damon.

Fletcher went to the table, looked thoughtfully along the row of algae cultures. "Have you run into any niobium on Sabria, Gene?"

"Niobium? No. Not in any appreciable concentration. There are traces in the ocean, naturally. I believe one of the corals shows a set of niobium lines." He cocked his head with birdlike inquisitiveness. "Why do you ask?"

"Just an idea, wild and random."

"I don't suppose Chrystal gave you any satisfaction?"

"None at all."

"Then what's the next move?"

Fletcher hitched himself up on the table. "I'm not sure. There's not much I can do. Unless—" he hesitated.

"Unless what?"

"Unless I make an underwater survey, myself."

Damon was appalled. "What do you hope to gain by that?"

Fletcher smiled. "If I knew, I wouldn't need to go. Remember, Chrystal went down, then came back up and stripped the micro-file."

"I realize that," said Damon. "Still, I think it's rather...well, fool-hardy, after what's happened."

"Perhaps, perhaps not." Fletcher slid off the table to the deck. "I'll let it ride till tomorrow, anyway."

He left Damon making out his daily check sheet, descended to the main deck.

Blue Murphy was waiting at the foot of the stairs. Fletcher said, "Well, Murphy?"

The round red face displayed a puzzled frown. "Agostino up there with you?"

Fletcher stopped short. "No."

"He should have relieved me half an hour ago. He's not in the dormitory; he's not in the mess hall."

"Good God," said Fletcher, "another one?"

Murphy looked over his shoulder at the ocean. "They saw him about an hour ago in the mess hall."

"Come on," said Fletcher. "Let's search the raft."

They looked everywhere—processing house, the cupola on the mast, all the nooks and crannies a man might take it into his head to explore. The barges were all at dock; the launch and catamaran swung at their moorings; the helicopter hulked on the deck with drooping blades.

Agostino was nowhere aboard the raft. No one knew where Agostino had gone; no one knew exactly when he had left.

The crew of the raft collected in the mess hall, making small nervous motions, looking out the portholes over the ocean.

Fletcher could think of very little to say. "Whatever is after us—and we don't know what it is—it can surprise us and it's watching. We've got to be careful—more than careful!"

Murphy pounded his fist softly on the table. "But what can we do? We can't just stand around like silly cows!"

"Sabria is theoretically a safe planet," said Damon. "According to Stryzkal and the Galactic Index, there are no hostile life forms here."

Murphy snorted, "I wish old Stryzkal was here now to tell me."

"He might be able to theorize back Raight and Agostino." Dave Jones looked at the calendar. "A month to go."

"We'll only run one shift," said Fletcher, "until we get replacements."

"Call them reinforcements," muttered Mahlberg.

"Tomorrow," said Fletcher, "I'm going to take the water-bug down, look around, and get an idea what's going on. In the meantime, everybody better carry hatchets or cleavers."

There was soft sound on the windows, on the deck outside. "Rain," said Mahlberg. He looked at the clock on the wall. "Midnight."

The rain hissed through the air, drummed on the walls; the decks ran with water and the mast-head lights glared through the slanting streaks.

Fletcher went to the streaming windows, looked toward the process house. "I guess we better button up for the night. There's no reason to—." He squinted through the window, then ran to the door and out into the rain.

Water pelted into his face, he could see very little but the glare of the lights in the rain. And a hint of white along the shining gray-black of the deck, like an old white plastic hose.

A snatch at his ankles: his feet were yanked from under him. He fell flat upon the streaming metal.

Behind him came the thud of feet; there were excited curses, a clang and scrape; the grip on Fletcher's ankles loosened.

Fletcher jumped up, staggered back against the mast. "Something's in the process house," he yelled.

The men pounded off through the rain; Fletcher came after.

But there was nothing in the process house. The doors were wide; the rooms were bright. The squat pulverizers stood on either hand, behind were the pressure tanks, the vats, the pipes of six different colors.

Fletcher pulled the master switch; the hum and grind of the machinery died. "Let's lock up and get back to the dormitory."

❋

Morning was the reverse of evening; first the green gloom of Atreus, warming to pink as Geideon rose behind the clouds. It was a blustery day, with squalls trailing dark curtains all around the compass.

Fletcher ate breakfast, dressed in a skin-tight coverall threaded with heating-filaments, then a waterproof garment with a plastic head-dome.

The water-bug hung on davits at the east edge of the raft, a shell of transparent plastic with the pumps sealed in a metal cell amidships. Submerging, the hull filled with water through valves, which then closed; the bug could submerge to four hundred feet, the hull resisting about half the pressure, the enclosed water the rest.

Fletcher lowered himself into the cockpit; Murphy connected the hoses from the air tanks to Fletcher's helmet, then screwed the port shut. Mahlberg and Hans Heinz winged out the davits. Murphy went to stand by the hoist-control; for a moment he hesitated, looking from the dark pink-dappled water to Fletcher, and back at the water.

Fletcher waved his hand. "Lower away." His voice came from the loudspeaker on the bulkhead behind them.

Murphy swung the handle. The bug eased down. Water gushed in through the valves, up around Fletcher's body, over his head. Bubbles rose from the helmet exhaust valve.

Fletcher tested the pumps, then cast off the grapples. The bug slant-ed down into the water.

165

Murphy sighed. "He's got more nerve than I'm ever likely to have."

"He can get away from whatever's after him," said Damon. "He might well be safer than we are here on the raft."

Murphy clapped him on the shoulder. "Damon, my lad—you can climb. Up on top of the mast you'll be safe; it's unlikely that they'll come there to tug you into the water." Murphy raised his eyes to the cupola a hundred feet over the deck. "And I think that's where I'd take myself—if only someone would bring me my food."

Heinz pointed to the water. "There go the bubbles. He went under the raft. Now he's headed north."

The day became stormy. Spume blew over the raft, and it meant a drenching to venture out on deck. The clouds thinned enough to show the outlines of Geideon and Atreus, a blood-orange and a lime.

Suddenly the winds died; the ocean flattened into an uneasy calm. The crew sat in the mess hall drinking coffee, talking in staccato uneasy voices.

Damon became restless and went up to his laboratory. He came running back down into the mess hall.

"Dekabrachs—they're under the raft! I saw them from the observation deck!"

Murphy shrugged. "They're safe from me."

"I'd like to get hold of one," said Damon. "Alive."

"Don't we have enough trouble already?" growled Dave Jones.

Damon explained patiently. "We know nothing about dekabrachs. They're a highly developed species. Chrystal destroyed all the data we had, and I should have at least one specimen."

Murphy rose to his feet. "I suppose we can scoop one up in a net."

"Good," said Damon. "I'll set up the big tank to receive it."

The crew went out on deck where the weather had turned sultry. The ocean was flat and oily; haze blurred sea and sky together in a smooth gradation of color, from dirty scarlet near the raft to pale pink overhead.

The boom was winged out, a parachute net was attached and lowered quietly into the water. Heinz stood by the winch; Murphy leaned over the rail, staring intently down into the water.

A pale shape drifted out from under the raft. "Lift!" bawled Murphy.

The line snapped taut; the net rose out of the water in a cascade of spray. In the center a six-foot dekabrach pulsed and thrashed, gill slits rasping for water.

The boom swung inboard; the net tripped; the dekabrach slid into the plastic tank.

It darted forward and backward; the plastic dented and bulged where it struck. Then it floated quiet in the center, head-tentacles folded back against the torso.

All hands crowded around the tank. The black eye-spot looked back through the transparent walls.

Murphy asked Damon, "Now what?"

"I'd like the tank lifted to the deck outside the laboratory where I can get at it."

"No sooner said than done."

The tank was hoisted and swung to the spot Damon had indicated; Damon went excitedly off to plan his research.

The crew watched the dekabrach for ten or fifteen minutes, then drifted back to the mess hall.

※

Time passed. Gusts of wind raked up the ocean into a sharp steep chop. At two o'clock the loudspeaker hissed; the crew stiffened, raised their heads.

Fletcher's voice came from the diaphragm. "Hello aboard the raft. I'm about two miles northwest. Stand by to haul me aboard."

"Hah!" cried Murphy, grinning. "He made it."

"I gave odds against him of four to one," Mahlberg said. "I'm lucky nobody took them."

"Get a move on; he'll be alongside before we're ready."

The crew trooped out to the landing. The water-bug came sliding over the ocean, its glistening back riding the dark disorder of the waters.

It slipped quietly up to the raft; grapples clamped to the plates fore and aft. The winch whined, the bug lifted from the sea, draining its ballast of water.

Fletcher, in the cockpit, looked tense and tired. He climbed stiffly out of the bug, stretched, unzipped the waterproof suit, pulled off the helmet.

"Well, I'm back." He looked around the group. "Surprised?"

"I'd have lost money on you," Mahlberg told him.

"What did you find out?" asked Damon. "Anything?"

Fletcher nodded. "Plenty. Let me get into clean clothes. I'm wringing wet—sweat." He stopped short, looking up at the tank on the laboratory deck. "When did that come aboard?"

"We netted it about noon," said Murphy. "Damon wanted to look one over."

Fletcher stood looking up at the tank with his shoulders drooping.

"Something wrong?" asked Damon.

"No," said Fletcher. "We couldn't have it worse than it is already." He turned away toward the dormitory.

The crew waited for him in the mess hall; twenty minutes later he appeared. He drew himself a cup of coffee, sat down.

"Well," said Fletcher. "I can't be sure—but it looks as if we're in trouble."

"Dekabrachs?" asked Murphy.

Fletcher nodded.

"I knew it!" Murphy cried in triumph. "You can tell by looking at the blatherskites they're up to no good."

Damon frowned, disapproving of emotional judgments. "Just what is the situation?" he asked Fletcher. "At least, as it appears to you?"

Fletcher chose his words carefully. "Things are going on that we've been unaware of. In the first place, the dekabrachs are socially organized."

"You mean to say—they're intelligent?"

Fletcher shook his head. "I don't know for sure. It's possible. It's equally possible that they live by instinct, like social insects."

"How in the world—" began Damon; Fletcher held up a hand. "I'll tell you just what happened; you can ask all the questions you like afterwards." He drank his coffee.

"When I went down under, naturally I was on the alert and kept my eyes peeled. I felt safe enough in the water-bug—but funny things have been happening, and I was a little nervous.

"As soon as I was in the water I saw the dekabrachs—five or six of them." Fletcher paused, sipped his coffee.

"What were they doing?" asked Damon.

"Nothing very much. Drifting near a big monitor which had attached itself to the seaweed. The arm was hanging down like a rope—clear out of sight. I edged the bug in just to see what the deks would do; they began backing away. I didn't want to waste too much time under the raft, so I swung off north, toward the Deeps. Halfway there I saw an odd thing; in fact I passed it, and swung around to take another look.

"There were about a dozen deks. They had a monitor—and this one was really big. A giant. It was hanging on a set of balloons or bubbles—

some kind of pods that kept it floating, and the deks were easing it along. In this direction."

"In this direction, eh?" mused Murphy.

"What did you do?" asked Manners.

"Well, perhaps it was all an innocent outing—but I didn't want to take any chances. The arm of this monitor would be like a hawser. I turned the bug at the bubbles, burst some, scattered the rest. The monitor dropped like a stone. The deks took off in different directions. I figured I'd won that round. I kept on going north, and pretty soon I came to where the slope starts down into the Deeps. I'd been traveling about twenty feet under; now I lowered to two hundred. I had to turn on the lights, of course—this red twilight doesn't penetrate water too well." Fletcher took another gulp of coffee. "All the way across the Shallows I'd been passing over coral banks and dodging forests of kelp. Where the shelf slopes down to the Deeps the coral gets to be something fantastic—I suppose there's more water movement, more nourishment, more oxygen. It grows a hundred feet high, in spires and towers, umbrellas, platforms, arches—white, pale blue, pale green.

"I came to the edge of a cliff. It was a shock—one minute my lights were on the coral, all these white towers and pinnacles—then there was nothing. I was over the Deeps. I got a little nervous." Fletcher grinned. "Irrational, of course. I checked the fathometer—bottom was twelve thousand feet down. I still didn't like it, and turned around, swung back. Then I noticed lights off to my right. I turned my own off, moved in to investigate. The lights spread out as if I was flying over a city—and that's just about what it was."

"Dekabrachs?" asked Damon.

Fletcher nodded. "Dekabrachs."

"You mean—they built it themselves? Lights and all?"

Fletcher frowned. "That's what I can't be sure of. The coral had grown into shapes that gave them little cubicles to swim in and out of, and do whatever they'd want to do in a house. Certainly they don't need protection from the rain. They hadn't built these coral grottoes in the sense that we build a house—but it didn't look like natural coral either. It's as if they made the coral grow to suit them."

Murphy said doubtfully, "Then they're intelligent."

"No, not necessarily. After all, wasps build complicated nests with no more equipment than a set of instincts."

"What's your opinion?" asked Damon. "Just what impression does it give?"

Fletcher shook his head. "I can't be sure. I don't know what kind of standards to apply. 'Intelligence' is a word that means lots of different things, and the way we generally use it is artificial and specialized."

"I don't get you," said Murphy. "Do you mean these deks are intelligent or don't you?"

Fletcher laughed. "Are men intelligent?"

"Sure. So they say, at least."

"Well, what I'm trying to get across is that we can't use man's intelligence as a measure of the dekabrach's mind. We've got to judge him by a different set of values—dekabrach values. Men use tools of metal, ceramic, fiber: inorganic stuff—at least, dead. I can imagine a civilization dependent upon living tools—specialized creatures the mastergroup uses for special purposes. Suppose the dekabrachs live on this basis? They force the coral to grow in the shape they want. They use the monitors for derricks or hoists, or snares, or to grab at something in the upper air."

"Apparently, then," said Damon, "you believe that the dekabrachs are intelligent."

Fletcher shook his head. "Intelligence is just a word—a matter of definition. What the deks do may not be susceptible to human definition."

"It's beyond me," said Murphy, settling back in his chair.

Damon pressed the subject. "I am not a metaphysicist or a semanticist. But it seems that we might apply, or try to apply, a crucial test."

"What difference does it make one way or the other?" asked Murphy.

Fletcher said, "It makes a big difference where the law is concerned."

"Ah," said Murphy, "the Doctrine of Responsibility."

Fletcher nodded. "We could be yanked off the planet for injuring or killing intelligent autochthones. It's been done."

"That's right," said Murphy. "I was on Alkaid Two when Graviton Corporation got in that kind of trouble."

"So if the deks are intelligent, we've got to watch our step. That's why I looked twice when I saw the dek in the tank."

"Well—are they or aren't they?" asked Mahlberg.

"There's one crucial test," Damon repeated.

The crew looked at him expectantly.

"Well?" asked Murphy. "Spill it."

"Communication."

Murphy nodded thoughtfully. "That seems to make sense." He looked at Fletcher. "Did you notice them communicating?"

Fletcher shook his head. "Tomorrow I'll take a camera out, and a sound recorder. Then we'll know for sure."

"Incidentally," said Damon, "why were you asking about niobium?"

Fletcher had almost forgotten. "Chrystal had a chunk on his desk. Or maybe he did—I'm not sure."

Damon nodded. "Well, it may be a coincidence, but the deks are loaded with it."

Fletcher stared.

"It's in their blood, and there's a strong concentration in the interior organs."

Fletcher sat with his cup halfway to his mouth. "Enough to make a profit on?"

Damon nodded. "Probably a hundred grams or more in the organism."

"Well, well," said Fletcher. "That's very interesting indeed."

Rain roared down during the night; a great wind came up, lifting and driving the rain and spume. Most of the crew had gone to bed: all except Dave Jones the steward and Manners the radio man, who sat up over a chess board.

A new sound rose over wind and rain—a metallic groaning, a creaking discord that presently became too loud to ignore. Manners jumped to his feet, went to the window.

"The mast!"

Dimly it could be seen through the rain, swaying like a reed, the arc of oscillation increasing with each swing.

"What can we do?" cried Jones.

One set of guy-lines snapped. "Nothing now."

"I'll call Fletcher." Jones ran for the passage to the dormitory.

The mast gave a sudden jerk, poised long seconds at an unlikely angle, then toppled across the process house.

Fletcher appeared, stared out the window. With the mast-head light no longer shining down, the raft was dark and ominous. Fletcher shrugged, turned away. "There's nothing we can do tonight. It's worth a man's life to go out on that deck."

In the morning, examination of the wreckage revealed that two of the guy-lines had been sawed or clipped cleanly through. The mast, of light-weight construction, was quickly cut apart, and the twisted segments dragged to a corner of the deck. The raft seemed bald and flat.

"Someone or something," said Fletcher, "is anxious to give us as much trouble as possible." He looked across the leaden-pink ocean to where the Pelagic Recoveries raft floated beyond the range of vision.

"Apparently," said Damon, "you refer to Chrystal."

"I have suspicions."

Damon glanced out across the water. "I'm practically certain."

"Suspicion isn't proof," said Fletcher. "In the first place, what would Chrystal hope to gain by attacking us?"

"What would the dekabrachs gain?"

"I don't know," said Fletcher. "I'd like to find out." He went to dress himself in the submarine suit.

The water-bug was made ready. Fletcher plugged a camera into the external mounting, connected a sound-recorder to a sensitive diaphragm in the skin. He seated himself, pulled the blister over his head.

The water-bug was lowered into the ocean. It filled with water, and its glistening back disappeared under the surface.

The crew patched the roof of the process house, jury-rigged an antenna.

The day passed; twilight came, and plum-colored evening.

The loudspeaker hissed and sputtered; Fletcher's voice, tired and tense, said, "Stand by; I'm coming in."

The crew gathered by the rail, straining their eyes through the dusk.

One of the dully glistening wave-fronts held its shape, drew closer, and became the water-bug.

The grapples were dropped; the water-bug drained its ballast and was hoisted into the chocks.

Fletcher jumped down to the deck, leaned limply against one of the davits. "I've had enough submerging to last me a while."

"What did you find out?" Damon asked anxiously.

"I've got it all on film. I'll run it off as soon as my head stops ringing."

Fletcher took a hot shower, then came down to the mess hall and ate the bowl of stew Jones put in front of him, while Manners transferred the film Fletcher had shot from camera to projector.

"I've made up my mind to two things," said Fletcher. "First—the deks are intelligent. Second, if they communicate with each other, it's by means imperceptible to human beings."

Damon blinked, surprised and dissatisfied. "That's almost a contradiction."

"Just watch," said Fletcher. "You can see for yourself."

Manners started the projector; the screen went bright.

"The first few feet show nothing very much," said Fletcher. "I drove directly out to the end of the shelf, and cruised along the edge of the Deeps. It drops away like the end of the world—straight down. I found a big colony about ten miles west of the one I found yesterday—almost a city."

"'City' implies civilization," Damon asserted in a didactic voice.

Fletcher shrugged. "If civilization means manipulation of environment—somewhere I've heard that definition—they're civilized."

"But they don't communicate?"

"Check the film for yourself."

The screen was dark with the color of the ocean. "I made a circle out over the Deeps," said Fletcher, "turned off my lights, started the camera and came in slow."

A pale constellation appeared in the center of the screen, separated into a swarm of sparks. They brightened and expanded; behind them appeared the outlines, tall and dim, of coral minarets, towers, spires, and spikes. They defined themselves as Fletcher moved closer. From the screen came Fletcher's recorded voice. "These formations vary in height from fifty to two hundred feet, along a front of about half a mile."

The picture expanded. Black holes showed on the face of the spires; pale dekabrach-shapes swam quietly in and out. "Notice," said the voice, "the area in front of the colony. It seems to be a shelf, or a storage yard. From up here it's hard to see; I'll drop down a hundred feet or so."

The picture changed; the screen darkened. "I'm dropping now— depth-meter reads three hundred sixty feet...Three eighty...I can't see too well; I hope the camera is getting it all."

Fletcher commented: "You're seeing it better now than I could; the luminous areas in the coral don't shine too strongly down there."

The screen showed the base of the coral structures and a nearly level bench fifty feet wide. The camera took a quick swing, peered down over the verge, into blackness.

"I was curious," said Fletcher. "The shelf didn't look natural. It isn't. Notice the outlines on down? They're just barely perceptible. The shelf is artificial—a terrace, a front porch."

The camera swung back to the bench, which now appeared to be marked off into areas vaguely differentiated in color.

Fletcher's voice said, "Those colored areas are like plots in a garden—there's a different kind of plant, or weed, or animal on each of them. I'll come in closer. Here are monitors." The screen showed two or three dozen heavy hemispheres, then passed on to what appeared to be eels with saw edges along their sides, attached to the bench by a sucker. Next were float-bladders, then a great number of black cones with very long loose tails.

Damon said in a puzzled voice, "What keeps them there?"

"You'll have to ask the dekabrachs," said Fletcher.

"I would if I knew how."

"I still haven't seen them do anything intelligent," said Murphy.

"Watch," said Fletcher.

Into the field of vision swam a pair of dekabrachs, black eye-spots staring out of the screen at the men in the mess hall.

"Dekabrachs," came Fletcher's voice from the screen.

"Up to now, I don't think they noticed me," Fletcher himself commented. "I carried no lights, and made no contrast against the background. Perhaps they felt the pump."

The dekabrachs turned together, dropped sharply for the shelf.

"Notice," said Fletcher. "They saw a problem, and the same solution occurred to both, at the same time. There was no communication."

The dekabrachs had diminished to pale blurs on one of the dark areas along the shelf.

"I didn't know what was happening," said Fletcher, "but I decided to move. And then—the camera doesn't show this—I felt bumps on the hull, as if someone were throwing rocks. I couldn't see what was going on until something hit the dome right in front of my face. It was a little torpedo, with a long nose like a knitting needle. I took off fast, before the deks tried something else."

The screen went black. Fletcher's voice said, "I'm out over the Deeps, running parallel with the edge of the Shallows." Indeterminate shapes swam across the screen, pale wisps blurred by watery distance. "I came back along the edge of the shelf," said Fletcher, "and found the colony I saw yesterday."

Once more the screen showed spires, tall structures, pale blue, pale green, ivory. "I'm going in close," came Fletcher's voice. "I'm going to look in one of those holes." The towers expanded; ahead was a dark hole.

"Right here I turned on the nose-light," said Fletcher. The black hole suddenly became a bright cylindrical chamber fifteen feet deep.

The walls were lined with glistening colored globes, like Christmas tree ornaments. A dekabrach floated in the center of the chamber. Translucent tendrils ending in knobs extended from the chamber walls and seemed to be punching and kneading the seal-smooth hide.

"I don't know what's going on," said Fletcher, "but the dek doesn't like me looking in on him."

The dekabrach backed to the rear of the chamber; the knobbed tendrils jerked away, into the walls.

"I looked into the next hole."

Another black hole became a bright chamber as the searchlight burnt in. A dekabrach floated quietly, holding a sphere of pink jelly before its eye. The wall-tendrils were not to be seen.

"This one didn't move," said Fletcher. "He was asleep or hypnotized or too scared. I started to take off—and there was the most awful thump. I thought I was a goner."

The screen gave a great lurch. Something dark hurtled past, and into the depths.

"I looked up," said Fletcher. "I couldn't see anything but about a dozen deks. Apparently they'd floated a big rock over me and dropped it. I started the pump and headed for home."

The screen went blank.

Damon was impressed. "I agree that they show patterns of intelligent behavior. Did you detect any sounds?"

"Nothing. I had the recorder going all the time. Not a vibration other than the bumps on the hull."

Damon's face was wry with dissatisfaction. "They must communicate somehow—how could they get along otherwise?"

"Not unless they're telepathic," said Fletcher. "I watched carefully. They make no sounds or motions to each other—none at all."

Manners asked, "Could they possibly radiate radio waves? Or infrared?"

Damon said glumly, "The one in the tank doesn't."

"Oh, come now," said Murphy, "are there no intelligent races that don't communicate?"

"None," said Damon. "They use different methods—sounds, signals, radiation—but all communicate."

"How about telepathy?" Heinz suggested.

"We've never come up against it; I don't believe we'll find it here," said Damon.

"My personal theory," said Fletcher, "is that they think alike, and so don't need to communicate."

Damon shook his head dubiously.

"Assume that they work on a basis of communal empathy," Fletcher went on, "that this is the way they've evolved. Men are individualistic; they need speech. The deks are identical; they're aware of what's going on without words." He reflected a few seconds. "I suppose, in a certain sense, they do communicate. For instance, a dek wants to extend the garden in front of its tower. It possibly waits till another dek comes near, then carries out a rock—indicating what it wants to do."

"Communication by example," said Damon.

"That's right—if you can call it communication. It permits a measure of cooperation—but clearly no small talk, no planning for the future or traditions of the past."

"Perhaps not even awareness of past or future; perhaps no awareness of time!" cried Damon.

"It's hard to estimate their native intelligence. It might be remarkably high, or it might be low; the lack of communication must be a terrific handicap."

"Handicap or not," said Mahlberg, "they've certainly got us on the run."

"And why?" cried Murphy, pounding the table with his big red fist. "That's the question. We've never bothered them. And all of a sudden, Raight's gone, and Agostino. Also our mast. Who knows what they'll think of tonight? Why? That's what I want to know."

"That," said Fletcher, "is a question I'm going to put to Ted Chrystal tomorrow."

Fletcher dressed himself in clean blue twill, ate a silent breakfast, and went out to the flight deck.

Murphy and Mahlberg had thrown the guy-lines off the helicopter and wiped the dome clean of salt-film.

Fletcher climbed into the cabin, twisted the inspection knob. Green light—everything in order.

Murphy said half-hopefully, "Maybe I better come with you, Sam— if there's any chance of trouble."

"Trouble? Why should there be trouble?"

"I wouldn't put much past Chrystal."

"I wouldn't either," said Fletcher. "But—there won't be any trouble."

He started the blades. The ram-tubes caught hold; the copter lifted, slanted up, away from the raft, and off into the northeast. Bio-Minerals became a bright tablet on the irregular wad of seaweed.

The day was dull, brooding, windless, apparently building up for one of the tremendous electrical storms which came every few weeks. Fletcher accelerated, thinking to get his errand over with as soon as possible.

Miles of ocean slid past; Pelagic Recoveries appeared ahead.

Twenty miles southwest from the raft, Fletcher overtook a small barge laden with raw material for Chrystal's macerators and leaching columns; he noticed that there were two men aboard, both huddled inside the plastic canopy. Pelagic Recoveries perhaps had its troubles too, thought Fletcher.

Chrystal's raft was little different from Bio-Minerals', except that the mast still rose from the central deck, and there was activity in the process house. They had not shut down, whatever their troubles.

Fletcher landed on the flight deck. As he stopped the blades, Chrystal came out of the office—a big blond man with a round jocular face.

Fletcher jumped down to the deck. "Hello, Ted," he said in a guarded voice.

Chrystal approached with a cheerful smile. "Hello, Sam! Long time since we've seen you." He shook hands briskly. "What's new at Bio-Minerals? Certainly too bad about Carl."

"That's what I want to talk about." Fletcher looked around the deck. Two of the crew stood watching. "Can we go to your office?"

"Sure, by all means." Chrystal led the way to the office, slid back the door. "Here we are."

Fletcher entered the office. Chrystal walked behind his desk. "Have a seat." He sat down in his own chair. "Now—what's on your mind? But first, how about a drink? You like Scotch, as I recall."

"Not today, thanks." Fletcher shifted in his chair. "Ted, we're up against a serious problem here on Sabria, and we might as well talk plainly about it."

"Certainly," said Chrystal. "Go right ahead."

"Carl Raight's dead. And Agostino."

Chrystal's eyebrows rose in shock. "Agostino too? How?"

"We don't know. He just disappeared."

Chrystal took a moment to digest the information. Then he shook his head in perplexity. "I can't understand it. We've never had trouble like this before."

"Nothing happening over here?"

Chrystal frowned. "Well—nothing to speak of. Your call put us on our guard."

"The dekabrachs seem to be responsible."

Chrystal blinked and pursed his lips, but said nothing.

"Have you been going out after dekabrachs, Ted?"

"Well now, Sam—" Chrystal hesitated, drumming his fingers on the desk. "That's hardly a fair question. Even if we were working with dekabrachs—or polyps or club-moss or wire-eels—I don't think I'd want to say, one way or the other."

"I'm not interested in your business secrets," said Fletcher. "The point is this: the deks appear to be an intelligent species. I have reason to believe that you're processing them for their niobium content. Apparently they're doing their best to retaliate and don't care who they hurt. They've killed two of our men. I've got a right to know what's going on."

Chrystal nodded. "I can understand your viewpoint—but I don't follow your chain of reasoning. For instance, you told me that a monitor had done for Raight. Now you say dekabrach. Also, what leads you to believe I'm going for niobium?"

"Let's not try to kid each other, Ted."

Chrystal looked shocked, then annoyed.

"When you were still working for Bio-Minerals," Fletcher went on, "you discovered that the deks were full of niobium. You wiped all that information out of the files, got financial backing, built this raft. Since then you've been hauling in dekabrachs."

Chrystal leaned back, surveyed Fletcher coolly. "Aren't you jumping to conclusions?"

"If I am, all you've got to do is deny it."

"Your attitude isn't very pleasant, Sam."

"I didn't come here to be pleasant. We've lost two men; also our mast. We've had to shut down."

"I'm sorry to hear that—" began Chrystal.

Fletcher interrupted: "So far, Chrystal, I've given you the benefit of the doubt."

Chrystal was surprised. "How so?"

"I'm assuming you didn't know the deks were intelligent, that they're protected by the Responsibility Act."

"Well?"

"Now you know. You don't have the excuse of ignorance."

Chrystal was silent for a few seconds. "Well, Sam—these are all rather astonishing statements."

"Do you deny them?"

"Of course I do!" said Chrystal with a flash of spirit.

"And you're not processing dekabrachs?"

"Easy, now. After all, Sam, this is my raft. You can't come aboard and chase me back and forth. It's high time you understood it."

Fletcher drew himself a little away, as if Chrystal's mere proximity were unpleasant. "You're not giving me a plain answer."

Chrystal leaned back in his chair, put his fingers together, puffed out his cheeks. "I don't intend to."

The barge that Fletcher had passed on his way was edging close to the raft. Fletcher watched it work against the mooring stage, snap its grapples. He asked, "What's on that barge?"

"Frankly, it's none of your business."

Fletcher rose to his feet, went to the window. Chrystal made uneasy protesting noises. Fletcher ignored him. The two barge-handlers had not emerged from the control cabin. They seemed to be waiting for a gangway which was being swung into position by the cargo boom.

Fletcher watched in growing curiosity and puzzlement. The gangway was built like a trough with high plywood walls.

He turned to Chrystal. "What's going on out there?"

Chrystal was chewing his lower lip, rather red in the face. "Sam, you came storming over here, making wild accusations, calling me dirty names—by implication—and I don't say a word. I try to allow for the strain you're under; I value the good will between our two outfits. I'll show you some documents that will prove once and for all—" he sorted through a sheaf of miscellaneous pamphlets.

Fletcher stood by the window, with half an eye for Chrystal, half for what was occurring out on deck.

The gangway was dropped into position; the barge-handlers were ready to disembark.

Fletcher decided to see what was going on. He started for the door.

Chrystal's face went stiff and cold. "Sam, I'm warning you, don't go out there!"

"Why not?"

"Because I say so."

Fletcher slid open the door; Chrystal made a motion to jump up from his chair; then he slowly sank back.

Fletcher walked out the door, crossed the deck toward the barge.

A man in the process house saw him through the window, and made urgent gestures.

Fletcher hesitated, then turned to look at the barge. A couple more steps and he could look into the hold. He stepped forward, craned his neck. From the corner of his eye, he saw the gestures becoming frantic. The man disappeared from the window.

The hold was full of limp white dekabrachs.

"Get back, you fool!" came a yell from the process house.

Perhaps a faint sound warned Fletcher; instead of backing away, he threw himself to the deck. A small object flipped over his head from the direction of the ocean, with a peculiar fluttering buzz. It struck a bulkhead, dropped—a fishlike torpedo, with a long needlelike proboscis. It came flapping toward Fletcher, who rose to his feet and ran crouching and dodging back toward the office.

Two more of the fishlike darts missed him by inches; Fletcher hurled himself through the door into the office.

Chrystal had not moved from the desk. Fletcher went panting up to him. "Pity I didn't get stuck, isn't it?"

"I warned you not to go out there."

Fletcher turned to look across the deck. The barge-handlers ran down the troughlike gangway to the process house. A glittering school of dart-fish flickered up out of the water, struck at the plywood.

Fletcher turned back to Chrystal. "I saw dekabrachs in that barge. Hundreds of them."

Chrystal had regained whatever composure he had lost. "Well? What if there are?"

"You know they're intelligent as well as I do."

Chrystal smilingly shook his head.

Fletcher's temper was going raw. "You're ruining Sabria for all of us!"

Chrystal held up his hand. "Easy, Sam. Fish are fish."

"Not when they're intelligent and kill men in retaliation."

Chrystal wagged his head. "*Are* they intelligent?"

Fletcher waited until he could control his voice. "Yes. They are."

Chrystal reasoned with him. "How do you know they are? Have you talked with them?"

"Naturally I haven't talked with them."

"They display a few social patterns. So do seals."

Fletcher came up closer, glared down at Chrystal. "I'm not going to argue definitions with you. I want you to stop hunting dekabrach, because you're endangering lives aboard both our rafts."

Chrystal leaned back a trifle. "Now, Sam, you know you can't intimidate me."

"You've killed two men; I've escaped by inches three times now. I'm not running that kind of risk to put money in your pocket."

"You're jumping to conclusions," Chrystal protested. "In the first place you've never proved—"

"I've proved enough! You've got to stop, that's all there is to it!"

Chrystal slowly shook his head. "I don't see how you're going to stop me, Sam." He brought his hand up from under the desk; it held a small gun. "Nobody's going to bulldoze me, not on my own raft."

Fletcher reacted instantly, taking Chrystal by surprise. He grabbed Chrystal's wrist, banged it against the angle of the desk. The gun flashed, seared a groove in the desk, fell from Chrystal's limp fingers to the floor. Chrystal hissed and cursed, bent to recover it, but Fletcher leaped over the desk, pushed him over backward in his chair. Chrystal kicked up at Fletcher's face, caught him a glancing blow on the cheek that sent Fletcher to his knees.

Both men dived for the gun; Fletcher reached it first, rose to his feet, backed to the wall. "Now we know where we stand."

"Put down that gun!"

Fletcher shook his head. "I'm putting you under arrest—civilian arrest. You're coming to Bio-Minerals until the inspector arrives."

Chrystal seemed dumfounded. "What?"

"I said I'm taking you to the Bio-Minerals raft. The inspector is due in three weeks, and I'll turn you over to him."

"You're crazy, Fletcher."

"Perhaps. But I'm taking no chances with you." Fletcher motioned with the gun. "Get going. Out to the copter."

Chrystal coolly folded his arms. "I'm not going to move. You can't scare me by waving a gun."

Fletcher raised his arm, sighted, pulled the trigger. The jet of fire grazed Chrystal's rump. Chrystal jumped, clapped his hand to the scorch.

"Next shot will be somewhat closer," said Fletcher.

Chrystal glared like a boar from a thicket. "You realize I can bring kidnapping charges against you?"

"I'm not kidnapping you. I'm placing you under arrest."

"I'll sue Bio-Minerals for everything they've got."

"Unless Bio-Minerals sues you first. Get going!"

❋

The entire crew met the helicopter: Damon, Blue Murphy, Manners, Hans Heinz, Mahlberg and Dave Jones.

Chrystal jumped haughtily to the deck, surveyed the men with whom he had once worked. "I've got something to say to you men."

The crew watched him silently.

Chrystal jerked his thumb at Fletcher. "Sam's got himself in a peck of trouble. I told him I'm going to throw the book at him and that's what I'm going to do." He looked from face to face. "If you men help him, you'll be accessories. I advise you, take that gun away from him and fly me back to my raft."

He looked around the circle, but met only coolness and hostility. He shrugged angrily. "Very well, you'll be liable for the same penalties as Fletcher. Kidnapping is a serious crime, don't forget."

Murphy asked Fletcher, "What shall we do with the varmint?"

"Put him in Carl's room; that's the best place for him. Come on, Chrystal."

Back in the mess hall, after locking the door on Chrystal, Fletcher told the crew, "I don't need to tell you—be careful of Chrystal. He's tricky. Don't talk to him. Don't run any errands of any kind. Call me if he wants anything. Everybody got that straight?"

Damon asked dubiously, "Aren't we getting in rather deep water?"

"Do you have an alternative suggestion?" asked Fletcher. "I'm certainly willing to listen."

Damon thought. "Wouldn't he agree to stop hunting Dekabrach?"

"No. He refused point-blank."

"Well," said Damon reluctantly, "I guess we're doing the right thing. But we've got to prove a criminal charge. The inspector won't care whether or not Chrystal's cheated Bio-Minerals."

Fletcher said, "If there's any backfire on this, I'll take full responsibility."

"Nonsense," said Murphy. "We're all in this together. I say you did just right. In fact, we ought to hand the sculpin over to the deks, and see what they'd say to him."

*

After a few minutes Fletcher and Damon went up to the laboratory to look at the captive dekabrach. It floated quietly in the center of the tank, the ten arms at right angles to its body, the black eye-area staring through the glass.

"If it's intelligent," said Fletcher, "it must be as interested in us as we are in it."

"I'm not so sure it's intelligent," said Damon stubbornly. "Why doesn't it try to communicate?"

"I hope the inspector doesn't think along the same lines," said Fletcher. "After all, we don't have an air-tight case against Chrystal."

Damon looked worried. "Bevington isn't a very imaginative man. In fact, he's rather official in his outlook."

Fletcher and the dekabrach examined each other. "I know it's intelligent—but how can I prove it?"

"If it's intelligent," Damon insisted doggedly, "it can communicate."

"If it can't," said Fletcher, "then it's our move."

"What do you mean?"

"We'll have to teach it."

Damon's expression became so perplexed and worried that Fletcher broke into laughter.

"I don't see what's funny," Damon complained. "After all, what you propose is...well, it's unprecedented."

"I suppose it is," said Fletcher. "But it's got to be done, nevertheless. How's your linguistic background?"

"Very limited."

"Mine is even more so."

They stood looking at the dekabrach.

"Don't forget," said Damon, "we've got to keep it alive. That means, we've got to feed it." He gave Fletcher a caustic glance. "I suppose you'll admit it eats."

"I know for sure it doesn't live by photosynthesis," said Fletcher. "There's just not enough light. I believe Chrystal mentioned on the micro-film that it ate coral fungus. Just a minute." He started for the door.

"Where are you going?"

"To check with Chrystal. He's certainly noted their stomach contents."

"He won't tell you," Damon said at Fletcher's back.

Fletcher returned ten minutes later.

"Well?" asked Damon in a skeptical voice.

Fletcher looked pleased with himself. "Coral fungus, mostly. Bits of tender young kelp shoots, stylax worms, sea-oranges."

"Chrystal told you all this?" asked Damon incredulously.

"That's right. I explained to him that he and the dekabrach were both our guests, that we planned to treat them exactly alike. If the dekabrach ate well, so would Chrystal. That was all he needed."

Later, Fletcher and Damon stood in the laboratory watching the dekabrach ingest black-green balls of fungus.

"Two days," said Damon sourly, "and what have we accomplished? Nothing."

Fletcher was less pessimistic. "We've made progress in a negative sense. We're pretty sure it has no auditory apparatus, that it doesn't react to sound, and apparently lacks means for making sound. Therefore, we've got to use visual methods to make contact."

"I envy you your optimism," Damon declared. "The beast has given no grounds to suspect either the capacity or the desire for communication."

"Patience," said Fletcher. "It still probably doesn't know what we're trying to do, and probably fears the worst."

"We not only have to teach it a language," grumbled Damon, "we've got to introduce it to the idea that communication is possible. And then invent a language."

Fletcher grinned. "Let's get to work."

"Certainly," said Damon. "But how?"

They inspected the dekabrach, and the black eye-area stared back through the wall of the tank. "We've got to work out a set of visual conventions," said Fletcher. "The ten arms are its most sensitive organs, and presumably are controlled by the most highly organized section of its brain. So—we work out a set of signals based on the dek's arm movements."

"Does that give us enough scope?"

"I should think so. The arms are flexible tubes of muscle. They can assume at least five distinct positions: straight forward, diagonal forward, perpendicular, diagonal back, and straight back. Since the beast has ten arms, evidently there are ten to the fifth power combinations—a hundred thousand."

"Certainly adequate."

"It's our job to work out syntax and vocabulary—a little difficult for an engineer and a biochemist, but we'll have a go at it."

Damon was becoming interested in the project. "It's merely a matter of consistency and sound basic structure. If the dek's got any comprehension whatever, we'll put it across."

"If we don't," said Fletcher, "we're gone geese—and Chrystal winds up taking over the Bio-Minerals raft."

They seated themselves at the laboratory table.

"We have to assume that the deks have no language," said Fletcher.

Damon grumbled uncertainly, and ran his fingers through his hair in annoyed confusion. "Not proven. Frankly, I don't think it's even likely. We can argue back and forth about whether they *could* get along on communal empathy, and such like—but that's a couple of light-years from answering the question whether they *do*.

"They *could* be using telepathy, as we said; they could also be emitting modulated X-rays, establishing long-and-short code-signals in some unknown-to-us subspace, hyperspace, or interspace—they *could* be doing almost anything we never heard of.

"As I see it, our best bet—and best hope—is that they *do* have some form of encoding system by which they communicate between themselves. Obviously, as you know, they have to have an internal coding-and-communication system; that's what a neuromuscular structure, with feedback loops, is. Any complex organism has to have communication internally. The whole point of this requirement of language as a means of classifying alien life forms is to distinguish between true communities of individual thinking entities, and the communal insect type of apparent-intelligence.

"Now, if they've got an ant- or bee-like city over there, we're sunk, and Chrystal wins. You can't teach an ant to talk; the nest-group has intelligence, but the individual doesn't.

"So we've got to assume they do have a language—or, to be more general, a formalized encoding system for intercommunication.

"We can also assume it uses a pathway not available to our organisms. That sound sensible to you?"

Fletcher nodded. "Call it a working hypothesis, anyway. We know we haven't seen any indication the dek has tried to signal us."

"Which suggests the creature is not intelligent."

Fletcher ignored the comment. "If we knew more about their habits, emotions, attitudes, we'd have a better framework for this new language."

"It seems placid enough."

The dekabrach moved its arms back and forth idly. The visual-surface studied the two men.

"Well," said Fletcher with a sigh, "first, a system of notation." He brought forward a model of the dekabrach's head, which Manners had constructed. The arms were of flexible conduit, and could be bent into various positions. "We number the arms 0 to 9 around the clock, starting with this one here at the top. The five positions—forward, diagonal forward, erect, diagonal back, and back—we call A, B, K, X, Y. K is normal position, and when an arm is at K, it won't be noted."

Damon nodded his agreement. "That's sound enough."

"The logical first step would seem to be numbers."

Together they worked out a system of numeration, and constructed a chart:

The colon (:) indicates a composite signal: i.e. two or more separate signals.

Number	0	1	2	et cetera
Signal	0Y	1Y	2Y	...
	10	11	12	...
	0Y,1Y	0Y,1Y:1Y	0Y,1Y:2Y	
	20	21	22	...
	0Y,2Y	0Y,2Y:1Y	0Y,2Y:2Y	
	100	101	102	...
	0X,1Y	0X,1Y:1Y	0X,1Y:2Y	
	110	111	112	...
	0X,1Y:0Y,1Y	0X,1Y:0Y,1Y:1Y	0X,1Y:0Y,1Y:2Y	
	120	121	122	...
	0X,1Y:0Y,2Y	0X,1Y:0Y,2Y:1Y	0X,1Y:0Y,2Y:2Y	
	200	201	202	...

```
0X,2Y          ...

1,000          ...
0B,1Y

2,000          ...
0B,2Y
```

Damon said, "It's consistent—but possibly cumbersome; for instance, to indicate five thousand, seven hundred sixty-six, it's necessary to make the signal...let's see: 0B, 5Y, then 0X, 7Y, then 0Y, 6Y, then 6Y."

"Don't forget that these are signals, not vocalizations," said Fletcher. "Even so, it's no more cumbersome than 'five thousand, seven hundred and sixty-six'."

"I suppose you're right."

"Now—words."

Damon leaned back in his chair. "We just can't build a vocabulary and call it a language."

"I wish I knew more linguistic theory," said Fletcher. "Naturally, we won't go into any abstractions."

"Our basic English structure might be a good idea," Damon mused, "with English parts of speech. That is, nouns are things, adjectives are attributes of things, verbs are the displacements which things undergo, or the absence of displacement."

Fletcher reflected. "We could simplify even further, to nouns, verbs and verbal modifiers."

"Is that feasible? How, for instance, would you say 'the large raft'?"

"We'd use a verb meaning 'to grow big'. 'Raft expanded'. Something like that."

"Humph," grumbled Damon. "You don't envisage a very expressive language."

"I don't see why it shouldn't be. Presumably the deks will modify whatever we give them to suit their own needs. If we get across just a basic set of ideas, they'll take it from there. Or by that time someone'll be out here who knows what he's doing."

"O.K.," said Damon, "get on with your Basic Dekabrach."

"First, let's list the ideas a dek would find useful and familiar."

"I'll take the nouns," said Damon. "You take the verbs; you can also have your modifiers." He wrote, 'No. 1: water.'

After considerable discussion and modification, a sparse list of basic nouns and verbs was agreed upon, and assigned signals.

The simulated dekabrach head was arranged before the tank, with a series of lights on a board nearby to represent numbers.

"With a coding machine we could simply type out our message," said Damon. "The machine would dictate the impulses to the arms of the model."

Fletcher agreed. "Fine, if we had the equipment and several weeks to tinker around with it. Too bad we don't. Now—let's start. The numbers first. You work the lights, I'll move the arms. Just one to nine for now."

Several hours passed. The dekabrach floated quietly, the black eye-spot observing.

Feeding time approached. Damon displayed the black-green fungus balls; Fletcher arranged the signal for 'food' on the arms of the model. A few morsels were dropped into the tank.

The dekabrach quietly sucked them into its oral tube.

Damon went through the pantomime of offering food to the model. Fletcher moved the arms to the signal 'food'. Damon ostentatiously placed the fungus ball in the model's oral tube, then faced the tank, and offered food to the dekabrach.

The dekabrach watched impassively.

Two weeks passed. Fletcher went up to Raight's old room to talk to Chrystal, whom he found reading a book from the micro-film library.

Chrystal extinguished the image of the book, swung his legs over the side of the bed, sat up.

Fletcher said, "In a very few days the inspector is due."

"So?"

"It's occurred to me that you might have made an honest mistake. At least I can see the possibility."

"Thanks," said Chrystal, "for nothing."

"I don't want to victimize you on what may be an honest mistake."

"Thanks again—but what do you want?"

"If you'll cooperate with me in having dekabrachs recognized as an intelligent life form, I won't press charges against you."

Chrystal raised his eyebrows. "That's big of you. And I'm supposed to keep my complaints to myself?"

"If the deks are intelligent, you don't have any complaints."

Chrystal looked keenly at Fletcher. "You don't sound too happy. The dek won't talk, eh?" Chrystal laughed at his joke.

Fletcher restrained his annoyance. "We're working on him."

"But you're beginning to suspect he's not so intelligent as you thought."

Fletcher turned to go. "This one only knows fourteen signals so far. But it's learning two or three a day."

"Hey!" called Chrystal. "Wait a minute!"

Fletcher stopped at the door. "What for?"

"I don't believe you."

"That's your privilege."

"Let me see this dek make signals."

Fletcher shook his head. "You're better off in here."

Chrystal glared. "Isn't that a rather unreasonable attitude?"

"I hope not." He looked around the room. "Anything you're lacking?"

"No." Chrystal turned the switch, and his book flashed once more on the ceiling.

Fletcher left the room; the door closed behind him; the bolts shot home. Chrystal sat up alertly, jumped to his feet with a peculiar lightness, went to the door, listened.

Fletcher's footfalls diminished down the corridor. Chrystal returned to the bed in two strides, reached under the pillow, brought out a length of electric cord, detached from a desk lamp. He had adapted two pencils as electrodes, notching through the wood to the lead, binding a wire around the graphite core so exposed. For resistance in the circuit he included a lamp bulb.

He went to the window. He could see the deck all the way down to the eastern edge of the raft, as well as behind the office to the storage bins at the back of the process house.

The deck was empty. The only movement was a white wisp of steam rising from the circulation flue, and the hurrying pink and scarlet clouds behind.

Chrystal went to work, whistling soundlessly between intently pursed lips. He plugged the cord into the baseboard strip, held the two pencils to the window, struck an arc, burnt at the groove which now ran nearly halfway around the window—the only means by which he could cut through the tempered beryl—silica glass.

It was slow work and very delicate. The arc was weak and fractious, fumes grated in Chrystal's throat. He persevered, blinking through watery eyes, twisting his head this way and that, until five-thirty, half an hour before his evening meal, when he put the equipment away. He dared not work after dark, for fear the flicker of light would arouse suspicion.

The days passed. Each morning Geideon and Atreus brought their respective flushes of scarlet and pale green to the dull sky; each evening they vanished in sad dark sunsets behind the western ocean.

A makeshift antenna had been jury-rigged from the top of the laboratory to a pole over the living quarters. Early one afternoon Manners blew the general alarm in short jubilant blasts to announce a signal from the LG-19, putting into Sabria on its regular six-months call. Tomorrow evening lighters would swing down from orbit, bringing the sector inspector, supplies, and new crews for both Bio-Minerals and Pelagic Recoveries.

Bottles were broken out in the mess hall; there was loud talk, brave plans, laughter.

Exactly on schedule the lighters—four of them—burst through the clouds. Two settled into the ocean beside Bio-Minerals, two more dropped down to the Pelagic Recoveries raft.

Lines were carried out by the launch, the lighters were warped against the dock.

First aboard the raft was Inspector Bevington, a brisk little man, immaculate in his dark-blue and white uniform. He represented the government, interpreted its multiplicity of rules, laws and ordinances; he was empowered to adjudicate minor offences, take custody of criminals, investigate violations of galactic law, check living conditions and safety practices, collect imposts, bonds and duties, and, in general, personify the government in all of its faces and phases.

The job might well have invited graft and petty tyranny, were not the inspectors themselves subject to minute inspection.

Bevington was considered the most conscientious and the most humorless man in the service. If he was not particularly liked, he was at least respected.

Fletcher met him at the edge of the raft. Bevington glanced at him sharply, wondering why Fletcher was grinning so broadly. Fletcher was thinking that now would be a dramatic moment for one of the dekabrach's monitors to reach up out of the sea and clutch Bevington's ankle. But there was no disturbance; Bevington leaped to the raft without interference.

He shook hands with Fletcher, seeking up and down the dock. "Where's Mr. Raight?"

Fletcher was taken aback; he had become accustomed to Raight's absence. "Why—he's dead."

It was Bevington's turn to be startled. "Dead?"

"Come along to the office," said Fletcher, "and I'll tell you about it. This last has been a wild month." He looked up to the window of Raight's old room where he expected to see Chrystal looking down. But the window was empty. Fletcher halted. Empty indeed! The window was vacant even of glass! He started down the deck.

"Here!" cried Bevington. "Where are you going?"

Fletcher paused long enough to call over his shoulder, "You'd better come with me!" then ran to the door leading into the mess hall. Bevington came after him, frowning in annoyance and surprise.

Fletcher looked into the mess hall, hesitated, came back out on deck, looked up at the vacant window. Where was Chrystal? As he had not come along the deck at the front of the raft, he must have headed for the process house.

"This way," said Fletcher.

"Just a minute!" protested Bevington. "I want to know just what and where—"

But Fletcher was on his way down the eastern side of the raft toward the process house, where the lighter crew was already looking over the cases of precious metal to be transshipped. They glanced up when Fletcher and Bevington came running up.

"Did anybody just come past?" asked Fletcher. "A big blond fellow?"

"He went in there." The lightermen pointed toward the process house.

Fletcher whirled, ran through the doorway. Beside the leaching columns he found Hans Heinz, looking ruffled and angry.

"Chrystal come through here?" Fletcher panted.

"Did he come through here! Like a hurricane. He gave me a push in the face."

"Where did he go?"

Heinz pointed. "Out on the front deck."

Fletcher and Bevington ran off, Bevington demanding petulantly, "Exactly what's going on here?"

"I'll explain in a minute," yelled Fletcher. He ran out on deck, looked toward the barges and launch.

No Ted Chrystal.

He could only have gone in one direction: back toward the living quarters, having led Fletcher and Bevington in a complete circle.

A sudden thought hit Fletcher. "The helicopter!"

But the helicopter stood undisturbed, with its guy-lines taut. Murphy came toward them, looking perplexedly over his shoulder.

"Seen Chrystal?" asked Fletcher.

Murphy pointed. "He just went up them steps."

"The laboratory!" cried Fletcher in sudden agony. Heart in his mouth he pounded up the steps, Murphy and Bevington at his heels. If only Damon were in the laboratory, not down on deck or in the mess hall.

The lab was empty—except for the tank with the dekabrach.

The water was cloudy, bluish. The dekabrach was thrashing from end to end of the tank, the ten arms kinked and knotted.

Fletcher jumped on a table, vaulted directly into the tank. He wrapped his arms around the writhing body, lifted. The supple shape squirmed out of his grasp. Fletcher grabbed again, heaved in desperation, raised it out of the tank.

"Grab hold," he hissed to Murphy between clenched teeth. "Lay it on the table."

Damon came rushing in. "What's going on?"

"Poison," said Fletcher. "Give Murphy a hand."

Damon and Murphy managed to lay the dekabrach on the table. Fletcher barked, "Stand back, flood coming!" He slid the clamps from the side of the tank, the flexible plastic collapsed; a thousand gallons of water gushed across the floor.

Fletcher's skin was beginning to burn. "Acid! Damon, get a bucket, wash off the dek. Keep him wet."

The circulatory system was still pumping brine into the tank. Fletcher tore off his trousers, which held the acid against his skin, gave himself a quick rinse, turned the brine-pipe around the tank, flushing off the acid.

The dekabrach lay limp, its propulsion vanes twitching. Fletcher felt sick and dull. "Try sodium carbonate," he told Damon. "Maybe we can neutralize some of the acid." On sudden thought he turned to Murphy, "Go get Chrystal. Don't let him get away."

This was the moment that Chrystal chose to stroll into the laboratory. He looked around the room in mild surprise, hopped up on a chair to avoid the water.

"What's going on in here?"

Fletcher said grimly, "You'll find out." To Murphy: "Don't let him get away."

"Murderer!" cried Damon in a voice that broke with strain and grief.

Chrystal raised his eyebrows in shock. "Murderer?"

Bevington looked back and forth between Fletcher, Chrystal and Damon. "Murderer? What's all this?"

"Just what the law specifies," said Fletcher. "Knowingly and willfully destroying one of an intelligent species. Murder."

The tank was rinsed; he clamped up the sides. The fresh brine began to rise up the sides.

"Now," said Fletcher. "Hoist the dek back in."

Damon shook his head hopelessly. "He's done for. He's not moving."

"We'll put him back in anyway," said Fletcher.

"I'd like to put Chrystal in there with him," Damon said with passionate bitterness.

"Come now," Bevington reproved him, "let's have no more talk like that. I don't know what's going on, but I don't like anything of what I hear."

Chrystal, looking amused and aloof, said, "I don't know what's going on either."

They lifted the dekabrach, lowered him into the tank.

The water was about six inches deep, rising too slowly to suit Fletcher.

"Oxygen," he called. Damon ran to the locker. Fletcher looked at Chrystal. "So you don't know what I'm talking about?"

"Your pet fish dies; don't try to pin it on me."

Damon handed Fletcher a breather-tube from the oxygen tank; Fletcher thrust it into the water beside the dekabrach's gills. Oxygen bubbled up; Fletcher agitated the water, urged it into the gill openings. The water was nine inches deep. "Sodium carbonate," Fletcher said over his shoulder. "Enough to neutralize what's left of the acid."

Bevington asked in an uncertain voice, "Is it going to live?"

"I don't know."

Bevington squinted sidewise at Chrystal, who shook his head. "Don't blame me."

The water rose. The dekabrach's arms lay limp, floating in all directions like Medusa locks.

Fletcher rubbed the sweat off his forehead. "If only I knew what to do! I can't give it a shot of brandy; I'd probably poison it."

The arms began to stiffen, extend. "Ah," breathed Fletcher, "that's better." He beckoned to Damon. "Gene, take over here—keep the oxygen going into the gills." He jumped to the floor where Murphy was flushing the area with buckets of water.

Chrystal was talking with great earnestness to Bevington. "I've gone in fear of my life these last three weeks! Fletcher is an absolute madman; you'd better send up for a doctor—or a psychiatrist." He caught Fletcher's eye, paused. Fletcher came slowly across the room. Chrystal returned to the inspector, whose expression was harassed Zand uneasy.

"I'm registering an official complaint," said Chrystal. "Against Bio-Minerals in general and Sam Fletcher in particular. As a representative of the law, I insist that you place Fletcher under arrest for criminal offenses against my person."

"Well," said Bevington, cautiously glancing at Fletcher. "I'll certainly make an investigation."

"He kidnapped me at the point of a gun," cried Chrystal. "He's kept me locked up for three weeks!"

"To keep you from murdering the dekabrachs," said Fletcher.

"That's the second time you've said that," Chrystal remarked ominously. "Bevington is a witness. You're liable for slander."

"Truth isn't slander."

"I've netted dekabrachs, so what? I also cut kelp and net coelacanths. You do the same."

"The deks are intelligent. That makes a difference." Fletcher turned to Bevington. "He knows it as well as I do. He'd process men for the calcium in their bones if he could make money at it!"

"You're a liar!" cried Chrystal.

Bevington held up his hands. "Let's have order here! I can't get to the bottom of this unless someone presents facts."

"He doesn't have facts," Chrystal insisted. "He's trying to run my raft off of Sabria—can't stand the competition!"

Fletcher ignored him. He said to Bevington, "You want facts. That's why the dekabrach is in that tank, and that's why Chrystal poured acid in on him."

"Let's get something straight," said Bevington, giving Chrystal a hard stare. "Did you pour acid into that tank?"

Chrystal folded his arms. "The question is completely ridiculous."

"Did you? No evasions now."

Chrystal hesitated, then said firmly, "No. And there's no vestige of proof that I did so."

Bevington nodded. "I see." He turned to Fletcher. "You spoke of facts. What facts?"

Fletcher went to the tank, where Damon still was swirling oxygenated water into the gills. "How's he coming?"

Damon shook his head dubiously. "He's acting peculiar. I wonder if the acid got him internally?"

Fletcher watched the long pale shape for a half minute. "Well, let's try him. That's all we can do."

He crossed the room, wheeled the model dekabrach forward. Chrystal laughed, turned away in disgust. "What do you plan to demonstrate?" asked Bevington.

"I'm going to show you that the dekabrach is intelligent and is able to communicate."

"Well, well," said Bevington. "This is something new, is it not?"

"Correct." Fletcher arranged his notebook.

"How did you learn his language?"

"It isn't his—it's a code we worked out between us."

Bevington inspected the model, looked down at the notebook. "These are the signals?"

Fletcher explained the system. "He's got a vocabulary of fifty-eight words, not counting numbers up to nine."

"I see." Bevington took a seat. "Go ahead. It's your show."

Chrystal turned. "I don't have to watch this fakery."

Bevington said, "You'd better stay here and protect your interests; if you don't, no one else will."

Fletcher moved the arms of the model. "This is admittedly a crude setup; with time and money we'll work out something better. Now, I'll start with numbers."

Chrystal said contemptuously, "I could train a rabbit to count that way."

"After a minute," said Fletcher, "I'll try something harder. I'll ask who poisoned him."

"Just a minute!" bawled Chrystal. "You can't tie me up that way!"

Bevington reached for the notebook. "How will you ask? What signals do you use?"

Fletcher pointed them out. "First, interrogation. The idea of interrogation is an abstraction which the dek still doesn't completely understand. We've established a convention of choice, or alternation, like, 'which do you want?' Maybe he'll catch on what I'm after."

"Very well—'interrogation'. Then what?"

"Dekabrach—receive—hot—water. ('Hot water' is for acid.) Interrogation: Man—give—hot—water?"

Bevington nodded. "That's fair enough. Go ahead."

Fletcher worked the signals. The black eye-area watched.

Damon said anxiously, "He's restless—very uneasy."

Fletcher completed the signals. The dekabrach's arms waved once or twice, gave a puzzled jerk.

Fletcher repeated the set of signals, added an extra 'interrogation—man?'

The arms moved slowly. "'Man'," read Fletcher. Bevington nodded. "Man. But which man?"

Fletcher said to Murphy, "Stand in front of the tank." And he signaled, "Man—give—hot—water—interrogation."

The dekabrach's arms moved. "'Null-zero'," read Fletcher. "No. Damon—step in front of the tank." He signaled the dekabrach. "Man—give—hot—water—interrogation."

"'Null'."

Fletcher turned to Bevington. "You stand in front of the tank." He signaled.

"'Null'."

Everyone looked at Chrystal. "Your turn," said Fletcher. "Step forward, Chrystal."

Chrystal came slowly forward, "I'm not a chump, Fletcher. I can see through your gimmick."

The dekabrach was moving its arms. Fletcher read the signals, Bevington looking over his shoulder at the notebook.

"'Man—give—hot—water.'"

Chrystal started to protest. Bevington quieted him. "Stand in front of the tank, Chrystal." To Fletcher: "Ask once again."

Fletcher signaled. The dekabrach responded. "'Man—give—hot—water. Yellow. Man. Sharp. Come. Give—hot—water. Go.'"

There was silence in the laboratory.

"Well," said Bevington flatly, "I think you've made your case, Fletcher."

"You're not going to get me that easy," said Chrystal.

"Quiet," rasped Bevington. "It's clear enough what's happened—"

"It's clear what's going to happen," said Chrystal in a voice husky with rage. He was holding Fletcher's gun. "I secured this before I came up here—and it looks as if—" he raised the gun toward the tank, squinted, his big white hand tightened on the trigger. Fletcher's heart went dead and cold.

"Hey!" shouted Murphy.

Chrystal jerked. Murphy threw his bucket; Chrystal fired at Murphy, missed. Damon jumped at him, Chrystal swung the gun. The white-hot jet pierced Damon's shoulder. Damon, screaming like a hurt horse, wrapped his bony arms around Chrystal. Fletcher and Murphy closed in, wrested away the gun, locked Chrystal's arms behind him.

Bevington said grimly, "You're in trouble now, Chrystal, even if you weren't before."

Fletcher said, "He's killed hundreds and hundreds of the deks. Indirectly he killed Carl Raight and John Agostino. He's got a lot to answer for."

❋

The replacement crew had moved down to the raft from the LG-19. Fletcher, Damon, Murphy and the rest of the old crew sat in the mess hall, six months of leisure ahead of them.

Damon's left arm hung in a sling; with his right he fiddled with his coffee cup. "I don't quite know what I'll be doing. I have no plans. The fact is, I'm rather up in the air."

Fletcher went to the window, looked out across the dark scarlet ocean. "I'm staying on."

"What?" cried Murphy. "Did I hear you right?"

Fletcher came back to the table. "I can't understand it myself."

Murphy shook his head in total lack of comprehension. "You can't be serious."

"I'm an engineer, a working man," said Fletcher. "I don't have a lust for power, or any desire to change the universe—but it seems as if Damon and I set something into motion—something important—and I want to see it through."

"You mean, teaching the deks to communicate?"

"That's right. Chrystal attacked them, forced them to protect themselves. He revolutionized their lives. Damon and I revolutionized the life of this one dek in an entirely new way. But we've just started. Think of the potentialities! Imagine a population of men in a fertile land—men like ourselves except that they never learned to talk. Then someone gives them contact with a new universe—an intellectual stimulus like nothing they'd ever experienced. Think of their reactions, their new attack on life! The deks are in that same position—except that we've just started with them. It's anybody's guess what they'll achieve—and somehow I want to be part of it. Even if I didn't, I couldn't leave with the job half-done."

Damon said suddenly, "I think I'll stay on, too."

"You two have gone stir-crazy," said Jones. "I can't get away fast enough."

The LG-19 had been gone three weeks; operations had become routine aboard the raft. Shift followed shift; the bins began to fill with new ingots, new blocks of precious metal.

Fletcher and Damon had worked long hours with the dekabrach; today would see the great experiment.

The tank was hoisted to the edge of the dock.

Fletcher signaled once again his final message. "Man show you signals. You bring many dekabrachs, man show signals. Interrogation."

The arms moved in assent. Fletcher backed away; the tank was hoisted, lowered over the side, submerged.

The dekabrach floated up, drifted a moment near the surface, slid down into the dark water.

"There goes Prometheus," said Damon, "bearing the gift of the gods."

"Better call it the gift of gab," said Fletcher grinning.

The pale shape had vanished from sight. "Ten gets you fifty he won't be back," Caldur, the new superintendent, offered them.

"I'm not betting," said Fletcher, "just hoping."

"What will you do if he doesn't come back?"

Fletcher shrugged. "Perhaps net another, teach him. After a while it's bound to take hold."

Three hours went by. Mists began to close in; rains blurred the sky. Damon, peering over the side, looked up. "I see a dek. But is it our dek?"

A dekabrach came to the surface. It moved its arms. "Many—dekabrachs. Show—signals."

"Professor Damon," said Fletcher, "your first class."

AFTERWORD TO "THE GIFT OF GAB"

I don't want [the early stories] to disappear, exactly, but I wish I wasn't reminded of them. They represent a process of learning the trade, so to speak. A good analogy might be this: suppose you were trying to learn oil painting. You'd start in by making lots of botches. You might come up with a recognizable tree, maybe, or a cat, or something of that sort...and then later in your life someone would rummage among these early productions and perhaps remark, for lack of anything better to say: "What a *charming* cat that is!" or "This particular thing has a nice airy quality about it."

Of course by this time you'd be trying something more advanced, and you'd only be conscious of the flaws in the early pieces...how crooked the cat's tail is...I re-read one of my early stories the other day, and the style now seems rather—well, journalistic.

—Jack Vance 1977

THE MIRACLE WORKERS

CHAPTER I

The war party from Faide Keep moved eastward across the downs: a column of a hundred armored knights, five hundred foot soldiers, a train of wagons. In the lead rode Lord Faide, a tall man in his early maturity, spare and catlike, with a sallow dyspeptic face. He sat in the ancestral car of the Faides, a boat-shaped vehicle floating two feet above the moss, and carried, in addition to his sword and dagger, his ancestral side weapons.

An hour before sunset a pair of scouts came racing back to the column, their club-headed horses loping like dogs. Lord Faide braked the motion of his car. Behind him the Faide kinsmen, the lesser knights, the leather-capped foot soldiers halted; to the rear the baggage train and the high-wheeled wagons of the jinxmen creaked to a stop.

The scouts approached at breakneck speed, at the last instant flinging their horses sidewise. Long shaggy legs kicked out, padlike hooves plowed through the moss. The scouts jumped to the ground, ran forward. "The way to Ballant Keep is blocked!"

Lord Faide rose in his seat, stood staring eastward over the gray-green downs. "How many knights? How many men?"

"No knights, no men, Lord Faide. The First Folk have planted a forest between North and South Wildwood."

Lord Faide stood a moment in reflection, then seated himself, pushed the control knob. The car wheezed, jerked, moved forward. The knights touched up their horses; the foot soldiers resumed their slouching gait. At the rear the baggage train creaked into motion, together with the six wagons of the jinxmen.

The sun, large, pale and faintly pink, sank in the west. North Wildwood loomed down from the left, separated from South Wildwood by an area of stony ground, only sparsely patched with moss. As the sun passed behind the horizon, the new planting became visible: a frail new growth connecting the tracts of woodland like a canal between two seas.

Lord Faide halted his car, stepped down to the moss. He appraised the landscape, then gave the signal to make camp. The wagons were ranged in a circle, the gear unloaded. Lord Faide watched the activity for a moment, eyes sharp and critical, then turned and walked out across the downs through the lavender and green twilight. Fifteen miles to the east his last enemy awaited him: Lord Ballant of Ballant Keep. Contemplating tomorrow's battle, Lord Faide felt reasonably confident of the outcome. His troops had been tempered by a dozen campaigns; his kinsmen were loyal and single-hearted. Head Jinxman to Faide Keep was Hein Huss, and associated with him were three of the most powerful jinxmen of Pangborn: Isak Comandore, Adam McAdam and the remarkable Enterlin, together with their separate troupes of cabalmen, spellbinders and apprentices. Altogether, an impressive assemblage. Certainly there were obstacles to be overcome: Ballant Keep was strong; Lord Ballant would fight obstinately; Anderson Grimes, the Ballant Head Jinxman, was efficient and highly respected. There was also this nuisance of the First Folk and the new planting which closed the gap between North and South Wildwood. The First Folk were a pale and feeble race, no match for human beings in single combat, but they guarded their forests with traps and deadfalls. Lord Faide cursed softly under his breath. To circle either North or South Wildwood meant a delay of three days, which could not be tolerated.

Lord Faide returned to the camp. Fires were alight, pots bubbled, orderly rows of sleep-holes had been dug into the moss. The knights groomed their horses within the corral of wagons; Lord Faide's own tent had been erected on a hummock, beside the ancient car.

Lord Faide made a quick round of inspection, noting every detail, speaking no word. The jinxmen were encamped a little distance apart from the troops. The apprentices and lesser spellbinders prepared food, while the jinxmen and cabalmen worked inside their tents, arranging cabinets and cases, correcting whatever disorder had been caused by the jolting of the wagons.

Lord Faide entered the tent of his Head Jinxman. Hein Huss was an enormous man, with arms and legs heavy as tree trunks, a torso like a barrel. His face was pink and placid, his eyes were water-clear; a stiff gray brush rose from his head, which was innocent of the cap jinxmen customarily wore against the loss of hair. Hein Huss disdained such precautions: it was his habit, showing his teeth in a face-splitting grin, to rumble, "Why should anyone hoodoo me, old Hein Huss? I am so inoffensive. Whoever tried would surely die, of shame and remorse."

Lord Faide found Huss busy at his cabinet. The doors stood wide, revealing hundreds of mannikins, each tied with a lock of hair, a bit of cloth, a fingernail clipping, daubed with grease, sputum, excrement, blood. Lord Faide knew well that one of these mannikins represented himself. He also knew that should he request it Hein Huss would deliver it without hesitation. Part of Huss' mana derived from his enormous confidence, the effortless ease of his power. He glanced at Lord Faide and read the question in his mind. "Lord Ballant did not know of the new planting. Anderson Grimes has now informed him, and Lord Ballant expects that you will be delayed. Grimes has communicated with Gisborne Keep and Castle Cloud. Three hundred men march tonight to reinforce Ballant Keep. They will arrive in two days. Lord Ballant is much elated."

Lord Faide paced back and forth across the tent. "Can we cross this planting?"

Hein Huss made a heavy sound of disapproval. "There are many futures. In certain of these futures you pass. In others you do not pass. I cannot ordain these futures."

Lord Faide had long learned to control his impatience at what sometimes seemed to be pedantic obfuscation. He grumbled, "They are either very stupid or very bold planting across the downs in this fashion. I cannot imagine what they intend."

Hein Huss considered, then grudgingly volunteered an idea. "What if they plant west from North Wildwood to Sarrow Copse? What if they plant west from South Wildwood to Old Forest?"

"Then Faide Keep is almost ringed by forest."

"And what if they join Sarrow Copse to Old Forest?"

Lord Faide stood stock-still, his eyes narrow and thoughtful. "Faide Keep would be surrounded by forest. We would be imprisoned...These plantings, do they proceed?"

"They proceed, so I have been told."

"What do they hope to gain?"

"I do not know. Perhaps they hope to isolate the keeps, to rid the planet of men. Perhaps they merely want secure avenues between the forests."

Lord Faide considered. Huss' final suggestion was reasonable enough. During the first centuries of human settlement, sportive young men had hunted First Folk with clubs and lances, eventually had driven them from their native downs into the forests. "Evidently they are more clever than we realize. Adam McAdam asserts that they do not think, but it seems that he is mistaken."

Hein Huss shrugged. "Adam McAdam equates thought to the human cerebral process. He cannot telepathize with the First Folk, hence he deduces that they do not 'think'. But I have watched them at Forest Market, and they trade intelligently enough." He raised his head, appeared to listen, then reached into his cabinet, delicately tightened a noose around the neck of one of the mannikins. From outside the tent came a sudden cough and a whooping gasp for air. Huss grinned, twitched open the noose. "That is Isak Comandore's apprentice. He hopes to complete a Hein Huss mannikin. I must say he works diligently, going so far as to touch its feet into my footprints whenever possible."

Lord Faide went to the flap of the tent. "We break camp early. Be alert, I may require your help." Lord Faide departed the tent.

Hein Huss continued the ordering of his cabinet. Presently he sensed the approach of his rival, Jinxman Isak Comandore, who coveted the office of Head Jinxman with all-consuming passion. Huss closed the cabinet and hoisted himself to his feet.

Comandore entered the tent, a man tall, crooked and spindly. His wedge-shaped head was covered with coarse russet ringlets; hot red-brown eyes peered from under his red eyebrows. "I offer my complete rights to Keyril, and will include the masks, the headdress, the amulets. Of all the demons ever contrived he has won the widest public acceptance.

To utter the name Keyril is to complete half the work of a possession. Keyril is a valuable property. I can give no more."

But Huss shook his head. Comandore's desire was the full simulacrum of Tharon Faide, Lord Faide's oldest son, complete with clothes, hair, skin, eyelashes, tears, excrement, sweat and sputum—the only one in existence, for Lord Faide guarded his son much more jealously than he did himself. "You offer convincingly," said Huss, "but my own demons suffice. The name Dant conveys fully as much terror as Keyril."

"I will add five hairs from the head of Jinxman Clarence Sears; they are the last, for he is now stark bald."

"Let us drop the matter; I will keep the simulacrum."

"As you please," said Comandore with asperity. He glanced out the flap of the tent. "That blundering apprentice. He puts the feet of the mannikin backwards into your prints."

Huss opened his cabinet, thumped a mannikin with his finger. From outside the tent came a grunt of surprise. Huss grinned. "He is young and earnest, and perhaps he is clever, who knows?" He went to the flap of the tent, called outside. "Hey, Sam Salazar, what do you do? Come inside."

Apprentice Sam Salazar came blinking into the tent, a thick-set youth with a round florid face, overhung with a rather untidy mass of straw-colored hair. In one hand he carried a crude pot-bellied mannikin, evidently intended to represent Hein Huss.

"You puzzle both your master and myself," said Huss. "There must be method in your folly, but we fail to perceive it. For instance, this moment you place my simulacrum backwards into my track. I feel a tug on my foot, and you pay for your clumsiness."

Sam Salazar showed small evidence of abashment. "Jinxman Comandore has warned that we must expect to suffer for our ambitions."

"If your ambition is jinxmanship," Comandore declared sharply, "you had best mend your ways."

"The lad is craftier than you know," said Hein Huss. "Look now." He took the mannikin from the youth, spit into its mouth, plucked a hair from his head, thrust it into a convenient crevice. "He has a Hein Huss mannikin, achieved at very small cost. Now, Apprentice Salazar, how will you hoodoo me?"

"Naturally, I would never dare. I merely want to fill the bare spaces in my cabinet."

Hein Huss nodded his approval. "As good a reason as any. Of course you own a simulacrum of Isak Comandore?"

Sam Salazar glanced uneasily sidewise at Isak Comandore. "He leaves none of his traces. If there is so much as an open bottle in the room, he breathes behind his hand."

"Ridiculous!" exclaimed Hein Huss. "Comandore, what do you fear?"

"I am conservative," said Comandore dryly. "You make a fine gesture, but some day an enemy may own that simulacrum; then you will regret your bravado."

"Bah. My enemies are all dead, save one or two who dare not reveal themselves." He clapped Sam Salazar a great buffet on the shoulder. "Tomorrow, Apprentice Salazar, great things are in store for you."

"What manner of great things?"

"Honor, noble self-sacrifice. Lord Faide must beg permission to pass Wildwood from the First Folk, which galls him. But beg he must. Tomorrow, Sam Salazar, I will elect you to lead the way to the parley, to deflect deadfalls, scythes and nettle-traps from the more important person who follows."

Sam Salazar shook his head and drew back. "There must be others more worthy; I prefer to ride in the rear with the wagons."

Comandore waved him from the tent. "You will do as ordered. Leave us; we have had enough apprentice talk."

Sam Salazar departed. Comandore turned back to Hein Huss. "In connection with tomorrow's battle, Anderson Grimes is especially adept with demons. As I recall, he has developed and successfully publicized Pont, who spreads sleep; Everid, a being of wrath; Deigne, a force of fear. We must take care that in countering these effects we do not neutralize each other."

"True," rumbled Huss. "I have long maintained to Lord Faide that a single jinxman—the Head Jinxman in fact—is more effective than a group at cross-purposes. But he is consumed by ambition and does not listen."

"Perhaps he wants to be sure that should advancing years overtake the Head Jinxman other equally effective jinxmen are at hand."

"The future has many paths," agreed Hein Huss. "Lord Faide is well-advised to seek early for my successor, so that I may train him over the years. I plan to assess all the subsidiary jinxmen, and select the most promising. Tomorrow I relegate to you the demons of Anderson Grimes."

Isak Comandore nodded politely. "You are wise to give over responsibility. When I feel the weight of my years I hope I may act with similar forethought. Good night, Hein Huss. I go to arrange my demon masks. Tomorrow Keyril must walk like a giant."

"Good night, Isak Comandore."

Comandore swept from the tent, and Huss settled himself on his stool. Sam Salazar scratched at the flap. "Well, lad?" growled Huss. "Why do you loiter?"

Sam Salazar placed the Hein Huss mannikin on the table. "I have no wish to keep this doll."

"Throw it in a ditch, then." Hein Huss spoke gruffly. "You must stop annoying me with stupid tricks. You efficiently obtrude yourself upon my attention, but you cannot transfer from Comandore's troupe without his express consent."

"If I gain his consent?"

"You will incur his enmity; he will open his cabinet against you. Unlike myself, you are vulnerable to a hoodoo. I advise you to be content. Isak Comandore is highly skilled and can teach you much."

Sam Salazar still hesitated. "Jinxman Comandore, though skilled, is intolerant of new thoughts."

Hein Huss shifted ponderously on his stool, examined Sam Salazar with his water-clear eyes. "What new thoughts are these? Your own?"

"The thoughts are new to me, and for all I know new to Isak Comandore. But he will say neither yes nor no."

Hein Huss sighed, settled his monumental bulk more comfortably. "Speak then, describe these thoughts, and I will assess their novelty."

"First, I have wondered about trees. They are sensitive to light, to moisture, to wind, to pressure. Sensitivity implies sensation. Might a man feel into the soul of a tree for these sensations? If a tree were capable of awareness, this faculty might prove useful. A man might select trees as sentinels in strategic sites, and enter into them as he chose."

Hein Huss was skeptical. "An amusing notion, but practically not feasible. The reading of minds, the act of possession, televoyance, all similar interplay, require psychic congruence as a basic condition. The minds must be able to become identities at some particular stratum. Unless there is sympathy, there is no linkage. A tree is at opposite poles from a man; the images of tree and man are incommensurable. Hence, anything more than the most trifling flicker of comprehension must be a true miracle of jinxmanship."

Sam Salazar nodded mournfully. "I realize this, and at one time hoped to equip myself with the necessary identification."

"To do this you must become a vegetable. Certainly the tree will never become a man."

"So I reasoned," said Sam Salazar. "I went alone into a grove of trees, where I chose a tall conifer. I buried my feet in the mold, I stood silent and naked—in the sunlight, in the rain; at dawn, noon, dusk, midnight. I closed my mind to man-thoughts, I closed my eyes to vision, my ears to sound. I took no nourishment except from rain and sun. I sent roots forth from my feet and branches from my torso. Thirty hours I stood, and two days later another thirty hours, and after two days another thirty hours. I made myself a tree, as nearly as possible to one of flesh and blood."

Hein Huss gave the great inward gurgle which signalized his amusement. "And you achieved sympathy?"

"Nothing useful," Sam Salazar admitted. "I felt something of the tree's sensations—the activity of light, the peace of dark, the coolness of rain. But visual and auditory experience—nothing. However, I do not regret the trial. It was a useful discipline."

"An interesting effort, even if inconclusive. The idea is by no means of startling originality, but the empiricism—to use an archaic word—of your method is bold, and no doubt antagonized Isak Comandore, who has no patience with the superstitions of our ancestors. I suspect that he harangued you against frivolity, metaphysics and inspirationalism."

"True," said Sam Salazar. "He spoke at length."

"You should take the lesson to heart. Isak Comandore is sometimes unable to make the most obvious truth seem credible. However, I cite you the example of Lord Faide who considers himself an enlightened man, free from superstition. Still, he rides in his feeble car, he carries a pistol sixteen hundred years old, he relies on Hellmouth to protect Faide Keep."

"Perhaps—unconsciously—he longs for the old magical times," suggested Sam Salazar thoughtfully.

"Perhaps," agreed Hein Huss. "And you do likewise?"

Sam Salazar hesitated. "There is an aura of romance, a kind of wild grandeur to the old days—but of course," he added quickly, "mysticism is no substitute for orthodox logic."

"Naturally not," agreed Hein Huss. "Now go; I must consider the events of tomorrow."

Sam Salazar departed, and Hein Huss, rumbling and groaning, hoisted himself to his feet. He went to the flap of his tent, surveyed the camp. All now was quiet. The fires were embers, the warriors lay in the pits they had cut into the moss. To north and south spread the woodlands. Among the trees and out on the downs were faint flickering luminosities, where the First Folk gathered spore-pods from the moss.

Hein Huss became aware of a nearby personality. He turned his head and saw approaching the shrouded form of Jinxman Enterlin, who concealed his face, who spoke only in whispers, who disguised his natural gait with a stiff stiltlike motion. By this means he hoped to reduce his vulnerability to hostile jinxmanship. The admission carelessly let fall of failing eyesight, of stiff joints, forgetfulness, melancholy, nausea might be of critical significance in controversy by hoodoo. Jinxmen therefore maintained the pose of absolute health and virility, even though they must grope blindly or limp doubled up from cramps.

Hein Huss called out to Enterlin, lifted back the flap to the tent. Enterlin entered; Huss went to the cabinet, brought forth a flask, poured liquor into a pair of stone cups. "A cordial only, free of overt significance."

"Good," whispered Enterlin, selecting the cup farthest from him. "After all, we jinxmen must relax into the guise of men from time to time." Turning his back on Huss, he introduced the cup through the folds of his hood, drank. "Refreshing," he whispered. "We need refreshment; tomorrow we must work."

Huss issued his reverberating chuckle. "Tomorrow Isak Comandore matches demons with Anderson Grimes. We others perform only subsidiary duties."

Enterlin seemed to make a quizzical inspection of Hein Huss through the black gauze before his eyes. "Comandore will relish this opportunity. His vehemence oppresses me, and his is a power which feeds on success. He is a man of fire, you are a man of ice."

"Ice quenches fire."

"Fire sometimes melts ice."

Hein Huss shrugged. "No matter. I grow weary. Time has passed all of us by. Only a moment ago a young apprentice showed me to myself."

"As a powerful jinxman, as Head Jinxman to the Faides, you have cause for pride."

Hein Huss drained the stone cup, set it aside. "No. I see myself at the top of my profession, with nowhere else to go. Only Sam Salazar the apprentice thinks to search for more universal lore; he comes to me for counsel, and I do not know what to tell him."

"Strange talk, strange talk!" whispered Enterlin. He moved to the flap of the tent. "I go now," he whispered. "I go to walk on the downs. Perhaps I will see the future."

"There are many futures."

Enterlin rustled away and was lost in the dark. Hein Huss groaned and grumbled, then took himself to his couch, where he instantly fell asleep.

CHAPTER II

The night passed. The sun, flickering with films of pink and green, lifted over the horizon. The new planting of the First Folk was silhouetted, a sparse stubble of saplings, against the green and lavender sky. The troops broke camp with practiced efficiency. Lord Faide marched to his car, leaped within; the machine sagged under his weight. He pushed a button, the car drifted forward, heavy as a waterlogged timber.

A mile from the new planting he halted, sent a messenger back to the wagons of the jinxmen. Hein Huss walked ponderously forward, followed by Isak Comandore, Adam McAdam and Enterlin. Lord Faide spoke to Hein Huss. "Send someone to speak to the First Folk. Inform them we wish to pass, offering them no harm, but that we will react savagely to any hostility."

"I will go myself," said Hein Huss. He turned to Comandore, "Lend me, if you will, your brash young apprentice. I can put him to good use."

"If he unmasks a nettle-trap by blundering into it, his first useful deed will be done," said Comandore. He signaled to Sam Salazar, who came reluctantly forward. "Walk in front of Head Jinxman Hein Huss that he may encounter no traps or scythes. Take a staff to probe the moss."

Without enthusiasm Sam Salazar borrowed a lance from one of the foot soldiers. He and Huss set forth, along the low rise that previously had separated North from South Wildwood. Occasionally outcroppings of stone penetrated the cover of moss; here and there grew bayberry trees, clumps of tarplant, ginger-tea and rosewort.

A half-mile from the planting Huss halted. "Now take care, for here the traps will begin. Walk clear of hummocks, these often conceal swing-scythes; avoid moss which shows a pale blue; it is dying or sickly and may cover a deadfall or a nettle-trap."

"Why cannot you locate the traps by clairvoyance?" asked Sam Salazar in a rather sullen voice. "It appears an excellent occasion for the use of these faculties."

"The question is natural," said Hein Huss with composure. "However you must know that when a jinxman's own profit or security is at stake his emotions play tricks on him. I would see traps everywhere and would never know whether clairvoyance or fear prompted me. In this case, that lance is a more reliable instrument than my mind."

Sam Salazar made a salute of understanding and set forth, with Hein Huss stumping behind him. At first he prodded with care, uncovering two traps, then advanced more jauntily; so swiftly indeed that Huss called out in exasperation, "Caution, unless you court death!"

Sam Salazar obligingly slowed his pace. "There are traps all around us, but I detect the pattern, or so I believe."

"Ah, ha, you do? Reveal it to me, if you will. I am only Head Jinxman, and ignorant."

"Notice. If we walk where the spore-pods have recently been harvested, then we are secure."

Hein Huss grunted. "Forward then. Why do you dally? We must do battle at Ballant Keep today."

Two hundred yards further, Sam Salazar stopped short. "Go on, boy, go on!" grumbled Hein Huss.

"The savages threaten us. You can see them just inside the planting. They hold tubes which they point toward us."

Hein Huss peered, then raised his head and called out in the sibilant language of the First Folk.

A moment or two passed, then one of the creatures came forth, a naked humanoid figure, ugly as a demon-mask. Foam-sacs bulged under its arms, orange-lipped foam-vents pointed forward. Its back was wrinkled and loose, the skin serving as a bellows to blow air through the foam-sacs. The fingers of the enormous hands ended in chisel-shaped blades, the head was sheathed in chitin. Billion-faceted eyes swelled from either side of the head, glowing like black opals, merging without definite limit into the chitin. This was a representative of the original inhabitants of the planet, who until the coming of man had inhabited the downs, burrowing in the moss, protecting themselves behind masses of foam exuded from the underarm sacs.

The creature wandered close, halted. "I speak for Lord Faide of Faide Keep," said Huss. "Your planting bars his way. He wishes that you guide him through, so that his men do not damage the trees, or spring the traps you have set against your enemies."

"Men are our enemies," responded the autochthon. "You may spring as many traps as you care to; that is their purpose." It backed away.

"One moment," said Hein Huss sternly. "Lord Faide must pass. He goes to battle Lord Ballant. He does not wish to battle the First Folk. Therefore it is wise to guide him across the planting without hindrance."

The creature considered a second or two. "I will guide him." He stalked across the moss toward the war party.

Behind followed Hein Huss and Sam Salazar. The autochthon, legs articulated more flexibly than a man's, seemed to weave and wander, occasionally pausing to study the ground ahead.

"I am puzzled," Sam Salazar told Hein Huss. "I cannot understand the creature's actions."

"Small wonder," grunted Hein Huss. "He is one of the First Folk, you are human. There is no basis for understanding."

"I disagree," said Sam Salazar seriously.

"Eh?" Hein Huss inspected the apprentice with vast disapproval. "You engage in contention with me, Head Jinxman Hein Huss?"

"Only in a limited sense," said Sam Salazar. "I see a basis for understanding with the First Folk in our common ambition to survive."

"A truism," grumbled Hein Huss. "Granting this community of interests with the First Folk, what is your perplexity?"

"The fact that it first refused, then agreed to conduct us across the planting."

Hein Huss nodded. "Evidently the information which intervened, that we go to fight at Ballant Keep, occasioned the change."

"This is clear," said Sam Salazar. "But think—"

"You exhort me to think?" roared Hein Huss.

"—here is one of the First Folk, apparently without distinction, who makes an important decision instantly. Is he one of their leaders? Do they live in anarchy?"

"It is easy to put questions," Hein Huss said gruffly. "It is not as easy to answer them."

"In short—"

"In short, I do not know. In any event, they are pleased to see us killing one another."

CHAPTER III

The passage through the planting was made without incident. A mile to the east the autochthon stepped aside and without formality returned to the forest. The war party, which had been marching in single file, regrouped into its usual formation. Lord Faide called Hein Huss and made the unusual gesture of inviting him up into the seat beside him. The ancient car dipped and sagged; the power-mechanism whined and chattered. Lord Faide, in high good spirits, ignored the noise. "I feared that we might be forced into a time-consuming wrangle. What of Lord Ballant? Can you read his thoughts?"

Hein Huss cast his mind forth. "Not clearly. He knows of our passage. He is disturbed."

Lord Faide laughed sardonically. "For excellent reason! Listen now, I will explain the plan of battle so that all may coordinate their efforts."

"Very well."

"We approach in a wide line. Ballant's great weapon is of course Volcano. A decoy must wear my armor and ride in the lead. The yellow-haired apprentice is perhaps the most expendable member of the party. In this way we will learn the potentialities of Volcano. Like our own Hellmouth, it was built to repel vessels from space and cannot command the ground immediately under the keep. Therefore we will advance in dispersed formation, to regroup two hundred yards from the keep. At this point the jinxmen will impel Lord Ballant forth from the keep. You no doubt have made plans to this end."

Hein Huss gruffly admitted that such was the case. Like other jinxmen, he enjoyed the pose that his power sufficed for extemporaneous control of any situation.

Lord Faide was in no mood for niceties and pressed for further information. Grudging each word, Hein Huss disclosed his arrangements. "I have prepared certain influences to discomfit the Ballant defenders and drive them forth. Jinxman Enterlin will sit at his cabinet, ready to retaliate if Lord Ballant orders a spell against you. Anderson Grimes undoubtedly will cast a demon—probably Everid—into the Ballant warriors; in return, Jinxman Comandore will possess an equal or a greater number of Faide warriors with the demon Keyril, who is even more ghastly and horrifying."

"Good. What more?"

"There is need for no more, if your men fight well."

"Can you see the future? How does today end?"

"There are many futures. Certain jinxmen—Enterlin for instance—profess to see the thread which leads through the maze; they are seldom correct."

"Call Enterlin here."

Hein Huss rumbled his disapproval. "Unwise, if you desire victory over Ballant Keep."

Lord Faide inspected the massive jinxman from under his black saturnine brows. "Why do you say this?"

"If Enterlin foretells defeat, you will be dispirited and fight poorly. If he predicts victory, you become overconfident and likewise fight poorly."

Lord Faide made a petulant gesture. "The jinxmen are loud in their boasts until the test is made. Then they always find reasons to retract, to qualify."

"Ha, ha!" barked Hein Huss. "You expect miracles, not honest jinxmanship. I spit—" He spat. "I predict that the spittle will strike the moss. The probabilities are high. But an insect might fly in the way. One of the First Folk might raise through the moss. The chances are slight. In the next instant there is only one future. A minute hence there are four futures. Five minutes hence, twenty futures. A billion futures could not express all the possibilities of tomorrow. Of these billion, certain are more probable than others. It is true that these probable futures sometimes send a delicate influence into the jinxman's brain. But unless he is completely impersonal and disinterested, his own desires overwhelm this influence. Enterlin is a strange man. He hides himself, he has no appetites. Occasionally his auguries are exact. Nevertheless, I advise against consulting him. You do better to rely on the practical and real uses of jinxmanship."

Lord Faide said nothing. The column had been marching along the bottom of a low swale; the car had been sliding easily downslope. Now they came to a rise, and the power-mechanism complained so vigorously that Lord Faide was compelled to stop the car. He considered. "Once over the crest we will be in view of Ballant Keep. Now we must disperse. Send the least valuable man in your troupe forward—the apprentice who tested out the moss. He must wear my helmet and corselet and ride in the car."

Hein Huss alighted, returned to the wagons, and presently Sam Salazar came forward. Lord Faide eyed the round, florid face with distaste. "Come close," he said crisply. Sam Salazar obeyed. "You will now ride in my place," said Lord Faide. "Notice carefully. This rod impels a forward motion. This arm steers—to right, to left. To stop, return the rod to its first position."

Sam Salazar pointed to some of the other arms, toggles, switches and buttons. "What of these?"

"They are never used."

"And these dials, what is their meaning?"

Lord Faide curled his lip, on the brink of one of his quick furies. "Since their use is unimportant to me, it is twenty times unimportant to you. Now. Put this cap on your head, and this helmet. See to it that you do not sweat."

Sam Salazar gingerly settled the magnificent black and green crest of Faide on his head, with a cloth cap underneath.

"Now this corselet."

The corselet was constructed of green and black metal sequins, with a pair of scarlet dragon-heads at either side of the breast.

"Now the cloak." Lord Faide flung the black cloak over Sam Salazar's shoulders. "Do not venture too close to Ballant Keep. Your purpose is to attract the fire of Volcano. Maintain a lateral motion around the keep, outside of dart range. If you are killed by a dart, the whole purpose of the deception is thwarted."

"You prefer me to be killed by Volcano?" inquired Sam Salazar.

"No. I wish to preserve the car and the crest. These are relics of great value. Evade destruction by all means possible. The ruse probably will deceive no one; but if it does, and if it draws the fire of Volcano, I must sacrifice the Faide car. Now—sit in my place."

Sam Salazar climbed into the car, settled himself on the seat.

"Sit straight," roared Lord Faide. "Hold your head up! You are simulating Lord Faide! You must not appear to slink!"

Sam Salazar heaved himself erect in the seat. "To simulate Lord Faide most effectively, I should walk among the warriors, with someone else riding in the car."

Lord Faide glared, then grinned sourly. "No matter. Do as I have commanded."

CHAPTER IV

Sixteen hundred years before, with war raging through space, a group of space captains, their home-bases destroyed, had taken refuge on Pangborn. To protect themselves against vengeful enemies, they built great forts armed with weapons from the dismantled spaceships.

The wars receded, Pangborn was forgotten. The newcomers drove the First Folk into the forests, planted and harvested the river valleys. Ballant Keep, like Faide Keep, Castle Cloud, Boghoten and the rest, overlooked one of these valleys. Four squat towers of a dense black substance supported an enormous parasol roof, and were joined by walls two-thirds as high as the towers. At the peak of the roof a cupola housed Volcano, the weapon corresponding to Faide's Hellmouth.

The Faide war party advancing over the rise found the great gates already secure, the parapets between the towers thronged with bowmen. According to Lord Faide's strategy, the war party advanced on a broad front. At the center rode Sam Salazar, resplendent in Lord Faide's armor. He made, however, small effort to simulate Lord Faide. Rather than sitting proudly erect, he crouched at the side of the seat, the crest canted at an angle. Lord Faide watched with disgust. Apprentice Salazar's reluctance to be demolished was understandable; if his impersonation failed to convince Lord Ballant, at least the Faide ancestral car might be spared. For a certainty Volcano was being manned; the Ballant gun-tender could be seen in the cupola, and the snout protruded at a menacing angle.

Apparently the tactic of dispersal, offering no single tempting target, was effective. The Faide war party advanced quickly to a point two hundred yards from the keep, below Volcano's effective field, without drawing fire; first the knights, then the foot soldiers, then the rumbling wagons of the magicians. The slow-moving Faide car was far outdistanced; any doubt as to the nature of the ruse must now be extinguished.

Apprentice Salazar, disliking the isolation, and hoping to increase the speed of the car, twisted one of the other switches, then another. From under the floor came a thin screeching sound; the car quivered and began to rise. Sam Salazar peered over the side, threw out a leg to jump. Lord Faide ran forward, gesturing and shouting. Sam Salazar hastily drew back his leg, returned the switches to their previous condition. The car dropped like a rock. He snapped the switches up again, cushioning the fall.

"Get out of that car!" roared Lord Faide. He snatched away the helmet, dealt Sam Salazar a buffet which toppled him head over heels. "Out of the armor; back to your duties!"

Sam Salazar hurried to the jinxmen's wagons where he helped erect Isak Comandore's black tent. Inside the tent a black carpet with red and yellow patterns was laid; Comandore's cabinet, his chair and his chest were carried in, and incense set burning in a censer. Directly in front of the main gate Hein Huss superintended the assembly of a rolling stage, forty feet tall and sixty feet long, the surface concealed from Ballant Keep by a tarpaulin.

Meanwhile, Lord Faide had dispatched an emissary, enjoining Lord Ballant to surrender. Lord Ballant delayed his response, hoping to delay the attack as long as possible. If he could maintain himself a day and a half, reinforcements from Gisborne Keep and Castle Cloud might force Lord Faide to retreat.

Lord Faide waited only until the jinxmen had completed their preparations, then sent another messenger, offering two more minutes in which to surrender.

One minute passed, two minutes. The envoys turned on their heels, marched back to the camp.

Lord Faide spoke to Hein Huss. "You are prepared?"

"I am prepared," rumbled Hein Huss.

"Drive them forth."

Huss raised his arm; the tarpaulin dropped from the face of his great display, to reveal a painted representation of Ballant Keep.

Huss retired to his tent, pulled the flaps together. Braziers burnt fiercely, illuminating the faces of Adam McAdam, eight cabalmen and six of the most advanced spellbinders. Each worked at a bench supporting several dozen dolls and a small glowing brazier. The cabalmen and spellbinders worked with dolls representing Ballant men-at-arms; Huss and Adam McAdam employed simulacra of the Ballant knights. Lord Ballant would not be hoodooed unless he ordered a jinx against Lord Faide—a courtesy the keep-lords extended each other.

Huss called out: "Sebastian!"

Sebastian, one of Huss' spellbinders, waiting at the flap to the tent, replied, "Ready, sir."

"Begin the display."

Sebastian ran to the stage, struck fire to a fuse. Watchers inside Ballant Keep saw the depicted keep take fire. Flame erupted from the windows, the roof glowed and crumbled. Inside the tent the two jinxmen, the cabalmen and the spellbinders methodically took dolls, dipped them into the heat of the braziers, concentrating, reaching out for the mind of the man whose doll they burnt. Within the keep men became uneasy. Many began to imagine burning sensations, which became more severe as their minds grew more sensitive to the idea of fire. Lord Ballant noted the uneasiness. He signaled to his chief jinxman Anderson Grimes. "Begin the counterspell."

Down the front of the keep unrolled a display even larger than Hein Huss', depicting a hideous beast. It stood on four legs and was shown picking up two men in a pair of hands, biting off their heads. Grimes' cabalmen meanwhile took up dolls representing the Faide warriors, inserted them into models of the depicted beast, closed the hinged jaws, all the while projecting ideas of fear and disgust. And the Faide warriors, staring at the depicted monster, felt a sense of horror and weakness.

Inside Huss' tent the braziers reeked and dolls smoked. Eyes stared, brows glistened. From time to time one of the workers gasped—signaling the entry of his projection into an enemy mind. Within the keep warriors began to mutter, to slap at burning skin, to eye each other fearfully, noting each other's symptoms. Finally one cried out, and tore at his armor. "I burn! The cursed witches burn me!" His pain aggravated the discomfort of the others; there was a growing sound throughout the keep.

Lord Ballant's oldest son, his mind penetrated by Hein Huss himself, struck his shield with his mailed fist. "They burn me! They burn us all! Better to fight than burn!"

"Fight! Fight!" came the voices of the tormented men.

Lord Ballant looked around at the twisted faces, some displaying blisters, scaldmarks. "Our own spell terrifies them; wait yet a moment!" he pleaded.

His brother called hoarsely, "It is not your belly that Hein Huss toasts in the flames, it is mine! We cannot win a battle of hoodoos; we must win a battle of arms!"

Lord Ballant cried desperately, "Wait, our own effects are working! They will flee in terror; wait, wait!"

His cousin tore off his corselet. "It's Hein Huss! I feel him! My leg's in the fire, the devil laughs at me. Next my head, he says. Fight, or I go forth to fight alone!"

"Very well," said Lord Ballant in a fateful voice. "We go forth to fight. First—the beast goes forth. Then we follow and smite them in their terror."

*

The gates to the keep swung suddenly wide. Out sprang what appeared to be the depicted monster: legs moving, arms waving, eyes rolling, issuing evil sounds. Normally the Faide warriors would have seen the monster for what it was: a model carried on the backs of three horses. But their minds had been influenced; they had been infected with horror; they drew back with arms hanging flaccid. From behind the monster the Ballant knights galloped, followed by the Ballant foot soldiers. The charge gathered momentum, tore into the Faide center. Lord Faide bellowed orders; discipline asserted itself. The Faide knights disengaged, divided into three platoons, engulfed the Ballant charge, while the foot soldiers poured darts into the advancing ranks.

There was the clatter and surge of battle; Lord Ballant, seeing that his sally had failed to overwhelm the Faide forces, and thinking to conserve his own forces, ordered a retreat. In good order the Ballant warriors began to back up toward the keep. The Faide knights held close contact, hoping to win to the courtyard. Close behind came a heavily loaded wagon pushed by armored horses, to be wedged against the gate.

Lord Faide called an order; a reserve platoon of ten knights charged from the side, thrust behind the main body of Ballant horsemen, rode through the foot soldiers fought into the keep, cut down the gate-tenders.

Lord Ballant bellowed to Anderson Grimes, "They have won inside; quick with your cursed demon! If he can help us, let him do so now!"

"Demon-possession is not a matter of an instant," muttered the jinxman. "I need time."

"You have no time! Ten minutes and we're all dead!"

"I will do my best. Everid, Everid, come swift!"

He hastened into his workroom, donned his demon-mask, tossed handful after handful of incense into the brazier. Against one wall stood a great form: black, slit-eyed, noseless. Great white fangs hung from its upper palate; it stood on heavy bent legs, arms reached forward to grasp. Anderson Grimes swallowed a cup of syrup, paced slowly back and forth. A moment passed.

"Grimes!" came Ballant's call from outside. "Grimes!"

A voice spoke. "Enter without fear."

Lord Ballant, carrying his ancestral side-arm, entered. He drew back with an involuntary sound. "Grimes!" he whispered.

"Grimes is not here," said the voice. "I am here. Enter."

Lord Ballant came forward stiff-legged. The room was dark except for the feeble glimmer of the brazier. Anderson Grimes crouched in a corner, head bowed under his demon-mask. The shadows twisted and pulsed with shapes and faces, forms struggling to become solid. The black image seemed to vibrate with life.

"Bring in your warriors," said the voice. "Bring them in five at a time, bid them look only at the floor until commanded to raise their eyes."

Lord Ballant retreated; there was no sound in the room.

A moment passed; then five limp and exhausted warriors filed into the room, eyes low.

"Look slowly up," said the voice. "Look at the orange fire. Breathe deeply. Then look at me. I am Everid, Demon of Hate. Look at me. Who am I?"

"You are Everid, Demon of Hate," quavered the warriors.

"I stand all around you, in a dozen forms…I come closer. Where am I?"

"You are close."

"Now I am you. We are together."

There was a sudden quiver of motion. The warriors stood straighter, their faces distorted.

"Go forth," said the voice. "Go quietly into the court. In a few minutes we march forth to slay."

The five stalked forth. Five more entered.

Outside the wall the Ballant knights had retreated as far as the gate; within, seven Faide knights still survived, and with their backs to the wall held the Ballant warriors away from the gate mechanism.

In the Faide camp Huss called to Comandore, "Everid is walking. Bring forth Keyril."

"Send the men," came Comandore's voice, low and harsh. "Send the men to me. I am Keyril."

Within the keep twenty warriors came marching into the courtyard. Their steps were cautious, tentative, slow. Their faces had lost individuality, they were twisted and distorted, curiously alike.

"Bewitched!" whispered the Ballant soldiers, drawing back. The seven Faide knights watched with sudden fright. But the twenty warriors, paying them no heed, marched out the gate. The Ballant knights parted; for an instant there was a lull in the fighting. The twenty sprang like tigers. Their swords glistened, twinkling in water-bright arcs. They crouched, jerked, jumped; Faide arms, legs, heads were hewed off. The twenty were cut and battered, but the blows seemed to have no effect.

The Faide attack faltered, collapsed. The knights, whose armor was no protection against the demoniac swords, retreated. The twenty possessed warriors raced out into the open toward the foot soldiers, running with great strides, slashing and rending. The Faide foot soldiers fought for a moment, then they too gave way and turned to flee.

From behind Comandore's tent appeared thirty Faide warriors, marching stiffly, slowly. Like the Ballant twenty their faces were alike— but between the Everid-possessed and the Keyril-possessed was the difference between the face of Everid and the face of Keyril.

Keyril and Everid fought, using the men as weapons, without fear, retreat, or mercy. Hack, chop, cut. Arms, legs, sundered torsos. Bodies fought headless for moments before collapsing. Only when a body was minced, hacked to bits, did the demoniac vitality depart. Presently there were no more men of Everid, and only fifteen men of Keyril. These hopped and limped and tumbled toward the keep where Faide knights still held the gate. The Ballant knights met them in despair, knowing that now was the decisive moment. Leaping, leering from chopped faces, slashing from tireless arms, the warriors cut a hole into the iron. The Faide knights, roaring victory cries, plunged after. Into the courtyard surged the battle, and now there was no longer doubt of the outcome. Ballant Keep was taken.

Back in his tent Isak Comandore took a deep breath, shuddered, flung down his demon-mask. In the courtyard the twelve remaining warriors dropped in their tracks, twitched, gasped, gushed blood and died.

Lord Ballant, in the last gallant act of a gallant life, marched forth brandishing his ancestral side-arm. He aimed across the bloody field at Lord Faide, pulled the trigger. The weapon spewed a brief gout of light; Lord Faide's skin prickled and hair rose from his head. The weapon crackled, turned cherry-red and melted. Lord Ballant threw down the weapon, drew his sword, marched forth to challenge Lord Faide.

Lord Faide, disinclined to unnecessary combat, signaled to his soldiers. A flight of darts ended Lord Ballant's life, saving him the discomfort of formal execution.

There was no further resistance. The Ballant defenders threw down their arms, marched grimly out to kneel before Lord Faide, while inside the keep the Ballant women gave themselves to mourning and grief.

CHAPTER V

Lord Faide had no wish to linger at Ballant Keep, for he took no relish in his victories. Inevitably, a thousand decisions had to be made. Six of the closest Ballant kinsmen were summarily stabbed and the title declared defunct. Others of the clan were offered a choice: an oath of lifelong fealty together with a moderate ransom, or death. Only two, eyes blazing hate, chose death and were instantly stabbed.

Lord Faide had now achieved his ambition. For over a thousand years the keep-lords had struggled for power; now one, now another gaining ascendancy. None before had ever extended his authority across the entire continent—which meant control of the planet, since all other land was either sun-parched rock or eternal ice. Ballant Keep had long thwarted Lord Faide's drive to power; now—success, total and absolute. It still remained to chastise the lords of Castle Cloud and Gisborne, both of whom, seeing opportunity to overwhelm Lord Faide, had ranged themselves behind Lord Ballant. But these were matters that might well be assigned to Hein Huss.

Lord Faide, for the first time in his life, felt a trace of uncertainty. Now what? No real adversaries remained. The First Folk must be whipped back, but here was no great problem; they were numerous, but no more than savages. He knew that dissatisfaction and controversy would ultimately arise among his kinsmen and allies. Inaction and boredom would breed irritability; idle minds would calculate the pros and cons of mischief. Even the most loyal would remember the campaigns with nostalgia and long for the excitement, the release, the license, of warfare. Somehow he must find means to absorb the energy of so many active and keyed-up men. How and where, this was the problem. The construction of roads? New farmland claimed from the downs? Yearly tournaments-at-arms? Lord Faide frowned at the inadequacy of his solutions, but his imagination was impoverished by the lack of tradition. The original settlers of Pangborn had been warriors, and had brought with them a certain amount of practical rule-of-thumb knowledge, but little else. The tales they passed down the generations described the great spaceships which moved with magic speed and certainty, the miraculous weapons, the wars in the void, but told nothing of human history or civilized achievement. And so Lord Faide, full of power and success, but with no goal toward which to turn his strength, felt more morose and saturnine than ever.

He gloomily inspected the spoils from Ballant Keep. They were of no great interest to him. Ballant's ancestral car was no longer used, but displayed behind a glass case. He inspected the weapon Volcano, but this could not be moved. In any event it was useless, its magic lost forever. Lord Faide now knew that Lord Ballant had ordered it turned against the Faide car, but that it had refused to spew its vaunted fire.

Lord Faide saw with disdainful amusement that Volcano had been sadly neglected. Corrosion had pitted the metal, careless cleaning had twisted the exterior tubing, undoubtedly diminishing the potency of the magic. No such neglect at Faide Keep! Jambart the weapon-tender cherished Hellmouth with absolute devotion. Elsewhere were other ancient devices, interesting but useless—the same sort of curios that cluttered shelves and cases at Faide Keep. (Peculiar, these ancient men! thought Lord Faide: at once so clever, yet so primitive and impractical. Conditions had changed; there had been enormous advances since the dark ages sixteen hundred years ago. For instance, the ancients had used intricate fetishes of metal and glass to communicate with each other. Lord Faide need merely voice his needs; Hein Huss could project his mind a hundred miles to see, to hear, to relay Lord Faide's words.) The ancients had contrived dozens of such objects, but the old magic had worn away and they never seemed to function. Lord Ballant's side-arm had melted, after merely stinging Lord Faide. Imagine a troop armed thus trying to cope with a platoon of demon-possessed warriors! Slaughter of the innocents!

❋

Among the Ballant trove Lord Faide noted a dozen old books and several reels of microfilm. The books were worthless, page after page of incomprehensible jargon; the microfilm was equally undecipherable. Again Lord Faide wondered skeptically about the ancients. Clever of course, but to look at the hard facts, they were little more advanced than the First Folk: neither had facility with telepathy or voyance or demon-command. And the magic of the ancients: might there not be a great deal of exaggeration in the legends? Volcano, for instance. A joke. Lord Faide wondered about his own Hellmouth. But no—surely Hellmouth was more trustworthy; Jambart cleaned and polished the weapon daily and washed the entire cupola with vintage wine every month. If human care could induce faithfulness, then Hellmouth was ready to defend Faide Keep!

Now there was no longer need for defense. Faide was supreme. Considering the future, Lord Faide made a decision. There should no longer be keep-lords on Pangborn; he would abolish the appellation. Habitancy of the keeps would gradually be transferred to trusted bailiffs on a yearly basis. The former lords would be moved to comfortable but indefensible manor houses, with the maintenance of private troops forbidden. Naturally they must be allowed jinxmen, but these would be made accountable to himself—perhaps through some sort of licensing provision. He must discuss the matter with Hein Huss. A matter for the future, however. Now he merely wished to settle affairs and return to Faide Keep.

There was little more to be done. The surviving Ballant kinsmen he sent to their homes after Hein Huss had impregnated fresh dolls with their essences. Should they default on their ransoms, a twinge of fire, a few stomach cramps would more than set them right. Ballant Keep itself Lord Faide would have liked to burn—but the material of the ancients was proof to fire. But in order to discourage any new pretenders to the Ballant heritage Lord Faide ordered all the heirlooms and relics brought forth into the courtyard, and then, one at a time, in order of rank, he bade his men choose. Thus the Ballant wealth was distributed. Even the jinxmen were invited to choose, but they despised the ancient trinkets as works of witless superstition. The lesser spellbinders and apprentices rummaged through the leavings, occasionally finding an overlooked bauble or some anomalous implement. Isak Comandore was irritated to find Sam Salazar staggering under a load of the ancient books. "And what is your purpose with these?" he barked. "Why do you burden yourself with rubbish?"

Sam Salazar hung his head. "I have no definite purpose. Undoubtedly there was wisdom—or at least knowledge—among the ancients; perhaps I can use these symbols of knowledge to sharpen my own understanding."

Comandore threw up his hands in disgust. He turned to Hein Huss who stood nearby. "First he fancies himself a tree and stands in the mud; now he thinks to learn jinxmanship through a study of ancient symbols."

Huss shrugged. "They were men like ourselves, and, though limited, they were not entirely obtuse. A certain simian cleverness is required to fabricate these objects."

"Simian cleverness is no substitute for sound jinxmanship," retorted Isak Comandore. "This is a point hard to overemphasize; I have drummed it into Salazar's head a hundred times. And now, look at him."

Huss grunted noncommittally. "I fail to understand what he hopes to achieve."

Sam Salazar tried to explain, fumbling for words to express an idea that did not exist. "I thought perhaps to decipher the writing, if only to understand what the ancients thought, and perhaps to learn how to perform one or two of their tricks."

Comandore rolled up his eyes. "What enemy bewitched me when I consented to take you as apprentice? I can cast twenty hoodoos in an hour, more than any of the ancients could achieve in a lifetime."

"Nevertheless," said Sam Salazar, "I notice that Lord Faide rides in his ancestral car, and that Lord Ballant sought to kill us all with Volcano."

"I notice," said Comandore with feral softness, "that my demon Keyril conquered Lord Ballant's Volcano, and that riding on my wagon I can outdistance Lord Faide in his car."

Sam Salazar thought better of arguing further. "True, Jinxman Comandore, very true. I stand corrected."

"Then discard that rubbish and make yourself useful. We return to Faide Keep in the morning."

"As you wish, Jinxman Comandore." Sam Salazar threw the books back into the trash.

CHAPTER VI

The Ballant clan had been dispersed, Ballant Keep was despoiled. Lord Faide and his men banqueted somberly in the great hall, tended by silent Ballant servitors.

Ballant Keep had been built on the same splendid scale as Faide Keep. The great hall was a hundred feet long, fifty feet wide, fifty feet high, paneled in planks sawed from pale native hardwood, rubbed and waxed to a rich honey color. Enormous black beams supported the ceiling; from these hung candelabra, intricate contrivances of green, purple and blue glass, knotted with ancient but still bright light-motes. On the far wall hung portraits of all the lords of Ballant Keep—one hundred and five grave faces in a variety of costumes. Below, a genealogical chart ten feet high detailed the descent of the Ballants and their connections with the other noble clans. Now there was a desolate air to the hall, and the one hundred and five dead faces were meaningless and empty.

Lord Faide dined without joy, and cast dour side-glance sat those of his kinsmen who reveled too gladly. Lord Ballant, he thought, had conducted himself only as he himself might have done under the same circumstances; coarse exultation seemed in poor taste, almost as if it were disrespect for Lord Faide himself. His followers were quick to catch his mood, and the banquet proceeded with greater decorum.

The jinxmen sat apart in a smaller room to the side. Anderson Grimes, erstwhile Ballant Head Jinxman, sat beside Hein Huss, trying to put a good face on his defeat. After all, he had performed creditably against four powerful adversaries, and had no cause to feel a diminution of mana. The five jinxmen discussed the battle, while the cabalmen and spellbinders listened respectfully. The conduct of the demon-possessed troops occasioned the most discussion. Anderson Grimes readily admitted that his conception of Everid was a force absolutely brutal and blunt, terrifying in its indomitable vigor. The other jinxmen agreed that he undoubtedly succeeded in projecting these qualities; Hein Huss however pointed out that Isak Comandore's Keyril, as cruel and vigorous as Everid, also combined a measure of crafty malice, which tended to make the possessed soldier a more effective weapon.

Anderson Grimes allowed that this might well be the case, and that in fact he had been considering such an augmentation of Everid's characteristics.

"To my mind," said Huss, "the most effective demon should be swift enough to avoid the strokes of the brute demons, such as Keyril and Everid. I cite my own Dant as example. A Dant-possessed warrior can easily destroy a Keyril or an Everid, simply through his agility. In an encounter of this sort the Keyrils and Everids presently lose their capacity to terrify, and thus half the effect is lost."

Isak Comandore pierced Huss with a hot russet glance. "You state a presumption as if it were fact. I have formulated Keyril with sufficient craft to counter any such displays of speed. I firmly believe Keyril to be the most fearsome of all demons."

"It may well be," rumbled Hein Huss thoughtfully. He beckoned to a steward, gave instructions. The steward reduced the light a trifle. "Behold," said Hein Huss. "There is Dant. He comes to join the banquet." To the side of the room loomed the tiger-striped Dant, a creature constructed of resilient metal, with four terrible arms, and a squat black head which seemed all gaping jaw.

"Look," came the husky voice of Isak Comandore. "There is Keyril." Keyril was rather more humanoid and armed with a cutlass. Dant spied Keyril. The jaws gaped wider, it sprang to the attack.

The battle was a thing of horror; the two demons rolled, twisted, bit, frothed, uttered soundless shrieks, tore each other apart. Suddenly

Dant sprang away, circled Keyril with dizzying speed, faster, faster; became a blur, a wild coruscation of colors that seemed to give off a high-pitched wailing sound, rising higher and higher in pitch. Keyril hacked brutally with his cutlass, then seemed to grow feeble and wan. The light that once had been Dant blazed white, exploded in a mental shriek; Keyril was gone and Isak Comandore lay moaning.

Hein Huss drew a deep breath, wiped his face, looked about him with a complacent grin. The entire company sat rigid as stones, staring, all except the apprentice Sam Salazar, who met Hein Huss' glance with a cheerful smile.

"So," growled Huss, panting from his exertion, "you consider yourself superior to the illusion; you sit and smirk at one of Hein Huss' best efforts."

"No, no," cried Sam Salazar, "I mean no disrespect! I want to learn, so I watched you rather than the demons. What could they teach me? Nothing!"

"Ah," said Huss, mollified. "And what did you learn?"

"Likewise, nothing," said Sam Salazar, "but at least I do not sit like a fish."

Comandore's voice came soft but crackling with wrath. "You see in me the resemblance to a fish?"

"I except you, Jinxman Comandore, naturally," Sam Salazar explained.

"Please go to my cabinet, Apprentice Salazar, and fetch me the doll that is your likeness. The steward will bring a basin of water, and we shall have some sport. With your knowledge of fish you perhaps can breathe under water. If not—you may suffocate."

"I prefer not, Jinxman Comandore," said Sam Salazar. "In fact, with your permission, I now resign your service."

Comandore motioned to one of his cabalmen. "Fetch me the Salazar doll. Since he is no longer my apprentice, it is likely indeed that he will suffocate."

"Come now, Comandore," said Hein Huss gruffly. "Do not torment the lad. He is innocent and a trifle addled. Let this be an occasion of placidity and ease."

"Certainly, Hein Huss," said Comandore. "Why not? There is ample time in which to discipline this upstart."

"Jinxman Huss," said Sam Salazar, "since I am now relieved of my duties to Jinxman Comandore, perhaps you will accept me into your service."

Hein Huss made a noise of vast distaste. "You are not my responsibility."

"There are many futures, Hein Huss," said Sam Salazar. "You have said as much yourself."

Hein Huss looked at Sam Salazar with his water-clear eyes. "Yes, there are many futures. And I think that tonight sees the full amplitude of jinxmanship...I think that never again will such power and skill gather at the same table. We shall die one by one and there shall be none to fill our shoes...Yes, Sam Salazar. I will take you as apprentice. Isak Comandore, do you hear? This youth is now of my company."

"I must be compensated," growled Comandore.

"You have coveted my doll of Tharon Faide, the only one in existence. It is yours."

"Ah, ha!" cried Isak Comandore leaping to his feet. "Hein Huss, I salute you! You are generous indeed! I thank you and accept!"

Hein Huss motioned to Sam Salazar. "Move your effects to my wagon. Do not show your face again tonight."

Sam Salazar bowed with dignity and departed the hall.

The banquet continued, but now something of melancholy filled the room. Presently a messenger from Lord Faide came to warn all to bed, for the party returned to Faide Keep at dawn.

CHAPTER VII

The victorious Faide troops gathered on the heath before Ballant Keep. As a parting gesture Lord Faide ordered the great gate torn off the hinges, so that ingress could never again be denied him. But even after sixteen hundred years the hinges were proof to all the force the horses could muster, and the gates remained in place.

Lord Faide accepted the fact with good grace and bade farewell to his cousin Renfroy, whom he had appointed bailiff. He climbed into his car, settled himself, snapped the switch. The car groaned and moved forward. Behind came the knights and the foot soldiers, then the baggage train, laden with booty, and finally the wagons of the jinxmen.

Three hours the column marched across the mossy downs. Ballant Keep dwindled behind; ahead appeared North and South Wildwood, darkening all the sweep of the western horizon. Where once the break had existed, the First Folk's new planting showed a smudge lower and less intense than the old woodlands.

Two miles from the woodlands Lord Faide called a halt and signaled up his knights. Hein Huss laboriously dismounted from his wagon, came forward.

"In the event of resistance," Lord Faide told the knights, "do not be tempted into the forest. Stay with the column and at all times be on your guard against traps."

Hein Huss spoke. "You wish me to parley with the First Folk once more?"

"No," said Lord Faide. "It is ridiculous that I must ask permission of savages to ride over my own land. We return as we came; if they interfere, so much the worse for them."

"You are rash," said Huss with simple candor.

Lord Faide glanced down at him with black eyebrows raised. "What damage can they do if we avoid their traps? Blow foam at us?"

"It is not my place to advise or to warn," said Hein Huss. "However, I point out that they exhibit a confidence which does not come from conscious weakness; also, that they carried tubes, apparently hollow grasswood shoots, which imply missiles."

Lord Faide nodded. "No doubt. However, the knights wear armor, the soldiers carry bucklers. It is not fit that I, Lord Faide of Faide Keep, choose my path to suit the whims of the First Folk. This must be made clear, even if the exercise involves a dozen or so First Folk corpses."

"Since I am not a fighting man," remarked Hein Huss, "I will keep well to the rear, and pass only when the way is secure."

"As you wish." Lord Faide pulled down the visor of his helmet. "Forward."

The column moved toward the forest, along the previous track, which showed plain across the moss. Lord Faide rode in the lead, flanked by his brother, Gethwin Faide and his cousin, Mauve Dermont-Faide.

A half-mile passed, and another. The forest was only a mile distant. Overhead the great sun rode at zenith; brightness and heat poured down; the air carried the oily scent of thorn and tarbush. The column moved on, more slowly; the only sound the clanking of armor, the muffled thud of hooves in the moss, the squeal of wagon wheels.

Lord Faide rose up in his car, watching for any sign of hostile preparation. A half-mile from the planting the forms of the First Folk, waiting in the shade along the forest's verge, became visible. Lord Faide ignored them, held a steady pace along the track they had traveled before.

The half-mile became a quarter-mile. Lord Faide turned to order the troops into single file and was just in time to see a hole open suddenly into the moss and his brother, Gethwin Faide, drop from sight. There was a rattle, a thud, the howling of the impaled horse; Gethwin's wild calls as the horse kicked and crushed him into the stakes. Mauve Dermont-Faide, riding beside Gethwin, could not control his own horse, which leaped aside from the pit and blundered upon a trigger. Up from the moss burst a tree trunk studded with foot-long thorns. It snapped, quick as a scorpion's tail; the thorns punctured Mauve Dermont-Faide's armor, his chest, whisked him from his horse to carry him suspended, writhing and screaming. The tip of the scythe pounded into Lord Faide's car, splintered against the hull. The car swung groaning through the air. Lord Faide clutched at the windscreen to prevent himself from falling.

The column halted; several men ran to the pit, but Gethwin Faide lay twenty feet below, crushed under his horse. Others took Mauve Dermont-Faide down from the swaying scythe, but he, too, was dead.

Lord Faide's skin tingled with a gooseflesh of hate and rage. He looked toward the forest. The First Folk stood motionless. He beckoned to Bernard, sergeant of the foot soldiers. "Two men with lances to try out the ground ahead. All others ready with darts. At my signal spit the devils."

Two men came forward, and marching before Lord Faide's car, probed at the ground. Lord Faide settled in his seat. "Forward."

The column moved slowly toward the forest, every man tense and ready. The lances of the two men in the vanguard presently broke through the moss, to disclose a nettle-trap—a pit lined with nettles, each frond ripe with globes of acid. Carefully they probed out a path to the side, and the column filed around, each man walking in the other's tracks.

At Lord Faide's side now rode his two nephews, Scolford and Edwin. "Notice," said Lord Faide in a voice harsh and tight. "These traps were laid since our last passage; an act of malice."

"But why did they guide us through before?"

Lord Faide smiled bitterly. "They were willing that we should die at Ballant Keep. But we have disappointed them."

"Notice, they carry tubes," said Scolford.

"Blowguns possibly," suggested Edwin.

Scolford disagreed. "They cannot blow through their foam-vents."

"No doubt we shall soon learn," said Lord Faide. He rose in his seat, called to the rear. "Ready with the darts!"

The soldiers raised their crossbows. The column advanced slowly, now only a hundred yards from the planting. The white shapes of the First Folk moved uneasily at the forest's edges. Several of them raised their tubes, seemed to sight along the length. They twitched their great hands.

One of the tubes was pointed toward Lord Faide. He saw a small black object leave the opening, flit forward, gathering speed. He heard a hum, waxing to a rasping, clicking flutter. He ducked behind the windscreen; the projectile swooped in pursuit, struck the windscreen like a thrown stone. It fell crippled upon the forward deck of the car— a heavy black insect like a wasp, its broken proboscis oozing ocher liquid, horny wings beating feebly, eyes like dumbbells fixed on Lord Faide. With his mailed fist, he crushed the creature.

Behind him other wasps struck knights and men; Corex Faide-Battaro took the prong through his visor into the eye, but the armor of the other knights defeated the wasps. The foot soldiers, however, lacked protection; the wasps half-buried themselves in flesh. The soldiers called out in pain, clawed away the wasps, squeezed the wounds. Corex Faide-Battaro toppled from his horse, ran blindly out over the heath, and after fifty feet fell into a trap. The stricken soldiers began to twitch, then fell on the moss, thrashed, leaped up to run with flapping arms, threw themselves in wild somersaults, forward, backward, foaming and thrashing.

In the forest, the First Folk raised their tubes again. Lord Faide bellowed, "Spit the creatures! Bowmen, launch your darts!"

There came the twang of crossbows, darts snapped at the quiet white shapes. A few staggered and wandered aimlessly away; most, however, plucked out the darts or ignored them. They took capsules from small sacks, put them to the end of their tubes.

"Beware the wasps!" cried Lord Faide. "Strike with your bucklers! Kill the cursed things in flight!"

The rasp of horny wings came again; certain of the soldiers found courage enough to follow Lord Faide's orders, and battered down the wasps. Others struck home as before; behind came another flight. The column became a tangle of struggling, crouching men.

"Footmen, retreat!" called Lord Faide furiously. "Footmen back! Knights to me!"

The soldiers fled back along the track, taking refuge behind the baggage wagons. Thirty of their number lay dying, or dead, on the moss.

Lord Faide cried out to his knights in a voice like a bugle. "Dismount, follow slow after me! Turn your helmets, keep the wasps from your eyes! One step at a time, behind the car! Edwin, into the car beside me, test the footing with your lance. Once in the forest there are no traps! Then attack!"

The knights formed themselves into a line behind the car. Lord Faide drove slowly forward, his kinsman Edwin prodding the ground ahead. The First Folk sent out a dozen more wasps, which dashed themselves vainly against the armor. Then there was silence…cessation of sound, activity. The First Folk watched impassively as the knights approached, step by step.

Edwin's lance found a trap, the column moved to the side. Another trap—and the column was diverted from the planting toward the forest. Step by step, yard by yard—another trap, another detour, and now the column was only a hundred feet from the forest. A trap to the left, a trap to the right: the safe path led directly toward an enormous heavy-branched tree. Seventy feet, fifty feet, then Lord Faide drew his sword.

"Prepare to charge, kill till your arms tire!"

From the forest came a crackling sound. The branches of the great tree trembled and swayed. The knights stared, for a moment frozen into place. The tree toppled forward, the knights madly tried to flee—to the rear, to the sides. Traps opened; the knights dropped upon sharp stakes. The tree fell; boughs cracked armored bodies like nuts; there was the hoarse yelling of pinned men, screams from the traps, the crackling subsidence of breaking branches. Lord Faide had been battered down into the car, and the car had been pressed groaning into the moss. His first instinctive act was to press the switch to rest position; then he staggered erect, clambered up through the boughs. A pale unhuman face peered at him; he swung his fist, crushed the faceted eye-bulge, and roaring with rage scrambled through the branches. Others of his knights were working themselves free, although almost a third were either crushed or impaled.

The First Folk came scrambling forward, armed with enormous thorns, long as swords. But now Lord Faide could reach them at close quarters. Hissing with vindictive joy he sprang into their midst, swinging his sword with both hands, as if demon-possessed. The surviving knights joined him and the ground became littered with dismembered First Folk. They drew back slowly, without excitement. Lord Faide reluctantly called back his knights. "We must succor those still pinned, as many as still are alive."

As well as possible branches were cut away, injured knights drawn forth. In some cases the soft moss had cushioned the impact of the tree. Six knights were dead, another four crushed beyond hope of recovery. To these Lord Faide himself gave the *coup de grâce*. Ten minutes further hacking and chopping freed Lord Faide's car, while the First Folk watched incuriously from the forest. The knights wished to charge once more, but Lord Faide ordered retreat. Without interference they returned the way they had come, back to the baggage train.

Lord Faide ordered a muster. Of the original war party, less than two-thirds remained. Lord Faide shook his head bitterly. Galling to think how easily he had been led into a trap! He swung on his heel, strode to the rear of the column, to the wagons of the magicians. The jinxmen sat around a small fire, drinking tea. "Which of you will hoodoo these white forest vermin? I want them dead—stricken with sickness, cramps, blindness, the most painful afflictions you can contrive!"

There was general silence. The jinxmen sipped their tea.

"Well?" demanded Lord Faide. "Have you no answer? Do I not make myself plain?"

Hein Huss cleared his throat, spat into the blaze. "Your wishes are plain. Unfortunately we cannot hoodoo the First Folk."

"And why?"

"There are technical reasons."

Lord Faide knew the futility of argument. "Must we slink home around the forest? If you cannot hoodoo the First Folk, then bring out your demons! I will march on the forest and chop out a path with my sword!"

"It is not for me to suggest tactics," grumbled Hein Huss.

"Go on, speak! I will listen."

"A suggestion has been put to me, which I will pass to you. Neither I nor the other jinxmen associate ourselves with it, since it recommends the crudest of physical principles."

"I await the suggestion," said Lord Faide.

"It is merely this. One of my apprentices tampered with your car, as you may remember."

"Yes, and I will see he gets the hiding he deserves."

"By some freak he caused the car to rise high into the air. The suggestion is this: that we load the car with as much oil as the baggage train affords, that we send the car aloft and let it drift over the planting. At a suitable moment, the occupant of the car will pour the oil over the trees, then hurl down a torch. The forest will burn. The First Folk will be at least discomfited; at best a large number will be destroyed."

Lord Faide slapped his hands together. "Excellent! Quickly, to work!" He called a dozen soldiers, gave them orders; four kegs of cooking oil, three buckets of pitch, six demijohns of spirit were brought and lifted into the car. The engines grated and protested, and the car sagged almost to the moss.

Lord Faide shook his head sadly. "A rude use of the relic, but all in good purpose. Now, where is that apprentice? He must indicate which switches and which buttons he turned."

"I suggest," said Hein Huss, "that Sam Salazar be sent up with the car."

Lord Faide looked sidewise at Sam Salazar's round, bland countenance. "An efficient hand is needed, a seasoned judgment. I wonder if he can be trusted?"

"I would think so," said Hein Huss, "inasmuch as it was Sam Salazar who evolved the scheme in the first place."

"Very well. In with you, Apprentice! Treat my car with reverence! The wind blows away from us; fire this edge of the forest, in as long a strip as you can manage. The torch, where is the torch?"

The torch was brought and secured to the side of the car.

"One more matter," said Sam Salazar. "I would like to borrow the armor of some obliging knight, to protect myself from the wasps. Otherwise—"

"Armor!" bawled Lord Faide. "Bring armor!"

At last, fully accoutered and with visor down, Sam Salazar climbed into the car. He seated himself, peered intently at the buttons and switches. In truth he was not precisely certain as to which he had manipulated before...He considered, reached forward, pushed, turned. The motors roared and screamed; the car shuddered, sluggishly rose into the air. Higher, higher, twenty feet, forty feet, sixty feet—a hundred, two hundred. The wind eased the car toward the forest; in the shade the First Folk watched. Several of them raised tubes, opened the shutters. The onlookers saw the wasps dart through the air to dash against Sam Salazar's armor.

The car drifted over the trees; Sam Salazar began ladling out the oil. Below, the First Folk stirred uneasily. The wind carried the car too far over the forest; Sam Salazar worked the controls, succeeded in guiding himself back. One keg was empty, and another; he tossed them out, presently emptied the remaining two, and the buckets of pitch. He soaked a rag in spirit, ignited it, threw it over the side, poured the spirit after.

The flaming rag fell into leaves. A crackle, fire blazed and sprang. The car now floated at a height of five hundred feet. Salazar poured over the remaining spirits, dropped the demijohns, guided the car back over the heath, and fumbling nervously with the controls dropped the car in a series of swoops back to the moss.

Lord Faide sprang forward, clapped him on the shoulder. "Excellently done! The forest blazes like tinder!"

The men of Faide Keep stood back, rejoicing to see the flames soar and lick. The First Folk scurried back from the heat, waving their arms; foam of a peculiar purple color issued from their vents as they ran, small useless puffs discharged as if by accident or through excitement. The flames ate through first the forest, then spread into the new planting, leaping through the leaves.

"Prepare to march!" called Lord Faide. "We pass directly behind the flames, before the First Folk return."

Off in the forest the First Folk perched in the trees, blowing out foam in great puffs and billows, building a wall of insulation. The flames had eaten half across the new planting, leaving behind smouldering saplings.

"Forward! Briskly!"

* * *

The column moved ahead. Coughing in the smoke, eyes smarting, they passed under still blazing trees and came out on the western downs.

Slowly the column moved forward, led by a pair of soldiers prodding the moss with lances. Behind followed Lord Faide with the knights, then came the foot soldiers, then the rumbling baggage train, and finally the six wagons of the jinxmen.

A thump, a creak, a snap. A scythe had broken up from the moss; the soldiers in the lead dropped flat; the scythe whipped past, a foot from Lord Faide's face. At the same time a plaintive cry came from the rear guard. "They pursue! The First Folk come!"

Lord Faide turned to inspect the new threat. A clot of First Folk, two hundred or more, came across the moss, moving without haste or urgency. Some carried wasp-tubes, others thorn-rapiers.

Lord Faide looked ahead. Another hundred yards should bring the army out upon safe ground; then he could deploy and maneuver. "Forward!"

The column proceeded, the baggage train and the jinxmen's wagons pressing close up against the soldiers. Behind and to the side came the First Folk, moving casually and easily.

At last Lord Faide judged they had reached secure ground. "Forward, now! Bring the wagons out, hurry now!"

The troops needed no urging; they trotted out over the heath, the wagons trundling after. Lord Faide ordered the wagons into a close double line, stationed the soldiers between, with the horses behind and protected from the wasps. The knights, now dismounted, waited in front.

The First Folk came listlessly, formlessly forward. Blank white faces stared; huge hands grasped tubes and thorns; traces of the purplish foam showed at the lips of their underarm orifices.

Lord Faide walked along the line of knights. "Swords ready. Allow them as close as they care to come. Then a quick charge." He motioned to the foot soldiers. "Choose a target...!" A volley of darts whistled overhead, to plunge into white bodies. With chisel-bladed fingers the First Folk plucked them out, discarded them with no evidence of vexation. One or two staggered, wandered confusedly across the line of approach. Others raised their tubes, withdrew the shutter. Out flew the insects, horny wings rasping, prongs thrust forward. Across the moss they flickered, to crush themselves against the armor of the knights, to drop to the ground, to be stamped upon. The soldiers cranked their crossbows back into tension, discharged another flight of darts, caused several more First Folk casualties.

The First Folk spread into a long line, surrounded the Faide troops. Lord Faide shifted half his knights to the other side of the wagons.

The First Folk wandered closer. Lord Faide called for a charge. The knights stepped smartly forward, swords swinging. The First Folk advanced a few more steps, then stopped short. The flaps of skin at their backs swelled, pulsed; white foam gushed through their vents; clouds and billows rose up around them. The knights halted uncertainly, prodding and slashing into the foam but finding nothing. The foam piled higher, rolling in and forward, pushing the knights back toward the wagons. They looked questioningly toward Lord Faide.

Lord Faide waved his sword. "Cut through to the other side! Forward!" Slashing two-handed with his sword, he sprang into the foam. He struck something solid, hacked blindly at it, pushed forward. Then his legs were seized; he was upended and fell with a spine-rattling jar. Now he felt the grate of a thorn searching his armor. It found a crevice under his corselet and pierced him. Cursing he raised on his hands and knees, plunged blindly forward. Enormous hard hands grasped him, heavy forms fell on his shoulders. He tried to breathe, the foam clogged his visor; he began to smother. Staggering to his feet he half-ran, half-fell out into the open air, carrying two of the First Folk with him. He had lost his sword, but managed to draw his dagger. The First Folk released him and stepped back into the foam. Lord Faide sprang to his feet. Inside the foam came the sounds of combat; some of his knights burst into the open; others called for help. Lord Faide motioned to the knights. "Back within; the devils slaughter our kinsmen! In and on to the center!"

He took a deep breath. Seizing his dagger he thrust himself back into the foam. A flurry of shapes came at him: he pounded with his fists, cut with his dagger, stumbled over a mass of living tissue. He kicked the softness, and stepped on metal. Bending, he grasped a leg but found it limp and dead. First Folk were on his back, another thorn found its mark; he groaned and thrust himself forward, and once again fell out into the open air.

A scant fifty of his knights had won back into the central clearing. Lord Faide cried out, "To the center; mount your horses!" Abandoning his car, he himself vaulted into a saddle. The foam boiled and billowed closer. Lord Faide waved his arm. "Forward, all; at a gallop! After us the wagons—out into the open!"

They charged, thrusting the frightened horses into the foam. There was white blindness, the feel of forms underneath, then the open air once again. Behind came the wagons, and the foot soldiers, running along the channel cut by the wagons. All won free—all but the knights who had fallen under the foam.

Two hundred yards from the great white clot of foam, Lord Faide halted, turned, looked back. He raised his fist, shook it in a passion. "My knights, my car, my honor! I'll burn your forests, I'll drive you into the sea, there'll be no peace till all are dead!" He swung around.

"Come," he called bitterly to the remnants of his war party. "We have been defeated. We retreat to Faide Keep."

CHAPTER VIII

Faide Keep, like Ballant Keep, was constructed of a black, glossy substance, half metal, half stone, impervious to heat, force and radiation. A parasol roof, designed to ward off hostile energy, rested on five squat outer towers, connected by walls almost as high as the lip of the overhanging roof.

The homecoming banquet was quiet and morose. The soldiers and knights ate lightly and drank much, but instead of becoming merry, lapsed into gloom. Lord Faide, overcome by emotion, jumped to his feet. "Everyone sits silent, aching with rage. I feel no differently. We shall take revenge. We shall put the forests to the torch. The cursed white savages will smother and burn. Drink now with good cheer; not a moment will be wasted. But we must be ready. It is no more than idiocy to attack as before. Tonight I take council with the jinxmen, and we will start a program of affliction."

The soldiers and knights rose to their feet, raised their cups and drank a somber toast. Lord Faide bowed and left the hall.

He went to his private trophy room. On the walls hung escutcheons, memorials, deathmasks, clusters of swords like many-petaled flowers; a rack of side-arms, energy pistols, electric stilettos; a portrait of the original Faide, in ancient spacefarer's uniform, and a treasured, almost unique, photograph of the great ship that had brought the first Faide to Pangborn.

Lord Faide studied the ancient face for several moments, then summoned a servant. "Ask the Head Jinxman to attend me."

Hein Huss presently stumped into the room. Lord Faide turned away from the portrait, seated himself, motioned to Hein Huss to do likewise. "What of the keep-lords?" he asked. "How do they regard the setback at the hands of the First Folk?"

"There are various reactions," said Hein Huss. "At Boghoten, Candelwade and Havve there is distress and anger."

Lord Faide nodded. "These are my kinsmen."

"At Gisborne, Graymar, Castle Cloud and Alder there is satisfaction, veiled calculation."

"To be expected," muttered Lord Faide. "These lords must be humbled; in spite of oaths and undertakings, they still think rebellion."

"At Star Home, Julian-Douray and Oak Hall I read surprise at the abilities of the First Folk, but in the main disinterest."

Lord Faide nodded sourly. "Well enough. There is no actual rebellion in prospect; we are free to concentrate on the First Folk. I will tell you what is in my mind. You report that new plantings are in progress between Wildwood, Old Forest, Sarrow Copse and elsewhere—possibly with the intent of surrounding Faide Keep." He looked inquiringly at Hein Huss, but no comment was forthcoming. Lord Faide continued. "Possibly we have underestimated the cunning of the savages. They seem capable of forming plans and acting with almost human persistence. Or, I should say, more than human persistence, for it appears that after sixteen hundred years they still consider us invaders and hope to exterminate us."

"That is my own conclusion," said Hein Huss.

"We must take steps to strike first. I consider this a matter for the jinxmen. We gain no honor dodging wasps, falling into traps, or groping through foam. It is a needless waste of lives. Therefore, I want you to assemble your jinxmen, cabalmen and spellbinders; I want you to formulate your most potent hoodoos—"

"Impossible."

Lord Faide's black eyebrows rose high. "'Impossible'?"

Hein Huss seemed vaguely uncomfortable. "I read the wonder in your mind. You suspect me of disinterest, irresponsibility. Not true. If the First Folk defeat you, we suffer likewise."

"Exactly," said Lord Faide dryly. "You will starve."

"Nevertheless, the jinxmen cannot help you." He hoisted himself to his feet, started for the door.

"Sit," said Lord Faide. "It is necessary to pursue this matter."

Hein Huss looked around with his bland, water-clear eyes. Lord Faide met his gaze. Hein Huss sighed deeply. "I see I must ignore the precepts of my trade, break the habits of a lifetime. I must explain." He took his bulk to the wall, fingered the side-arms in the rack, studied the portrait of the ancestral Faide. "These miracle workers of the old times—unfortunately we cannot use their magic! Notice the bulk of the spaceship! As heavy as Faide Keep." He turned his gaze on the table, teleported a candelabra two or three inches. "With considerably less effort they gave that spaceship enormous velocity, using ideas and forces they knew to be imaginary and irrational. We have advanced since then, of course. We no longer employ mysteries, arcane constructions, wild nonhuman forces. We are rational and practical—but we cannot achieve the effects of the ancient magicians."

Lord Faide watched Hein Huss with saturnine eyes. Hein Huss gave his deep rumbling laugh. "You think that I wish to distract you with talk? No, this is not the case. I am preparing to enlighten you." He returned to his seat, lowered his bulk with a groan. "Now I must talk at length, to which I am not accustomed. But you must be given to understand what we jinxmen can do and what we cannot do.

"First, unlike the ancient magicians, we are practical men. Naturally there is difference in our abilities. The best jinxman combines great telepathic facility, implacable personal force, intimate knowledge of his fellow humans. He knows their acts, motives, desires and fears; he understands the symbols that most vigorously represent these qualities. Jinxmanship in the main is drudgery—dangerous, difficult and unromantic—with no mystery except that which we employ to confuse our enemies." Hein Huss glanced at Lord Faide to encounter the same saturnine gaze. "Ha! I still have told you nothing; I still have spent many words talking around my inability to confound the First Folk. Patience."

"Speak on," said Lord Faide.

"Listen then. What happens when I hoodoo a man? First I must enter into his mind telepathically. There are three operational levels: the conscious, the unconscious, the cellular. The most effective jinxing is done if all three levels are influenced. I feel into my victim, I learn as much as possible, supplementing my previous knowledge of him, which is part of my stock in trade. I take up his doll, which carries his traces. The doll is highly useful but not indispensable. It serves as a focus for my attention; it acts as a pattern, or a guide, as I fix upon the mind of the victim, and he is bound by his own telepathic capacity to the doll which bears his traces.

"So! Now! Man and doll are identified in my mind, and at one or more levels in the victim's mind. Whatever happens to the doll the victim feels to be happening to himself. There is no more to simple hoodooing than that, from the standpoint of the jinxman. But naturally the victims differ greatly. Susceptibility is the key idea here. Some men are more susceptible than others. Fear and conviction breed susceptibility. As a jinxman succeeds he becomes ever more feared, and consequently the more efficacious he becomes. The process is self-generative.

"Demon-possession is a similar technique. Susceptibility is again essential; again conviction creates susceptibility. It is easiest and most dramatic when the characteristics of the demon are well known, as in the case of Comandore's Keyril. For this reason, demons can be exchanged or traded among jinxmen. The commodity actually traded is public acceptance and familiarity with the demon."

"Demons then do not actually exist?" inquired Lord Faide half-incredulously.

Hein Huss grinned vastly, showing enormous yellow teeth. "Telepathy works through a superstratum. Who knows what is created in this superstratum? Maybe the demons live on after they have been conceived; maybe they now are real. This of course is speculation, which we jinxmen shun.

"So much for demons, so much for the lesser techniques of jinxmanship. I have explained sufficient to serve as background to the present situation."

"Excellent," said Lord Faide. "Continue."

"The question, then, is: How does one cast a hoodoo into a creature of an alien race?" He looked inquiringly at Lord Faide. "Can you tell me?"

"I?" asked Lord Faide surprised. "No."

"The method is basically the same as in the hoodooing of men. It is necessary to make the creature believe, in every cell of his being, that he suffers or dies. This is where the problems begin to arise. Does the creature think—that is to say, does he arrange the processes of his life in the same manner as men? This is a very important distinction. Certain creatures of the universe use methods other than the human nerve-node system to control their environments. We call the human system 'intelligence'—a word which properly should be restricted to human activity. Other creatures use different agencies, different systems, arriving sometimes at similar ends. To bring home these generalities, I cannot hope to merge my mind with the corresponding capacity in the First Folk. The key will not fit the lock. At least, not altogether. Once or twice when I watched the First Folk trading with men at Forest Market, I felt occasional weak significances. This implies that the First Folk mentality creates something similar to human telepathic impulses. Nevertheless, there is no real sympathy between the two races.

"This is the first and the least difficulty. If I were able to make complete telepathic contact—what then? The creatures are different from us. They have no words for 'fear', 'hate', 'rage', 'pain', 'bravery', 'cowardice'.

One may deduce that they do not feel these emotions. Undoubtedly they know other sensations, possibly as meaningful. Whatever these may be, they are unknown to me, and therefore I cannot either form or project symbols for these sensations."

Lord Faide stirred impatiently. "In short, you tell me that you cannot efficiently enter these creatures' minds; and that if you could, you do not know what influences you could plant there to do them harm."

"Succinct," agreed Hein Huss. "Substantially accurate."

Lord Faide rose to his feet. "In that case you must repair these deficiencies. You must learn to telepathize with the First Folk; you must find what influences will harm them. As quickly as possible."

Hein Huss stared reproachfully at Lord Faide. "But I have gone to great lengths to explain the difficulties involved! To hoodoo the First Folk is a monumental task! It would be necessary to enter Wildwood, to live with the First Folk, to become one of them, as my apprentice thought to become a tree. Even then an effective hoodoo is improbable! The First Folk must be susceptible to conviction! Otherwise there would be no bite to the hoodoo! I could guarantee no success. I would predict failure. No other jinxman would dare tell you this, no other would risk his mana. I dare because I am Hein Huss, with life behind me."

"Nevertheless we must attempt every weapon at hand," said Lord Faide in a dry voice. "I cannot risk my knights, my kinsmen, my soldiers against these pallid half-creatures. What a waste of good flesh and blood to be stuck by a poison insect! You must go to Wildwood; you must learn how to hoodoo the First Folk."

Hein Huss heaved himself erect. His great round face was stony; his eyes were like bits of water-worn glass. "It is likewise a waste to go on a fool's errand. I am no fool, and I will not undertake a hoodoo which is futile from the beginning."

"In that case," said Lord Faide, "I will find someone else." He went to the door, summoned a servant. "Bring Isak Comandore here."

Hein Huss lowered his bulk into the chair. "I will remain during the interview, with your permission."

"As you wish."

Isak Comandore appeared in the doorway, tall, loosely articulated, head hanging forward. He darted a glance of swift appraisal at Lord Faide, at Hein Huss, then stepped into the room.

Lord Faide crisply explained his desires. "Hein Huss refuses to undertake the mission. Therefore I call on you."

Isak Comandore calculated. The pattern of his thinking was clear: he possibly could gain much mana; there was small risk of diminution, for had not Hein Huss already dodged away from the project? Comandore nodded. "Hein Huss has made clear the difficulties; only a very clever and very lucky jinxman can hope to succeed. But I accept the challenge, I will go."

"Good," said Hein Huss. "I will go, too." Isak Comandore darted him a sudden hot glance. "I wish only to observe. To Isak Comandore goes the responsibility and whatever credit may ensue."

"Very well," said Comandore presently. "I welcome your company. Tomorrow morning we leave. I go to order our wagon."

Late in the evening Apprentice Sam Salazar came to Hein Huss where he sat brooding in his workroom. "What do you wish?" growled Huss.

"I have a request to make of you, Head Jinxman Huss."

"Head Jinxman in name only," grumbled Hein Huss. "Isak Comandore is about to assume my position."

Sam Salazar blinked, laughed uncertainly. Hein Huss fixed wintry-pale eyes on him. "What do you wish?"

"I have heard that you go on an expedition to Wildwood, to study the First Folk."

"True, true. What then?"

"Surely they will now attack all men?"

Hein Huss shrugged. "At Forest Market they trade with men. At Forest Market men have always entered the forest. Perhaps there will be change, perhaps not."

"I would go with you, if I may," said Sam Salazar.

"This is no mission for apprentices."

"An apprentice must take every opportunity to learn," said Sam Salazar. "Also you will need extra hands to set up tents, to load and unload cabinets, to cook, to fetch water and other such matters."

"Your argument is convincing," said Hein Huss. "We depart at dawn; be on hand."

CHAPTER IX

As the sun lifted over the heath the jinxmen departed Faide Keep. The high-wheeled wagon creaked north over the moss, Hein Huss and Isak Comandore riding the front seat, Sam Salazar with his legs hanging over the tail. The wagon rose and fell with the dips and mounds of the moss, wheels wobbling, and presently passed out of sight behind Skywatcher's Hill.

Five days later, an hour before sunset, the wagon reappeared. As before, Hein Huss and Isak Comandore rode the front seat, with Sam Salazar perched behind. They approached the keep, and without giving so much as a sign or a nod, drove through the gate into the courtyard.

Isak Comandore unfolded his long legs, stepped to the ground like a spider; Hein Huss lowered himself with a grunt. Both went to their quarters, while Sam Salazar led the wagon to the jinxmen's warehouse.

Somewhat later Isak Comandore presented himself to Lord Faide, who had been waiting in his trophy room, forced to a show of indifference through considerations of position, dignity and protocol. Isak Comandore stood in the doorway, grinning like a fox. Lord Faide eyed him with sour dislike, waiting for Comandore to speak. Hein Huss might have stationed himself an entire day, eyes placidly fixed on Lord Faide, awaiting the first word; Isak Comandore lacked the absolute serenity. He came a step forward. "I have returned from Wildwood."

"With what results?"

"I believe that it is possible to hoodoo the First Folk."

Hein Huss spoke from behind Comandore. "I believe that such an undertaking, if feasible, would be useless, irresponsible and possibly dangerous." He lumbered forward.

Isak Comandore's eyes glowed hot red-brown; he turned back to Lord Faide. "You ordered me forth on a mission; I will render a report."

"Seat yourselves. I will listen."

Isak Comandore, nominal head of the expedition, spoke. "We rode along the river bank to Forest Market. Here was no sign of disorder or of hostility. A hundred First Folk traded timber, planks, posts and poles for knife blades, iron wire, and copper pots. When they returned to their barge we followed them aboard, wagon, horses and all. They showed no surprise—"

"Surprise," said Hein Huss heavily, "is an emotion of which they have no knowledge."

Isak Comandore glared briefly. "We spoke to the barge-tenders, explaining that we wished to visit the interior of Wildwood. We asked if the First Folk would try to kill us to prevent us from entering the forest. They professed indifference as to either our well-being or our destruction. This was by no means a guarantee of safe conduct; however, we

244

accepted it as such, and remained aboard the barge." He spoke on with occasional emendations from Hein Huss.

They had proceeded up the river, into the forest, the First Folk poling against the slow current. Presently they put away the poles; nevertheless the barge moved as before. The mystified jinxmen discussed the possibility of teleportation, or symbological force, and wondered if the First Folk had developed jinxing techniques unknown to men. Sam Salazar, however, noticed that four enormous water beetles, each twelve feet long with oil-black carapaces and blunt heads, had risen from the river bed and pushed the barge from behind—apparently without direction or command. The First Folk stood at the bow, turning the nose of the barge this way or that to follow the winding of the river. They ignored the jinxmen and Sam Salazar as if they did not exist.

The beetles swam tirelessly; the barge moved for four hours as fast as a man could walk. Occasionally, First Folk peered from the forest shadows, but none showed interest or concern in the barge's unusual cargo. By midafternoon the river widened, broke into many channels and became a marsh; a few minutes later the barge floated out into the open water of a small lake. Along the shore, behind the first line of trees appeared a large settlement. The jinxmen were interested and surprised. It had always been assumed that the First Folk wandered at random through the forest, as they had originally lived in the moss of the downs.

The barge grounded; the First Folk walked ashore, the men followed with the horses and wagon. Their immediate impressions were of swarming numbers, of slow but incessant activity, and they were attacked by an overpoweringly evil smell.

Ignoring the stench the men brought the wagon in from the shore, paused to take stock of what they saw. The settlement appeared to be a center of many diverse activities. The trees had been stripped of lower branches, and supported blocks of hardened foam three hundred feet long, fifty feet high, twenty feet thick, with a space of a man's height intervening between the underside of the foam and the ground. There were a dozen of these blocks, apparently of cellular construction. Certain of the cells had broken open and seethed with small white fish-like creatures—the First Folk young.

Below the blocks masses of First Folk engaged in various occupations, in the main unfamiliar to the jinxmen. Leaving the wagon in the care of Sam Salazar, Hein Huss and Isak Comandore moved forward among the First Folk, repelled by the stench and the pressure of alien flesh, but drawn by curiosity. They were neither heeded nor halted; they wandered everywhere about the settlement. One area seemed to be an enormous zoo, divided into a number of sections. The purpose of one of these sections—a kind of range two hundred feet long—was all too clear. At one end three or four First Folk released wasps from tubes; at the other end a human corpse hung on a rope—a Faide casualty from the battle at the new planting. Certain of the wasps flew straight at the corpse; just before contact they were netted and removed. Others flew up and away or veered toward the First Folk who stood along the side of the range. These latter also were netted and killed at once.

The purpose of the business was clear enough. Examining some of the other activity in this new light, the jinxmen were able to interpret much that had hitherto puzzled them.

They saw beetles tall as dogs with heavy saw-toothed pincers attacking objects resembling horses; pens of insects even larger, long, narrow, segmented, with dozens of heavy legs and nightmare heads. All these creatures—wasps, beetles, centipedes—in smaller and less formidable form were indigenous to the forest; it was plain that the First Folk had been practicing selective breeding for many years, perhaps centuries.

Not all the activity was warlike. Moths were trained to gather nuts, worms to gnaw straight holes through timber; in another section caterpillars chewed a yellow mash, molded it into identical spheres. Much of the evil odor emanated from the zoo; the jinxmen departed without reluctance, and returned to the wagon. Sam Salazar pitched the tent and built a fire, while Hein Huss and Isak Comandore discussed the settlement.

Night came; the blocks of foam glowed with imprisoned light; the activity underneath proceeded without cessation. The jinxmen retired to the tent and slept, while Sam Salazar stood guard.

The following day Hein Huss was able to engage one of the First Folk in conversation: the first attention of any sort given to them.

The conversation was long; Hein Huss reported only the gist of it to Lord Faide. (Isak Comandore turned away, ostentatiously disassociating himself from the matter.)

Hein Huss first of all had inquired as to the purpose of the sinister preparations: the wasps, beetles, centipedes and the like.

"We intend to kill men," the creature had reported ingenuously. "We intend to return to the moss. This has been our purpose ever since men appeared on the planet."

Huss had stated that such an ambition was shortsighted, that there was ample room for both men and First Folk on Pangborn. "The First Folk," said Hein Huss, "should remove their traps and cease their efforts to surround the keeps with forest."

"No," came the response, "men are intruders. They mar the beautiful moss. All will be killed."

Isak Comandore returned to the conversation. "I noticed here a significant fact. All the First Folk within sight had ceased their work; all looked toward us, as if they, too, participated in the discussion. I reached the highly important conclusion that the First Folk are not complete individuals but components of a larger unity, joined to a greater or less extent by a telepathic phase not unlike our own."

Hein Huss continued placidly, "I remarked that if we were attacked, many of the First Folk would perish. The creature showed no concern, and in fact implied much of what Jinxman Comandore had already induced: 'There are always more in the cells to replace the elements which die. But if the community becomes sick, all suffer. We have been forced into the forests, into a strange existence. We must arm ourselves and drive away the men, and to this end we have developed the methods of men to our own purposes!'"

Isak Comandore spoke. "Needless to say, the creature referred to the ancient men, not ourselves."

"In any event," said Lord Faide, "they leave no doubt as to their intentions. We should be fools not to attack them at once, with every weapon at our disposal."

Hein Huss continued imperturbably. "The creature went on at some length. 'We have learned the value of irrationality.' 'Irrationality' of course was not his word or even his meaning. He said something like 'a series of vaguely motivated trials'—as close as I can translate. He said, 'We have learned to change our environment. We use insects and trees and plants and water-slugs. It is an enormous effort for us who would prefer a placid life in the moss. But you men have forced this life on us, and now you must suffer the consequences.' I pointed out once more that men were not helpless, that many First Folk would die. The creature seemed unworried. 'The community persists.' I asked a delicate question, 'If your purpose is to kill men, why do you allow us here?' He said, 'The entire community of men will be destroyed.' Apparently they believe the human society to be similar to their own, and therefore regard the killing of three wayfaring individuals as pointless effort."

Lord Faide laughed grimly. "To destroy us they must first win past Hellmouth, then penetrate Faide Keep. This they are unable to do."

Isak Comandore resumed his report. "At this time I was already convinced that the problem was one of hoodooing not an individual but an entire race. In theory this should be no more difficult than hoodooing one. It requires no more effort to speak to twenty than to one. With this end in view I ordered the apprentice to collect substances associated with the creatures. Skinflakes, foam, droppings, all other exudations obtainable. While he did so, I tried to put myself in rapport with the creatures. It is difficult, for their telepathy works across a different stratum than ours. Nevertheless, to a certain extent I have succeeded."

"Then you can hoodoo the First Folk?" asked Lord Faide.

"I vouchsafe nothing until I try. Certain preparations must be made."

"Go then; make your preparations."

Comandore rose to his feet and with a sly side-glance for Hein Huss left the room. Huss waited, pinching his chin with heavy fingers. Lord Faide looked at him coldly. "You have something to add?"

Huss grunted, hoisted himself to his feet. "I wish that I did. But my thoughts are confused. Of the many futures, all seem troubled and angry. Perhaps our best is not good enough."

Lord Faide looked at Hein Huss with surprise; the massive Head Jinxman had never before spoken in terms so pessimistic and melancholy. "Speak then; I will listen."

Hein Huss said gruffly, "If I knew any certainties I would speak gladly. But I am merely beset by doubts. I fear that we can no longer depend on logic and careful jinxmanship. Our ancestors were miracle workers, magicians. They drove the First Folk into the forest. To put us to flight in our turn the First Folk have adopted the ancient methods: random trial and purposeless empiricism. I am dubious. Perhaps we must turn our backs on sanity and likewise return to the mysticism of our ancestors."

Lord Faide shrugged. "If Isak Comandore can hoodoo the First Folk, such a retreat may be unnecessary."

"The world changes," said Hein Huss. "Of so much I feel sure: the old days of craft and careful knowledge are gone. The future is for men of cleverness, of imagination untroubled by discipline; the unorthodox Sam Salazar may become more effective than I. The world changes."

Lord Faide smiled his sour dyspeptic smile. "When that day comes I will appoint Sam Salazar Head Jinxman and also name him Lord Faide, and you and I will retire together to a hut on the downs."

Hein Huss made a heavy fateful gesture and departed.

CHAPTER X

Two days later Lord Faide, coming upon Isak Comandore, inquired as to his progress. Comandore took refuge in generalities. After another two days Lord Faide inquired again and this time insisted on particulars. Comandore grudgingly led the way to his workroom, where a dozen cabalmen, spellbinders and apprentices worked around a large table, building a model of the First Folk settlement in Wildwood.

"Along the lakeshore," said Comandore, "I will range a great number of dolls, daubed with First Folk essences. When this is complete I will work up a hoodoo and blight the creatures."

"Good. Perform well." Lord Faide departed the workroom, mounted to the topmost pinnacle of the keep, to the cupola where the ancestral weapon Hellmouth was housed. "Jambart! Where are you?"

Weapon-tender Jambart, short, blue-jowled, red-nosed and big-bellied, appeared. "My lord?"

"I come to inspect Hellmouth. Is it prepared for instant use?"

"Prepared, my lord, and ready. Oiled, greased, polished, scraped, burnished, tended—every part smooth as an egg."

Lord Faide made a scowling examination of Hellmouth—a heavy cylinder six feet in diameter, twelve feet long, studded with half-domes interconnected with tubes of polished copper. Jambart undoubtedly had been diligent. No trace of dirt or rust or corrosion showed; all was gleaming metal. The snout was covered with a heavy plate of metal and tarred canvas; the ring upon which the weapon swiveled was well-greased.

Lord Faide surveyed the four horizons. To the south was fertile Faide Valley; to the west open downs; to north and east the menacing loom of Wildwood.

He turned back to Hellmouth and pretended to find a smear of grease. Jambart boiled with expostulations and protestations; Lord Faide uttered a grim warning, enjoining less laxity, then descended to the workroom of Hein Huss. He found the Head Jinxman reclining on a couch, staring at the ceiling. At a bench stood Sam Salazar surrounded by bottles, flasks and dishes.

Lord Faide stared balefully at the confusion. "What are you doing?" he asked the apprentice.

Sam Salazar looked up guiltily. "Nothing in particular, my lord."

"If you are idle, go then and assist Isak Comandore."

"I am not idle, Lord Faide."

"Then what do you do?"

Sam Salazar gazed sulkily at the bench. "I don't know."

"Then you are idle!"

"No, I am occupied. I pour various liquids on this foam. It is First Folk foam. I wonder what will happen. Water does not dissolve it, nor spirits. Heat chars and slowly burns it, emitting a foul smoke."

Lord Faide turned away with a sneer. "You amuse yourself as a child might. Go to Isak Comandore; he can find use for you. How do you expect to become a jinxman, dabbling and prattling like a baby among pretty rocks?"

Hein Huss gave a deep sound: a mingling of sigh, snort, grunt and clearing of the throat. "He does no harm, and Isak Comandore has hands enough. Salazar will never become a jinxman; that has been clear a long time."

Lord Faide shrugged. "He is your apprentice, and your responsibility. Well, then. What news from the keeps?"

Hein Huss, groaning and wheezing, swung his legs over the edge of the couch. "The lords share your concern, to greater or less extent. Your close allies will readily place troops at your disposal; the others likewise if pressure is brought to bear."

Lord Faide nodded in dour satisfaction. "For the moment there is no urgency. The First Folk hold to their forests. Faide Keep of course is impregnable, although they might ravage the valley..." he paused thoughtfully. "Let Isak Comandore cast his hoodoo. Then we will see."

From the direction of the bench came a hiss, a small explosion, a whiff of acrid gas. Sam Salazar turned guiltily to look at them, his eyebrows singed. Lord Faide gave a snort of disgust and strode from the room.

"What did you do?" Hein Huss inquired in a colorless voice.

"I don't know."

Now Hein Huss likewise snorted in disgust. "Ridiculous. If you wish to work miracles, you must remember your procedures. Miracle-working is not jinxmanship, with established rules and guides. In matters so complex it is well that you take notes, so that the miracles may be repeated."

Sam Salazar nodded in agreement and turned back to the bench.

CHAPTER XI

Late during the day, news of new First Folk truculence reached Faide Keep. On Honeymoss Hill, not far west of Forest Market, a camp of shepherds had been visited by a wandering group of First Folk, who began to kill the sheep with thorn-swords. When the shepherds protested they, too, were attacked, and many were killed. The remainder of the sheep were massacred.

The following day came other news: four children swimming in Brastock River at Gilbert Ferry had been seized by enormous water-beetles and cut into pieces. On the other side of Wildwood, in the foothills immediately below Castle Cloud, peasants had cleared several hillsides and planted them to vines. Early in the morning they had discovered a horde of black disklike flukes devouring the vines—leaves, branches, trunks and roots. They set about killing the flukes with spades and at once were stung to death by wasps.

Adam McAdam reported the incidents to Lord Faide, who went to Isak Comandore in a fury. "How soon before you are prepared?"

"I am prepared now. But I must rest and fortify myself. Tomorrow morning I work the hoodoo."

"The sooner the better! The creatures have left their forest; they are out killing men!"

Isak Comandore pulled his long chin. "That was to be expected; they told us as much."

Lord Faide ignored the remark. "Show me your tableau."

Isak Comandore took him into his workroom. The model was now complete, with the masses of simulated First Folk properly daubed and sensitized, each tied with a small wad of foam. Isak Comandore pointed to a pot of dark liquid. "I will explain the basis of the hoodoo. When I visited the camp I watched everywhere for powerful symbols. Undoubtedly there were many at hand, but I could not discern them. However, I remembered a circumstance from the battle at the planting: when the creatures were attacked, threatened with fire and about to die, they spewed foam of dull purple color. Evidently this purple foam is associated with death. My hoodoo will be based upon this symbol."

"Rest well, then, so that you may hoodoo to your best capacity."

The following morning Isak Comandore dressed in long robes of black, set a mask of the demon Nard on his head to fortify himself. He entered his workroom, closed the door.

An hour passed, two hours. Lord Faide sat at breakfast with his kin, stubbornly maintaining a pose of cynical unconcern. At last he could contain himself no longer and went out into the courtyard where Comandore's underlings stood fidgeting and uneasy. "Where is Hein Huss?" demanded Lord Faide. "Summon him here."

Hein Huss came stumping out of his quarters. Lord Faide motioned to Comandore's workshop. "What is happening? Is he succeeding?"

Hein Huss looked toward the workshop. "He is casting a powerful hoodoo. I feel confusion, anger—"

"In Comandore, or in the First Folk?"

"I am not in rapport. I think he has conveyed a message to their minds. A very difficult task, as I explained to you. In this preliminary aspect he has succeeded."

"'Preliminary'? What else remains?"

"The two most important elements of the hoodoo: the susceptibility of the victim and the appropriateness of the symbol."

Lord Faide frowned. "You do not seem optimistic."

"I am uncertain. Isak Comandore may be right in his assumption. If so, and if the First Folk are highly susceptible, today marks a great victory, and Comandore will achieve tremendous mana!"

Lord Faide stared at the door to the workshop. "What now?"

Hein Huss' eyes went blank with concentration. "Isak Comandore is near death. He can hoodoo no more today."

Lord Faide turned, waved his arm to the cabalmen. "Enter the workroom! Assist your master!"

The cabalmen raced to the door, flung it open. Presently they emerged supporting the limp form of Isak Comandore, his black robe spattered with purple foam. Lord Faide pressed close. "What did you achieve? Speak!"

Isak Comandore's eyes were half-closed, his mouth hung loose and wet. "I spoke to the First Folk, to the whole race. I sent the symbol into their minds—" His head fell limply sidewise.

Lord Faide moved back. "Take him to his quarters. Put him on his couch." He turned away, stood indecisively, chewing at his drooping lower lip. "Still we do not know the measure of his success."

"Ah," said Hein Huss, "but we do!"

Lord Faide jerked around. "What is this? What do you say?"

"I saw into Comandore's mind. He used the symbol of purple foam; with tremendous effort he drove it into their minds. Then he learned that purple foam means not death—purple foam means fear for the safety of the community, purple foam means desperate rage."

"In any event," said Lord Faide after a moment, "there is no harm done. The First Folk can hardly become more hostile."

Three hours later a scout rode furiously into the courtyard, threw himself off his horse, ran to Lord Faide. "The First Folk have left the forest! A tremendous number! Thousands! They are advancing on Faide Keep!"

"Let them advance!" said Lord Faide. "The more the better! Jambart, where are you?"

"Here, sir."

"Prepare Hellmouth! Hold all in readiness!"

"Hellmouth is always ready, sir!"

Lord Faide struck him across the shoulders. "Off with you! Bernard!"

The sergeant of the Faide troops came forward. "Ready, Lord Faide."

"The First Folk attack. Armor your men against wasps, feed them well. We will need all our strength."

Lord Faide turned to Hein Huss. "Send to the keeps, to the manor houses, order our kinsmen to join us, with all their troops and all their armor. Send to Bellgard Hall, to Boghoten, Camber and Candelwade. Haste, haste, it is only hours from Wildwood."

Huss held up his hand. "I have already done so. The keeps are warned. They know your need."

"And the First Folk—can you feel their minds?"

"No."

Lord Faide walked away. Hein Huss lumbered out the main gate, walked around the keep, casting appraising glances up the black walls of the squat towers, windowless and proof even against the ancient miracle-weapons. High on top the great parasol roof Jambart the weapon-tender worked in the cupola, polishing that which already glistened, greasing surfaces already heavy with grease.

Hein Huss returned within. Lord Faide approached him, mouth hard, eyes bright. "What have you seen?"

"Only the keep, the walls, the towers, the roof, and Hellmouth."

"And what do you think?"

"I think many things."

"You are noncommittal; you know more than you say. It is best that you speak, because if Faide Keep falls to the savages you die with the rest of us."

Hein Huss' water-clear eyes met the brilliant black gaze of Lord Faide. "I know only what you know. The First Folk attack. They have proved they are not stupid. They intend to kill us. They are not jinx-men; they cannot afflict us or force us out. They cannot break in the walls. To burrow under, they must dig through solid rock. What are their plans? I do not know. Will they succeed? Again, I do not know. But the day of the jinxman and his orderly array of knowledge is past. I think that again we must grope for miracles, blindly and foolishly, like Salazar pouring liquids on foam."

A troop of armored horsemen rode in through the gates: warriors from nearby Bellgard Hall. And as the hours passed contingents from other keeps came to Faide Keep, until the courtyard was dense with troops and horses.

Two hours before sunset the First Folk were sighted across the downs. They seemed a very large company, moving in an undisciplined clot with a number of stragglers, forerunners and wanderers out on the flanks.

The hot-bloods from outside keeps came clamoring to Lord Faide, urging a charge to cut down the First Folk; they found no seconding voices among the veterans of the battle at the planting. Lord Faide, however, was pleased to see the dense mass of First Folk. "Let them approach only a mile more—and Hellmouth will take them! Jambart!"

"At your call, Lord Faide."

"Come, Hellmouth speaks!" He strode away with Jambart after. Up to the cupola they climbed.

"Roll forth Hellmouth, direct it against the savages!"

Jambart leaped to the glistening array of wheels and levers. He hesitated in perplexity, then tentatively twisted a wheel. Hellmouth responded by twisting slowly around on its radial track, to the groan and chatter of long-frozen bearings. Lord Faide's brows lowered into a menacing line. "I hear evidence of neglect."

"Neglect, my lord, never! Find one spot of rust, a shadow of grime, you may have me whipped!"

"What of the sound?"

"That is internal and invisible—none of my responsibility."

Lord Faide said nothing. Hellmouth now pointed toward the great pale tide from Wildwood. Jambart twisted a second wheel and Hellmouth thrust forth its heavy snout. Lord Faide, in a voice harsh with anger, cried, "The cover, fool!"

"An oversight, my lord, easily repaired." Jambart crawled out along the top of Hellmouth, clinging to the protuberances for dear life, with below only the long smooth sweep of roof. With considerable difficulty he tore the covering loose, then grunting and cursing, inched himself back, jerking with his knees, rearing his buttocks.

The First Folk had slowed their pace a trifle, the main body only a half-mile distant.

"Now," said Lord Faide in high excitement, "before they disperse, we exterminate them!" He sighted through a telescopic tube, squinting through the dimness of internal films and incrustations, signaled to Jambart for the final adjustments. "Now! Fire!"

Jambart pulled the firing lever. Within the great metal barrel came a sputter of clicking sounds. Hellmouth whined, roared. Its snout glowed red, orange, white, and out poured a sudden gout of blazing purple radiation—which almost instantly died. Hellmouth's barrel quivered with heat, fumed, seethed, hissed. From within came a faint pop. Then there was silence.

A hundred yards in front of the First Folk a patch of moss burnt black where the bolt had struck. The aiming device was inaccurate. Hellmouth's bolt had killed perhaps twenty of the First Folk vanguard.

Lord Faide made feverish signals. "Quick! Raise the barrel. Now! Fire again!"

Jambart pulled the firing arm, to no avail. He tried again, with the same lack of success. "Hellmouth evidently is tired."

"Hellmouth is dead," cried Lord Faide. "You have failed me. Hellmouth is extinct."

"No, no," protested Jambart. "Hellmouth rests! I nurse it as my own child! It is polished like glass! Whenever a section wears off or breaks loose, I neatly remove the fracture, and every trace of cracked glass."

Lord Faide threw up his arms, shouted in vast inarticulate grief, ran below. "Huss! Hein Huss!"

Hein Huss presented himself. "What is your will?"

"Hellmouth has given up its fire. Conjure me more fire for Hellmouth, and quickly!"

"Impossible."

"Impossible!" cried Lord Faide. "That is all I hear from you! Impossible, useless, impractical! You have lost your ability. I will consult Isak Comandore."

"Isak Comandore can put no more fire into Hellmouth than can I."

"What sophistry is this? He put demons into men, surely he can put fire into Hellmouth!"

"Come, Lord Faide, you are overwrought. You know the difference between jinxmanship and miracle-working."

Lord Faide motioned to a servant. "Bring Isak Comandore here to me!"

Isak Comandore, face haggard, skin waxy, limped into the courtyard. Lord Faide waved peremptorily. "I need your skill. You must restore fire to Hellmouth."

Comandore darted a quick glance at Hein Huss, who stood solid and cold. Comandore decided against dramatic promises that could not be fulfilled. "I cannot do this, my lord."

"What! You tell me this, too?"

"Remark the difference, Lord Faide, between man and metal. A man's normal state is something near madness; he is at all times balanced on a knife-edge between hysteria and apathy. His senses tell him far less of the world than he thinks they do. It is a simple trick to deceive a man, to possess him with a demon, to drive him out of his mind, to kill him. But metal is insensible; metal reacts only as its shape and condition dictates, or by the working of miracles."

"Then you must work miracles!"

"Impossible."

Lord Faide drew a deep breath, collected himself. He walked swiftly across the court. "My armor, my horse. We attack."

The column formed, Lord Faide at the head. He led the knights through the portals, with armored footmen behind.

"Beware the foam!" called Lord Faide. "Attack, strike, cut, draw back. Keep your visors drawn against the wasps! Each man must kill a hundred! Attack!"

The troop rode forth against the horde of First Folk, knights in the lead. The hooves of the horses pounded softly over the thick moss; in the west the large pale sun hung close to the horizon.

Two hundred yards from the First Folk the knights touched the club-headed horses into a lope. They raised their swords, and shouting, plunged forward, each man seeking to be first. The clotted mass of First Folk separated: black beetles darted forth and after them long segmented centipede creatures. They dashed among the horses, mandibles clicking, snouts slashing. Horses screamed, reared, fell over backwards; beetles cut open armored knights as a dog cracks a bone. Lord Faide's horse threw him and ran away; he picked himself up, hacked at a nearby beetle, lopped off its front leg. It darted forward, he lopped off the leg opposite; the heavy head dipped, tore up the moss. Lord Faide cut off the remaining legs, and it lay helpless.

"Retreat," he bellowed. "Retreat!"

The knights moved back, slashing and hacking at beetles and centipedes, killing or disabling all which attacked.

"Form into a double line, knights and men. Advance slowly, supporting each other!"

The men advanced. The First Folk dispersed to meet them, armed with their thorn-swords and carrying pouches. Ten yards from the men they reached into the pouches, brought forth dark balls which they threw at the men. The balls broke and spattered on the armor.

"Charge!" bawled Lord Faide. The men sprang forward into the mass of First Folk, cutting, slashing, killing. "Kill!" called Lord Faide in exultation. "Leave not one alive!"

A pang struck him, a sting inside his armor, followed by another and another. Small things crawled inside the metal, stinging, biting, crawling. He looked about: on all sides were harassed expressions, faces working in anguish. Sword arms fell limp as hands beat on the metal, futilely trying to scratch, rub. Two men suddenly began to tear off their armor.

"Retreat," cried Lord Faide. "Back to the keep!"

The retreat was a rout, the soldiers shedding articles of armor as they ran. After them came a flight of wasps—a dozen or more, and half as many men cried out as the poison prongs struck into their backs.

Inside the keep stormed the disorganized company, casting aside the last of their armor, slapping their skin, scratching, rubbing, crushing the ferocious red mites that infested them.

"Close the gates," roared Lord Faide.

The gates slid shut. Faide Keep was besieged.

CHAPTER XII

During the night the First Folk surrounded the keep, forming a ring fifty yards from the walls. All night there was motion, ghostly shapes coming and going in the starlight.

Lord Faide watched from a parapet until midnight, with Hein Huss at his side. Repeatedly, he asked, "What of the other keeps? Do they send further reinforcements?" to which Hein Huss each time gave the same reply: "There is confusion and doubt. The keep-lords are anxious to help but do not care to throw themselves away. At this moment they consider and take stock of the situation."

Lord Faide at last left the parapet, signaling Hein Huss to follow. He went to his trophy room, threw himself into a chair, motioned Hein Huss to be seated. For a moment he fixed the jinxman with a cool, calculating stare. Hein Huss bore the appraisal without discomfort.

"You are Head Jinxman," said Lord Faide finally. "For twenty years you have worked spells, cast hoodoos, performed auguries—more effectively than any other jinxman of Pangborn. But now I find you inept and listless. Why is this?"

"I am neither inept nor listless. I am unable to achieve beyond my abilities. I do not know how to work miracles. For this you must consult my apprentice Sam Salazar, who does not know either, but who earnestly tries every possibility and many impossibilities."

"You believe in this nonsense yourself! Before my very eyes you become a mystic!"

Hein Huss shrugged. "There are limitations to my knowledge. Miracles occur—that we know. The relics of our ancestors lie everywhere. Their methods were supernatural, repellent to our own mental processes—but think! Using these same methods the First Folk threaten to destroy us. In the place of metal they use living flesh—but the result is similar. The men of Pangborn, if they assemble and accept casualties, can drive the First Folk back to Wildwood—but for how long? A year? Ten years? The First Folk plant new trees, dig more traps—and presently come forth again, with more terrible weapons: flying beetles, large as a horse; wasps strong enough to pierce armor, lizards to scale the walls of Faide Keep."

Lord Faide pulled at his chin. "And the jinxmen are helpless?"

"You saw for yourself. Isak Comandore intruded enough into their consciousness to anger them, no more."

"So then—what must we do?"

Hein Huss held out his hands. "I do not know. I am Hein Huss, jinxman. I watch Sam Salazar with fascination. He learns nothing, but he is either too stupid or too intelligent to be discouraged. If this is the way to work miracles, he will work them."

Lord Faide rose to his feet. "I am deathly tired. I cannot think, I must sleep. Tomorrow we will know more."

Hein Huss left the trophy room, returned to the parapet. The ring of First Folk seemed closer to the walls, almost within dart-range. Behind them and across the moors stretched a long pale column of marching First Folk. A little back from the keep a pile of white material began to grow, larger and larger as the night proceeded.

* * *

Hours passed, the sky lightened; the sun rose in the east. The First Folk tramped the downs like ants, bringing long bars of hardened foam down from the north, dropping them into piles around the keep, returning into the north once more.

Lord Faide came up on the parapet, haggard and unshaven. "What is this? What do they do?"

Bernard the sergeant responded. "They puzzle us all, my lord."

"Hein Huss! What of the other keeps?"

"They have armed and mounted; they approach cautiously."

"Can you communicate our urgency?"

"I can, and I have done so. I have only accentuated their caution."

"Bah!" cried Lord Faide in disgust. "Warriors they call themselves! Loyal and faithful allies!"

"They know of your bitter experience," said Hein Huss. "They ask themselves, reasonably enough, what they can accomplish which you who are already here cannot do first."

Lord Faide laughed sourly. "I have no answer for them. In the meantime we must protect ourselves against the wasps. Armor is useless; they drive us mad with mites...Bernard!"

"Yes, Lord Faide."

"Have each of your men construct a frame two-feet square, fixed with a short handle. To these frames should be sewed a net of heavy mesh. When these frames are built we will sally forth, two soldiers to guard one half-armored knight on foot."

"In the meantime," said Hein Huss, "the First Folk proceed with their plans."

Lord Faide turned to watch. The First Folk came close up under the walls carrying rods of hardened foam. "Bernard! Put your archers to work! Aim for the heads!"

Along the walls bowmen cocked their weapons. Darts spun down into the First Folk. A few were affected, turned and staggered away; others plucked away the bolts without concern. Another flight of bolts, a few more First Folk were disabled. The others planted the rods in the moss, exuded foam in great gushes, their back-flaps vigorously pumping air. Other First Folk brought more rods, pushed them into the foam. Entirely around the keep, close under the walls, extended the mound of foam. The ring of First Folk now came close and all gushed foam; it bulked up swiftly. More rods were brought, thrust into the foam, reinforcing and stiffening the mass.

"More darts!" barked Lord Faide. "Aim for the heads! Bernard— your men, have they prepared the wasp-nets?"

"Not yet, Lord Faide. The project requires some little time."

Lord Faide became silent. The foam, now ten feet high, rapidly piled higher. Lord Faide turned to Hein Huss. "What do they hope to achieve?"

Hein Huss shook his head. "For the moment I am uncertain."

The first layer of foam had hardened; on top of this the First Folk spewed another layer, reinforcing again with the rods, crisscrossing, horizontal and vertical. Fifteen minutes later, when the second layer was hard the First Folk emplaced and mounted rude ladders to raise a third layer. Surrounding the keep now was a ring of foam thirty feet high and forty feet thick at the base.

"Look," said Hein Huss. He pointed up. The parasol roof overhanging the walls ended only thirty feet above the foam. "A few more layers and they will reach the roof."

"So then?" asked Lord Faide. "The roof is as strong as the walls."

"And we will be sealed within."

Lord Faide studied the foam in the light of this new thought. Already the First Folk, climbing laboriously up ladders along the outside face of their wall of foam, were preparing to lay on a fourth layer. First—rods, stiff and dry, then great gushes of white. Only twenty feet remained between roof and foam.

Lord Faide turned to the sergeant. "Prepare the men to sally forth."

"What of the wasp-nets, sir?"

"Are they almost finished?"

"Another ten minutes, sir."

"Another ten minutes will see us smothering. We must force a passage through the foam."

Ten minutes passed, and fifteen. The First Folk created ramps behind their wall: first, dozens of the rods, then foam, and on top, to distribute the weight, reed mats.

Bernard the sergeant reported to Lord Faide. "We are ready."

"Good." Lord Faide descended into the courtyard. He faced the men, gave them their orders. "Move quickly, but stay together; we must not lose ourselves in the foam. As we proceed, slash ahead and to the sides. The First Folk see through the foam; they have the advantage of us. When we break through, we use the wasp-nets. Two foot soldiers must guard each knight. Remember, quickly through the foam, that we do not smother. Open the gates."

The gates slid back, the troops marched forth. They faced an unbroken blank wall of foam. No enemy could be seen.

Lord Faide waved his sword. "Into the foam." He strode forward, pushed into the white mass, now crisp and brittle and harder than he had bargained for. It resisted him; he cut and hacked. His troops joined him, carving a way into the foam. First Folk appeared above them, crawling carefully on the mats. Their back flaps puffed, pumped; foam issued from their vents, falling in a cascade over the troops.

Hein Huss sighed. He spoke to Apprentice Sam Salazar. "Now they must retreat, otherwise they smother. If they fail to win through, we all smother."

Even as he spoke the foam, piling up swiftly, in places reached the roof. Below, bellowing and cursing, Lord Faide backed out from under, wiped his face clear. Once again, in desperation, he charged forward, trying at a new spot.

The foam was friable and cut easily, but the chunks detached still blocked the opening. And again down tumbled a cascade of foam, covering the soldiers.

Lord Faide retreated, waved his men back into the keep. At the same moment First Folk crawling on mats on the same level as the parapet over the gate laid rods up from the foam to rest against the projecting edge of the roof. They gushed foam; the view of the sky was slowly blocked from the view of Hein Huss and Sam Salazar.

"In an hour, perhaps two, we will die," said Hein Huss. "They have now sealed us in. There are many men here in the keep, and all will now breathe deeply."

Sam Salazar said nervously, "There is a possibility we might be able to survive—or at least not smother."

"Ah?" inquired Hein Huss with heavy sarcasm. "You plan to work a miracle?"

"If a miracle, the most trivial sort. I observed that water has no effect on the foam, nor a number of other liquids: milk, spirits, wine, or caustic. Vinegar, however, instantly dissolves the foam."

"Aha," said Hein Huss. "We must inform Lord Faide."

"Better that you do so," said Sam Salazar. "He will pay me no heed."

CHAPTER XIII

Half an hour passed. Light filtered into Faide Keep only as a dim gray gloom. Air tasted flat, damp and heavy. Out from the gates sallied the troops. Each carried a crock, a jug, a skin, or a pan containing strong vinegar.

"Quickly now," called Lord Faide, "but careful! Spare the vinegar, don't throw it wildly. In close formation now—forward."

The soldiers approached the wall, threw ladles of vinegar ahead. The foam crackled, melted.

"Waste no vinegar," shouted Lord Faide. "Forward, quickly now; bring forward the vinegar!"

Minutes later they burst out upon the downs. The First Folk stared at them, blinking.

"Charge," croaked Lord Faide, his throat thick with fumes. "Mind now, wasp-nets! Two soldiers to each knight! Charge, double-quick. Kill the white beasts."

The men dashed ahead. Wasp-tubes were leveled. "Halt!" yelled Lord Faide. "Wasps!"

The wasps came, wings rasping. Nets rose up; wasps struck with a thud. Down went the nets; hard feet crushed the insects. The beetles and the lizard-centipedes appeared, not so many as of the last evening, for a great number had been killed. They darted forward, and a score of men died, but the insects were soon hacked into chunks of reeking brown flesh. Wasps flew, and some struck home; the agonies of the dying men were unnerving. Presently the wasps likewise decreased in number, and soon there were no more.

The men faced the First Folk, armed only with thorn-swords and their foam, which now came purple with rage.

Lord Faide waved his sword; the men advanced and began to kill the First Folk, by dozens, by hundreds.

Hein Huss came forth and approached Lord Faide. "Call a halt."

"A halt? Why? Now we kill these bestial things."

"Far better not. Neither need kill the other. Now is the time to show great wisdom."

"They have besieged us, caught us in their traps, stung us with their wasps! And you say halt?"

"They nourish a grudge sixteen hundred years old. Best not to add another one."

Lord Faide stared at Hein Huss. "What do you propose?"

"Peace between the two races, peace and cooperation."

"Very well. No more traps, no more plantings, no more breeding of deadly insects."

"Call back your men. I will try."

Lord Faide cried out, "Men, fall back. Disengage."

Reluctantly the troops drew back. Hein Huss approached the huddled mass of purple-foaming First Folk. He waited a moment. They watched him intently. He spoke in their language.

"You have attacked Faide Keep; you have been defeated. You planned well, but we have proved stronger. At this moment we can kill you. Then we can go on to fire the forest, starting a hundred blazes. Some of the fires you can control. Others not. We can destroy Wildwood. Some First Folk may survive, to hide in the thickets and breed new plans to kill men. This we do not want. Lord Faide has agreed to peace, if you likewise agree. This means no more death-traps. Men will freely approach and pass through the forests. In your turn you may freely come out on the moss. Neither race shall molest the other. Which do you choose? Extinction—or peace?"

The purple foam no longer dribbled from the vents of the First Folk. "We choose peace."

"There must be no more wasps, beetles. The death-traps must be disarmed and never replaced."

"We agree. In our turn we must be allowed freedom of the moss."

"Agreed. Remove your dead and wounded, haul away the foam rods."

Hein Huss returned to Lord Faide. "They have chosen peace."

Lord Faide nodded. "Very well. It is for the best." He called to his men. "Sheathe your weapons. We have won a great victory." He ruefully surveyed Faide Keep, swathed in foam and invisible except for the parasol roof. "A hundred barrels of vinegar will not be enough."

Hein Huss looked off into the sky. "Your allies approach quickly. Their jinxmen have told them of your victory."

Lord Faide laughed his sour laugh. "To my allies will fall the task of removing the foam from Faide Keep."

CHAPTER XIV

In the hall of Faide Keep, during the victory banquet, Lord Faide called jovially across to Hein Huss. "Now, Head Jinxman, we must deal with your apprentice, the idler and the waster Sam Salazar."

"He is here, Lord Faide. Rise, Sam Salazar, take cognizance of the honor being done you."

Sam Salazar rose to his feet, bowed.

Lord Faide proffered him a cup. "Drink, Sam Salazar, enjoy yourself. I freely admit that your idiotic tinkerings saved the lives of us all. Sam Salazar, we salute you, and thank you. Now, I trust that you will put frivolity aside, apply yourself to your work, and learn honest jinxmanship. When the time comes, I promise that you shall find a lifetime of employment at Faide Keep."

"Thank you," said Sam Salazar modestly. "However, I doubt if I will become a jinxman."

"No? You have other plans?"

Sam Salazar stuttered, grew faintly pink in the face, then straightened himself, spoke as clearly and distinctly as he could. "I prefer to continue what you call my frivolity. I hope I can persuade others to join me."

"Frivolity is always attractive," said Lord Faide. "No doubt you can find other idlers and wasters, runaway farm boys, and the like."

Sam Salazar said staunchly, "This frivolity might become serious. Undoubtedly the ancients were barbarians. They used symbols to control entities they were unable to understand. We are methodical and rational; why can't we systematize and comprehend the ancient miracles?"

"Well, why can't we?" asked Lord Faide. "Does anyone have an answer?"

No one responded, although Isak Comandore hissed between his teeth and shook his head.

"I personally may never be able to work miracles; I suspect it is more complicated than it seems," said Sam Salazar. "However, I hope that you will arrange for a workshop where I and others who might share my views can make a beginning. In this matter I have the encouragement and the support of Head Jinxman Hein Huss."

Lord Faide lifted his goblet. "Very well, Apprentice Sam Salazar. Tonight I can refuse you nothing. You shall have exactly what you wish, and good luck to you. Perhaps you will produce a miracle during my lifetime."

Isak Comandore said huskily to Hein Huss, "This is a sad event! It signalizes intellectual anarchy, the degradation of jinxmanship, the prostitution of logic. Novelty has a way of attracting youth; already I see apprentices and spellbinders whispering in excitement. The jinxmen of the future will be sorry affairs. How will they go about demon-possession? With a cog, a gear and a push-button. How will they cast a hoodoo? They will find it easier to strike their victim with an axe."

"Times change," said Hein Huss. "There is now the one rule of Faide on Pangborn, and the keeps no longer need to employ us. Perhaps I will join Sam Salazar in his workshop."

"You depict a depressing future," said Isak Comandore with a sniff of disgust.

"There are many futures, some of which are undoubtedly depressing."

Lord Faide raised his glass. "To the best of your many futures, Hein Huss. Who knows? Sam Salazar may conjure a spaceship to lead us back to home-planet."

"Who knows?" said Hein Huss. He raised his goblet. "To the best of the futures!"

AFTERWORD TO "THE MIRACLE WORKERS"

Strange things happen. Almost everyone has had some sort of brush with the paranormal, even the most resistant and skeptical of persons. The range of events is wide and only roughly amenable to classification. In olden times angels and demons were held responsible; to date no one has produced a more reasonable explanation. Phenomena such as telepathy and poltergeists may well be manifestations of different and distinct principles; there may be two, three, four, or more such realms of knowledge, each at least as rich and intricate as physics or astronomy. There is little systematic study. Conventional scientists shy away from the field because they are, in fact, conventional; because they fear to compromise their careers; because the subject is difficult to get a grip on; because scientists are as susceptible to awe and eeriness as anyone else. So: the mysteries persist; the lore accumulates, and we know for sure no more than our remote ancestors, if as much…"The Miracle Workers" [has a] definite psionic orientation, and [makes] at least a superficial inquiry into certain aspects and implications of telekinesis and demon-possession. I can't pretend to offer enlightenment; there isn't any to be had. The [story], in any event, [was] not conceived as [an] argumentative [vehicle], but simply [reflects] my own fascination with the vast and wonderful reaches of the unknown.

—Jack Vance 1970

GUYAL OF SFERE

Guyal of Sfere had been born one apart from his fellows and early proved a source of vexation for his sire. Normal in outward configuration, there existed within his mind a void which ached for nourishment. It was as if a spell had been cast upon his birth, a harassment visited on the child in a spirit of sardonic mockery, so that every occurrence, no matter how trifling, became a source of wonder and amazement. Even as young as four seasons he was expounding such inquiries as:

"Why do squares have more sides than triangles?"

"How will we see when the sun goes dark?"

"Do flowers grow under the ocean?"

"Do stars hiss and sizzle when rain comes by night?"

To which his impatient sire gave such answers as:

"So it was ordained by the Pragmatica; squares and triangles must obey the rote."

"We will be forced to grope and feel our way."

"I have never verified this matter; only the Curator would know."

"By no means, since the stars are high above the rain, higher even than the highest clouds, and swim in rarified air where rain will never breed."

As Guyal grew to youth, this void in his mind, instead of becoming limp and waxy, seemed to throb with a more violent ache. And so he asked:

"Why do people die when they are killed?"

"Where does beauty vanish when it goes?"

"How long have men lived on Earth?"

"What is beyond the sky?"

To which his sire, biting acerbity back from his lips, would respond:

"Death is the heritage of life; a man's vitality is like air in a bladder. Poinct this bubble and away, away, away, flees life, like the color of fading dream."

"Beauty is a luster which love bestows to guile the eye. Therefore it may be said that only when the brain is without love will the eye look and see no beauty."

"Some say men rose from the earth like grubs in a corpse; others aver that the first men desired residence and so created Earth by sorcery. The question is shrouded in technicality; only the Curator may answer with exactness."

"An endless waste."

And Guyal pondered and postulated, proposed and expounded until he found himself the subject of surreptitious humor. The demesne was visited by a rumor that a gleft, coming upon Guyal's mother in labor, had stolen part of Guyal's brain, which deficiency he now industriously sought to restore.

Guyal therefore drew himself apart and roamed the grassy hills of Sfere in solitude. But ever was his mind acquisitive, ever did he seek to exhaust the lore of all around him, until at last his father in vexation refused to hear further inquiries, declaring that all knowledge had been known, that the trivial and useless had been discarded, leaving a residue which was all that was necessary to a sound man.

At this time Guyal was in his first manhood, a slight but well-knit youth with wide clear eyes, a penchant for severely elegant dress, and a hidden trouble which showed itself in the clamps at the corner of his mouth.

Hearing his father's angry statement Guyal said, "One more question, then I ask no more."

"Speak," declared his father. "One more question I grant you."

"You have often referred me to the Curator; who is he, and where may I find him, so as to allay my ache for knowledge?"

A moment the father scrutinized the son, whom he now considered past the verge of madness. Then he responded in a quiet voice, "The Curator guards the Museum of Man, which antique legend places in the Land of the Falling Wall—beyond the mountains of Fer Aquila and north of Ascolais. It is not certain that either Curator or Museum still exist; still it would seem that if the Curator knows all things, as is the legend, then surely he would know the wizardly foil to death."

Guyal said, "I would seek the Curator, and the Museum of Man, that I likewise may know all things."

The father said with patience, "I will bestow on you my fine white horse, my Expansible Egg for your shelter, my Scintillant Dagger to illuminate the night. In addition, I lay a blessing along the trail, and danger will slide you by so long as you never wander from the trail."

Guyal quelled the hundred new questions at his tongue, including an inquisition as to where his father had learned these manifestations of sorcery, and accepted the gifts: the horse, the magic shelter, the dagger with the luminous pommel, and the blessing to guard him from the disadvantageous circumstances which plagued travelers along the dim trails of Ascolais.

He caparisoned the horse, honed the dagger, cast a last glance around the old manse at Sfere, and set forth to the north, with the void in his mind athrob for the soothing pressure of knowledge.

He ferried the River Scaum on an old barge. Aboard the barge and so off the trail, the blessing lost its puissance and the barge-tender, who coveted Guyal's rich accoutrements, sought to cudgel him with a knoblolly. Guyal fended off the blow and kicked the man into the murky deep, where he drowned.

Mounting the north bank of the Scaum he saw ahead the Porphiron Scar, the dark poplars and white columns of Kaiin, the dull gleam of Sanreale Bay.

Wandering the crumbled streets, he put the languid inhabitants such a spate of questions that one in wry jocularity commended him to a professional augur.

This one dwelled in a booth painted with the Signs of the Aumoklopelastianic Cabal. He was a lank brownman with red-rimmed eyes and a stained white beard.

"What are your fees?" inquired Guyal cautiously.

"I respond to three questions," stated the augur. "For twenty terces I phrase the answer in clear and actionable language; for ten I use the language of cant, which occasionally admits of ambiguity; for five, I speak a parable which you must interpret as you will; and for one terce, I babble in an unknown tongue."

"First I must inquire, how profound is your knowledge?"

"I know all," responded the augur. "The secrets of red and the secrets of black, the lost spells of Grand Motholam, the way of the fish and the voice of the bird."

"And where have you learned all these things?"

"By pure induction," explained the augur. "I retire into my booth, I closet myself with never a glint of light, and, so sequestered, I resolve the profundities of the world."

"With all this precious knowledge at hand," ventured Guyal, "why do you live so meagerly, with not an ounce of fat to your frame and these miserable rags to your back?"

The augur stood back in fury. "Go along, go along! Already I have wasted fifty terces of wisdom on you, who have never a copper to your pouch. If you desire free enlightenment," and he cackled in mirth, "seek out the Curator." And he sheltered himself in his booth.

Guyal took lodging for the night, and in the morning continued north. The ravaged acres of the Old Town passed to his left, and the trail took to the fabulous forest.

For many a day Guyal rode north, and, heedful of danger, held to the trail. By night he surrounded himself and his horse in his magical habiliment, the Expansible Egg—a membrane impermeable to thew, claw, ensorcelment, pressure, sound and chill—and so rested at ease despite the efforts of the avid creatures of the dark.

The great dull globe of the sun fell behind him; the days became wan and the nights bitter, and at last the crags of Fer Aquila showed as a tracing on the north horizon.

The forest had become lower and less dense, and the characteristic tree was the daobado, a rounded massy construction of heavy gnarled branches, these a burnished russet bronze, clumped with dark balls of foliage. Beside a giant of the species Guyal came upon a village of turf huts. A gaggle of surly louts appeared and surrounded him with expressions of curiosity. Guyal, no less than the villagers, had questions to ask, but none would speak till the hetman strode up—a burly man who wore a shaggy fur hat, a cloak of brown fur and a bristling beard, so that it was hard to see where one ended and the other began. He exuded a rancid odor which displeased Guyal, who, from motives of courtesy, kept his distaste concealed.

"Where go you?" asked the hetman.

"I wish to cross the mountains to the Museum of Man," said Guyal. "Which way does the trail lead?"

The hetman pointed out a notch on the silhouette of the mountains. "There is Omona Gap, which is the shortest and best route, though there is no trail. None comes and none goes, since when you pass the Gap, you walk an unknown land. And with no traffic there manifestly need be no trail."

The news did not cheer Guyal.

"How then is it known that Omona Gap is on the way to the Museum?"

The hetman shrugged. "Such is our tradition."

Guyal turned his head at a hoarse snuffling and saw a pen of woven wattles. In a litter of filth and matted straw stood a number of hulking men eight or nine feet tall. They were naked, with shocks of dirty yellow hair and watery blue eyes. They had waxy faces and expressions of crass stupidity. As Guyal watched, one of them ambled to a trough and noisily began gulping gray mash.

Guyal said, "What manner of things are these?"

The hetman blinked in amusement at Guyal's naïveté. "Those are our oasts, naturally." And he gestured in disapprobation at Guyal's white horse. "Never have I seen a stranger oast than the one you bestride. Ours carry us easier and appear to be less vicious; in addition no flesh is more delicious than oast properly braised and kettled."

Standing close, he fondled the metal of Guyal's saddle and the red and yellow embroidered quilt. "Your deckings however are rich and of superb quality. I will therefore bestow you my large and weighty oast in return for this creature with its accoutrements."

Guyal politely declared himself satisfied with his present mount, and the hetman shrugged his shoulders.

A horn sounded. The hetman looked about, then turned back to Guyal. "Food is prepared; will you eat?"

Guyal glanced toward the oast-pen. "I am not presently hungry, and I must hasten forward. However, I am grateful for your kindness."

He departed; as he passed under the arch of the great daobado, he turned a glance back toward the village. There seemed an unwonted activity among the huts. Remembering the hetman's covetous touch at his saddle, and aware that no longer did he ride the protected trail, Guyal urged his horse forward and pounded fast under the trees.

As he neared the foothills the forest dwindled to a savannah, floored with a dull, jointed grass that creaked under the horse's hooves. Guyal glanced up and down the plain. The sun, old and red as an autumn pomegranate, wallowed in the south-west; the light across the plain was dim and watery; the mountains presented a curiously artificial aspect, like a tableau planned for the effect of eery desolation.

Guyal glanced once again at the sun. Another hour of light, then the dark night of the latter-day Earth. Guyal twisted in the saddle, looked behind him, feeling lone, solitary, vulnerable. Four oasts, carrying men on their shoulders, came trotting from the forest. Sighting Guyal, they broke into a lumbering run. With a crawling skin Guyal wheeled his horse and eased the reins, and the white horse loped across the plain toward Omona Gap. Behind came the oasts, bestraddled by the fur-cloaked villagers.

As the sun touched the horizon, another forest ahead showed as an indistinct line of murk. Guyal looked back to his pursuers, bounding now a mile behind, turned his gaze back to the forest. An ill place to ride by night...

The darkling foliage loomed above him; he passed under the first gnarled boughs. If the oasts were unable to sniff out a trail, they might now be eluded. He changed directions, turned once, twice, a third time, then stood his horse to listen. Far away a crashing in the brake reached his ears. Guyal dismounted, led the horse into a deep hollow where a bank of foliage made a screen. Presently the four men on their hulking oasts passed in the afterglow above him, black double-shapes in attitudes suggestive of ill-temper and disappointment.

The thud and pad of feet dwindled and died.

The horse moved restlessly; the foliage rustled.

A damp air passed down the hollow and chilled the back of Guyal's neck. Darkness rose from old Earth like ink in a basin.

Guyal shivered: best to ride away through the forest, away from the dour villagers and their numb mounts. Away...

He turned his horse up to the height where the four had passed and sat listening. Far down the wind he heard a hoarse call. Turning in the opposite direction he let the horse choose its own path.

Branches and boughs knit patterns on the fading purple over him; the air smelt of moss and dank mould. The horse stopped short. Guyal, tensing in every muscle, leaned a little forward, head twisted, listening. There was a feel of danger on his cheek. The air was still, uncanny; his eyes could plumb not ten feet into the black. Somewhere near was death—grinding, roaring death, to come as a sudden shock.

Sweating cold, afraid to stir a muscle, he forced himself to dismount. Stiffly he slid from the saddle, brought forth the Expansible Egg, and flung it around his horse and himself. Ah, now...Guyal released the pressure of his breath. Safety.

Wan red light slanted through the branches from the east. Guyal's breath steamed in the air when he emerged from the Egg. After a handful of dried fruit for himself and a sack of meal for the horse, he mounted and set out toward the mountains.

The forest passed, and Guyal rode out on an upland. He scanned the line of mountains. Suffused with rose sunlight, the gray, sage green, dark green range rambled far to the west toward the Melantine, far to the east into the Falling Wall country. Where was Omona Gap?

Guyal of Sfere searched in vain for the notch which had been visible from the village of the fur-cloaked murderers.

He frowned and turned his eyes up the height of the mountains. Weathered by the rains of earth's duration, the slopes were easy and the crags rose like the stumps of rotten teeth. Guyal turned his horse uphill and rode the trackless slope into the mountains of Fer Aquila.

Guyal of Sfere had lost his way in a land of wind and naked crags. As night came he slouched numbly in the saddle while his horse took him where it would. Somewhere the ancient way through Omona Gap led to the northern tundra, but now, under a chilly overcast, north, east, south and west were alike under the lavender-metal sky. Guyal reined his horse and, rising in the saddle, searched the landscape. The crags rose, tall, remote; the ground was barren of all but clumps of dry shrub. He slumped back in the saddle, and his white horse jogged forward.

Head bowed to the wind rode Guyal, and the mountains slanted along the twilight like the skeleton of a fossil god.

The horse halted, and Guyal found himself at the brink of a wide valley. The wind had died; the valley was quiet. Guyal leaned forward staring. Below spread a dark and lifeless city. Mist blew along the streets and the afterglow fell dull on slate roofs.

The horse snorted and scraped the stony ground.

"A strange town," said Guyal, "with no lights, no sound, no smell of smoke...Doubtless an abandoned ruin from ancient times..."

He debated descending to the streets. At times the old ruins were haunted by peculiar distillations, but such a ruin might be joined to the tundra by a trail. With this thought in mind he started his horse down the slope.

He entered the town and the hooves rang loud and sharp on the cobbles. The buildings were framed of stone and dark mortar and seemed in uncommonly good preservation. A few lintels had cracked and sagged, a few walls gaped open, but for the most part the stone houses had successfully met the gnaw of time...Guyal scented smoke. Did people live here still? He would proceed with caution.

Before a building which seemed to be a hostelry flowers bloomed in an urn. Guyal reined his horse and reflected that flowers were rarely cherished by persons of hostile disposition.

"Hallo!" he called—once, twice.

No heads peered from the doors, no orange flicker brightened the windows. Guyal slowly turned and rode on.

The street widened and twisted toward a large hall, where Guyal saw a light. The building had a high facade, broken by four large windows, each of which had its two blinds of patined bronze filigree, and each over-looked a small balcony. A marble balustrade fronting the terrace shimmered bone-white, and, behind, the hall's portal of massive wood stood slightly ajar; from here came the beam of light and also a strain of music.

Guyal of Sfere, halting, gazed not at the house nor at the light through the door. He dismounted and bowed to the young woman who sat pensively along the course of the balustrade. Though it was very cold, she wore but a simple gown, yellow-orange, a daffodil's color. Topaz hair fell loose to her shoulders and gave her face a cast of gravity and thoughtfulness.

As Guyal straightened from his greeting the woman nodded, smiled slightly, and absently fingered the hair by her cheek.

"A bitter night for travelers."

"A bitter night for musing on the stars," responded Guyal.

She smiled again. "I am not cold. I sit and dream...I listen to the music."

"What place is this?" inquired Guyal, looking up the street, down the street, and once more to the girl. "Are there any here but yourself?"

"This is Carchasel," said the girl, "abandoned by all ten thousand years ago. Only I and my aged uncle live here, finding this place a refuge from the Saponids of the tundra."

Guyal thought: this woman may or may not be a witch.

"You are cold and weary," said the girl, "and I keep you standing in the street." She rose to her feet. "Our hospitality is yours."

"Which I gladly accept," said Guyal, "but first I must stable my horse."

"He will be content in the house yonder. We have no stable." Guyal, following her finger, saw a low stone building with a door opening into blackness.

He took the white horse thither and removed the bridle and saddle; then, standing in the doorway, he listened to the music he had noted before, the piping of a weird and ancient air.

"Strange, strange," he muttered, stroking the horse's muzzle. "The uncle plays music, the girl stares alone at the stars of the night..." He considered a moment. "I may be over suspicious. If witch she be, there is naught to be gained from me. If they be simple refugees as she says, and lovers of music, they may enjoy the airs from Ascolais; it will repay, in some measure, their hospitality." He reached into his saddlebag, brought forth his flute, and tucked it inside his jerkin.

He ran back to where the girl awaited him.

"You have not told me your name," she reminded him, "that I may introduce you to my uncle."

"I am Guyal of Sfere, by the River Scaum in Ascolais. And you?"

She smiled, pushing the portal wider. Warm yellow light fell into the cobbled street.

"I have no name. I need none. There has never been any but my uncle; and when he speaks, there is no one to answer but I."

Guyal stared in astonishment; then, deeming his wonder too apparent for courtesy, he controlled his expression. Perhaps she suspected him of wizardry and feared to pronounce her name lest he make magic with it.

They entered a flagged hall, and the sound of piping grew louder.

"I will call you Ameth, if I may," said Guyal. "That is a flower of the south, as golden and kind and fragrant as you seem to be."

She nodded. "You may call me Ameth."

They entered a tapestry-hung chamber, large and warm. A great fire glowed at one wall, and here stood a table bearing food. On a bench sat the musician—an old man, untidy, unkempt. His white hair hung tangled down his back; his beard, in no better case, was dirty and yellow. He wore a ragged kirtle, by no means clean, and the leather of his sandals had broken into dry cracks. Strangely, he did not take the flute from his mouth, but kept up his piping; and the girl in yellow, so Guyal noted, seemed to move in rhythm to the tones.

"Uncle Ludowik," she cried in a gay voice, "I bring you a guest, Sir Guyal of Sfere."

Guyal looked into the man's face and wondered. The eyes though somewhat rheumy with age, were gray and bright—feverishly bright and intelligent; and, so Guyal thought, awake with a strange joy. This joy further puzzled Guyal, for the lines of the face indicated nothing other than years of misery.

"Perhaps you play?" inquired Ameth. "My uncle is a great musician, and this is his time for music. He has kept the routine for many years..." She turned and smiled at Ludowik the musician. Guyal nodded politely.

Ameth motioned to the bounteous table. "Eat, Guyal, and I will pour you wine. Afterwards perhaps you will play the flute for us."

"Gladly," said Guyal, and he noticed how the joy on Ludowik's face grew more apparent, quivering around the corners of his mouth.

He ate and Ameth poured him golden wine until his head went to reeling. And never did Ludowik cease his piping—now a tender melody of running water, again a grave tune that told of the lost ocean to the west, another time a simple melody such as a child might sing at his games. Guyal noted with wonder how Ameth fitted her mood to the music—grave and gay as the music led her. Strange! thought Guyal. But then—people thus isolated were apt to develop peculiar mannerisms, and they seemed kindly withal.

He finished his meal and stood erect, steadying himself against the table. Ludowik was playing a lilting tune, a melody of glass birds swinging round and round on a red string in the sunlight. Ameth came dancing over to him and stood close—very close—and he smelled the warm perfume of her loose golden hair. Her face was happy and wild...Peculiar how Ludowik watched so grimly, and yet without a word. Perhaps he misdoubted a stranger's intent. Still...

"Now," breathed Ameth, "perhaps you will play the flute; you are so strong and young." Then she said quickly, as she saw Guyal's eyes widen, "I mean you will play on the flute for old uncle Ludowik, and he will be happy and go off to bed—and then we will sit and talk far into the night."

"Gladly will I play the flute," said Guyal. Curse the tongue of his, at once so fluent and yet so numb. It was the wine. "Gladly will I play. I am accounted quite skillful at my home manse at Sfere."

He glanced at Ludowik, then stared at the expression of crazy gladness he had surprised. Marvellous that a man should be so fond of music.

"Then—play!" breathed Ameth, urging him a little toward Ludowik and the flute.

"Perhaps," suggested Guyal, "I had better wait till your uncle pauses. I would seem discourteous—"

"No, as soon as you indicate that you wish to play, he will let off. Merely take the flute. You see," she confided, "he is rather deaf."

"Very well," said Guyal, "except that I have my own flute." And he brought it out from under his jerkin. "Why—what is the matter?" For a startling change had come over the girl and the old man. A quick light had risen in her eyes, and Ludowik's strange gladness had gone, and there was but dull hopelessness in his eyes, stupid resignation.

Guyal slowly stood back, bewildered. "Do you not wish me to play?"

There was a pause. "Of course," said Ameth, young and charming once more. "But I'm sure that Uncle Ludowik would enjoy hearing you play his flute. He is accustomed to the pitch—another scale might be unfamiliar…"

Ludowik nodded, and hope again shone in the rheumy old eyes. It was indeed a fine flute, Guyal saw, a rich piece of white metal, chased and set with gold, and Ludowik clutched this flute as if he would never let go.

"Take the flute," suggested Ameth. "He will not mind in the least." Ludowik shook his head, to signify the absence of his objections. But Guyal, noting with distaste the long stained beard, also shook his head. "I can play any scale, any tone on my flute. There is no need for me to use that of your uncle and possibly distress him. Listen," and he raised his instrument. "Here is a song of Kaiin, called 'The Opal, the Pearl and the Peacock'."

He put the pipe to his lips and began to play, very skillfully indeed, and Ludowik followed him, filling in gaps, making chords. Ameth, forgetting her vexation, listened with eyes half-closed, and moved her arm to the rhythm.

"Did you enjoy that?" asked Guyal, when he had finished.

"Very much. Perhaps you would try it on Uncle Ludowik's flute? It is a fine flute to play, very soft and easy to the breath."

"No," said Guyal, with sudden obstinacy. "I am able to play only my own instrument." He blew again, and it was a dance of the festival, a quirking carnival air. Ludowik, playing with supernal skill, ran merry phrases as might fit, and Ameth, carried away by the rhythm, danced a dance of her own, a merry step in time to the music.

Guyal played a wild tarantella of the peasant folk, and Ameth danced wilder and faster, flung her arms, wheeled, jerked her head in a fine display. And Ludowik's flute played a brilliant obbligato, hurtling over, now under, chording, veering, warping little silver strings of sound around Guyal's melody, adding urgent little grace-phrases.

Ludowik's eyes now clung to the whirling figure of the dancing girl. And suddenly he struck up a theme of his own, a tune of wildest abandon, of a frenzied beating rhythm; and Guyal, carried away by the force of the music, blew as he never had blown before, invented trills and runs, gyrating arpeggios, blew high and shrill, loud and fast and clear.

It was as nothing to Ludowik's music. His eyes were starting; sweat streamed from his seamed old forehead; his flute tore the air into quivering ecstatic shreds.

Ameth danced frenzy; she was no longer beautiful, she appeared grotesque and unfamiliar. The music became something more than the senses could bear. Guyal's own vision turned pink and gray; he saw Ameth fall in a faint, in a foaming fit; and Ludowik, fiery-eyed, staggered erect, hobbled to her body and began a terrible intense concord, slow measures of most solemn and frightening meaning.

Ludowik played death.

Guyal of Sfere turned and ran wide-eyed from the hall. Ludowik, never noticing, continued his terrible piping, played as if every note were a skewer through the twitching girl's shoulder-blades.

Guyal ran through the night, and cold air bit at him like sleet. He burst into the shed, and the white horse softly nickered at him. On with the saddle, on with the bridle, away down the streets of old Carchasel, past the gaping black windows, ringing down the starlit cobbles, away from the music of death!

Guyal of Sfere galloped up the mountain with the stars in his face, and not until he came to the shoulder did he turn in the saddle to look back.

The verging of dawn trembled into the stony valley. Where was Carchasel? There was no city—only a crumble of ruins...

Hark! A far sound?..

No. All was silence.

And yet...

No. Only crumbled stones in the floor of the valley.

Guyal, fixed of eye, turned and went his way, along the trail which stretched north before him.

The walls of the defile which led the trail were steep gray granite, stained scarlet and black by lichen, mildewed blue. The horse's hooves made a hollow clop-clop-clop on the stone, loud to Guyal's ears, hypnotic to his brain, and after the sleepless night he found his frame sagging. His eyes grew dim and warm with drowsiness, but the trail ahead led to unseen vistas, and the void in Guyal's brain drove him without surcease.

The lassitude became such that Guyal slipped halfway from his saddle. Rousing himself, he resolved to round one more bend in the trail and then take rest.

The rock beetled above and hid the sky where the sun had passed the zenith. The trail twisted around a shoulder of rock; ahead shone a patch of indigo heaven. One more turning, Guyal told himself. The defile fell open, the mountains were at his back and he looked out across a hundred miles of steppe. It was a land shaded with subtle colors, washed with delicate shadows, fading and melting into the lurid haze at the horizon. He saw a lone eminence cloaked by a dark company of trees, the glisten of a lake at its foot. To the other side a ranked mass of gray-white ruins was barely discernible. The Museum of Man?...After a moment of vacillation, Guyal dismounted and sought sleep within the Expansible Egg.

The sun rolled in sad sumptuous majesty behind the mountains; murk fell across the tundra. Guyal awoke and refreshed himself in a rill nearby. Giving meal to his horse, he ate dry fruit and bread; then he mounted and rode down the trail. The plain spread vastly north before him, into desolation; the mountains lowered black above and behind; a slow cold breeze blew in his face. Gloom deepened; the plain sank from sight like a drowned land. Hesitant before the murk, Guyal reined his horse. Better, he thought, to ride in the morning. If he lost the trail in the dark, who could tell what he might encounter?

A mournful sound. Guyal stiffened and turned his face to the sky. A sigh? A moan? A sob?...Another sound, closer, the rustle of cloth, a loose garment. Guyal cringed into his saddle. Floating slowly down through the darkness came a shape robed in white. Under the cowl and glowing with eer-light looked a drawn face with eyes like the holes in a skull.

It breathed its sad sound and drifted away on high...There was only the blow of the wind past Guyal's ears.

He drew a shuddering breath and slumped against the pommel. His shoulders felt exposed, naked. He slipped to the ground and established the shelter of the Egg about himself and his horse. Preparing his pallet, he lay himself down; presently, as he lay staring into the dark, sleep came on him and so the night passed.

He awoke before dawn and once more set forth. The trail was a ribbon of white sand between banks of gray furze and the miles passed swiftly.

The trail led toward the tree-clothed eminence Guyal had noted from above; now he thought to see roofs through the heavy foliage and

smoke on the sharp air. And presently to right and left spread cultivated fields of spikenard, callow and mead-apple. Guyal continued with
eyes watchful for men.

To one side appeared a fence of stone and black timber: the stone
chiseled and hewn to the semblance of four globes beaded on a central
pillar, the black timbers which served as rails fitted in sockets and
carved in precise spirals. Behind this fence a region of bare earth lay
churned, pitted, cratered, burnt and wrenched, as if visited at once by
fire and the blow of a tremendous hammer. In wondering speculation
Guyal gazed and so did not notice the three men who came quietly
upon him.

The horse started nervously; Guyal, turning, saw the three. They
barred his road and one held the bridle of his horse.

They were tall, well-formed men, wearing tight suits of somber
leather bordered with black. Their headgear was heavy maroon cloth
crumpled in precise creases, and leather flaps extended horizontally
over each ear. Their faces were long and solemn, with clear golden-
ivory skin, golden eyes and jet-black hair. Clearly they were not savages: they moved with a silky control, they eyed Guyal with critical
appraisal, their garb implied the discipline of an ancient convention.

The leader stepped forward. His expression was neither threat nor
welcome. "Greetings, stranger; whither bound?"

"Greetings," replied Guyal cautiously. "I go as my star directs…You
are the Saponids?"

"That is our race, and before you is our town Saponce." He inspected Guyal with frank curiosity. "By the color of your custom I suspect
your home to be in the south."

"I am Guyal of Sfere, by the River Scaum in Ascolais."

"The way is long," observed the Saponid. "Terrors beset the traveler. Your impulse must be most intense, and your star must draw with
fervent allure."

"I come," said Guyal, "on a pilgrimage for the ease of my spirit; the
road seems short when it attains its end."

The Saponid offered polite acquiescence. "Then you have crossed
the Fer Aquilas?"

"Indeed; through cold wind and desolate stone." Guyal glanced
back at the looming mass. "Only yesterday at night-fall did I leave the
gap. And then a ghost hovered above till I thought the grave was marking me for its own."

He paused in surprise; his words seemed to have released a powerful emotion in the Saponids. Their features lengthened, their mouths grew white and clenched. The leader, his polite detachment a trifle diminished, searched the sky with ill-concealed apprehension. "A ghost...In a white garment, thus and so, floating on high?"

"Yes; is it a known familiar of the region?"

There was a pause.

"In a certain sense," said the Saponid. "It is a signal of woe...But I interrupt your tale."

"There is little to tell. I took shelter for the night, and this morning I fared down to the plain."

"Were you not molested further? By Koolbaw the Walking Serpent, who ranges the slopes like fate?"

"I saw neither walking serpent nor crawling lizard; further, a blessing protects my trail and I come to no harm so long as I keep my course."

"Interesting, interesting."

"Now," said Guyal, "permit me to inquire of you, since there is much I would learn; what is this ghost and what evil does he commemorate?"

"You ask beyond my certain knowledge," replied the Saponid cautiously. "Of this ghost it is well not to speak lest our attention reinforce his malignity."

"As you will," replied Guyal. "Perhaps you will instruct me..." He caught his tongue. Before inquiring for the Museum of Man, it would be wise to learn in what regard the Saponids held it, lest, learning his interest, they seek to prevent him from knowledge.

"Yes?" inquired the Saponid. "What is your lack?"

Guyal indicated the seared area behind the fence of stone and timber. "What is the portent of this devastation?"

The Saponid stared across the area with a blank expression and shrugged. "It is one of the ancient places; so much is known, no more. Death lingers here, and no creature may venture across the place without succumbing to a most malicious magic which raises virulence and angry sores. Here is where those whom we kill are sent...But away. You will desire to rest and refresh yourself at Saponce. Come; we will guide you."

He turned down the trail toward the town, and Guyal, finding neither words nor reasons to reject the idea, urged his horse forward.

As they approached the tree-shrouded hill the trail widened to a road. To the right hand the lake drew close, behind low banks of purple reeds. Here were docks built of heavy black baulks and boats rocked to the wind-feathered ripples. They were built in the shape of sickles, with bow and stern curving high from the water.

Up into the town, and the houses were hewn timber, ranging in tone from golden brown to weathered black. The construction was intricate and ornate, the walls rising three stories to steep gables overhanging front and back. Pillars and piers were carved with complex designs: meshing ribbons, tendrils, leaves, lizards, and the like. The screens which guarded the windows were likewise carved, with foliage patterns, animal faces, radiant stars: rich textures in the mellow wood. It was clear that much expressiveness had been expended on the carving.

Up the steep lane, under the gloom cast by the trees, past the houses half-hidden by the foliage, and the Saponids of Saponce came forth to stare. They moved quietly and spoke in low voices, and their garments were of an elegance Guyal had not expected to see on the northern steppe.

His guide halted and turned to Guyal. "Will you oblige me by waiting till I report to the Voyevode, that he may prepare a suitable reception?"

The request was framed in candid words and with guileless eyes. Guyal thought to perceive ambiguity in the phrasing, but since the hooves of his horse were planted in the center of the road, and since he did not propose leaving the road, Guyal assented with an open face. The Saponid disappeared and Guyal sat musing on the pleasant town perched so high above the plain.

A group of girls approached to glance at Guyal with curious eyes. Guyal returned the inspection, and now found a puzzling lack about their persons, a discrepancy which he could not instantly identify. They wore graceful garments of woven wool, striped and dyed various colors; they were supple and slender, and seemed not lacking in coquetry. And yet...

The Saponid returned. "Now, Sir Guyal, may we proceed?"

Guyal, endeavoring to remove any flavor of suspicion from his words, said, "You will understand, Sir Saponid, that by the very nature of my father's blessing I dare not leave the delineated course of the trail; for then, instantly, I would become liable to any curse, which, placed on me along the way, might be seeking just such occasion for leeching close on my soul."

The Saponid made an understanding gesture. "Naturally; you follow a sound principle. Let me reassure you. I but conduct you to a reception by the Voyevode who even now hastens to the plaza to greet a stranger from the far south."

Guyal bowed in gratification, and they continued up the road.

A hundred paces and the road levelled, crossing a common planted with small, fluttering, heart shaped leaves, colored in all shades of purple, red, green and black.

The Saponid turned to Guyal. "As a stranger I must caution you never to set foot on the common. It is one of our sacred places, and tradition requires that a severe penalty be exacted for transgressions and sacrilege."

"I note your warning," said Guyal. "I will respectfully obey your law."

They passed a dense thicket; with hideous clamor a bestial shape sprang from concealment, a creature staring-eyed with tremendous fanged jaws. Guyal's horse shied, bolted, sprang out on to the sacred common and trampled the fluttering leaves.

A number of Saponid men rushed forth, grasped the horse, seized Guyal and dragged him from the saddle.

"Ho!" cried Guyal. "What means this? Release me!"

The Saponid who had been his guide advanced, shaking his head in reproach. "Indeed, and only had I just impressed upon you the gravity of such an offense!"

"But the monster frightened my horse!" said Guyal. "I am no wise responsible for this trespass; release me, let us proceed to the reception."

The Saponid said, "I fear that the penalties prescribed by tradition must come into effect. Your protests, though of superficial plausibility, will not bear serious examination. For instance, the creature you term a monster is in reality a harmless domesticated beast. Secondly, I observe the animal you bestride; he will not make a turn or twist without the twitch of the reins. Thirdly, even if your postulates were conceded, you thereby admit to guilt by virtue of negligence and omission. You should have secured a mount less apt to unpredictable action, or upon learning of the sanctitude of the common, you should have considered such a contingency as even now occurred, and therefore dismounted, leading your beast. Therefore, Sir Guyal, though loath, I am forced to believe you guilty of impertinence, impiety, disregard and impudicity. Therefore, as Castellan and Sergeant-Reader of the Litany, so responsible for the detention of law-breakers, I must order you secured, contained, pent, incarcerated and confined until such time as the penalties will be exacted."

"The entire episode is mockery!" raged Guyal. "Are you savages, then, thus to mistreat a lone wayfarer?"

"By no means," replied the Castellan. "We are a highly civilized people, with customs bequeathed us by the past. Since the past was more glorious than the present, what presumption we would show by questioning these laws!"

Guyal fell quiet. "And what are the usual penalties for my act?"

The Castellan made a reassuring motion. "The rote prescribes three acts of penance, which in your case, I am sure will be nominal. But— the forms must be observed, and it is necessary that you be constrained in the Felon's Caseboard." He motioned to the men who held Guyal's arm. "Away with him; cross neither track nor trail, for then your grasp will be nerveless and he will be delivered from justice."

Guyal was pent in a well-aired but poorly lighted cellar of stone. The floor he found dry, the ceiling free of crawling insects. He had not been searched, nor had his Scintillant Dagger been removed from his sash. With suspicions crowding his brain he lay on the rush bed and, after a period, slept.

Now ensued the passing of a day. He was given food and drink; and at last the Castellan came to visit him.

"You are indeed fortunate," said the Saponid, "in that, as a witness, I was able to suggest your delinquencies to be more the result of negligence than malice. The last penalties exacted for the crime were stringent; the felon was ordered to perform the following three acts: first, to cut off his toes and sew the severed members into the skin at his neck; second, to revile his forbears for three hours, commencing with a Common Bill of Anathema, including feigned madness and hereditary disease, and at last defiling the hearth of his clan with ordure; and third, walking a mile under the lake with leaded shoes in search of the Lost Book of Qualls." And the Castellan regarded Guyal with complacency.

"What deeds must I perform?" inquired Guyal drily.

The Castellan joined the tips of his fingers together. "As I say, the penances are nominal, by decree of the Voyevode. First you must swear never again to repeat your crime."

"That I gladly do," said Guyal, and so bound himself.

"Second," said the Castellan with a slight smile, "you must adjudicate at a Grand Pageant of Pulchritude among the maids of the village and select her whom you deem the most beautiful."

"Scarcely an arduous task," commented Guyal. "Why does it fall to my lot?"

The Castellan looked vaguely to the ceiling. "There are a number of concomitants to victory in this contest...Every person in the town would find relations among the participants—a daughter, a sister, a niece—and so would hardly be considered unprejudiced. The charge of favoritism could never be levelled against you; therefore you make an ideal selection for this important post."

Guyal seemed to hear the ring of sincerity in the Saponid's voice; still he wondered why the selection of the town's loveliest was a matter of such import.

"And third?" he inquired.

"That will be revealed after the contest, which occurs this afternoon."

The Saponid departed the cell.

Guyal, who was not without vanity, spent several hours restoring himself and his costume from the ravages of travel. He bathed, trimmed his hair, shaved his face, and, when the Castellan came to unlock the door, he felt that he made no discreditable picture.

He was led out upon the road and directed up the hill toward the summit of the terraced town of Saponce. Turning to the Castellan he said, "How is it that you permit me to walk the trail once more? You must know that now I am safe from molestation..."

The Castellan shrugged. "True. But you would gain little by insisting upon your temporary immunity. Ahead the trail crosses a bridge, which we could demolish; behind we need but breach the dam to Peilvemchal Torrent; then, should you walk the trail, you would be swept to the side and so rendered vulnerable. No, Sir Guyal of Sfere, once the secret of your immunity is abroad then you are liable to a variety of stratagems. For instance, a large wall might be placed athwart the way, before and behind you. No doubt the spell would preserve you from thirst and hunger, but what then? So would you sit till the sun went out."

Guyal said no word. Across the lake he noticed a trio of the crescent boats approaching the docks, prows and sterns rocking and dipping into the shaded water with a graceful motion. The void in his mind made itself known. "Why are boats constructed in such fashion?"

The Castellan looked blankly at him. "It is the only practicable method. Do not the oe-pods grow thusly to the south?"

"Never have I seen oe-pods."

"They are the fruit of a great vine, and grow in scimitar-shape. When sufficiently large, we cut and clean them, slit the inner edge, grapple end to end with strong line and constrict till the pod opens as is desirable. Then when cured, dried, varnished, carved, burnished, and lacquered; fitted with deck, thwarts and gussets—then have we our boats."

They entered the plaza, a flat area at the summit surrounded on three sides by tall houses of carved dark wood. The fourth side was open to a vista across the lake and beyond to the loom of the mountains. Trees overhung all and the sun shining through made a scarlet pattern on the sandy floor.

To Guyal's surprise there seemed to be no preliminary ceremonies or formalities to the contest, and small spirit of festivity was manifest among the townspeople. Indeed they seemed beset by subdued despondency and eyed him without enthusiasm.

A hundred girls stood gathered in a disconsolate group in the center of the plaza. It seemed to Guyal that they had gone to few pains to embellish themselves for beauty. To the contrary, they wore shapeless rags, their hair seemed deliberately misarranged, their faces dirty and scowling.

Guyal stared and turned to his guide. "These girls seem not to relish the garland of pulchritude."

The Castellan nodded wryly. "As you see, they are by no means jealous for distinction; modesty has always been a Saponid trait."

Guyal hesitated. "What is the form of procedure? I do not desire in my ignorance to violate another of your arcane apochrypha."

The Castellan said with a blank face, "There are no formalities. We conduct these pageants with expedition and the least possible ceremony. You need but pass among these maidens and point out her whom you deem the most attractive."

Guyal advanced to his task, feeling more than half-foolish. Then he reflected: this is a penalty for contravening an absurd tradition; I will conduct myself with efficiency and so the quicker rid myself of the obligation.

He stood before the hundred girls, who eyed him with hostility and anxiety, and Guyal saw that his task would not be simple, since, on the whole, they were of a comeliness which even the dirt, grimacing and rags could not disguise.

"Range yourselves, if you please, into a line," said Guyal. "In this way, none will be at disadvantage."

Sullenly the girls formed a line.

Guyal surveyed the group. He saw at once that a number could be eliminated: the squat, the obese, the lean, the pocked and coarse-featured—perhaps a quarter of the group. He said suavely, "Never have I seen such unanimous loveliness; each of you might legitimately claim the cordon. My task is arduous; I must weigh fine imponderables; in the end my choice will undoubtedly be based on subjectivity and those of

real charm will no doubt be the first discharged from the competition."
He stepped forward. "Those whom I indicate may retire."

He walked down the line, pointing, and the ugliest, with expressions of unmistakable relief, hastened to the sidelines.

A second time Guyal made his inspection, and now, somewhat more familiar with those he judged, he was able to discharge those who, while suffering no whit from ugliness, were merely plain.

Roughly a third of the original group remained. These stared at Guyal with varying degrees of apprehension and truculence as he passed before them, studying each in turn...All at once his mind was determined, and his choice definite. Somehow the girls felt the change in him, and in their anxiety and tension left off the expressions they had been wearing to daunt and bemuse him.

Guyal made one last survey down the line. No, he had been accurate in his choice. There were girls here as comely as the senses could desire, girls with opal-glowing eyes and hyacinth features, girls as lissome as reeds, with hair silky and fine despite the dust which they seemed to have rubbed upon themselves.

The girl whom Guyal had selected was slighter than the others and possessed of a beauty not at once obvious. She had a small triangular face, great wistful eyes and thick black hair cut raggedly short at the ears. Her skin was of a transparent paleness, like the finest ivory; her form slender, graceful, and of a compelling magnetism, urgent of intimacy. She seemed to have sensed his decision and her eyes widened.

Guyal took her hand, led her forward, and turned to the Voyevode—an old man sitting stolidly in a heavy chair.

"This is she whom I find the loveliest among your maidens."

There was silence through the square. Then there came a hoarse sound, a cry of sadness from the Castellan and Sergeant-Reader. He came forward, sagging of face, limp of body. "Guyal of Sfere, you have wrought a great revenge for my tricking you. This is my beloved daughter, Shierl, whom you have designated for dread."

Guyal turned in wonderment from the Castellan to the girl Shierl, in whose eyes he now recognized a film of numbness, a gazing into a great depth.

Returning to the Castellan, Guyal stammered, "I meant but complete impersonality. This your daughter Shierl I find one of the loveliest creatures of my experience; I cannot understand where I have offended."

"No, Guyal," said the Castellan, "you have chosen fairly, for such indeed is my own thought."

"Well then," said Guyal, "reveal to me now my third task that I may have done and continue my pilgrimage."

The Castellan said, "Three leagues to the north lies the ruin which tradition tells us to be the olden Museum of Man."

"Ah," said Guyal, "go on, I attend."

"You must, as your third charge, conduct this my daughter Shierl to the Museum of Man. At the portal you will strike on a copper gong and announce to whomever responds: 'We are those summoned from Saponce.'"

Guyal started, frowned. "How is this? 'We'?"

"Such is your charge," said the Castellan in a voice like thunder.

Guyal looked to left, right, forward and behind. But he stood in the center of the plaza surrounded by the hardy men of Saponce.

"When must this charge be executed?" he inquired in a controlled voice.

The Castellan said in a voice bitter as oak-wort: "Even now Shierl goes to clothe herself in yellow. In one hour shall she appear, in one hour shall you set forth for the Museum of Man."

"And then?"

"And then—for good or for evil, it is not known. You fare as thirteen thousand have fared before you."

Down from the plaza, down the leafy lanes of Saponce came Guyal, indignant and clamped of mouth, though the pit of his stomach felt tender and heavy with trepidation. The ritual carried distasteful overtones: execution or sacrifice. Guyal's step faltered.

The Castellan seized his elbow with a hard hand. "Forward."

Execution or sacrifice... The faces along the lane swam with morbid curiosity, inner excitement; gloating eyes searched him deep to relish his fear and horror, and the mouths half-drooped, half-smiled in the inner hugging for joy not to be the one walking down the foliage streets, and forth to the Museum of Man.

The eminence, with the tall trees and carved dark houses, was at his back; they walked out into the claret sunlight of the tundra. Here were eighty women in white chlamys with ceremonial buckets of woven straw over their heads; around a tall tent of yellow silk they stood.

The Castellan halted Guyal and beckoned to the Ritual Matron. She flung back the hangings at the door of the tent; the girl within, Shierl, came slowly forth, eyes wide and dark with fright.

She wore a stiff gown of yellow brocade, and the wand of her body seemed pent and constrained within. The gown came snug under her chin, left her arms bare and raised past the back of her head in a stiff spear-headed cowl. She was frightened as a small animal trapped is frightened; she stared at Guyal, at her father, as if she had never seen them before.

The Ritual Matron put a gentle hand on her waist, propelled her forward. Shierl stepped once, twice, irresolutely halted. The Castellan brought Guyal forward and placed him at the girl's side; now two children, a boy and a girl, came hastening up with cups which they proffered to Guyal and Shierl. Dully she accepted the cup. Guyal took his and glanced suspiciously at the murky brew. He looked up to the Castellan. "What is the nature of this potion?"

"Drink," said the Castellan. "So will your way seem the shorter; so will terror leave you behind, and you will march to the Museum with a steadier step."

"No," said Guyal. "I will not drink. My senses must be my own when I meet the Curator. I have come far for the privilege; I would not stultify the occasion stumbling and staggering." And he handed the cup back to the boy.

Shierl stared dully at the cup she held. Said Guyal: "I advise you likewise to avoid the drug; so will we come to the Museum of Man with our dignity to us."

Hesitantly she returned the cup. The Castellan's brow clouded, but he made no protest.

An old man in a black costume brought forward a satin pillow on which rested a whip with a handle of carved steel. The Castellan now lifted this whip, and advancing, laid three light strokes across the shoulders of both Shierl and Guyal.

"Now, I charge thee, get hence and go from Saponce, outlawed forever; thou art waifs forlorn. Seek succor at the Museum of Man. I charge thee, never look back, leave all thoughts of past and future here at North Garden. Now and forever are you sundered from all bonds, claims, relations, and kinships, together with all pretenses to amity, love, fellowship and brotherhood with the Saponids of Saponce. Go, I exhort; go, I command; go, go, go!"

Shierl sunk her teeth into her lower lip; tears freely coursed her cheek though she made no sound. With hanging head she started across the lichen of the tundra, and Guyal, with a swift stride, joined her.

Now there was no looking back. For a space the murmurs, the nervous sounds followed their ears; then they were alone on the plain. The limitless north lay across the horizon; the tundra filled the foreground and background, an expanse dreary, dun and moribund. Alone marring the region, the white ruins—once the Museum of Man—rose a league before them, and along the faint trail they walked without words.

Guyal said in a tentative tone, "There is much I would understand."

"Speak," said Shierl. Her voice was low but composed.

"Why are we forced and exhorted to this mission?"

"It is thus because it has always been thus. Is not this reason enough?"

"Sufficient possibly for you," said Guyal, "but for me the causality is unconvincing. I must acquaint you with the void in my mind, which lusts for knowledge as a lecher yearns for carnality; so pray be patient if my inquisition seems unnecessarily thorough."

She glanced at him in astonishment. "Are all to the south so strong for knowing as you?"

"In no degree," said Guyal. "Everywhere normality of the mind may be observed. The habitants adroitly perform the motions which fed them yesterday, last week, a year ago. I have been informed of my aberration well and full. 'Why strive for a pedant's accumulation?' I have been told. 'Why forego merriment, music, and revelry for the abstract and abstruse?'"

"Indeed," said Shierl. "Well do they counsel; such is the consensus at Saponce."

Guyal shrugged. "The rumor goes that I am demon-bereft of my senses. Such may be. In any event the effect remains and the obsession haunts me."

Shierl indicated understanding and acquiescence. "Ask on then; I will endeavor to ease these yearnings."

He glanced at her sidelong, studied the charming triangle of her face, the heavy black hair, the great lustrous eyes, dark as yu-sapphires. "In happier circumstances, there would be other yearnings I would beseech you likewise to ease."

"Ask," replied Shierl of Saponce. "The Museum of Man is close; there is occasion for naught but words."

"Why are we thus dismissed and charged, with tacit acceptance of our doom?"

"The immediate cause is the ghost you saw on the hill. When the ghost appears, then we of Saponce know that the most beautiful maiden and the most handsome youth of the town must be despatched to the Museum. The prime behind the custom I do not know. So it is; so it has been; so it will be till the sun gutters like a coal in the rain and darkens Earth, and the winds blow snow over Saponce."

"But what is our mission? Who greets us, what is our fate?"

"Such details are unknown."

Guyal mused, "The likelihood of pleasure seems small...There are discordants in the episode. You are beyond doubt the loveliest creature of the Saponids, the loveliest creature of Earth—but I, I am a casual stranger, and hardly the most well-favored youth of the town."

She smiled a trifle. "You are not uncomely."

Guyal said somberly, "Over-riding the condition of my person is the fact that I am a stranger and so bring little loss to the town of Saponce."

"That aspect has no doubt been considered," the girl said.

Guyal searched the horizon. "Let us then avoid the Museum of Man, let us circumvent this unknown fate and take to the mountains, and so south to Ascolais. Lust for enlightenment will never fly me in the face of destruction so clearly implicit."

She shook her head. "Do you suppose that we would gain by the ruse? The eyes of a hundred warriors follow us till we pass through the portals of the Museum; should we attempt to scamp our duty we should be bound to stakes, stripped of our skins by the inch, and at last be placed in bags with a thousand scorpions poured around our heads. Such is the traditional penalty; twelve times in history has it been invoked."

Guyal threw back his shoulders and spoke in a nervous voice. "Ah, well—the Museum of Man has been my goal for many years. On this motive I set forth from Sfere, so now I would seek the Curator and satisfy my obsession for brainfilling."

"You are blessed with great fortune," said Shierl, "for you are being granted your heart's desire."

Guyal could find nothing to say, so for a space they walked in silence. Then he spoke. "Shierl."

"Yes, Guyal of Sfere?"

"Do they separate us and take us apart?"

"I do not know."

"Shierl."

"Yes?"

"Had we met under a happier star..." He paused.

Shierl walked in silence.

He looked at her coolly. "You speak not."

"But you ask nothing," she said in surprise. Guyal turned his face ahead, to the Museum of Man.

Presently she touched his arm. "Guyal, I am greatly frightened."

Guyal gazed at the ground beneath his feet, and a blossom of fire sprang alive in his brain. "See the marking through the lichen?"

"Yes; what then?"

"Is it a trail?"

Dubiously she responded, "It is a way worn by the passage of many feet. So then—it is a trail."

Guyal said in restrained jubilation, "Here is safety, if I never permit myself to be cozened from the way. But you—ah, I must guard you; you must never leave my side, you must swim in the charm which protects me; perhaps then we will survive."

Shierl said sadly, "Let us not delude our reason, Guyal of Sfere."

But as they walked, the trail grew plainer, and Guyal became correspondingly sanguine. And ever larger bulked the crumble which marked the Museum of Man, presently to occupy all their vision.

If a storehouse of knowledge had existed here, little sign of it remained. There was a great flat floor, flagged in white stone, now chalky, broken and inter-thrust by weeds. Around this floor rose a series of monoliths, pocked and worn, and toppled off at various heights. These at one time had supported a vast roof; now of roof there was none and the walls were but dreams of the far past.

So here was the flat floor bounded by the broken stumps of pillars, bare to the winds of time and the glare of cool red sun. The rains had washed the marble, the dust from the mountains had been laid on and swept off, laid on and swept off, and those who had built the Museum were less than a mote of this dust, so far and forgotten were they.

"Think," said Guyal, "think of the vastness of knowledge which once was gathered here and which is now one with the soil—unless, of course, the Curator has salvaged and preserved."

Shierl looked about apprehensively. "I think rather of the portal, and that which awaits us...Guyal," she whispered, "I fear, I fear greatly...Suppose they tear us apart? Suppose there is torture and death for us? I fear a tremendous impingement, the shock of horror..."

Guyal's own throat was hot and full. He looked about with challenge. "While I still breathe and hold power in my arms to fight, there will be none to harm us."

Shierl groaned softly. "Guyal, Guyal, Guyal of Sfere—why did you choose me?"

"Because," said Guyal, "my eye went to you like the nectar moth flits to the jacynth; because you were the loveliest and I thought nothing but good in store for you."

With a shuddering breath Shierl said, "I must be courageous; after all, if it were not I it would be some other maid equally fearful...And there is the portal."

Guyal inhaled deeply, inclined his head, and strode forward. "Let us be to it, and know..."

The portal opened into a nearby monolith, a door of flat black metal. Guyal followed the trail to the door, and rapped staunchly with his fist on the small copper gong to the side.

The door groaned wide on its hinges, and cool air, smelling of the under-earth, billowed forth. In the black gape their eyes could find nothing.

"Hola within!" cried Guyal.

A soft voice, full of catches and quavers, as if just after weeping, said, "Come ye, come ye forward. You are desired and awaited."

Guyal leaned his head forward, straining to see. "Give us light, that we may not wander from the trail and bottom ourselves."

The breathless quaver of a voice said, "Light is not needed; anywhere you step, that will be your trail, by an arrangement so agreed with the Way-Maker."

"No," said Guyal, "we would see the visage of our host. We come at his invitation; the minimum of his guest-offering is light; light there must be before we set foot inside the dungeon. Know we come as seekers after knowledge; we are visitors to be honored."

"Ah, knowledge, knowledge," came the sad breathlessness. "That shall be yours, in full plentitude—knowledge of many strange affairs; oh, you shall swim in a tide of knowledge—"

Guyal interrupted the sad, sighing voice. "Are you the Curator? Hundreds of leagues have I come to bespeak the Curator and put him my inquiries. Are you he?"

"By no means. I revile the name of the Curator as a treacherous non-essential."

"Who then may you be?"

"I am no one, nothing. I am an abstraction, an emotion, the ooze of terror, the sweat of horror, the shake in the air when a scream has departed."

"You speak the voice of man."

"Why not? Such things as I speak lie in the closest and dearest center of the human brain."

Guyal said in a subdued voice, "You do not make your invitation as enticing as might be hoped."

"No matter, no matter; enter you must, into the dark and on the instant, as my lord, who is myself, waxes warm and languorous."

"If light there be, we enter."

"No light, no insolent scorch is ever found in the Museum."

"In this case," said Guyal, drawing forth his Scintillant Dagger, "I innovate a welcome reform. For see, now there is light!"

From the under-pommel issued a searching glare; the ghost tall before them screeched and fell into twinkling ribbons like pulverized tinsel. There were a few vagrant motes in the air; he was gone.

Shierl, who had stood stark and stiff as one mesmerized, gasped a soft warm gasp and fell against Guyal. "How can you be so defiant?"

Guyal said in a voice half-laugh, half-quaver, "In truth I do not know...perhaps I find it incredible that Destiny would direct me from pleasant Sfere, through forest and crag, into the northern waste, merely to play the role of cringing victim. Disbelieving so inconclusive a destiny, I am bold."

He moved the dagger to right and left, and they saw themselves to be at the portal of a keep, cut from concreted rock. At the back opened a black depth. Crossing the floor swiftly, Guyal kneeled and listened.

He heard no sound. Shierl, at his back, stared with eyes as black and deep as the pit itself, and Guyal, turning, received a sudden irrational impression of a sprite of the olden times—a creature small and delicate, heavy with the weight of her charm, pale, sweet, clean.

Leaning with his glowing dagger, he saw a crazy rack of stairs voyaging down into the dark, and his light showed them and their shadows in so confusing a guise that he blinked and drew back.

Shierl said, "What do you fear?"

Guyal rose, turned to her. "We are momentarily untended here in the Museum of Man, and we are impelled forward by various forces; you by the will of your people; I, by that which has driven me since I first tasted air...If we stay here we shall be once more arranged in harmony with the hostile pattern. If we go forward boldly, we may so come to a position of strategy and advantage. I propose that we set forth in all courage, descend these stairs and seek the Curator."

"But does he exist?"

"The ghost spoke fervently against him."

"Let us go then," said Shierl. "I am resigned."

Guyal said gravely, "We go in the mental frame of adventure, aggressiveness, zeal. Thus does fear vanish and the ghosts become creatures of mind-weft; thus does our élan burst the under-earth terror."

"We go."

They started down the stairs.

Back, forth, back, forth, down flights at varying angles, stages of varying heights, treads at varying widths, so that each step was a matter for concentration. Back, forth, down, down, down, and the black-barred shadows moved and jerked in bizarre modes on the walls.

The flight ended, they stood in a room similar to the entry above. Before them was another black portal, polished at one spot by use; on the walls to either side were inset brass plaques bearing messages in unfamiliar characters.

Guyal pushed the door open against a slight pressure of cold air, which, blowing through the aperture, made a slight rush, ceasing when Guyal opened the door farther.

"Listen."

It was a far sound, an intermittent clacking, and it held enough fell significance to raise the hairs at Guyal's neck. He felt Shierl's hand gripping his with clammy pressure.

Dimming the dagger's glow to a glimmer, Guyal passed through the door, with Shierl coming after. From afar came the evil sound, and by the echoes they knew they stood in a great hall.

Guyal directed the light to the floor: it was of a black resilient material. Next the wall: polished stone. He permitted the light to glow in the direction opposite to the sound, and a few paces distant they saw a bulky black case, studded with copper bosses, topped by a shallow glass tray in which could be seen an intricate concourse of metal devices.

With the purpose of the black cases not apparent, they followed the wall, and as they walked similar cases appeared, looming heavy and dull, at regular intervals. The clacking receded as they walked; then they came to a right angle, and turning the corner, they seemed to approach the sound. Black case after black case passed; slowly, tense as foxes, they walked, eyes groping for sight through the darkness.

The wall made another angle, and here there was a door.

Guyal hesitated. To follow the new direction of the wall would mean approaching the source of the sound. Would it be better to discover the worst quickly or to reconnoitre as they went?

He propounded the dilemma to Shierl, who shrugged. "It is all one; sooner or later the ghosts will flit down to pluck at us; then we are lost."

"Not while I possess light to stare them away to wisps and shreds," said Guyal. "Now I would find the Curator, and possibly he is to be found behind this door. We will so discover."

He laid his shoulder to the door; it eased ajar with a crack of golden light. Guyal peered through. He sighed, a muffled sound of wonder.

Now he opened the door further; Shierl clutched at his arm.

"This is the Museum," said Guyal in rapt tone. "Here there is no danger...He who dwells in beauty of this sort may never be other than beneficent..." He flung wide the door.

The light came from an unknown source, from the air itself, as if leaking from the discrete atoms; every breath was luminous, the room floated full of invigorating glow. A great rug pelted the floor, a monster tabard woven of gold, brown, bronze, two tones of green, fuscous red and smalt blue. Beautiful works of human fashioning ranked the walls. In glorious array hung panels of rich woods, carved, chased, enameled; scenes of olden times painted on woven fiber; formulas of color, designed to convey emotion rather than reality. To one side hung plats of wood laid on with slabs of soapstone, malachite and jade in rectangular patterns, richly varied and subtle, with miniature flecks of cinnabar, rhodochrosite and coral for warmth. Beside was a section given to disks of luminous green, flickering and fluorescent with varying blue films and moving dots of scarlet and black. Here were representations of three hundred marvellous flowers, blooms of a forgotten age, no longer extant on waning Earth; there were as many starburst patterns, rigidly conventionalized in form, but each of subtle distinction. All these and a multitude of other creations, selected from the best of human fervor.

The door thudded softly behind them; staring, every inch of skin atingle, the two from Earth's final time moved forward through the hall.

"Somewhere near must be the Curator," whispered Guyal. "There is a sense of careful tending and great effort here in the gallery."

"Look."

Opposite were two doors, laden with the sense of much use. Guyal strode quickly across the room but was unable to discern the means for opening the door, for it bore no latch, key, handle, knob or bar. He rapped with his knuckles and waited; no sound returned.

Shierl tugged at his arm. "These are private regions. It is best not to venture too rudely."

Guyal turned away and they continued down the gallery. Past the real expression of man's brightest dreamings they walked, until the concentration of so much fire and spirit and creativity put them into awe. "What great minds lie in the dust," said Guyal in a low voice. "What gorgeous souls have vanished into the buried ages; what marvellous creatures are lost past the remotest memory...Nevermore will there be the like; now in the last fleeting moments, humanity festers rich as rotten fruit. Rather than master and overpower our world, our highest aim is to cheat it through sorcery."

Shierl said, "But you, Guyal—you are apart. You are not like this..."

"I would know," declared Guyal with fierce emphasis. "In all my youth this ache has driven me, and I have journeyed from the old manse at Sfere to learn from the Curator...I am dissatisfied with the mindless accomplishments of the magicians, who have all their lore by rote."

Shierl gazed at him with a marvelling expression, and Guyal's soul throbbed with love. She felt him quiver and whispered recklessly, "Guyal of Sfere, I am yours, I melt for you..."

"When we win to peace," said Guyal, "then our world will be of gladness..."

The room turned a corner, widened. And now the clacking sound they had noticed in the dark outer hall returned, louder, more suggestive of unpleasantness. It seemed to enter the gallery through an arched doorway opposite.

Guyal moved quietly to this door, with Shierl at his heels, and so they peered into the next chamber.

A great face looked from the wall, a face taller than Guyal, as tall as Guyal might reach with hands on high. The chin rested on the floor, the scalp slanted back into the panel.

Guyal stared, taken aback. In this pageant of beautiful objects, the grotesque visage was the disparity and dissonance a lunatic might have created. Ugly and vile was the face, of a gut-wrenching silly obscenity. The skin shone a gun-metal sheen, the eyes gazed dully from slanting folds of greenish tissue. The nose was a small lump, the mouth a gross pulpy slash.

In sudden uncertainty Guyal turned to Shierl. "Does this not seem an odd work so to be honored here in the Museum of Man?"

Shierl was staring with eyes agonized and wide. Her mouth opened, quivered, wetness streaked her chin. With hands jerking, shaking, she grabbed his arm, staggered back into the gallery.

"Guyal," she cried, "Guyal, come away!" Her voice rose to a pitch. "Come away, come away!"

He faced her in surprise. "What are you saying?"

"That horrible thing in there—"

"It is but the diseased effort of an elder artist."

"It lives."

"How is this!"

"It lives!" she babbled. "It looked at me, then turned and looked at you. And it moved—and then I pulled you away…"

Guyal shrugged off her hand; in stark disbelief he faced through the doorway.

"Ahhhh…" breathed Guyal.

The face had changed. The torpor had evaporated; the glaze had departed the eyes. The mouth squirmed; a hiss of escaping gas sounded. The mouth opened; a great gray tongue lolled forth. And from this tongue darted a tendril slimed with mucus. It terminated in a grasping hand, which groped for Guyal's ankle. He jumped aside; the hand missed its clutch, the tendril coiled.

Guyal, in an extremity, with his bowels clenched by sick fear, sprang back into the gallery. The hand seized Shierl, grasped her ankle. The eyes glistened; and now the flabby tongue swelled another wen, sprouted a new member…Shierl stumbled, fell limp, her eyes staring, foam at her lips. Guyal, shouting in a voice he could not hear, shouting high and crazy, ran forward slashing with his dagger. He cut at the gray wrist, but his knife sprang away as if the steel itself were horrified. His gorge at his teeth, he seized the tendril; with a mighty effort he broke it against his knee.

The face winced, the tendril jerked back. Guyal leapt forward, dragged Shierl into the gallery, lifted her, carried her back, out of reach.

Through the doorway now, Guyal glared in hate and fear. The mouth had closed; it sneered disappointment and frustrated lust. And now Guyal saw a strange thing: from the dank nostril oozed a wisp of white which swirled, writhed, formed a tall thing in a white robe—a thing with a drawn face and eyes like holes in a skull. Whimpering and mewing in distaste for the light, it wavered forward into the gallery, moving with curious little pauses and hesitancies.

Guyal stood still. Fear had exceeded its power; fear no longer had meaning. A brain could react only to the maximum of its intensity; how could this thing harm him now? He would smash it with his hands, beat it into sighing fog.

"Hold, hold, hold!" came a new voice. "Hold, hold, hold. My charms and tokens, an ill day for Thorsingol...But then, avaunt, you ghost, back to the orifice, back and avaunt, avaunt, I say! Go, else I loose the actinics; trespass is not allowed, by supreme command from the Lycurgat; aye, the Lycurgat of Thorsingol. Avaunt, so then."

The ghost wavered, paused, staring in fell passivity at the old man who had hobbled into the gallery.

Back to the snoring face wandered the ghost, and let itself be sucked up into the nostril.

The face rumbled behind its lips, then opened the great gray gape and belched a white fiery lick that was like flame but not flame. It sheeted, flapped at the old man, who moved not an inch. From a rod fixed high on the door frame came a whirling disk of golden sparks. It cut and dismembered the white sheet, destroyed it back to the mouth of the face, whence now issued a black bar. This bar edged into the whirling disk and absorbed the sparks. There was an instant of dead silence.

Then the old man crowed, "Ah, you evil episode; you seek to interrupt my tenure. But no, there is no validity in your purpose; my clever baton holds your unnatural sorcery in abeyance; you are as naught; why do you not disengage and retreat into Jeldred?"

The rumble behind the large lips continued. The mouth opened wide: a gray viscous cavern was so displayed. The eyes glittered in titanic emotion. The mouth yelled, a roaring wave of violence, a sound to buffet the head and drive shock like a nail into the mind.

The baton sprayed a mist of silver. The sound curved and centralized and sucked into the metal fog; the sound was captured and consumed; it was never heard. The fog balled, lengthened to an arrow, plunged with intense speed at the nose, and buried itself in the pulp. There was a heavy sound, an explosion; the face seethed in pain and the nose was a blasted clutter of shredded gray plasms. They waved like starfish arms and grew together once more, and now the nose was pointed like a cone.

The old man said, "You are captious today, my demoniac visitant—a vicious trait. You would disturb poor old Kerlin in his duties? So. You are ingenuous and neglectful. So ho. Baton," and he turned and peered at the rod, "you have tasted that sound? Spew out a fitting penalty, smear the odious face with your infallible retort."

A flat sound, a black flail which curled, slapped the air and smote home to the face. A glowing weal sprang into being. The face sighed and the eyes twisted up into their folds of greenish tissue.

Kerlin the Curator laughed, a shrill yammer on a single tone. He stopped short and the laugh vanished as if it had never begun. He turned to Guyal and Shierl, who stood pressed together in the door-frame.

"How now, how now? You are after the gong; the study hours are long ended. Why do you linger?" He shook a stern finger. "The Museum is not the site for roguery; this I admonish. So now be off, home to Thorsingol; be more prompt the next time; you disturb the established order..." He paused and threw a fretful glance over his shoulder. "The day has gone ill; the Nocturnal Key-keeper is inexcusably late...Surely I have waited an hour on the sluggard; the Lycurgat shall be so informed. I would be home to couch and hearth; here is ill use for old Kerlin, thus to detain him for the careless retard of the night-watch...And, further, the encroachment of you two laggards; away now, and be off; out into the twilight!" And he advanced, making directive motions with his hands.

Guyal said, "My lord Curator, I must speak words with you."

The old man halted, peered. "Eh? What now? At the end of a long day's effort? No, no, you are out of order; regulation must be observed. Attend my audiarium at the fourth circuit tomorrow morning; then we shall hear you. So go now, go."

Guyal fell back nonplussed. Shierl fell on her knees. "Sir Curator, we beg you for help; we have no place to go."

Kerlin the Curator looked at her blankly. "No place to go! What folly you utter! Go to your domicile, or to the Pubescentarium, or to the Temple, or to the Outward Inn. Forsooth, Thorsingol is free with lodging; the Museum is no casual tavern."

"My lord," cried Guyal desperately, "will you hear me? We speak from emergency."

"Say on then."

"Some malignancy has bewitched your brain. Will you credit this?"

"Ah, indeed?" ruminated the Curator.

"There is no Thorsingol. There is naught but dark waste. Your city is an eon gone."

The Curator smiled benevolently. "Ah, sad...A sad case. So it is with these younger minds. The frantic drive of life is the Prime Unhinger." He shook his head. "My duty is clear. Tired bones, you must wait your well-deserved rest. Fatigue—begone; duty and simple humanity make demands; here is madness to be countered and cleared. And in any event the Nocturnal Key-keeper is not here to relieve me of my tedium." He beckoned. "Come."

Hesitantly Guyal and Shierl followed him. He opened one of his doors, passed through muttering and expostulating with doubt and watchfulness. Guyal and Shierl came after.

The room was cubical, floored with dull black stuff, walled with myriad golden knobs on all sides. A hooded chair occupied the center of the room, and beside it was a chest-high lectern whose face displayed a number of toggles and knurled wheels.

"This is the Curator's own Chair of Knowledge," explained Kerlin. "As such it will, upon proper adjustment, impose the Pattern of Hynomeneural Clarity. So—I demand the correct sometsyndic arrangement—" he manipulated the manuals "—and now, if you will compose yourself, I will repair your hallucination. It is beyond my normal call of duty, but I am humane and would not be spoken of as mean or unwilling."

Guyal inquired anxiously, "Lord Curator, this Chair of Clarity, how will it affect me?"

Kerlin the Curator said grandly, "The fibers of your brain are twisted, snarled, frayed, and so make contact with unintentional areas. By the marvellous craft of our modern cerebrologists, this hood will compose your synapses with the correct readings from the library—those of normality, you must understand—and so repair the skein, and make you once more a whole man."

"Once I sit in the chair," Guyal inquired, "what will you do?"

"Merely close this contact, engage this arm, throw in this toggle—then you daze. In thirty seconds, this bulb glows, signaling the success and completion of the treatment. Then I reverse the manipulation, and you arise a creature of renewed sanity."

Guyal looked at Shierl. "Did you hear and comprehend?"

"Yes, Guyal," in a small voice.

"Remember." Then to the Curator: "Marvellous. But how must I sit?"

"Merely relax in the seat. Then I pull the hood slightly forward, to shield the eyes from distraction."

Guyal leaned forward, peered gingerly into the hood. "I fear I do not understand."

The Curator hopped forward impatiently. "It is an act of the utmost facility. Like this." He sat in the chair.

"And how will the hood be applied?"

"In this wise." Kerlin seized a handle, pulled the shield over his face.

"Quick," said Guyal to Shierl. She sprang to the lectern; Kerlin the Curator made a motion to release the hood; Guyal seized the spindly frame, held it. Shierl flung the switches; the Curator relaxed, sighed.

Shierl gazed at Guyal, dark eyes wide and liquid as the great water-flamerian of South Almery. "Is he—dead?"

"I hope not."

They gazed uncertainly at the relaxed form. Seconds passed.

A clanging noise sounded from afar—a crush, a wrench, an exultant bellow, lesser halloos of wild triumph.

Guyal rushed to the door. Prancing, wavering, sidling into the gallery came a multitude of ghosts; through the open door behind, Guyal could see the great head. It was shoving out, pushing into the room. Great ears appeared, part of a bull-neck, wreathed with purple wattles. The wall cracked, sagged, crumbled. A great hand thrust through, a forearm...

Shierl screamed. Guyal, pale and quivering, slammed the door in the face of the nearest ghost. It seeped in around the jamb, slowly, wisp by wisp.

Guyal sprang to the lectern. The bulb showed dullness. Guyal's hands twitched along the controls. "Only Kerlin's awareness controls the magic of the baton," he panted. "So much is clear." He stared into the bulb with agonized urgency. "Glow, bulb, glow..."

By the door the ghost seeped and billowed.

"Glow, bulb, glow..."

The bulb glowed. With a sharp cry Guyal returned the switches to neutrality, jumped down, flung up the hood.

Kerlin the Curator sat looking at him.

Behind the ghost formed itself—a tall white thing in white robes, and the dark eye-holes stared like outlets into non-imagination.

Kerlin the Curator sat looking.

The ghost moved under the robes. A hand like a bird's foot appeared, holding a clod of dingy matter. The ghost cast the matter to the floor; it exploded into a puff of black dust. The motes of the cloud grew, became a myriad of wriggling insects. With one accord they darted across the floor, growing as they spread, and became scuttling creatures with monkey-heads.

Kerlin the Curator moved. "Baton," he said. He held up his hand. It held his baton. The baton spat an orange gout—red dust. It puffed before the rushing horde and each mote became a red scorpion. So ensued a ferocious battle; and little shrieks and chittering sounds rose from the floor.

The monkey-headed things were killed, routed. The ghost sighed, moved his claw-hand once more. But the baton spat forth a ray of purest light and the ghost sloughed into nothingness.

"Kerlin!" cried Guyal. "The demon is breaking into the gallery."

Kerlin flung open the door, stepped forth.

"Baton," said Kerlin, "perform thy utmost intent."

The demon said, "No, Kerlin, hold the magic; I thought you dazed. Now I retreat."

With a vast quaking and heaving he pulled back until once more only his face showed through the hole.

"Baton," said Kerlin, "be you on guard."

The baton disappeared from his hand.

Kerlin turned and faced Guyal and Shierl.

"There is need for many words, for now I die. I die, and the Museum shall lie alone. So let us speak quickly, quickly, quickly…"

Kerlin moved with feeble steps to a portal which snapped aside as he approached. Guyal and Shierl, speculating on the probable trends of Kerlin's disposition, stood hesitantly to the rear.

"Come, come," said Kerlin in sharp impatience. "My strength flags, I die. You have been my death."

Guyal moved slowly forward, with Shierl half a pace behind. Suitable response to the accusation escaped him; words seemed without conviction.

Kerlin surveyed them with a thin grin. "Halt your misgivings and hasten; the necessities to be accomplished in the time available thereto make the task like trying to write the Tomes of Kae in a minim of ink. I wane; my pulsing comes in shallow tides, my sight flickers…"

He waved a despairing hand, then, turning, led them into the inner chamber, where he slumped into a great chair. With many uneasy glances at the door, Guyal and Shierl settled upon a padded couch.

Kerlin jeered in a feeble voice, "You fear the white phantasms? Poh, they are pent from the gallery by the baton, which contains their every effort. Only when I am smitten out of mind—or dead—will the baton cease its function. You must know," he added with somewhat more vigor, "that the energies and dynamics do not channel from my brain but from the central potentium of the Museum, which is perpetual; I merely direct and order the rod."

"But this demon—who or what is he? Why does he come to look through the walls?"

Kerlin's face settled into a bleak mask. "He is Blikdak, Ruler-Divinity of the demon-world Jeldred. He wrenched the hole intent on gulfing the knowledge of the Museum into his mind, but I forestalled him; so he sits waiting in the hole till I die. Then he will glut himself with erudition to the great disadvantage of men."

"Why cannot this demon be exhorted hence and the hole abolished?"

Kerlin the Curator shook his head. "The fires and furious powers I control are not valid in the air of the demon-world, where substance and form are of different entity. So far as you see him, he has brought his environment with him; so far he is safe. When he ventures further into the Museum, the power of Earth dissolves the Jeldred mode; then may I spray him with prismatic fervor from the potentium…But stay, enough of Blikdak for the nonce; tell me, who are you, why are you ventured here, and what is the news of Thorsingol?"

Guyal said in a halting voice, "Thorsingol is passed beyond memory. There is naught above but arid tundra and the old town of the Saponids. I am of the southland; I have coursed many leagues so that I might speak to you and fill my mind with knowledge. This girl Shierl is of the Saponids, and victim of an ancient custom which sends beauty into the Museum at the behest of Blikdak's ghosts."

"Ah," breathed Kerlin, "have I been so aimless? I recall these youthful shapes which Blikdak employed to relieve the tedium of his vigil…They flit down my memory like may-flies along a panel of glass…I put them aside as creatures of his own conception, postulated by his own imagery…"

Shierl shrugged in bewilderment. "But why? What use to him are human creatures?"

Kerlin said dully, "Girl, you are all charm and freshness; the monstrous urges of the demon-lord Blikdak are past your conceiving. These youths of both sexes are his play, on whom he practices various junctures, joinings, coiti, perversions, sadisms, nauseas, antics and at last struggles to the death. Then he sends forth a ghost demanding further youth and beauty."

Shierl whispered, "This was to have been I…"

Guyal said in puzzlement, "I cannot understand. Such acts, in my understanding, are the characteristic derangements of humanity. They are anthropoid by the very nature of the functioning sacs, glands and organs. Since Blikdak is a demon…"

"Consider him!" spoke Kerlin. "His lineaments, his apparatus. He is nothing else but anthropoid, and such is his origin, together with all the demons, frits and winged glowing-eyed creatures that infest latter-day Earth. Blikdak, like the others, is from the mind of man. The sweaty condensation, the stench and vileness, the cloacal humors, the brutal delights, the rapes and sodomies, the scatophiliac whims, the manifold tittering lubricities that have drained through humanity formed a vast tumor; so Blikdak assumed his being, so now this is he. You have seen how he molds his being, so he performs his enjoyments. But of Blikdak, enough. I die, I die!" He sank into the chair with heaving chest.

"See me! My eyes vary and waver. My breath is shallow as a bird's, my bones are the pith of an old vine. I have lived beyond knowledge; in my madness I knew no passage of time. Where there is no knowledge there are no somatic consequences. Now I remember the years and centuries, the millennia, the epochs—they are like quick glimpses through a shutter. So, curing my madness, you have killed me."

Shierl blinked, drew back. "But when you die? What then? Blikdak..."

Guyal asked, "In the Museum of Man is there no knowledge of the exorcisms necessary to dissolve this demon? He is clearly our first antagonist, our immediacy."

"Blikdak must be eradicated," said Kerlin. "Then will I die in ease; then must you assume the care of the Museum." He licked his white lips. "An ancient principle specifies that, in order to destroy a substance, the nature of the substance must be determined. In short, before Blikdak may be dissolved, we must discover his elemental nature." And his eyes moved glassily to Guyal.

"Your pronouncement is sound beyond argument," admitted Guyal, "but how may this be accomplished? Blikdak will never allow such an investigation."

"No; there must be subterfuge, some instrumentality..."

"The ghosts are part of Blikdak's stuff?"

"Indeed."

"Can the ghosts be stayed and prevented?"

"Indeed; in a box of light, the which I can effect by a thought. Yes, a ghost we must have." Kerlin raised his head. "Baton! one ghost; admit a ghost!"

A moment passed; Kerlin held up his hand. There was a faint scratch at the door, and a soft whine could be heard without. "Open," said a voice, full of sobs and catches and quavers. "Open and let forth the youthful creatures to Blikdak. He finds boredom and lassitude in his vigil; so let the two come forth to negate his unease."

Kerlin laboriously rose to his feet. "It is done."

From behind the door came a sad voice, "I am pent, I am snared in scorching brilliance!"

"Now we discover," said Guyal. "What dissolves the ghost dissolves Blikdak."

"True indeed," assented Kerlin.

"Why not light?" inquired Shierl. "Light parts the fabric of the ghosts like a gust of wind tatters the fog."

"But merely for their fragility; Blikdak is harsh and solid, and can withstand the fiercest radiance safe in his demon-land alcove." And Kerlin mused. After a moment he gestured to the door. "We go to the image-expander; there we will explode the ghost to macroid dimension; so shall we find his basis. Guyal of Sfere, you must support my frailness; in truth my limbs are weak as wax."

On Guyal's arm he tottered forward, and with Shierl close at their heels they gained the gallery. Here the ghost wept in its cage of light, and searched constantly for a dark aperture to seep his essence through.

Paying him no heed Kerlin hobbled and limped across the gallery. In their wake followed the box of light and perforce the ghost.

"Open the great door," cried Kerlin in a voice beset with cracking and hoarseness. "The great door into the Cognative Repository!"

Shierl ran ahead and thrust her force against the door; it slid aside, and they looked into the great dark hall, and the golden light from the gallery dwindled into the shadows and was lost.

"Call for Lumen," Kerlin said.

"Lumen!" cried Guyal. "Lumen, attend!"

Light came to the great hall, and it proved so tall that the pilasters along the wall dwindled to threads, and so long and wide that a man might be winded to fatigue in running a dimension. Spaced in equal rows were the black cases with the copper bosses that Guyal and Shierl had noted on their entry. And above each hung five similar cases, precisely fixed, floating without support.

"What are these?" asked Guyal in wonder.

"Would my poor brain encompassed a hundredth part of what these banks know," panted Kerlin. "They are great brains crammed with all that is known, experienced, achieved, or recorded by man. Here is all the lost lore, early and late, the fabulous imaginings, the history of ten million cities, beginnings of time and the presumed finalities; the reason for human existence and the reason for the reason. Daily I have labored and toiled in these banks; my achievement has been a synopsis of the most superficial sort: a panorama across a wide and multifarious country."

Said Shierl, "Would not the craft to destroy Blikdak be contained here?"

"Indeed, indeed; our task would be merely to find the information. Under which casing would we search? Consider these categories: Demonlands; Killings and Mortefactions; Expositions and Dissolutions of Evil; History of Granvilunde (where such an entity was repelled); Attractive and Detractive Hyperordnets; Therapy for Hallucinants and Ghost-takers; Constructive Journal, item for regeneration of burst walls, sub-division for invasion by demons; Procedural Suggestions in Time of Risk...Aye, these and a thousand more. Somewhere is knowledge of how to smite Blikdak's abhorred face back into his quasiplace. But where to look? There is no Index Major; none except the poor synopsis of my compilation. He who seeks specific knowledge must often go on an extended search..." His voice trailed off. Then: "Forward! Forward through the banks to the Mechanismus."

So through the banks they went, like roaches in a maze, and behind drifted the cage of light with the wailing ghost. At last they entered a chamber smelling of metal; again Kerlin instructed Guyal and Guyal called, "Attend us, Lumen, attend!"

Through intricate devices walked the three, Guyal lost and rapt beyond inquiry, even though his brain ached with the want of knowing.

At a tall booth Kerlin halted the cage of light. A pane of vitrean dropped before the ghost. "Observe now," Kerlin said, and manipulated the activants.

They saw the ghost, depicted and projected: the flowing robe, the haggard visage. The face grew large, flattened; a segment under the vacant eye became a scabrous white place. It separated into pustules, and a single pustule swelled to fill the pane. The crater of the pustule was an intricate stippled surface, a mesh as of fabric, knit in a lacy pattern.

"Behold!" said Shierl. "He is a thing woven as if by thread."

Guyal turned eagerly to Kerlin; Kerlin raised a finger for silence. "Indeed, indeed, a goodly thought, especially since here beside us is a rotor of extreme swiftness, used in reeling the cognitive filaments of the cases...Now then observe: I reach to this panel, I select a mesh, I withdraw a thread, and note! The meshes ravel and loosen and part. And now to the bobbin on the rotor, and I wrap the thread, and now with a twist we have the cincture made..."

Shierl said dubiously, "Does not the ghost observe and note your doing?"

"By no means," asserted Kerlin. "The pane of vitrean shields our actions; he is too exercised to attend. And now I dissolve the cage and he is free."

The ghost wandered forth, cringing from the light.

"Go!" cried Kerlin. "Back to your genetrix; back, return and go!"

The ghost departed. Kerlin said to Guyal, "Follow; find when Blikdak snuffs him up."

Guyal at a cautious distance watched the ghost seep up into the black nostril, and returned to where Kerlin waited by the rotor. "The ghost has once more become part of Blikdak."

"Now then," said Kerlin, "we cause the rotor to twist, the bobbin to whirl, and we shall observe."

The rotor whirled to a blur; the bobbin (as long as Guyal's arm) became spun with ghost-thread, at first glowing pastel polychrome, then nacre, then fine milk-ivory.

The rotor spun, a million times a minute, and the thread drawn unseen and unknown from Blikdak thickened on the bobbin.

The rotor spun; the bobbin was full—a cylinder shining with glossy silken sheen. Kerlin slowed the rotor; Guyal snapped a new bobbin into place, and the unraveling of Blikdak continued.

Three bobbins—four—five—and Guyal, observing Blikdak from afar, found the giant face quiescent, the mouth working and sucking, creating the clacking sound which had first caused them apprehension.

Eight bobbins. Blikdak opened his eyes, stared in puzzlement around the chamber.

Twelve bobbins: a discolored spot appeared on the sagging cheek, and Blikdak quivered in uneasiness.

Twenty bobbins: the spot spread across Blikdak's visage, across the slanted fore-dome, and his mouth hung lax; he hissed and fretted.

Thirty bobbins: Blikdak's head seemed stale and putrid; the gun-metal sheen had become an angry maroon, the eyes bulged, the mouth hung open, the tongue lolled limp.

Fifty bobbins: Blikdak collapsed. His dome lowered against the febrile mouth; his eyes shone like feverish coals.

Sixty bobbins: Blikdak was no more.

And with the dissolution of Blikdak so dissolved Jeldred, the demonland created for the housing of evil. The breach in the wall gave on barren rock, unbroken and rigid.

And in the Mechanismus sixty shining bobbins lay stacked neat; the evil so disorganized glowed with purity and iridescence.

Kerlin fell back against the wall. "I expire; my time has come. I have guarded well the Museum; together we have won it away from Blikdak...Attend me now. Into your hands I pass the curacy; now the Museum is your charge to guard and preserve."

"For what end?" asked Shierl. "Earth expires, almost as you...Wherefore knowledge?"

"More now than ever," gasped Kerlin. "Attend: the stars are bright, the stars are fair; the banks know blessed magic to fleet you to youthful climes. Now—I go. I die."

"Wait!" cried Guyal. "Wait, I beseech!"

"Why wait?" whispered Kerlin. "The way to peace is on me; you call me back?"

"How do I extract from the banks?"

"The key to the index is in my chambers, the index of my life..." And Kerlin died.

<hr />

Guyal and Shierl climbed to the upper ways and stood outside the portal on the ancient flagged floor. It was night; the marble shone faintly underfoot, the broken columns loomed on the sky.

Across the plain the yellow lights of Saponce shone warm through the trees; above in the sky shone the stars.

Guyal said to Shierl, "There is your home; there is Saponce. Do you wish to return?"

She shook her head. "Together we have looked through the eyes of knowledge. We have seen old Thorsingol, and the Sherrit Empire before it, and Golwan Andra before that and the Forty Kades even before. We have seen the warlike green-men, and the knowledgeable Pharials and the Clambs who departed Earth for the stars, as did the Merioneth before them and the Gray Sorcerers still earlier. We have seen oceans rise and fall, the mountains crust up, peak and melt in the beat of rain; we have looked on the sun when it glowed hot and full and yellow...No, Guyal, there is no place for me at Saponce..."

Guyal, leaning back on the weathered pillar, looked up to the stars. "Knowledge is ours, Shierl—all of knowing to our call. And what shall we do?"

Together they looked up to the white stars.

"What shall we do..."

AFTERWORD TO "GUYAL OF SFERE"

I wrote while I was at sea. I did this Dying Earth thing...I wrote that, sitting looking out over the water, and then I got tired of that particular life for various reasons.

—Jack Vance 1983

NOISE

I

Captain Hess placed a notebook on the desk and hauled a chair up under his sturdy buttocks. Pointing to the notebook, he said, "That's the property of your man Evans. He left it aboard the ship."

Galispell asked in faint surprise, "There was nothing else? No letter?"

"No, sir, not a thing. That notebook was all he had when we picked him up."

Galispell rubbed his fingers along the scarred fibers of the cover. "Understandable, I suppose." He flipped back the cover. "Hmmmm."

Hess said tentatively, "What's been your opinion of Evans? Rather a strange chap?"

"Howard Evans? No, not at all. He's been a very valuable man to us." He considered Captain Hess reflectively. "Exactly how do you mean 'strange'?"

Hess frowned, searching for the precise picture of Evans' behavior. "I guess you might say erratic, or maybe emotional."

Galispell was genuinely startled. "Howard Evans?"

Hess' eyes went to the notebook. "I took the liberty of looking through his log, and—well—"

"And you got the impression he was—strange."

Hess flushed stubbornly. "Maybe everything he writes is true. But I've been poking into odd corners of space all my life and I've never seen anything like it."

"Peculiar situation," said Galispell in a neutral voice. He looked thoughtfully at the notebook.

II

Journal of Howard Charles Evans

I commence this journal without pessimism but certainly without optimism. I feel as if I have already died once. My time in the lifeboat was at least a foretaste of death. I flew on and on through the dark, and a coffin could be only slightly more cramped. The stars were above, below, ahead, astern. I have no clock, and I can put no duration to my drifting. It was more than a week, it was less than a year.

So much for space, the lifeboat, the stars. There are not too many pages in this journal. I will need them all to chronicle my life on this world which, rising up under me, gave me life.

There is much to tell and many ways in the telling. There is myself, my own response to this rather dramatic situation. But lacking the knack for tracing the contours and contortions of my psyche, I will try to detail events as objectively as possible.

I landed the lifeboat on as favorable a spot as I had opportunity to select. I tested the atmosphere, temperature, pressure and biology; then I ventured outside. I rigged an antenna and dispatched my first SOS.

Shelter is no problem; the lifeboat serves me as a bed, and, if necessary, a refuge. From sheer boredom later on I may fell a few of these trees and build a house. But I will wait; there is no urgency.

A stream of pure water trickles past the lifeboat; I have abundant concentrated food. As soon as the hydroponic tanks begin to produce there will be fresh fruits and vegetables and yeast proteins—

Survival seems no particular problem.

The sun is a ball of dark crimson, and casts hardly more light than the full moon of Earth. The lifeboat rests on a meadow of thick black-green creeper, very pleasant underfoot. A hundred yards distant in the direction I shall call south lies a lake of inky water, and the meadow slopes smoothly down to the water's edge. Tall sprays of rather pallid vegetation—I had best use the word 'trees'—bound the meadow on either side.

Behind is a hillside, which possibly continues into a range of mountains; I can't be sure. This dim red light makes vision uncertain after the first few hundred feet.

The total effect is one of haunted desolation and peace. I would enjoy the beauty of the situation if it were not for the uncertainties of the future.

The breeze drifts across the lake, smelling pleasantly fragrant, and it carries a whisper of sound from off the waves.

I have assembled the hydroponic tanks and set out cultures of yeast. I shall never starve nor die of thirst. The lake is smooth and inviting; perhaps in time I will build a little boat. The water is warm, but I dare not swim. What could be more terrible than to be seized from below and dragged under?

There is probably no basis for my misgivings. I have seen no animal life of any kind: no birds, fish, insects, crustacea. The world is one of absolute quiet, except for the whispering breeze.

The scarlet sun hangs in the sky, remaining in place during many of my sleeps. I see it is slowly westering; after this long day how long and how monotonous will be the night!

I have sent off four SOS sequences; somewhere a monitor station must catch them.

A machete is my only weapon, and I have been reluctant to venture far from the lifeboat. Today (if I may use the word) I took my courage in my hands and started around the lake. The trees are rather like birches, tall and supple. I think the bark and leaves would shine a clear silver in light other than this wine-colored gloom. Along the lakeshore they stand in a line, almost as if long ago they had been planted by a wandering gardener. The tall branches sway in the breeze, glinting scarlet with purple overtones, a strange and wonderful picture which I am alone to see.

I have heard it said that enjoyment of beauty is magnified in the presence of others: that a mysterious rapport comes into play to reveal subtleties which a single mind is unable to grasp. Certainly as I walked along the avenue of trees with the lake and the scarlet sun behind, I would have been grateful for companionship—but I believe that something of peace, the sense of walking in an ancient abandoned garden, would be lost.

The lake is shaped like an hour-glass; at the narrow waist I could look across and see the squat shape of the lifeboat. I sat down under a bush, which continually nodded red and black flowers in front of me.

Mist fibrils drifted across the lake and the wind made low musical sounds.

I rose to my feet, continued around the lake.

I passed through forests and glades and came once more to my lifeboat.

I went to tend my hydroponic tanks, and I think the yeast had been disturbed, prodded at curiously.

The dark red sun is sinking. Every day—it must be clear that I use 'day' as the interval between my sleeps—finds it lower in the sky. Night is almost upon me, long night. How shall I spend my time in the dark?

I have no gauge other than my mind, but the breeze seems colder. It brings long mournful chords to my ears, very sad, very sweet. Mist-wraiths go fleeting across the meadow.

Wan stars already show themselves, nameless ghost-lamps without significance.

I have been considering the slope behind my meadow; tomorrow I think I will make the ascent.

*

I have plotted the position of every article I possess. I will be gone some hours; and—if a visitor meddles with my goods, I will know his presence for certain.

The sun is low, the air pinches at my cheeks. I must hurry if I wish to return while light still shows me the landscape. I picture myself lost; I see myself wandering the face of this world, groping for my precious lifeboat, my tanks, my meadow.

Anxiety, curiosity, obstinacy all spurring me, I set off up the slope at a half-trot.

Becoming winded almost at once, I slowed my pace. The turf of the lakeshore had disappeared; I was walking on bare rock and lichen. Below me the meadow became a patch, my lifeboat a gleaming spindle. I watched for a moment. Nothing stirred anywhere in my range of vision.

I continued up the slope and finally breasted the ridge. A vast rolling valley fell off below me. Far away a range of great mountains stood into the dark sky. The wine-colored light slanting in from the west lit the prominences, the frontal sallies and bluffs, left the valleys in gloom: an alternate sequence of red and black beginning far in the west, continuing past, far to the east.

I looked down behind me, down to my own meadow, and was hard put to find it in the fading light. Ah, there it was! And there, the lake, a sprawling hour-glass. Beyond was dark forest, then a strip of old rose savannah, then a dark strip of woodland, then delicate laminae of colorings to the horizon.

The sun touched the edge of the mountains, and with what seemed almost a sudden lurch, fell half below the horizon. I turned down-slope; a terrible thing to be lost in the dark. My eye fell upon a white object,

314

a hundred yards along the ridge. I stared, and walked nearer. Gradually it assumed form: a thimble, a cone, a pyramid—a cairn of white rocks. I walked forward with feet achingly heavy.

A cairn, certainly. I stood looking down on it.

I turned, looked over my shoulder. Nothing in view. I looked down to the meadow. Swift shapes? I strained through the gathering murk. Nothing.

I tore at the cairn, threw rocks aside. What was below?

Nothing.

In the ground a faintly-marked rectangle three feet long was perceptible. I stood back. No power I knew of could induce me to dig into that soil.

The sun was disappearing. Already at the south and north the afterglow began, lees of wine: the sun moved with astounding rapidity; what manner of sun was this, dawdling at the meridian, plunging below the horizon?

I turned down-slope, but darkness came faster. The scarlet sun was gone; in the west was the sad sketch of departed flame. I stumbled, I fell. I looked into the east. A marvellous zodiacal light was forming, a strengthening blue triangle.

I watched, from my hands and knees. A cusp of bright blue lifted into the sky. A moment later a flood of sapphire washed the landscape. A new sun of intense indigo rose into the sky.

The world was the same and yet different; where my eyes had been accustomed to red and the red subcolors, now I saw the intricate cycle of blue.

When I returned to my meadow the breeze carried a new sound: bright chords that my mind could almost form into melody. For a moment I so amused myself, and thought to see dance-motion in the wisps of vapor which for the last few days had been noticeable over my meadow.

In what I will call a peculiar frame of mind I crawled into the lifeboat and went to sleep.

I crawled blinking out of the lifeboat into an electric world. I listened. Surely that was music—faint whispers drifting in on the wind like a fragrance.

I went down to the lake, as blue as a ball of that cobalt dye so aptly known as bluing.

The music came louder; I could catch snatches of melody—sprightly quick-step phrases carried like colored tinsel on a flow of cream.

I put my hands to my ears; if I were experiencing hallucinations, the music would continue. The sound diminished, but did not fade entirely; my test was not definitive. But I felt sure it was real. And where music was there must be musicians...I ran forward, shouted, "Hello!"

"Hello!" came the echo from across the lake.

The music faded a moment, as a cricket chorus quiets when disturbed, then gradually I could hear it again—distant music, 'horns of elf-land faintly blowing'.

It went completely out of perception. I was left standing haggard in the blue light, alone on my meadow.

I washed my face, returned to the lifeboat, sent out another set of SOS signals.

Possibly the blue day is shorter than the red day; with no clock I can't be sure. But with my new fascination, the music and its source, the blue day seems to pass swifter.

Never have I caught sight of the musicians. Is the sound generated by the trees, by diaphanous insects crouching out of my vision?

One day I glanced across the lake, and wonder of wonders! a gay town spread along the opposite shore. After a first dumbfounded gaze, I ran down to the water's edge, stared as if it were the most precious sight of my life.

Pale silk swayed and rippled: pavilions, tents, fantastic edifices...Who inhabited these places? I waded knee-deep into the lake, the breath catching and creaking in my throat, and thought to see flitting shapes.

I ran like a madman around the shore. Plants with pale blue blossoms succumbed to my feet; I left the trail of an elephant through a patch of delicate reeds.

And when I came panting and exhausted to the shore opposite my meadow, what was there? Nothing.

The city had vanished like a dream, like spectres blown on a wind. I sat down on a rock. Music came clear for an instant, as if a door had momentarily opened.

I jumped to my feet. Nothing to be seen. I looked back across the lake. There—on my meadow—a host of gauzy shapes moved like Mayflies over a still pond.

When I returned, my meadow was vacant. The shore across the lake was bare.

So goes the blue day; and now there is amazement to my life. Whence comes the music? Who and what are these flitting shapes, never quite real but never entirely out of mind? Four times an hour I press a hand to my forehead, fearing the symptoms of a mind turning in on itself...If music actually exists on this world, actually vibrates the air, why should it come to my ears as Earth music? These chords I hear might be struck on familiar instruments; the harmonies are not at all alien...And these pale plasmic wisps that I forever seem to catch from the corner of my eye: the style is that of gay and playful humanity. The tempo of their movement is the tempo of the music: tarantella, sarabande, farandole...

So goes the blue day. Blue air, blue-black turf, ultramarine water, and the bright blue star bent to the west...How long have I lived on this planet? I have broadcast the SOS sequence until now the batteries hiss with exhaustion; soon there will be an end to power. Food, water are no problem to me, but what use is a lifetime of exile on a world of blue and red?

The blue day is at its close. I would like to mount the slope and watch the blue sun's passing—but the remembrance of the red sunset still provokes a queasiness in my stomach. So I will watch from my meadow, and then, if there is darkness, I will crawl into the lifeboat like a bear into a cave, and wait the coming of light.

The blue day goes. The sapphire sun wanders into the western forest, the sky glooms to blue-black, the stars show like unfamiliar home-places.

For some time now I have heard no music; perhaps it has been so all-present that I neglect it.

The blue star is gone, the air chills. I think that deep night is on me indeed...I hear a throb of sound, plangent, plaintive; I turn my head. The east glows pale pearl. A silver globe floats up into the night like a lotus drifting on a lake: a great ball like six of Earth's full moons. Is this a sun, a satellite, a burnt-out star? What a freak of cosmology I have chanced upon!

The silver sun—I must call it a sun, although it casts a cool satin light—moves in an aureole like oyster-shell. Once again the color of the planet changes. The lake glistens like quicksilver, the trees are hammered metal...The silver star passes over a high wrack of clouds, and the music seems to burst forth as if somewhere someone flung wide curtains: the music of moonlight, medieval marble, piazzas with slim fluted colonnades, soft sighing strains...

I wander down to the lake. Across on the opposite shore once more I see the town. It seems clearer, more substantial; I note details that shimmered away to vagueness before—a wide terrace beside the lake, spiral columns, a row of urns. The silhouette is, I think, the same as when I saw it under the blue sun: great silken tents; shimmering, reflecting cusps of light; pillars of carved stone, lucent as milk-glass; fantastic fixtures of no obvious purpose...Barges drift along the dark quicksilver lake like moths, great sails bellying idly, the rigging a mesh of cobweb. Nodules of light, like fairy lanterns, hang on the stays, along the masts...On sudden thought, I turn, look up to my own meadow. I see a row of booths as at an old-time fair, a circle of pale stone set in the turf, a host of filmy shapes.

Step by step I edge toward my lifeboat. The music waxes, chords and structures of wonderful sweetness. I peer at one of the shapes, but the outlines waver. It moves to the emotion of the music—or does the motion of the shape generate the music?

I run forward, shouting hoarsely. One of the shapes slips past me, and I look into a blur where a face might be. I come to a halt, panting hard; I stand on the marble circle. I stamp; it rings solid. I walk toward the booths, they seem to display complex things of pale cloth and dim metal—but as I look my eyes mist over as with tears. The music goes far far away, my meadow lies bare and quiet. My feet press into silver-black turf; in the sky hangs the silver-black star.

I am sitting with my back to the lifeboat, staring across the lake, which is still as a mirror. I have arrived at a set of theories.

My primary proposition is that I am sane—a necessary article of faith; why bother even to speculate otherwise? So—events occurring outside my own mind cause everything I have seen and heard. But—note this!—these sights and sounds do not obey the laws of classical science; in many respects they seem particularly subjective.

It must be, I tell myself, that both objectivity and subjectivity enter into the situation. I receive impressions which my brain finds unfamiliar, and so translates to the concept most closely related. By this theory the inhabitants of this world are constantly close; I move unknowingly through their palaces and arcades; they dance incessantly around me. As my mind gains sensitivity, I verge upon rapport with their way of life and I see them. More exactly, I sense something which creates an image in the visual region of my brain. Their emotions, the pattern of their life sets up a kind of vibration which sounds in my brain as music...The reality of these creatures I am sure I will never know. They are diaphane, I am flesh; they live in a world of spirit, I plod the turf with my heavy feet.

*

These last days I have neglected to broadcast the SOS. Small lack; the batteries are about done.

The silver sun is at the zenith, and leans westward. What comes next? Back to the red sun? Or darkness? Certainly this is no ordinary planetary system; the course of this world along its orbit must resemble one of the pre-Copernican epicycles.

I believe that my brain is gradually tuning into phase with this world, reaching a new high level of sensitivity. If my theory is correct, the élan vital of the native beings expresses itself in my brain as music. On Earth we would perhaps use the word 'telepathy'...So I am practicing, concentrating, opening my consciousness wide to these new perceptions. Ocean mariners know a trick of never looking directly at a far light lest it strike the eyes' blind spot. I am using a similar device of never staring directly at one of the gauzy beings. I allow the image to establish itself, build itself up, and by this technique they appear quite definitely human. I sometimes think I can glimpse the features. The women are like sylphs, achingly beautiful; the men—I have not seen one in detail, but their carriage, their form is hauntingly familiar.

The music is always part of the background, just as rustling of leaves is part of a forest. The mood of these creatures seems to change with their sun, so I hear music to suit. The red sun gave them passionate melancholy, the blue sun merriment. Under the silver star they are delicate, imaginative, wistful, and in my mind sounds Debussy's La Mer and Les Sirènes.

The silver day is on the wane. Today I sat beside the lake with the trees a screen of silver filigree, watching the moth-barges drift back and forth. What is their function? Can life such as this be translated in terms of economies, ecology, sociology? I doubt it. The word intelligence may not even enter the picture; is not our brain a peculiarly anthropoid characteristic, and is not intelligence a function of our peculiarly anthropoid brain?...A portly barge sways near, with swamp-globes of orange and blue in the rigging, and I forget my hypotheses. I can never know the truth, and it is perfectly possible that these creatures are no more aware of me than I originally was aware of them.

Time goes by; I return to the lifeboat. A young woman-shape whirls past. I pause, peer into her face; she tilts her head, her eyes burn into mine as she passes, mocking topaz, not unkindly...I try an SOS—listlessly, because I suspect the batteries to be dank and dead.

And indeed they are.

※

The silver star is like an enormous Christmas tree bauble, round and glistening. It floats low, and once more I stand irresolute, half-expecting night.

The star falls; the forest receives it. The sky dulls, and night has come.

I face the east, my back pressed to the pragmatic hull of my lifeboat. Nothing.

I have no conception of the passage of time. Darkness, timelessness. Somewhere clocks turn minute hands, second hands, hour hands—I stand staring into the night, perhaps as slow as a sandstone statue, perhaps as feverish as a salamander.

In the darkness there is a peculiar cessation of sound. The music has dwindled; down through a series of wistful chords, a forlorn last cry...

A glow in the east, a green glow, spreading. Up rises a magnificent green sphere, the essence of all green, the tincture of emeralds, glowing as grass, fresh as mint, deep as the sea.

A throb of sound: rhythmical strong music, swinging and veering.

The green light floods the planet, and I prepare for the green day.

I am almost one with the native things. I wander among their pavilions, I pause by their booths to ponder their stuffs and wares: silken medallions, spangles and circlets of woven metal, cups of fluff and iridescent puff, puddles of color and wafts of light-shot gauze. There are chains of green glass; captive butterflies; spheres which seem to hold all the heavens, all the clouds, all the stars.

And to all sides of me go the flicker and flit of the dream-people. The men are all vague, but familiar; the women turn me smiles of ineffable provocation. But I will drive myself mad with temptations; what I see is no more than the formulation of my own brain, an interpretation...And this is tragedy, for there is one creature so unutterably lovely that whenever I see the shape that is she, my throat aches and I run forward, to peer into her eyes that are not eyes...

Today I clasped my arms around her, expecting yielding wisp. Surprisingly there was the feel of supple flesh. I kissed her, cheek, chin, mouth. Such a look of perplexity on the sweet face as I have never seen; Heaven knows what strange act the creature thought me to be performing.

She went her way, but the music is strong and triumphant: the voice of cornets, the shoulder of resonant bass below.

A man comes past; something in his stride, his posture, plucks at my memory. I step forward; I will gaze into his face, I will plumb the vagueness.

He whirls past like a figure on a carousel; he wears flapping ribbons of silk and pompoms of spangled satin. I pound after him, I plant myself in his path. He strides past with a side-glance, and I stare into the rigid mask-like face.

It is my own face.

He wears my face, he walks with my stride. He is I.

Already is the green day gone?

The green sun goes, and the music takes on depth. No cessation now; there is preparation, imminence...What is that other sound? A far spasm of something growling and clashing like a broken gear-box.

It fades out.

The green sun goes down in a sky like a peacock's tail. The music is slow, exalted.

The west fades, the east glows. The music goes toward the east, to the great bands of rose, yellow, orange, lavender. Cloud-flecks burst into flame. A golden glow consumes the sky, north and south.

The music takes on volume, a liturgical chanting.

Up rises the new sun—a gorgeous golden ball. The music swells into a paean of light, fulfillment, regeneration...Hark! A second time the harsh sound grates across the music.

Into the sky, across the sun, drifts the shape of a spaceship. It hovers over my meadow, the landing jets come down like plumes.

The ship lands.

I hear the mutter of voices—men's voices.

The music is vanished; the marble carvings, the tinsel booths, the wonderful silken cities are gone.

III

Galispell looked up, rubbed his chin.

Captain Hess asked anxiously, "What do you think of it?"

For a moment Galispell made no reply; then he said, "It's a strange document..." He looked for a long moment out the window. "What happened after you picked him up? Did you see any of these phenomena he talks about?"

"Not a thing." Captain Hess solemnly shook his big round head. "Sure, the system was a fantastic gaggle of dark stars and fluorescent planets and burnt-out old suns; maybe all these things played hob with his mind. He didn't seem too overjoyed to see us, that's a fact—just stood there, staring at us as if we were trespassers. 'We got your SOS,' I told him. 'Jump aboard, wrap yourself around a good meal!' He came walking forward as if his feet were dead.

"Well, to make a long story short, he finally came aboard. We loaded on his lifeboat and took off.

"During the voyage back he had nothing to do with anybody—just kept to himself, walking up and down the promenade.

"He had a habit of putting his hands to his head; one time I asked him if he was sick, if he wanted the medic to look him over. He said no, there was nothing wrong with him. That's about all I know of the man.

"We made Sun, and came down toward Earth. Personally, I didn't see what happened because I was on the bridge, but this is what they tell me:

"As Earth got bigger and bigger Evans began to act more restless than usual, wincing and turning his head back and forth. When we were about a thousand miles out, he gave a kind of furious jump.

"'The noise!' he yelled. 'The horrible noise!' And with that he ran astern, jumped into his lifeboat, cast off, and they tell me disappeared back the way we came.

"And that's all I got to tell you, Mr. Galispell. It's too bad, after our taking all that trouble to get him, Evans decided to pull up stakes—but that's the way it goes."

"He took off back along your course?"

"That's right. If you're wanting to ask, could he have made the planet where we found him, the answer is, not likely."

"But there's a chance?" persisted Galispell.

"Oh, sure," said Captain Hess. "There's a chance."

AFTERWORD TO "NOISE"

Today is a wonderful time to be alive—the most exciting and color-ful age in the whole tremendous history of man. We are in a period of change-over, from a civilization based of European ideas that has lost its momentum and grown tired, to a new civilization on whose basic patterns we are still working. No one could call this an era of calm; quite the reverse. Events come at us with a rapidity that bewilders most people and alarms not a few. Science fiction provides a primary educa-tion for this new age exactly as history and geography books have edu-cated us for the present. Science fiction gives us a head start at fitting ourselves to the new conditions, and we have an enormous advantage over people who ignore the future.

—Jack Vance 1953

THE KOKOD WARRIORS

I

Magnus Ridolph sat on the Glass Jetty at Providencia, fingering a quarti-quartino of Blue Ruin. At his back rose Granatee Head; before him spread Mille-Iles Ocean and the myriad little islands, each with its trees and neo-classic villa. A magnificent blue sky extended overhead; and beneath his feet, under the glass floor of the jetty, lay Coral Canyon, with schools of sea-moths flashing and flickering like metal snowflakes. Magnus Ridolph sipped his liqueur and considered a memorandum from his bank describing a condition barely distinguishable from poverty.

He had been perhaps too trusting with his money. A few months previously, the Outer Empire Investment and Realty Society, to which he had entrusted a considerable sum, was found to be bankrupt. The Chairman of the Board and the General Manager, a Mr. See and a Mr. Holpers, had been paying each other unexpectedly large salaries, most of which had been derived from Magnus Ridolph's capital investment.

Magnus Ridolph sighed, glanced at his liqueur. This would be the last of these; hereafter he must drink *vin ordinaire*, a fluid rather like tarragon vinegar, prepared from the fermented rind of a local cactus.

A waiter approached. "A lady wishes to speak to you, sir."

Magnus Ridolph preened his neat white beard. "Show her over, by all means."

The waiter returned; Magnus Ridolph's eyebrows went S-shape as he saw his guest: a woman of commanding presence, with an air of militant and dignified virtue. Her interest in Magnus Ridolph was clearly professional.

She came to an abrupt halt. "You are Mr. Magnus Ridolph?"

He bowed. "Will you sit down?"

The woman rather hesitantly took a seat. "Somehow, Mr. Ridolph, I expected someone more—well…"

Magnus Ridolph's reply was urbane. "A younger man, perhaps? With conspicuous biceps, a gun on his hip, a space helmet on his head? Or perhaps my beard alarms you?"

"Well, not exactly that, but my business—"

"Ah, you came to me in a professional capacity?"

"Well, yes. I would say so."

In spite of the memorandum from his bank—which now he folded and tucked into his pocket—Magnus Ridolph spoke with decision. "If your business requires feats of physical prowess, I beg you hire elsewhere. My janitor might satisfy your needs: an excellent chap who engages his spare time moving bar-bells from one elevation to another."

"No, no," said the woman hastily. "I'm sure you misunderstand; I merely pictured a different sort of individual…"

Magnus Ridolph cleared his throat. "What is your problem?"

"Well—I am Martha Chickering, secretary of the Women's League Committee for the Preservation of Moral Values. We are fighting a particularly disgraceful condition that the law refuses to abate. We have appealed to the better nature of the persons involved, but I'm afraid that financial gain means more to them than decency."

"Be so kind as to state your problem."

"Are you acquainted with the world—" she spoke it as if it were a social disease "—Kokod?"

Magnus Ridolph nodded gravely, stroked his neat white beard. "Your problem assumes form."

"Can you help us, then? Every right-thinking person condemns the goings-on—brutal, undignified, nauseous…"

Magnus Ridolph nodded. "The exploitation of the Kokod natives is hardly commendable."

"Hardly commendable!" cried Martha Chickering. "It's despicable! It's trafficking in blood! We execrate the sadistic beasts who patronize bull-fights—but we condone, even encourage the terrible things that take place on Kokod while Holpers and See daily grow wealthier."

"Ha, ha!" exclaimed Magnus Ridolph. "Bruce Holpers and Julius See?"

"Why, yes." She looked at him questioningly. "Perhaps you know them?"

Magnus Ridolph sat back in his chair, turned the liqueur down his throat. "To some slight extent. We had what I believe is called a business connection. But no matter, please continue. Your problem has acquired a new dimension, and beyond question the situation is deplorable."

"Then you agree that the Kokod Syndicate should be broken up? You will help us?"

Magnus Ridolph spread his arms in a fluent gesture. "Mrs. Chickering, my good wishes are freely at your disposal; active participation in the crusade is another matter and will be determined by the fee your organization is prepared to invest."

Mrs. Chickering spoke stiffly. "Well, we assume that a man of principle might be willing to make certain sacrifices—"

Magnus Ridolph sighed. "You touch me upon a sensitive spot, Mrs. Chickering. I shall indeed make a sacrifice. Rather than the extended rest I had promised myself, I will devote my abilities to your problem...Now let us discuss my fee—no, first, what do you require?"

"We insist that the gaming at Shadow Valley Inn be halted. We want Bruce Holpers and Julius See prosecuted and punished. We want an end put to the Kokod wars."

Magnus Ridolph looked off into the distance and for a moment was silent. When at last he spoke, his voice was grave. "You list your requirements on a descending level of feasibility."

"I don't understand you, Mr. Ridolph."

"Shadow Valley Inn might well be rendered inoperative by means of a bomb or an epidemic of Mayerheim's Bloat. To punish Holpers and See, we must demonstrate that a non-existent law has been criminally violated. And to halt the Kokod wars, it will be necessary to alter the genetic heritage, glandular make-up, training, instinct, and general outlook on life, of each of the countless Kokod warriors."

Mrs. Chickering blinked and stammered; Magnus Ridolph held up a courteous hand. "However, that which is never attempted never transpires; I will bend my best efforts to your requirements. My fee—well, in view of the altruistic ends in prospect, I will be modest; a thousand munits a week and expenses. Payable, if you please, in advance."

Magnus Ridolph left the jetty, mounted Granatee Head by steps cut into the green-veined limestone. On top, he paused by the wrought-iron balustrade to catch his breath and enjoy the vista over the ocean. Then he turned and entered the blue lace and silver filigree lobby of the Hotel des Mille Iles.

Presenting a bland face to the scrutiny of the desk clerk he sauntered into the library, where he selected a cubicle, settled himself before the mnemiphot. Consulting the index for Kokod, he punched the appropriate keys.

The screen came to life. Magnus Ridolph inspected first a series of charts which established that Kokod was an exceedingly small world of high specific gravity.

Next appeared a projection of the surface, accompanied by a slow-moving strip of descriptive matter:

Although a small world, Kokod's gravity and atmosphere make it uniquely habitable for men. It has never been settled, due to an already numerous population of autochthones and a lack of valuable minerals.

Tourists are welcomed at Shadow Valley Inn, a resort hotel at Shadow Valley. Weekly packets connect Shadow Valley Inn with Starport.

Kokod's most interesting feature is its population.

The chart disappeared, to be replaced by a picture entitled, 'Typical Kokod Warrior (from Rock River Tumble)', and displaying a man-like creature two feet tall. The head was narrow and peaked; the torso was that of a bee—long, pointed, covered with yellow down. Scrawny arms gripped a four-foot lance, a stone knife hung at the belt. The chitinous legs were shod with barbs. The creature's expression was mild, almost reproachful.

A voice said, "You will now hear the voice of Sam 192 Rock River."

The Kokod warrior inhaled deeply; wattles beside his chin quivered. From the mnemiphot screen issued a high-pitched stridency. Interpretation appeared on a panel to the right.

"I am Sam 192, squadronite, Company 14 of the Advance Force, in the service of Rock River Tumble. Our valor is a source of wonder to all; our magnificent stele is rooted deep, and exceeded in girth only by the steles of Rose Slope Tumble and crafty Shell Strand Tumble.

"This day I have come at the invitation of the (untranslatable) of Small Square Tumble, to tell of our victories and immensely effective strategies."

Another sound made itself heard: a man speaking falsetto in the Kokod language. The interpretation read:

●

Question: Tell us about life in Rock River Tumble.

Sam 192: It is very companionable.

Q: What is the first thing you do in the morning?

A: We march past the matrons, to assure ourselves of a properly martial fecundity.

Q: What do you eat?

A: We are nourished in the fields.

(Note: The Kokod metabolism is not entirely understood; apparently they ferment organic material in a crop, and oxidize the resultant alcohols.)

Q: Tell us about your daily life.

A: We practice various disciplines, deploy in the basic formations, hurl weapons, train the kinderlings, elevate the veterans.

Q: How often do you engage in battle?

A: When it is our time: when the challenge has issued and the appropriate Code of Combat agreed upon with the enemy.

Q: You mean, you fight in various styles?

A: There are 97 conventions of battle which may be employed: for instance, Code 48, by which we overcame strong Black Glass Tumble, allows the lance to be grasped only by the left hand and permits no severing of the leg tendons with the dagger. Code 69, however, insists that the tendons must be cut before the kill is made and the lances are used thwart-wise, as bumpers.

Q: Why do you fight? Why are there wars?

A: Because the steles of the other tumbles would surpass ours in size, did we not fight and win victories.

(Note: the stele is a composite tree growing in each tumble. Each victory is celebrated by the addition of a shoot, which joins and augments the main body of the stele. The Rock River Stele is 17 feet in diameter, and is estimated to be 4,000 years old. The Rose Slope Stele is 18 feet in diameter, and the Shell Strand Stele is almost 20 feet in diameter.)

Q: What would happen if warriors from Frog Pond Tumble cut down Rock River Stele?

Sam 192 made no sound. His wattles blew out; his head bobbed. After a moment he turned, marched out of view.

Into the screen came a man wearing shoulder tabs of Commonwealth Control. He looked after Sam 192 with an expression of patronizing good humor that Magnus Ridolph considered insufferable.

"The Kokod warriors are well known through the numerous sociological studies published on Earth, of which the most authoritative is perhaps the Carlisle Foundation's *Kokod: A Militaristic Society,* mnemiphot code AK-SK-RD-BP.

"To summarize, let me state that there are 81 tumbles or castles on Kokod, each engaged in highly formalized warfare with all the others. The evolutionary function of this warfare is the prevention of overpopulation on a small world. The Tumble Matrons are prolific, and only these rather protean measures assure a balanced ecology.

"I have been asked repeatedly whether the Kokod warriors fear death? My belief is that identification with the home tumble is so intense that the warriors have small sense of individuality. Their sole ambition is winning battles, swelling the girth of their stele and so glorifying their tumble."

The man spoke on. Magnus Ridolph reached out, speeded up the sequence.

On the screen appeared Shadow Valley Inn—a luxurious building under six tall parasol trees. The commentary read: "At Shadow Valley Inn, genial co-owners Julius See and Bruce Holpers greet tourists from all over the universe."

Two cuts appeared—a dark man with a lowering broad face, a mouth uncomfortably twisted in a grin; the other, lanky, with a long head sparsely thatched with red excelsior. 'See' and 'Holpers' read the sub-headings.

Magnus Ridolph halted the progression of the program, studied the faces for a few seconds, then allowed the sequence to continue.

"Mr. See and Mr. Holpers," ran the script, "have ingeniously made use of the incessant wars as a means of diverting their guests. A sheet quotes odds on each day's battle—a pastime which arouses enthusiasm among sporting visitors."

Magnus Ridolph turned off the mnemiphot, sat back in the chair, stroked his beard reflectively. "Where odds exist," he said to himself, "there likewise exists the possibility of upsetting the odds…Luckily, my obligation to Mrs. Chickering will in no way interfere with a certain measure of subsidiary profits. Or better, let us say, recompense."

II

Alighting from the Phoenix Line packet, the Hesperornis, Ridolph was startled momentarily by the close horizons of Kokod. The sky seemed to begin almost at his feet.

Waiting to transfer the passengers to the inn was an over-decorated charabanc. Magnus Ridolph gingerly took a seat, and when the vehicle lurched forward a heavy woman scented with musk was thrust against him. "Really!" complained the woman.

"A thousand apologies," replied Magnus Ridolph, adjusting his position. "Next time I will take care to move out of your way."

The woman brushed him with a contemptuous glance and turned to her companion, a woman with the small head and robust contour of a peacock.

"Attendant!" the second woman called presently.

"Yes, Madame."

"Tell us about these native wars, we've heard so much about them."

"They're extremely interesting, Madame. The little fellows are quite savage."

"I hope there's no danger for the onlookers?"

"None whatever; they reserve their unfriendliness for each other."

"What time are the excursions?"

"I believe the Ivory Dune and the Eastern Shield Tumbles march tomorrow; the scene of battle no doubt will center around Muscadine Meadow, so there should be three excursions. To catch the deployments, you leave the inn at 5 A.M.; for the onslaught, at 6 A.M.; and 7 or 8 for the battle proper."

"It's ungodly early," the matron commented. "Is nothing else going on?"

"I'm not certain, Madame. The Green Ball and the Shell Strand might possibly war tomorrow, but they would engage according to Convention 4, which is hardly spectacular."

"Isn't there anything close by the inn?"

"No, Madame. Shadow Valley Tumble only just finished a campaign against Marble Arch, and are occupied now in repairing their weapons."

"What are the odds on the first of these—the Ivory Dune and the Eastern Shield?"

"I believe eight gets you five on Ivory Dune, and five gets you four on Eastern Shield."

"That's strange. Why aren't the odds the same both ways?"

"All bets must be placed through the inn management, Madame."

The carry-all rattled into the courtyard of the inn. Magnus Ridolph leaned forward. "Kindly brace yourself, Madame; the vehicle is about to stop, and I do not care to be held responsible for a second unpleasant incident."

The woman made no reply. The charabanc halted; Magnus Ridolph climbed to the ground. Before him was the inn and behind a mountainside, dappled with succulent green flowers on lush violet bushes. Along the ridge grew tall, slender trees like poplars, vivid black and red. A most colorful world, decided Magnus Ridolph, and turning, inspected the view down the valley. There were bands and layers of colors—pink, violet, yellow, green, graying into a distant dove color. Where the mouth of the valley gave on the river peneplain, Magnus Ridolph glimpsed a tall conical edifice. "One of the tumbles?" he inquired of the charabanc attendant.

"Yes sir—the Meadow View Tumble. Shadow Valley Tumble is further up the valley, behind the inn."

Magnus Ridolph turned to enter the inn. His eyes met those of a man in a severe black suit—a short man with a dumpy face that looked as if it had been compressed in a vise. Ridolph recognized the countenance of Julius See. "Well, well, this is a surprise indeed," said Magnus.

See nodded grimly. "Quite a coincidence..."

"After the unhappy collapse of Outer Empire Realty and Investment I feared—indeed, I dreaded—that I should never see you again." And Magnus Ridolph watched Julius See with mild blue eyes blank as a lizard's.

"No such luck," said See. "As a matter of fact I run this place. Er, may I speak to you a moment inside?"

"Certainly, by all means."

Ridolph followed his host through the well-appointed lobby into an office. A thin-faced man with thin red hair and squirrel teeth rose quickly to his feet. "You'll remember my partner, Bruce Holpers," said See with no expression in his voice.

"Of course," said Ridolph. "I am flattered that you honor me with your personal attention."

See cut the air with his hand—a small petulant gesture. "Forget the smart talk, Ridolph...What's your game?"

Magnus Ridolph laughed easily. "Gentlemen, gentlemen—"

"Gentlemen my foot! Let's get down to brass tacks. If you've got any ideas left over from that Outer Empire deal, put them away."

"I assure you—"

"I've heard stories about you, Ridolph, and what I brought you in to tell you was that we're running a nice quiet place here, and we don't want any disturbance."

"Of course not," agreed Ridolph.

"Maybe you came for a little clean fun, betting on these native chipmunks; maybe you came on a party that we won't like."

Ridolph held out his hands guilelessly. "I can hardly say I'm flattered. I appear at your inn, an accredited guest; instantly you take me aside and admonish me."

"Ridolph," said See, "you have a funny reputation, and a normal sharpshooter never knows what side you're working on."

"Enough of this," said Magnus sternly. "Open the door, or I shall institute a strong protest."

"Look," said See ominously, "we own this hotel. If we don't like your looks, you'll camp out and rustle your own grub until the next packet—which is a week away."

Magnus Ridolph said coldly, "You will become liable to extensive damages if you seek to carry out your threat; in fact, I defy you, put me out if you dare!"

The lanky red-haired Holpers laid a nervous hand on See's arm. "He's right, Julie. We can't refuse service or the Control yanks our charter."

"If he misbehaves or performs any mischief, we can put him out."

"You have evidence, then, that I am a source of annoyance?"

See stood back, hands behind him. "Call this little talk a warning, Ridolph. You've just had your warning."

Returning to the lobby, Magnus Ridolph ordered his luggage sent to his room, and inquired the whereabouts of the Commonwealth Control officer.

"He's established on the edge of Black Bog, sir; you'll have to take an air-car unless you care for an all-night hike."

"You may order out an air-car," said Magnus Ridolph.

※

Seated in the well-upholstered tonneau, Ridolph watched Shadow Valley Inn dwindle below. The sun, Pi Sagittarius, which had already set, once more came into view as the car rose to clear Basalt Mountain, then sank in a welter of purples, greens and reds—a phoenix dying in its many-colored blood. Kokod twilight fell across the planet.

Below passed a wonderfully various landscape: lakes and parks, meadows, cliffs, crags, sweeping hillside slopes, river valleys. Here and there Ridolph sensed shapes in the fading light—the hive-like tumbles. As evening deepened into dove-colored night, the tumbles flickered with dancing orange sparks of illumination.

The air-car slanted down, slid under a copse of trees shaped like feather-dusters. Magnus Ridolph alighted, stepped around to the pilot's compartment.

"Who is the Control officer?"

"His name is Clark, sir, Everley Clark."

Magnus Ridolph nodded. "I'll be no more than twenty minutes. Will you wait, please?"

"Yes, sir. Very well, sir."

Magnus Ridolph glanced sharply at the man: a suggestion of insolence behind the formal courtesy?...He strode to the frame building. The upper half of the door hung wide; cheerful yellow light poured out into the Kokod night. Within, Magnus Ridolph glimpsed a tall pink man in neat tan gabardines. Something in the man's physiognomy struck a chord of memory; where had he seen this round pink face before? He rapped smartly on the door; the man turned his head and rather glumly arose. Magnus Ridolph saw the man to be he of the mnemiphot presentation on Kokod, the man who had interviewed the warrior, Sam 192.

Everley Clark came to the door. "Yes? What can I do for you?"

"I had hoped for the privilege of a few words with you," replied Magnus Ridolph.

Clark blew out his cheeks, fumbled with the door fastenings. "By all means," he said hollowly. "Come in, sir." He motioned Magnus Ridolph to a chair. "Won't you sit down? My name is Everley Clark."

"I am Magnus Ridolph."

Clark evinced no flicker of recognition, responding with only a blank stare of inquiry.

Ridolph continued a trifle frostily. "I assume that our conversation can be considered confidential?"

"Entirely, sir. By all means." Clark showed a degree of animation, went to the fireplace, stood warming his hands at an imaginary blaze.

Ridolph chose his words for their maximum weight. "I have been employed by an important organization which I am not at liberty to name. The members of this organization—who I may say exert a not negligible political influence—feel that Control's management of Kokod business has been grossly inefficient and incorrect."

"Indeed!" Clark's official affability vanished as if a pink spotlight had been turned off.

Magnus Ridolph continued soberly. "In view of these charges, I thought it my duty to confer with you and learn your opinions."

Clark said grimly. "What do you mean—'charges'?"

"First, it is claimed that the gambling operations at Shadow Valley Inn are—if not illegal—explicitly, shamelessly and flagrantly unmoral."

"Well?" said Clark bitterly. "What do you expect me to do? Run out waving a Bible? I can't interfere with tourist morals. They can play merry hell, run around naked, beat their dogs, forge checks—as long as they leave the natives alone, they're out of my jurisdiction."

Magnus Ridolph nodded sagely. "I see your position clearly. But a second and more serious allegation is that in allowing the Kokod wars to continue day in and day out, Control condones and tacitly encourages a type of brutality which would not be allowed on any other world of the Commonwealth."

Clark seated himself, sighed deeply. "If you'll forgive me for saying so, you sound for all the world like one of the form letters I get every day from women's clubs, religious institutes and anti-vivisectionist societies." He shook his round pink face with sober emphasis. "Mr. Ridolph, you just don't know the facts. You come up here in a lather of indignation, you shoot off your mouth and sit back with a pleased expression—good deed for the day. Well, it's not right! Do you think I enjoy seeing these little creatures tearing each other apart? Of course not—although I admit I've become used to it. When Kokod was first visited, we tried to stop the wars. The natives considered us damn fools, and went on fighting. We enforced peace, by threatening to cut down the steles. This meant something to them; they gave up the wars. And you never saw a sadder set of creatures in your life. They sat around in the dirt; they contracted a kind of roup and died by the droves. None of them cared enough to drag the corpses away. Four tumbles were wiped out; Cloud Crag, Yellow Bush, Sunset Ridge and Vinegrass. You can see them today, colonies thousands of years old, destroyed in a few months. And all this time the Tumble-matrons were producing young. No one had the spirit to feed them, and they starved or ran whimpering around the planet like naked little rats."

"Ahem," said Magnus Ridolph. "A pity."

"Fred Exman was adjutant here then. On his own authority he ordered the ban removed, told them to fight till they were blue in the face. The wars began half an hour later, and the natives have been happy and healthy ever since."

"If what you say is true," Magnus Ridolph remarked mildly, "I have fallen into the common fault of wishing to impose my personal tenor of living upon creatures constitutionally disposed to another."

Clark said emphatically, "I don't like to see those sadistic bounders at the hotel capitalizing on the wars, but what can I do about it? And the tourists are no better: morbid unhealthy jackals, enjoying the sight of death…"

Magnus Ridolph suggested cautiously, "Then it would be safe to say that, as a private individual, you would not be averse to a cessation of the gambling at Shadow Valley Inn?"

"Not at all," said Everley Clark. "As a private citizen, I've always thought that Julius See, Bruce Holpers and their guests represented mankind at its worst."

"One more detail," said Magnus Ridolph. "I believe you speak and understand the Kokod language?"

"After a fashion—yes." Clark grimaced in apprehension. "You realize I can't compromise Control officially?"

"I understand that very well."

"Just what do you plan, then?"

"I'll know better after I witness one or two of these campaigns."

III

Soft chimes roused Magnus Ridolph; he opened his eyes into the violet gloom of a Kokod dawn. "Yes?"

The hotel circuit said, "Five o'clock, Mr. Ridolph. The first party for today's battle leaves in one hour."

"Thank you." Ridolph swung his bony legs over the edge of the air-cushion, sat a reflective moment. He gained his feet, gingerly performed a set of calisthenic exercises.

In the bathroom he rinsed his mouth with tooth-cleanser, rubbed depilatory on his cheeks, splashed his face with cold water, applied tonic to his trim white beard.

Returning to the bedroom, he selected a quiet gray and blue outfit, with a rather dashing cap.

His room opened upon a terrace facing the mountainside; as he strolled forth, the two women whom he had encountered in the charabanc the day previously came past. Magnus Ridolph bowed, but the women passed without even a side glance.

"Cut me dead, by thunder," said Magnus Ridolph to himself. "Well, well." And he adjusted his cap to an even more rakish angle.

In the lobby a placard announced the event of the day:

IVORY DUNE TUMBLE

vs.

EASTERN SHIELD TUMBLE

at Muscadine Meadow

All bets must be placed with the attendant.
Odds against Ivory Dune: 8:13
Odds against Eastern Shield: 5:4
In the last hundred battles Ivory Dune has won 41 engagements, Eastern Shield has won 59.
Excursions leave as follows:
For deployment: 6 A.M.
For onslaught: 7 A.M.
For battle proper: 8 A.M.
It is necessary that no interference be performed in the vicinity of the battle. Any guest infringing on this rule will be barred from further wagering. There will be no exceptions.

At a booth nearby, two personable young women were issuing betting vouchers. Magnus Ridolph passed quietly into the restaurant, where he breakfasted lightly on fruit juice, rolls and coffee, finishing in ample time to secure a place with the first excursion.

The observation vehicle was of that peculiar variety used in conveying a large number of people across a rough terrain. The car proper was suspended by a pair of cables from a kite-copter which flew five hundred feet overhead. The operator, seated in the nose of the car, worked pitch and attack by remote control, and so could skim quietly five feet over the ground, hover over waterfalls, ridges, ponds, other areas of scenic beauty with neither noise nor the thrash of driven air to disturb the passengers.

Muscadine Meadow was no small distance away; the operator lofted the ship rather abruptly over Basalt Mountain, then slid on a long slant into the northeast. Pi Sagittarius rolled up into the sky like a melon, and the grays, greens, reds, purples of the Kokod countryside shone up from below, rich as Circassian tapestry.

"We are near the Eastern Shield," the attendant announced in a mellifluous baritone. "The tumble is a trifle to the right, beside that bold face of granite whence it derives its name. If you look closely you will observe the Eastern Shield armies already on the march."

Bending forward studiously, Magnus Ridolph noticed a brown and yellow column winding across the mountainside. To their rear he saw first the tall stele, rising two hundred feet, spraying over at the top into a fountain of pink, black and light green foliage; then below, the conical tumble.

The car sank slowly, drifted over a wooded patch of broken ground, halted ten feet above a smooth green meadow.

"This is the Muscadine," announced the guide. "At the far end you can see Muscadine Tumble and Stele, currently warring against Opal Grotto, odds 9 to 7 both ways...If you will observe along the line of bamboo trees you will see the green caps of the Ivory Dune warriors. We can only guess their strategy, but they seem to be preparing a rather intricate offensive pattern—"

A woman's voice said peevishly, "Can't you take the car up higher so we can see everything?"

"Certainly, if you wish, Mrs. Chaim."

Five hundred feet above, copter blades slashed the air; the car wafted up like thistledown.

The guide continued, "The Eastern Shield warriors can be seen coming over the hill...It seems as if they surmise the Ivory Dune strategy and will attempt to attack the flank...There!" His voice rose animatedly. "By the bronze tree! The scouts have made a brush...Eastern Shield lures the Ivory Dune scouts into ambush...They're gone. Apparently today's code is 4, or possibly 36, allowing all weapons to be used freely, without restriction."

An old man with a nose like a raspberry said, "Put us down, driver. From up here we might as well be back at the inn."

"Certainly, Mr. Pilby."

The car sank low. Mrs. Chaim sniffed and glared.

The meadow rose from below; the car grounded gently on glossy dark green creepers. The guide said, "Anyone who wishes may go further on foot. For safety's sake, do not approach the battle more closely than three hundred feet; in any event the inn assumes no responsibility of any sort whatever."

"Hurry," said Mr. Pilby sharply. "The onslaught will be over before we're in place."

The guide good-naturedly shook his head. "They're still sparring for position, Mr. Pilby. They'll be dodging and feinting half an hour yet; that's the basis of their strategy—neither side wants to fight until they're assured of the best possible advantage." He opened the door. With Pilby in the lead, several dozen of the spectators stepped down on Muscadine Meadow, among them Magnus Ridolph, Mrs. Chaim and her peacock-shaped friend whom she addressed as "Mrs. Borgage".

"Careful, ladies and gentlemen," called the guide, "Not too close to the battle."

"I've got my money on Eastern Shield," said Mrs. Borgage with heavy archness. "I'm going to make sure there's no funny business."

Magnus Ridolph inspected the scene of battle. "I'm afraid you are doomed to disappointment, Mrs. Borgage. In my opinion, Ivory Dune has selected the stronger position; if they hold on their right flank, give a trifle at the center, and catch the Eastern Shield forces on two sides when they close in, there should be small doubt as to the outcome of today's encounter."

"It must be wonderful to be so penetrating," said Mrs. Borgage in a sarcastic undertone to Mrs. Chaim.

Mr. Pilby said, "I don't think you see the battleground in its entire perspective, sir. The Eastern Shield merely needs to come in around that line of trees to catch the whole rear of the Ivory Dune line—"

"But by so doing," Magnus Ridolph pointed out, "they leave their rear unguarded; clearly Ivory Dune has the advantage of maneuver."

To the rear a second excursion boat landed. The doors opened, there was a hurrying group of people. "Has anything happened yet?" "Who's winning?"

"The situation is fluid," declared Pilby.

"Look, they're closing in!" came the cry. "It's the onslaught!"

Now rose the piping of Kokod war hymns: from Ivory Dune throats the chant sacred and long-beloved at Ivory Dune Tumble, and countering, the traditional paean of the Eastern Shield.

Down the hill came the Eastern Shield warriors, half-bent forward.

A thud and clatter—battle. The shock of small bodies, the dry whisper of knife against lance, the hoarse orders of leg-leaders and squadronites.

Forward and backward, green and black mingled with orange and white. Small bodies were hacked apart, dryly dismembered; small black eyes went dead and dim; a hundred souls raced all together, pell-mell, for the Tumble Beyond the Sky.

Forward and backward moved the standard-bearers—those who carried the sapling from the sacred stele, whose capture would mean defeat for one and victory for the other.

On the trip back to the inn, Mrs. Chaim and Mrs. Borgage sat glum and solitary while Mr. Pilby glowered from the window.

Magnus Ridolph said affably to Pilby, "In a sense, an amateur strategist, such as myself, finds these battles a trifle tedious. He needs no more than a glance at the situation, and his training indicates the logical outcome. Naturally none of us are infallible, but given equal forces and equal leadership, we can only assume that the forces in the better position will win."

Pilby lowered his head, chewed the corners of his mustache. Mrs. Chaim and Mrs. Borgage studied the landscape with fascinated absorption.

"Personally," said Ridolph, "I never gamble. I admire a dynamic attack on destiny, rather than the suppliance and passivity of the typical gambler; nevertheless I feel for you all in your losses, which I hope were not too considerable?"

There was no reply. Magnus Ridolph might have been talking to empty air. After a moment Mrs. Chaim muttered inaudibly to the peacock-shaped Mrs. Borgage, and Mr. Pilby slouched even deeper in his seat. The remainder of the trip was passed in silence.

After a modest dinner of cultivated Bylandia protein, a green salad, and cheese, Magnus Ridolph strolled into the lobby, inspected the morrow's scratch sheet.

The announcement read:

TOMORROW'S FEATURED BATTLE:
VINE HILL TUMBLE
vs.

ROARING CAPE TUMBLE
near Pink Stone Table.

Odds against Vine Hill Tumble: 1:3
Odds against Roaring Cape Tumble: 4:1
All bets must be placed with the attendant.

In the last hundred engagements Vine Hill Tumble has won 77, Roaring Cape has won 23.

Turning away, Magnus Ridolph bumped into Julius See, who was standing, rocking on his heels, his hands behind his back.

"Well, Ridolph, think you'll maybe take a flyer?"

Magnus Ridolph nodded. "A wager on Roaring Cape Tumble might prove profitable."

"That's right."

"On the other hand, Vine Hill is a strong favorite."

"That's what the screamer says."

"What would be your own preference, Mr. See?" asked Magnus Ridolph ingenuously.

"I don't have any preference. I work 23 to 77."

"Ah, you're not a gambling man, then?"

"Not any way you look at it."

Ridolph rubbed his beard and looked reflectively toward the ceiling. "Normally I should say the same of myself. But the wars offer an amateur strategist an unprecedented opportunity to test his abilities, and I may abandon the principles of a lifetime to back my theories."

Julius See turned away. "That's what we're here for."

"Do you impose a limit on the bets?"

See paused, looked over his shoulder. "We usually call a hundred thousand munits our maximum pay-off."

Magnus Ridolph nodded. "Thank you." He crossed the lobby, entered the library. On one wall was a map of the planet, with red discs indicating the location of each tumble.

Magnus Ridolph located Vine Hill and Roaring Cape Tumbles, and found Pink Stone Table, the latter near an arm of Drago Bay. Magnus Ridolph went to a rack, found a large scale physiographic map of the area under his consideration. He took it to a table and spent half an hour in deep concentration.

He rose, replaced the map, sauntered through the lobby and out the side entrance. The pilot who had flown him the previous evening rose to his feet smartly. "Good evening, Mr. Ridolph. Intending another ride?"

"As a matter of fact, I am," Magnus Ridolph admitted. "Are you free?"

"In a moment, as soon as I turn in my day's report."

Ridolph looked thoughtfully after the pilot's hurrying figure. He quietly stepped around to the front entrance. From the vantage of the open door he watched the pilot approach Bruce Holpers and speak hastily.

Holpers ran a lank white hand through his red hair, gave a series of nervous instructions. The pilot nodded sagely, turned away. Magnus Ridolph returned by the route he had come.

He found the pilot waiting beside the ship. "I thought I had better notify Clark that I was coming," said Ridolph breezily. "In case the car broke down, or there were any accident, he would understand the situation and know where to look for me."

The pilot's hands hesitated on the controls. Magnus Ridolph said, "Is there game of any sort on Kokod?"

"No sir, none whatever."

"A pity. I am carrying with me a small target pistol with which I had hoped to bag a trophy or two...Perhaps I'll be able to acquire one or two of the native weapons."

"That's quite unlikely, sir."

"In any case," said Magnus Ridolph cheerily, "you might be mistaken, so I will hold my weapon ready."

The pilot looked straight ahead.

Magnus Ridolph climbed into the back seat. "To the Control office, then."

"Yes, Mr. Ridolph."

IV

Everley Clark greeted his visitor cautiously; when Ridolph sat back in a basket chair, Clark's eyes went everywhere in the room but to those of his guest.

Magnus Ridolph lit an *aromatique*. "Those shields on the wall are native artifacts, I presume?"

"Yes," said Clark quickly. "Each tumble has its distinct colors and insignia."

"To Earthly eyes, the patterns seem fortuitous, but naturally and inevitably Kokod symbology is unique...A magnificent display. Does the collection have a price?"

Clark looked doubtfully at the shields. "I'd hate to let them go—although I suppose I could get others. These shields are hard to come by; each requires many thousand hours of work. They make the lacquer by a rather painstaking method, grinding pigment into a vehicle prepared from the boiled-down dead."

Ridolph nodded. "So that's how they dispose of the corpses."

"Yes; it's quite a ritual."

"About those shields—would you take ten thousand munits?"

Clark's face mirrored indecision. Abruptly he lit a cigarette. "Yes, I'd have to take ten thousand munits; I couldn't afford to refuse."

"It would be a shame to deprive you of a possession you obviously value so highly," said Magnus Ridolph. He examined the backs of his hands critically. "If ten thousand munits means so much to you, why do you not gamble at the inn? Surely with your knowledge of Kokod ways, your special information..."

Clark shook his head. "You can't beat that kind of odds. It's a sucker's game, betting at the inn."

"Hmm." Magnus Ridolph frowned. "It might be possible to influence the course of a battle. Tomorrow, for instance, the Vine Hill and Roaring Cape Tumbles engage each other, on Pink Stone Table, and the odds against Roaring Cape seem quite attractive."

Clark shook his head. "You'd lose your shirt betting on Roaring Cape. All their veterans went in the Pyrite campaign."

Magnus Ridolph said thoughtfully, "The Roaring Cape might win, if they received a small measure of assistance."

Clark's pink face expanded in alarm like a trick mask. "I'm an officer of the Commonwealth! I couldn't be party to a thing like that! It's unthinkable!"

Magnus Ridolph said judiciously, "Certainly the proposal is not one to enter upon hastily; it must be carefully considered. In a sense, the Commonwealth might be best served by the ousting of Shadow Valley Inn from the planet, or at least the present management. Financial depletion is as good a weapon as any. If, incidentally, we were to profit, not an eyebrow in the universe could be justifiably raised. Especially since the part that you might play in the achievement would be carefully veiled..."

Clark shoved his hands deep in his pockets, stared a long moment at Magnus Ridolph. "I could not conceivably put myself in the position of siding with one tumble against another. If I did so, what little influence I have on Kokod would go up in smoke."

Magnus Ridolph shook his head indulgently. "I fear you imagine the two of us carrying lances, marching in step with the warriors, fighting in the first ranks. No, no, my friend, I assure you I intend nothing quite so broad."

"Well," snapped Clark, "just what do you intend?"

"It occurred to me that if we set out a few pellets of a sensitive explosive, such as fulminate of mercury, no one could hold us responsible if tomorrow the Vine Hill armies blundered upon them, and were thereby thrown into confusion."

"How would we know where to set out these pellets? I should think—"

Magnus Ridolph made an easy gesture. "I profess an amateur's interest in military strategy; I will assume responsibility for that phase of the plan."

"But I have no fulminate of mercury," cried Clark, "no explosive of any kind!"

"But you do have a laboratory?"

Clark assented reluctantly. "Rather a makeshift affair."

"Your reagents possibly include fuming nitric acid and iodine?"

"Well—yes."

"Then to work. Nothing could suit our purpose better than nitrogen iodide."

The following afternoon Magnus Ridolph sat in the outdoor café overlooking the vista of Shadow Valley. His right hand clasped an eggshell goblet of Methedeon wine, his left held a mild cigar. Turning his head, he observed the approach of Julius See and, a few steps behind, like a gaunt red-headed ghost, his partner Bruce Holpers.

See's face was compressed into layers: a smear of black hair, creased forehead, barred eyebrows, eyes like a single dark slit, pale upper lip, mouth, wide sallow chin. Magnus Ridolph nodded affably. "Good evening gentlemen."

See came to a halt, as two steps later, did Bruce Holpers.

"Perhaps you can tell me the outcome of today's battle?" asked Magnus Ridolph. "I indulged myself in a small wager, breaking the habit of many years, but so far I have not learned whether the gods of chance have favored me."

"Well, well," said See throatily. "'The gods of chance' you call yourself."

Magnus Ridolph turned him a glance of limpid inquiry. "Mr. See, you appear disturbed; I hope nothing is wrong?"

"Nothing special, Ridolph. We had a middling bad day—but they average out with the good ones."

"Unfortunate…I take it, then, that the favorite won? If so, my little wager has been wiped out."

"Your little 25,000 munit wager, eh? And half a dozen other 25,000 munit wagers placed at your suggestion?"

Magnus Ridolph stroked his beard soberly. "I believe I did mention that I thought the odds against Roaring Cape interesting, but now you tell me that Vine Hill has swept the field."

Bruce Holpers uttered a dry cackle. See said harshly, "Come off it, Ridolph. I suppose you're completely unaware that a series of mysterious explosions—" "Land mines," interrupted Holpers, "that's what they were." "—threw Vine Hill enough off stride so that Roaring Cape mopped up Pink Stone Table with them."

Magnus Ridolph sat up.

"Is that right, indeed? Then I have won after all!"

Julius See became suddenly silky, and Bruce Holpers, teetering on heel and toe, glanced skyward. "Unfortunately, Mr. Ridolph, so many persons had placed large bets on Roaring Cape that on meeting the odds, we find ourselves short on cash. We'll have to ask you to take your winnings out in board and room."

"But gentlemen!" protested Magnus Ridolph. "A hundred thousand munits! I'll be here until doomsday!"

See shook his head. "Not at our special Ridolph rates. The next packet is due in five days. Your bill comes to 20,000 munits a day. Exactly 100,000 munits."

"I'm afraid I find your humor a trifle heavy," said Magnus Ridolph frostily.

"It wasn't intended to make you laugh," said See. "Only us. I'm getting quite a kick out of it. How about you, Bruce?"

"Ha, ha, ha," laughed Holpers.

Magnus Ridolph rose to his feet. "There remains to me the classical recourse. I shall leave your exorbitant premises."

See permitted a grin to widen his lips. "Where are you going to leave to?"

"He's going to Roaring Cape Tumble," snickered Holpers. "They owe him a lot."

"In connection with the hundred thousand munits owed me, I'll take a note, an IOU. Oddly enough, a hundred thousand munits is almost exactly what I lost in the Outer Empire Realty and Investment failure."

See grinned sourly. "Forget it, Ridolph, give it up—an angle that didn't pay off."

Magnus Ridolph bowed, marched away. See and Holpers stood looking after him. Holpers made an adenoidal sound. "Think he'll move out?"

See grunted. "There's no reason why he should. He's not getting the hundred thousand anyway; he'd be smarter sitting tight."

"I hope he does go; he makes me nervous. Another deal like today would wipe us out. Six hundred thousand munits—a lot of scratch to go in ten minutes."

"We'll get it back…Maybe we can rig a battle or two ourselves."

Holpers' long face dropped, and his teeth showed. "I'm not so sure that's a good idea. First thing you know Commonwealth Control would be—"

"Pah!" spat See. "What's Control going to do about it? Clark has all the fire and guts of a Leghorn pullet."

"Yes, but—"

"Just leave it to me."

They returned to the lobby. The desk clerk made an urgent motion. "Mr. Ridolph has just checked out! I don't understand where—"

See cut him off with a brusque motion. "He can camp under a stele for all I care."

Magnus Ridolph sat back in the most comfortable of Everley Clark's armchairs and lit a cigarette. Clark watched him with an expression at once wary and obstinate. "We have gained a tactical victory," said Magnus Ridolph, "and suffered a strategic defeat."

Everley Clark knit his brows uneasily. "I don't quite follow you. I should think—"

"We have diminished the financial power of Shadow Valley Inn, and hence, done serious damage. But the blow was not decisive and the syndicate is still viable. I was unable to collect my hundred thousand munits, and also have been forced from the scene of maximum engagement. By this token we may fairly consider that our minimum objectives have not been gained."

"Well," said Clark, "I know it hurts to have to admit defeat, but we've done our best and no one can do more. Considering my position, perhaps it's just as well that—"

"If conditions were to be allowed to rest on the present basis," said Magnus Ridolph, "there might be reason for some slight relaxation. But I fear that See and Holpers have been too thoroughly agitated by their losses to let the matter drop."

Everley Clark eyed Magnus Ridolph in perturbation. "But what can they do? Surely I never—"

Magnus Ridolph shook his head gravely. "I must admit that both See and Holpers accused me of setting off the explosions which routed the Vine Hill Tumble. Admission of guilt would have been ingenuous; naturally I maintained that I had done nothing of the sort. I claimed that I had no opportunity to do so, and further, that the Ecologic Examiner aboard the Hesperornis who checked my luggage would swear that I had no chemicals whatsoever among my effects. I believe that I made a convincing protestation."

Everley Clark clenched his fists in alarm, hissed through his teeth.

Magnus Ridolph, looking thoughtfully across the room, went on. "I fear that they will ask themselves the obvious questions: 'Who has Magnus Ridolph most intimately consorted with, since his arrival on Kokod?' 'Who, besides Ridolph, has expressed disapproval of Shadow Valley Inn?'"

Everley Clark rose to his feet, paced back and forth. Ridolph continued in a dispassionate voice: "I fear that they will include these questions and whatever answers come to their minds in the complaint which they are preparing for the Chief Inspector at Methedeon."

Clark slumped into a chair, sat staring glassily at Magnus Ridolph. "Why did I let you talk me into this?" he asked hollowly.

Magnus Ridolph rose to his feet in his turn, paced slowly, tugging at his beard. "Certainly, events have not taken the trend we would have chosen, but strategists, amateur or otherwise, must expect occasional setbacks."

"Setbacks!" bawled Clark. "I'll be ruined! Disgraced! Drummed out of the Control!"

"A good strategist is necessarily flexible," mused Magnus Ridolph. "Beyond question, we now must alter our thinking; our primary objective becomes saving you from disgrace, expulsion, and possible prosecution."

Clark ran his hands across his face. "But—what can we do?"

"Very little, I fear," Magnus Ridolph said frankly. He puffed a moment on his cigarette, shook his head doubtfully. "There is one line of attack which might prove fruitful…Yes, I think I see a ray of light."

"How? In what way? You're not planning to confess?"

"No," said Magnus Ridolph. "We gain little, if anything, by that ruse. Our only hope is to discredit Shadow Valley Inn. If we can demonstrate that they do not have the best interests of the Kokod natives at heart, I think we can go a long way toward weakening their allegations."

"That might well be, but—"

"If we could obtain iron-clad proof, for instance, that Holpers and See are callously using their position to wreak physical harm upon the natives, I think you might consider yourself vindicated."

"I suppose so…But doesn't the idea seem—well, impractical? See and Holpers have always fallen over backwards to avoid anything of that sort."

"So I would imagine. Er, what is the native term for Shadow Valley Inn?"

"Big Square Tumble, they call it."

"As the idea suggests itself to me, we must arrange that a war is conducted on the premises of Shadow Valley Inn, that Holpers and See are required to take forcible measures against the warriors!"

V

Everley Clark shook his head. "Devilish hard. You don't quite get the psychology of these tribes. They'll fight till they fall apart to capture the rallying standard of another tumble—that's a sapling from the sacred stele of course—but they won't be dictated to, or led or otherwise influenced."

"Well, well," said Magnus Ridolph. "In that case, your position is hopeless." He came to a halt before Clark's collection of shields. "Let us talk of pleasanter matters."

Everley Clark gave no sign that he had heard.

Magnus Ridolph stroked one of the shields with reverent fingertips. "Remarkable technique, absolutely unique in my experience. I assume that this rusty orange is one of the ochers?"

Everley Clark made an ambiguous sound.

"A truly beautiful display," said Magnus Ridolph. "I suppose there's no doubt that—if worse comes to worst in our little business—you will be allowed to decorate your cell at the Regional Penitentiary as you desire."

Everley Clark said in a thick voice, "Do you think they'll go that far?"

Ridolph considered. "I sincerely hope not. I don't see how we can prevent it unless—" he held up a finger "—unless—"

"What?" croaked Clark.

"It is farcically simple; I wonder at our own obtuseness."

"What? What? For Heaven's sake, man—"

"I conceive one certain means by which the warriors can be persuaded to fight at Shadow Valley Inn."

Everley Clark's face fell. "Oh. Well, how, then?"

"Shadow Valley Inn or Big Square Tumble, if you like, must challenge the Kokod warriors to a contest of arms."

Everley Clark's expression became more bewildered than ever. "But that's out of the question. Certainly Holpers and See would never..."

Magnus Ridolph rose to his feet. "Come," he said, with decision. "We will act on their behalf."

Clark and Magnus Ridolph walked down Shell Strand. On their right the placid blue-black ocean transformed itself into surf of mingled meringue and whipped-cream; on the left bulked the Hidden Hills. Behind towered the magnificent stele of the Shell Strand Tumble; ahead soared the almost equally impressive stele of the Sea Stone Tumble, toward which they bent their steps. Corps of young warriors drilled along the beach; veterans of a hundred battles who had grown stiff, hard and knobby came down from the forest bearing faggots of lance-stock. At the door to the tumble, infant warriors scampered in the dirt like rats.

Clark said huskily, "I don't like this, I don't like it a bit...If it ever gets out—"

"Is such a supposition logically tenable?" asked Magnus Ridolph. "You are the only living man who speaks the Kokod language."

"Suppose there is killing—slaughter?"

"I hardly think it likely."

"It's not impossible. And think of these little warriors—they'll be bearing the brunt—"

Magnus Ridolph said patiently, "We have discussed these points at length."

Clark muttered, "I'll go through with it...But God forgive us both if—"

"Come, come," exclaimed Magnus Ridolph. "Let us approach the matter with confidence; apologizing in advance to your deity hardly maximizes our morale...Now, what is protocol at arranging a war?"

Clark pointed out a dangling wooden plate painted with one of the traditional Kokod patterns. "That's the Charter Board: all I need to do is—well, watch me."

He strode up to the board, took a lance from the hands of a blinking warrior, smartly struck the object. It resonated a dull musical note.

Clark stepped back, and through his nose passed the bagpipe syllables of the Kokod language.

From the door of the tumble stepped a dozen blank-faced warriors, listening attentively.

Clark wound up his speech, turned, scuffed dirt toward the magnificent Sea Stone stele.

The warriors watched impassively. From within the stele came a torrent of syllables. Clark replied at length, then turned on his heel and rejoined Magnus Ridolph. His forehead was damp. "Well, that's that. It's all set. Tomorrow morning at Big Square Tumble."

"Excellent," said Magnus Ridolph briskly. "Now to Shell Strand Tumble, then Rock River, and next Rainbow Cleft."

Clark groaned. "You'll have the entire planet at odds."

"Exactly," said Magnus Ridolph. "After our visit to Rainbow Cleft, you can drop me off near Shadow Valley Inn, where I have some small business."

Clark darted him a suspicious side-glance. "What kind of business?"

"We must be practical," said Magnus Ridolph. "One of the necessary appurtenances to a party at war on Kokod is a rallying standard, a sacred sapling, a focus of effort for the opposing force. Since we can expect neither Holpers nor See to provide one, I must see to the matter myself."

Ridolph strolled up Shadow Valley, approached the hangar where the inn's aircraft were housed. From the shadow of one of the fantastic Kokod trees, he counted six vehicles: three carry-alls, two air-cars like the one which had conveyed him originally to the Control station, and a sleek red sportster evidently the personal property of either See or Holpers.

Neither the hangar-men nor the pilots were in evidence; it might well be their dinner hour. Magnus Ridolph sauntered carelessly forward, whistling an air currently being heard along far-off boulevards.

He cut his whistle off sharply, moved at an accelerated rate. Fastidiously protecting his hands with a bit of rag, he snapped the repair panels from each of the observation cars, made a swift abstraction from each, did likewise for the air-cars. At the sleek sportster he paused, inspected the lines critically.

"An attractive vehicle," he said to himself, "one which might creditably serve the purposes for which I intend it."

He slid back the door, looked inside. The starter key was absent.

Steps sounded behind him. "Hey," said a rough voice, "what are you doing with Mr. See's car?"

Magnus Ridolph withdrew without haste.

"Offhand," he said, "what would you estimate the value of this vehicle?"

The hangarman paused, glowering and suspicious. "Too much not to be taken care of."

Magnus Ridolph nodded. "Thirty thousand munits, possibly."

"Thirty thousand on Earth. This is Kokod."

"I'm thinking of offering See a hundred thousand munits."

The hangarman blinked. "He'd be crazy not to take it."

"I suppose so," sighed Magnus Ridolph. "But first, I wanted to satisfy myself as to the craft's mechanical condition. I fear it has been neglected."

The hangarman snorted in indignation. "Not on your life."

Magnus Ridolph frowned. "That tube is certainly spitting. I can tell by the patina along the enamel."

"No such thing!" roared the hangarman. "That tube flows like a dream."

Ridolph shook his head. "I can't offer See good money for a defective vehicle...He'll be angry to lose the sale."

The hangarman's tone changed. "I tell you, that tube's good as gold...Wait, I'll show you."

He pulled a key-ring from his pocket, plugged it into the starter socket. The car quivered free of the ground, eager for flight. "See? Just what I told you."

Magnus Ridolph said doubtfully. "It seems to be working fairly well now...You get on the telephone and tell Mr. See that I am taking his car for a trial spin, a final check..."

The mechanic looked dumbly at Magnus Ridolph, slowly turned to the speaker on the wall.

Magnus Ridolph jumped into the seat. The mechanic's voice was loud. "The gentleman that's buying your boat is giving it the once-over; don't let him feed you no line about a bum tube; the ship is running like oil down a four mile bore, don't take nothing else...What?...Sure he's here; he said so himself...A little schoolteacher guy with a white beard like a nanny-goat..." The sound from the telephone caused him to jump back sharply. Anxiously, he turned to look where he had left Magnus Ridolph and Julius See's sleek red air-car.

Both had disappeared.

Mrs. Chaim roused her peacock-shaped friend Mrs. Borgage rather earlier than usual. "Hurry, Altamira; we've been so late these last few mornings, we've missed the best seats in the observation car."

Mrs. Borgage obliged by hastening her toilet; in short order the two ladies appeared in the lobby. By a peculiar coincidence both wore costumes of dark green, a color which each thought suited the other not at all. They paused by the announcement of the day's war in order to check the odds, then turned into the dining room.

They ate a hurried breakfast, set out for the loading platform. Mrs. Borgage, pausing to catch her breath and enjoy the freshness of the morning, glanced toward the roof of the inn. Mrs. Chaim rather impatiently looked over her shoulder. "Whatever are you staring at, Altamira?"

Mrs. Borgage pointed. "It's that unpleasant little man Ridolph...I can't fathom what he's up to...He seems to be fixing some sort of branch to the roof."

Mrs. Chaim sniffed. "I thought the management had turned him out."

"Isn't that Mr. See's air-car on the roof behind him?"

"I really couldn't say," replied Mrs. Chaim. "I know very little of such things." She turned away toward the loading platform, and Mrs. Borgage followed.

Once more they met interruption; this time in the form of the pilot. His clothes were disarranged; his face had suffered scratching and contusion. Running wild-eyed, he careened into the two green-clad ladies, disengaged himself and continued without apology.

Mrs. Chaim bridled in outrage. "Well, I never!" She turned to look after the pilot. "Has the man gone mad?"

Mrs. Borgage, peering ahead to learn the source of the pilot's alarm, uttered a sharp cry.

"What is it?" asked Mrs. Chaim irritatedly.

Mrs. Borgage clasped her arm with bony fingers. "Look..."

VI

During the subsequent official investigation, Commonwealth Control Agent Everley Clark transcribed the following eye-witness account:

"I am Joe 234, Leg-leader of the Fifteenth Brigade, the Fanatics, in the service of the indomitable Shell Strand Tumble.

"We are accustomed to the ruses of Topaz Tumble and the desperate subtleties of Star Throne; hence the ambush prepared by the giant warriors of Big Square Tumble took us not at all by surprise.

"Approaching by Primary Formation 17, we circled the flat space occupied by several flying contrivances, where we flushed out a patrol spy. We thrashed him with our lances, and he fled back toward his own forces.

"Continuing, we encountered a first line of defense consisting of two rather ineffectual warriors accoutred in garments of green cloth. These we beat, also, according to Convention 22, in force during the day. Uttering terrible cries, the two warriors retreated, luring us toward prepared positions inside the tumble itself. High on the roof the standard of Big Square Tumble rose, plain to see. No deception there, at least! Our strategic problem assumed a clear form: how best to beat down resistance and win to the roof.

"Frontal assault was decided upon; the signal to advance was given. We of the Fifteenth were first past the outer defense—a double panel of thick glass which we broke with rocks. Inside we met a spirited defense which momentarily threw us back.

"At this juncture occurred a diversion in the form of troops from the Rock River Tumble, which, as we now know, the warriors of the Big Square Tumble had rashly challenged for the same day. The Rock River warriors entered by a row of flimsy doors facing the mountain, and at this time the Big Square defenders violated Convention 22, which requires that the enemy be subdued by blows of the lance. Flagrantly they hurled glass cups and goblets, and by immemorial usage we were allowed to retaliate in kind.

"At the failure of this tactic, the defending warriors withdrew to an inner bastion, voicing their war-cries.

"The siege began in earnest; and now the Big Square warriors began to pay the price of their arrogance. Not only had they pitted themselves against Shell Strand and Rock River, but they likewise had challenged the redoubtable Rainbow Cleft and Sea Stone, conquerors of Rose Slope and Dark Fissure. The Sea Stone warriors, led by their Throw-away Legion, poured through a secret rear-entrance, while the Rainbow Cleft Special Vanguard occupied the Big Square main council hall.

"A terrible battle raged for several minutes in a room designed for the preparation of nourishments, and again the Big Square warriors broke code by throwing fluids, pastes, and powders—a remission which the alert Shell Strand warriors swiftly copied.

"I led the Fanatic Fifteenth outside, hoping to gain exterior access to the roof, and thereby win the Big Square standard. The armies of Shell Strand, Sea Stone, Rock River and Rainbow Cleft now completely surrounded Big Square Tumble, a magnificent sight which shall live in my memory till at last I lay down my lance.

"In spite of our efforts, the honor of gaining the enemy standard went to a daredevil squad from Sea Stone, which scaled a tree to the roof and so bore away the trophy. The defenders, ignorant of, or ignoring the fact that the standard had been taken, broke the code yet again, this time by using tremendous blasts of water. The next time Shell Strand wars with Big Square Tumble we shall insist on one of the Conventions allowing any and all weapons; otherwise we place ourselves at a disadvantage.

"Victorious, our army, together with the troops of Sea Stone, Rock River and Rainbow Cleft, assembled in the proper formations and marched off to our home tumbles. Even as we departed, the great Black Comet Tumble dropped from the sky to vomit further warriors for Big Square. However, there was no pursuit, and unmolested we returned to the victory rituals."

Captain Bussey of the Phoenix Line packet *Archaeornyx*, which had arrived as the Kokod warriors marched away, surveyed the wreckage with utter astonishment. "What in God's name happened to you?"

Julius See stood panting, his forehead clammy with sweat. "Get me guns," he cried hoarsely. "Get me a blaster; I'll wipe out every damn hive on the planet…"

Holpers came loping up, arms flapping the air. "They've completely demolished us; you should see the lobby, the kitchen, the day rooms! A shambles—"

Captain Bussey shook his head in bewilderment. "Why in the world should they attack you? They're supposed to be a peaceable race…except toward each other, of course."

"Well, something got into them," said See, still breathing hard. "They came at us like tigers—beating us with their damn little sticks…I finally washed them out with fire-hoses."

"What about your guests?" asked Captain Bussey in sudden curiosity.

See shrugged. "I don't know what happened to them. A bunch ran off up the valley, smack into another army. I understand they got beat up as good as those that stayed."

"We couldn't even escape in our aircraft," complained Holpers. "Not one of them would start…"

A mild voice interrupted. "Mr. See, I have decided against purchasing your air-car, and have returned it to the hangar."

See slowly turned, the baleful aura of his thoughts almost tangible. "You, Ridolph…I'm beginning to see daylight…"

"I beg your pardon?"

"Come on, spill it!" See took a threatening step forward. Captain Bussey said, "Careful, See, watch your temper." See ignored him. "What's your part in all this, Ridolph?"

Magnus Ridolph shook his head in bewilderment. "I'm completely at a loss. I rather imagine that the natives learned of your gambling on events they considered important, and decided to take punitive steps."

The ornamental charabanc from the ship rolled up; among the passengers was a woman of notable bust, correctly tinted, massaged, coiffed, scented and decorated. "Ah!" said Magnus Ridolph. "Mrs. Chickering! Charming!"

"I could stay away no longer," said Mrs. Chickering. "I had to know how—our business was proceeding."

Julius See leaned forward curiously. "What kind of business do you mean?"

Mrs. Chickering turned him a swift contemptuous glance; then her attention was attracted by two women who came hobbling from the direction of the inn. She gasped, "Olga! Altamira! What on Earth—"

"Don't stand there gasping," snapped Mrs. Chaim. "Get us clothes. Those frightful savages tore us to shreds."

Mrs. Chickering turned in confusion to Magnus Ridolph. "Just what has happened! Surely you can't have—"

Magnus Ridolph cleared his throat. "Mrs. Chickering, a word with you aside." He drew her out of earshot of the others. "Mrs. Chaim and Mrs. Borgage—they are friends of yours?"

Mrs. Chickering cast an anxious glance over her shoulder. "I can't understand the situation at all," she muttered feverishly. "Mrs. Chaim is the president of the Woman's League and Mrs. Borgage is treasurer...I can't understand them running around with their clothing in shreds..."

Magnus Ridolph said candidly, "Well, Mrs. Chickering, in carrying out your instructions, I allowed scope to the natural combativeness of the natives, and perhaps they—"

"Martha," came Mrs. Chaim's grating voice close at hand, "what is your connection with this man? I have reason to suspect that he is mixed up in this terrible attack...look at him!" Her voice rose furiously. "They haven't laid a finger on him! And the rest of us—"

Martha Chickering licked her lips. "Well, Olga dear, this is Magnus Ridolph. In accordance with last month's resolution, we hired him to close down the gambling here at the inn."

Magnus Ridolph said in his suavest tones, "Following which, Mrs. Chaim and Mrs. Borgage naturally thought it best to come out and study the situation at first hand; am I right?"

Mrs. Chaim and Mrs. Borgage glared. Mrs. Chaim said, "If you think, Martha Chickering, that the Woman's League will in any way recognize this rogue—"

"My dear Mrs. Chaim," protested Magnus Ridolph.

"But, Olga—I promised him a thousand munits a week!"

Magnus Ridolph waved his hand airily. "My dear Mrs. Chickering, I prefer that any sums due me be distributed among worthy charities. I have profited during my short stay here—"

"See!" came Captain Bussey's voice. "For God's sake, man, control yourself!"

Magnus Ridolph, turning, found See struggling in the grasp of Captain Bussey. "Try and collect!" See cried out to Magnus Ridolph. He angrily thrust Captain Bussey's arms aside, stood with hands clenching and unclenching. "Just try and collect!"

"My dear Mr. See, I have already collected."

"You've done nothing of the sort—and if I catch you in my boat again, I'll break your scrawny little neck!"

Magnus Ridolph held up his hand. "The hundred thousand munits I wrote off immediately; however, there were six other bets which I placed by proxy; these were paid, and my share of the winnings came to well over three hundred thousand munits. Actually, I regard this sum as return of the capital which I placed with the Outer Empire Investment and Realty Society, plus a reasonable profit. Everything considered, it was a remunerative as well as instructive investment."

"Ridolph," muttered See, "one of these days—"

Mrs. Chaim shouldered forward. "Did I hear you say 'Outer Empire Realty and Investment Society'?"

Magnus Ridolph nodded. "I believe that Mr. See and Mr. Holpers were responsible officials of the concern."

Mrs. Chaim took two steps forward. See frowned uneasily; Bruce Holpers began to edge away. "Come back here!" cried Mrs. Chaim. "I have a few words to say before I have you arrested."

Magnus Ridolph turned to Captain Bussey. "You return to Methedeon on schedule, I assume?"

"Yes," said Captain Bussey dryly.

Magnus Ridolph nodded. "I think I will go aboard at once, since there will be considerable demand for passage."

"As you wish," said Captain Bussey.

"I believe No. 12 is your best cabin?"

"I believe so," said Captain Bussey.

"Then kindly regard Cabin No. 12 as booked."

"Very well, Mr. Ridolph."

Magnus Ridolph looked up the mountainside. "I noticed Mr. Pilby running along the ridge a few minutes ago. I think it would be a real kindness if he were notified that the war is over."

"I think so too," said Captain Bussey. They looked around the group. Mrs. Chaim was still engaged with Julius See and Bruce Holpers. Mrs. Borgage was displaying her bruises to Mrs. Chickering. No one seemed disposed to act on Magnus Ridolph's suggestion.

Magnus Ridolph shrugged, climbed the gangway into the *Archaeornyx.* "Well, no matter. In due course he will very likely come by himself."

AFTERWORD TO "THE KOKOD WARRIORS"

It hasn't come easy. It's been a matter of plugging away, finding what I can do, and then trying to do it properly. I'm not one of these chaps who was an instant success. There was a long period in which I wrote a lot of junk, as an apprentice, learning my trade. I found out I was no good at gadget stories, or at least they were very boring to me, and I found out that I didn't enjoy writing whimsy, and I finally blundered into this thing which I keep on doing, which is essentially a history of the human future.

—Jack Vance 1983

THE OVERWORLD

On the heights above the river Xzan, at the site of certain ancient ruins, Iucounu the Laughing Magician had built a manse to his private taste: an eccentric structure of steep gables, balconies, sky-walks, cupolas, together with three spiral green glass towers through which the red sunlight shone in twisted glints and peculiar colors.

Behind the manse and across the valley, low hills rolled away like dunes to the limit of vision. The sun projected shifting crescents of black shadow; otherwise the hills were unmarked, empty, solitary. The Xzan, rising in the Old Forest to the east of Almery, passed below, then three leagues to the west made junction with the Scaum. Here was Azenomei, a town old beyond memory, notable now only for its fair, which attracted folk from all the region. At Azenomei Fair Cugel had established a booth for the sale of talismans.

Cugel was a man of many capabilities, with a disposition at once flexible and pertinacious. He was long of leg, deft of hand, light of finger, soft of tongue. His hair was the blackest of black fur, growing low down his forehead, coving sharply back above his eyebrows. His darting eye, long inquisitive nose and droll mouth gave his somewhat lean and bony face an expression of vivacity, candor, and affability. He had known many vicissitudes, gaining therefrom a suppleness, a fine discretion, a mastery of both bravado and stealth. Coming into the possession of an ancient lead coffin—after discarding the contents—he had formed a number of leaden lozenges. These, stamped with appropriate seals and runes, he offered for sale at the Azenomei Fair.

Unfortunately for Cugel, not twenty paces from his booth a certain Fianosther had established a larger booth with articles of greater variety and more obvious efficacy, so that whenever Cugel halted a passerby to enlarge upon the merits of his merchandise, the passerby would like as not display an article purchased from Fianosther and go his way.

On the third day of the fair Cugel had disposed of only four periapts, at prices barely above the cost of the lead itself, while Fianosther was hard put to serve all his customers. Hoarse from bawling futile inducements, Cugel closed down his booth and approached Fianosther's place of trade, in order to inspect the mode of construction and the fastenings at the door.

Fianosther, observing, beckoned him to approach. "Enter, my friend, enter. How goes your trade?"

"In all candor, not too well," said Cugel. "I am both perplexed and disappointed, for my talismans are not obviously useless."

"I can resolve your perplexity," said Fianosther. "Your booth occupies the site of the old gibbet, and has absorbed unlucky essences. But I thought to notice you examining the manner in which the timbers of my booth are joined. You will obtain a better view from within, but first I must shorten the chain of the captive erb which roams the premises during the night."

"No need," said Cugel. "My interest was cursory."

"As to the disappointment you suffer," Fianosther went on, "it need not persist. Observe these shelves. You will note that my stock is seriously depleted."

Cugel acknowledged as much. "How does this concern me?"

Fianosther pointed across the way to a man wearing garments of black. This man was small, yellow of skin, bald as a stone. His eyes resembled knots in a plank; his mouth was wide and curved in a grin of chronic mirth. "There stands Iucounu the Laughing Magician," said Fianosther. "In a short time he will come into my booth and attempt to buy a particular red libram, the casebook of Dibarcas Maior, who studied under Great Phandaal. My price is higher than he will pay, but he is a patient man, and will remonstrate for at least three hours. During this time his manse stands untenanted. It contains a vast collection of thaumaturgical artifacts, instruments, and activants, as well as curiosa, talismans, amulets and librams. I am anxious to purchase such items. Need I say more?"

"This is all very well," said Cugel, "but would Iucounu leave his manse without guard or attendant?"

Fianosther held wide his hands. "Why not? Who would dare steal from Iucounu the Laughing Magician?"

"Precisely this thought deters me," Cugel replied. "I am a man of resource, but not insensate recklessness."

"There is wealth to be gained," stated Fianosther. "Dazzles and displays, marvels beyond worth, as well as charms, puissances, and elixirs. But remember, I urge nothing, I counsel nothing; if you are apprehended, you have only heard me exclaiming at the wealth of Iucounu the Laughing Magician! But here he comes. Quick: turn your back so that he may not see your face. Three hours he will be here, so much I guarantee!"

Iucounu entered the booth, and Cugel bent to examine a bottle containing a pickled homunculus.

"Greetings, Iucounu!" called Fianosther. "Why have you delayed? I have refused munificent offers for a certain red libram, all on your account! And here—note this casket! It was found in a crypt near the site of old Karkod. It is yet sealed and who knows what wonder it may contain? My price is a modest twelve thousand terces."

"Interesting," murmured Iucounu. "The inscription—let me see…Hmm. Yes, it is authentic. The casket contains calcined fish-bone, which was used throughout Grand Motholam as a purgative. It is worth perhaps ten or twelve terces as a curio. I own caskets aeons older, dating back to the Age of Glow."

Cugel sauntered to the door, gained the street, where he paced back and forth, considering every detail of the proposal as explicated by Fianosther. Superficially the matter seemed reasonable: here was Iucounu; there was the manse, bulging with encompassed wealth. Certainly no harm could result from simple reconnaissance. Cugel set off eastward along the banks of the Xzan.

The twisted turrets of green glass rose against the dark blue sky, scarlet sunlight engaging itself in the volutes. Cugel paused, made a careful appraisal of the countryside. The Xzan flowed past without a sound. Nearby, half-concealed among black poplars, pale green larch, drooping pall-willow, was a village—a dozen stone huts inhabited by barge-men and tillers of the river terraces: folk engrossed in their own concerns.

Cugel studied the approach to the manse: a winding way paved with dark brown tile. Finally he decided that the more frank his approach the less complex need be his explanations, if such were demanded. He began the climb up the hillside, and Iucounu's manse reared above him.

Gaining the courtyard, he paused to search the landscape. Across the river hills rolled away into the dimness, as far as the eye could reach.

Cugel marched briskly to the door, rapped, but evoked no response. He considered. If Iucounu, like Fianosther, maintained a guardian beast, it might be tempted to utter a sound if provoked. Cugel called out in various tones: growling, mewing, yammering.

Silence within.

He walked gingerly to a window and peered into a hall draped in pale gray, containing only a tabouret on which, under a glass bell jar, lay a dead rodent. Cugel circled the manse, investigating each window as he came to it, and finally reached the great hall of the ancient castle. Nimbly he climbed the rough stones, leapt across to one of Iucounu's fanciful parapets and in a trice had gained access to the manse.

He stood in a bed chamber. On a dais six gargoyles supporting a couch turned heads to glare at the intrusion. With two stealthy strides Cugel gained the arch which opened into an outer chamber. Here the walls were green and the furnishings black and pink. He left the room for a balcony circling a central chamber, light streaming through oriels high in the walls. Below were cases, chests, shelves and racks containing all manner of objects: Iucounu's marvelous collection.

Cugel stood poised, tense as a bird, but the quality of the silence reassured him: the silence of an empty place. Still, he trespassed upon the property of Iucounu the Laughing Magician, and vigilance was appropriate.

Cugel strode down a sweep of circular stairs into a great hall. He stood enthralled, paying Iucounu the tribute of unstinted wonder. But his time was limited; he must rob swiftly and be on his way. Out came his sack; he roved the hall, fastidiously selecting those objects of small bulk and great value: a small pot with antlers, which emitted clouds of remarkable gases when the prongs were tweaked; an ivory horn through which sounded voices from the past; a small stage where costumed imps stood ready to perform comic antics; an object like a cluster of crystal grapes, each affording a blurred view into one of the demon-worlds; a baton sprouting sweetmeats of assorted flavor; an ancient ring engraved with runes; a black stone surrounded by nine zones of impalpable color. He passed by hundreds of jars of powders and liquids, likewise forbore from the vessels containing preserved heads. Now he came to shelves stacked with volumes, folios and librams, where he selected with care, taking for preference those bound in purple velvet, Phandaal's characteristic color. He likewise selected folios of drawings and ancient maps, and the disturbed leather exuded a musty odor.

He circled back to the front of the hall past a case displaying a score of small metal chests, sealed with corroded bands of great age. Cugel selected three at random; they were unwontedly heavy. He passed by several massive engines whose purpose he would have liked to explore, but time was advancing, and best he should be on his way, back to Azenomei and the booth of Fianosther...

Cugel frowned. In many respects the prospect seemed impractical. Fianosther would hardly choose to pay full value for his goods, or, more accurately, Iucounu's goods. It might be well to bury a certain proportion of the loot in an isolated place...Here was an alcove Cugel had not previously noted. A soft light welled like water against the crystal pane, which separated alcove from hall. A niche to the rear displayed a complicated object of great charm. As best Cugel could distinguish, it seemed a miniature carousel on which rode a dozen beautiful dolls of seeming vitality. The object was clearly of great value, and Cugel was pleased to find an aperture in the crystal pane. He stepped through, but two feet before him a second pane blocked his way, establishing an avenue which evidently led to the magic whirligig. Cugel proceeded confidently, only to be stopped by another pane which he had not seen until he bumped into it. Cugel retraced his steps and to his gratification found the doubtlessly correct entrance a few feet back. But this new avenue led him by several right angles to another blank pane. Cugel decided to forego acquisition of the carousel and depart the castle. He turned, but discovered himself to be a trifle confused. He had come from his left—or was it his right?...Cugel was still seeking egress when in due course Iucounu returned to his manse.

Pausing by the alcove Iucounu gave Cugel a stare of humorous astonishment. "What have we here? A visitor? And I have been so remiss as to keep you waiting! Still, I see you have amused yourself, and I need feel no mortification." Iucounu permitted a chuckle to escape his lips. He then pretended to notice Cugel's bag. "What is this? You have brought objects for my examination? Excellent! I am always anxious to enhance my collection, in order to keep pace with the attrition of the years. You would be astounded to learn of the rogues who seek to despoil me! That merchant of clap-trap in his tawdry little booth, for instance—you could not conceive his frantic efforts in this regard! I tolerate him because to date he has not been bold enough to venture himself into my manse. But come, step out here into the hall, and we will examine the contents of your bag."

Cugel bowed graciously. "Gladly. As you assume, I have indeed been waiting for your return. If I recall correctly, the exit is by this passage..." He stepped forward, but again was halted. He made a gesture of rueful amusement. "I seem to have taken a wrong turning."

"Apparently so," said Iucounu. "Glancing upward, you will notice a decorative motif upon the ceiling. If you heed the flexion of the lunules you will be guided to the hall."

"Of course!" And Cugel briskly stepped forward in accordance with the directions.

"One moment!" called Iucounu. "You have forgotten your sack!"

Cugel reluctantly returned for the sack, once more set forth, and presently emerged into the hall.

Iucounu made a suave gesture. "If you will step this way I will be glad to examine your merchandise."

Cugel glanced reflectively along the corridor toward the front entrance. "It would be a presumption upon your patience. My little knick-knacks are below notice. With your permission I will take my leave."

"By no means!" declared Iucounu heartily. "I have few visitors, most of whom are rogues and thieves. I handle them severely, I assure you! I insist that you at least take some refreshment. Place your bag on the floor."

Cugel carefully set down the bag. "Recently I was instructed in a small competence by a sea-hag of White Alster. I believe you will be interested. I require several ells of stout cord."

"You excite my curiosity!" Iucounu extended his arm; a panel in the wainscoting slid back; a coil of rope was tossed to his hand. Rubbing his face as if to conceal a smile, Iucounu handed the rope to Cugel who shook it out with great care. "I will ask your cooperation," said Cugel. "A small matter of extending one arm and one leg."

"Yes, of course." Iucounu held out his hand, pointed a finger. The rope coiled around Cugel's arms and legs, pinning him so that he was unable to move. Iucounu's grin nearly split his great soft head. "This is a surprising development! By error I called forth Thief-taker! For your own comfort, do not strain, as Thief-taker is woven of wasp-legs. Now then, I will examine the contents of your bag." He peered into Cugel's sack and emitted a soft cry of dismay. "You have rifled my collection! I note certain of my most treasured valuables!"

Cugel grimaced. "Naturally! But I am no thief; Fianosther sent me here to collect certain objects, and therefore—"

Iucounu held up his hand. "The offense is far too serious for flippant disclaimers. I have stated my abhorrence for plunderers and thieves, and now I must visit upon you justice in its most unmitigated rigor—unless, of course, you can suggest an adequate requital."

"Some such requital surely exists," Cugel averred. "This cord however rasps upon my skin, so that I find cogitation impossible."

"No matter. I have decided to apply the Charm of Forlorn Encystment, which constricts the subject in a pore some forty-five miles below the surface of the earth."

Cugel blinked in dismay. "Under these conditions, requital could never be made."

"True," mused Iucounu. "I wonder if after all there is some small service which you can perform for me."

"The villain is as good as dead!" declared Cugel. "Now remove these abominable bonds!"

"I had no specific assassination in mind," said Iucounu. "Come."

The rope relaxed, allowing Cugel to hobble after Iucounu into a side chamber hung with intricately embroidered tapestry. From a cabinet Iucounu brought a small case and laid it on a floating disk of glass. He opened the case, gestured to Cugel, who perceived that the box showed two indentations lined with scarlet fur, where reposed a single small hemisphere of filmed violet glass.

"As a knowledgeable and traveled man," suggested Iucounu, "you doubtless recognize this object. No? You are familiar, of course, with the Cutz Wars of the Eighteenth Aeon? No?" Iucounu hunched up his shoulders in astonishment. "During these ferocious events the demon Unda-Hrada—he is listed as 16-04 Green in Thrump's Almanac— thought to assist his principals, and to this end thrust certain agencies up from the sub-world La-Er. In order that they might perceive, they were tipped with cusps similar to the one you see before you. When events went amiss, the demon snatched himself back to La-Er. The hemispheres were dislodged and broadcast across Cutz. One of these, as you see, I own. You must procure its mate and bring it to me, whereupon your trespass shall be overlooked."

Cugel reflected. "The choice, if it lies between a sortie into the demon-world La-Er and the Spell of Forlorn Encystment, is moot. Frankly, I am at a loss for decision."

Iucounu's laugh almost split the big yellow bladder of his head. "A visit to La-Er perhaps will prove unnecessary. You may secure the article in that land once known as Cutz."

"If I must, I must," growled Cugel, thoroughly displeased by the manner in which the day's work had ended. "Who guards this violet hemisphere? What is its function? How do I go and how return? What necessary weapons, talismans and other magical adjuncts do you undertake to fit me out with?"

"All in good time," said Iucounu. "First I must ensure that, once at liberty, you conduct yourself with unremitting loyalty, zeal and singleness of purpose."

"Have no fear," declared Cugel, "my word is my bond."

"Excellent!" cried Iucounu. "This knowledge represents a basic security which I do not in the least take lightly. The act now to be performed is doubtless supererogatory."

He departed the chamber and after a moment returned with a covered glass bowl containing a small white creature, all claws, prongs, barbs and hooks, now squirming angrily. "This," said Iucounu, "is my friend Firx, from the star Achernar, who is far wiser than he seems. Firx is annoyed at being separated from his comrade with whom he shares a vat in my workroom. He will assist you in the expeditious discharge of your duties." Iucounu stepped close, deftly thrust the creature against Cugel's abdomen. It merged into his viscera, took up a vigilant post clasped around Cugel's liver.

Iucounu stood back, laughing in that immoderate glee which had earned him his cognomen. Cugel's eyes bulged from his head. He opened his mouth to utter an objurgation, but instead clenched his jaw, rolled up his eyes.

The rope uncoiled itself. Cugel stood quivering, every muscle knotted.

Iucounu's mirth dwindled to a thoughtful grin. "You spoke of magical adjuncts. What of those talismans whose efficacy you proclaimed from your booth in Azenomei? Will they not immobilize enemies, dissolve iron, impassion virgins, confer immortality?"

"These talismans are not uniformly dependable," said Cugel. "I will require further competences."

"You have them," said Iucounu, "in your sword, your crafty persuasiveness and the agility of your feet. Still, you have aroused my concern and I will help you to this extent." He hung a small square tablet about Cugel's neck. "You now may put aside all fear of starvation. A touch of this potent object will induce nutriment into wood, bark, grass, even discarded clothing. It will also sound a chime in the presence of poison. So now—there is nothing to delay us! Come, we will go. Rope? Where is Rope?"

Obediently the rope looped around Cugel's neck, and Cugel was forced to march along behind Iucounu.

They came out upon the roof of the antique castle. Darkness had long since fallen over the land. Up and down the valley of the Xzan glimmered faint lights, while the Xzan itself was an irregular width darker than dark.

Iucounu pointed to a cage. "This will be your conveyance. Inside."

Cugel hesitated. "It might be preferable to dine well, to sleep and rest, to set forth tomorrow refreshed."

"What?" spoke Iucounu in a voice like a horn. "You dare stand before me and state preferences? You, who came skulking into my house, pillaged my valuables and left all in disarray? Do you understand your luck? Perhaps you prefer the Forlorn Encystment?"

"By no means!" protested Cugel nervously. "I am anxious only for the success of the venture!"

"Into the cage then."

Cugel turned despairing eyes around the castle roof, slowly went to the cage and stepped within.

"I trust you suffer no deficiency of memory," said Iucounu. "But even if this becomes the case, and if you neglect your prime responsibility, which is to say, the procuring of the violet cusp, Firx is on hand to remind you."

Cugel said, "Since I am now committed to this enterprise, and unlikely to return, you may care to learn my appraisal of yourself and your character. In the first place—"

But Iucounu held up his hand. "I do not care to listen; obloquy injures my self-esteem and I am skeptical of praise. So now—be off!" He drew back, stared up into the darkness, then shouted that invocation known as Thasdrubal's Laganetic Transfer. From high came a thud and a buffet, a muffled bellow of rage.

Iucounu retreated a few steps, shouted up words in an archaic language; and the cage with Cugel crouching within was snatched aloft and hurled through the air.

❁

Cold wind bit Cugel's face. The cage swung back and forth. From above came a flapping and creaking of vast wings and dismal lamentation. Below all was dark, a blackness like a pit. By the disposition of the stars Cugel perceived that the course was to the north, and presently he sensed the thrust of the Maurenron Mountains below; and then they flew over that wilderness known as the Land of the Falling Wall. Once or twice Cugel glimpsed the lights of an isolated castle, and once he noted a great bonfire. For a period a winged sprite came to flap alongside the cage and peer within. It seemed to find Cugel's plight amusing, and when Cugel sought information as to the land below, it merely uttered raucous cries of mirth. It became fatigued and sought to cling to the cage, but Cugel kicked it away, and it fell off into the wind with a scream of envy.

The east flushed the red of old blood, and presently the sun appeared, trembling like an old man with a chill. The ground was shrouded by mist; Cugel was barely able to see that they crossed a land of black mountains and dark chasms. Presently the mist parted once more to reveal a leaden sea. Once or twice he peered up but the roof of the cage concealed the demon except for the tips of the leathern wings.

At last the demon reached the north shore of the ocean. Swooping to the beach it vented a vindictive croak, and allowed the cage to fall from a height of fifteen feet.

Cugel crawled from the broken cage. Nursing his bruises he called a curse after the departing demon, then plodded back through sand and dank yellow spinifex, and climbed the slope of the foreshore. To the north were marshy barrens and a far huddle of low hills; to east and west ocean and dreary beach. Cugel shook his fist to the south. Somehow, at some time, in some manner, he would visit revenge upon the Laughing Magician! so much he vowed.

A few hundred yards to the west was the trace of an ancient seawall. Cugel thought to inspect it, but hardly moved three steps before Firx clamped prongs into his liver. Cugel, rolling up his eyes in agony, reversed his direction and set out along the shore to the east.

Presently he hungered, and bethought himself of the charm furnished by Iucounu. He picked up a piece of driftwood and rubbed it with the tablet, hoping to see a transformation into a tray of sweetmeats or a roast fowl. But the driftwood merely softened to the texture of cheese, retained the flavor of driftwood. Cugel ate with snaps and gulps. Another score against Iucounu! How the Laughing Magician would pay!

The scarlet globe of the sun slid across the southern sky. Night approached, and at last Cugel came upon human habitation: a rude village beside a small river. The huts were like bird's-nests of mud and sticks, and smelled vilely of ordure and filth. Among them wandered a people as unlovely and graceless as the huts. They were squat, brutish and obese; their hair was a coarse yellow tangle; their features were lumps. Their single noteworthy attribute—one in which Cugel took an instant and keen interest—was their eyes: blind-seeming violet hemispheres, similar in every respect to that object required by Iucounu.

Cugel approached the village cautiously but the inhabitants took small interest in him. If the hemisphere coveted by Iucounu were identical to the violet eyes of these folk, then a basic uncertainty of the mission was resolved, and procuring the violet cusp became merely a matter of tactics.

Cugel paused to observe the villagers, and found much to puzzle him. In the first place they carried themselves not as the ill-smelling loons they were, but with a remarkable loftiness and a dignity which verged at times upon hauteur. Cugel watched in puzzlement: were they a tribe of dotards? In any event they seemed to pose no threat, and he advanced into the main avenue of the village, walking gingerly to avoid the more noxious heaps of refuse. One of the villagers now deigned to notice him, and addressed him in grunting guttural voice. "Well sirrah: what is your wish? Why do you prowl the outskirts of our city Smolod?"

"I am a wayfarer," said Cugel. "I ask only to be directed to the inn, where I may find food and lodging."

"We have no inn; travelers and wayfarers are unknown to us. Still, you are welcome to share our plenty. Yonder is a manse with appointments sufficient for your comfort." The man pointed to a dilapidated hut. "You may eat as you will; merely enter the refectory yonder and select what you wish; there is no stinting at Smolod."

"I thank you gratefully," said Cugel, and would have spoken further except that his host had strolled away.

Cugel gingerly looked into the shed, and after some exertion cleaned out the most inconvenient debris, and arranged a trestle on which to sleep. The sun was now at the horizon and Cugel went to that storeroom which had been identified as the refectory. The villager's description of the bounty available, as Cugel had suspected, was in the nature of hyperbole. To one side of the storeroom was a heap of smoked fish; to the other a bin containing lentils mingled with various seeds and cereals. Cugel took a portion to his hut, where he made a glum supper.

The sun had set; Cugel went forth to see what the village offered in the way of entertainment, but found the streets deserted. In certain of the huts lamps burned, and Cugel peering through the cracks saw the residents dining upon smoked fish or engaged in discourse. He returned to his shed, built a small fire against the chill and composed himself for sleep.

The following day Cugel renewed his observation of the village Smolod and its violet-eyed folk. None, he noticed, went forth to work, nor did there seem to be fields near at hand. The discovery caused Cugel dissatisfaction. In order to secure one of the violet eyes, he would be obliged to kill its owner, and for this purpose freedom from officious interference was essential.

He made tentative attempts at conversation among the villagers, but they looked at him in a manner which presently began to jar at Cugel's equanimity: it was almost as if they were gracious lords and he the ill-smelling lout!

During the afternoon he strolled south, and about a mile along the shore came upon another village. The people were much like the inhabitants of Smolod, but with ordinary-seeming eyes. They were likewise industrious; Cugel watched them till fields and fish the ocean.

He approached a pair of fishermen on their way back to the village, their catch slung over their shoulders. They stopped, eyed Cugel with no great friendliness. Cugel introduced himself as a wayfarer and asked concerning the lands to the east, but the fishermen professed ignorance other than the fact that the land was barren, dreary and dangerous.

"I am currently a guest at the village Smolod," said Cugel. "I find the folk pleasant enough, but somewhat odd. For instance, why are their eyes as they are? What is the nature of their affliction? Why do they conduct themselves with such aristocratic self-assurance and suavity of manner?"

"The eyes are magic cusps," stated the older of the fishermen in a grudging voice. "They afford a view of the Overworld; why should not the owners behave as lords? So will I when Radkuth Vomin dies, for I inherit his eyes."

"Indeed!" exclaimed Cugel, marveling. "Can these magic cusps be detached at will and transferred as the owner sees fit?"

"They can, but who would exchange the Overworld for this?" The fisherman swung his arm around the dreary landscape. "I have toiled long and at last it is my turn to taste the delights of the Overworld. After this there is nothing, and the only peril is death through a surfeit of bliss."

"Vastly interesting!" remarked Cugel. "How might I qualify for a pair of these magic cusps?"

"Strive as do all the others of Grodz: place your name on the list, then toil to supply the lords of Smolod with sustenance. Thirty-one years have I sown and reaped lentils and emmer and netted fish and dried them over slow fires, and now the name of Bubach Angh is at the head of the list, and you must do the same."

"Thirty-one years," mused Cugel. "A period of not negligible duration." And Firx squirmed restlessly, causing Cugel's liver no small discomfort.

The fishermen proceeded to their village Grodz; Cugel returned to Smolod. Here he sought out that man to whom he had spoken upon his arrival to the village. "My lord," said Cugel, "as you know I am a traveler from a far land, attracted here by the magnificence of the city Smolod."

"Understandable," grunted the other. "Our splendor cannot help but inspire emulation."

"What then is the source of the magic cusps?"

The elder turned the violet hemispheres upon Cugel as if seeing him for the first time. He spoke in a surly voice. "It is a matter we do not care to dwell upon, but there is no harm in it, now that the subject has been broached. At a remote time the demon Underherd sent up tentacles to look across Earth, each tipped with a cusp. Simbilis the Sixteenth pained the monster, which jerked back to his sub-world and the cusps became dislodged. Four hundred and twelve of the cusps were gathered and brought to Smolod, then as splendid as now it appears to me. Yes, I realize that I see but a semblance, but so do you, and who is to say which is real?"

"I do not look through magic cusps," said Cugel.

"True." The elder shrugged. "It is a matter I prefer to overlook. I dimly recall that I inhabit a sty and devour the coarsest of food—but the subjective reality is that I inhabit a glorious palace and dine on splendid viands among the princes and princesses who are my peers. It is explained thus: the demon Underherd looked from the sub-world to this one; we look from this to the Overworld, which is the quintessence of human hope, visionary longing, and beatific dream. We who inhabit this world—how can we think of ourselves as other than splendid lords? This is how we are."

"It is inspiring!" exclaimed Cugel. "How may I obtain a pair of these magic cusps?"

"There are two methods. Underherd lost four hundred and fourteen cusps; we control four hundred and twelve. Two were never found, and evidently lie on the floor of the ocean's deep. You are at liberty to secure these. The second means is to become a citizen of Grodz, and furnish the lords of Smolod with sustenance till one of us dies, as we do infrequently."

"I understand that a certain Lord Radkuth Vomin is ailing."

"Yes, that is he." The elder indicated a pot-bellied old man with a slack drooling mouth, sitting in filth before his hut. "You see him at his ease in the pleasaunce of his palace. Lord Radkuth strained himself with a surfeit of lust, for our princesses are the most ravishing creations of human inspiration, just as I am the noblest of princes. But Lord Radkuth indulged himself too copiously, and thereby suffered a mortification. It is a lesson for us all."

"Perhaps I might make special arrangements to secure his cusps?" ventured Cugel.

"I fear not. You must go to Grodz and toil as do the others. As did I, in a former existence which now seems dim and inchoate...To think I suffered so long! But you are young; thirty or forty or fifty years is not too long a time to wait."

Cugel put his hand to his abdomen to quiet the fretful stirrings of Firx. "In the space of so much time, the sun may well have waned. Look!" He pointed as a black flicker crossed the face of the sun and seemed to leave a momentary crust. "Even now it ebbs!"

"You are over-apprehensive," stated the elder. "To us who are lords of Smolod, the sun puts forth a radiance of exquisite colors."

"This may well be true at the moment," said Cugel, "but when the sun goes dark, what then? Will you take an equal delight in the gloom and the chill?"

But the elder no longer attended him. Radkuth Vomin had fallen sideways into the mud, and appeared to be dead.

Toying indecisively with his knife Cugel went to look down at the corpse. A deft cut or two—no more than the work of a moment—and he would have achieved his goal. He swayed forward, but already the fugitive moment had passed. Other lords of the village had approached to jostle Cugel aside; Radkuth Vomin was lifted and carried with the most solemn nicety into the ill-smelling precincts of his hut.

Cugel stared wistfully through the doorway, calculating the chances of this ruse and that.

"Let lamps be brought!" intoned the elder. "Let a final effulgence surround Lord Radkuth on his gem-encrusted bier! Let the golden clarion sound from the towers; let the princesses don robes of samite; let their tresses obscure the faces of delight Lord Radkuth loved so well! And now we must keep vigil! Who will guard the bier?"

Cugel stepped forward. "I would deem it honor indeed."

The elder shook his head. "This is a privilege reserved for his peers. Lord Maulfag, Lord Glus: perhaps you will act in this capacity." Two of the villagers approached the bench on which Lord Radkuth Vomin lay.

"Next," declared the elder, "the obsequies must be proclaimed, and the magic cusps transferred to Bubach Angh that most deserving squire of Grodz. Who, again, will go to notify this squire?"

"Again," said Cugel, "I offer my services, if only to requite in some small manner the hospitality I have enjoyed at Smolod."

"Well spoken!" intoned the elder. "So, then, at speed to Grodz; return with that squire who by his faith and dutiful toil deserves advancement."

Cugel bowed, ran off across the barrens toward Grodz. As he approached the outermost fields he moved cautiously, skulking from tussock to copse, and presently found that which he sought: a peasant turning the dank soil with a mattock.

Cugel crept quietly forward, struck down the loon with a gnarled root. He stripped off the best garments, the leather hat, the leggings and foot-gear; with his knife he hacked off the stiff straw-colored beard. Taking all and leaving the peasant lying dazed and naked in the mud he fled on long strides back toward Smolod. In a secluded spot he dressed himself in the stolen garments. He examined the hacked-off beard with some perplexity, and finally, by tying up tufts of the coarse yellow hair and tying tuft to tuft, contrived to bind enough together to make a straggling false beard for himself. That hair which remained he tucked up under the brim of the flapping leather hat.

Now the sun had set; plum-colored gloom obscured the land. Cugel returned to Smolod. Oil lamps flickered before the hut of Radkuth Vomin, where the obese and misshapen village women wailed and groaned.

Cugel stepped cautiously forward, wondering what might be expected of him. As for his disguise: it would either prove effective or it would not. To what extent the violet cusps befuddled perception was a matter of doubt; he could only hazard a trial.

Cugel marched boldly up to the door of the hut. Pitching his voice as low as possible, he called, "I am here, revered princes of Smolod: Squire Bubach Angh of Grodz, who for thirty-one years has heaped the choicest of delicacies into the Smolod larders. Now I appear, beseeching elevation to the estate of nobility."

"As is your right," said the Chief Elder. "But you seem a man different to that Bubach Angh who so long has served the princes of Smolod."

"I have been transfigured—through grief at the passing of Prince Radkuth Vomin and through rapture at the prospect of elevation."

"This is clear and understandable. Come then—prepare yourself for the rites."

"I am ready as of this instant," said Cugel. "Indeed, if you will but tender me the magic cusps I will take them quietly aside and rejoice."

The Chief Elder shook his head indulgently. "This is not in accord with the rites. To begin with you must stand naked here on the pavilion of this mighty castle, and the fairest of the fair will anoint you in aromatics. Then comes the invocation to Eddith Bran Maur. And then—"

"Revered," stated Cugel, "allow me one boon. Before the ceremonies begin, fit me with the magic cusps so that I may understand the full portent of the ceremony."

The Chief Elder considered. "The request is unorthodox, but reasonable. Bring forth the cusps!"

There was a wait, during which Cugel stood first on one foot then the other. The minutes dragged; the garments and the false beard itched intolerably. And now at the outskirts of the village he saw the approach of several new figures, coming from the direction of Grodz. One was almost certainly Bubach Angh, while another seemed to have been shorn of his beard.

The Chief Elder appeared, holding in each hand a violet cusp. "Step forward!"

Cugel called loudly, "I am here, sir."

"I now apply the potion which sanctifies the junction of magic cusp to right eye."

At the back of the crowd Bubach Angh raised his voice. "Hold! What transpires?"

Cugel turned, pointed. "What jackal is this that interrupts solemnities? Remove him: hence!"

"Indeed!" called the Chief Elder peremptorily. "You demean yourself and the dignity of the ceremony."

Bubach Angh crouched back, momentarily cowed.

"In view of the interruption," said Cugel, "I had as lief merely take custody of the magic cusps until these louts can properly be chastened."

"No," said the Chief Elder. "Such a procedure is impossible." He shook drops of rancid fat in Cugel's right eye. But now the peasant of the shorn beard set up an outcry: "My hat! My blouse! My beard! Is there no justice?"

"Silence!" hissed the crowd. "This is a solemn occasion!"

"But I am Bu—"

Cugel called, "Insert the magic cusp, lord; let us ignore these louts."

"A lout, you call me?" roared Bubach Angh. "I recognize you now, you rogue. Hold up proceedings!"

The Chief Elder said inexorably, "I now invest you with the right cusp. You must temporarily hold this eye closed to prevent a discord which would strain the brain, and cause stupor. Now the left eye." He stepped forward with the ointment, but Bubach Angh and the beardless peasant no longer would be denied. "Hold up proceedings! You ennoble an impostor! I am Bubach Angh, the worthy squire! He who stands before you is a vagabond!"

The Chief Elder inspected Bubach Angh with puzzlement. "For a fact you resemble that peasant who for thirty-one years has carted supplies to Smolod. But if you are Bubach Angh, who is this?"

The beardless peasant lumbered forward. "It is the soulless wretch who stole the clothes from my back and the beard from my face."

"He is a criminal, a bandit, a vagabond—"

"Hold!" called the Chief Elder. "The words are ill-chosen. Remember that he has been exalted to the rank of prince of Smolod."

"Not altogether!" cried Bubach Angh. "He has one of my eyes. I demand the other!"

"An awkward situation," muttered the Chief Elder. He spoke to Cugel: "Though formerly a vagabond and cutthroat, you are now a prince, and a man of responsibility. What is your opinion?"

"I suggest a hiding for these obstreperous louts. Then—"

Bubach Angh and the beardless peasant, uttering shouts of rage, sprang forward. Cugel, leaping away, could not control his right eye. The lid flew open; into his brain crashed such a wonder of exaltation that his breath caught in his throat and his heart almost stopped from astonishment. But concurrently his left eye showed the reality of Smolod, the dissonance was too wild to be tolerated; he stumbled and fell against a hut. Bubach Angh stood over him with mattock raised high, but now the Chief Elder stepped between.

"Do you take leave of your senses? This man is a prince of Smolod!"

"A man I will kill, for he has my eye! Do I toil thirty-one years for the benefit of a vagabond?"

"Calm yourself, Bubach Angh, if that be your name, and remember the issue is not yet entirely clear. Possibly an error has been made—undoubtedly an honest error, for this man is now a prince of Smolod, which is to say, justice and sagacity personified."

"He was not that before he received the cusp," argued Bubach Angh, "which is when the offense was committed."

"I cannot occupy myself with casuistic distinctions," replied the elder. "In any event, your name heads the list and on the next fatality—"

"Ten or twelve years hence?" cried Bubach Angh. "Must I toil yet longer, and receive my reward just as the sun goes dark? No, no, this cannot be!"

The beardless peasant made a suggestion: "Take the other cusp. In this way you will have at least half of your rights, and so prevent the interloper from cheating you totally."

Bubach Angh agreed. "I will start with my one magic cusp; I will then kill that knave and take the other, and all will be well."

"Now then," said the Chief Elder haughtily, "this is hardly the tone to take in reference to a prince of Smolod!"

"Bah!" snorted Bubach Angh. "Remember the source of your viands! We of Grodz will not toil to no avail."

"Very well," said the Chief Elder. "I deplore your uncouth bluster, but I cannot deny that you have a measure of reason on your side. Here is the left cusp of Radkuth Vomin. I will dispense with the invocation, anointment and the congratulatory paean. If you will be good enough to step forward and open your left eye—so."

As Cugel had done, Bubach Angh looked through both eyes together and staggered back in a daze. But clapping his hand to his left eye he recovered himself, and advanced upon Cugel. "You now must see the futility of your trick. Extend me that cusp and go your way, for you will never have the use of the two."

"It matters very little," said Cugel. "Thanks to my friend Firx I am well content with the one."

Bubach Angh ground his teeth. "Do you think to trick me again? Your life has approached its end: not just I but all Grodz goes warrant for this!"

"Not in the precincts of Smolod!" warned the Chief Elder. "There must be no quarrels among the princes: I decree amity! You who have shared the cusps of Radkuth Vomin must also share his palace, his robes, appurtenances, jewels and retinue, until that hopefully remote occasion when one or the other dies, whereupon the survivor shall take all. This is my judgment; there is no more to be said."

"The moment of the interloper's death is hopefully near at hand," rumbled Bubach Angh. "The instant he sets foot from Smolod will be his last! The citizens of Grodz will maintain a vigil of a hundred years, if necessary!"

Firx squirmed at this news and Cugel winced at the discomfort. In a conciliatory voice he addressed Bubach Angh. "A compromise might be arranged: to you shall go the entirety of Radkuth Vomin's estate: his palace, appurtenances, retinue. To me shall devolve only the magic cusps."

But Bubach Angh would have none of it. "If you value your life, deliver that cusp to me this moment."

"This cannot be done," said Cugel.

Bubach Angh turned away, spoke to the beardless peasant, who nodded and departed. Bubach Angh glowered at Cugel, then went to Radkuth Vomin's hut and sat on the heap of rubble before the door. Here he experimented with his new cusp, cautiously closing his right eye, opening the left to stare in wonder at the Overworld. Cugel thought to take advantage of his absorption and sauntered off toward the edge of town. Bubach Angh appeared not to notice. Ha! thought Cugel. It was to be so easy then! Two more strides and he would be lost into the darkness! Jauntily he stretched his long legs to take those two strides. A slight sound—a grunt, a scrape, a rustle of clothes—caused him to jerk aside; down swung a mattock blade, cutting the air where his head had been. In the faint glow cast by the Smolod lamps Cugel glimpsed the beardless peasant's vindictive countenance. Behind him Bubach Angh came loping, heavy head thrust forward like a bull. Cugel dodged, ran with agility back into the heart of Smolod. Slowly and in vast disappointment Bubach Angh returned, to seat himself once more. "You will never escape," he told Cugel. "Give over the cusp and preserve your life!"

"By no means," replied Cugel with spirit. "Rather fear for your own sodden vitality, which goes in even greater peril!"

From the hut of the Chief Elder came an admonitory call. "Cease the bickering! I am indulging the exotic whims of a beautiful princess and must not be distracted."

Cugel, recalling the oleaginous wads of flesh, the leering slab-sided visages, the matted verminous hair, the wattles and wens, the evil odors, which characterized the women of Smolod, marveled anew at the power of the cusps. Bubach Angh was once more testing the vision of his left eye. Cugel composed himself on a bench and attempted the use of his right eye, first holding his hand before his left...

Cugel wore a shirt of supple silver scales, tight scarlet trousers, a dark blue cloak. He sat on a marble bench before a row of spiral marble columns overgrown with dark foliage and white flowers. To either side the palaces of Smolod towered into the night, one behind the other, with soft lights accenting the arches and windows. The sky was a soft dark blue, hung with great glowing stars; among the palaces were gardens of cypress, myrtle, jasmine, sphade, thyssam; the air was pervaded with the perfume of flowers and flowing water. From somewhere came a wisp of music: a murmur of soft chords, a sigh of melody. Cugel took a deep breath, rose to his feet. He stepped forward, moved across the terrace. Palaces and gardens shifted perspective; on a dim lawn three girls in gowns of white gauze watched him over their shoulders.

Cugel took an involuntary step forward, then recalling the malice of Bubach Angh, paused to check on his whereabouts. Across the plaza rose a palace of seven stories, each level with its terrace garden, with vines and flowers trailing down the walls. Through the windows Cugel glimpsed rich furnishings, lustrous chandeliers, the soft movement of liveried chamberlains. On the pavilion before the palace stood a hawk-featured man with a cropped golden beard in robes of ocher and black, with gold epaulettes and black buskins. He stood one foot on a stone griffin, arms on bent knee, gazing toward Cugel with an expression of brooding dislike. Cugel marveled: could this be the pig-faced Bubach Angh? Could the magnificent seven-tiered palace be the hovel of Radkuth Vomin?

Cugel moved slowly off across the plaza, and now came upon a pavilion lit by candelabra. Tables supported meats, jellies, pastries of every description; and Cugel's belly, nourished only by driftwood and smoked fish, urged him forward. He passed from table to table, sampling morsels from every dish, and found all to be of the highest quality.

"Smoked fish and lentils I may still be devouring," Cugel told himself, "but there is much to be said for the enchantment by which they become such exquisite delicacies. Indeed a man might do far worse than spend the rest of his life here in Smolod."

Almost as if Firx had been anticipating the thought, he instantly inflicted upon Cugel's liver a series of agonizing pangs, and Cugel bitterly reviled Iucounu the Laughing Magician and repeated his vows of vengeance.

Recovering his composure, he sauntered to that area where the formal gardens surrounding the palaces gave way to parkland. He looked over his shoulder to find the hawk-faced prince in ocher and black approaching, with manifestly hostile intent. In the dimness of the park Cugel noted other movement and thought to spy a number of armoured warriors.

Cugel returned to the plaza and Bubach Angh followed, once more to stand glowering at Cugel in front of Radkuth Vomin's palace.

"Clearly," said Cugel aloud, for the benefit of Firx, "there will be no departure from Smolod tonight. Naturally I am anxious to convey the cusp to Iucounu, but if I am killed then neither the cusp nor the admirable Firx will ever return to Almery."

Firx made no further demonstration. Now, thought Cugel, where to pass the night? The seven-tiered palace of Radkuth Vomin manifestly offered ample and spacious accommodation for both himself and Bubach Angh. In essence however the two would be crammed together in a one-roomed hut, with a single heap of damp reeds for a couch. Thoughtfully, regretfully, Cugel closed his right eye, opened his left.

Smolod was as before. The surly Bubach Angh crouched before the door to Radkuth Vomin's hut. Cugel stepped forward, kicked Bubach Angh smartly. In surprise and shock, both Bubach Angh's eyes opened, and the rival impulses colliding in his brain induced paralysis. Back in the darkness the beardless peasant roared and came charging forward, mattock on high, and Cugel relinquished his plan to cut Bubach Angh's throat. He skipped inside the hut, closed and barred the door.

He now closed his left eye, opened his right. He found himself in the magnificent entry hall of Radkuth Vomin's palace, the portico of which was secured by a portcullis of forged iron. Without, the golden-haired prince in ocher and black, holding his hand over one eye, was lifting himself in cold dignity from the pavement of the plaza. Raising one arm in noble defiance Bubach Angh swung his cloak over his shoulder, marched off to join his warriors.

Cugel sauntered through the palace, inspecting the appointments with pleasure. If it were not for the importunities of Firx, there would be no haste in trying the perilous journey back to the Valley of the Xzan.

Cugel selected a luxurious chamber facing to the south, doffed his rich garments for satin nightwear, settled upon a couch with sheets of pale blue silk, and instantly fell asleep.

In the morning there was a degree of difficulty remembering which eye to open, and Cugel thought it might be well to fashion a patch to wear over that eye not currently in use.

By day the palaces of Smolod were more grand than ever, and now the plaza was thronged with princes and princesses, all of utmost beauty.

Cugel dressed himself in handsome garments of black, with a jaunty green cap and green sandals. He descended to the entry hall, raised the portcullis with a gesture of command and went forth into the plaza.

There was no sign of Bubach Angh. The other inhabitants of Smolod greeted him with courtesy and the princesses displayed noticeable warmth, as if they found him of good address. Cugel responded politely, but without fervor: not even the magic cusp could persuade him against the sour wads of fat, flesh, grime and hair which were the Smolod women.

He breakfasted on delightful viands at the pavilion, then returned to the plaza to consider his next course of action. A cursory inspection of the parklands revealed Grodz warriors on guard. There was no immediate prospect of escape.

The nobility of Smolod applied themselves to their diversions. Some wandered the meadows; others went boating upon the delightful waterways to the north. The Chief Elder, a prince of sagacious and noble visage, sat alone on an onyx bench, deep in reverie.

Cugel approached; the Chief Elder aroused himself and gave Cugel a salute of measured cordiality. "I am not easy in my mind," he declared. "In spite of all judiciousness, and allowing for your unavoidable ignorance of our customs, I feel a certain inequity has been done, and I am at a loss as how to repair it."

"It seems to me," said Cugel, "that Squire Bubach Angh, though doubtless a worthy man, exhibits a lack of discipline unfitting the dignity of Smolod. In my opinion he would be all the better for a few years more seasoning at Grodz."

"There is something in what you say," replied the elder. "Small personal sacrifices are sometimes essential to the welfare of the group. I feel certain that you, if the issue arose, would gladly offer up your cusp and enroll anew at Grodz. What are a few years? They flutter past like butterflies."

Cugel made a suave gesture. "Or a trial by lot might be arranged, in which all who see with two cusps participate, the loser of the trial donating one of his cusps to Bubach Angh. I myself will make do with one."

The elder frowned. "Well—the contingency is remote. Meanwhile you must participate in our merry-making. If I may say so, you cut a personable figure and certain of the princesses have been casting sheep's eyes in your direction. There, for instance, the lovely Udela Narshag—and there, Zokoxa of the Rose-Petals, and beyond the vivacious Ilviu Lasmal. You must not be backward; here in Smolod we live an uncircumscribed life."

"The charm of these ladies has not escaped me," said Cugel. "Unluckily I am bound by a vow of continence."

"Unfortunate man!" exclaimed the Chief Elder. "The princesses of Smolod are nonpareil! And notice—yet another soliciting your attention!"

"Surely it is you she summons," said Cugel, and the elder went to confer with the young woman in question, who had come riding into the plaza in a magnificent boat-shaped car which walked on six swan-feet. The princess reclined on a couch of pink down and was beautiful enough to make Cugel rue the fastidiousness of his recollection, which projected every matted hair, mole, dangling underlip, sweating seam and wrinkle of the Smolod women to the front of his memory. This princess was indeed the essence of a day-dream: slender and supple, with skin like still cream, a delicate nose, lucent brooding eyes, a mouth of delightful flexibility. Her expression intrigued Cugel, for it was more complex than that of the other princesses: pensive, yet wilful; ardent yet dissatisfied.

Into the plaza came Bubach Angh, accoutered in military wise, with corselet, morion and sword. The Chief Elder went to speak to him; and now to Cugel's irritation the princess in the walking boat signaled to him.

He went forward. "Yes, princess; you saluted me, I believe?"

The princess nodded. "I speculate on your presence up here in these northern lands." She spoke in a soft clear voice like music.

Cugel said, "I am here on a mission; I stay but a short while at Smolod, and then must continue east and south."

"Indeed!" said the princess. "What is the nature of your mission?"

"To be candid, I was brought here by the malice of a magician. It was by no means a yearning of my own."

The princess laughed softly. "I see few strangers. I long for new faces and new talk. Perhaps you will come to my palace and we will talk of magic, and the strange circumstances which throng the dying earth."

Cugel bowed stiffly. "Your offer is kind. But you must seek elsewhere; I am bound by a vow of continence. Control your displeasure, for it applies not only to you but to Udela Narshag yonder, to Zokoxa, and to Ilviu Lasmal."

The princess raised her eyebrows, sank back on her down-covered couch. She smiled faintly. "Indeed, indeed. You are a harsh man, a stern relentless man, thus to refuse yourself to so many imploring women."

"This is the case, and so it must be." Cugel turned away to face the Chief Elder who approached with Bubach Angh at his back.

"Sorry circumstances," announced the Chief Elder in a troubled voice. "Bubach Angh speaks for the village of Grodz. He declares that no more victuals will be furnished until justice is done, and this they define as the surrender of your cusp to Bubach Angh, and your person to a punitive committee who waits in the parkland yonder."

Cugel laughed uneasily. "What a distorted view! You assured them of course that we of Smolod would eat grass and destroy the cusps before agreeing to such detestable provisions?"

"I fear that I temporized," stated the Chief Elder. "I feel that the others of Smolod favor a more flexible course of action."

The implication was clear, and Firx began to stir in exasperation. In order to appraise circumstances in the most forthright manner possible, Cugel shifted the patch to look from his left eye.

Certain citizens of Grodz, armed with scythes, mattocks and clubs waited at a distance of fifty yards: evidently the punitive committee to which Bubach Angh had referred. To one side were the huts of Smolod; to the other the walking boat and the princess of such—Cugel stared in astonishment. The boat was as before, walking on six bird-legs, and sitting in the pink down was the princess—if possible, more beautiful than ever. But now her expression, rather than faintly smiling, was cool and still.

Cugel drew a deep breath, took to his heels. Bubach Angh shouted an order to halt, but Cugel paid no heed. Across the barrens he raced, with the punitive committee in pursuit.

Cugel laughed gleefully. He was long of limb, sound of wind; the peasants were stumpy, knot-muscled, phlegmatic. He could easily run two miles to their one. He paused, and turned to wave farewell. To his dismay two legs from the walking boat detached themselves and leapt after him. Cugel ran for his life. In vain. The legs came bounding past, one on either side. They swung around, kicked him to a halt.

Cugel sullenly walked back, the legs hopping behind. Just before he reached the outskirts of Smolod he reached under the patch and pulled loose the magic cusp. As the punitive committee bore down on him, he held it aloft. "Stand back—or I break the cusp to fragments!"

"Hold! Hold!" called Bubach Angh. "This must not be! Come, give me the cusp and accept your just deserts."

"Nothing has yet been decided," Cugel reminded him. "The Chief Elder has ruled for no one."

The girl rose from her seat in the boat. "I will rule; I am Derwe Coreme, of the House of Domber. Give me the violet glass, whatever it is."

"By no means," said Cugel. "Take the cusp from Bubach Angh."

"Never!" exclaimed the squire from Grodz.

"What? You both have a cusp and both want two? What are these precious objects? You wear them as eyes? Give them to me."

Cugel drew his sword. "I prefer to run, but I fight if I must."

"I cannot run," said Bubach Angh. "I prefer to fight." He pulled the cusp from his own eye. "Now then, vagabond, prepare to die."

"A moment," said Derwe Coreme. From one of the legs of the boat thin arms reached to seize the wrists of both Cugel and Bubach Angh. The cusps fell to earth; that of Cugel was caught and conveyed to Derwe Coreme; that of Bubach Angh struck a stone and shivered to fragments. He howled in anguish, leapt upon Cugel, who gave ground before the attack.

Bubach Angh knew nothing of swordplay; he hacked and slashed as if he were cleaning fish. The fury of his attack, however, was unsettling and Cugel was hard put to defend himself. In addition to Bubach Angh's sallies and slashes, Firx was deploring the loss of the cusp.

Derwe Coreme had lost interest in the affair. The boat started off across the barrens, moving faster and ever faster. Cugel slashed out with his sword, leapt back, leapt back once more, and for the second time fled across the barrens, and the folk of Smolod and Grodz shouted curses after him.

The boat-car jogged along at a leisurely rate. Lungs throbbing, Cugel gained upon it, and with a great bound leapt up, caught the downy gunwale, pulled himself astride.

It was as he expected. Derwe Coreme had looked through the cusp and lay back in a daze. The violet cusp reposed in her lap.

Cugel seized it then for a moment stared down into the exquisite face and wondered if he dared more. Firx thought not. Already Derwe Coreme was sighing and moving her head.

Cugel leapt from the boat, and only just in time. Had she seen him? He ran to a clump of reeds which grew by a pond, flung himself in the water. From here he saw the walking-boat halt while Derwe Coreme rose to her feet. She felt through the pink down for the cusp, then she looked all around the countryside. But the blood-red light of the low sun was in her eyes when she looked toward Cugel, and she saw only the reeds and the reflection of sun on water.

Angry and sullen as never before, she set the boat into motion. It walked, then cantered, then loped to the south.

Cugel emerged from the water, inspected the magic cusp, tucked it into his pouch, looked back toward Smolod. He started to walk south, then paused. He took the cusp from his pocket, closed his left eye, held the cusp to his right. There rose the palaces, tier on tier, tower above tower, the gardens hanging down the terraces…Cugel would have stared a long time but Firx became restive.

Cugel returned the cusp to his pouch and once again set his face to the south, for the long journey back to Almery.

AFTERWORD TO "THE OVERWORLD"

I was one of those precocious, highly intelligent kids, old beyond my years. I had lots of brothers and sisters, but I was isolated from them in a certain kind of way. I just read and read and read. One of the things I read was the old *Weird Tales* magazine, which published Clark Ashton Smith. He was one of the generative geniuses of fantasy…Smith is a little clumsy at times, but at least his prose is always readable.

When I wrote my first fantasies, I was no longer aware of Smith—it had sunk so far into my subconscious. But when it was pointed out to me, I could very readily see the influence.

—Jack Vance 1983

THE MEN RETURN

The Relict came furtively down the crag, a shambling gaunt creature with tortured eyes. He moved in a series of quick dashes using panels of dark air for concealment, running behind each passing shadow, at times crawling on all fours, head low to the ground. Arriving at the final low outcrop of rock, he halted and peered across the plain.

Far away rose low hills, blurring into the sky, which was mottled and sallow like poor milk-glass. The intervening plain spread like rotten velvet, black-green and wrinkled, streaked with ocher and rust. A fountain of liquid rock jetted high in the air, branched out into black coral. In the middle distance a family of gray objects evolved with a sense of purposeful destiny: spheres melted into pyramids, became domes, tufts of white spires, sky-piercing poles; then, as a final tour de force, tesseracts.

The Relict cared nothing for this; he needed food and out on the plain were plants. They would suffice in lieu of anything better. They grew in the ground, or sometimes on a floating lump of water, or surrounding a core of hard black gas. There were dank black flaps of leaf, clumps of haggard thorn, pale green bulbs, stalks with leaves and contorted flowers. There were no recognizable species, and the Relict had no means of knowing if the leaves and tendrils he had eaten yesterday would poison him today.

He tested the surface of the plain with his foot. The glassy surface (though it likewise seemed a construction of red and gray-green pyramids) accepted his weight, then suddenly sucked at his leg. In a frenzy he tore himself free, jumped back, squatted on the temporarily solid rock.

Hunger rasped at his stomach. He must eat. He contemplated the plain. Not too far away a pair of Organisms played—sliding, diving, dancing, striking flamboyant poses. Should they approach he would try to kill one of them. They resembled men, and so should make a good meal.

He waited. A long time? A short time? It might have been either; duration had neither quantitative nor qualitative reality. The sun had vanished, and there was no standard cycle or recurrence. 'Time' was a word blank of meaning.

Matters had not always been so. The Relict retained a few tattered recollections of the old days, before system and logic had been rendered obsolete. Man had dominated Earth by virtue of a single assumption: that an effect could be traced to a cause, itself the effect of a previous cause.

Manipulation of this basic law yielded rich results; there seemed no need for any other tool or instrumentality. Man congratulated himself on his generalized structure. He could live on desert, on plain or ice, in forest or in city; Nature had not shaped him to a special environment.

He was unaware of his vulnerability. Logic was the special environment; the brain was the special tool.

Then came the terrible hour when Earth swam into a pocket of non-causality, and all the ordered tensions of cause-effect dissolved. The special tool was useless; it had no purchase on reality. From the two billions of men, only a few survived—the mad. They were now the Organisms, lords of the era, their discords so exactly equivalent to the vagaries of the land as to constitute a peculiar wild wisdom. Or perhaps the disorganized matter of the world, loose from the old organization, was peculiarly sensitive to psycho-kinesis.

A handful of others, the Relicts, managed to exist, but only through a delicate set of circumstances. They were the ones most strongly charged with the old causal dynamic. It persisted sufficiently to control the metabolism of their bodies, but could extend no further. They were fast dying out, for sanity provided no leverage against the environment. Sometimes their own minds sputtered and jangled, and they would go raving and leaping out across the plain.

The Organisms observed with neither surprise nor curiosity; how could surprise exist? The mad Relict might pause by an Organism, and try to duplicate the creature's existence. The Organism ate a mouthful of plant; so did the Relict. The Organism rubbed his feet with crushed water; so did the Relict. Presently the Relict would die of poison or rent bowels or skin lesions, while the Organism relaxed in the dank black grass. Or the Organism might seek to eat the Relict; and the Relict would run off in terror, unable to abide any part of the world—running, bounding, breasting the thick air; eyes wide, mouth open, calling and gasping until finally he foundered in a pool of black iron or blundered into a vacuum pocket, to bat around like a fly in a bottle.

The Relicts now numbered very few. Finn, he who crouched on the rock overlooking the plain, lived with four others. Two of these were old men and soon would die. Finn likewise would die unless he found food.

Out on the plain one of the Organisms, Alpha, sat down, caught a handful of air, a globe of blue liquid, a rock, kneaded them together, pulled the mixture like taffy, gave it a great heave. It uncoiled from his hand like rope. The Relict crouched low. No telling what deviltry would occur to the creature. He and all the rest of them—unpredictable! The Relict valued their flesh as food; but the Organisms would eat him if opportunity offered. In the competition he was at a great disadvantage. Their random acts baffled him. If, seeking to escape, he ran, the worst terror would begin. The direction he set his face was seldom the direction the varying frictions of the ground let him move. But the Organisms were as random and uncommitted as the environment, and the double set of disorders sometimes compounded, sometimes canceled each other. In the latter case the Organism might catch him…It was inexplicable. But then, what was not? The word 'explanation' had no meaning.

They were moving toward him; had they seen him? He flattened himself against the sullen yellow rock.

The two Organisms paused not far away. He could hear their sounds, and crouched, sick from conflicting pangs of hunger and fear.

Alpha sank to his knees, lay flat on his back, arms and legs flung out at random, addressing the sky in a series of musical cries, sibilants, guttural groans. It was a personal language he had only now improvised, but Beta understood him well.

"A vision," cried Alpha. "I see past the sky. I see knots, spinning circles. They tighten into hard points; they will never come undone."

Beta perched on a pyramid, glanced over his shoulder at the mottled sky.

"An intuition," chanted Alpha, "a picture out of the other time. It is hard, merciless, inflexible."

Beta poised on the pyramid, dove through the glassy surface, swam under Alpha, emerged, lay flat beside him.

"Observe the Relict on the hillside. In his blood is the whole of the old race—the narrow men with minds like cracks. He has exuded the intuition. Clumsy thing—a blunderer," said Alpha.

"They are all dead, all of them," said Beta. "Although three or four remain." (When past, present and future are no more than ideas left over from another era, like boats on a dry lake—then the completion of a process can never be defined.)

Alpha said, "This is the vision. I see the Relicts swarming the Earth; then whisking off to nowhere, like gnats in the wind. This is behind us."

The Organisms lay quiet, considering the vision.

A rock, or perhaps a meteor, fell from the sky, struck into the surface of the pond. It left a circular hole which slowly closed. From another part of the pool a gout of fluid splashed into the air, floated away.

Alpha spoke: "Again—the intuition comes strong! There will be lights in the sky."

The fever died in him. He hooked a finger into the air, hoisted himself to his feet.

Beta lay quiet. Slugs, ants, flies, beetles were crawling on him, boring, breeding. Alpha knew that Beta could arise, shake off the insects, stride off. But Beta seemed to prefer passivity. That was well enough. He could produce another Beta should he choose, or a dozen of him. Sometimes the world swarmed with Organisms, all sorts, all colors, tall as steeples, short and squat as flower-pots. Sometimes they hid quietly in deep caves, and sometimes the tentative substance of Earth would shift, and perhaps one, or perhaps thirty, would be shut in the subterranean cocoon, and all would sit gravely waiting, until such time as the ground would open and they could peer blinking and pallid out into the light.

"I feel a lack," said Alpha. "I will eat the Relict." He set forth, and sheer chance brought him near to the ledge of yellow rock. Finn the Relict sprang to his feet in panic.

Alpha tried to communicate so that Finn might pause while Alpha ate. But Finn had no grasp for the many-valued overtones of Alpha's voice. He seized a rock, hurled it at Alpha. The rock puffed into a cloud of dust, blew back into the Relict's face.

Alpha moved closer, extended his long arms. The Relict kicked. His feet went out from under him and he slid out on the plain. Alpha ambled complacently behind him. Finn began to crawl away. Alpha moved off to the right—one direction was as good as another. He collided with Beta, and began to eat Beta instead of the Relict. The Relict hesitated; then approached, and joining Alpha, pushed chunks of pink flesh into his mouth.

Alpha said to the Relict, "I was about to communicate an intuition to him whom we dine upon. I will speak to you."

Finn could not understand Alpha's personal language. He ate as rapidly as possible.

Alpha spoke on. "There will be lights in the sky. The great lights."

Finn rose to his feet and warily watching Alpha, seized Beta's legs, began to pull him toward the hill. Alpha watched with quizzical unconcern.

It was hard work for the spindly Relict. Sometimes Beta floated; sometimes he wafted off on the air; sometimes he adhered to the terrain. At last he sank into a knob of granite which froze around him. Finn tried to jerk Beta loose, and then to pry him up with a stick, without success.

He ran back and forth in an agony of indecision. Beta began to collapse, wither, like a jellyfish on hot sand. The Relict abandoned the hulk. Too late, too late! Food going to waste! The world was a hideous place of frustration!

Temporarily his belly was full. He started back up the crag, and presently found the camp, where the four other Relicts waited—two ancient males, two females. The females, Gisa and Reak, like Finn, had been out foraging. Gisa had brought in a slab of lichen; Reak a bit of nameless carrion.

The old men, Boad and Tagart, sat quietly waiting either for food or for death.

The women greeted Finn sullenly. "Where is the food you went forth to find?"

"I had a whole carcass," said Finn. "I could not carry it."

Boad had slyly stolen the slab of lichen and was cramming it into his mouth. It came alive, quivered and exuded a red ichor which was poison, and the old man died.

"Now there is food," said Finn. "Let us eat."

But the poison created a putrescence; the body seethed with blue foam, flowed away of its own energy.

The women turned to look at the other old man, who said in a quavering voice, "Eat me if you must—but why not choose Reak, who is younger than I?"

Reak, the younger of the women, gnawing on the bit of carrion, made no reply.

Finn said hollowly, "Why do we worry ourselves? Food is ever more difficult, and we are the last of all men."

"No, no," spoke Reak, "not the last. We saw others on the green mound."

"That was long ago," said Gisa. "Now they are surely dead."

"Perhaps they have found a source of food," suggested Reak.

Finn rose to his feet, looked across the plain. "Who knows? Perhaps there is a more pleasant land beyond the horizon."

"There is nothing anywhere but waste and evil creatures," snapped Gisa.

"What could be worse than here?" Finn argued calmly.

No one could find grounds for disagreement.

"Here is what I propose," said Finn. "Notice this tall peak. Notice the layers of hard air. They bump into the peak, they bounce off, they float in and out and disappear past the edge of sight. Let us all climb this peak, and when a sufficiently large bank of air passes, we will throw ourselves on top, and allow it to carry us to the beautiful regions which may exist just out of sight."

There was argument. The old man Tagart protested his feebleness; the women derided the possibility of the bountiful regions Finn envisioned, but presently, grumbling and arguing, they began to clamber up the pinnacle.

It took a long time; the obsidian was soft as jelly and Tagart several times professed himself at the limit of his endurance. But still they climbed, and at last reached the pinnacle. There was barely room to stand. They could see in all directions, far out over the landscape, till vision was lost in the watery gray.

The women bickered and pointed in various directions, but there was small sign of happier territory. In one direction blue-green hills shivered like bladders full of oil. In another direction lay a streak of black—a gorge or a lake of clay. In another direction were blue-green hills—the same they had seen in the first direction; somehow there had been a shift. Below was the plain, gleaming like an iridescent beetle, here and there pocked with black velvet spots, overgrown with questionable vegetation.

They saw Organisms, a dozen shapes loitering by ponds, munching vegetable pods or small rocks or insects. There came Alpha. He moved slowly, still awed by his vision, ignoring the other Organisms. Their play went on, but presently they stood quiet, sharing the oppression.

On the obsidian peak, Finn caught hold of a passing filament of air, drew it in. "Now—all on, and we sail away to the Land of Plenty."

"No," protested Gisa, "there is no room, and who knows if it will fly in the right direction?"

"Where is the right direction?" asked Finn. "Does anyone know?"

No one knew, but the women still refused to climb aboard the filament. Finn turned to Tagart. "Here, old one, show these women how it is; climb on!"

"No, no," he cried. "I fear the air; this is not for me."

"Climb on, old man, then we follow."

Wheezing and fearful, clenching his hands deep into the spongy mass, Tagart pulled himself out onto the air, spindly shanks hanging over into nothing. "Now," spoke Finn, "who next?"

The women still refused. "You go then, yourself," cried Gisa.

"And leave you, my last guarantee against hunger? Aboard now!"

"No, the air is too small; let the old one go and we will follow on a larger."

"Very well." Finn released his grip. The air floated off over the plain, Tagart straddling and clutching for dear life.

They watched him curiously. "Observe," said Finn, "how fast and easily moves the air. Above the Organisms, over all the slime and uncertainty."

But the air itself was uncertain, and the old man's raft dissolved. Clutching at the departing wisps, Tagart sought to hold his cushion together. It fled from under him, and he fell.

On the peak the three watched the spindly shape flap and twist on its way to earth far below.

"Now," Reak exclaimed in vexation, "we even have no more meat."

"None," said Gisa, "except the visionary Finn himself."

They surveyed Finn. Together they would more than outmatch him.

"Careful," cried Finn. "I am the last of the Men. You are my women, subject to my orders."

They ignored him, muttering to each other, looking at him from the side of their faces.

"Careful!" cried Finn. "I will throw you both from this peak."

"That is what we plan for you," said Gisa. They advanced with sinister caution.

"Stop! I am the last man!"

"We are better off without you."

"One moment! Look at the Organisms!"

The women looked. The Organisms stood in a knot, staring at the sky.

"Look at the sky!"

The women looked; the frosted glass was cracking, breaking, curling aside.

"The blue! The blue sky of old times!"

A terribly bright light burnt down, seared their eyes. The rays warmed their naked backs.

"The sun," they said in awed voices. "The sun has come back to Earth."

The shrouded sky was gone; the sun rode proud and bright in a sea of blue. The ground below churned, cracked, heaved, solidified. They felt the obsidian harden under their feet; its color shifted to glossy black. The Earth, the sun, the galaxy, had departed the region of freedom; the other time with its restrictions and logic was once more with them.

"This is Old Earth,"cried Finn. "We are Men of Old Earth! The land is once again ours!"

"And what of the Organisms?"

"If this is the Earth of old, then let the Organisms beware!"

The Organisms stood on a low rise of ground beside a runnel of water that was rapidly becoming a river flowing out onto the plain.

Alpha cried, "Here is my intuition! It is exactly as I knew. The freedom is gone; the tightness, the constriction are back!"

"How will we defeat it?" asked another Organism.

"Easily," said a third. "Each must fight a part of the battle. I plan to hurl myself at the sun, and blot it from existence." And he crouched, threw himself into the air. He fell on his back and broke his neck.

"The fault," said Alpha, "is in the air; because the air surrounds all things."

Six Organisms ran off in search of air, and stumbling into the river, drowned.

"In any event," said Alpha, "I am hungry." He looked around for suitable food. He seized an insect which stung him. He dropped it. "My hunger remains."

He spied Finn and the two women descending from the crag. "I will eat one of the Relicts," he said. "Come, let us all eat."

Three of them started off—as usual in random directions. By chance Alpha came face to face with Finn. He prepared to eat, but Finn picked up a rock. The rock remained a rock: hard, sharp, heavy. Finn swung it down, taking joy in the inertia. Alpha died with a crushed skull. One of the other Organisms attempted to step across a crevasse twenty feet wide and was engulfed; the other sat down, swallowed rocks to assuage his hunger, and presently went into convulsions.

Finn pointed here and there around the fresh new land. "In that quarter, the new city, like that of the legends. Over here the farms, the cattle."

"We have none of these," protested Gisa.

"No," said Finn. "Not now. But once more the sun rises and sets, once more rock has weight and air has none. Once more water falls as rain and flows to the sea." He stepped forward over the fallen Organism. "Let us make plans."

AFTERWORD TO "THE MEN RETURN"

Going back to the painting analogy; if you're painting seascapes, you'd use a lot of blues and greens. If you're painting the inside of an old Genoese tavern, you'd use blacks, browns and golds.

Essentially, I try to use the tools appropriate to the job; the tools being words and style. I don't plan these things ahead of time, they simply occur.

—Jack Vance 1977

THE SORCERER PHARESM

The mountains were behind: the dark defiles, the tarns, the echoing stone heights—all now a sooty bulk to the north. For a time Cugel wandered a region of low rounded hills the color and texture of old wood, with groves of blue-black trees dense along the ridges, then came upon a faint trail which took him south by long swings and slants, and at last broke out over a vast dim plain. A half-mile to the right rose a line of tall cliffs, which instantly attracted his attention, bringing him a haunting pang of déjà-vu. He stared mystified. At some time in the past he had known these cliffs: how? when? His memory provided no response. He settled himself upon a low lichen-covered rock to rest, but now Firx, the monitor which Iucounu the Laughing Magician had implanted in Cugel's viscera, became impatient and inflicted a stimulating pang. Cugel leapt to his feet, groaning with weariness and shaking his fist to the southwest, the presumable direction of Almery. "Iucounu, Iucounu! If I could repay a tenth of your offenses, the world would think me harsh!"

He set off down the trail, under the cliffs which had affected him with such poignant but impossible recollections. Far below spread the plain, filling three-quarters of the horizon with colors much like those of the lichened rock Cugel had just departed: black patches of woodland; a gray crumble where ruins filled an entire valley; nondescript streaks of gray-green, lavender, gray-brown; the leaden glint of two great rivers disappearing into the haze of distance.

Cugel's brief rest had only served to stiffen his joints; he limped, and the pouch chafed his hip. Even more distressing was the hunger gripping his belly. Another tally against Iucounu who had sent Cugel to the northern wastes on a mission of wanton frivolity: Iucounu, it must be allowed had furnished an amulet converting such normally inedible substances as grass, wood, horn, hair, humus and the like into a nutritious paste. Unfortunately—and this was a measure of Iucounu's mordant humor—the paste retained the flavor of the native substance, and during his passage of the mountains Cugel had tasted little better than spurge, cullion, blackwort, oak-twigs and galls, and on one occasion, when all else failed, certain refuse discovered in the cave of a bearded thawn. Cugel had eaten only minimally; his long spare frame had become gaunt; his cheek-bones protruded like sponsons; the black eyebrows which once had crooked so jauntily now lay flat and dispirited. Truly, truly, Iucounu had much to answer for! And Cugel, as he proceeded, debated the exact quality of revenge he would take if ever he found his way back to Almery.

The trail swung down upon a wide stony flat where the wind had carved a thousand grotesque figures. Surveying the area Cugel thought to perceive regularity among the eroded shapes, and halted to rub his long chin in appraisal. The pattern displayed an extreme subtlety—so subtle indeed, that Cugel wondered if it had not been projected by his own mind. Moving closer, he discerned further complexities, and elaborations upon complexities: twists, spires, volutes; disks, saddles, wrenched spheres; torsions and flexions; spindles, cardioids, lanciform pinnacles: the most laborious, painstaking and intricate rock-carving conceivable, manifestly no random effort of the elements. Cugel frowned in perplexity, unable to imagine a motive for so complex an undertaking.

He went on and a moment later heard voices, together with the clank of tools. He stopped short, listened cautiously, then proceeded, to come upon a gang of about fifty men ranging in stature from three inches to well over twelve feet. Cugel approached on tentative feet, but after a glance the workers paid him no heed, continuing to chisel, grind, scrape, probe and polish with dedicated zeal.

Cugel watched for several minutes, then approached the overseer, a man three feet in height who stood at a lectern consulting the plans spread before him, comparing them to the work in progress by means of an ingenious optical device. He appeared to note everything at once, calling instructions, chiding, exhorting against error, instructing the least deft in the use of their tools. To exemplify his remarks he used a wonderfully extensible forefinger, which reached forth thirty feet to tap at a section of rock, to scratch a quick diagram, then as swiftly retract.

The foreman drew back a pace or two, temporarily satisfied with the work in progress, and Cugel came forward. "What intricate effort is this and what is its object?"

"The work is as you see," replied the foreman in a voice of penetrating compass. "From natural rock we produce specified shapes, at the behest of the sorcerer Pharesm...Now then! Now then!" The cry was addressed to a man three feet taller than Cugel, who had been striking the stone with a pointed maul. "I detect overconfidence!" The forefinger shot forth. "Use great care at this juncture; note how the rock tends to cleave? Strike here a blow of the sixth intensity at the vertical, using a semi-clenched grip; at this point a fourth-intensity blow groin-wise; then employ a quarter-gauge bant-iron to remove the swange."

With the work once more going correctly, he fell to studying his plans, shaking his head with a frown of dissatisfaction. "Much too slow! The craftsmen toil as if in a drugged torpor, or else display a mulish stupidity. Only yesterday Dadio Fessadil, he of three ells with the green kerchief yonder, used a nineteen-gauge feezing-bar to groove the bead of a small inverted quatrefoil."

Cugel shook his head in surprise, as if never had he heard of so egregious a blunder. And he asked: "What prompts this inordinate rock-hewing?"

"I cannot say," replied the foreman. "The work has been in progress three hundred and eighteen years, but during this time Pharesm has never clarified his motives. They must be pointed and definite, for he makes a daily inspection and is quick to indicate errors." Here he turned aside to consult with a man as tall as Cugel's knee, who voiced uncertainty as to the pitch of a certain volute. The foreman, consulting an index, resolved the matter; then he turned back to Cugel, this time with an air of frank appraisal. "You appear both astute and deft; would you care to take employment? We lack several craftsmen of the half-ell category, or, if you prefer more forceful manifestations, we can nicely use an apprentice stone-breaker of sixteen ells. Your stature is adjusted in either direction, there is identical scope for advancement. As you see I am a man of four ells. I reached the position of Striker in one year, Molder of Forms in three, Assistant Chade in ten, and I have now served as Chief Chade for nineteen years. My predecessor was of two ells, and the Chief Chade before him was a ten-ell man." He went on to enumerate advantages of the work, which included sustenance, shelter, narcotics of choice, nympharium privileges, a stipend starting at ten terces a day, various other benefits including Pharesm's services as diviner and exorciser. "Additionally, Pharesm maintains a conservatory where all may enrich their intellects. I myself take instruction in Insect Identification, the Heraldry of the Kings of Old Gomaz, Unison Chanting, Practical Catalepsy and Orthodox Doctrine. You will never find a master more generous than Pharesm the Sorcerer!"

Cugel restrained a smile for the Chief Chade's enthusiasm; still, his stomach was roiling with hunger and he did not reject the proffer out of hand. "I had never before considered such a career," he said. "You cite advantages of which I was unaware."

"True; they are not generally known."

"I cannot immediately say yes or no. It is a decision of consequence which I feel I should consider in all its aspects."

The Chief Chade gave a nod of profound agreement. "We encourage deliberation in our craftsmen, when every stroke must achieve the desired effect. To repair an inaccuracy of as much as a fingernail's width the entire block must be removed, a new block fitted into the socket of the old, whereupon all begins anew. Until the work has reached its previous stage nympharium privileges are denied to all. Hence, we wish no opportunistic or impulsive newcomers to the group."

Firx, suddenly apprehending that Cugel proposed a delay, made representations of a most agonizing nature. Clasping his abdomen, Cugel took himself aside and while the Chief Chade watched in perplexity, argued heatedly with Firx. "How may I proceed without sustenance?" Firx's response was an incisive motion of the barbs. "Impossible!" exclaimed Cugel. "The amulet of Iucounu theoretically suffices, but I can stomach no more spurge; remember, if I fall dead in the trail, you will never rejoin your comrade in Iucounu's vats!"

Firx saw the justice of the argument and reluctantly became quiet. Cugel returned to the lectern, where the Chief Chade had been distracted by the discovery of a large tourmaline opposing the flow of a certain complicated helix. Finally Cugel was able to engage his attention. "While I weigh the proffer of employment and the conflicting advantages of diminution versus elongation, I will need a couch on which to recline. I also wish to test the perquisites you describe, perhaps for the period of a day or more."

"Your prudence is commendable," declared the Chief Chade. "The folk of today tend to commit themselves rashly to courses they later regret. It was not so in my youth, when sobriety and discretion prevailed.

I will arrange for your admission into the compound, where you may verify each of my assertions. You will find Pharesm stern but just, and only the man who hacks the rock willy-nilly has cause to complain. But observe! Here is Pharesm the Sorcerer on his daily inspection!"

Up the trail came a man of imposing stature wearing a voluminous white robe. His countenance was benign; his hair was like yellow down; his eyes were turned upward as if rapt in the contemplation of an ineffable sublimity. His arms were sedately folded, and he moved without motion of his legs. The workers, doffing their caps and bowing in unison, chanted a respectful salute, to which Pharesm returned an inclination of the head. Spying Cugel, he paused, made a swift survey of the work so far accomplished, then glided without haste to the lectern.

"All appears reasonably exact," he told the Chief Chade. "I believe the polish on the underside of Epi-projection 56-16 is uneven and I detect a minute chip on the secondary cinctor of the nineteenth spire. Neither circumstance seems of major import and I recommend no disciplinary action."

"The deficiencies shall be repaired and the careless artisans reprimanded: this at the very least!" exclaimed the Chief Chade in an angry passion. "Now I wish to introduce a possible recruit to our work-force. He claims no experience at the trade, and will deliberate before deciding to join our group. If he so elects, I envision the usual period as rubble-gatherer, before he is entrusted with tool-sharpening and preliminary excavation."

"Yes; this would accord with our usual practice. However..." Pharesm glided effortlessly forward, took Cugel's left hand and performed a swift divination upon the fingernails. His bland countenance became sober. "I see contradictions of four varieties. Still it is clear that your optimum bent lies elsewhere than in the hewing and shaping of rock. I advise that you seek another and more compatible employment."

"Well spoken!" cried the Chief Chade. "Pharesm the Sorcerer demonstrates his infallible altruism! In order that I do not fall short of the mark I hereby withdraw my proffer of employment! Since no purpose can now be served by reclining upon a couch or testing the perquisites, you need waste no more irreplaceable time."

Cugel made a sour face. "So casual a divination might well be inaccurate."

The Chief Chade extended his forefinger thirty feet vertically in outraged remonstrance, but Pharesm gave a placid nod. "This is quite correct, and I will gladly perform a more comprehensive divination, though the process requires six to eight hours."

"So long?" asked Cugel in astonishment.

"This is the barest minimum. First you are swathed head to foot in the intestines of fresh-killed owls, then immersed in a warm bath containing a number of secret organic substances. I must, of course, char the small toe of your left foot, and dilate your nose sufficiently to admit an explorer beetle, that he may study the conduits leading to and from your sensorium. But let us return to my divinatory, that we may commence the process in good time."

Cugel pulled at his chin, torn this way and that. Finally he said, "I am a cautious man, and even must ponder the advisability of undertaking such a divination; hence, I will require several days of calm and meditative somnolence. Your compound and the adjacent nympharium appear to afford the conditions requisite to such a state; hence—"

Pharesm indulgently shook his head. "Caution, like any other virtue, can be carried to an extreme. The divination must proceed at once."

Cugel attempted to argue further but Pharesm was adamant, and presently glided off down the trail.

Cugel disconsolately went to the side, considering first this stratagem, then that. The sun neared the zenith, and the workmen began to speculate as to the nature of the viands to be served for their mid-day meal. At last the Chief Chade signaled; all put down their tools and gathered about the cart which contained the repast.

Cugel jocularly called out that he might be persuaded to share the meal, but the Chief Chade would not hear of it. "As in all of Pharesm's activities, an exactitude of consequence must prevail. It is an unthinkable discrepancy that fifty-four men should consume the food intended for fifty-three."

Cugel could contrive no apposite reply, and sat in silence while the rock-hewers munched at meat pies, cheeses and salt fish. All ignored him save for one, a quarter-ell man whose generosity far exceeded his stature, and who undertook to reserve for Cugel a certain portion of his food. Cugel replied that he was not at all hungry, and rising to his feet wandered off through the project, hoping to discover some forgotten cache of food. He prowled here and there, but the rubble-gatherers had removed every trace of substance extraneous to the pattern. With appetite unassuaged Cugel arrived at the center of the work where, sprawled on a carved disk, he spied a most peculiar creature: essentially a gelatinous globe swimming with luminous particles from which a number of transparent tubes or tentacles dwindled away to nothing. Cugel bent to examine the creature, which pulsed with a slow internal rhythm. He prodded it with his finger, and bright little flickers rippled away from the point of contact. Interesting: a creature of unique capabilities!

Removing a pin from his garments, he prodded a tentacle, which emitted a peevish pulse of light, while the golden flecks in its substance surged back and forth. More intrigued than ever, Cugel hitched himself close, and gave himself to experimentation, probing here and there, watching the angry flickers and sparkles with great amusement.

A new thought occurred to Cugel. The creature displayed qualities reminiscent of both coelenterate and echinoderm. A terrene nudibranch? A mollusc deprived of its shell? More importantly, was the creature edible?

Cugel brought forth his amulet, applied it to the central globe and to each of the tentacles. He heard neither chime nor buzz: the creature was non-poisonous. He unsheathed his knife, sought to excise one of the tentacles, but found the substance too resilient and tough to be cut. There was a brazier nearby, kept aglow for forging and sharpening the workers' tools. He lifted the creature by two of its tentacles, carried it to the brazier and arranged it over the fire. He toasted it carefully and when he deemed it sufficiently cooked, sought to eat it. Finally, after various undignified efforts, he crammed the entire creature down his throat, finding it without taste or sensible nutritive volume.

The stone-carvers were returning to their work. With a significant glance for the foreman Cugel set off down the trail.

Not far distant was the dwelling of Pharesm the Sorcerer: a long low building of melted rock surmounted by eight oddly shaped domes of copper, mica, and bright blue glass. Pharesm himself sat at leisure before the dwelling, surveying the valley with a serene and all-inclusive magnanimity. He held up a hand in calm salute. "I wish you pleasant travels and success in all future endeavors."

"The sentiment is naturally valued," said Cugel with some bitterness. "You might however have rendered a more meaningful service by extending a share of your noon meal."

Pharesm's placid benevolence was as before. "This would have been an act of mistaken altruism. Too fulsome a generosity corrupts the recipient and stultifies his resource."

Cugel gave a bitter laugh. "I am a man of iron principle, and I will not complain, even though, lacking any better fare, I was forced to

devour a great transparent insect which I found at the heart of your
rock-carving."

Pharesm swung about with a suddenly intent expression. "A great
transparent insect, you say?"

"Insect, epiphyte, mollusc—who knows? It resembled no creature
I have yet seen, and its flavor, even after carefully grilling at the brazier,
was not distinctive."

Pharesm floated seven feet into the air, to turn the full power of his
gaze down at Cugel. He spoke in a low harsh voice: "Describe this creature in detail!"

Wondering at Pharesm's severity, Cugel obeyed. "It was thus and
thus as to dimension." He indicated with his hands. "In color it was a
gelatinous transparency shot with numberless golden specks. These
flickered and pulsed when the creature was disturbed. The tentacles
seemed to grow flimsy and disappear rather than terminate. The creature
evinced a certain sullen determination, and ingestion proved difficult."

Pharesm clutched at his head, hooking his fingers into the yellow
down of his hair. He rolled his eyes upward and uttered a tragic cry. "Ah!
Five hundred years I have toiled to entice this creature, despairing, doubt-
ing, brooding by night, yet never abandoning hope that my calculations
were accurate and my great talisman cogent. Then, when finally it appears,
you fall upon it for no other reason than to sate your repulsive gluttony!"

Cugel, somewhat daunted by Pharesm's wrath, asserted his absence
of malicious intent. Pharesm would not be mollified. He pointed out
that Cugel had committed trespass and hence had forfeited the option
of pleading innocence. "Your very existence is a mischief, compounded
by bringing the unpleasant fact to my notice. Benevolence prompted
me to forbearance, which now I perceive for a grave mistake."

"In this case," stated Cugel with dignity, "I will depart your presence at once. I wish you good fortune for the balance of the day, and
now, farewell."

"Not so fast," said Pharesm in the coldest of voices. "Exactitude has
been disturbed; the wrong which has been committed demands a counter-act to validate the Law of Equipoise. I can define the gravity of your
act in this manner: should I explode you on this instant into the most
minute of your parts the atonement would measure one ten-millionth of
your offense. A more stringent retribution becomes necessary."

Cugel spoke in great distress. "I understand that an act of consequence was performed, but remember! my participation was basically

casual. I categorically declare first my absolute innocence, second my lack of criminal intent, and third my effusive apologies. And now, since I have many leagues to travel, I will—"

Pharesm made a peremptory gesture. Cugel fell silent. Pharesm drew a deep breath. "You fail to understand the calamity you have visited upon me. I will explain, so that you may not be astounded by the rigors which await you. As I have adumbrated, the arrival of the creature was the culmination of my great effort. I determined its nature through a perusal of forty-two thousand librams, all written in cryptic language: a task requiring a hundred years. During a second hundred years I evolved a pattern to draw it in upon itself and prepared exact specification. Next I assembled stone-cutters, and across a period of three hundred years gave solid form to my pattern. Since like subsumes like, the variates and intercongeles create a suprapullulation of all areas, qualities and intervals into a crystorrhoid whorl, eventually exciting the ponentiation of a pro-ubietal chute. Today occurred the concatenation; the 'creature', as you call it, pervolved upon itself; in your idiotic malice you devoured it."

Cugel, with a trace of haughtiness, pointed out that the "idiotic malice" to which the distraught sorcerer referred was in actuality simple hunger. "In any event, what is so extraordinary about the 'creature'? Others equally ugly may be found in the net of any fisherman."

Pharesm drew himself to his full height, glared down at Cugel. "The 'creature'," he said in a grating voice, "is TOTALITY. The central globe is all of space, viewed from the inverse. The tubes are vortices into various eras, and what terrible acts you have accomplished with your prodding and poking, your boiling and chewing, are impossible to imagine!"

"What of the effects of digestion?" inquired Cugel delicately. "Will the various components of space, time and existence retain their identity after passing the length of my inner tract?"

"Bah. The concept is jejune. Enough to say that you have wreaked damage and created a serious tension in the ontological fabric. Inexorably you are required to restore equilibrium."

Cugel held out his hands. "Is it not possible a mistake has been made? That the 'creature' was no more than pseudo-TOTALITY? Or is it conceivable that the 'creature' may by some means be lured forth once more?"

"The first two theories are untenable. As to the last, I must confess that certain frantic expedients have been forming in my mind." Pharesm made a sign, and Cugel's feet became attached to the soil. "I must go to my divinatory and learn the full significance of the distressing events. In due course I will return."

"At which time I will be feeble with hunger," said Cugel fretfully. "Indeed, a crust of bread and a bite of cheese would have averted all the events for which I am now reproached."

"Silence!" thundered Pharesm. "Do not forget that your penalty remains to be fixed; it is the height of impudent recklessness to hector a person already struggling to maintain his judicious calm!"

"Allow me to say this much," replied Cugel. "If you return from your divining to find me dead and desiccated here on the path, you will have wasted much time fixing upon a penalty."

"The restoration of vitality is a small task," said Pharesm. "A variety of deaths by contrasting processes may well enter into your judgment." He started toward his divinatory, then turned back and made an impatient gesture. "Come, it is easier to feed you than return to the road."

Cugel's feet were once more free and he followed Pharesm through a wide arch into the divinatory. In a broad room with splayed gray walls, illuminated by three-colored polyhedra, Cugel devoured the food Pharesm caused to appear. Meanwhile Pharesm secluded himself in his workroom, where he occupied himself with his divinations. As time passed Cugel grew restless, and on three occasions approached the arched entrance. On each occasion a Presentment came to deter him, first in the shape of a leaping ghoul, next as a zig-zag blaze of energy, and finally as a score of glittering purple wasps.

Discouraged, Cugel went to a bench, and sat waiting with elbows on long legs, hands under his chin.

Pharesm at last reappeared, his robe wrinkled, the fine yellow down of his hair disordered into a multitude of small spikes. Cugel slowly rose to his feet.

"I have learned the whereabouts of TOTALITY," said Pharesm, in a voice like the strokes of a great gong. "In indignation, removing itself from your stomach, it has recoiled a million years into the past."

Cugel gave his head a solemn shake. "Allow me to offer my sympathy, and my counsel, which is: never despair! Perhaps the 'creature' will choose to pass this way again."

"An end to your chatter! TOTALITY must be recovered. Come."

Cugel reluctantly followed Pharesm into a small room walled with blue tile, roofed with a tall cupola of blue and orange glass. Pharesm pointed to a black disk at the center of the floor. "Stand there."

Cugel glumly obeyed. "In a certain sense, I feel that—"

"Silence!" Pharesm came forward. "Notice this object!" He displayed an ivory sphere the size of two fists, carved in exceedingly fine detail. "Here you see the pattern from which my great work is derived. It expresses the symbolic significance of NULLITY to which TOTALITY must necessarily attach itself, by Kratinjae's Second Law of Cryptorrhoid Affinities, with which you are possibly familiar."

"Not in every aspect," said Cugel. "But may I ask your intentions?"

Pharesm's mouth moved in a cool smile. "I am about to attempt one of the most cogent spells ever evolved: a spell so fractious, harsh, and coactive, that Phandaal, Ranking Sorcerer of Grand Motholam, barred its use. If I am able to control it, you will be propelled one million years into the past. There you will reside until you have accomplished your mission, when you may return."

Cugel stepped quickly from the black disk. "I am not the man for this mission, whatever it may be. I fervently urge the use of someone else!"

Pharesm ignored the expostulation. "The mission, of course, is to bring the symbol into contact with TOTALITY." He brought forth a wad of tangled gray tissue. "In order to facilitate your search, I endow you with this instrument which relates all possible vocables to every conceivable system of meaning." He thrust the net into Cugel's ear, where it swiftly engaged itself with the nerve of consonant expression. "Now," said Pharesm, "you need listen to a strange language for but three minutes when you become proficient in its use. And now, another article to enhance the prospect of success: this ring. Notice the jewel: should you approach to within a league of TOTALITY, darting lights within the gem will guide you. Is all clear?"

Cugel gave a reluctant nod. "There is another matter to be considered. Assume that your calculations are incorrect and that TOTALITY has returned only nine hundred thousand years into the past: what then? Must I dwell out my life in this possibly barbarous era?"

Pharesm frowned in displeasure. "Such a situation involves an error of ten percent. My system of reckoning seldom admits of deviation greater than one per cent."

Cugel began to make calculations, but now Pharesm signaled to the black disk. "Back! And do not again move hence, or you will be the worse for it!"

Sweat oozing from his glands, knees quivering and sagging, Cugel returned to the place designated.

Pharesm retreated to the far end of the room, where he stepped into a coil of gold tubing, which sprang spiraling up to clasp his body. From a desk he took four black disks, which he began to shuffle and juggle with such fantastic dexterity that they blurred in Cugel's sight. Pharesm at last flung the disks away; spinning and wheeling they hung in the air, gradually drifting toward Cugel.

Pharesm next took up a white tube, pressed it tight against his lips and spoke an incantation. The tube swelled and bulged into a great globe. Pharesm twisted the end shut and shouting a thunderous spell, hurled the globe at the spinning disks, and all exploded. Cugel was surrounded, seized, jerked in all directions outward, compressed with equal vehemence: the net result, a thrust in a direction contrary to all, with an impetus equivalent to the tide of a million years. Among dazzling lights and distorted visions Cugel was transported beyond his consciousness.

Cugel awoke in a glare of orange-gold sunlight, of a radiance he had never known before. He lay on his back looking up into a sky of warm blue, of lighter tone and softer texture than the indigo sky of his own time.

He tested arms and legs and finding no damage, sat upright, then slowly rose to his feet, blinking in the unfamiliar radiance.

The topography had changed only slightly. The mountains to the north were taller and of harsher texture, and Cugel could not identify the way he had come—or, more properly—the way he would come. The site of Pharesm's project was now a low forest of feather-light green trees, on which hung clusters of red berries. The valley was as before, though the rivers flowed by different courses and three great cities were visible at varying distances. The air drifting up from the valley carried a strange tart fragrance mingled with an antique exhalation of moulder and must, and it seemed to Cugel that a peculiar melancholy hung in the air; in fact, he thought to hear music: a slow plaintive melody, so sad as to bring tears to his eyes. He searched for the source of the music, but it faded and disappeared even as he sought it, and only when he ceased to listen did it return.

For the first time Cugel looked toward the cliffs which rose to the west, and now the sense of déjà-vu was stronger than ever. Cugel pulled at his chin in puzzlement. The time was a million years previous to that other occasion on which he had seen the cliffs, and hence, by definition, must be the first. But it was also the second time, for he well remembered his initial experience of the cliffs. On the other hand, the logic of time could not be contravened, and by such reckoning this view preceded the other. A paradox, thought Cugel: a puzzle indeed! Which experience had provided the background to the poignant sense of familiarity he had felt on both occasions?...Cugel dismissed the subject as unprofitable and started to turn away when movement caught his eye. He looked back up the face of the cliffs, and the air was suddenly full and rich with the music he had heard before, music of anguish and exalted despair. Cugel stared in wonder. A great winged creature wearing white robes flapped on high along the face of the cliff. The wings were long, ribbed with black chitin, sheathed with gray membrane. Cugel watched in awe as it swooped into a cave high up in the face of the cliff.

A gong tolled, from a direction Cugel could not determine. Overtones shuddered across the air, and when they died, the unheard music became almost audible. From far over the valley came one of the Winged Beings, carrying a human form, of what age and sex Cugel could not determine. It hovered beside the cliff and dropped its burden. Cugel thought to hear a faint cry and the music was sad, stately, sonorous. The body seemed to fall slowly down the great height and struck at last at the base of the cliff. The Winged Being, after dropping the body, glided to a high ledge, where it folded its wings and stood like a man, staring over the valley. Cugel shrank back behind a rock. Had he been seen? He could not be sure. He heaved a deep sigh. This sad golden world of the past was not to his liking; the sooner he could leave the better. He examined the ring which Pharesm had furnished, but the gem shone like dull glass, with none of the darting glitters which would point the direction to TOTALITY. It was as Cugel feared. Pharesm had erred in his calculations and Cugel could never return to his own time.

The sound of flapping wings caused him to look into the sky. He shrank back into such concealment as the rock offered. The music of woe swelled and sighed away, as in the light of the setting sun the winged creature hovered beside the cliff and dropped its victim. Then it landed on a ledge with a great flapping of wings and entered a cave.

Cugel rose to his feet and ran crouching down the path through the amber dusk.

The path presently entered a grove of trees and here Cugel paused to catch his breath, after which he proceeded more circumspectly. He crossed a patch of cultivated ground on which stood a vacant hut. Cugel considered it as shelter for the night, but thought to see a dark shape watching from the interior and passed it by.

The trail led away from the cliffs, across rolling downs, and just before the twilight gave way to night Cugel came to a village standing on the banks of a pond.

Cugel approached warily, but was encouraged by the signs of tidiness and good husbandry. In a park beside the pond stood a pavilion possibly intended for music, miming or declamation; surrounding the park were small narrow houses with high gables, the ridges of which were raised in decorative scallops. Opposite the pond was a larger building, with an ornate front of woven wood and enameled plaques of red, blue and yellow. Three tall gables served as its roof, the central ridge supporting an intricate carved panel, while those to either side bore a series of small spherical blue lamps. At the front was a wide pergola sheltering benches, tables and an open space, all illuminated by red and green fire-fans. Here towns-folk took their ease, inhaling incense and drinking wine, while youths and maidens cavorted in an eccentric high-kicking dance, to the music of pipes and a concertina.

Emboldened by the placidity of the scene, Cugel approached. The villagers were of a type he had never before encountered, of no great stature, with generally large heads and long restless arms. Their skin was a rich pumpkin orange; their eyes and teeth were black; their hair, likewise black, hung smoothly down beside the faces of the men to terminate in a fringe of blue beads, while the women wound their hair around white rings and pegs, to arrive at a coiffure of no small complexity. The features were heavy at jaw and cheek-bone; the long widespaced eyes drooped in a droll manner at the outer corners. The noses and ears were long and were under considerable muscular control, endowing the faces with great vivacity. The men wore flounced black kirtles, brown surcoats, headgear consisting of a wide black disk, a black cylinder, another lesser disk, surmounted by a gilded ball. The women wore black trousers, brown jackets with enameled disks at the navel, and at each buttock a simulated tail of green or red plumes, possibly an indication as to marital status.

Cugel stepped into the light of the fire-fans; instantly all talk ceased. Noses became rigid, eyes stared, ears twisted about in curiosity. Cugel smiled to left and right, waved his hands in a debonair all-inclusive greeting, and took a seat at an empty table.

There were mutters of astonishment at the various tables, too quiet to reach Cugel's ears. Presently one of the elders arose and approaching Cugel's table spoke a sentence, which Cugel found unintelligible, for with insufficient scope, Pharesm's mesh as yet failed to yield meaning. Cugel smiled politely, held wide his hands in a gesture of well-meaning helplessness. The elder spoke once more, in a rather sharper voice, and again Cugel indicated his inability to understand. The elder gave his ears a sharp disapproving jerk and turned away. Cugel signaled to the proprietor, pointed to the bread and wine on a nearby table and signified his desire that the same be brought to him.

The proprietor voiced a query which, for all its unintelligibility, Cugel was able to interpret. He brought forth a gold coin, and, satisfied, the proprietor turned away.

Conversation recommenced at the various tables and before long the vocables conveyed meaning to Cugel. When he had eaten and drunk, he rose to his feet and walked to the table of the elder who had first spoken to him, where he bowed respectfully. "Do I have permission to join you at your table?"

"Certainly; if you are so inclined. Sit." The elder indicated a seat. "From your behavior I assumed that you were not only deaf and dumb, but also guilty of mental retardation. It is now clear, at least, that you hear and speak."

"I profess rationality as well," said Cugel. "As a traveler from afar, ignorant of your customs, I thought it best to watch quietly a few moments, lest in error I commit a solecism."

"Ingenious but peculiar," was the elder's comment. "Still, your conduct offers no explicit contradiction to orthodoxy. May I inquire the urgency which brings you to Farwan?"

Cugel glanced at his ring; the crystal was dull and lifeless: TOTALITY was clearly elsewhere. "My homeland is uncultured; I travel that I may learn the modes and styles of more civilized folk."

"Indeed!" The elder mulled the matter over for a moment, and nodded in qualified approval. "Your garments and physiognomy are of a type unfamiliar to me; where is this homeland of yours?"

"It lies in a region so remote," said Cugel, "that never till this instant had I knowledge of the land of Farwan!"

The elder flattened his ears in surprise. "What? Glorious Farwan, unknown? The great cities Impergos, Tharuwe, Rhaverjand—all unheard of? What of the illustrious Sembers? Surely the fame of the

Sembers has reached you? They expelled the star-pirates; they brought the sea to the Land of Platforms; the splendor of Padara Palace is beyond description!"

Cugel sadly shook his head. "No rumor of this extraordinary magnificence has come to my ears."

The elder gave his nose a saturnine twitch. Cugel was clearly a dolt. He said shortly: "Matters are as I state."

"I doubt nothing," said Cugel. "In fact I admit to ignorance. But tell me more, for I may be forced to abide long in this region. For instance, what of the Winged Beings that reside in the cliff? What manner of creature are they?"

The elder pointed toward the sky. "If you had the eyes of a nocturnal titvit you might note a dark moon which reels around the earth, and which cannot be seen except when it casts its shadow upon the sun. The Winged Beings are denizens of this dark world and their ultimate nature is unknown. They serve the Great God Yelisea in this fashion: whenever comes the time for man or woman to die, the Winged Beings are informed by a despairing signal from the dying person's norn. They thereupon descend upon the unfortunate and convey him to their caves, which in actuality constitute a magic opening into the blessed land Byssom."

Cugel leaned back, black eyebrows raised in a somewhat quizzical arch. "Indeed, indeed," he said, in a voice which the elder found insufficiently earnest.

"There can be no doubt as to the truth of the facts as I have stated them. Orthodoxy derives from this axiomatic foundation, and the two systems are mutually reinforcing: hence each is doubly validated."

Cugel frowned. "The matter undoubtedly goes as you aver—but are the Winged Beings consistently accurate in their choice of victim?"

The elder rapped the table in annoyance. "The doctrine is irrefutable, for those whom the Winged Beings take never survive, even when they appear in the best of health. Admittedly the fall upon the rocks conduces toward death, but it is the mercy of Yelisea which sees fit to grant a speedy extinction, rather than the duration of a possibly agonizing canker. The system is wholly beneficent. The Winged Beings summon only the moribund, which are then thrust through the cliff into the blessed land Byssom. Occasionally a heretic argues otherwise and in this case—but I am sure that you share the orthodox view?"

"Wholeheartedly," Cugel asserted. "The tenets of your belief are demonstrably accurate." And he drank deep of his wine. Even as he set down the goblet a murmur of music whispered through the air: a concord infinitely sweet, infinitely melancholy. All sitting under the pergola became silent—though Cugel was unsure that he in fact had heard music.

The elder huddled forward a trifle, and drank from his own goblet. Only then did he glance up. "The Winged Beings are passing over even now."

Cugel pulled thoughtfully at his chin. "How does one protect himself from the Winged Beings?"

The question was ill-put; the elder glared, an act which included the curling forward of his ears. "If a person is about to die, the Winged Beings appear. If not, he need have no fear."

Cugel nodded several times. "You have clarified my perplexity. Tomorrow—since you and I are manifestly in the best of health—let us walk up the hill and saunter back and forth near the cliff."

"No," said the elder, "and for this reason: the atmosphere at such an elevation is insalubrious; a person is likely to inhale a noxious fume, which entails damage to the health."

"I comprehend perfectly," said Cugel. "Shall we abandon this dismal topic? For the nonce we are alive and concealed to some extent by the vines which shroud the pergola. Let us eat and drink and watch the merry-making. The youths of the village dance with great agility."

The elder drained his goblet and rose to his feet. "You may do as you please; as for me, it is time for my Ritual Abasement, this act being an integral part of our belief."

"I will perform something of a like nature by and by," said Cugel. "I wish you the enjoyment of your rite."

The elder departed the pergola and Cugel was left by himself. Presently certain youths, attracted by curiosity, joined him, and Cugel explained his presence once again, though with less emphasis upon the barbaric crudity of his native land, for several girls had joined the group, and Cugel was stimulated by their exotic coloring and the vivacity of their attitudes. Much wine was served and Cugel was persuaded to attempt the kicking, jumping local dance, which he performed without discredit. The exercise brought him into close proximity with an especially beguiling girl, who announced her name to be Zhiaml Vraz. At the conclusion of the dance, she put her arm around his waist, conducted him back to the table, and settled herself upon his lap. This act of familiarity excited no apparent disapproval among the others of the group, and Cugel was emboldened further. "I have not yet arranged for a bed-chamber; perhaps I should do so before the hour grows late."

411

The girl signaled the inn-keeper. "Perhaps you have reserved a chamber for this chisel-faced stranger?"

"Indeed; I will display it for his approval."

He took Cugel to a pleasant chamber on the ground floor, furnished with couch, commode, rug and lamp. On one wall hung a tapestry woven in purple and black; on another was a representation of a peculiarly ugly baby which seemed trapped or compressed in a transparent globe. The room suited Cugel; he announced as much to the innkeeper and returned to the pergola, where now the merry-makers were commencing to disperse. The girl Zhiaml Vraz yet remained, and she welcomed Cugel with a warmth which undid the last vestige of his caution. After another goblet of wine, he leaned close to her ear. "Perhaps I am over-prompt; perhaps I over-indulge my vanity; perhaps I contravene the normal decorum of the village—but is there reason why we should not repair to my chamber, and there amuse ourselves?"

"None whatever," said the girl. "I am unwed and until this time may conduct myself as I wish, for this is our custom."

"Excellent," said Cugel. "Do you care to precede me, or walk discreetly to the rear?"

"We shall go together; there is no need for furtiveness!"

Together they went to the chamber and performed a number of erotic exercises, after which Cugel collapsed into a sleep of utter exhaustion, for his day had been taxing.

During the middle hours he awoke to find Zhiaml Vraz departed from the chamber, a fact which in his drowsiness caused him no distress and he once more returned to sleep.

The sound of the door angrily flung ajar aroused him; he sat up on the couch to find the sun not yet arisen, and a deputation led by the elder regarding him with horror and disgust.

The elder pointed a long quivering finger through the gloom. "I thought to detect heretical opinion; now the fact is known! Notice: he sleeps with neither head-covering nor devotional salve on his chin. The girl Zhiaml Vraz reports that at no time in their congress did the villain call out for the approval of Yelisea!"

"Heresy beyond a doubt!" declared the others of the deputation.

"What else could be expected of an outlander?" asked the elder contemptuously. "Look! even now he refuses to make the sacred sign."

"I do not know the sacred sign!" Cugel expostulated. "I know nothing of your rites! This is not heresy, it is simple ignorance!"

"I cannot believe this," said the elder. "Only last night I outlined the nature of orthodoxy."

"The situation is grievous," said another in a voice of portentous melancholy. "Heresy exists only through putrefaction of the Lobe of Correctitude."

"This is an incurable and fatal mortification," stated another, no less dolefully.

"True! Alas, too true!" sighed one who stood by the door. "Unfortunate man!"

"Come!" called the elder. "We must deal with the matter at once."

"Do not trouble yourself," said Cugel. "Allow me to dress myself and I will depart the village never to return."

"To spread your detestable doctrine elsewhere? By no means!"

And now Cugel was seized and hauled naked from the chamber. Out across the park he was marched, and to the pavilion at the center. Several of the group erected an enclosure formed of wooden posts on the platform of the pavilion and into this enclosure Cugel was thrust. "What do you do?" he cried out. "I wish no part of your rites!"

He was ignored, and stood peering between the interstices of the enclosure while certain of the villagers sent aloft a large balloon of green paper buoyed by hot air, carrying three green fire-fans below.

Dawn showed sallow in the west. The villagers, with all arranged to their satisfaction, withdrew to the edge of the park. Cugel attempted to climb from the enclosure, but the wooden rods were of such dimension and spacing as to allow him no grip.

The sky lightened; high above burnt the green fire-fans. Cugel, hunched and in goose-flesh from the morning chill, walked back and forth the length of the enclosure. He stopped short, as from afar came the haunting music. It grew louder, seeming to reach the very threshold of audibility. High in the sky appeared a Winged Being, white robes trailing and flapping. Down it settled, and Cugel's joints became limp and loose. The Winged Being hovered over the enclosure, dropped, enfolded Cugel in its white robe, endeavored to bear him aloft. But Cugel had seized a bar of the enclosure and the Winged Being flapped in vain. The bar creaked, groaned, cracked. Cugel fought free of the stifling cloak, tore at the bar with hysterical strength; it snapped and splintered. Cugel seized a fragment, stabbed at the Winged Being. The sharp stick punctured the white cloak, and the Winged Being buffeted Cugel with a wing. Cugel seized one of the chitin ribs and with a mighty effort twisted it around backward, so that the substance cracked and broke and the wing hung torn. The Winged Being, aghast, gave a great bound which carried both it and Cugel out upon the pavilion, and now it hopped through the village trailing its broken wing.

Cugel ran behind belaboring it with a cudgel he had seized up. He glimpsed the villagers staring in awe; their mouths were wide and wet, and they might have been screaming but he heard nothing. The Winged Being hopped faster, up the trail toward the cliff, with Cugel wielding the cudgel with all his strength. The golden sun rose over the far mountains; the Winged Being suddenly turned to face Cugel, and Cugel felt the glare of its eyes, though the visage, if such there were, was concealed beneath the hood of the cloak. Abashed and panting, Cugel stood back, and now it occurred to him that he stood almost defenseless should others drop on him from on high. So now he shouted an imprecation at the creature and turned back to the village.

All had fled. The village was deserted. Cugel laughed aloud. He went to the inn, dressed himself in his garments, buckled on his sword. He went out into the taproom, and looking into the till, found a number of coins which he transferred to his pouch, alongside the ivory representation of NULLITY. He returned outdoors: best to depart while none were on hand to detain him. A flicker of light attracted his attention: the ring on his finger glinted with dozens of streaming sparks, and all pointed up the trail, toward the cliffs.

Cugel shook his head wearily, checked the darting lights once again. Without ambiguity they directed him back the way he had come. Pharesm's calculations, after all, had been accurate. He had best act with decision, lest TOTALITY once more drift beyond his reach.

He delayed only long enough to find an axe, and hastened up the trail, following the glittering sparks of the ring.

Not far from where he had left it, he came upon the maimed Winged Being, now sitting on a rock beside the road, the hood drawn over its head. Cugel picked up a stone, heaved it at the creature, which collapsed into sudden dust, leaving only a tumble of white cloth to signal the fact of its existence.

Cugel continued up the road, keeping to such cover as offered itself, but to no avail. Overhead hovered Winged Beings, flapping and swooping. Cugel made play with the axe, striking at the wings, and the creatures flew high, circling above.

Cugel consulted the ring and was led on up the trail, with the Winged Beings hovering just above. The ring coruscated with the intensity of its message: there was TOTALITY, resting blandly on a rock!

Cugel restrained the cry of exultation which rose in his throat. He brought forth the ivory symbol of NULLITY, ran forward and applied it to the gelatinous central globe.

As Pharesm had asserted, adherence was instant. With the contact Cugel could feel the spell which bound him to the olden time dissolving.

A swoop, a buffet of great wings! Cugel was knocked to the ground. White cloth enveloped him, and with one hand holding NULLITY he was unable to swing his axe. This was now wrenched from his grasp. He released NULLITY, gripped a rock, kicked, somehow freed himself, and sprang for his axe. The Winged Being seized NULLITY and with TOTALITY attached, bore it aloft and toward a cave high in the cliffs.

Great forces were pulling at Cugel, whirling in all directions at once. There was a roaring in his ears, a flutter of violet lights, and Cugel fell a million years into the future.

He recovered consciousness in the blue-tiled room with the sting of an aromatic liquor at his lips. Pharesm, bending over him, patted his face, poured more of the liquor into his mouth. "Awake! Where is TOTALITY? How are you returned?"

Cugel pushed him aside, and sat up on the couch.

"TOTALITY!" roared Pharesm. "Where is it? Where is my talisman?"

"I will explain," said Cugel in a thick voice. "I had it in my grasp, and it was wrenched away by winged creatures in the service of Great God Yelisea."

"Tell me, tell me!"

Cugel recounted the circumstances which had led first to gaining and then losing that which Pharesm sought. As he talked, Pharesm's face became damp with grief and his shoulders sagged. At last he marched Cugel outside, into the dim red light of late afternoon. Together they scrutinized the cliffs which now towered desolate and lifeless above them. "To which cave did the creature fly?" asked Pharesm. "Point it out, if you are able!"

Cugel pointed. "There, or so it would seem. All was confusion, all a tumble of wings and white robes..."

"Remain here." Pharesm went inside the workroom and presently returned. "I give you light," he said, and he handed Cugel a cold white flame tied into a silver chain. "Prepare yourself."

At Cugel's feet he cast a pellet which broke into a vortex, and Cugel was carried dizzily aloft to that crumbling ledge which he had indicated to Pharesm. Nearby was the dark opening into a cave. Cugel turned the flame within. He saw a dusty passage, three strides wide and higher than he could reach. It led back into the cliff, twisting slightly to the side. It seemed barren of all life.

Holding the lamp before him Cugel slowly moved along the passage, heart thumping for dread of something he could not define. He stopped short: music? The memory of music? He listened and could hear nothing: but when he tried to step forward fear clamped his legs. He held high the lantern and peered down the dusty passage. Where did it lead? What lay beyond? Dusty cave? Demonland? The blessed land Byssom? Cugel slowly proceeded, every sense alert. On a ledge he spied a shriveled brown spheroid: the talisman he had carried into the past. TOTALITY had long since disengaged itself and departed.

Cugel carefully lifted the object, which was brittle with the age of a million years, and returned to the ledge. The vortex, at a command from Pharesm, conveyed Cugel back to the ground.

Dreading the wrath of Pharesm, Cugel tendered the withered talisman.

Pharesm took it, held it between thumb and forefinger. "This was all?"

"There was nothing more."

Pharesm let the object fall. It struck and instantly became dust. Pharesm looked at Cugel, took a deep breath, then turned with a gesture of unspeakable frustration and marched back to his divinatory.

Cugel gratefully moved off down the trail, past the workmen standing in an anxious group waiting for orders. They eyed Cugel sullenly and a two-ell man hurled a rock. Cugel shrugged and continued south along the trail. Presently he passed the site of the village, now a waste overgrown with gnarled old trees. The pond had disappeared and the ground was hard and dry. In the valley below were ruins, but none of these marked the sites of the ancient cities Impergos, Tharuwe and Rhaverjand, now gone beyond memory.

Cugel walked south. Behind him the cliffs merged with haze and presently were lost to view.

AFTERWORD TO "THE SORCERER PHARESM"

Motivations are naturally the important components of any story—the dynamic essence, so to speak. Lacking motivations—obsessions, lust, greed, fear, revenge—the story becomes a pastoral idyll, an impressionistic sketch. It should be noted that no one seems interested in reading about virtue.

Frank Herbert had...a formula. He wrote it out, P-R-E-S-S-U-R-E. Coincidentally, at the time he mentioned this to me, he had just published a story called *Under Pressure*. He felt then that at all times your characters have to be under pressure to move, to be forced to move one way or the other. Well, this is no doubt true. As for myself, I don't adhere to formulas of any sort. I don't trust them. I don't think you can write on the basis of rules. If you keep some slogan in front of your mind while you're writing, you'll be limiting yourself.

—Jack Vance 1977

THE NEW PRIME

Music, carnival lights, the slide of feet on waxed oak, perfume, muffled talk and laughter.

Arthur Caversham of 20-century Boston felt air along his skin, and discovered himself to be stark naked.

It was at Janice Paget's coming out party: three hundred guests in formal evening-wear surrounded him.

For a moment he felt no emotion beyond vague bewilderment. His presence seemed the outcome of logical events, but his memory was fogged and he could find no definite anchor of certainty.

He stood a little apart from the rest of the stag line, facing the red and gold calliope where the orchestra sat. The buffet, the punch-bowl, the champagne wagons, tended by clowns, were to his right; to the left, through the open flap of the circus tent, lay the garden, now lit by strings of colored lights, red, green, yellow, blue, and he caught a glimpse of a merry-go-round across the lawn.

Why was he here? He had no recollection, no sense of purpose…The night was warm. The other young men in the full-dress suits must feel rather sticky, he thought…An idea tugged at a corner of his mind, nagged, teased. There was a significant aspect to the affair which he was overlooking. Refusing to surface, the idea lay like an irritant just below the level of his conscious mind.

He noticed that the young men nearby had moved away from him. He heard chortles of amusement, astonished exclamations. A girl dancing past saw him over the arm of her escort; she gave a startled squeak, jerked her eyes away, giggling and blushing.

Something was wrong. These young men and women were startled and amazed by his naked skin to the point of embarrassment. The gnaw of urgency came closer to the surface. He must do something. Taboos felt with such intensity might not be violated without unpleasant consequences; such was his understanding. He was lacking garments; these he must obtain.

He looked about him, inspecting the young men who watched him with ribald delight, disgust or curiosity. To one of these latter he addressed himself.

"Where can I get some clothing?"

The young man shrugged. "Where did you leave it?"

Two heavy-set men in dark blue uniforms entered the tent; Arthur Caversham saw them from the corner of his eye, and his mind worked with desperate intensity.

This young man seemed typical of those around him. What sort of appeal would have meaning for him? Like any other human being, he could be moved to action if the right chord were struck. By what method could he be moved?

Sympathy?

Threats?

The prospect of advantage or profit?

Caversham rejected all of these. By violating the taboo he had forfeited his claim to sympathy. A threat would excite derision, and he had no profit or advantage to offer. The stimulus must be more devious...He reflected that young men customarily banded together in secret societies. In the thousand cultures he had studied this was almost infallibly true. Long-houses, drug-cults, tongs, instruments of sexual initiation—whatever the name, the external aspects were near-identical: painful initiation, secret signs and passwords, uniformity of group conduct, obligation to service. If this young man were a member of such an association, he might react to an appeal to this group-spirit.

Arthur Caversham said, "I've been put in this taboo situation by the brotherhood; in the name of the brotherhood, find me some suitable garments."

The young man stared, taken aback. "Brotherhood?...You mean fraternity?" Enlightenment spread over his face. "Is this some kind of hell-week stunt?" He laughed. "If it is, they sure go all the way."

"Yes," said Arthur Caversham. "My fraternity."

The young man said, "This way then—and hurry, here comes the law. We'll take off under the tent. I'll lend you my topcoat till you make it back to your house."

The two uniformed men, pushing quietly through the dancers, were almost upon them. The young man lifted the flap of the tent, Arthur Caversham ducked under, his friend followed. Together they ran through the many-colored shadows to a little booth painted with gay red and white stripes near the entrance to the tent.

"You stay back, out of sight," said the young man. "I'll check out my coat."

"Fine," said Arthur Caversham.

The young man hesitated. "What's your house? Where do you go to school?"

Arthur Caversham desperately searched his mind for an answer. A single fact reached the surface.

"I'm from Boston."

"Boston U.? Or M.I.T.? Or Harvard?"

"Harvard."

"Ah." The young man nodded. "I'm Washington and Lee myself. What's your house?"

"I'm not supposed to say."

"Oh," said the young man, puzzled but satisfied. "Well—just a minute..."

Bearwald the Halforn halted, numb with despair and exhaustion. The remnants of his platoon sank to the ground around him, and they stared back to where the rim of the night flickered and glowed with fire. Many villages, many wood-gabled farmhouses had been given the torch, and the Brands from Mount Medallion reveled in human blood.

The pulse of a distant drum touched Bearwald's skin, a deep thrumm-thrumm-thrumm, almost inaudible. Much closer he heard a hoarse human cry of fright, then exultant killing-calls, not human. The Brands were tall, black, man-shaped but not men. They had eyes like lamps of red glass, bright white teeth, and tonight they seemed bent on slaughtering all the men of the world.

"Down," hissed Kanaw, his right arm-guard, and Bearwald crouched. Across the flaring sky marched a column of tall Brand warriors, rocking jauntily, without fear.

Bearwald said suddenly, "Men—we are thirteen. Fighting arm to arm with these monsters we are helpless. Tonight their total force is down from the mountain; the hive must be near-deserted. What can we lose if we undertake to burn the home-hive of the Brands? Only our lives, and what are these now?"

Kanaw said, "Our lives are nothing; let us be off at once."

"May our vengeance be great," said Broctan the left arm-guard. "May the home-hive of the Brands be white ashes this coming morn..."

Mount Medallion loomed overhead; the oval hive lay in Pangborn Valley. At the mouth of the valley, Bearwald divided the platoon into two halves, and placed Kanaw in the van of the second. "We move silently twenty yards apart; thus if either party rouses a Brand, the other may attack from the rear and so kill the monster before the vale is roused. Do all understand?"

"We understand."

"Forward, then, to the hive."

The valley reeked with an odor like sour leather. From the direction of the hive came a muffled clanging. The ground was soft, covered with runner moss; careful feet made no sound. Crouching low, Bearwald could see the shapes of his men against the sky—here indigo with a violet rim. The angry glare of burning Echevasa lay down the slope to the south.

A sound. Bearwald hissed, and the columns froze. They waited. *Thud thud thud thud* came the steps—then a hoarse cry of rage and alarm.

"Kill, kill the beast!" yelled Bearwald.

The Brand swung his club like a scythe, lifting one man, carrying the body around with the after-swing. Bearwald leapt close, struck with his blade, slicing as he hewed; he felt the tendons part, smelled the hot gush of Brand blood.

The clanging had stopped now, and Brand cries carried across the night.

"Forward," panted Bearwald. "Out with your tinder, strike fire to the hive. Burn, burn, burn—"

Abandoning stealth he ran forward; ahead loomed the dark dome. Immature Brands came surging forth, squeaking and squalling, and with them came the genetrices—twenty-foot monsters crawling on hands and feet, grunting and snapping as they moved.

"Kill!" yelled Bearwald the Halforn. "Kill! Fire, fire, fire!"

He dashed to the hive, crouched, struck spark to tinder, puffed. The rag, soaked with saltpeter, flared; Bearwald fed it straw, thrust it against the hive. The reed-pulp and withe crackled.

He leapt up as a horde of young Brands darted at him. His blade rose and fell; they were cleft, no match for his frenzy. Creeping close came the great Brand genetrices, three of them, swollen of abdomen, exuding an odor vile to his nostrils.

"Out with the fire!" yelled the first. "Fire, out. The Great Mother is tombed within; she lies too fecund to move...Fire, woe, destruction!" And they wailed, "Where are the mighty? Where are our warriors?"

Thrumm-thrumm-thrumm came the sound of skin-drums. Up the valley rolled the echo of hoarse Brand voices.

Bearwald stood back to the blaze. He darted forward, severed the head of a creeping genetrix, jumped back...Where were his men? "Kanaw!" he called. "Laida! Theyat! Gyorg! Broctan!"

He craned his neck, saw the flicker of fires. "Men! Kill the creeping mothers!" And leaping forward once more, he hacked and hewed, and another genetrix sighed and groaned and rolled flat.

The Brand voices changed to alarm; the triumphant drumming halted; the thud of footsteps came loud.

At Bearwald's back the hive burnt with a pleasant heat. Within came a shrill keening, a cry of vast pain.

In the leaping blaze he saw the charging Brand warriors. Their eyes glared like embers, their teeth shone like white sparks. They came forward, swinging their clubs, and Bearwald gripped his sword, too proud to flee.

After grounding his air-sled Ceistan sat a few minutes inspecting the dead city Therlatch: a wall of earthen brick a hundred feet high, a dusty portal, and a few crumbled roofs lifting above the battlements. Behind the city the desert spread across the near, middle and far distance to the hazy shapes of the Altilune Mountains at the horizon, pink in the light of the twin suns Mig and Pag.

Scouting from above he had seen no sign of life, nor had he expected any, after a thousand years of abandonment. Perhaps a few sandcrawlers wallowed in the heat of the ancient bazaar, perhaps a few leobars inhabited the crumbled masonry. Otherwise the streets would feel his presence with great surprise.

Jumping from the air-sled, Ceistan advanced toward the portal. He passed under, stood looking right and left with interest. In the parched air the brick buildings stood almost eternal. The wind smoothed and rounded all harsh angles; the glass had been cracked by the heat of day and chill of night; heaps of sand clogged the passageways.

Three streets led away from the portal and Ceistan could find nothing to choose between them. Each was dusty, narrow, and each twisted out of his line of vision after a hundred yards.

Ceistan rubbed his chin thoughtfully. Somewhere in the city lay a brass-bound coffer, containing the Crown and Shield Parchment. This, according to tradition, set a precedent for the fief-holder's immunity from energy-tax. Glay, who was Ceistan's liege-lord, having cited the parchment as justification for his delinquency, had been challenged to show validity. Now he lay in prison on charge of rebellion, and in the morning he would be nailed to the bottom of an air-sled and sent drifting into the west, unless Ceistan returned with the Parchment.

After a thousand years, there was small cause for optimism, thought Ceistan. However, the lord Glay was a fair man and he would leave no stone unturned…If it existed, the chest presumably would lie in state, in the town's Legalic, or the Mosque, or in the Hall of Relicts, or possibly in the Sumptuar. He would search all of these, allowing two hours per building; the eight hours so used would see the end to the pink daylight.

At random he entered the street in the center and shortly came to a plaza at whose far end rose the Legalic, the Hall of Records and Decisions. At the façade Ceistan paused, for the interior was dim and gloomy. No sound came from the dusty void save the sigh and whisper of the dry wind. He entered.

The great hall was empty. The walls were illuminated with frescoes of red and blue, as bright as if painted yesterday. There were six to each wall, the top half displaying a criminal act and the bottom half the penalty.

Ceistan passed through the hall, into the chambers behind. He found but dust and the smell of dust. Into the crypts he ventured, and these were lit by oubliettes. There was much litter and rubble, but no brass coffer.

Up and out into the clean air he went, and strode across the plaza to the Mosque, where he entered under the massive architrave.

The Nunciator's Confirmatory lay wide and bare and clean, for the tesselated floor was swept by a powerful draft. A thousand apertures opened from the low ceiling, each communicating with a cell overhead; thus arranged so that the devout might seek counsel with the Nunciator as he passed below without disturbing their attitudes of supplication. In the center of the pavilion a disk of glass roofed a recess. Below was a coffer and in the coffer rested a brass-bound chest. Ceistan sprang down the steps in high hopes.

But the chest contained jewels—the tiara of the Old Queen, the chest vellopes of the Gonwand Corps, the great ball, half emerald, half ruby, which in the ancient ages was rolled across the plaza to signify the passage of the old year.

Ceistan tumbled them all back in the coffer. Relicts on this planet of dead cities had no value, and synthetic gems were infinitely superior in luminosity and water.

Leaving the Mosque, he studied the height of the suns. The zenith was past, the moving balls of pink fire leaned to the west. He hesitated, frowning and blinking at the hot earthen walls, considering that not impossibly both coffer and parchment were fable, like so many others regarding dead Therlatch.

A gust of wind swirled across the plaza and Ceistan choked on a dry throat. He spat and an acrid taste bit his tongue. An old fountain opened in the wall nearby; he examined it wistfully, but water was not even a memory along these dead streets.

Once again he cleared his throat, spat, turned across the city toward the Hall of Relics.

He entered the great nave, past square pillars built of earthen brick. Pink shafts of light struck down from the cracks and gaps in the roof, and he was like a midge in the vast space. To all sides were niches cased in glass, and each held an object of ancient reverence: the Armor in which Plange the Forewarned led the Blue Flags; the coronet of the First Serpent; an array of antique Padang skulls; Princess Thermosteraliam's bridal gown of woven cobweb palladium, as fresh as the day she wore it; the original Tablets of Legality; the great conch throne of an early dynasty; a dozen other objects. But the coffer was not among them.

Ceistan sought for entrance to a possible crypt, but except where the currents of dusty air had channeled grooves in the porphyry, the floor was smooth.

Out once more into the dead streets, and now the suns had passed behind the crumbled roofs, leaving the streets in magenta shadow.

With leaden feet, burning throat and a sense of defeat, Ceistan turned to the Sumptuar, on the citadel. Up the wide steps, under the verdigris-fronted portico into a lobby painted with vivid frescoes. These depicted the maidens of ancient Therlatch at work, at play, amid sorrow and joy: slim creatures with short black hair and glowing ivory skin, as graceful as water-vanes, as round and delectable as chermoyan plums. Ceistan passed through the lobby with many side-glances, thinking sadly that these ancient creatures of delight were now the dust he trod under his feet.

He walked down a corridor which made a circuit of the building, and from which the chambers and apartments of the Sumptuar might be entered. The wisps of a wonderful rug crunched under his feet, and the walls displayed moldy tatters, once tapestries of the finest weave. At the entrance to each chamber a fresco pictured the Sumptuar maiden and the sign she served; at each of these chambers Ceistan paused, made a quick investigation, and so passed on to the next. The beams slanting in through the cracks served him as a gauge of time, and they flattened ever more toward the horizontal.

Chamber after chamber after chamber. There were chests in some, altars in others, cases of manifestos, triptychs, and fonts in others. But never the chest he sought.

And ahead was the lobby where he had entered the building. Three more chambers were to be searched, then the light would be gone.

He came to the first of these, and this was hung with a new curtain. Pushing it aside, he found himself looking into an outside court, full in the long light of the twin suns. A fountain of water trickled down across steps of apple-green jade into a garden as soft and fresh and green as any in the north. And rising in alarm from a couch was a maiden, as vivid and delightful as any in the frescoes. She had short dark hair, a face as pure and delicate as the great white frangipani she wore over her ear.

For an instant Ceistan and the maiden stared eye to eye; then her alarm faded and she smiled shyly.

"Who are you?" Ceistan asked in wonder. "Are you a ghost or do you live here in the dust?"

"I am real," she said. "My home is to the south, at the Palram Oasis, and this is the period of solitude to which all maidens of the race submit when aspiring for Upper Instruction...So without fear may you come beside me, and rest, and drink of fruit wine and be my companion through the lonely night, for this is my last week of solitude and I am weary of my own aloneness."

Ceistan took a step forward, then hesitated. "I must fulfill my mission. I seek the brass coffer containing the Crown and Shield Parchment. Do you know of this?"

She shook her head. "It is nowhere in the Sumptuar." She rose to her feet, stretching her ivory arms as a kitten stretches. "Abandon your search, and come let me refresh you."

Ceistan looked at her, looked up at the fading light, looked down the corridor to the two doors yet remaining. "First I must complete my search; I owe duty to my lord Glay, who will be nailed under an air-sled and sped west unless I bring him aid."

The maiden said with a pout, "Go then to your dusty chamber; and go with a dry throat. You will find nothing, and if you persist so stubbornly, I will be gone when you return."

"So let it be," said Ceistan.

He turned away, marched down the corridor. The first chamber was bare and dry as a bone. In the second and last, a man's skeleton lay tumbled in a corner; this Ceistan saw in the last rosy light of the twin suns.

There was no brass coffer, no parchment. So Glay must die, and Ceistan's heart hung heavy.

He returned to the chamber where he had found the maiden, but she had departed. The fountain had been stopped, and moisture only filmed the stones.

Ceistan called, "Maiden, where are you? Return; my obligation is at an end…"

There was no response.

Ceistan shrugged, turned to the lobby and so outdoors, to grope his way through the deserted twilight street to the portal and his air-sled.

Dobnor Daksat became aware that the big man in the embroidered black cloak was speaking to him.

Orienting himself to his surroundings, which were at once familiar and strange, he also became aware that the man's voice was condescending, supercilious.

"You are competing in a highly advanced classification," he said. "I marvel at your—ah, confidence." And he eyed Daksat with a gleaming and speculative eye.

Daksat looked down at the floor, frowned at the sight of his clothes. He wore a long cloak of black-purple velvet, swinging like a bell around his ankles. His trousers were of scarlet corduroy, tight at the waist, thigh and calf, with a loose puff of green cloth between calf and ankle. The clothes were his own, obviously: they looked wrong and right at once, as did the carved gold knuckle-guards he wore on his hands.

The big man in the dark cloak continued speaking, looking at a point over Daksat's head, as if Daksat were nonexistent.

"Clauktaba has won Imagist honors over the years. Bel-Washab was the Korsi Victor last month; Tol Morabait is an acknowledged master of the technique. And there is Ghisel Ghang of West Ind, who knows no peer in the creation of fire-stars, and Pulakt Havjorska, the Champion of the Island Realm. So it becomes a matter of skepticism whether you, new, inexperienced, without a fund of images, can do more than embarrass us all with your mental poverty."

Daksat's brain was yet wrestling with his bewilderment, and he could feel no strong resentment at the big man's evident contempt. He said, "Just what is all this? I'm not sure that I understand my position."

The man in the black cloak inspected him quizzically. "So, now you commence to experience trepidation? Justly, I assure you." He sighed, waved his hands. "Well, well—young men will be impetuous, and perhaps you have formed images you considered not discreditable. In any event, the public eye will ignore you for the glories of Clauktaba's geometrics and Ghisel Ghang's star-bursts. Indeed, I counsel you, keep your images small, drab and confined: you will so avoid the faults of bombast and discord...Now, it is time to go to your imagicon. This way, then. Remember, greys, browns, lavenders, perhaps a few tones of ocher and rust; then the spectators will understand that you compete for the schooling alone, and do not actively challenge the masters. This way then..."

He opened a door and led Dobnor Daksat up a stair and so out into the night.

They stood in a great stadium, facing six great screens forty feet high. Behind them in the dark sat tier upon tier of spectators—thousands and thousands, and their sounds came as a soft crush. Daksat turned to see them, but all their faces and their individualities had melted into the entity as a whole.

"Here," said the big man, "this is your apparatus. Seat yourself and I will adjust the ceretemps."

Daksat suffered himself to be placed in a heavy chair, so soft and deep that he felt himself to be floating. Adjustments were made at his head and neck and the bridge of his nose. He felt a sharp prick, a pressure, a throb, and then a soothing warmth. From the distance, a voice called out over the crowd:

"Two minutes to grey mist! Two minutes to grey mist! Attend, imagists, two minutes to grey mist!"

The big man stooped over him. "Can you see well?"

Daksat raised himself a trifle. "Yes...All is clear."

"Very well. At 'grey mist', this little filament will glow. When it dies, then it is your screen, and you must imagine your best."

The far voice said, "One minute to grey mist! The order is Pulakt Havjorska, Tol Morabait, Ghisel Ghang, Dobnor Daksat, Clauktaba and Bel-Washab. There are no handicaps; all colors and shapes are permitted. Relax then, ready your lobes, and now—grey mist!"

The light glowed on the panel of Daksat's chair, and he saw five of the six screens light to a pleasant pearl-grey, swirling a trifle as if agitated, excited. Only the screen before him remained dull. The big man who stood behind him reached down, prodded. "Grey mist, Daksat; are you deaf and blind?"

Daksat thought grey mist, and instantly his screen sprang to life, displaying a cloud of silver-grey, clean and clear.

"Humph," he heard the big man snort. "Somewhat dull and without interest—but I suppose good enough...See how Clauktaba's rings with hints of passion already, quivers with emotion."

And Daksat, noting the screen to his right, saw this to be true. The grey, without actually displaying color, flowed and filmed as if suppressing a vast flood of light.

Now to the far left, on Pulakt Havjorska's screen, color glowed. It was a gambit image, modest and restrained—a green jewel dripping a rain of blue and silver drops which struck a black ground and disappeared in little orange explosions.

Then Tol Morabait's screen glowed; a black and white checkerboard with certain of the squares flashing suddenly green, red, blue and yellow—warm searching colors, pure as shafts from a rainbow. The image disappeared in a flush mingled of rose and blue.

Ghisel Ghang wrought a circle of yellow which quivered, brought forth a green halo, which in turn bulging, gave rise to a larger band of brilliant black and white. In the center formed a complex kaleidoscopic pattern. The pattern suddenly vanished in a brilliant flash of light; on the screen for an instant or two appeared the identical pattern in a complete new suit of colors. A ripple of sound from the spectators greeted this *tour de force*.

The light on Daksat's panel died. Behind him he felt a prod. "Now."

Daksat eyed the screen and his mind was blank of ideas. He ground his teeth. Anything. Anything. A picture…He imagined a view across the meadowlands beside the river Melramy.

"Hm," said the big man behind him. "Pleasant. A pleasant fantasy, and rather original."

Puzzled, Daksat examined the picture on the screen. So far as he could distinguish, it was an uninspired reproduction of a scene he knew well. Fantasy? Was that what was expected? Very well, he'd produce fantasy. He imagined the meadows glowing, molten, white-hot. The vegetation, the old cairns slumped into a viscous seethe. The surface smoothed, became a mirror which reflected the Copper Crags.

Behind him the big man grunted. "A little heavy-handed, that last, and thereby you destroyed the charming effect of those unearthly colors and shapes…"

Daksat slumped back in his chair, frowning, eager for his turn to come again.

Meanwhile Clauktaba created a dainty white blossom with purple stamens on a green stalk. The petals wilted, the stamens discharged a cloud of swirling yellow pollen.

Then Bel-Washab, at the end of the line, painted his screen a luminous underwater green. It rippled, bulged, and a black irregular blot marred the surface. From the center of the blot seeped a trickle of hot gold which quickly meshed and veined the black blot.

Such was the first passage.

There was a pause of several seconds. "Now," breathed the voice behind Daksat, "now the competition begins."

On Pulakt Havjorska's screen appeared an angry sea of color: waves of red, green, blue, an ugly mottling. Dramatically a yellow shape appeared at the lower right, vanquished the chaos. It spread over the screen, the center went lime-green. A black shape appeared, split, bowed softly and easily to both sides. Then turning, the two shapes wandered into the background, twisting, bending with supple grace. Far down a perspective they merged, darted forward like a lance, spread out into a series of lances, formed a slanting pattern of slim black bars.

"Superb!" hissed the big man. "The timing, so just, so exact!"

Tol Morabait replied with a fuscous brown field threaded with crimson lines and blots. Vertical green hatching formed at the left, strode across the screen to the right. The brown field pressed forward, bulged through the green bars, pressed hard, broke, and segments flitted forward to leave the screen. On the black background behind the green hatching, which now faded, lay a human brain, pink, pulsing. The brain sprouted six insect-like legs, scuttled crabwise back into the distance.

Ghisel Ghang brought forth one of his fire-bursts—a small pellet of bright blue exploding in all directions, the tips working and writhing through wonderful patterns in the five colors, blue, violet, white, purple and light green.

Dobnor Daksat, rigid as a bar, sat with hands clenched and teeth grinding into teeth. Now! Was not his brain as excellent as those of the far lands? Now!

On the screen appeared a tree, conventionalized in greens and blues, and each leaf was a tongue of fire. From these fires wisps of smoke arose on high to form a cloud which worked and swirled, then emptied a cone of rain about the tree. The flames vanished and in their places appeared star-shaped white flowers. From the cloud came a bolt of lightning, shattering the tree to agonized fragments of glass. Another bolt into the brittle heap and the screen exploded in a great gout of white, orange and black.

The voice of the big man said doubtfully, "On the whole well done, but mind my warning, and create more modest images, since—"

"Silence!" said Dobnor Daksat in a harsh voice.

So the competition went, round after round of spectacles, some sweet as canmel honey, others as violent as the storms which circle the poles. Color strove with color, patterns evolved and changed, sometimes in glorious cadence, sometimes in the bitter discord necessary to the strength of the image.

And Daksat built dream after dream, while his tension vanished, and he forgot all save the racing pictures in his mind and on the screen, and his images became as complex and subtle as those of the masters.

"One more passage," said the big man behind Daksat, and now the imagists brought forth the master-dreams: Pulakt Havjorska, the growth and decay of a beautiful city; Tol Morabait, a quiet composition of green and white interrupted by a marching army of insects who left a dirty wake, and who were joined in battle by men in painted leather armor and tall hats, armed with short swords and flails. The insects were destroyed and chased off the screen; the dead warriors became bones and faded to twinkling blue dust. Ghisel Ghang created three fire-bursts simultaneously, each different, a gorgeous display.

Daksat imagined a smooth pebble, magnified it to a block of marble, chipped it away to create the head of a beautiful maiden. For a moment she stared forth and varying emotions crossed her face—joy at her sudden existence, pensive thought, and at last fright. Her eyes turned milky opaque blue, the face changed to a laughing sardonic mask, black-cheeked with a fleering mouth. The head tilted, the mouth spat into the air. The head flattened into a black background, the drops of spittle shone like fire, became stars, constellations, and one of these expanded, became a planet with configurations dear to Daksat's heart. The planet hurtled off into darkness, the constellations faded. Dobnor Daksat relaxed. His last image. He sighed, exhausted.

The big man in the black cloak removed the harness in brittle silence. At last he asked, "The planet you imagined in that last screening, was that a creation or a remembrance of actuality? It was none of our system here, and it rang with the clarity of truth."

Dobnor Daksat stared at him puzzled, and the words faltered in his throat. "But it is—home! This world! Was it not this world?"

The big man looked at him strangely, shrugged, turned away. "In a moment now the winner of the contest will be made known and the jeweled brevet awarded."

The day was gusty and overcast, the galley was low and black, manned by the oarsmen of Belaclaw. Ergan stood on the poop, staring across the two miles of bitter sea to the coast of Racland, where he knew the sharp-faced Racs stood watching from the headlands.

A gout of water erupted a few hundred yards astern.

Ergan spoke to the helmsman. "Their guns have better range than we bargained for. Better stand offshore another mile and we'll take our chances with the current."

Even as he spoke, there came a great whistle and he glimpsed a black pointed projectile slanting down at him. It struck the waist of the galley, exploded. Timber, bodies, metal, flew everywhere, and the galley laid its broken back into the water, doubled up and sank.

Ergan, jumping clear, discarded his sword, casque and greaves almost as he hit the chill grey water. Gasping from the shock, he swam in circles, bobbing up and down in the chop; then, finding a length of timber, he clung to it for support.

From the shores of Racland a longboat put forth and approached, bow churning white foam as it rose and fell across the waves. Ergan turned loose the timber and swam as rapidly as possible from the wreck. Better drowning than capture; there would be more mercy from the famine-fish which swarmed the waters than from the pitiless Racs.

So he swam, but the current took him to the shore, and at last, struggling feebly, he was cast upon a pebbly beach.

Here he was discovered by a gang of Rac youths and marched to a nearby command post. He was tied and flung into a cart and so conveyed to the city Korsapan.

In a grey room he was seated facing an intelligence officer of the Rac secret police, a man with the grey skin of a toad, a moist grey mouth, eager, searching eyes.

"You are Ergan," said the officer. "Emissary to the Bargee of Salomdek. What was your mission?"

Ergan stared back eye to eye, hoping that a happy and convincing response would find his lips. None came, and the truth would incite an immediate invasion of both Belaclaw and Salomdek by the tall thin-headed Rac soldiers, who wore black uniforms and black boots.

Ergan said nothing. The officer leaned forward. "I ask you once more; then you will be taken to the room below." He said "Room Below" as if the words were capitalized, and he said it with soft relish.

Ergan, in a cold sweat, for he knew of the Rac torturers, said, "I am not Ergan; my name is Ervard; I am an honest trader in pearls."

"This is untrue," said the Rac. "Your aide was captured and under the compression pump he blurted up your name with his lungs."

"I am Ervard," said Ergan, his bowels quaking.

The Rac signaled. "Take him to the Room Below."

A man's body, which has developed nerves as outposts against danger, seems especially intended for pain, and cooperates wonderfully with the craft of the torturer. These characteristics of the body had been studied by the Rac specialists, and other capabilities of the human nervous system had been blundered upon by accident. It had been found that certain programs of pressure, heat, strain, friction, torque, surge, jerk, sonic and visual shock, vermin, stench and vileness created cumulative effects, whereas a single method, used to excess, lost its stimulation thereby.

All this lore and cleverness was lavished upon Ergan's citadel of nerves, and they inflicted upon him the entire gamut of pain: the sharp twinges, the dull lasting joint-aches which groaned by night, the fiery flashes, the assaults of filth and lechery, together with shocks of occasional tenderness when he would be allowed to glimpse the world he had left.

Then back to the Room Below.

But always: "I am Ervard the trader." And always he tried to goad his mind over the tissue barrier to death, but always the mind hesitated at the last toppling step, and Ergan lived.

The Racs tortured by routine, so that the expectation, the approach of the hour, brought with it as much torment as the act itself. And then the heavy unhurried steps outside the cell, the feeble thrashing around to evade, the harsh laughs when they cornered him and carried him forth, and the harsh laughs when three hours later they threw him sobbing and whimpering back to the pile of straw that was his bed.

"I am Ervard," he said, and trained his mind to believe that this was the truth, so that never would they catch him unaware. "I am Ervard! I am Ervard, I trade in pearls!"

He tried to strangle himself on straw, but a slave watched always, and this was not permitted.

He attempted to die by self-suffocation, and would have been glad to succeed, but always as he sank into blessed numbness, so did his mind relax and his motor nerves take up the mindless business of breathing once more.

He ate nothing, but this meant little to the Racs, as they injected him full of tonics, sustaining drugs and stimulants, so that he might always be keyed to the height of his awareness.

"I am Ervard," said Ergan, and the Racs gritted their teeth angrily. The case was now a challenge; he defied their ingenuity, and they puzzled long and carefully upon refinements and delicacies, new shapes to the iron tools, new types of jerk ropes, new directions for the strains and pressures. Even when it was no longer important whether he was Ergan or Ervard, since war now raged, he was kept and maintained as a problem, an ideal case; so he was guarded and cosseted with even more than usual care, and the Rac torturers mulled over their techniques, making changes here, improvements there.

Then one day the Belaclaw galleys landed and the feather-crested soldiers fought past the walls of Korsapan.

The Racs surveyed Ergan with regret. "Now we must go, and still you will not submit to us."

"I am Ervard," croaked that which lay on the table. "Ervard the trader."

A splintering crash sounded overhead.

"We must go," said the Racs. "Your people have stormed the city. If you tell the truth, you may live. If you lie, we kill you. So there is your choice. Your life for the truth."

"The truth?" muttered Ergan. "It is a trick—" And then he caught the victory chant of the Belaclaw soldiery. "The truth? Why not?...Very well." And he said, "I am Ervard," for now he believed this to be the truth.

✸

Galactic Prime was a lean man with reddish-brown hair sparse across a fine arch of skull. His face, undistinguished otherwise, was given power by great dark eyes flickering with a light like fire behind smoke. Physically he had passed the peak of his youth; his arms and legs were thin and loose-jointed; his head inclined forward as if weighted by the intricate machinery of his brain.

Arising from the couch, smiling faintly, he looked across the arcade to the eleven Elders. They sat at a table of polished wood, backs to a wall festooned with vines. They were grave men, slow in their motions, and their faces were lined with wisdom and insight. By the ordained system, Prime was the executive of the universe, the Elders the deliberative body, invested with certain restrictive powers.

"Well?"

The Chief Elder without haste raised his eyes from the computer. "You are the first to arise from the couch."

Prime turned a glance up the arcade, still smiling faintly. The others lay variously: some with arms clenched, rigid as bars; others huddled in foetal postures. One had slumped from the couch half to the floor; his eyes were open, staring at remoteness.

Prime returned to the Chief Elder, who watched him with detached curiosity. "Has the optimum been established?"

The Chief Elder consulted the computer. "Twenty-six thirty-seven is the optimum score."

Prime waited, but the Chief Elder said no more. Prime stepped to the alabaster balustrade beyond the couches. He leaned forward, looked out across the vista—miles and miles of sunny haze, with a twinkling sea in the distance. A breeze blew past his face, ruffling the scant russet strands of his hair. He took a deep breath, flexed his fingers and hands, for the memory of the Rac torturers was still heavy on his mind. After a moment he swung around, leaned back, resting his elbows upon the balustrade. He glanced once more down the line of couches; there were still no signs of vitality from the candidates.

"Twenty-six thirty-seven," he muttered. "I venture to estimate my own score at twenty-five ninety. In the last episode I recall an incomplete retention of personality."

"Twenty-five seventy-four," said the Chief Elder. "The computer judged Bearwald the Halforn's final defiance of the Brand warriors unprofitable."

Prime considered. "The point is well made. Obstinacy serves no purpose unless it advances a predetermined end. It is a flaw I must seek to temper." He looked along the line of Elders, from face to face. "You make no enunciations, you are curiously mute."

He waited; the Chief Elder made no response.

"May I enquire the high score?"

"Twenty-five seventy-four."

Prime nodded. "Mine."

"Yours is the high score," said the Chief Elder.

Prime's smile disappeared; a puzzled line appeared across his brow. "In spite of this, you are still reluctant to confirm my second span of authority; there are still doubts among you."

"Doubts and misgivings," replied the Chief Elder.

Prime's mouth pulled in at the corners, although his brows were still raised in polite inquiry. "Your attitude puzzles me. My record is one of selfless service. My intelligence is phenomenal, and in this final test, which I designed to dispel your last doubts, I attained the highest score. I have proved my social intuition and flexibility, my leadership, devotion to duty, imagination and resolution. In every commensurable aspect, I fulfill best the qualifications for the office I hold."

The Chief Elder looked up and down the line of his fellows. There were none who wished to speak. The Chief Elder squared himself in his chair, sat back.

"Our attitude is difficult to represent. Everything is as you say. Your intelligence is beyond dispute, your character is exemplary, you have served your term with honor and devotion. You have earned our respect, admiration and gratitude. We realize also that you seek this second term from praiseworthy motives: you regard yourself as the man best able to coordinate the complex business of the galaxy."

Prime nodded grimly. "But you think otherwise."

"Our position is perhaps not quite so blunt."

"Precisely what is your position?" Prime gestured along the couches. "Look at these men. They are the finest of the galaxy. One man is dead. That one stirring on the third couch has lost his mind; he is a lunatic. The others are sorely shaken. And never forget that this test has been expressly designed to measure the qualities essential to the Galactic Prime."

"This test has been of great interest to us," said the Chief Elder mildly. "It has considerably affected our thinking."

Prime hesitated, plumbing the unspoken overtones of the words. He came forward, seated himself across from the line of Elders. With a narrow glance he searched the faces of the eleven men, tapped once, twice, three times with his fingertips on the polished wood, leaned back in the chair.

"As I have pointed out, the test has gauged each candidate for the exact qualities essential to the optimum conduct of office, in this fashion: Earth of the twentieth century is a planet of intricate conventions; on Earth the candidate, as Arthur Caversham, is required to use his social intuition—a quality highly important in this galaxy of two billion suns. On Belotsi, Bearwald the Halforn is tested for courage and the ability to conduct positive action. At the dead city Therlatch on Praesepe Three, the candidate, as Ceistan, is rated for devotion to duty, and as Dobnor Daksat at the Imagicon on Staff, his creative conceptions are rated against the most fertile imaginations alive. Finally as Ergan, on Chankozar, his will, persistence and ultimate fiber are explored to their extreme limits.

"Each candidate is placed in the identical set of circumstances by a trick of temporal, dimensional and cerebro-neural meshing, which is rather complicated for the present discussion. Sufficient that each candidate is objectively rated by his achievements, and that the results are commensurable."

He paused, looked shrewdly along the line of grave faces. "I must emphasize that although I myself designed and arranged the test, I thereby gained no advantage. The mnemonic synapses are entirely disengaged from incident to incident, and only the candidate's basic personality acts. All were tested under precisely the same conditions. In my opinion the scores registered by the computer indicate an objective and reliable index of the candidate's ability for the highly responsible office of Galactic Executive."

The Chief Elder said, "The scores are indeed significant."

"Then—you approve my candidacy?"

The Chief Elder smiled. "Not so fast. Admittedly you are intelligent, admittedly you have accomplished much during your term as Prime. But much remains to be done."

"Do you suggest that another man would have achieved more?"

The Chief Elder shrugged. "I have no conceivable way of knowing. I point out your achievements, such as the Glenart civilization, the Dawn Time on Masilis, the reign of King Karal on Aevir, the suppression of the Arkid Revolt. There are many such examples. But there are also shortcomings: the totalitarian governments on Earth, the savagery on Belotsi and Chankozar, so pointedly emphasized in your test. Then there is the decadence of the planets in the Eleven Hundred Ninth Cluster, the rise of the Priest-kings on Fiir, and much else."

Prime clenched his mouth and the fires behind his eyes burnt more brightly.

The Chief Elder continued. "One of the most remarkable phenomena of the galaxy is the tendency of humanity to absorb and manifest the personality of the Prime. There seems to be a tremendous resonance which vibrates from the brain of the Prime through the minds of man from Center to the outer fringes. It is a matter which should be studied, analyzed and subjected to control. The effect is as if every thought of the Prime is magnified a billion-fold, as if every mood sets the tone for a thousand civilizations, every facet of his personality reflects in the ethics of a thousand cultures."

Prime said tonelessly, "I have remarked this phenomenon and have thought much on it. Prime's commands are promulgated in such a way as to exert subtle rather than overt influence; perhaps here is the background of the matter. In any event, the fact of this influence is even more reason to select for the office a man of demonstrated virtue."

"Well put," said the Chief Elder. "Your character is indeed beyond reproach. However, we of the Elders are concerned by the rising tide of authoritarianism among the planets of the galaxy. We suspect that this principle of resonance is at work. You are a man of intense and indomitable will, and we feel that your influence has unwittingly prompted an irruption of autarchies."

Prime was silent a moment. He looked down the line of couches where the other candidates were recovering awareness. They were men of various races: a pale Northkin of Palast, a stocky red Hawolo, a grey-haired grey-eyed Islander from the Sea Planet—each the outstanding man of the planet of his birth. Those who had returned to consciousness sat quietly, collecting their wits, or lay back on the couch, trying to expunge the test from their minds. There had been a toll taken: one lay dead, another bereft of his wits crouched whimpering beside his couch.

The Chief Elder said, "The objectionable aspects of your character are perhaps best exemplified by the test itself."

Prime opened his mouth; the Chief Elder held up his hand. "Let me speak; I will try to deal fairly with you. When I am done, you may say your say.

"I repeat that your basic direction is displayed by the details of the test that you devised. The qualities you measured were those which you considered the most important: that is, those ideals by which you guide your own life. This arrangement I am sure was completely unconscious, and hence completely revealing. You conceive the essential characteristics of the Prime to be social intuition, aggressiveness, loyalty, imagination and dogged persistence. As a man of strong character you seek to exemplify these ideals in your own conduct; therefore it is not at all surprising that in this test, designed by you, with a scoring system calibrated by you, your score should be highest.

"Let me clarify the idea by an analogy. If the Eagle were conducting a test to determine the King of Beasts, he would rate all the candidates on their ability to fly; necessarily he would win. In this fashion the Mole would consider ability to dig important; by his system of testing he would inevitably emerge King of Beasts."

Prime laughed sharply, ran a hand through his sparse red-brown locks. "I am neither Eagle nor Mole."

The Chief Elder shook his head. "No. You are zealous, dutiful, imaginative, indefatigable—so you have demonstrated, as much by specifying tests for these characteristics as by scoring high in these same tests. But conversely, by the very absence of other tests you demonstrate deficiencies in your character."

"And these are?"

"Sympathy. Compassion. Kindness." The Chief Elder settled back in his chair. "Strange. Your predecessor two times removed was rich in these qualities. During his term, the great humanitarian systems based on the idea of human brotherhood sprang up across the universe. Another example of resonance—but I digress."

Prime said with a sardonic twitch of his mouth, "May I ask this: have you selected the next Galactic Prime?"

The Chief Elder nodded. "A definite choice has been made."

"What was his score in the test?"

"By your scoring system—seventeen eighty. He did poorly as Arthur Caversham; he tried to explain the advantages of nudity to the policeman.

He lacked the ability to concoct an instant subterfuge; he has little of your quick craft. As Arthur Caversham he found himself naked. He is sincere and straightforward, hence tried to expound the positive motivations for his state, rather than discover the means to evade the penalties."

"Tell me more about this man," said Prime shortly.

"As Bearwald the Halforn, he led his band to the hive of the Brands on Mount Medallion, but instead of burning the hive, he called forth to the queen, begging her to end the useless slaughter. She reached out from the doorway, drew him within and killed him. He failed—but the computer still rated him highly on his forthright approach.

"At Therlatch, his conduct was as irreproachable as yours, and at the Imagicon his performance was adequate. Yours approached the brilliance of the Master Imagists, which is high achievement indeed.

"The Rac tortures are the most trying element of the test. You knew well you could resist limitless pain; therefore you ordained that all other candidates must likewise possess this attribute. The new Prime is sadly deficient here. He is sensitive, and the idea of one man intentionally inflicting pain upon another sickens him. I may add that none of the candidates achieved a perfect count in the last episode. Two others equaled your score—"

Prime evinced interest. "Which are they?"

The Chief Elder pointed them out—a tall hard-muscled man with rock-hewn face standing by the alabaster balustrade gazing moodily out across the sunny distance, and a man of middle age who sat with his legs folded under him, watching a point three feet before him with an expression of imperturbable placidity.

"One is utterly obstinate and hard," said the Chief Elder. "He refused to say a single word. The other assumes an outer objectivity when unpleasantness overtakes him. Others among the candidates fared not so well; mental readjustment and therapy will be necessary in almost all cases."

Their eyes went to the witless creature with vacant eyes who padded up and down the aisle, muttering quietly to himself.

"The tests were by no means valueless," said the Chief Elder. "We learned a great deal. By your system of scoring, the competition rated you most high. By other standards which we Elders postulated, your place was lower."

With a tight mouth Prime inquired, "Who is this paragon of altruism, kindliness, sympathy and generosity?"

The lunatic wandered close, fell on his hands and knees, crawled whimpering to the wall. He pressed his face to the cool stone, stared blankly up at Prime. His mouth hung loose, his chin was wet, his eyes rolled apparently free of each other.

The Chief Elder smiled in great compassion; he stroked the mad creature's head. "This is he. Here is the man we select."

The old Galactic Prime sat silent, mouth compressed, eyes burning like far volcanoes.

At his feet the new Prime, Lord of Two Billion Suns, found a dead leaf, put it into his mouth, and began to chew.

AFTERWORD TO "THE NEW PRIME"

Science fiction in the far to medium distant past concerned itself with scientific processes, or the consequences of some scientific quirk. Often the writers were pretty much ahead of the scientists. They "invented" any number of things which today are showing up around us. As of today, "science" is so *vast* in scope that no writer—unless he makes it his full-time job—can keep up.

Unless he confines himself to generalities, the producing writer can make terrible blunders if he tries to deal too intimately with "modern science." For instance, if I were to write a story where the gimmick was the behavior of "quarks" or the various kinds of "charm"—I'd just be using jargon. It's not much fun doing that. That is just one aspect—point A. Point B is that many stories of the 40's and 50's, some of my own included, often used little known or misunderstood facts of science to provide the denouement of the story. I remember once using superconductivity in this manner. This isn't a very firm foundation for a story. Readers today are not so interested in these tricks. They're amusing, but they certainly can't provide the basis for an extended work. What a reader wants is to discover a situation with which he can identify. So in this case, that old-type science fiction story—the idea story—falls flat.

—Jack Vance 1977

THE SECRET

Sunbeams slanted through chinks in the wall of the hut; from the lagoon came shouts and splashing of the village children. Rona ta Inga at last opened his eyes. He had slept far past his usual hour of arising, far into the morning. He stretched his legs, cupped hands behind his head, stared absently up at the ceiling of thatch. In actuality he had awakened at the usual hour, to drift off again into a dreaming doze—a habit to which lately he had become prone. Only lately. Inga frowned and sat up with a jerk. What did this mean? Was it a sign? Perhaps he should inquire from Takti Tai…But it was all so ridiculous. He had slept late for the most ordinary of reasons: he enjoyed lazing and drowsing and dreaming.

On the mat beside him were crumpled flowers, where Mai Mio had lain. Inga gathered the blossoms and laid them on the shelf which held his scant possessions. An enchanting creature, this Mai Mio. She laughed no more and no less than other girls; her eyes were like other eyes, her mouth like all mouths; but her quaint and charming mannerisms made her absolutely unique: the single Mai Mio in all the universe. Inga had loved many maidens. All in some way were singular, but Mai Mio was a creature delightfully, exquisitely apart from the others. There was considerable difference in their ages. Mai Mio only recently had become a woman—even now from a distance she might be mistaken for a boy—while Inga was older by at least five or six seasons. He was not quite sure. It mattered little in any event. It mattered very little, he told himself again, quite emphatically. This was his village, his island; he had no desire to leave. Ever!

443

The children came up the beach from the lagoon. Two or three darted under his hut, swinging on one of the poles, chanting nonsense-words. The hut trembled; the outcry jarred upon Inga's nerves. He shouted in irritation. The children became instantly silent, in awe and astonishment, and trotted away looking over their shoulders.

Inga frowned; for the second time this morning he felt dissatisfied with himself. He would gain an unenviable reputation if he kept on in such a fashion. What had come over him? He was the same Inga that he was yesterday...Except for the fact that a day had elapsed and he was a day older.

He went out on the porch before his hut, stretched in the sunlight. To right and left were forty or fifty other such huts as his own, with intervening trees; ahead lay the lagoon blue and sparkling in the sunlight. Inga jumped to the ground, walked to the lagoon, swam, dived far down among the glittering pebbles and ocean growths which covered the lagoon floor. Emerging he felt relaxed and at peace—once more himself: Rona ta Inga, as he had always been, and always would be!

Squatting on his porch he breakfasted on fruit and cold baked fish from last night's feast and considered the day ahead. There was no urgency, no duty to fulfil, no need to satisfy. He could join the party of young bucks now on their way into the forest, hoping to snare fowl. He could fashion a brooch of carved shell and goana-nut for Mai Mio. He could lounge and gossip; he could fish. Or he could visit his best friend Takti Tai, who was building a boat. Inga rose to his feet. He would fish. He walked along the beach to his canoe, checked equipment, pushed off, paddled across the lagoon to the opening in the reef. The winds blew to the west as always. Leaving the lagoon Inga turned a swift glance downwind—an almost furtive glance—then bent his neck into the wind and paddled east.

Within the hour he had caught six fine fish, and drifted back along the reef to the lagoon entrance. Everyone was swimming when he returned. Maidens, young men, children. Mai Mio paddled to the canoe, hooked her arms over the gunwales, grinned up at him, water glistening on her cheeks. "Rona ta Inga! did you catch fish? Or am I bad luck?"

"See for yourself."

She looked. "Five—no, six! All fat silver-fins! I am good luck! May I sleep often in your hut?"

"So long as I catch fish the following day."

She dropped back into the water, splashed him, sank out of sight. Through the undulating surface Inga could see her slender brown form skimming off across the bottom. He beached the canoe, wrapped the fish in big sipi-leaves and stored them in a cool cistern, then ran down to the lagoon to join the swimming.

Later he and Mai Mio sat in the shade; she plaiting a decorative cord of coloured bark which later she would weave into a basket; he leaning back, looking across the water. Artlessly Mai Mio chattered—of the new song Ama ta Lalau had composed, of the odd fish she had seen while swimming underwater, of the change which had come over Takti Tai since he had started building his boat.

Inga made an absent-minded sound, but said nothing.

"We have formed a band," Mai Mio confided. "There are six of us: Ipa, Tuiti, Hali sai Iano, Zoma, Oiu Ngo and myself. We have pledged never to leave the island. Never, never, never. There is too much joy here. Never will we sail west—never. Whatever the secret, we do not wish to know."

Inga smiled, a rather wistful smile. "There is much wisdom in the pledge you have made."

She stroked his arm. "Why do you not join us in our pledge? True, we are six girls—but a pledge is a pledge."

"True."

"Do you want to sail west?"

"No."

Mai Mio excitedly rose to her knees. "I will call together the band, and all of us, all together: we will recite the pledge again, never will we leave our island! And to think, you are the oldest of all the village!"

"Takti Tai is older," said Inga.

"But Takti Tai is building his boat! He hardly counts any more!"

"Vai Ona is as old as I. Almost as old."

"Do you know something? Whenever Vai Ona goes out to fish, he always looks to the west. He wonders."

"Everyone wonders."

"Not I!" Mai Mio jumped to her feet. "Not I—not any of the band. Never, never, never—never will we leave the island! We have pledged ourselves!" She reached down, patted Inga's cheek, ran off to where a group of her friends were sharing a basket of fruit.

Inga sat quietly for five minutes. Then he made an impatient gesture, rose and walked along the shore to the platform where Takti Tai worked on his boat. This was a catamaran with a broad deck, a shelter of woven withe thatched with sipi-leaf, a stout mast. In silence Inga helped Takti

Tai shape the mast, scraping a tall well-seasoned pasiao-tui sapling with sharp shells. Inga presently paused, laid aside the shell. He said, "Long ago there were four of us. You, me, Akara and Zan. Remember?"

Takti Tai continued to scrape. "Of course I remember."

"One night we sat on the beach around a fire—the four of us. Remember?"

Takti Tai nodded.

"We pledged never to leave the island. We swore never to weaken, we spilled blood to seal the pact. Never would we sail west."

"I remember."

"Now you sail," said Inga. "I will be the last of the group."

Takti Tai paused in his scraping, looked at Inga, as if he would speak, then bent once more over the mast. Inga presently returned up the beach to his hut, where squatting on the porch he carved at the brooch for Mai Mio.

A youth came to sit beside him. Inga, who had no particular wish for companionship, continued with his carving. But the youth, absorbed in his own problems, failed to notice. "Advise me, Rona ta Inga. You are the oldest of the village and very sage."

Inga raised his eyebrows, then scowled, but said nothing.

"I love Hali sai Iano, I long for her desperately, but she laughs at me and runs off to throw her arms about the neck of Hopu. What should I do?"

"The situation is quite simple," said Inga. "She prefers Hopu. You need merely select another girl. What of Talau Io? She is pretty and affectionate, and seems to like you."

The youth vented a sigh. "Very well. I will do as you suggest. After all, one girl is much like another." He departed, unaware of the sardonic look Inga directed at his back. He asked himself, why do they come to me for advice? I am only two or three, or at most four or five, seasons their senior. It is as if they think me the fount and source of all sagacity!

During the evening a baby was born. The mother was Omei Ni Io, who for almost a season had slept in Inga's hut. Since it was a boy-child she named it Inga ta Omei. There was a naming ceremony at which Inga presided. The singing and dancing lasted until late, and if it were not for the fact that the child was his own, with his name, Inga would have crept off early to his hut. He had attended many naming ceremonies.

A week later Takti Tai sailed west, and there was a ceremony of a different sort. Everyone came to the beach to touch the hull of the boat and bless it with water. Tears ran freely down all cheeks, including Takti

Tai's. For the last time he looked around the lagoon, into the faces of those he would be leaving. Then he turned, signaled; the young men pushed the boat away from the beach, then jumping into the water, towed it across the lagoon, guided it out into the ocean. Takti Tai cut brails, tightened halyards; the big square sail billowed in the wind. The boat surged west. Takti Tai stood on the platform, gave a final flourish of the hand, and those on the beach waved farewell. The boat moved out into the afternoon, and when the sun sank, it could be seen no more.

During the evening meal the talk was quiet; everyone stared into the fire. Mai Mio finally jumped to her feet. "Not I," she chanted. "Not I—ever, ever, ever!"

"Nor I," shouted Ama ta Lalau, who of all the youths was the most proficient musician. He reached for the guitar which he had carved from a black soa-gum trunk, struck chords, began to sing.

Inga watched quietly. He was now the oldest on the island, and it seemed as if the others were treating him with a new respect. Ridiculous! What nonsense! So little older was he that it made no difference whatever! But he noticed that Mai Mio was laughingly attentive to Ama ta Lalau, who responded to the flirtation with great gallantry. Inga watched with a heavy feeling around the heart, and presently went off to his hut. That night, for the first time in weeks Mai Mio did not sleep beside him. No matter, Inga told himself: one girl is much like another.

The following day he wandered up the beach to the platform where Takti Tai had built his boat. The area was clean and tidy, and tools were hung carefully in a nearby shed. In the forest beyond grew fine makara trees, from which the staunchest hulls were fashioned.

Inga turned away. He took his canoe out to catch fish, and leaving the lagoon looked to the west. There was nothing to see but empty horizon, precisely like the horizon to east, to north and to south—except that the western horizon concealed the secret...The rest of the day he felt uneasy. During the evening meal he looked from face to face. None were the faces of his dear friends; they all had built their boats and had sailed. His friends had departed; his friends knew the secret.

The next morning, without making a conscious decision, Inga sharpened the tools and felled two fine makara trees. He was not precisely building a boat—so he assured himself—but it did no harm for wood to season.

Nevertheless the following day he trimmed the trees, cut the trunks to length, and the next day assembled all the young men to help carry the trunks to the platform. No one seemed surprised; everyone knew that Rona ta Inga was building his boat. Mai Mio had now frankly taken up with Ama ta Lalau and as Inga worked on his boat he watched them play in the water, not without a lump of bitterness in his throat. Yes, he told himself, it would be pleasure indeed to join his true friends—the youths and maidens he had known since he dropped his milk-name, whom he had sported with, who now were departed, and for whom he felt an aching loneliness. Diligently he hollowed the hulls, burning, scraping, chiseling. Then the platform was secured, the little shelter woven and thatched to protect him from rain. He scraped a mast from a flawless pasiao-tui sapling, stepped and stayed it. He gathered bast, wove a coarse but sturdy sail, hung it to stretch and season. Then he began to provision the boat. He gathered nutmeats, dried fruit, smoked fish wrapped in sipi-leaf. He filled blow-fish bladders with water. How long was the trip to the west? No one knew. Best not to go hungry, best to stock the boat well: once down the wind there was no turning back.

One day he was ready. It was a day much like all the other days of his life. The sun shone warm and bright, the lagoon glittered and rippled up and down the beach in little gushes of play-surf. Rona ta Inga's throat felt tense and stiff; he could hardly trust his voice. The young folk came to line the beach; all blessed the boat with water. Inga gazed into each face, then along the line of huts, the trees, the beaches, the scenes he loved with such intensity...Already they seemed remote. Tears were coursing his cheeks. He held up his hand, turned away. He felt the boat leave the beach, float free on the water. Swimmers thrust him out into the ocean. For the last time he turned to look back at the village, fighting a sudden maddening urge to jump from the boat, to swim back to the village. He hoisted the sail, the wind thrust deep into the hollow. Water surged under the hulls and he was coasting west, with the island astern.

Up the blue swells, down into the long troughs, the wake gurgling, the bow rising and falling. The long afternoon waned and became golden; sunset burned and ebbed and became a halcyon dusk. The stars appeared, and Inga, sitting silently by his rudder, held the sail full to the wind. At midnight he lowered the sail and slept, the boat drifting quietly.

In the morning he was completely alone, the horizons blank. He raised the sail and scudded west, and so passed the day, and the next, and others. And Inga became thankful that he had provisioned the boat with generosity. On the sixth day he seemed to notice that a chill had come into the wind; on the eighth day he sailed under a high overcast, the like of which he had never seen before. The ocean changed from blue to grey and presently took on a green tinge. Now the water was cold. The wind blew with great force, bellying his bast sail, and Inga huddled in the shelter to avoid the harsh spray. On the morning of the ninth day he thought to see a dim dark shape loom ahead, which at noon became a line of tall cliffs with surf beating against jagged rocks, roaring back and forth across coarse shingle. In mid-afternoon he ran his boat up on one of the shingle beaches, jumped gingerly ashore. Shivering in the whooping gusts, he took stock of the situation. There was no living thing to be seen along the foreshore but three or four grey gulls. A hundred yards to his right lay a battered hulk of another boat, and beyond was a tangle of wood and fibre which might have been still another.

Inga carried ashore what provisions remained, bundled them together, and by a faint trail climbed the cliffs. He came out on an expanse of rolling grey-green downs. Two or three miles inland rose a line of low hills, toward which the trail seemed to lead.

Inga looked right and left; again there was no living creature in sight other than gulls. Shouldering his bundle he set forth along the trail.

Nearing the hills he came upon a hut of turf and stone, beside a patch of cultivated soil. A man and a woman worked in the field. Inga peered closer. What manner of creatures were these? They resembled human beings; they had arms and legs and faces—but how seamed and seared and grey they were! How shrunken were their hands, how they bent and hobbled as they worked! He walked quickly by, and they did not appear to notice him.

Now Inga hastened, as the end of the day was drawing on and the hills loomed before him. The trail led along a valley grown with gnarled oak and low purple-green shrubs, then slanted up the hillside through a stony gap, where the wind generated whistling musical sounds. From the gap Inga looked out over a flat valley. He saw copses of low trees, plots of tilled land, a group of huts. Slowly he walked down the trail. In a nearby field a man raised his head. Inga paused, thinking to recognize him. Was this not Oma ta Akara who had sailed west ten or twelve seasons back? It seemed impossible. This man was fat, the hair had almost departed his head, his cheeks hung loose at the jawline. No, this could not be lithe Oma ta Akara! Hurriedly Inga turned away, and presently entered the village. Before a nearby hut stood one whom he recognized with joy. "Takti Tai!"

Takti Tai nodded. "Rona ta Inga. I knew you'd be coming soon."

"I'm delighted to see you! But let us leave this terrible place; let us return to the island!"

Takti Tai smiled a little, shook his head.

Inga protested heatedly, "Don't tell me you prefer this dismal land? Come! My boat is still seaworthy. If somehow we can back it off the beach, gain the open sea…"

The wind sang down over the mountains, strummed through the trees. Inga's words died in his throat. It was clearly impossible to work the boat off the foreshore.

"Not only the wind," said Takti Tai. "We could not go back now. We know the secret."

Inga stared in wonderment. "The secret? Not I."

"Come. Now you will learn."

Takti Tai took him through the village to a structure of stone, with a high-gabled roof shingled with slate. "Enter, and you will know the secret."

Hesitantly Rona ta Inga entered the stone structure. On a stone table lay a still figure surrounded by six tall candles. Inga stared at the shrunken white face, at the white sheet which lay motionless over the narrow chest. "Who is this? A man? How thin he is. Does he sleep? Why do you show me such a thing?"

"This is the secret," said Takti Tai. "It is called 'death'."

AFTERWORD TO "THE SECRET"

An interesting footnote to my connection with *Worlds Beyond* concerns "The Secret," the second story I sold Damon [Knight]. When *World's Beyond* folded it carried with it into oblivion the still unpublished story which thereupon mysteriously vanished and was seen no more. About five years later I rewrote the story, using the same title. Again "The Secret" disappeared, somewhere after leaving Scott Meredith's office, but before finding a market. I have searched high and low for carbons to these stories without success; both versions have vanished without a trace. I can surmise only that I brushed upon an elemental verity, most truly secret indeed, and that one or another of the

Upper Forces saw fit to expunge the dangerous knowledge before it gained currency. I will not attempt a third version; I value my life and sanity, and can take a hint.

—Jack Vance 1976

THE MOON MOTH

The houseboat had been built to the most exacting standards of Sirenese craftsmanship, which is to say, as close to the absolute as human eye could detect. The planking of waxy dark wood showed no joints, the fastenings were platinum rivets countersunk and polished flat. In style, the boat was massive, broad-beamed, steady as the shore itself, without ponderosity or slackness of line. The bow bulged like a swan's breast, the stem rising high, then crooking forward to support an iron lantern. The doors were carved from slabs of a mottled black-green wood; the windows were many-sectioned, paned with squares of mica, stained rose, blue, pale green and violet. The bow was given to service facilities and quarters for the slaves; amidships were a pair of sleeping cabins, a dining saloon and a parlor saloon, opening upon an observation deck at the stern.

Such was Edwer Thissell's houseboat, but ownership brought him neither pleasure nor pride. The houseboat had become shabby. The carpeting had lost its pile; the carved screens were chipped; the iron lantern at the bow sagged with rust. Seventy years ago the first owner, on accepting the boat, had honored the builder and had been likewise honored; the transaction (for the process represented a great deal more than simple giving and taking) had augmented the prestige of both. That time was far gone; the houseboat now commanded no prestige whatever. Edwer Thissell, resident on Sirene only three months, recognized the lack but could do nothing about it: this particular houseboat was the best he could get. He sat on the rear deck practising the *ganga*, a zither-like instrument not much larger than his hand. A hundred yards inshore, surf defined a strip of white beach; beyond rose jungle, with the silhouette of craggy black hills against the sky. Mireille shone hazy and white overhead, as if through a tangle of spider-web; the face of the ocean pooled and puddled with mother-of-pearl luster. The scene had become as familiar, though not as boring, as the *ganga*, at which he had worked two hours, twanging out the Sirenese scales, forming chords, traversing simple progressions. Now he put down the *ganga* for the *zachinko,* this a small sound-box studded with keys, played with the right hand. Pressure on the keys forced air through reeds in the keys themselves, producing a concertina-like tone. Thissell ran off a dozen quick scales, making very few mistakes. Of the six instruments he had set himself to learn, the *zachinko* had proved the least refractory (with the exception, of course, of the *hymerkin,* that clacking, slapping, clattering device of wood and stone used exclusively with the slaves).

Thissell practised another ten minutes, then put aside the *zachinko.* He flexed his arms, wrung his aching fingers. Every waking moment since his arrival had been given to the instruments: the *hymerkin,* the *ganga,* the *zachinko,* the *kiv,* the *strapan,* the *gomapard.* He had practised scales in nineteen keys and four modes, chords without number, intervals never imagined on the Home Planets. Trills, arpeggios, slurs, click-stops and nasalization; damping and augmentation of overtones; vibratos and wolf-tones; concavities and convexities. He practised with a dogged, deadly diligence, in which his original concept of music as a source of pleasure had long become lost. Looking over the instruments Thissell resisted an urge to fling all six into the Titanic.

He rose to his feet, went forward through the parlor saloon, the dining-saloon, along a corridor past the galley and came out on the foredeck. He bent over the rail, peered down into the underwater pens where Toby and Rex, the slaves, were harnessing the dray-fish for the weekly trip to Fan, eight miles north. The youngest fish, either playful or captious, ducked and plunged. Its streaming black muzzle broke water, and Thissell, looking into its face felt a peculiar qualm: the fish wore no mask!

Thissell laughed uneasily, fingering his own mask, the Moon Moth. No question about it, he was becoming acclimated to Sirene! A significant stage had been reached when the naked face of a fish caused him shock!

The fish were finally harnessed; Toby and Rex climbed aboard, red bodies glistening, black cloth masks clinging to their faces. Ignoring

Thissell they stowed the pen, hoisted anchor. The dray-fish strained, the harness tautened, the houseboat moved north.

Returning to the after-deck, Thissell took up the *strapan*—this a circular sound-box eight inches in diameter. Forty-six wires radiated from a central hub to the circumference where they connected to either a bell or a tinkle-bar. When plucked, the bells rang, the bars chimed; when strummed, the instrument gave off a twanging, jingling sound. When played with competence, the pleasantly acid dissonances produced an expressive effect; in an unskilled hand, the results were less felicitous, and might even approach random noise. The *strapan* was Thissell's weakest instrument and he practised with concentration during the entire trip north.

In due course the houseboat approached the floating city. The dray-fish were curbed, the houseboat warped to a mooring. Along the dock a line of idlers weighed and gauged every aspect of the houseboat, the slaves and Thissell himself, according to Sirenese habit. Thissell, not yet accustomed to such penetrating inspection, found the scrutiny unsettling, all the more so for the immobility of the masks. Self-consciously adjusting his own Moon Moth, he climbed the ladder to the dock.

A slave rose from where he had been squatting, touched knuckles to the black cloth at his forehead, and sang on a three-tone phrase of interrogation: "The Moon Moth before me possibly expresses the identity of Ser Edwer Thissell?"

Thissell tapped the *hymerkin* which hung at his belt and sang: "I am Ser Thissell."

"I have been honored by a trust," sang the slave. "Three days from dawn to dusk I have waited on the dock; three nights from dusk to dawn I have crouched on a raft below this same dock listening to the feet of the Night-men. At last I behold the mask of Ser Thissell."

Thissell evoked an impatient clatter from the *hymerkin*. "What is the nature of this trust?"

"I carry a message, Ser Thissell. It is intended for you."

Thissell held out his left hand, playing the *hymerkin* with his right. "Give me the message."

"Instantly, Ser Thissell."

The message bore a heavy superscription:

EMERGENCY COMMUNICATION!
RUSH!

Thissell ripped open the envelope. The message was signed by Castel Cromartin, Chief Executive of the Interworld Policies Board, and after the formal salutation read:

> ABSOLUTELY URGENT the following orders be executed! Aboard *Carina Cruzeiro*, destination Fan, date of arrival January 10 U.T., is notorious assassin, Haxo Angmark. Meet landing with adequate authority, effect detention and incarceration of this man. These instructions must be successfully implemented. Failure is unacceptable.
>
> ATTENTION! Haxo Angmark is superlatively dangerous. Kill him without hesitation at any show of resistance.

Thissell considered the message with dismay. In coming to Fan as Consular Representative he had expected nothing like this; he felt neither inclination nor competence in the matter of dealing with dangerous assassins. Thoughtfully he rubbed the fuzzy gray cheek of his mask. The situation was not completely dark; Esteban Rolver, Director of the Space-Port, would doubtless cooperate, and perhaps furnish a platoon of slaves.

More hopefully, Thissell reread the message. January 10, Universal Time. He consulted a conversion calendar. Today, 40th in the Season of Bitter Nectar—Thissell ran his finger down the column, stopped. January 10. Today.

A distant rumble caught his attention. Dropping from the mist came a dull shape: the lighter returning from contact with the *Carina Cruzeiro*.

Thissell once more re-read the note, raised his head, studied the descending lighter. Aboard would be Haxo Angmark. In five minutes he would emerge upon the soil of Sirene. Landing formalities would detain him possibly twenty minutes. The landing field lay a mile and a half distant, joined to Fan by a winding path through the hills.

Thissell turned to the slave. "When did this message arrive?"

The slave leaned forward uncomprehendingly. Thissell reiterated his question, singing to the clack of the *hymerkin:* "This message: you have enjoyed the honor of its custody how long?"

The slave sang: "Long days have I waited on the wharf, retreating only to the raft at the onset of dusk. Now my vigil is rewarded; I behold Ser Thissell."

Thissell turned away, walked furiously up the dock. Ineffective, inefficient Sirenese! Why had they not delivered the message to his houseboat? Twenty-five minutes—twenty-two now...

At the esplanade Thissell stopped, looked right, left, hoping for a miracle: some sort of air-transport to whisk him to the space-port, where with Rolver's aid, Haxo Angmark might still be detained. Or better yet, a second message canceling the first. Something, anything...But air-cars were not to be found on Sirene, and no second message appeared.

Across the esplanade rose a meager row of permanent structures, built of stone and iron and so proof against the efforts of the Nightmen. A hostler occupied one of these structures, and as Thissell watched a man in a splendid pearl and silver mask emerged riding one of the lizard-like mounts of Sirene.

Thissell sprang forward. There was still time; with luck he might yet intercept Haxo Angmark. He hurried across the esplanade.

Before the line of stalls stood the hostler, inspecting his stock with solicitude, occasionally burnishing a scale or whisking away an insect. There were five of the beasts in prime condition, each as tall as a man's shoulder, with massive legs, thick bodies, heavy wedge-shaped heads. From their fore-fangs, which had been artificially lengthened and curved into near-circles, gold rings depended. Their scales had been stained in diaper-pattern: purple and green, orange and black, red and blue, brown and pink, yellow and silver.

Thissell came to a breathless halt in front of the hostler. He reached for his *kiv**, then hesitated. Could this be considered a casual personal encounter? The *zachinko* perhaps? But the statement of his needs hardly seemed to demand the formal approach. Better the *kiv* after all. He struck a chord, but by error found himself stroking the *ganga*. Beneath his mask Thissell grinned apologetically; his relationship with this hostler was by no means on an intimate basis. He hoped that the hostler was of sanguine disposition, and in any event the urgency of the occasion allowed no time to select an exactly appropriate instrument. He struck a second chord, and playing as well as agitation, breathlessness and lack of skill allowed, sang out a request: "Ser Hostler, I have immediate need of a swift mount. Allow me to select from your herd."

*Kiv: five banks of resilient metal strips, fourteen to the bank, played by touching, twisting, twanging.

The hostler wore a mask of considerable complexity which Thissell could not identify: a construction of varnished brown cloth, pleated gray leather and high on the forehead two large green and scarlet globes, minutely segmented like insect eyes. He inspected Thissell a long moment, then, rather ostentatiously selecting his *stimic**, executed a brilliant progression of trills and rounds, of an import Thissell failed to grasp. The hostler sang, "Ser Moon Moth, I fear that my steeds are unsuitable to a person of your distinction."

Thissell earnestly twanged at the *ganga*. "By no means: they all seem adequate. I am in great haste and will gladly accept any of the group."

The hostler played a brittle cascading crescendo. "Ser Moon Moth," he sang, "the steeds are ill and dirty. I am flattered that you consider them adequate to your use. I cannot accept the merit you offer me. And—" here, switching instruments, he struck a cool tinkle from his *krodatch*** "—somehow I fail to recognize the boon companion and co-craftsman who accosts me so familiarly with his *ganga.*"

The implication was clear. Thissell would receive no mount. He turned, set off at a run for the landing field. Behind him sounded a clatter of the hostler's *hymerkin*—whether directed toward the hostler's slaves, or toward himself Thissell did not pause to learn.

The previous Consular Representative of the Home Planets on Sirene had been killed at Zundar. Masked as a Tavern Bravo he had accosted a girl beribboned for the Equinoctial Attitudes, a solecism for which he had been instantly beheaded by a Red Demiurge, a Sun Sprite and a Magic Hornet. Edwer Thissell, recently graduated from the Institute, had been named his successor, and allowed three days to prepare himself. Normally of a contemplative, even cautious disposition, Thissell had regarded the appointment as a challenge. He learned the

---

*Stimic: three flute-like tubes equipped with plungers. Thumb and forefinger squeeze a bag to force air across the mouth-pieces; the second, third and fourth little fingers manipulate the slide. The stimic is an instrument well-adapted to the sentiments of cool withdrawal, or even disapproval.

**Krodatch: a small square sound-box strung with resined gut. The musician scratches the strings with his fingernail, or strokes them with his fingertips, to produce a variety of quietly formal sounds. The krodatch is also used as an instrument of insult.

Sirenese language by sub-cerebral techniques, and found it uncompli-
cated. Then, in the *Journal of Universal Anthropology,* he read:

> The population of the Titanic littoral is highly individualis-
> tic, possibly in response to a bountiful environment which puts
> no premium upon group activity. The language, reflecting this
> trait, expresses the individual's mood, and his emotional atti-
> tude toward a given situation. Factual information is regarded
> as a secondary concomitant. Moreover, the language is sung,
> characteristically to the accompaniment of a small instrument.
> As a result, there is great difficulty in ascertaining fact from a
> native of Fan, or the forbidden city Zundar. One will be regaled
> with elegant arias and demonstrations of astonishing virtuosity
> upon one or another of the numerous musical instruments. The
> visitor to this fascinating world, unless he cares to be treated
> with the most consummate contempt, must therefore learn to
> express himself after the approved local fashion.

Thissell made a note in his memorandum book: 'Procure small
musical instrument, together with directions as to use.' He read on.

> There is everywhere and at all times a plenitude, not to say,
> a superfluity, of food, and the climate is benign. With a fund of
> racial energy and a great deal of leisure time, the population
> occupies itself with intricacy. Intricacy in all things: intricate
> craftsmanship, such as the carved panels which adorn the
> houseboats; intricate symbolism, as exemplified in the masks
> worn by everyone; the intricate half-musical language which
> admirably expresses subtle moods and emotions, and above all
> the fantastic intricacy of inter-personal relationships. Prestige,
> face, *mana,* repute, glory: the Sirenese word is *strakh.* Every
> man has his characteristic *strakh,* which determines whether,
> when he needs a houseboat, he will be urged to avail himself of
> a floating palace, rich with gems, alabaster lanterns, peacock
> faience and carved wood, or grudgingly permitted an aban-
> doned shack on a raft. There is no medium of exchange on
> Sirene; the single and sole currency is *strakh*...

Thissell rubbed his chin and read further.

Masks are worn at all times, in accordance with the philosophy that a man should not be compelled to use a similitude foisted upon him by factors beyond his control; that he should be at liberty to choose that semblance most consonant with his *strakh*. In the civilized areas of Sirene—which is to say the Titanic littoral—a man literally never shows his face; it is his basic secret.

Gambling, by this token, is unknown on Sirene; it would be catastrophic to Sirenese self-respect to gain advantage by means other than the exercise of *strakh*. The word 'luck' has no counterpart in the Sirenese language.

Thissell made another note: 'Get mask. Museum? Drama guild?'

He finished the article, hastened forth to complete his preparations, and the next day embarked aboard the *Robert Astroguard* for the first leg of the passage to Sirene.

The lighter settled upon the Sirenese space-port, a topaz disk isolated among the black, green and purple hills. The lighter grounded, and Edwer Thissell stepped forth. He was met by Esteban Rolver, the local agent for Spaceways. Rolver threw up his hands, stepped back. "Your mask," he cried huskily. "Where is your mask?"

Thissell held it up rather self-consciously. "I wasn't sure—"

"Put it on," said Rolver, turning away. He himself wore a fabrication of dull green scales, blue-lacquered wood. Black quills protruded at the cheeks, and under his chin hung a black and white checked pom-pom, the total effect creating a sense of sardonic supple personality.

Thissell adjusted the mask to his face, undecided whether to make a joke about the situation or to maintain a reserve suitable to the dignity of his post.

"Are you masked?" Rolver inquired over his shoulder.

Thissell replied in the affirmative and Rolver turned. The mask hid the expression of his face, but his hand unconsciously flicked a set of keys strapped to his thigh. The instrument sounded a trill of shock and polite consternation. "You can't wear that mask!" sang Rolver. "In fact—how, where, did you get it?"

"It's copied from a mask owned by the Polypolis museum," declared Thissell stiffly. "I'm sure it's authentic."

Rolver nodded, his own mask more sardonic-seeming than ever. "It's authentic enough. It's a variant of the type known as the Sea-Dragon Conqueror, and is worn on ceremonial occasions by persons of enormous prestige: princes, heroes, master craftsmen, great musicians."

"I wasn't aware—"

Rolver made a gesture of languid understanding. "It's something you'll learn in due course. Notice my mask. Today I'm wearing a Tarn Bird. Persons of minimal prestige—such as you, I, any other out-worlder—wear this sort of thing."

"Odd," said Thissell, as they started across the field toward a low concrete blockhouse. "I assumed that a person wore whatever he liked."

"Certainly," said Rolver. "Wear any mask you like—if you can make it stick. This Tarn Bird for instance. I wear it to indicate that I presume nothing. I make no claims to wisdom, ferocity, versatility, musicianship, truculence, or any of a dozen other Sirenese virtues."

"For the sake of argument," said Thissell, "what would happen if I walked through the streets of Zundar in this mask?"

Rolver laughed, a muffled sound behind his mask. "If you walked along the docks of Zundar—there are no streets—in any mask, you'd be killed within the hour. That's what happened to Benko, your predecessor. He didn't know how to act. None of us out-worlders know how to act. In Fan we're tolerated—so long as we keep our place. But you couldn't even walk around Fan in that regalia you're sporting now. Somebody wearing a Fire Snake or a Thunder Goblin—masks, you understand—would step up to you. He'd play his *krodatch*, and if you failed to challenge his audacity with a passage on the *skaranyi**, a dev-ilish instrument, he'd play his *hymerkin*—the instrument we use with the slaves. That's the ultimate expression of contempt. Or he might ring his dueling-gong and attack you then and there."

"I had no idea that people here were quite so irascible," said Thissell in a subdued voice.

Rolver shrugged and swung open the massive steel door into his office. "Certain acts may not be committed on the Concourse at Polypolis without incurring criticism."

---

*Skaranyi: a miniature bag-pipe, the sac squeezed between thumb and palm, the four fingers controlling the stops along four tubes.

"Yes, that's quite true," said Thissell. He looked around the office. "Why the security? The concrete, the steel?"

"Protection against the savages," said Rolver. "They come down from the mountains at night, steal what's available, kill anyone they find ashore." He went to a closet, brought forth a mask. "Here. Use this Moon Moth; it won't get you in trouble."

Thissell unenthusiastically inspected the mask. It was constructed of mouse-colored fur; there was a tuft of hair at each side of the mouth-hole, a pair of feather-like antennae at the forehead. White lace flaps dangled beside the temples and under the eyes hung a series of red folds, creating an effect at once lugubrious and comic.

Thissell asked, "Does this mask signify any degree of prestige?"

"Not a great deal."

"After all, I'm Consular Representative," said Thissell. "I represent the Home Planets, a hundred billion people—"

"If the Home Planets want their representative to wear a Sea-Dragon Conqueror mask, they'd better send out a Sea-Dragon Conqueror type of man."

"I see," said Thissell in a subdued voice. "Well, if I must..."

Rolver politely averted his gaze while Thissell doffed the Sea-Dragon Conqueror and slipped the more modest Moon Moth over his head. "I suppose I can find something just a bit more suitable in one of the shops," Thissell said. "I'm told a person simply goes in and takes what he needs, correct?"

Rolver surveyed Thissell critically. "That mask—temporarily, at least—is perfectly suitable. And it's rather important not to take any-thing from the shops until you know the *strakh* value of the article you want. The owner loses prestige if a person of low *strakh* makes free with his best work."

Thissell shook his head in exasperation. "Nothing of this was explained to me! I knew of the masks, of course, and the painstaking integrity of the craftsmen, but this insistence on prestige—*strakh*, what-ever the word is..."

"No matter," said Rolver. "After a year or two you'll begin to learn your way around. I suppose you speak the language?"

"Oh, indeed. Certainly."

"And what instruments do you play?"

"Well—I was given to understand that any small instrument was adequate, or that I could merely sing."

"Very inaccurate. Only slaves sing without accompaniment. I suggest that you learn the following instruments as quickly as possible: the *hymerkin* for your slaves. The *ganga* for conversation between intimates or one a trifle lower than yourself in *strakh*. The *kiv* for casual polite intercourse. The *zachinko* for more formal dealings. The *strapan* or the *krodatch* for your social inferiors—in your case, should you wish to insult someone. The *gomapard** or the *double-kamanthil*** for ceremonials." He considered a moment. "The *crebarin,* the water-lute and the *slobo* are highly useful also—but perhaps you'd better learn the other instruments first. They should provide at least a rudimentary means of communication."

"Aren't you exaggerating?" suggested Thissell. "Or joking?"

Rolver laughed his saturnine laugh. "Not at all. First of all, you'll need a houseboat. And then you'll want slaves."

Rolver took Thissell from the landing field to the docks of Fan, a walk of an hour and a half along a pleasant path under enormous trees loaded with fruit, cereal pods, sacs of sugary sap.

"At the moment," said Rolver, "there are only four out-worlders in Fan, counting yourself. I'll take you to Welibus, our Commercial Factor. I think he's got an old houseboat he might let you use."

Cornely Welibus had resided fifteen years in Fan, acquiring sufficient *strakh* to wear his South Wind mask with authority. This consisted of a blue disk inlaid with cabochons of lapis-lazuli, surrounded by an aureole of shimmering snake-skin. Heartier and more cordial than Rolver, he not only provided Thissell with a houseboat, but also a score of various musical instruments and a pair of slaves.

Embarrassed by the largesse, Thissell stammered something about payment, but Welibus cut him off with an expansive gesture. "My dear fellow, this is Sirene. Such trifles cost nothing."

---

*Gomapard: one of the few electric instruments used on Sirene. An oscillator produces an oboe-like tone which is modulated, choked, vibrated, raised and lowered in pitch by four keys.

**Double-kamanthil: an instrument similar to the ganga, except the tones are produced by twisting and inclining a disk of resined leather against one or more of the forty-six strings.

"But a houseboat—"

Welibus played a courtly little flourish on his *kiv.* "I'll be frank, Ser Thissell. The boat is old and a trifle shabby. I can't afford to use it; my status would suffer." A graceful melody accompanied his words. "Status as yet need not concern you. You require merely shelter, comfort and safety from the Night-men."

"'Night-men'?"

"The cannibals who roam the shore after dark."

"Oh yes. Ser Rolver mentioned them."

"Horrible things. We won't discuss them." A shuddering little trill issued from his kiv. "Now, as to slaves." He tapped the blue disk of his mask with a thoughtful forefinger. "Rex and Toby should serve you well." He raised his voice, played a swift clatter on the hymerkin. *"Avan esx trobu!"*

A female slave appeared wearing a dozen tight bands of pink cloth, and a dainty black mask sparkling with mother-of-pearl sequins.

"Fascu etz Rex ae Toby."

Rex and Toby appeared, wearing loose masks of black cloth, russet jerkins. Welibus addressed them with a resonant clatter of *hymerkin,* enjoining them to the service of their new master, on pain of return to their native islands. They prostrated themselves, sang pledges of servitude to Thissell in soft husky voices. Thissell laughed nervously and essayed a sentence in the Sirenese language. "Go to the houseboat, clean it well, bring aboard food."

Toby and Rex stared blankly through the holes in their masks. Welibus repeated the orders with hymerkin accompaniment. The slaves bowed and departed.

Thissell surveyed the musical instruments with dismay. "I haven't the slightest idea how to go about learning these things."

Welibus turned to Rolver. "What about Kershaul? Could he be persuaded to give Ser Thissell some basic instruction?"

Rolver nodded judicially. "Kershaul might undertake the job."

Thissell asked, "Who is Kershaul?"

"The fourth of our little group of expatriates," replied Welibus, "an anthropologist. You've read *Zundar the Splendid? Rituals of Sirene? The Faceless Folk?* No? A pity. All excellent works. Kershaul is high in prestige, and I believe visits Zundar from time to time. Wears a Cave Owl, sometimes a Star Wanderer or even a Wise Arbiter."

"He's taken to an Equatorial Serpent," said Rolver. "The variant with the gilt tusks."

"Indeed!" marveled Welibus. "Well, I must say he's earned it. A fine fellow, good chap indeed." And he strummed his *zachinko* thoughtfully.

✸

Three months passed. Under the tutelage of Mathew Kershaul, Thissell practised the *hymerkin,* the *ganga,* the *strapan,* the *kiv,* the *gomapard,* and the *zachinko.* The others could wait, said Kershaul, until Thissell had mastered the six basic instruments. He lent Thissell recordings of noteworthy Sirenese conversing in various moods and to various accompaniments, so that Thissell might learn the melodic conventions currently in vogue, and perfect himself in the niceties of intonation, the various rhythms, cross-rhythms, compound rhythms, implied rhythms and suppressed rhythms. Kershaul professed to find Sirenese music a fascinating study, and Thissell admitted that it was a subject not readily exhausted. The quarter-tone tuning of the instruments admitted the use of twenty-four tonalities which, multiplied by the five modes in general use, resulted in one hundred and twenty separate scales. Kershaul, however, advised that Thissell primarily concentrate on learning each instrument in its fundamental tonality, using only two of the modes.

With no immediate business at Fan except the weekly visits to Mathew Kershaul, Thissell took his houseboat eight miles south and moored it in the lee of a rocky promontory. Here, if it had not been for the incessant practising, Thissell lived an idyllic life. The sea was calm and crystal-clear; the beach, ringed by the gray, green and purple foliage of the forest, lay close at hand if he wanted to stretch his legs.

Toby and Rex occupied a pair of cubicles forward, Thissell had the after-cabins to himself. From time to time he toyed with the idea of a third slave, possibly a young female, to contribute an element of charm and gaiety to the menage, but Kershaul advised against the step, fearing that the intensity of Thissell's concentration might somehow be diminished. Thissell acquiesced and devoted himself to the study of the six instruments.

The days passed quickly. Thissell never became bored with the pageantry of dawn and sunset; the white clouds and blue sea of noon; the night sky blazing with the twenty-nine stars of Cluster SI 1-715. The weekly trip to Fan broke the tedium, Toby and Rex foraged for food; Thissell visited the luxurious houseboat of Mathew Kershaul for instruction and advice. Then, three months after Thissell's arrival, came the message completely disorganizing the routine: Haxo Angmark, assassin, *agent provocateur,* ruthless and crafty criminal, had come to Sirene. 'Effect detention and incarceration of this man!' read the orders. 'Attention! Haxo Angmark is superlatively dangerous. Kill without hesitation!'

✸

Thissell was not in the best of condition. He trotted fifty yards until his breath came in gasps, then walked: through low hills crowned with white bamboo and black tree-ferns; across meadows yellow with grass-nuts, through orchards and wild vineyards. Twenty minutes passed, twenty-five minutes passed, twenty-five minutes; with a heavy sensation in his stomach Thissell knew that he was too late. Haxo Angmark had landed, and might be traversing this very road toward Fan. But along the way Thissell met only four persons: a boy-child in a mock-fierce Alk Islander mask; two young women wearing the Red Bird and the Green Bird; a man masked as a Forest Goblin. Coming upon the man, Thissell stopped short. Could this be Angmark?

Thissell essayed a stratagem. He went boldly to the man, stared into the hideous mask. "Angmark," he called in the language of the Home Planets, "you are under arrest!"

The Forest Goblin stared uncomprehendingly, then started forward along the track.

Thissell put himself in the way. He reached for his ganga, then recalling the hostler's reaction, instead struck a chord on the *zachinko.* "You travel the road from the space-port," he sang. "What have you seen there?"

The Forest Goblin grasped his hand-bugle, an instrument used to deride opponents on the field of battle, to summon animals, or occasionally to evince a rough and ready truculence. "Where I travel and what I see are the concern solely of myself. Stand back or I walk upon your face." He marched forward, and had not Thissell leapt aside the Forest Goblin might well have made good his threat.

Thissell stood gazing after the retreating back. Angmark? Not likely, with so sure a touch on the hand-bugle. Thissell hesitated, then turned and continued on his way.

Arriving at the space-port, he went directly to the office. The heavy door stood ajar; as Thissell approached, a man appeared in the doorway. He wore a mask of dull green scales, mica plates, blue-lacquered wood and black quills—the Tarn Bird.

"Ser Rolver," Thissell called out anxiously, "who came down from the *Carina Cruzeiro?*"

Rolver studied Thissell a long moment. "Why do you ask?"

"Why do I ask?" demanded Thissell. "You must have seen the space-gram I received from Castel Cromartin!"

"Oh yes," said Rolver. "Of course. Naturally."

"It was delivered only half an hour ago," said Thissell bitterly. "I rushed out as fast as I could. Where is Angmark?"

"In Fan, I assume," said Rolver.

Thissell cursed softly. "Why didn't you delay him?"

Rolver shrugged. "I had neither authority, inclination nor the capability to stop him."

Thissell fought back his annoyance. In a voice of studied calm he said, "On the way I passed a man in rather a ghastly mask—saucer eyes, red wattles."

"A Forest Goblin," said Rolver. "Angmark brought the mask with him."

"But he played the hand-bugle," Thissell protested. "How could Angmark—"

"He's well-acquainted with Sirene; he spent five years here in Fan."

Thissell grunted in annoyance. "Cromartin made no mention of this."

"It's common knowledge," said Rolver with a shrug. "He was Commercial Representative before Welibus took over."

"Were he and Welibus acquainted?"

Rolver laughed shortly. "Naturally. But don't suspect poor Welibus of anything more venal than juggling his accounts; I assure you he's no consort of assassins."

"Speaking of assassins," said Thissell, "do you have a weapon I might borrow?"

Rolver inspected him in wonder. "You came out here to take Angmark bare-handed?"

"I had no choice," said Thissell. "When Cromartin gives orders he expects results. In any event you were here with your slaves."

"Don't count on me for help," Rolver said testily. "I wear the Tarn Bird and make no pretensions of valor. But I can lend you a power pistol. I haven't used it recently; I won't guarantee its charge."

Rolver went into the office and a moment later returned with the gun. "What will you do now?"

Thissell shook his head wearily. "I'll try to find Angmark in Fan. Or might he head for Zundar?"

Rolver considered. "Angmark might be able to survive in Zundar. But he'd want to brush up on his musicianship. I imagine he'll stay in Fan a few days."

"But how can I find him? Where should I look?"

"That I can't say," replied Rolver. "You might be safer not finding him. Angmark is a dangerous man."

Thissell returned to Fan the way he had come.

Where the path swung down from the hills into the esplanade a thick-walled *pisé-de-terre* building had been constructed. The door was carved from a solid black plank; the windows were guarded by enfoliated bands of iron. This was the office of Cornely Welibus, Commercial Factor, Importer and Exporter. Thissell found Welibus sitting at his ease on the tiled verandah, wearing a modest adaptation of the Waldemar mask. He seemed lost in thought and might or might not have recognized Thissell's Moon Moth; in any event he gave no signal of greeting.

Thissell approached the porch. "Good morning, Ser Welibus."

Welibus nodded abstractedly and said in a flat voice, plucking at his *krodatch,* "Good morning."

Thissell was rather taken aback. This was hardly the instrument to use toward a friend and fellow out-worlder, even if he did wear the Moon Moth.

Thissell said coldly, "May I ask how long you have been sitting here?"

Welibus considered half a minute, and now when he spoke he accompanied himself on the more cordial *crebarin.* But the recollection of the *krodatch* chord still rankled in Thissell's mind.

"I've been here fifteen or twenty minutes. Why do you ask?"

"I wonder if you noticed a Forest Goblin pass?"

Welibus nodded. "He went on down the esplanade—turned into that first mask shop, I believe."

Thissell hissed between his teeth. This would naturally be Angmark's first move. "I'll never find him once he changes masks," he muttered.

"Who is this Forest Goblin?" asked Welibus, with no more than casual interest.

Thissell could see no reason to conceal the name. "A notorious criminal: Haxo Angmark."

"Haxo Angmark!" croaked Welibus, leaning back in his chair. "You're sure he's here?"

"Reasonably sure."

Welibus rubbed his shaking hands together. "This is bad news—bad news indeed! He's an unscrupulous scoundrel."

"You knew him well?"

"As well as anyone." Welibus was now accompanying himself with the *kiv*. "He held the post I now occupy. I came out as an inspector and found that he was embezzling some four thousand UMIs a month. I'm sure he feels no great gratitude toward me." Welibus glanced nervously up the esplanade. "I hope you catch him."

"I'm doing my best. He went into the mask shop, you say?"

"I'm sure of it."

Thissell turned away. As he went down the path he heard the black plank door thud shut behind him.

He walked down the esplanade to the mask-maker's shop, paused outside as if admiring the display: a hundred miniature masks, carved from rare woods and minerals, dressed with emerald flakes, spider-web silk, wasp wings, petrified fish scales and the like. The shop was empty except for the mask-maker, a gnarled knotty man in a yellow robe, wearing a deceptively simple Universal Expert mask, fabricated from over two thousand bits of articulated wood.

Thissell considered what he would say, how he would accompany himself, then entered. The mask-maker, noting the Moon Moth and Thissell's diffident manner, continued with his work.

Thissell, selecting the easiest of his instruments, stroked his *strapan*—possibly not the most felicitous choice, for it conveyed a certain degree of condescension. Thissell tried to counteract this flavor by singing in warm, almost effusive, tones, shaking the *strapan* whimsically when he struck a wrong note: "A stranger is an interesting person to deal with; his habits are unfamiliar, he excites curiosity. Not twenty minutes ago a stranger entered this fascinating shop, to exchange his drab Forest Goblin for one of the remarkable and adventurous creations assembled on the premises."

The mask-maker turned Thissell a side glance, and without words he played a progression of chords on an instrument Thissell had never seen before: a flexible sac gripped in the palm with three short tubes leading between the fingers. When the tubes were squeezed almost shut and air forced through the slit, an oboe-like tone ensued. To Thissell's developing ear the instrument seemed difficult, the mask-maker expert, and the music conveyed a profound sense of disinterest.

Thissell tried again, laboriously manipulating the *strapan*. He sang, "To an out-worlder on a foreign planet, the voice of one from his home is like water to a wilting plant. A person who could unite two such persons might find satisfaction in such an act of mercy."

The mask-maker casually fingered his own *strapan,* and drew forth a set of rippling scales, his fingers moving faster than the eyes could follow. He sang in the formal style: "An artist values his moments of concentration; he does not care to spend time exchanging banalities with persons of at best average prestige." Thissell attempted to insert a counter melody, but the mask-maker struck a new set of complex chords whose portent evaded Thissell's understanding, and continued: "Into the shop comes a person who evidently has picked up for the first time an instrument of unparalleled complication, for the execution of his music is open to criticism. He sings of home-sickness and longing for the sight of others like himself. He dissembles his enormous *strakh* behind a Moon Moth, for he plays the *strapan* to a Master Craftsman, and sings in a voice of contemptuous raillery. The refined and creative artist ignores the provocation. He plays a polite instrument, remains noncommittal, and trusts that the stranger will tire of his sport and depart."

Thissell took up his *kiv.* "The noble mask-maker completely misunderstands me—"

He was interrupted by staccato rasping of the mask-maker's *strapan.* "The stranger now sees fit to ridicule the artist's comprehension."

Thissell scratched furiously at his *strapan:* "To protect myself from the heat, I wander into a small and unpretentious mask-shop. The artisan, though still distracted by the novelty of his tools, gives promise of development. He works zealously to perfect his skill, so much so that he refuses to converse with strangers, no matter what their need."

The mask-maker carefully laid down his carving tool. He rose to his feet, went behind a screen, and shortly returned wearing a mask of gold and iron, with simulated flames licking up from the scalp. In one hand he carried a *skaranyi,* in the other a *scimitar.* He struck off a brilliant series of wild tones, and sang: "Even the most accomplished artist can augment his *strakh* by killing sea-monsters, Night-men and importunate idlers. Such an occasion is at hand. The artist delays his attack exactly ten seconds, because the offender wears a Moon Moth." He twirled his scimitar, spun it in the air.

Thissell desperately pounded the *strapan.* "Did a Forest Goblin enter the shop? Did he depart with a new mask?"

"Five seconds have elapsed," sang the mask-maker in steady ominous rhythm.

Thissell departed in frustrated rage. He crossed the square, stood looking up and down the esplanade. Hundreds of men and women sauntered along the docks, or stood on the decks of their houseboats, each wearing a mask chosen to express his mood, prestige and special attributes, and everywhere sounded the twitter of musical instruments.

Thissell stood at a loss. The Forest Goblin had disappeared. Haxo Angmark walked at liberty in Fan, and Thissell had failed the urgent instructions of Castel Cromartin.

Behind him sounded the casual notes of a *kiv.* "Ser Moon Moth Thissell, you stand engrossed in thought."

Thissell turned, to find beside him a Cave Owl, in a somber cloak of black and gray. Thissell recognized the mask, which symbolized erudition and patient exploration of abstract ideas; Mathew Kershaul had worn it on the occasion of their meeting a week before.

"Good morning, Ser Kershaul," muttered Thissell.

"And how are the studies coming? Have you mastered the C-Sharp Plus scale on the *gomapard*? As I recall, you were finding those inverse intervals puzzling."

"I've worked on them," said Thissell in a gloomy voice. "However, since I'll probably be recalled to Polypolis, it may be all time wasted."

"Eh? What's this?"

Thissell explained the situation in regard to Haxo Angmark. Kershaul nodded gravely. "I recall Angmark. Not a gracious personality, but an excellent musician, with quick fingers and a real talent for new instruments." Thoughtfully he twisted the goatee of his Cave Owl mask. "What are your plans?"

"They're non-existent," said Thissell, playing a doleful phrase on the *kiv.* "I haven't any idea what masks he'll be wearing, and if I don't know what he looks like, how can I find him?"

Kershaul tugged at his goatee. "In the old days he favored the Exo Cambian Cycle, and I believe he used an entire set of Nether Denizens. Now of course his tastes may have changed."

"Exactly," Thissell complained. "He might be twenty feet away and I'd never know it." He glanced bitterly across the esplanade toward the mask-maker's shop. "No one will tell me anything. I doubt if they care that a murderer is walking their docks."

"Quite correct," Kershaul agreed. "Sirenese standards are different from ours."

"They have no sense of responsibility," declared Thissell. "I doubt if they'd throw a rope to a drowning man."

"It's true that they dislike interference," Kershaul agreed. "They emphasize individual responsibility and self-sufficiency."

"Interesting," said Thissell, "but I'm still in the dark about Angmark."

Kershaul surveyed him gravely. "And should you locate Angmark, what will you do then?"

"I'll carry out the orders of my superior," said Thissell doggedly.

"Angmark is a dangerous man," mused Kershaul. "He's got a number of advantages over you."

"I can't take that into account. It's my duty to send him back to Polypolis. He's probably safe, since I haven't the remotest idea how to find him."

Kershaul reflected. "An out-worlder can't hide behind a mask, not from the Sirenese at least. There are four of us here at Fan—Rolver, Welibus, you and me. If another out-worlder tries to set up housekeeping the news will get around in short order."

"What if he heads for Zundar?"

Kershaul shrugged. "I doubt if he'd dare. On the other hand—" Kershaul paused, then noting Thissell's sudden inattention, turned to follow Thissell's gaze.

A man in a Forest Goblin mask came swaggering toward them along the esplanade. Kershaul laid a restraining hand on Thissell's arm, but Thissell stepped out into the path of the Forest Goblin, his borrowed gun ready. "Haxo Angmark," he cried, "don't make a move, or I'll kill you. You're under arrest."

"Are you sure this is Angmark?" asked Kershaul in a worried voice.

"I'll find out," said Thissell. "Angmark, turn around, hold up your hands."

The Forest Goblin stood rigid with surprise and puzzlement. He reached to his *zachinko*, played an interrogatory arpeggio, and sang, "Why do you molest me, Moon Moth?"

Kershaul stepped forward and played a placatory phrase on his *slobo*. "I fear that a case of confused identity exists, Ser Forest Goblin. Ser Moon Moth seeks an out-worlder in a Forest Goblin mask."

The Forest Goblin's music became irritated, and he suddenly switched to his *stimic*. "He asserts that I am an out-worlder? Let him prove his case, or he has my retaliation to face."

Kershaul glanced in embarrassment around the crowd which had gathered and once more struck up an ingratiating melody. "I am positive that Ser Moon Moth—"

The Forest Goblin interrupted with a fanfare of *skaranyi* tones. "Let him demonstrate his case or prepare for the flow of blood."

Thissell said, "Very well, I'll prove my case." He stepped forward, grasped the Forest Goblin's mask. "Let's see your face, that'll demonstrate your identity!"

The Forest Goblin sprang back in amazement. The crowd gasped, then set up an ominous strumming and toning of various instruments.

The Forest Goblin reached to the nape of his neck, jerked the cord to his duel-gong, and with his other hand snatched forth his scimitar.

Kershaul stepped forward, playing the *slobo* with great agitation. Thissell, now abashed, moved aside, conscious of the ugly sound of the crowd.

Kershaul sang explanations and apologies; the Forest Goblin answered; Kershaul spoke over his shoulder to Thissell: "Run for it, or you'll be killed! Hurry!"

Thissell hesitated; the Forest Goblin put up his hand to thrust Kershaul aside. "Run!" screamed Kershaul. "To Welibus' office, lock yourself in!"

Thissell took to his heels. The Forest Goblin pursued him a few yards, then stamped his feet, sent after him a set of raucous and derisive blasts of the hand-bugle, while the crowd produced a contemptuous counterpoint of clacking *hymerkins*.

There was no further pursuit. Instead of taking refuge in the Import-Export office, Thissell turned aside and after cautious reconnaissance proceeded to the dock where his houseboat was moored.

The hour was not far short of dusk when he finally returned aboard. Toby and Rex squatted on the forward deck, surrounded by the provisions they had brought back: reed baskets of fruit and cereal, blue-glass jugs containing wine, oil and pungent sap, three young pigs in a wicker pen. They were cracking nuts between their teeth, spitting the shells over the side. They looked up at Thissell, and it seemed that they rose to their feet with a new casualness. Toby muttered something under his breath; Rex smothered a chuckle.

Thissell clacked his *hymerkin* angrily. He sang, "Take the boat offshore; tonight we remain at Fan."

In the privacy of his cabin he removed the Moon Moth, stared into a mirror at his almost unfamiliar features. He picked up the Moon

Moth, examined the detested lineaments: the furry gray skin, the blue spines, the ridiculous lace flaps. Hardly a dignified presence for the Consular Representative of the Home Planets. If, in fact, he still held the position when Cromartin learned of Angmark's winning free!

Thissell flung himself into a chair, stared moodily into space. Today he'd suffered a series of setbacks, but he wasn't defeated yet; not by any means. Tomorrow he'd visit Mathew Kershaul; they'd discuss how best to locate Angmark. As Kershaul had pointed out, another out-world establishment could not be camouflaged; Haxo Angmark's identity would soon become evident. Also, tomorrow he must procure another mask. Nothing extreme or vainglorious, but a mask which expressed a modicum of dignity and self-respect.

At this moment one of the slaves tapped on the door-panel, and Thissell hastily pulled the hated Moon Moth back over his head.

Early next morning, before the dawn-light had left the sky, the slaves sculled the houseboat back to that section of the dock set aside for the use of out-worlders. Neither Rolver nor Welibus nor Kershaul had yet arrived and Thissell waited impatiently. An hour passed, and Welibus brought his boat to the dock. Not wishing to speak to Welibus, Thissell remained inside his cabin.

A few moments later Rolver's boat likewise pulled in alongside the dock. Through the window Thissell saw Rolver, wearing his usual Tarn Bird, climb to the dock. Here he was met by a man in a yellow-tufted Sand Tiger mask, who played a formal accompaniment on his *gomapard* to whatever message he brought Rolver.

Rolver seemed surprised and disturbed. After a moment's thought he manipulated his own *gomapard,* and as he sang he indicated Thissell's houseboat. Then, bowing, he went on his way.

The man in the Sand Tiger mask climbed with rather heavy dignity to the float and rapped on the bulwark of Thissell's houseboat.

Thissell presented himself. Sirenese etiquette did not demand that he invite a casual visitor aboard, so he merely struck an interrogation on his *zachinko*.

The Sand Tiger played his *gomapard* and sang. "Dawn over the bay of Fan is customarily a splendid occasion; the sky is white with yellow and green colors; when Mireille rises, the mists burn and writhe like flames. He who sings derives a greater enjoyment from the hour when the floating corpse of an out-worlder does not appear to mar the serenity of the view."

Thissell's *zachinko* gave off a startled interrogation almost of its own accord; the Sand Tiger bowed with dignity. "The singer acknowledges no peer in steadfastness of disposition; however, he does not care to be plagued by the antics of a dissatisfied ghost. He therefore has ordered his slaves to attach a thong to the ankle of the corpse, and while we have conversed they have linked the corpse to the stern of your houseboat. You will wish to administer whatever rites are prescribed in the Out-world. He who sings wishes you a good morning and now departs."

Thissell rushed to the stern of his houseboat. There, near-naked and mask-less, floated the body of a mature man, supported by air trapped in his pantaloons.

Thissell studied the dead face, which seemed characterless and vapid—perhaps in direct consequence of the mask-wearing habit. The body appeared of medium stature and weight, and Thissell estimated the age as between forty-five and fifty. The hair was nondescript brown, the features bloated by the water. There was nothing to indicate how the man had died.

This must be Haxo Angmark, thought Thissell. Who else could it be? Mathew Kershaul? Why not? Thissell asked himself uneasily. Rolver and Welibus had already disembarked and gone about their business. He searched across the bay to locate Kershaul's houseboat, and discovered it already tying up to the dock. Even as he watched, Kershaul jumped ashore, wearing his Cave Owl mask.

He seemed in an abstracted mood, for he passed Thissell's houseboat without lifting his eyes from the dock.

Thissell turned back to the corpse. Angmark then, beyond a doubt. Had not three men disembarked from the houseboats of Rolver, Welibus and Kershaul, wearing masks characteristic of these men? Obviously, the corpse of Angmark...The easy solution refused to sit quiet in Thissell's mind. Kershaul had pointed out that another out-worlder would be quickly identified. How else could Angmark maintain himself unless he...Thissell brushed the thought aside. The corpse was obviously Angmark.

And yet...

Thissell summoned his slaves, gave orders that a suitable container be brought to the dock, that the corpse be transferred therein, and conveyed to a suitable place of repose. The slaves showed no enthusiasm for the task and Thissell was forced to thunder forcefully, if not skillfully, on the *hymerkin* to emphasize his orders.

He walked along the dock, turned up the esplanade, passed the office of Cornely Welibus and set out along the pleasant little lane to the landing field.

When he arrived, he found that Rolver had not yet made an appearance. An over-slave, given status by a yellow rosette on his black cloth mask, asked how he might be of service. Thissell stated that he wished to dispatch a message to Polypolis.

There was no difficulty here, declared the slave. If Thissell would set forth his message in clear block-print it would be dispatched immediately. Thissell wrote:

OUT-WORLDER FOUND DEAD, POSSIBLY ANGMARK. AGE 48, MEDIUM PHYSIQUE, BROWN HAIR. OTHER MEANS OF IDENTIFICATION LACKING. AWAIT ACKNOWLEDGEMENT AND/OR INSTRUCTIONS.

He addressed the message to Castel Cromartin at Polypolis and handed it to the over-slave. A moment later he heard the characteristic sputter of trans-space discharge.

An hour passed. Rolver made no appearance. Thissell paced restlessly back and forth in front of the office. There was no telling how long he would have to wait: trans-space transmission time varied unpredictably. Sometimes the message snapped through in micro-seconds; sometimes it wandered through unknowable regions for hours; and there were several authenticated examples of messages being received before they had been transmitted.

Another half-hour passed, and Rolver finally arrived, wearing his customary Tarn Bird. Coincidentally Thissell heard the hiss of the incoming message.

Rolver seemed surprised to see Thissell. "What brings you out so early?"

Thissell explained. "It concerns the body which you referred to me this morning. I'm communicating with my superiors about it."

Rolver raised his head and listened to the sound of the incoming message. "You seem to be getting an answer. I'd better attend to it."

"Why bother?" asked Thissell. "Your slave seems efficient."

"It's my job," declared Rolver. "I'm responsible for the accurate transmission and receipt of all space-grams."

"I'll come with you," said Thissell. "I've always wanted to watch the operation of the equipment."

"I'm afraid that's irregular," said Rolver. He went to the door which led into the inner compartment. "I'll have your message in a moment."

Thissell protested, but Rolver ignored him and went into the inner office. Five minutes later he reappeared, carrying a small yellow envelope. "Not too good news," he announced with unconvincing commiseration.

Thissell glumly opened the envelope. The message read:

BODY NOT ANGMARK. ANGMARK HAS BLACK HAIR. WHY DID YOU NOT MEET LANDING? SERIOUS INFRACTION, HIGHLY DISSATISFIED. RETURN TO POLYPOLIS NEXT OPPORTUNITY.
CASTEL CROMARTIN

Thissell put the message in his pocket. "Incidentally, may I inquire the color of your hair?"

Rolver played a surprised little trill on his *kiv*. "I'm quite blond. Why do you ask?"

"Mere curiosity."

Rolver played another run on the kiv. "Now I understand. My dear fellow, what a suspicious nature you have! Look!" He turned and parted the folds of his mask at the nape of his neck. Thissell saw that Rolver was blond indeed.

"Are you reassured?" asked Rolver jocularly.

"Oh, indeed," said Thissell. "Incidentally, have you another mask you could lend me? I'm sick of this Moon Moth."

"I'm afraid not," said Rolver. "But you need merely go into a mask-maker's shop and make a selection."

"Yes, of course," said Thissell. He took his leave of Rolver and returned along the trail to Fan. Passing Welibus' office he hesitated, then turned in. Today Welibus wore a dazzling confection of green glass prisms and silver beads, a mask Thissell had never seen before.

Welibus greeted him cautiously to the accompaniment of a *kiv*. "Good morning, Ser Moon Moth."

"I won't take too much of your time," said Thissell, "but I have a rather personal question to put to you. What color is your hair?"

Welibus hesitated a fraction of a second, then turned his back, lifted the flap of his mask. Thissell saw heavy black ringlets. "Does that answer your question?" inquired Welibus.

"Completely," said Thissell. He crossed the esplanade, went out on the dock to Kershaul's houseboat. Kershaul greeted him without enthusiasm, and invited him aboard with a resigned wave of the hand.

"A question I'd like to ask," said Thissell; "What color is your hair?"

Kershaul laughed woefully. "What little remains is black. Why do you ask?"

"Curiosity."

"Come, come," said Kershaul with an unaccustomed bluffness. "There's more to it than that."

Thissell, feeling the need of counsel, admitted as much. "Here's the situation. A dead out-worlder was found in the harbor this morning. His hair was brown. I'm not entirely certain, but the chances are—let me see, yes, two out of three that Angmark's hair is black."

Kershaul pulled at the Cave Owl's goatee. "How do you arrive at that probability?"

"The information came to me through Rolver's hands. He has blond hair. If Angmark has assumed Rolver's identity, he would naturally alter the information which came to me this morning. Both you and Welibus admit to black hair."

"Hm," said Kershaul. "Let me see if I follow your line of reasoning. You feel that Haxo Angmark has killed either Rolver, Welibus or myself and assumed the dead man's identity. Right?"

Thissell looked at him in surprise. "You yourself emphasized that Angmark could not set up another out-world establishment without revealing himself! Don't you remember?"

"Oh, certainly. To continue. Rolver delivered a message to you stating that Angmark was dark, and announced himself to be blond."

"Yes. Can you verify this? I mean for the old Rolver?"

"No," said Kershaul sadly. "I've seen neither Rolver nor Welibus without their masks."

"If Rolver is not Angmark," Thissell mused, "if Angmark indeed has black hair, then both you and Welibus come under suspicion."

"Very interesting," said Kershaul. He examined Thissell warily. "For that matter, you yourself might be Angmark. What color is your hair?"

"Brown," said Thissell curtly. He lifted the gray fur of the Moon Moth mask at the back of his head.

"But you might be deceiving me as to the text of the message," Kershaul put forward.

"I'm not," said Thissell wearily. "You can check with Rolver if you care to."

Kershaul shook his head. "Unnecessary. I believe you. But another matter: what of voices? You've heard all of us before and after Angmark arrived. Isn't there some indication there?"

"No. I'm so alert for any evidence of change that you all sound rather different. And the masks muffle your voices."

Kershaul tugged the goatee. "I don't see any immediate solution to the problem." He chuckled. "In any event, need there be? Before Angmark's advent, there were Rolver, Welibus, Kershaul and Thissell. Now—for all practical purposes—there are still Rolver, Welibus, Kershaul and Thissell. Who is to say that the new member may not be an improvement upon the old?"

"An interesting thought," agreed Thissell, "but it so happens that I have a personal interest in identifying Angmark. My career is at stake."

"I see," murmured Kershaul. "The situation then becomes an issue between yourself and Angmark."

"You won't help me?"

"Not actively. I've become pervaded with Sirenese individualism. I think you'll find that Rolver and Welibus will respond similarly." He sighed. "All of us have been here too long."

Thissell stood deep in thought. Kershaul waited patiently a moment, then said, "Do you have any further questions?"

"No," said Thissell. "I have merely a favor to ask you."

"I'll oblige if I possibly can," Kershaul replied courteously.

"Give me, or lend me, one of your slaves, for a week or two."

Kershaul played an exclamation of amusement on the *ganga*. "I hardly like to part with my slaves; they know me and my ways—"

"As soon as I catch Angmark you'll have him back."

"Very well," said Kershaul. He rattled a summons on his *hymerkin*, and a slave appeared. "Anthony," sang Kershaul, "you are to go with Ser Thissell and serve him for a short period."

The slave bowed, without pleasure.

Thissell took Anthony to his houseboat, and questioned him at length, noting certain of the responses upon a chart. He then enjoined Anthony to say nothing of what had passed, and consigned him to the care of Toby and Rex. He gave further instructions to move the houseboat away from the dock and allow no one aboard until his return.

He set forth once more along the way to the landing field, and found Rolver at a lunch of spiced fish, shredded bark of the salad tree, and a bowl of native currants. Rolver clapped an order on the *hymerkin,* and a slave set a place for Thissell. "And how are the investigations proceeding?"

"I'd hardly like to claim any progress," said Thissell. "I assume that I can count on your help?"

Rolver laughed briefly. "You have my good wishes."

"More concretely," said Thissell, "I'd like to borrow a slave from you. Temporarily."

Rolver paused in his eating. "Whatever for?"

"I'd rather not explain," said Thissell. "But you can be sure that I make no idle request."

Without graciousness Rolver summoned a slave and consigned him to Thissell's service.

On the way back to his houseboat, Thissell stopped at Welibus' office.

Welibus looked up from his work. "Good afternoon, Ser Thissell."

Thissell came directly to the point. "Ser Welibus, will you lend me a slave for a few days?"

Welibus hesitated, then shrugged. "Why not?" He clacked his *hymerkin;* a slave appeared. "Is he satisfactory? Or would you prefer a young female?" He chuckled—rather offensively, to Thissell's way of thinking.

"He'll do very well. I'll return him in a few days."

"No hurry." Welibus made an easy gesture and returned to his work.

Thissell continued to his houseboat, where he separately interviewed each of his two new slaves and made notes upon his chart.

Dusk came soft over the Titanic Ocean. Toby and Rex sculled the houseboat away from the dock, out across the silken waters. Thissell sat on the deck listening to the sound of soft voices, the flutter and tinkle of musical instruments. Lights from the floating houseboats glowed yellow and wan watermelon-red. The shore was dark; the Night-men would presently come slinking to paw through refuse and stare jealously across the water.

In nine days the *Buenaventura* came past Sirene on its regular schedule; Thissell had his orders to return to Polypolis. In nine days, could he locate Haxo Angmark?

Nine days weren't too many, Thissell decided, but they might possibly be enough.

Two days passed, and three and four and five. Every day Thissell went ashore and at least once a day visited Rolver, Welibus and Kershaul.

Each reacted differently to his presence. Rolver was sardonic and irritable; Welibus formal and at least superficially affable; Kershaul mild and suave, but ostentatiously impersonal and detached in his conversation.

Thissell remained equally bland to Rolver's dour jibes, Welibus' jocundity, Kershaul's withdrawal. And every day, returning to his houseboat he made marks on his chart.

The sixth, the seventh, the eighth day came and passed. Rolver, with rather brutal directness, inquired if Thissell wished to arrange for passage on the *Buenaventura*. Thissell considered, and said, "Yes, you had better reserve passage for one."

"Back to the world of faces," shuddered Rolver. "Faces! Everywhere pallid, fish-eyed faces. Mouths like pulp, noses knotted and punctured; flat, flabby faces. I don't think I could stand it after living here. Luckily you haven't become a real Sirenese."

"But I won't be going back," said Thissell.

"I thought you wanted me to reserve passage."

"I do. For Haxo Angmark. He'll be returning to Polypolis in the brig."

"Well, well," said Rolver. "So you've picked him out."

"Of course," said Thissell. "Haven't you?"

Rolver shrugged. "He's either Welibus or Kershaul, that's as close as I can make it. So long as he wears his mask and calls himself either Welibus or Kershaul, it means nothing to me."

"It means a great deal to me," said Thissell. "What time tomorrow does the lighter go up?"

"Eleven twenty-two sharp. If Haxo Angmark's leaving, tell him to be on time."

"He'll be here," said Thissell.

He made his usual call upon Welibus and Kershaul, then returning to his houseboat, put three final marks on his chart.

The evidence was here, plain and convincing. Not absolutely incontrovertible evidence, but enough to warrant a definite move. He checked over his gun. Tomorrow: the day of decision. He could afford no errors.

The day dawned bright white, the sky like the inside of an oyster shell; Mireille rose through iridescent mists. Toby and Rex sculled the houseboat to the dock. The remaining three out-world houseboats floated somnolently on the slow swells.

One boat Thissell watched in particular, that whose owner Haxo Angmark had killed and dropped into the harbor. This boat presently moved toward the shore, and Haxo Angmark himself stood on the front deck, wearing a mask Thissell had never seen before: a construction of scarlet feathers, black glass and spiked green hair.

Thissell was forced to admire his poise. A clever scheme, cleverly planned and executed—but marred by an insurmountable difficulty.

Angmark returned within. The houseboat reached the dock. Slaves flung out mooring lines, lowered the gang-plank. Thissell, his gun ready in the pocket flap of his robes, walked down the dock, went aboard. He pushed open the door to the saloon. The man at the table raised his red, black and green mask in surprise.

Thissell said, "Angmark, please don't argue or make any—"

Something hard and heavy tackled him from behind; he was flung to the floor, his gun wrested expertly away.

Behind him the *hymerkin* clattered; a voice sang, "Bind the fool's arms."

The man sitting at the table rose to his feet, removed the red, black and green mask to reveal the black cloth of a slave. Thissell twisted his head. Over him stood Haxo Angmark, wearing a mask Thissell recognized as a Dragon Tamer, fabricated from black metal, with a knife-blade nose, socketed eyelids, and three crests running back over the scalp.

The mask's expression was unreadable, but Angmark's voice was triumphant. "I trapped you very easily."

"So you did," said Thissell. The slave finished knotting his wrists together. A clatter of Angmark's *hymerkin* sent him away. "Get to your feet," said Angmark. "Sit in that chair."

"What are we waiting for?" inquired Thissell.

"Two of our fellows still remain out on the water. We won't need them for what I have in mind."

"Which is?"

"You'll learn in due course," said Angmark. "We have an hour or so on our hands."

Thissell tested his bonds. They were undoubtedly secure.

Angmark seated himself. "How did you fix on me? I admit to being curious...Come, come," he chided as Thissell sat silently. "Can't you recognize that I have defeated you? Don't make affairs unpleasant for yourself."

Thissell shrugged. "I operated on a basic principle. A man can mask his face, but he can't mask his personality."

"Aha," said Angmark. "Interesting. Proceed."

"I borrowed a slave from you and the other two out-worlders, and I questioned them carefully. What masks had their masters worn during the month before your arrival? I prepared a chart and plotted their responses. Rolver wore the Tarn Bird about eighty percent of the time, the remaining twenty percent divided between the Sophist Abstraction and the Black Intricate. Welibus had a taste for the heroes of Kan Dachan Cycle. He wore the Chalekun, the Prince Intrepid, the Seavain most of the time: six days out of eight. The other two days he wore his South Wind or his Gay Companion. Kershaul, more conservative, preferred the Cave Owl, the Star Wanderer, and two or three other masks he wore at odd intervals.

"As I say, I acquired this information from possibly its most accurate source, the slaves. My next step was to keep watch upon the three of you. Every day I noted what masks you wore and compared it with my chart. Rolver wore his Tarn Bird six times, his Black Intricate twice. Kershaul wore his Cave Owl five times, his Star Wanderer once, his Quincunx once and his Ideal of Perfection once. Welibus wore the Emerald Mountain twice, the Triple Phoenix three times, the Prince Intrepid once and the Shark God twice."

Angmark nodded thoughtfully. "I see my error. I selected from Welibus' masks, but to my own taste—and as you point out, I revealed myself. But only to you." He rose and went to the window. "Kershaul and Rolver are now coming ashore; they'll soon be past and about their business—though I doubt if they'd interfere in any case; they've both become good Sirenese."

Thissell waited in silence. Ten minutes passed. Then Angmark reached to a shelf and picked up a knife. He looked at Thissell. "Stand up."

Thissell slowly rose to his feet. Angmark approached from the side, reached out, lifted the Moon Moth from Thissell's head. Thissell gasped and made a vain attempt to seize it. Too late; his face was bare and naked.

Angmark turned away, removed his own mask, donned the Moon Moth. He struck a call on his hymerkin. Two slaves entered, stopped in shock at the sight of Thissell.

Angmark played a brisk tattoo, sang, "Carry this man up to the dock."

"Angmark," cried Thissell. "I'm maskless!"

The slaves seized him and in spite of Thissell's desperate struggles, conveyed him out on the deck, along the float and up on the dock.

Angmark fixed a rope around Thissell's neck. He said, "You are now Haxo Angmark, and I am Edwer Thissell. Welibus is dead, you shall soon be dead. I can handle your job without difficulty. I'll play musical instruments like a Night-man and sing like a crow. I'll wear the Moon Moth till it rots and then I'll get another. The report will go to Polypolis, Haxo Angmark is dead. Everything will be serene."

Thissell barely heard. "You can't do this," he whispered. "My mask, my face..." A large woman in a blue and pink flower mask walked down the dock. She saw Thissell and emitted a piercing shriek, flung herself prone on the dock.

"Come along," said Angmark brightly. He tugged at the rope, and pulled Thissell down the dock. A man in a Pirate Captain mask coming up from his houseboat stood rigid in amazement.

Angmark played the *zachinko* and sang, "Behold the notorious criminal Haxo Angmark. Through all the outer-worlds his name is reviled. Now he is captured and led in shame to his death. Behold Haxo Angmark!"

They turned into the esplanade. A child screamed in fright, a man called hoarsely. Thissell stumbled; tears tumbled from his eyes; he could see only disorganized shapes and colors. Angmark's voice belled out richly: "Everyone behold: the criminal of the out-worlds, Haxo Angmark! Approach and observe his execution!"

Thissell feebly cried out, "I'm not Angmark; I'm Edwer Thissell; he's Angmark." But no one listened to him; there were only cries of dismay, shock, disgust at the sight of his face. He called to Angmark, "Give me my mask, a slave-cloth..."

Angmark sang jubilantly, "In shame he lived, in maskless shame he dies."

A Forest Goblin stood before Angmark. "Moon Moth, we meet once more."

Angmark sang, "Stand aside, friend Goblin, I must execute this criminal. In shame he lived, in shame he dies!"

A crowd had formed around the group; masks stared in morbid titillation at Thissell.

The Forest Goblin jerked the rope from Angmark's hand, threw it to the ground. The crowd roared. Voices cried, "No duel, no duel! Execute the monster!"

A cloth was thrown over Thissell's head. Thissell awaited the thrust of a blade. But instead his bonds were cut. Hastily he adjusted the cloth, hiding his face, peering between the folds.

Four men clutched Haxo Angmark. The Forest Goblin confronted him, playing the *skaranyi*. "A week ago you reached to divest me of my mask; you have now achieved your perverse aim!"

"But he is a criminal," cried Angmark. "He is notorious, infamous!"

"What are his misdeeds?" sang the Forest Goblin.

"He has murdered, betrayed; he has wrecked ships; he has tortured, blackmailed, robbed, sold children into slavery; he has—"

The Forest Goblin stopped him. "Your religious differences are of no importance. We can vouch however for your present crimes!"

The hostler stepped forward. He sang fiercely, "This insolent Moon Moth nine days ago sought to pre-empt my choicest mount!"

Another man pushed close. He wore a Universal Expert, and sang, "I am a Master Mask-maker; I recognize this Moon Moth out-worlder! Only recently he entered my shop and derided my skill. He deserves death!"

"Death to the out-world monster!" cried the crowd. A wave of men surged forward. Steel blades rose and fell, the deed was done.

Thissell watched, unable to move. The Forest Goblin approached, and playing the stimic sang sternly, "For you we have pity, but also contempt. A true man would never suffer such indignities!"

Thissell took a deep breath. He reached to his belt and found his *zachinko*. He sang, "My friend, you malign me! Can you not appreciate true courage? Would you prefer to die in combat or walk maskless along the esplanade?"

The Forest Goblin sang, "There is only one answer. First I would die in combat; I could not bear such shame."

Thissell sang. "I had such a choice. I could fight with my hands tied, and so die—or I could suffer shame, and through this shame conquer my enemy. You admit that you lack sufficient *strakh* to achieve this deed. I have proved myself a hero of bravery! I ask, who here has courage to do what I have done?"

"Courage?" demanded the Forest Goblin. "I fear nothing, up to and beyond death at the hands of the Night-men!"

"Then answer."

The Forest Goblin stood back. He played his *double-kamanthil*. "Bravery indeed, if such were your motives."

The hostler struck a series of subdued *gomapard* chords and sang, "Not a man among us would dare what this maskless man has done."

The crowd muttered approval.

The mask-maker approached Thissell, obsequiously stroking his *double-kamanthil*. "Pray, Lord Hero, step into my nearby shop, exchange this vile rag for a mask befitting your quality."

Another mask-maker sang, "Before you choose, Lord Hero, examine my magnificent creations!"

A man in a Bright-Sky Bird mask approached Thissell reverently. "I have only just completed a sumptuous houseboat; seventeen years of toil have gone into its fabrication. Grant me the good fortune of accepting and using this splendid craft; aboard waiting to serve you are alert slaves and pleasant maidens; there is ample wine in storage and soft silken carpets on the decks."

"Thank you," said Thissell, striking the *zachinko* with vigor and confidence. "I accept with pleasure. But first a mask."

The mask-maker struck an interrogative trill on the *gomapard*. "Would the Lord Hero consider a Sea-Dragon Conqueror beneath his dignity?"

"By no means," said Thissell. "I consider it suitable and satisfactory. We shall go now to examine it."

AFTERWORD TO "THE MOON MOTH"

The symbolic adjuncts used to enlarge the human personality are of course numerous. Clothes comprise a most important category of these symbols and sometimes when people are gathered together it is amusing to examine garments, unobtrusively of course, and to reflect that each article has been selected with solicitous care with the intention of creating some particular effect.

Despite the symbolic power of clothes, men and women are judged, by and large, by circumstances more difficult to control: posture, accent, voice timbre, the shape and color of their bodies, and most significant of all, their faces. Voices can be modulated, diets and exercise, theoretically at least, force the body into socially acceptable contours. What can be done to the face? Enormous effort has been expended in this direction. Jowls are hoisted, eyebrows attached or eliminated, noses cropped, de-hooked, de-humped. The hair is tormented into a thousand styles: puffed, teased, wet, dried, hung this way or that: all to formulate a fashionable image. Nonetheless, all pretenses are transparent: nature-fakery yields to the critical eye. No matter what our inclinations, whether or not we like our faces, we are forced to live with them, and to accept whatever favor, censure or derision we willy-nilly incur.

Except those intricate and intelligent folk of the world Sirene, whose unorthodox social habits are considered in the [preceding] pages.

—Jack Vance 1976

THE BAGFUL OF DREAMS

The River Isk, departing Lumarth, wandered in wide curves across the Plain of Red Flowers, bearing generally south. For six halcyon days Cugel sailed his skiff down the brimming river, stopping by night at one or another of the river-bank inns.

On the seventh day the river swung to the west, and passed by erratic sweeps and reaches through that land of rock spires and forested hillocks known as the Chaim Purpure. The wind blew, if at all, in unpredictable gusts, and Cugel, dropping the sail, was content to drift with the current, guiding the craft with an occasional stroke of the oars.

The villages of the plain were left behind; the region was uninhabited. In view of the crumbled tombs along the shore, the groves of cypress and yew, the quiet conversations to be overheard by night, Cugel was pleased to be afloat rather than afoot, and drifted out of the Chaim Purpure with great relief.

At the village Troon, the river emptied into the Tsombol Marsh, and Cugel sold the skiff for ten terces. To repair his fortunes he took employment with the town butcher, performing the more distasteful tasks attendant upon the trade. However, the pay was adequate and Cugel steeled himself to his undignified duties. He worked to such good effect that he was called upon to prepare the feast served at an important religious festival.

Through oversight, or stress of circumstance, Cugel used two sacred beasts in the preparation of his special ragout. Halfway through the banquet the mistake was discovered and once again Cugel left town under a cloud.

After hiding all night behind the abattoir to evade the hysterical mobs, Cugel set off at best speed across the Tsombol Marsh.

The road went by an indirect route, swinging around bogs and stagnant ponds, veering to follow the bed of an ancient highway, in effect doubling the length of the journey. A wind from the north blew the sky clear of all obscurity, so that the landscape showed in remarkable clarity. Cugel took no pleasure in the view, especially when, looking ahead, he spied a far pelgrane cruising down the wind.

As the afternoon advanced the wind abated, leaving an unnatural stillness across the marsh. From behind tussocks water-wefkins called out to Cugel, using the sweet voices of unhappy maidens: "Cugel, oh Cugel! Why do you travel in haste? Come to my bower and comb my beautiful hair!"

And: "Cugel, oh Cugel! Where do you go? Take me with you, to share your joyous adventures!"

And: "Cugel, beloved Cugel! The day is dying; the year is at an end! Come visit me behind the tussock, and we will console each other without constraint!"

Cugel only walked the faster, anxious to discover shelter for the night.

As the sun trembled at the edge of Tsombol Marsh Cugel came upon a small inn, secluded under five dire oaks. He gratefully took lodging for the night, and the innkeeper served a fair supper of stewed herbs, spitted reed-birds, seed-cake and thick burdock beer.

As Cugel ate, the innkeeper stood by with hands on hips. "I see by your conduct that you are a gentleman of high place; still you hop across Tsombol Marsh on foot like a bumpkin. I am puzzled by the incongruity."

"It is easily explained," said Cugel. "I consider myself the single honest man in a world of rogues and blackguards, present company excepted. In these conditions it is hard to accumulate wealth."

The innkeeper pulled at his chin, and turned away. When he came to serve Cugel a dessert of currant cake, he paused long enough to say: "Your difficulties have aroused my sympathy. Tonight I will reflect on the matter."

The innkeeper was as good as his word. In the morning, after Cugel had finished his breakfast, the innkeeper took him into the stable-yard and displayed a large dun-colored beast with powerful hind legs and a tufted tail, already bridled and saddled for riding.

"This is the least I can do for you," said the innkeeper. "I will sell this beast at a nominal figure. Agreed, it lacks elegance, and in fact is a hybrid of dounge and felukhary. Still, it moves with an easy stride; it feeds upon inexpensive wastes, and is notorious for its stubborn loyalty."

Cugel moved politely away. "I appreciate your altruism, but for such a creature any price whatever is excessive. Notice the sores at the base of its tail, the eczema along its back, and, unless I am mistaken, it lacks an eye. Also, its odor is not all it might be."

"Trifles!" declared the innkeeper. "Do you want a dependable steed to carry you across the Plain of Standing Stones, or an adjunct to your vanity? The beast becomes your property for a mere thirty terces."

Cugel jumped back in shock. "When a fine Cambalese wheriot sells for twenty? My dear fellow, your generosity outreaches my ability to pay!"

The innkeeper's face expressed only patience. "Here, in the middle of Tsombol Marsh, you will buy not even the smell of a dead wheriot."

"Let us discard euphemism," said Cugel. "Your price is an outrage."

For an instant the innkeeper's face lost its genial cast and he spoke in a grumbling voice: "Every person to whom I sell this steed takes the same advantage of my kindliness."

Cugel was puzzled by the remark. Nevertheless, sensing irresolution, he pressed his advantage. "In spite of a dozen misgivings, I offer a generous twelve terces!"

"Done!" cried the innkeeper almost before Cugel had finished speaking. "I repeat, you will discover this beast to be totally loyal, even beyond your expectations."

Cugel paid over twelve terces and gingerly mounted the creature. The landlord gave him a benign farewell. "May you enjoy a safe and comfortable journey!"

Cugel replied in like fashion. "May your enterprises prosper!"

In order to make a brave departure, Cugel tried to rein the beast up and around in a caracole, but it merely squatted low to the ground, then padded out upon the road.

Cugel rode a mile in comfort, and another, and taking all with all, was favorably impressed with his acquisition. "No question but what the beast walks on soft feet; now let us discover if it will canter at speed."

He shook out the reins; the beast set off down the road, its gait a unique prancing strut, with tail arched and head held high.

Cugel kicked his heels into the creature's heaving flanks. "Faster then! Let us test your mettle!"

The beast sprang forward with great energy, and the breeze blew Cugel's cloak flapping behind his shoulders.

A massive dire oak stood beside a bend in the road: an object which the beast seemed to identify as a landmark. It increased its pace, only to stop short and elevate its hind-quarters, thus projecting Cugel into the ditch. When he managed to stagger back up on the road, he discovered the beast cavorting across the marsh, in the general direction of the inn.

"A loyal creature indeed!" grumbled Cugel. "It is unswervingly faithful to the comfort of its barn." He found his green velvet cap, clapped it back upon his head and once more trudged south along the road.

During the late afternoon Cugel came to a village of a dozen mud huts populated by a squat long-armed folk, distinguished by great shocks of whitewashed hair.

Cugel gauged the height of the sun, then examined the terrain ahead, which extended in a dreary succession of tussock and pond to the edge of vision. Putting aside all qualms he approached the largest and most pretentious of the huts.

The master of the house sat on a bench to the side, whitewashing the hair of one of his children into radiating tufts like the petals of a white chrysanthemum, while other urchins played nearby in the mud.

"Good afternoon," said Cugel. "Are you able to provide me food and lodging for the night? I naturally intend adequate payment."

"I will feel privileged to do so," replied the householder. "This is the most commodious hut of Samsetiska, and I am known for my fund of anecdotes. Do you care to inspect the premises?"

"I would be pleased to rest an hour in my chamber before indulging myself in a hot bath."

His host blew out his cheeks, and wiping the whitewash from his hands beckoned Cugel into the hut. He pointed to a heap of reeds at the side of the room. "There is your bed; recline for as long as you like. As for a bath, the ponds of the swamp are infested with threlkoids and wire-worms, and cannot be recommended."

"In that case I must do without," said Cugel. "However, I have not eaten since breakfast, and I am willing to take my evening meal as soon as possible."

"My spouse has gone trapping in the swamp," said his host. "It is premature to discuss supper until we learn what she has gleaned from her toil."

In due course the woman returned carrying a sack and a wicker basket. She built up a fire and prepared the evening meal, while Erwig the householder brought forth a two-string guitar and entertained Cugel with ballads of the region.

At last the woman called Cugel and Erwig into the hut, where she served bowls of gruel, dishes of fried moss and ganions, with slices of coarse black bread.

After the meal Erwig thrust his spouse and children out into the night, explaining: "What we have to say is unsuitable for unsophisticated ears. Cugel is an important traveler and does not wish to measure his every word."

Bringing out an earthenware jug, Erwig poured two tots of arrak, one of which he placed before Cugel, then disposed himself for conversation. "Whence came you and where are you bound?"

Cugel tasted the arrak, which scorched the entire interior of his glottal cavity. "I am native to Almery, to which I now return."

Erwig scratched his head in perplexity. "I cannot divine why you go so far afield, only to retrace your steps."

"Certain enemies worked mischief upon me," said Cugel. "Upon my return, I intend an appropriate revenge."

"Such acts soothe the spirit like no others," agreed Erwig. "An immediate obstacle is the Plain of Standing Stones, by reason of asms which haunt the area. I might add that pelgrane are also common."

Cugel gave his sword a nervous twitch. "What is the distance to the Plain of Standing Stones?"

"Four miles south the ground rises and the Plain begins. The track proceeds from sarsen to sarsen for a distance of fifteen miles. A stout-hearted traveler will cross the plain in four to five hours, assuming that he is not delayed or devoured. The town Cuirnif lies another two hours beyond."

"An inch of foreknowledge is worth ten miles of afterthought—"

"Well spoken!" cried Erwig, swallowing a gulp of arrak. "My own opinion, to an exactitude! Cugel, you are astute!"

"—and in this regard, may I inquire your opinion of Cuirnif?"

"The folk are peculiar in many ways," said Erwig. "They preen themselves upon the gentility of their habits, yet they refuse to whitewash their hair, and they are slack in their religious observances. For instance, they make obeisance to Divine Wiulio with the right hand, not on the buttock, but on the abdomen, which we here consider a slipshod practice. What are your own views?"

"The rite should be conducted as you describe," said Cugel. "No other method carries weight."

Erwig refilled Cugel's glass. "I consider this an important endorsement of our views!"

The door opened and Erwig's spouse looked into the hut. "The night is dark. A bitter wind blows from the north, and a black beast prowls at the edge of the marsh."

"Stand among the shadows; divine Wiulio protects his own. It is unthinkable that you and your brats should annoy our guest."

The woman grudgingly closed the door and returned into the night. Erwig pulled himself forward on his stool and swallowed a quantity of arrak. "The folk of Cuirnif, as I say, are strange enough, but their ruler, Duke Orbal, surpasses them in every category. He devotes himself to the study of marvels and prodigies, and every jack-leg magician with two spells in his head is feted and celebrated and treated to the best of the city."

"Most odd!" declared Cugel.

Again the door opened and the woman looked into the hut. Erwig put down his glass and frowned over his shoulder. "What is it this time?"

"The beast is now moving among the huts. For all we know it may also worship Wiulio."

Erwig attempted argument, but the woman's face became obdurate. "Your guest might as well forego his niceties now as later, since we all, in any event, must sleep on the same heap of reeds." She opened wide the door and commanded her urchins into the hut. Erwig, assured that no further conversation was possible, threw himself down upon the reeds, and Cugel followed soon after.

In the morning Cugel breakfasted on ash-cake and herb tea, and prepared to take his departure. Erwig accompanied him to the road. "You have made a favorable impression upon me, and I will assist you across the Plain of Standing Stones. At the first opportunity take up a pebble the size of your fist and make the trigrammatic sign upon it. If you are attacked, hold high the pebble and cry out: 'Stand aside! I carry a sacred object!' At the first sarsen, deposit the stone and select another from the pile, again make the sign and carry it to the second sarsen, and so across the plain."

"So much is clear," said Cugel. "But perhaps you should show me the most powerful version of the sign, and thus refresh my memory."

Erwig scratched a mark in the dirt. "Simple, precise, correct! The folk of Cuirnif omit this loop and scrawl in every which direction."

"Slackness, once again!" said Cugel.

"So then, Cugel: farewell! The next time you pass be certain to halt at my hut! My crock of arrak has a loose stopper!"

"I would not forego the pleasure for a thousand terces. And now, as to my indebtedness—"

Erwig held up his hand. "I accept no terces from my guests!" He jerked and his eyes bulged as his spouse came up and prodded him in the ribs. "Ah well," said Erwig. "Give the woman a terce or two; it will cheer her as she performs her tasks."

Cugel paid over five terces, to the woman's enormous satisfaction, and so departed the village.

After four miles the road angled up to a gray plain studded at intervals with twelve-foot pillars of gray stone. Cugel found a large pebble, and placing his right hand on his buttock made a profound salute to the object. He scratched upon it a sign somewhat similar to that drawn for him by Erwig and intoned: "I commend this pebble to the attention of Wiulio! I request that it protect me across this dismal plain!"

He scrutinized the landscape, but aside from the sarsens and the long black shadows laid by the red morning sun, he discovered nothing worthy of attention, and thankfully set off along the track.

He had traveled no more than a hundred yards when he felt a presence and whirling about discovered an asm of eight fangs almost on his heels. Cugel held high the pebble and cried out: "Away with you! I carry a sacred object and I do not care to be molested!"

The asm spoke in a soft blurred voice: "Wrong! You carry an ordinary pebble. I watched and you scamped the rite. Flee if you wish! I need the exercise."

The asm advanced. Cugel threw the stone with all his force. It struck the black forehead between the bristling antennae, and the asm fell flat; before it could rise Cugel had severed its head.

He started to proceed, then turned back and took up the stone. "Who knows who guided the throw so accurately? Wiulio deserves the benefit of the doubt."

At the first sarsen he exchanged stones as Erwig had recommended, and this time he made the trigrammatic sign with care and precision.

Without interference he crossed to the next sarsen and so continued across the plain.

The sun made its way to the zenith, rested a period, then descended into the west. Cugel marched unmolested from sarsen to sarsen. On several occasions he noted pelgrane sliding across the sky, and each time flung himself flat to avoid attention.

The Plain of Standing Stones ended at the brink of a scarp overlooking a wide valley. With safety close at hand Cugel relaxed his vigilance, only to be startled by a scream of triumph from the sky. He darted a horrified glance over his shoulder, then plunged over the edge of the scarp into a ravine, where he dodged among rocks and pressed himself into the shadows. Down swooped the pelgrane, past and beyond Cugel's hiding place. Warbling in joy, it alighted at the base of the scarp, to evoke instant outcries and curses from a human throat.

Keeping to concealment Cugel descended the slope, to discover that the pelgrane now pursued a portly black-haired man in a suit of black and white diaper. This person at last took nimble refuge behind a thick-boled olophar tree, and the pelgrane chased him first one way, then another, clashing its fangs and snatching with its clawed hands.

For all his rotundity, the man showed remarkable deftness of foot and the pelgrane began to scream in frustration. It halted to glare through the crotch of the tree and snap out with its long maw.

On a whimsical impulse Cugel stole out upon a shelf of rock; then, selecting an appropriate moment, he jumped to land with both feet on the creature's head, forcing the neck down into the crotch of the olophar tree. He called out to the startled man: "Quick! Fetch a stout cord! We will bind this winged horror in place!"

The man in the black and white diaper cried out: "Why show mercy? It must be killed and instantly! Move your foot, so that I may hack away its head."

"Not so fast," said Cugel. "For all its faults, it is a valuable specimen by which I hope to profit."

"Profit?" The idea had not occurred to the portly gentleman. "I must assert my prior claim! I was just about to stun the beast when you interfered."

Cugel said: "In that case I will take my weight off the creature's neck and go my way."

The man in the black-and-white suit made an irritable gesture. "Certain persons will go to any extreme merely to score a rhetorical point. Hold fast then! I have a suitable cord over yonder."

The two men dropped a branch over the pelgrane's head and bound it securely in place. The portly gentleman, who had introduced himself as Iolo the Dream-taker, asked: "Exactly what value do you place upon this horrid creature, and why?"

Cugel said: "It has come to my attention that Orbal, Duke of Ombalique, is an amateur of oddities. Surely he would pay well for such a monster, perhaps as much as a hundred terces."

"Your theories are sound," Iolo admitted. "Are you sure that the bonds are secure?"

As Cugel tested the ropes he noticed an ornament consisting of a blue glass egg on a golden chain attached to the creature's crest. As he removed the object, Iolo's hand darted out, but Cugel shouldered him aside. He disengaged the amulet, but Iolo caught hold of the chain and the two glared eye to eye.

"Release your grip upon my property," said Cugel in an icy voice.

Iolo protested vigorously. "The object is mine since I saw it first."

"Nonsense! I took it from the crest and you tried to snatch it from my hand."

Iolo stamped his foot. "I will not be domineered!" He sought to wrest the blue egg from Cugel's grasp. Cugel lost his grip and the object was thrown against the hillside where it broke in a bright blue explosion to create a hole into the hillside. Instantly a golden-gray tentacle thrust forth and seized Cugel's leg.

Iolo sprang back and from a safe distance watched Cugel's efforts to avoid being drawn into the hole. Cugel saved himself at the last moment by clinging to a stump. He called out: "Iolo, make haste! Fetch a cord and tie the tentacle to this stump; otherwise it will drag me into the hill!"

Iolo folded his arms and spoke in a measured voice: "Avarice has brought this plight upon you. It may be a divine judgment and I am reluctant to interfere."

"What? When you fought tooth and nail to wrench the object from my hand?"

Iolo frowned and pursed his lips. "In any case I own a single rope: that which ties my pelgrane."

"Kill the pelgrane!" panted Cugel. "Put the cord to its most urgent use!"

"You yourself valued this pelgrane at a hundred terces. The worth of the rope is ten terces."

"Very well," said Cugel through gritted teeth. "Ten terces for the rope, but I cannot pay a hundred terces for a dead pelgrane, since I carry only forty-five."

"So be it. Pay over the forty-five terces. What surety can you offer for the remainder?"

Cugel managed to toss over his purse of terces. He displayed the opal ear-bangle which Iolo promptly demanded, but which Cugel refused to relinquish until the tentacle had been tied to the stump.

With poor grace Iolo hacked the head off the pelgrane, then brought over the rope and secured the tentacle to the stump, thus easing the strain upon Cugel's leg.

"The ear-bangle, if you please!" said Iolo, and he poised his knife significantly near the rope.

Cugel tossed over the jewel. "There you have it: all my wealth. Now, please free me from this tentacle."

"I am a cautious man," said Iolo. "I must consider the matter from several perspectives." He set about making camp for the night.

Cugel called out a plaintive appeal: "Do you remember how I rescued you from the pelgrane?"

"Indeed I do! An important philosophical question has thereby been raised. You disturbed a stasis and now a tentacle grips your leg, which is, in a sense, the new stasis. I will reflect carefully upon the matter."

Cugel argued to no avail. Iolo built up a campfire over which he cooked a stew of herbs and grasses, which he ate with half a cold fowl and draughts of wine from a leather bottle.

Leaning back against a tree he gave his attention to Cugel. "No doubt you are on your way to Duke Orbal's Grand Exposition of Marvels?"

"I am a traveler, no more," said Cugel. "What is this 'Grand Exposition'?"

Iolo gave Cugel a pitying glance for his stupidity. "Each year Duke Orbal presides over a competition of wonder-workers. This year the prize is one thousand terces, which I intend to win with my 'Bagful of Dreams'."

"Your 'Bagful of Dreams' I assume to be a jocularity, or something on the order of a romantic metaphor?"

"Nothing of the sort!" declared Iolo in scorn.

"A kaleidoscopic projection? A program of impersonations? A hallucinatory gas?"

"None of these. I carry with me a number of pure unadulterated dreams, coalesced and crystallized."

From his satchel Iolo brought a sack of soft brown leather, from which he took an object resembling a pale blue snowflake an inch in diameter. He held it up into the firelight where Cugel could admire its fleeting lusters. "I will ply Duke Orbal with my dreams, and how can I fail to win over all other contestants?"

"Your chances would seem to be good. How do you gather these dreams?"

"The process is secret; still I can describe the general procedure. I live beside Lake Lelt in the Land of Dai-Passant. On calm nights the surface of the water thickens to a film which reflects the stars as small globules of shine. By using a suitable cantrap, I am able to lift up impalpable threads composed of pure starlight and water-skein. I weave this thread into nets and then I go forth in search of dreams. I hide under valances and in the leaves of outdoor bowers; I crouch on roofs; I wander through sleeping houses. Always I am ready to net the dreams as they drift past. Each morning I carry these wonderful wisps to my laboratory and there I sort them out and work my processes. In due course I achieve a crystal of a hundred dreams, and with these confections I hope to enthrall Duke Orbal."

"I would offer congratulations were it not for this tentacle gripping my leg," said Cugel.

"That is a generous emotion," said Iolo. He fed several logs into the fire, chanted a spell of protection against creatures of the night, and composed himself for sleep.

An hour passed. Cugel tried by various means to ease the grip of the tentacle, without success, nor could he draw his sword or bring 'Spatterlight' from his pouch.

At last he sat back and considered new approaches to the solution of his problem.

By dint of stretching and straining he obtained a twig, with which he dragged close a long dead branch, which allowed him to reach another of equal length. Tying the two together with a string from his pouch, he contrived a pole exactly long enough to reach Iolo's recumbent form.

Working with care Cugel drew Iolo's satchel across the ground, finally to within reach of his fingers. First he brought out Iolo's wallet, to find two hundred terces, which he transferred to his own purse; next the opal ear-bangle, which he dropped into the pocket of his shirt; then the bagful of dreams.

The satchel contained nothing more of value, save that portion of cold fowl which Iolo had reserved for his breakfast and the leather bottle of wine, both of which Cugel put aside for his own use. He returned the satchel to where he had found it, then separated the branches and tossed them aside. Lacking a better hiding place for the bagful of dreams, Cugel tied the string to the bag and lowered it into the mysterious hole. He ate the fowl and drank the wine, then made himself as comfortable as possible.

The night wore on. Cugel heard the plaintive call of a night-jar and also the moan of a six-legged shamb, at some distance.

In due course the sky glowed purple and the sun appeared. Iolo roused himself, yawned, ran his fingers through his tousled hair, blew up the fire and gave Cugel a civil greeting. "And how passed the night?"

"As well as could be expected. It is useless, after all, to complain against inexorable reality."

"Exactly so. I have given considerable thought to your case, and I have arrived at a decision which will please you. This is my plan. I shall proceed into Cuirnif and there drive a hard bargain for the ear-bangle. After satisfying your account, I will return and pay over to you whatever sums may be in excess."

Cugel suggested an alternative scheme. "Let us go into Cuirnif together; then you will be spared the inconvenience of a return trip."

Iolo shook his head. "My plan must prevail." He went to the satchel for his breakfast and so discovered the loss of his property. He uttered a plangent cry and stared at Cugel. "My terces, my dreams! They are gone, all gone! How do you account for this?"

"Very simply. At approximately four minutes after midnight a robber came from the forest and made off with the contents of your satchel."

Iolo tore at his beard with the fingers of both hands. "My precious dreams! Why did you not cry out an alarm?"

Cugel scratched his head. "In all candor I did not dare disturb the stasis."

Iolo jumped to his feet and looked through the forest in all directions. He turned back to Cugel. "What sort of man was this robber?"

"In certain respects he seemed a kindly man; after taking possession of your belongings, he presented me with half a cold fowl and a bottle of wine, which I consumed with gratitude."

"You consumed my breakfast!"

Cugel shrugged. "I could not be sure of this, and in fact I did not inquire. We held a brief conversation and I learned that like ourselves he is bound for Cuirnif and the Exposition of Marvels."

"Ah, ah ha! Would you recognize this person were you to see him again?"

"Without a doubt."

Iolo became instantly energetic. "Let us see as to this tentacle. Perhaps we can pry it loose." He seized the tip of the golden-gray member and bracing himself worked to lift it from Cugel's leg. For several minutes he toiled, kicking and prying, paying no heed to Cugel's cries of pain. Finally the tentacle relaxed and Cugel crawled to safety.

With great caution Iolo approached the hole and peered down into the depths. "I see only a glimmer of far lights. The hole is mysterious!...What is this bit of string which leads into the hole?"

"I tied a rock to the string and tried to plumb the bottom of the hole," Cugel explained. "It amounts to nothing."

Iolo tugged at the string, which first yielded, then resisted, then broke, and Iolo was left looking at the frayed end. "Odd! The string is corroded, as if through contact with some acrid substance."

"Most peculiar!" said Cugel.

Iolo threw the string back into the hole. "Come, we can waste no more time! Let us hasten into Cuirnif and seek out the scoundrel who stole my valuables."

The road left the forest and passed through a district of fields and orchards. Peasants looked up in wonder as the two passed by: the portly Iolo dressed in black and white diaper and the lank Cugel with a black cloak hanging from his spare shoulders and a fine dark green cap gracing his saturnine visage.

Along the way Iolo put ever more searching questions in regard to the robber. Cugel had lost interest in the subject and gave back ambiguous, even contradictory, answers, and Iolo's questions became ever more searching.

Upon entering Cuirnif, Cugel noticed an inn which seemed to offer comfortable accommodation. He told Iolo: "Here our paths diverge, since I plan to stop at the inn yonder."

"The Five Owls? It is the dearest inn of Cuirnif! How will you pay your account?"

Cugel made a confident gesture. "Is not a thousand terces the grand prize at the Exposition?"

"Certainly, but what marvel do you plan to display? I warn you, the Duke has no patience with charlatans."

"I am not a man who tells all he knows," said Cugel. "I will disclose none of my plans at this moment."

"But what of the robber?" cried Iolo. "Were we not to search Cuirnif high and low?"

"The Five Owls is as good a vantage as any, since the robber will surely visit the common room to boast of his exploits and squander your terces on drink. Meanwhile, I wish you easy roofs and convenient dreams." Cugel bowed politely and took his leave of Iolo.

At the Five Owls Cugel selected a suitable chamber, where he refreshed himself and ordered his attire. Then, repairing to the common room, he made a leisurely meal upon the best the house could provide.

The innkeeper stopped by to make sure that all was in order and Cugel complimented him upon his table. "In fact, all taken with all, Cuirnif must be considered a place favored by the elements. The prospect is pleasant, the air is bracing, and Duke Orbal would seem to be an indulgent ruler."

The innkeeper gave a somewhat noncommital assent. "As you indicate, Duke Orbal is never exasperated, truculent, suspicious, nor harsh unless in his wisdom he feels so inclined, whereupon all mildness is put aside in the interests of justice. Glance up to the crest of the hill; what do you see?"

"Four tubes, or stand-pipes, approximately thirty yards tall and one yard in diameter."

"Your eye is accurate. Into these tubes are dropped insubordinate members of society, without regard for who stands below or who may be coming after. Hence, while you may converse with Duke Orbal or even venture a modest pleasantry, never ignore his commands. Criminals, of course, are given short shrift."

Cugel, from habit, looked uneasily over his shoulder. "Such strictures will hardly apply to me, a stranger in town."

The innkeeper gave a skeptical grunt. "I assume that you came to witness the Exposition of Marvels?"

"Quite so! I may even try for the grand prize. In this regard, can you recommend a dependable hostler?"

"Certainly." The innkeeper provided explicit directions.

"I also wish to hire a gang of strong and willing workers," said Cugel. "Where may these be recruited?"

The innkeeper pointed across the square to a dingy tavern. "In the yard of the 'Howling Dog' all the riffraff in town take counsel together. Here you will find workers sufficient to your purposes."

"While I visit the hostler, be good enough to send a boy across to hire twelve of these sturdy fellows."

"As you wish."

At the hostler's Cugel rented a large six-wheeled wagon and a team of strong farlocks. When he returned with the wagon to the Five Owls, he found waiting a work-force of twelve individuals of miscellaneous sort, including a man not only senile but also lacking a leg. Another, in the throes of intoxication, fought away imaginary insects. Cugel discharged these two on the spot. The group also included Iolo the Dream-taker, who scrutinized Cugel with the liveliest suspicion.

Cugel asked: "My dear fellow, what do you do in such sordid company?"

"I take employment so that I may eat," said Iolo. "May I ask how you came by the funds to pay for so much skilled labor? Also, I notice that from your ear hangs that gem which only last night was my property!"

"It is the second of a pair," said Cugel. "As you know, the robber took the first along with your other valuables."

Iolo curled his lip. "I am more than ever anxious to meet this quixotic robber who takes my gem but leaves you in possession of yours."

"He was indeed a remarkable person. I believe that I glimpsed him not an hour ago, riding hard out of town."

Iolo again curled his lip. "What do you propose to do with this wagon?"

"If you care to earn a wage, you will soon find out for yourself."

Cugel drove the wagon and the gang of workers out of Cuirnif along the road to the mysterious hole, where he found all as before. He ordered trenches dug into the hillside; crating was installed, after which that block of soil surrounding and including the hole, the stump and the tentacle, was dragged up on the bed of the wagon.

During the middle stages of the project Iolo's manner changed. He began calling orders to the workmen and addressed Cugel with cordiality. "A noble idea, Cugel! We shall profit greatly!"

Cugel raised his eyebrows. "I hope indeed to win the grand prize. Your wage, however, will be relatively modest, even scant, unless you work more briskly."

"What!" stormed Iolo. "Surely you agree that this hole is half my property!"

"I agree to nothing of the sort. Say no more of the matter, or you will be discharged on the spot."

Grumbling and fuming Iolo returned to work. In due course Cugel conveyed the block of soil, with the hole, stump and tentacle, back to Cuirnif. Along the way he purchased an old tarpaulin with which he concealed the hole, the better to magnify the eventual effect of his display.

At the site of the Grand Exposition Cugel slid his exhibit off the wagon and into the shelter of a pavilion, after which he paid off his men, to the dissatisfaction of those who had cultivated extravagant hopes.

Cugel refused to listen to complaints. "The pay is sufficient! If it were ten times as much, every last terce would still end up in the till at the 'Howling Dog'."

"One moment!" cried Iolo. "You and I must arrive at an understanding!"

Cugel merely jumped up on the wagon and drove it back to the hostelry. Some of the men pursued him a few steps; others threw stones, without effect.

On the following day trumpets and gongs announced the formal opening of the exposition. Duke Orbal arrived at the plaza wearing a splendid robe of magenta plush trimmed with white feathers, and a hat of pale blue velvet three feet in diameter, with silver tassels around the brim and a cockade of silver puff.

Mounting a rostrum, Duke Orbal addressed the crowd. "As all know, I am considered an eccentric, what with my enthusiasm for marvels and prodigies, but, after all, when the preoccupation is analyzed, is it all so absurd? Think back across the aeons to the times of the Vapurials, the Green and Purple College, the mighty magicians among whose number we include Amberlin, the second Chidule of Porphyrhyncos, Morreion, Calanctus the Calm, and of course the Great Phandaal. These were the days of power, and they are not likely to return except in nostalgic recollection. Hence this, my Grand Exposition of Marvels, and withal, a pale recollection of the way things were.

"Still, all taken with all, I see by my schedule that we have a stimulating program, and no doubt I will find difficulty in awarding the grand prize."

Duke Orbal glanced at a paper. "We will inspect Zaraflam's 'Nimble Squadrons', Bazzard's 'Unlikely Musicians', Xallops and his 'Compendium of Universal Knowledge'. Iolo will offer his 'Bagful of Dreams', and, finally, Cugel will present for our amazement that to which he gives the tantalizing title: 'Nowhere'. A most provocative program! And now without further ado we will proceed to evaluate Zaraflam's 'Nimble Squadrons'."

The crowd surged around the first pavilion and Zaraflam brought forth his 'Nimble Squadrons': a parade of cockroaches smartly turned out in red, white, and black uniforms. The sergeants brandished cutlasses; the foot soldiers carried muskets; the squadrons marched and countermarched in intricate evolutions.

"Halt!" bawled Zaraflam.

The cockroaches stopped short.

"Present arms!"

The cockroaches obeyed.

"Fire a salute in honor of Duke Orbal!"

The sergeants raised their cutlasses; the footmen elevated their muskets. Down came the cutlasses; the muskets exploded, emitting little puffs of white smoke.

"Excellent!" declared Duke Orbal. "Zaraflam, I commend your painstaking accuracy!"

"A thousand thanks, your Grace! Have I won the grand prize?"

"It is still too early to predict. Now, to Bazzard and his 'Unlikely Musicians'!"

The spectators moved on to the second pavilion where Bazzard presently appeared, his face woebegone. "Your Grace and noble citizens of Cuirnif! My 'Unlikely Musicians' were fish from the Cantic Sea and I felt sure of the grand prize when I brought them to Cuirnif. However, during the night a leak drained the tank dry. The fish are dead and their music is lost forever! I still wish to remain in contention for the prize; hence I will simulate the songs of my former troupe. Please adjudicate the music on this basis."

Duke Orbal made an austere sign. "Impossible. Bazzard's exhibit is hereby declared invalid. We now move on to Xallops and his remarkable 'Compendium'."

Xallops stepped forward from his pavilion. "Your Grace, ladies and gentlemen of Cuirnif! My entry at this exposition is truly remarkable; however, unlike Zaraflam and Bazzard, I can take no personal credit for its existence. By trade I am a ransacker of ancient tombs, where the risks are great and rewards few. By great good luck I chanced upon that crypt where several aeons ago the sorcerer Zinqzin was laid to rest. From this dungeon I rescued the volume which I now display to your astounded eyes."

Xallops whisked away a cloth to reveal a great book bound in black leather. "On command this volume must reveal information of any and every sort; it knows each trivial detail, from the time the stars first caught fire to the present date. Ask; you shall be answered!"

"Remarkable!" declared Duke Orbal. "Present before us the Lost Ode of Psyrme!"

"Certainly," said the book in a rasping voice. It threw back its covers to reveal a page covered with crabbed and interlocked characters.

Duke Orbal put a perplexed question: "This is beyond my comprehension; you may furnish a translation."

"The request is denied," said the book. "Such poetry is too sweet for ordinary ears."

Duke Orbal glanced at Xallops, who spoke quickly to the book: "Show us scenes from aeons past."

"As you like. Reverting to the Nineteenth Aeon of the Fifty-second Cycle, I display a view across Linxfade Valley, toward Kolghut's Tower of Frozen Blood."

"The detail is both notable and exact!" declared Duke Orbal. "I am curious to gaze upon the semblance of Kolghut himself."

"Nothing could be easier. Here is the terrace of the Temple at Tanutra. Kolghut stands beside the flowering wail-bush. In the chair sits the Empress Noxon, now in her hundred and fortieth year. She has tasted no water in her entire lifetime, and eats only bitter blossom, with occasionally a morsel of boiled eel."

"Bah!" said Duke Orbal. "A most hideous old creature! Who are those gentlemen ranked behind her?"

"They constitute her retinue of lovers. Every month one of their number is executed and a new stalwart is recruited to take his place. Competition is keen to win the affectionate regard of the Empress."

"Bah!" muttered Duke Orbal. "Show us rather a beautiful court lady of the Yellow Age."

The book spoke a petulant syllable in an unknown language. The page turned to reveal a travertine promenade beside a slow river.

"This view reveals to good advantage the topiary of the time. Notice here, and here!" With a luminous arrow the book indicated a row of massive trees clipped into globular shapes. "Those are irix, the sap of which may be used as an effective vermifuge. The species is now extinct. Along the concourse you will observe a multitude of persons. Those with black stockings and long white beards are Alulian slaves, whose ancestors arrived from far Canopus. They are also extinct. In the middle distance stands a beautiful woman named Jiao Jaro. She is indicated by a red dot over her head, although her face is turned toward the river."

"This is hardly satisfactory," grumbled Duke Orbal. "Xallops, can you not control the perversity of your exhibit?"

"I fear not, your Grace."

Duke Orbal gave a sniff of displeasure. "A final question! Who among the folk now residing in Cuirnif presents the greatest threat to the welfare of my realm?"

"I am a repository of information, not an oracle," stated the book. "However, I will remark that among those present stands a fox-faced vagabond with a crafty expression, whose habits would bring a blush to the cheeks of the Empress Noxon herself. His name—"

Cugel leapt forward and pointed across the plaza. "The robber! There he goes now! Summon the constables! Sound the gong!"

While everyone turned to look, Cugel slammed shut the book and dug his knuckles into the cover. The book grunted in annoyance.

Duke Orbal turned back with a frown of perplexity. "I saw no robber."

"In that case, I was surely mistaken. But yonder waits Iolo with his famous 'Bagful of Dreams'!"

The Duke moved on to Iolo's pavilion, followed by the enthralled onlookers. Duke Orbal said: "Iolo the Dream-taker, your fame has preceded you all the distance from Dai-Passant! I hereby tender you an official welcome!"

Iolo answered in an anguished voice: "Your Grace, I have sorry news to relate. For the whole of one year I prepared for this day, hoping to win the grand prize. The blast of midnight winds, the outrage of householders, the terrifying attentions of ghosts, shrees, roof-runners and fermins: all of these have caused me discomfort! I have roamed the dark hours in pursuit of my dreams! I have lurked beside dormers, crawled through attics, hovered over couches; I have suffered scratches and contusions; but never have I counted the cost if through my enterprise I were able to capture some particularly choice specimen.

"Each dream trapped in my net I carefully examined; for every dream cherished and saved I released a dozen, and finally from my store of superlatives I fashioned my wonderful crystals, and these I brought down the long road from Dai-Passant. Then, only last night, under the most mysterious circumstances, my precious goods were stolen by a robber only Cugel claims to have seen.

"I now point out that the dreams, whether near or far, represent marvels of truly superlative quality, and I feel that a careful description of the items—"

Duke Orbal held up his hand. "I must reiterate the judgment rendered upon Bazzard. A stringent rule stipulates that neither imaginary nor purported marvels qualify for the competition. Perhaps we will have the opportunity to adjudicate your dreams on another occasion. Now we must pass on to Cugel's pavilion and investigate his provocative 'Nowhere'."

Cugel stepped up on the dais before his exhibit. "Your Grace, I present for your inspection a legitimate marvel: not a straggle of insects, not a pedantic almanac, but an authentic miracle." Cugel whisked away the cloth. "Behold!"

The Duke made a puzzled sound. "A pile of dirt? A stump? What is that odd-looking member emerging from the hole?"

"Your Grace, I have here an opening into an unknown space, with the arm of one of its denizens. Inspect this tentacle! It pulses with the life of another cosmos! Notice the golden luster of the dorsal surface, the green and lavender of these encrustations. On the underside you will discover three colors of a sort never before seen!"

With a nonplussed expression Duke Orbal pulled at his chin. "This is all very well, but where is the rest of the creature? You present not a marvel, but the fraction of a marvel! I can make no judgment on the basis of a tail, or a hindquarters, or a proboscis, whatever the member may be. Additionally, you claim that the hole enters a far cosmos; still I see only a hole, resembling nothing so much as the den of a wysen-imp."

Iolo thrust himself forward. "May I venture an opinion? As I reflect upon events, I have become convinced that Cugel himself stole my Dreams!"

"Your remarks interest no one," said Cugel. "Kindly hold your tongue while I continue my demonstration."

Iolo was not to be subdued so easily. He turned to Duke Orbal and cried in a poignant voice: "Hear me out, if you will! I am convinced that the 'robber' is no more than a figment of Cugel's imagination! He took my dreams and hid them, and where else but in the hole itself? For evidence I cite that length of string which leads into the hole."

Duke Orbal inspected Cugel with a frown. "Are these charges true? Answer exactly, since all can be verified."

Cugel chose his words with care. "I can only affirm what I myself know. Conceivably the robber hid Iolo's dreams in the hole while I was otherwise occupied. For what purpose? Who can say?"

Duke Orbal asked in a gentle voice: "Has anyone thought to search the hole for this elusive 'bag of dreams'?"

Cugel gave an indifferent shrug. "Iolo may enter now and search to his heart's content."

"You claim this hole!" retorted Iolo. "It therefore becomes your duty to protect the public!"

For several minutes an animated argument took place, until Duke Orbal intervened. "Both parties have raised persuasive points; I feel, however, that I must rule against Cugel. I therefore decree that he search his premises for the missing dreams and recover them if possible."

Cugel disputed the decision with such vigor that Duke Orbal turned to glance along the skyline, whereupon Cugel moderated his position. "The judgment of your Grace of course must prevail, and if I must, I will cast about for Iolo's lost dreams, although his theories are clearly absurd."

"Please do so, at once."

Cugel obtained a long pole, to which he attached a grapple. Gingerly thrusting his contrivance into the hole, he raked back and forth, but succeeded only in stimulating the tentacle, which thrashed from side to side.

Iolo suddenly cried out in excitement. "I notice a remarkable fact! The block of earth is at most six feet in breadth, yet Cugel plunged into the hole a pole twelve feet in length! What trickery does he practice now?"

Cugel replied in even tones: "I promised Duke Orbal a marvel and a wonderment, and I believe that I have done so."

Duke Orbal nodded gravely. "Well said, Cugel! Your exhibit is provocative! Still, you offer us only a tantalizing glimpse: a bottomless hole, a length of tentacle, a strange color, a far-off light—to the effect that your exhibit seems somewhat makeshift and impromptu. Contrast, if you will, the precision of Zaraflam's cockroaches!" He held up his hand as Cugel started to protest. "You display a hole: admitted, and a fine hole it is. But how does this hole differ from any other? Can I in justice award the prize on such a basis?"

"The matter may be resolved in a manner to satisfy us all," said Cugel. "Let Iolo enter the hole, to assure himself that his dreams are indeed elsewhere. Then, on his return, he will bear witness to the truly marvelous nature of my exhibit."

Iolo made an instant protest. "Cugel claims the exhibit; let him make the exploration!"

Duke Orbal raised his hand for silence. "I pronounce a decree to the effect that Cugel must immediately enter his exhibit in search of Iolo's properties, and likewise make a careful study of the environment, for the benefit of us all."

"Your Grace!" protested Cugel. "This is no simple matter! The tentacle almost fills the hole!"

"I see sufficient room for an agile man to slide past."

"Your Grace, to be candid, I do not care to enter the hole, by reason of extreme fear."

Duke Orbal again glanced up at the tubes which stood in a row along the skyline. He spoke over his shoulder to a burly man in a maroon and black uniform. "Which of the tubes is most suitable for use at this time?"

"The second tube from the right, your Grace, is only one-quarter occupied."

Cugel declared in a trembling voice: "I fear, but I have conquered my fear! I will seek Iolo's lost dreams!"

"Excellent," said Duke Orbal with a tight-lipped grin. "Please do not delay; my patience wears thin."

Cugel tentatively thrust a leg into the hole, but the motion of the tentacle caused him to snatch it out again. Duke Orbal muttered a few words to his constable, who brought up a winch. The tentacle was hauled forth from the hole a good five yards.

Duke Orbal instructed Cugel: "Straddle the tentacle, seize it with hands and legs and it will draw you back through the hole."

In desperation Cugel clambered upon the tentacle. The tension of the winch was relaxed and Cugel was pulled into the hole.

The light of Earth curled away from the opening and made no entrance; Cugel was plunged into a condition of near-total darkness, where, however, by some paradoxical condition he was able to sense the scope of his new environment in detail.

He stood on a surface at once flat, yet rough, with rises and dips and hummocks like the face of a windy sea. The black spongy stuff underfoot showed small cavities and tunnels in which Cugel sensed the motion of innumerable near-invisible points of light. Where the sponge rose high, the crest curled over like breaking surf, or stood ragged and crusty; in either case, the fringes glowed red, pale blue and several colors Cugel had never before observed. No horizon could be detected and the local concepts of distance, proportion, and size were not germane to Cugel's understanding.

Overhead hung dead Nothingness. The single feature of note, a large disk the color of rain, floated at the zenith, an object so dim as to be almost invisible. At an indeterminate distance—a mile? ten miles? a hundred yards?—a hummock of some bulk overlooked the entire panorama. On closer inspection Cugel saw this hummock to be a prodigious mound of gelatinous flesh, inside which floated a globular organ apparently analogous to an eye. From the base of this creature a hundred tentacles extended far and wide across the black sponge. One of these tentacles passed near Cugel's feet, through the intracosmic gap, and out upon the soil of Earth.

Cugel discovered Iolo's sack of dreams, not three feet distant. The black sponge, bruised by the impact, had welled a liquid which had dissolved a hole in the leather, allowing the star-shaped dreams to spill out upon the sponge. In groping with the pole, Cugel had damaged a growth of brown palps. The resulting exudation had dripped upon the dreams and when Cugel picked up one of the fragile flakes, he saw that its edges glowed with eery fringes of color. The combination of oozes which had permeated the object caused his fingers to itch and tingle.

A score of small luminous nodes swarmed around his head, and a soft voice addressed him by name. "Cugel, what a pleasure that you have come to visit us! What is your opinion of our pleasant land?"

Cugel looked about in wonder; how could a denizen of this place know his name? At a distance of ten yards he noticed a small hummock of plasm not unlike the monstrous bulk with the floating eye.

Luminous nodes circled his head and the voice sounded in his ears: "You are perplexed, but remember, here we do things differently. We transfer our thoughts in small modules; if you look closely you will see them speeding through the fluxion: dainty little animalcules eager to unload their weight of enlightenment. There! Notice! Directly before your eyes hovers an excellent example. It is a thought of your own regarding which you are dubious; hence it hesitates, and awaits your decision."

"What if I speak?" asked Cugel. "Will this not facilitate matters?"

"To the contrary! Sound is considered offensive and everyone deplores the slightest murmur."

"This is all very well," grumbled Cugel, "but—"

"Silence, please! Send forth animalcules only!"

Cugel dispatched a whole host of luminous purports: "I will do my best. Perhaps you can inform me how far this land extends?"

"Not with certainty. At times I send forth animalcules to explore the far places; they report an infinite landscape similar to that which you see."

"Duke Orbal of Ombalique has commanded me to gather information and he will be interested in your remarks. Are valuable substances to be found here?"

"To a certain extent. There is proscedel and diphany and an occasional coruscation of zamanders."

"My first concern, of course, is to collect information for Duke Orbal, and I must also rescue Iolo's dreams; still I would be pleased to acquire a valuable trinket or two, if only to remind myself of our pleasant association."

"Understandable! I sympathize with your objectives."

"In that case, how may I obtain a quantity of such substances?"

"Easily. Simply send off animalcules to gather up your requirements." The creature emitted a whole host of pale plasms which darted away in all directions and presently returned with several dozen small spheres sparkling with a frosty blue light. "Here are zamanders of the first water," said the creature. "Accept them with my compliments."

Cugel placed the gems in his pouch. "This is a most convenient system for gaining wealth. I also wish to obtain a certain amount of diphany."

"Send forth animalcules! Why exert yourself needlessly?"

"We think along similar lines." Cugel dispatched several hundred animalcules which presently returned with twenty small ingots of the precious metal.

Cugel examined his pouch. "I still have room for a quantity of proscedel. With your permission I will send out the requisite animalcules."

"I would not dream of interfering," asserted the creature.

The animalcules sped forth, and before long returned with sufficient proscedel to fill Cugel's pouch. The creature said thoughtfully: "This is at least half of Uthaw's treasure; however, he appears not to have noticed its absence."

"'Uthaw'?" inquired Cugel. "Do you refer to yonder monstrous hulk?"

"Yes, that is Uthaw, who sometimes is both coarse and irascible."

Uthaw's eye rolled toward Cugel and bulged through the outer membrane. A tide of animalcules arrived pulsing with significance. "I notice that Cugel has stolen my treasure, which I denounce as a breach of hospitality! In retribution, he must dig twenty-two zamanders from below the Shivering Trillows. He must then sift eight pounds of prime proscedel from the Dust of Time. Finally he must scrape eight acres of diphany bloom from the face of the High Disk."

Cugel sent forth animalcules. "Lord Uthaw, the penalty is harsh but just. A moment while I go to fetch the necessary tools!" He gathered up the dreams and sprang to the aperture. Seizing the tentacle he cried through the hole: "Pull the tentacle, work the winch! I have rescued the dreams!"

The tentacle convulsed and thrashed, effectively blocking the opening. Cugel turned and putting his fingers to his mouth emitted a piercing whistle. Uthaw's eye rolled upward and the tentacle fell limp.

The winch heaved at the tentacle and Cugel was drawn back through the hole. Uthaw, recovering his senses, jerked his tentacle so violently that the rope snapped; the winch was sent flying; and several persons were swept from their feet. Uthaw jerked back his tentacle and the hole immediately closed.

Cugel cast the sack of dream-flakes contemptuously at the feet of Iolo. "There you are, ingrate! Take your vapid hallucinations and go your way! Let us hear no more of you!"

Cugel turned to Duke Orbal. "I am now able to render a report upon the other cosmos. The ground is composed of a black spongelike substance and flickers with a trillion infinitesimal glimmers. My research discovered no limits to the extent of the land. A pale disk, barely visible, covers a quarter of the sky. The denizens are, first and foremost, an ill-natured hulk named Uthaw, and others more or less similar. No sound is allowed and meaning is conveyed by animalcules, which also procure the necessities of life. In essence, these are my discoveries, and now, with utmost respect, I claim the grand prize of one thousand terces."

From behind his back Cugel heard Iolo's mocking laughter. Duke Orbal shook his head. "My dear Cugel, what you suggest is impossible. To what exhibit do you refer? The boxful of dirt yonder? It lacks all pretensions to singularity."

"But you saw the hole! With your winch you pulled the tentacle! In accordance with your orders, I entered the hole and explored the region!"

"True enough, but hole and tentacle are both vanished. I do not for a moment suggest mendacity, but your report is not easily verified. I can hardly award honors to an entity so fugitive as the memory of a nonexistent hole! I fear that on this occasion I must pass you by. The prize will be awarded to Zaraflam and his remarkable cockroaches."

"A moment, your Grace!" Iolo called out. "Remember, I am entered in the competition! At last I am able to display my products! Here is a particularly choice item, distilled from a hundred dreams captured early in the morning from a bevy of beautiful maidens asleep in a bower of fragrant vines."

"Very well," said Duke Orbal. "I will delay the award until I test the quality of your visions. What is the procedure? Must I compose myself for slumber?"

"Not at all! The ingestion of the dream during waking hours produces not a hallucination, but a mood: a sensibility fresh, new and sweet: an allurement of the faculties, an indescribable exhilaration. Still, why should you not be comfortable as you test my dreams? You there! Fetch a couch! And you, a cushion for his Grace's noble head. You! Be good enough to take his Grace's hat."

Cugel saw no profit in remaining. He moved to the outskirts of the throng.

Iolo brought forth his dream and for a moment seemed puzzled by the ooze still adhering to the object, then decided to ignore the matter, and paid no further heed, except to rub his fingers as if after contact with some viscid substance.

Making a series of grand gestures, Iolo approached the great chair where Duke Orbal sat at his ease. "I will arrange the dream for its most convenient ingestion," said Iolo. "I place a quantity into each ear; I insert a trifle up each nostril; I arrange the balance under your Grace's illustrious tongue. Now, if your Grace will relax, in half a minute the quintessence of a hundred exquisite dreams will be made known."

Duke Orbal became rigid. His fingers clenched the arms of the chair. His back arched and his eyes bulged from their sockets. He turned over backward, then rolled, jerked, jumped and bounded about the plaza before the amazed eyes of his subjects.

Iolo called out in a brassy voice: "Where is Cugel? Fetch that scoundrel Cugel!"

But Cugel had already departed Cuirnif and was nowhere to be found.

AFTERWORD TO "THE BAGFUL OF DREAMS"

The less a writer discusses his work—and himself—the better. The master chef slaughters no chickens in the dining room; the doctor writes prescriptions in Latin; the magician hides his hinges, mirrors, and trapdoors with the utmost care. Recently I read of a surgeon who, after performing a complicated abortion, displayed to the ex-mother the fetus in a jar of formaldehyde. The woman went into hysterics and sued him, and I believe collected. No writer has yet been hauled into court on similar grounds, but the day may arrive.

—Jack Vance 1975

THE MITR

A rocky headland made a lee for the bay and the wide empty beach. The water barely rose and fell. A high overcast grayed the sky, stilled the air. The bay shone with a dull luster, like old pewter.

Dunes bordered the beach, breaking into a nearby forest of pitchy black-green cypress. The forest was holding its own, matting down the drifts with whiskery roots.

Among the dunes were ruins: glass walls ground milky by salt breeze and sand. In the center of these walls a human being had brought grass and ribbon-weed for her bed. Her name was Mitr, or so the beetles called her. For want of any other, she had taken the word for a name.

The name, the grass bed, a length of brown cloth stolen from the beetles were her only possessions. Possibly her belongings might be said to include a mouldering heap of bones which lay a hundred yards back in the forest. They interested her strongly, and she vaguely remembered a connection with herself. In the old days when her arms and legs had been short and round she had not marked the rather grotesque correspondence of form. Now she had lengthened and the resemblance was plain. Eyeholes like her eyes, a mouth like her own, teeth, jaw, skull, shoulders, ribs, legs, feet. From time to time she would wander back into the forest and stand wondering, though of late she had not been regular in her visits.

Today was dreary and gray. She felt bored, uneasy, and after some thought decided that she was hungry. Wandering out on the dunes she listlessly ate a number of grass-pods. Perhaps she was not hungry after all.

517

She walked down to the beach, stood looking out across the bay. A damp wind flapped the brown cloth, rumpled her hair. Perhaps it would rain. She looked anxiously at the sky. Rain made her wet and miserable. She could always take shelter among the rocks of the headland but—sometimes it was better to be wet.

She wandered down along the beach, caught and ate a small shellfish. There was little satisfaction in the salty flesh. Apparently she was not hungry. She picked up a sharp stick and drew a straight line in the damp sand—fifty feet—a hundred feet long. She stopped, looked back over her work with pleasure. She walked back, drawing another line parallel to the first, a hand's-breadth distant. Very interesting effect. Fired by sudden enthusiasm she drew more lines up and down the beach until she had created an extensive grate of parallel lines.

She looked over her work with satisfaction. Making such marks on the smooth sand was pleasant and interesting. Some other time she would do it again, and perhaps use curving lines or cross-hatching. But enough for now. She dropped the stick. The feeling of hunger that was not hunger came over her again. She caught a sand-locust but threw it away without eating it.

She began to run at full speed along the beach. This was better, the flash of her legs below her, the air clean in her lungs. Panting, she came to a halt, flung herself down in the sand.

Presently she caught her breath, sat up. She wanted to run some more, but felt a trifle languid. She grimaced, jerked uneasily. Maybe she should visit the beetles over the headland; perhaps the old gray creature called Ti-Sri-Ti would speak to her.

Tentatively she rose to her feet and started back along the beach. The plan gave her no real pleasure. Ti-Sri-Ti had little of interest to say. He answered no questions, but recited interminable data concerned with the colony: how many grubs would be allowed to mature, how many pounds of spider-eggs had been taken to storage, the condition of his mandibles, antennae, eyes...

She hesitated, but after a moment went on. Better Ti-Sri-Ti than no one, better the sound of a voice than the monotonous crash of gray surf. And perhaps he might say something interesting; on occasions his conversation went far afield and then Mitr listened with absorption: "The mountains are ruled by wild lizards and beyond are the Mercaloid Mechanvikis, who live under the ground with only fuming chimneys and slag-runs to tell of activity below. The beetles live along the shore and of the Mitr only one remains by old Glass City, the last of the Mitr."

She had not quite understood, since the flux and stream of time, the concepts of before and after, meant nothing to her. The universe was static; day followed day, not in a series, but as a duplication.

Ti-Sri-Ti had droned on: "Beyond the mountains is endless desert, then endless ice, then endless waste, then a land of seething fire, then the great water and once more the land of life, the rule and domain of the beetles, where every solstice a new acre of leaf mulch is chewed and laid..." And then there had been an hour dealing with beetle fungi-culture.

Mitr wandered along the beach. She passed the beautiful grate she had scratched in the damask sand, passed her glass walls, climbed the first shelves of black rock. She stopped, listened. A sound?

She hesitated, then went on. There was a rush of many feet. A long brown and black beetle sprang upon her, pressed her against the rocks. She fought feebly, but the fore-feet pinned her shoulders, arched her back. The beetle pressed his proboscis to her neck, punctured her skin. She stood limp, staring into his red eyes while he drank.

He finished, released her. The wound closed of itself, smarted and ached. The beetle climbed up over the rocks.

Mitr sat for an hour regaining her strength. The thought of listening to Ti-Sri-Ti now gave her no pleasure.

She wandered listlessly back along the beach, ate a few bits of seaweed and a small fish which had been trapped in a tide-pool.

She walked to the water's edge and stared out past the headland to the horizon. She wanted to cry out, to yell; something of the same urge which had driven her to run so swiftly along the beach. She raised her voice, called, a long musical note. The damp mild breeze seemed to muffle the sound. She turned away discouraged.

She wandered down the shore to the little stream of fresh water. Here she drank and ate some of the blackberries that grew in rank thickets.

She jerked upright, raised her head. A vast high sound filled the sky, seemed part of all the air. She stood rigid, then craned her neck, searching the overcast, legs half-bent for flight.

A long black sky-fish dropped into view, snorting puffs of fire. Terrified, she backed into the blackberry bushes. The brambles tore her legs, brought her to awareness. She dodged into the forest, crouched under a leaning cypress trunk.

The sky-fish dropped with astounding rapidity, lowered to the beach, settled with a quiet final belch and sigh. Mitr watched in frozen fascination. Never had she known of such a thing, never would she walk the beach again without watching the heavens.

The sky-fish opened. She saw the glint of metal, glass. From the interior jumped three creatures. Her head moved forward in wonder. They were something like herself, but large, red, burly. Strange, frightening things. They made a great deal of noise, talking in hoarse rough voices. One of them saw the glass walls, and for a space they examined the ruins with great interest.

The brown and black beetle which had drank her blood chose this moment to scuttle down the rocks to the beach. One of the newcomers set up a loud halloo and the beetle, bewildered and resentful, ran back up toward the rocks. The stranger held a shiny thing in his hand. It spat a lance of fire and the beetle burst into a thousand incandescent pieces. The three cried out in loud voices, laughing; Mitr shrank back under the tree trunk, making herself as small as possible.

One of the strangers noticed the place on the beach where she had drawn her grating. He called his companions and they looked with every display of attention, studying her footprints with extreme interest. One of them made a comment which caused the others to break into loud laughter. Then they all turned and searched up and down the beach.

They were seeking her, thought Mitr. She crouched so far under the trunk that the bark bruised her flesh.

Presently their interest waned and they went back to the sky-fish. One of them brought forth a long black tube which he took down to the edge of the surf and threw far out into the leaden water. The tube stiffened, pulsed, made sucking sounds. The sky-fish was thirsty and was drinking through his proboscis, thought Mitr.

The three strangers now walked along the beach toward the fresh-water stream. Mitr watched their approach with apprehension. Were they following her tracks? Her hands were sweating, her skin tingled.

They stopped at the water's edge, drank, only a few paces away. Mitr could see them plainly. They had bright copper hair and little hair-wisps around their mouths. They wore shining red carapaces around their chests, gray cloth on their legs, metal foot-wrappings. They were much like herself—but somehow different. Bigger, harder, more energetic. They were cruel, too; they had burnt the brown and black beetle. Mitr watched them fascinatedly. Where was their home? Were there others like them, like her, in the sky?

She shifted her position; the foliage crackled. Tingles of excitement and fear ran along her back. Had they heard? She peered out, ready to flee. No, they were walking back down the beach toward the sky-fish.

Mitr jumped up from under the tree-trunk, stood watching from behind the foliage. Plainly they cared little that another like themselves lived nearby. She became angry. Now she wanted to chide them, and order them off her beach.

She held back. It would be foolish to show herself. They might easily throw a lance of flame to burn her as they had the beetle. In any event they were rough and brutal. Strange creatures.

She stole through the forest, flitting from trunk to trunk, falling flat when necessary until she had approached the sky-fish as closely as shelter allowed.

The strangers were standing close around the base of the monster and showed no further disposition to explore.

The tube into the bay grew limp. They pulled it back into the sky-fish. Did that mean that they were about to leave? Good. They had no right on her beach. They had committed an outrage, landing so arrogantly, and killing one of her beetles. She almost stepped forward to upbraid them; then remembered how rough and hard and cruel they were, and held back with a tingling skin.

Stand quietly. Presently they will go, and you will be left in possession of your beach.

She moved restlessly. Rough red brutes. Don't move or they will see you. And then? She shivered.

They were making preparations for leaving. A lump came into her throat. They had seen her tracks and had never bothered to search. They could have found her so easily, she had hid herself almost in plain sight. And now she was closer than ever. If she moved forward only a step, then they would see her.

Skin tingling, she moved a trifle out from behind the tree-trunk. Just a little bit. Then she jumped back, heart thudding.

Had they seen her? With a sudden fluttering access of fright she hoped not. What would they do?

She looked cautiously around the trunk. One of the strangers was staring in a puzzled manner, as if he might have glimpsed movement. Even now he didn't see her. He looked straight into her eyes.

She heard him call out, then she was fleeing through the forest. He charged after her, and after him came the other two, battering down the undergrowth.

They left her, bruised and bleeding, in a bed of ferns, and marched back through the forest toward the beach, laughing and talking in their rough hoarse voices.

She lay quiet for a while. Their voices grew faint. She rose to her feet, staggered, limped after them.

A great glare lit the sky. Through the trees she saw the sky-fish thunder up—higher, higher, higher. It vanished through the overcast. There was silence along the beach, only the endless mutter of the surf.

She walked down to the water's edge, where the tide was coming in. The overcast was graying with evening.

She looked for many minutes into the sky, listening. No sound. The damp wind blew in her face, ruffling her hair. She sighed, turned back toward the ruined glass walls with tears on her cheeks.

The tide was washing up over the grate of straight lines she had drawn so carefully in the sand. Another few minutes and it would be entirely gone.

AFTERWORD TO "THE MITR"

I think everything I've ever read contributes to the background from which I write…for instance, when I was awfully young, I read all the Oz books. They were an enormous influence on me. And then there [were] the Edward Stratemeyer fiction-factory writers. [Howard R. Garis and other writers] had a pseudonym of Roy Rockwood and [they] wrote different kinds of science fiction stories…

Later, I loved P.G. Wodehouse. I thought he was a marvelous writer. I still do to this day. I think he hasn't been appreciated enough for his magnificent creativity and his beautiful writing. Oh, they laugh at him, but they don't take him seriously because he seems frivolous. He did what he set out to do and he did it beautifully.

Then there was a writer called Jeffrey Farnol, who wrote in the early '20s. He wrote magnificent adventure stories, which I read in my teens, I guess. I was fascinated by their mastery of atmosphere and pace, excitement and derring-do. He's dated a little bit. He's kind of sentimental in his attitudes towards ladies and old people. He's very courtly… Those are two men that I admire.

Then there was Clark Ashton Smith, who wrote for *Weird Tales* and who had a wild imagination. He wasn't a very talented writer, but his imagination was wonderful. Also Edgar Rice Burroughs. I don't think he had any influence on my writing at all, but I loved his work when I was young...Burroughs could generate atmosphere, especially the Barsoom books.

These are just the tip of the iceberg, because I read and read and read. I read everything.

—Jack Vance 2002

MORREION

1

The archveult Xexamedes, digging gentian roots in Were Wood, became warm with exertion. He doffed his cloak and returned to work, but the glint of blue scales was noticed by Herark the Harbinger and the diabolist Shrue. Approaching by stealth they leapt forth to confront the creature. Then, flinging a pair of nooses about the supple neck, they held him where he could do no mischief.

After great effort, a hundred threats and as many lunges, twists and charges on the part of Xexamedes, the magicians dragged him to the castle of Ildefonse, where other magicians of the region gathered in high excitement.

In times past Ildefonse had served the magicians as preceptor and he now took charge of the proceedings. He first inquired the archveult's name.

"I am Xexamedes, as well you know, old Ildefonse!"

"Yes," said Ildefonse, "I recognize you now, though my last view was your backside, as we sent you fleeting back to Jangk. Do you realize that you have incurred death by returning?"

"Not so, Ildefonse, since I am no longer an archveult of Jangk. I am an immigrant of Earth; I declare myself reverted to the estate of a man. Even my fellows hold me in low esteem."

"Well and good," said Ildefonse. "However, the ban was and is explicit. Where do you now house yourself?" The question was casual, and Xexamedes made an equally bland response.

"I come, I go; I savor the sweet airs of Earth, so different from the chemical vapors of Jangk."

Ildefonse was not to be put off. "What appurtenances did you bring: specifically, how many IOUN stones?"

"Let us talk of other matters," suggested Xexamedes. "I now wish to join your local coterie, and, as a future comrade to all present, I find these nooses humiliating."

The short-tempered Hurtiancz bellowed, "Enough impudence! What of the IOUN stones?"

"I carry a few such trinkets," replied Xexamedes with dignity.

"Where are they?"

Xexamedes addressed himself to Ildefonse. "Before I respond, may I inquire your ultimate intentions?"

Ildefonse pulled at his white beard and raised his eyes to the chandelier. "Your fate will hinge upon many factors. I suggest that you produce the IOUN stones."

"They are hidden under the floorboards of my cottage," said Xexamedes in a sulky voice.

"Which is situated where?"

"At the far edge of Were Wood."

Rhialto the Marvellous leapt to his feet. "All wait here! I will verify the truth of the statement!"

The sorcerer Gilgad held up both arms. "Not so fast! I know the region exactly! I will go!"

Ildefonse spoke in a neutral voice. "I hereby appoint a committee to consist of Rhialto, Gilgad, Mune the Mage, Hurtiancz, Kilgas, Ao of the Opals, and Barbanikos. This group will go to the cottage and bring back all contraband. The proceedings are adjourned until your return."

2

The adjuncts of Xexamedes were in due course set forth on a sideboard in Ildefonse's great hall, including thirty-two IOUN stones: spheres, ellipsoids, spindles, each approximately the size of a small plum, each displaying inner curtains of pale fire. A net prevented them from drifting off like dream-bubbles.

"We now have a basis for further investigation," said Ildefonse. "Xexamedes, exactly what is the source of these potent adjuncts?"

Xexamedes jerked his tall black plumes in surprise, either real or simulated. He was yet constrained by the two nooses. Haze of Wheary Water held one rope, Barbanikos the other, to ensure that Xexamedes could touch neither. Xexamedes inquired, "What of the indomitable Morreion? Did he not reveal his knowledge?"

Ildefonse frowned in puzzlement. "'Morreion'? I had almost forgotten the name…What were the circumstances?"

Herark the Harbinger, who knew lore of twenty aeons, stated: "After the archveults were defeated, a contract was made. The archveults were given their lives, and in turn agreed to divulge the source of the IOUN stones. The noble Morreion was ordered forth to learn the secret and was never heard from since."

"He was instructed in all the procedures," declared Xexamedes. "If you wish to learn—seek out Morreion!"

Ildefonse asked, "Why did he not return?"

"I cannot say. Does anyone else wish to learn the source of the stones? I will gladly demonstrate the procedure once again."

For a moment no one spoke. Then Ildefonse suggested, "Gilgad, what of you? Xexamedes has made an interesting proposal."

Gilgad licked his thin brown lips. "First, I wish a verbal description of the process."

"By all means," said Xexamedes. "Allow me to consult a document." He stepped toward the sideboard, drawing Haze and Barbanikos together; then he leaped back. With the slack thus engendered he grasped Barbanikos and exuded a galvanic impulse. Sparks flew from Barbanikos' ears; he jumped into the air and fell down in a faint. Xexamedes snatched the rope from Haze and before anyone could prevent him, he fled from the great hall.

"After him!" bawled Ildefonse. "He must not escape!"

The magicians gave chase to the fleet archveult. Across the Scaum hills, past Were Wood ran Xexamedes; like hounds after a fox came the magicians. Xexamedes entered Were Wood and doubled back, but the magicians suspected a trick and were not deceived.

Leaving the forest Xexamedes approached Rhialto's manse and took cover beside the aviary. The bird-women set up an alarm and old Funk, Rhialto's servitor, hobbled forth to investigate.

Gilgad now spied Xexamedes and exerted his Instantaneous Electric Effort—a tremendous many-pronged dazzle which not only shivered Xexamedes but destroyed Rhialto's aviary, shattered his antique way-post and sent poor old Funk dancing across the sward on stilts of crackling blue light.

3

A linden leaf clung to the front door of Rhialto's manse, pinned by a thorn. A prank of the wind, thought Rhialto, and brushed it aside. His new servant Puiras, however, picked it up and, in a hoarse grumbling voice, read:

NOTHING THREATENS MORREION

"What is this regarding Morreion?" demanded Rhialto. Taking the leaf he inspected the minute silver characters. "A gratuitous reassurance." A second time he discarded the leaf and gave Puiras his final instructions. "At midday prepare a meal for the Minuscules—gruel and tea will suffice. At sunset serve out the thrush pâté. Next, I wish you to scour the tile of the great hall. Use no sand, which grinds at the luster of the glaze. Thereafter, clear the south sward of debris; you may use the aeolus, but take care; blow only down the yellow reed; the black reed summons a gale, and we have had devastation enough. Set about the aviary; salvage all useful material. If you find corpses, deal with them appropriately. Is so much clear?"

Puiras, a man spare and loose-jointed, with a bony face and lank black hair, gave a dour nod. "Except for a single matter. When I have accomplished all this, what else?"

Rhialto, drawing on his cloth-of-gold gauntlets, glanced sidewise at his servant. Stupidity? Zeal? Churlish sarcasm? Puiras' visage offered no clue. Rhialto spoke in an even voice. "Upon completion of these tasks, your time is your own. Do not tamper with the magical engines; do not, for your life, consult the portfolios, the librams or the compendiary. In due course, I may instruct you in a few minor dints; until then, be cautious!"

"I will indeed."

Rhialto adjusted his six-tiered black satin hat, donned his cloak with that flourish which had earned him his soubriquet 'the Marvellous'. "I go to visit Ildefonse. When I pass the outer gate impose the boundary curse; under no circumstances lift it until I signal. Expect me at sunset: sooner, if all goes well."

Making no effort to interpret Puiras' grunt, Rhialto sauntered to the north portal, averting his eyes from the wreckage of his wonderful aviary. Barely had he passed the portal by, when Puiras activated the curse, prompting Rhialto to jump hastily forward. Rhialto adjusted the set of his hat. The ineptitude of Puiras was but one in a series of misfortunes, all attributable to the archveult Xexamedes. His aviary destroyed, the way-post shattered, old Funk dead! From some source compensation must be derived!

4

Ildefonse lived in a castle above the River Scaum: a vast and complex structure of a hundred turrets, balconies, elevated pavilions and pleasaunces. During the final ages of the 21st Aeon, when Ildefonse had served as preceptor, the castle had seethed with activity. Now only a single wing of this monstrous edifice was in use, with the rest abandoned to dust, owls and archaic ghosts.

Ildefonse met Rhialto at the bronze portal. "My dear colleague, splendid as usual! Even on an occasion like that of today! You put me to shame!" Ildefonse stood back the better to admire Rhialto's austerely handsome visage, his fine blue cloak and trousers of rose velvet, his glossy boots. Ildefonse himself, for reasons obscure, presented himself in the guise of a jovial sage, with bald pate, a lined countenance, pale blue eyes, an irregular white beard—conceivably a natural condition which vanity would not let him discard.

"Come in, then," cried Ildefonse. "As always, with your sense of drama, you are last to arrive!"

They proceeded to the great hall. On hand were fourteen sorcerers: Zilifant, Perdustin, Herark the Harbinger, Haze of Wheary Water, Ao of the Opals, Eshmiel, Kilgas, Byzant the Necrope, Gilgad, Vermoulian the Dream-walker, Barbanikos, the diabolist Shrue, Mune the Mage, Hurtiancz. Ildefonse called out, "The last of our cabal has arrived: Rhialto the Marvellous, at whose manse the culminating stroke occurred!"

Rhialto doffed his hat to the group. Some returned the salute; others, Gilgad, Byzant the Necrope, Mune the Mage, Kilgas, merely cast cool glances over their shoulders.

Ildefonse took Rhialto by the arm and led him to the buffet. Rhialto accepted a goblet of wine, which he tested with his amulet.

In mock chagrin Ildefonse protested: "The wine is sound; have you yet been poisoned at my board?"

"No. But never have circumstances been as they are today."

Ildefonse made a sign of wonder. "The circumstances are favorable! We have vanquished our enemy; his IOUN stones are under our control!"

"True," said Rhialto. "But remember the damages I have suffered! I claim corresponding benefits, of which my enemies would be pleased to deprive me."

"Tush," scolded Ildefonse. "Let us talk on a more cheerful note. How goes the renewal of your way-post? The Minuscules carve with zest?"

"The work proceeds," Rhialto replied. "Their tastes are by no means coarse. For this single week their steward has required two ounces of honey, a gill of Misericord, a dram and a half of malt spirits, all in addition to biscuit, oil and a daily ration of my best thrush pâté."

Ildefonse shook his head in disapproval. "They become ever more splendid, and who must pay the score? You and I. So the world goes." He turned away to refill the goblet of the burly Hurtiancz.

"I have made investigation," said Hurtiancz ponderously, "and I find that Xexamedes had gone among us for years. He seems to have been a renegade, as unwelcome on Jangk as on Earth."

"He may still be the same," Ildefonse pointed out. "Who found his corpse? No one! Haze here declares that electricity to an archveult is like water to a fish."

"This is the case," declared Haze of Wheary Water, a hot-eyed wisp of a man.

"In that event, the damage done to my property becomes more irresponsible than ever!" cried Rhialto. "I demand compensation before any other general adjustments are made."

Hurtiancz frowned. "I fail to comprehend your meaning."

"It is elegantly simple," said Rhialto. "I suffered serious damage; the balance must be restored. I intend to claim the IOUN stones."

"You will find yourself one among many," said Hurtiancz.

Haze of Wheary Water gave a sardonic snort. "Claim as you please."

Mune the Mage came forward. "The archveult is barely dead; must we bicker so quickly?"

Eshmiel asked, "Is he dead after all? Observe this!" He displayed a linden leaf. "I found it on my blue tile kurtivan. It reads, 'NOTHING THREATENS MORREION'."

"I also found such a leaf!" declared Haze.

"And I!" said Hurtiancz.

"How the centuries roll, one past the other!" mused Ildefonse. "Those were the days of glory, when we sent the archveults flitting like a band of giant bats! Poor Morreion! I have often puzzled as to his fate."

Eshmiel frowned down at his leaf. "'NOTHING THREATENS MORREION'—so we are assured. If such is the case, the notice would seem superfluous and over-helpful."

"It is quite clear," Gilgad grumbled. "Morreion went forth to learn the source of the IOUN stones; he did so, and now is threatened by nothing."

"A possible interpretation," said Ildefonse in a pontifical voice. "There is certainly more here than meets the eye."

"It need not trouble us now," said Rhialto. "To the IOUN stones in present custody, however, I now put forward a formal claim, as compensation for the damage I took in the common cause."

"The statement has a specious plausibility," remarked Gilgad. "Essentially, however, each must benefit in proportion to his contribution. I do not say this merely because it was my Instantaneous Electric Effort which blasted the archveult."

Ao of the Opals said sharply, "Another casuistic assumption which must be rejected out-of-hand, especially since the providential energy allowed Xexamedes to escape!"

The argument continued an hour. Finally a formula proposed by Ildefonse was put to vote and approved by a count of fifteen to one. The goods formerly owned by the archveult Xexamedes were to be set out for inspection. Each magician would list the items in order of choice; Ildefonse would collate the lists. Where conflict occurred determination must be made by lot. Rhialto, in recognition of his loss, was granted a free selection after Choice five had been determined; Gilgad was accorded the same privilege after Choice ten.

Rhialto made a final expostulation: "What value to me is Choice five? The archveult owned nothing but the stones, a few banal adjuncts and these roots, herbs and elixirs."

His views carried no weight. Ildefonse distributed sheets of paper; each magician listed the articles he desired; Ildefonse examined each list in turn. "It appears," he said, "that all present declare their first choice to be the IOUN stones."

Everyone glanced towards the stones; they winked and twinkled with pale white fire.

"Such being the case," said Ildefonse, "determination must be made by chance."

He set forth a crockery pot and sixteen ivory disks. "Each will indite his sign upon one of the chips and place it into the pot, in this fashion." Ildefonse marked one of the chips, dropped it into the pot. "When all have done so, I will call in a servant, who will bring forth a single chip."

"A moment!" exclaimed Byzant. "I apprehend mischief; it walks somewhere near."

Ildefonse turned the sensitive Necrope a glance of cold inquiry. "To what mischief do you refer?"

"I detect a contradiction, a discord; something strange walks among us; there is someone here who should not be here."

"Someone moves unseen!" cried Mune the Mage. "Ildefonse, guard the stones!"

Ildefonse peered here and there through the shadowy old hall. He made a secret signal and pointed to a far corner: "Ghost! Are you on hand?"

A soft sad whisper said, "I am here."

"Respond: who walks unseen among us?"

"Stagnant eddies of the past. I see faces: the less-than-ghosts, the ghosts of dead ghosts...They glimmer and glimpse, they look and go."

"What of living things?"

"No harsh blood, no pulsing flesh, no strident hearts."

"Guard and watch." Ildefonse returned to Byzant the Necrope. "What now?"

"I feel a strange flavor."

"What do you suggest then?"

Byzant spoke softly, to express the exquisite delicacy of his concepts. "Among all here, I alone am sufficiently responsive to the subtlety of the IOUN stones. They should be placed in my custody."

"Let the drawing proceed!" Hurtiancz called out. "Byzant's plan will never succeed."

"Be warned!" cried Byzant. With a black glance towards Hurtiancz, he moved to the rear of the group.

Ildefonse summoned one of his maidens. "Do not be alarmed. You must reach into the pot, thoroughly stir the chips, and bring forth one, which you will then lay upon the table. Do you understand?"

"Yes, Lord Magician."

"Do as I bid."

The girl went to the pot. She reached forth her hand. At this precise instant Rhialto activated a spell of Temporal Stasis, with which, in anticipation of some such emergency, he had come prepared.

Time stood still for all but Rhialto. He glanced around the chamber, at the magicians in their frozen attitudes, at the servant girl with one hand over the pot, at Ildefonse staring at the girl's elbow.

Rhialto leisurely sauntered over to the IOUN stones. He could now take possession, but such an act would arouse a tremendous outcry and all would league themselves against him. A less provocative system was in order. He was startled by a soft sound from the corner of the room, when there should be no sound in still air.

"Who moves?" called Rhialto.

"I move," came the soft voice of the ghost.

"Time is at a standstill. You must not move, or speak, or watch, or know."

"Time, no-time—it is all one. I know each instant over and over."

Rhialto shrugged and turned to the urn. He brought out the chips. To his wonder each was indited 'Ildefonse'.

"Aha!" exclaimed Rhialto. "Some crafty rascal selected a previous instant for his mischief! Is it not always the case? At the end of this, he and I will know each other the better!" Rhialto rubbed out Ildefonse's signs and substituted his own. Then he replaced all in the pot.

Resuming his former position, he revoked the spell.

Noise softly filled the room. The girl reached into the pot. She stirred the chips, brought forth one of them which she placed upon the table. Rhialto leaned over the chip, as did Ildefonse. It gave a small jerk. The sign quivered and changed before their eyes.

Ildefonse lifted it and in a puzzled voice read, "Gilgad!"

Rhialto glanced furiously at Gilgad, who gave back a bland stare. Gilgad had also halted time, but Gilgad had waited until the chip was actually upon the table.

Ildefonse said in a muffled voice, "That is all. You may go." The girl departed. Ildefonse poured the chips on the table. They were correctly indited; each bore the sign or the signature of one of the magicians present. Ildefonse pulled at his white beard. He said, "It seems that Gilgad has availed himself of the IOUN stones."

Gilgad strode to the table. He emitted a terrible cry. "The stones! What has been done to them?" He held up the net, which now sagged under the weight of its contents. The brooding translucence was gone; the objects in the net shone with a vulgar vitreous glitter. Gilgad took one and dashed it to the floor, where it shattered into splinters. "These are not the IOUN stones! Knavery is afoot!"

"Indeed!" declared Ildefonse. "So much is clear."

"I demand my stones," raved Gilgad. "Give them to me at once or I loose a spell of anguish against all present!"

"One moment," growled Hurtiancz. "Delay your spell. Ildefonse, bring forth your ghost; learn what transpired."

Ildefonse gave his beard a dubious tug, then raised his finger towards the far corner. "Ghost! Are you at hand?"

"I am."

"What occurred while we drew chips from the pot?"

"There was motion. Some moved, some stayed. When the chip at last was laid on the table, a strange shape passed into the room. It took the stones and was gone."

"What manner of strange shape?"

"It wore a skin of blue scales; black plumes rose from its head, still it carried a soul of man."

"Archveult!" muttered Hurtiancz. "I suspect Xexamedes!"

Gilgad cried, "So then, what of my stones, my wonderful stones? How will I regain my property? Must I always be stripped of my valued possessions?"

"Cease your keening!" snapped the diabolist Shrue. "The remaining items must be distributed. Ildefonse, be so good as to consult the lists."

Ildefonse took up the papers. "Since Gilgad won the first draw, his list will now be withdrawn. For second choice—"

He was interrupted by Gilgad's furious complaint. "I protest this intolerable injustice! I won nothing but a handful of glass gewgaws!"

Ildefonse shrugged. "It is the robber-archveult to whom you must complain, especially when the drawing was attended by certain temporal irregularities, to which I need make no further reference."

Gilgad raised his arms in the air; his saturnine face knotted to the surge and counter-surge of his passions. His colleagues watched with dispassionate faces. "Proceed, Ildefonse," said Vermoulian the Dream-walker.

Ildefonse spread out the papers. "It appears that among the group only Rhialto has selected, for second choice, this curiously shaped device, which appears to be one of Houlart's Preterite Recordiums. I therefore make this award and place Rhialto's list with Gilgad's.

Perdustin, Barbanikos, Ao of the Opals, and I myself have evinced a desire for this Casque of Sixty Directions, and we must therefore undertake a trial by lot. The jar, four chips—"

"On this occasion," said Perdustin, "let the maid be brought here now. She will put her hand over the mouth of the pot; we will insert the chips between her fingers; thus we ensure against a disruption of the laws of chance."

Ildefonse pulled at his white whiskers, but Perdustin had his way. In this fashion all succeeding lots were drawn. Presently it became Rhialto's turn to make a free choice.

"Well then, Rhialto," said Ildefonse. "What do you select?"

Rhialto's resentment boiled up in his throat. "As restitution for my seventeen exquisite bird-women, my ten-thousand-year-old way-post, I am supposed to be gratified with this packet of Stupefying Dust?"

Ildefonse spoke soothingly. "Human interactions, stimulated as they are by disequilibrium, never achieve balance. In even the most favorable transaction, one party—whether he realizes it or not—must always come out the worse."

"The proposition is not unknown to me," said Rhialto in a more reasonable voice. "However—"

Zilifant uttered a sudden startled cry. "Look!" He pointed to the great mantel-piece; here, camouflaged by the carving, hung a linden leaf. With trembling fingers Ildefonse plucked it down. Silver characters read:

> MORREION LIVES A DREAM.
> NOTHING IS IMMINENT !

"Ever more confusing," muttered Hurtiancz. "Xexamedes persists in reassuring us that all is well with Morreion: an enigmatic exercise!"

"It must be remembered," the ever cautious Haze pointed out, "that Xexamedes, a renegade, is enemy to all."

Herark the Harbinger held up a black-enameled forefinger. "My habit is to make each problem declare its obverse. The first message, 'NOTHING THREATENS MORREION', becomes 'SOMETHING DOES NOT THREATEN MORREION'; and again, 'NOTHING DOES THREATEN MORREION'."

"Verbiage, prolixity!" grumbled the practical Hurtiancz.

"Not so fast!" said Zilifant. "Herark is notoriously profound!

'NOTHING' might be intended as a delicate reference to death; a niceness of phrase, so to speak."

"Was Xexamedes famous for his exquisite good taste?" asked Hurtiancz with heavy sarcasm. "I think not. Like myself, when he meant 'death' he said 'death'."

"My point exactly!" cried Herark. "I ask myself: What is the 'Nothing', which threatens Morreion? Shrue, what or where is 'Nothing'?"

Shrue hunched his thin shoulders. "It is not to be found among the demon-lands."

"Vermoulian, in your peregrine palace you have traveled far. Where or what is 'Nothing'?"

Vermoulian the Dream-walker declared his perplexity. "I have never discovered such a place."

"Mune the Mage: What or where is 'Nothing'?"

"Somewhere," reflected Mune the Mage, "I have seen a reference to 'Nothing', but I cannot recall the connection."

"The key word is 'reference'," stated Herark. "Ildefonse, be so good as to consult the Great Gloss."

Ildefonse selected a volume from a shelf, threw back the broad covers. "'Nothing'. Various topical references...a metaphysical description...a place? 'Nothing: the nonregion beyond the end of the cosmos.'"

Hurtiancz suggested, "For good measure, why not consult the entry 'Morreion'?"

Somewhat reluctantly Ildefonse found the reference. He read: "'Morreion: A legendary hero of the 21st Aeon, who vanquished the archveults and drove them, aghast, to Jangk. Thereupon they took him as far as the mind can reach, to the shining fields where they win their ioun stones. His erstwhile comrades, who had vowed their protection, put him out of mind, and thereafter nought can be said.' A biased and inaccurate statement, but interesting nonetheless."

Vermoulian the Dream-walker rose to his feet. "I have been planning an extended journey in my palace; this being the case I will take it upon myself to seek Morreion."

Gilgad gave a croak of fury and dismay. "You think to explore the 'shining fields'! It is I who has earned the right, not you!"

Vermoulian, a large man, sleek as a seal, with a pallid inscrutable face, declared: "My exclusive purpose is to rescue the hero Morreion; the IOUN stones to me are no more than an idle afterthought."

Ildefonse spoke: "Well said! But you will work more efficaciously with a very few trusted colleagues; perhaps myself alone."

"Precisely correct!" asserted Rhialto. "But a third person of proved resource is necessary in the event of danger. I also will share the hardships; otherwise I would think ill of myself."

Hurtiancz spoke with truculent fervor. "I never have been one to hold back! You may rely on me."

"The presence of a Necrope is indispensable," stated Byzant. "I must therefore accompany the group."

Vermoulian asserted his preference for traveling alone, but no one would listen. Vermoulian at last capitulated, with a peevish droop to his usually complacent countenance. "I leave at once. If any are not at the palace within the hour I will understand that they have changed their minds."

"Come, come!" chided Ildefonse. "I need three-and-a-half hours simply to instruct my staff! We require more time."

"The message declared, 'Nothing is imminent'," said Vermoulian. "Haste is of the essence!"

"We must take the word in its context," said Ildefonse. "Morreion has known his present condition several aeons; the word 'imminent' may well designate a period of five hundred years."

With poor grace Vermoulian agreed to delay his departure until the following morning.

5

The ancient sun sank behind the Scaum hills; thin black clouds hung across the maroon afterlight. Rhialto arrived at the outer portal to his domain. He gave a signal and waited confidently for Puiras to lift the boundary curse.

The manse showed no responsive sign.

Rhialto made another signal, stamping impatiently. From the nearby forest of sprawling kang trees came the moaning of a grue, arousing the hairs at the back of Rhialto's neck. He flashed his finger-beams once more: where was Puiras? The white jade tiles of the roof loomed pale through the twilight. He saw no lights. From the forest the grue moaned again and in a plaintive voice called out for solace. Rhialto tested the boundary with a branch, to discover no curse, no protection whatever.

Flinging down the branch, he strode to the manse. All seemed to be in order, though Puiras was nowhere to be found. If he had scoured the hall the effort was not noticeable. Shaking his head in deprecation, Rhialto went to examine the way-post, which was being repaired by his Minuscules. The superintendent flew up on a mosquito to render his report; it seemed that Puiras had neglected to set out the evening victuals. Rhialto did so now and added half an ounce of jellied eel at his own expense.

With a dram of Blue Ruin at his elbow, Rhialto examined the convoluted tubes of bronze which he had brought from the castle of Ildefonse: the so-called Preterite Recordium. He tried to trace the course of the tubes but they wound in and out in a most confusing fashion. He gingerly pressed one of the valves, to evoke a sibilant whispering from the horn. He touched another, and now he heard a far-off guttural song. The sound came not from the horn, but from the pathway, and a moment later Puiras lurched through the door. He turned a vacuous leer toward Rhialto and staggered off toward his quarters.

Rhialto called sharply: "Puiras!"

The servitor lurched about. "What then?"

"You have taken too much to drink; in consequence you are drunk."

Puiras ventured a knowing smirk. "Your perspicacity is keen, your language is exact. I take no exception to either remark."

Rhialto said, "I have no place for an irresponsible or bibulous servant. You are hereby discharged."

"No, you don't!" cried Puiras in a coarse voice, and emphasized the statement with a belch. "They told me I'd have a good post if I stole no more than old Funk and praised your noble airs. Well then! Tonight I stole only moderately, and from me the lack of insult is high praise. So there's the good post and what's a good post without a walk to the village?"

"Puiras, you are dangerously intoxicated," said Rhialto. "What a disgusting sight you are indeed!"

"No compliments!" roared Puiras. "We can't all be fine magicians with fancy clothes at the snap of a finger."

In outrage Rhialto rose to his feet. "Enough! Be off to your quarters before I inflict a torment upon you!"

"That's where I was going when you called me back," replied Puiras sulkily.

Rhialto conceived a further rejoinder to be beneath his dignity. Puiras stumbled away, muttering under his breath.

6

At rest upon the ground, Vermoulian's wonderful peregrine palace, together with its loggias, formal gardens and entrance pavilion, occupied an octagonal site some three acres in extent. The plan of the palace proper was that of a four-pointed star, with a crystal spire at each apex and a spire, somewhat taller, at the center, in which Vermoulian maintained his private chambers. A marble balustrade enclosed the forward pavilion. At the center a fountain raised a hundred jets of water; to either side grew lime trees with silver blossoms and silver fruit. The quadrangles to the right and left were laid out as formal gardens; the area at the rear was planted with herbs and salads for the palace kitchen.

Vermoulian's guests occupied suites in the wings; under the central spire were the various salons, the morning and afternoon rooms, the library, the music chamber, the formal dining room and the lounge.

An hour after sunrise the magicians began to arrive, with Gilgad first on the scene and Ildefonse the last. Vermoulian, his nonchalance restored, greeted each magician with carefully measured affability. After inspecting their suites the magicians gathered in the grand salon. Vermoulian addressed the group. "It is my great pleasure to entertain so distinguished a company! Our goal: the rescue of the hero Morreion! All present are keen and dedicated—but do all understand that we must wander far regions?" Vermoulian turned his placid gaze from face to face. "Are all prepared for tedium, discomfort and danger? Such may well eventuate, and if any have doubts or if any pursue subsidiary goals, such as a search for IOUN stones, now is the time for these persons to return to their respective manses, castles, caves, and eyries. Are any so inclined? No? We depart."

Vermoulian bowed to his now uneasy guests. He mounted to the control belvedere where he cast a spell of buoyancy upon the palace; it rose to drift on the morning breeze like a pinnacled cloud. Vermoulian consulted his Celestial Almanac and made note of certain symbols; these he inscribed upon the carnelian mandate-wheel, which he set into rotation; the signs were spun off into the interflux, to elucidate a route across the universe. Vermoulian fired a taper and held it to the speed-incense; the palace departed; ancient Earth and the waning sun were left behind.

Beside the marble balustrade stood Rhialto. Ildefonse came to join him; the two watched Earth dwindle to a rosy-pink crescent. Ildefonse spoke in a melancholy voice: "When one undertakes a journey of this sort, where the event is unknown, long thoughts come of their own accord. I trust that you left your affairs in order?"

"My household is not yet settled," said Rhialto. "Puiras has proved unsatisfactory; when drunk he sings and performs grotesque capers; when sober he is as surly as a leech on a corpse. This morning I demoted him to Minuscule."

Ildefonse nodded absently. "I am troubled by what I fear to be cross-purposes among our colleagues, worthy fellows though they may be."

"You refer to the 'shining fields' of IOUN stones?" Rhialto put forward delicately.

"I do. As Vermoulian categorically declared, we fare forth to the rescue of Morreion. The IOUN stones can only prove a distraction. Even if a supply were discovered, I suspect that the interests of all might best be served by a highly selective distribution, the venal Gilgad's complaints notwithstanding."

"There is much to be said for this point of view," Rhialto admitted. "It is just as well to have a prior understanding upon a matter so inherently controversial. Vermoulian of course must be allotted a share."

"This goes without saying."

At this moment Vermoulian descended to the pavilion where he was approached by Mune the Mage, Hurtiancz and the others. Mune raised a question regarding their destination. "The question of ultimates becomes important. How, Vermoulian, can you know that this precise direction will take us to Morreion?"

"A question well put," said Vermoulian. "To respond, I must cite an intrinsic condition of the universe. We set forth in any direction which seems convenient; each leads to the same place: the end of the universe."

"Interesting!" declared Zilifant. "In this case, we must inevitably find Morreion; an encouraging prospect!"

Gilgad was not completely satisfied. "What of the 'shining fields' in the reference? Where are these located?"

"A matter of secondary or even tertiary concern," Ildefonse reminded him. "We must think only of the hero Morreion."

"Your solicitude is late by several aeons," said Gilgad waspishly. "Morreion may well have grown impatient."

"Other circumstances intervened," said Ildefonse with a frown of annoyance. "Morreion will certainly understand the situation."

Zilifant remarked. "The conduct of Xexamedes becomes ever more puzzling! As a renegade archveult, he has no ostensible reason to oblige either Morreion, the archveults, or ourselves."

"The mystery in due course will be resolved," said Herark the Harbinger.

7

So went the voyage. The palace drifted through the stars, under and over clouds of flaming gas, across gulfs of deep black space. The magicians meditated in the pergolas, exchanged opinions in the salons over goblets of liquor, lounged upon the marble benches of the pavilion, leaned on the balustrade to look down at the galaxies passing below. Breakfasts were served in the individual suites, luncheons were usually set forth al fresco on the pavilion, the dinners were sumptuous and formal and extended far into the night. To enliven these evenings Vermoulian called forth the most charming, witty and beautiful women of all the past eras, in their quaint and splendid costumes. They found the peregrine palace no less remarkable than the fact of their own presence aboard. Some thought themselves dreaming; others conjectured their own deaths; a few of the more sophisticated made the correct presumption. To facilitate social intercourse Vermoulian gave them command of contemporary language, and the evenings frequently became merry affairs. Rhialto became enamored of a certain Mersei from the land of Mith, long since foundered under the waters of the Shan Ocean. Mersei's charm resided in her slight body, her grave pale face behind which thoughts could be felt but not seen. Rhialto plied her with all gallantry, but she failed to respond, merely looking at him in disinterested silence, until Rhialto wondered if she were slack-witted, or possibly more subtle than himself. Either case made him uncomfortable, and he was not sorry when Vermoulian returned this particular group to oblivion.

Through clouds and constellations they moved, past bursting galaxies and meandering star-streams; through a region where the stars showed a peculiar soft violet and hung in clouds of pale green gas; across a desolation where nothing whatever was seen save a few far luminous clouds. Then presently they came to a new region, where blazing white giants seemed to control whirlpools of pink, blue and white gas, and the magicians lined the balustrade looking out at the spectacle.

At last the stars thinned; the great star-streams were lost in the distance. Space seemed darker and heavier, and finally there came a time when all the stars were behind and nothing lay ahead but darkness. Vermoulian made a grave announcement. "We are now close to the end of the universe! We must go with care. 'Nothing' lies ahead."

"Where then is Morreion?" demanded Hurtiancz. "Surely he is not to be found wandering vacant space."

"Space is not yet vacant," stated Vermoulian. "Here there and roundabout are dead stars and wandering star-hulks; in a sense, we traverse the refuse-heap of the universe, where the dead stars come to await a final destiny; and notice, yonder, far ahead, a single star, the last in the universe. We must approach with caution; beyond lies 'Nothing'."

"'Nothing' is not yet visible," remarked Ao of the Opals.

"Look more closely!" said Vermoulian. "Do you see that dark wall? That is 'Nothing'."

"Again," said Perdustin, "the question arises: where is Morreion? Back at Ildefonse's castle, when we formed conjectures, the end of the universe seemed a definite spot. Now that we are here, we find a considerable latitude of choice."

Gilgad muttered, half to himself, "The expedition is a farce. I see no 'fields', shining or otherwise."

Vermoulian said, "The solitary star would seem an initial object of investigation. We approach at a rash pace; I must slake the speed-incense."

The magicians stood by the balustrade watching as the far star waxed in brightness. Vermoulian called down from the belvedere to announce a lone planet in orbit around the sun.

"A possibility thereby exists," stated Mune the Mage, "that on this very planet we may find Morreion."

8

The palace moved down to the solitary star and the lone planet became a disk the color of moth-wing. Beyond, clearly visible in the wan sunlight, stood the ominous black wall. Hurtiancz said, "Xexamedes' warning now becomes clear—assuming, of course, that Morreion inhabits this drab and isolated place."

The world gradually expanded, to show a landscape dreary and worn. A few decayed hills rose from the plains; as many ponds gleamed sullenly in the sunlight. The only other features of note were the ruins of once-extensive cities; a very few buildings had defied the ravages of time sufficiently to display a squat and distorted architecture.

The palace settled close above one of the ruins; a band of small weasel-like rodents bounded away into the scrub; no other sign of life was evident. The palace continued west around the planet. Vermoulian presently called down from the belvedere: "Notice the cairn; it marks an ancient thoroughfare."

Other cairns at three-mile intervals appeared, mounds of carefully fitted stones six feet high; they marked a way around the planet.

At the next tumble of ruins Vermoulian, observing a level area, allowed the palace to settle so that the ancient city and its cluster of surviving structures might be explored.

The magicians set off in various directions, the better to pursue their investigations. Gilgad went towards the desolate plaza, Perdustin and Zilifant to the civic amphitheatre, Hurtiancz into a nearby tumble of sandstone blocks. Ildefonse, Rhialto, Mune the Mage and Herark the Harbinger wandered at random, until a raucous chanting brought them up short.

"Peculiar!" exclaimed Herark. "It sounds like the voice of Hurtiancz, the most dignified of men!"

The group entered a cranny through the ruins, which opened into a large chamber, protected from sifting sand by massive blocks of rock. Light filtered through various chinks and apertures; down the middle ran a line of six long slabs. At the far end sat Hurtiancz, watching the entry of the magicians with an imperturbable gaze. On the slab in front of him stood a globe of dark brown glass, or glazed stone. A rack behind him held other similar bottles.

"It appears," said Ildefonse, "that Hurtiancz has stumbled upon the site of the ancient tavern."

"Hurtiancz!" Rhialto called out. "We heard your song and came to investigate. What have you discovered?"

Hurtiancz hawked and spat on the ground. "Hurtiancz!" cried Rhialto. "Do you hear me? Or have you taken too much of this ancient tipple to be sensible?"

Hurtiancz replied in a clear voice, "In one sense I have taken too much: in another, not enough."

Mune the Mage picked up the brown glass bottle and smelled the contents. "Astringent, tart, herbal." He tasted the liquid. "It is quite refreshing."

Ildefonse and Herark the Harbinger each took a brown glass globe from the rack and broke open the bung; they were joined by Rhialto and Mune the Mage.

Ildefonse, as he drank, became garrulous, and presently he fell to speculating in regard to the ancient city: "Just as from one bone the skilled palaeontologist deduces an entire skeleton, so from a single artifact the qualified scholar reconstructs every aspect of the responsible race. As I taste this liquor, as I examine this bottle, I ask myself, What do the dimensions, textures, colors and flavors betoken? No intelligent act is without symbolic significance."

Hurtiancz, upon taking drink, tended to become gruff and surly. Now he stated in an uncompromising voice, "The subject is of small import."

Ildefonse was not to be deterred. "Here the pragmatic Hurtiancz and I, the man of many parts, are at variance. I was about to carry my argument a step farther, and in fact I will do so, stimulated as I am by this elixir of a vanished race. I therefore suggest that in the style of the previous examples, a natural scientist, examining a single atom, might well be able to asseverate the structure and history of the entire universe!"

"Bah!" muttered Hurtiancz. "By the same token, a sensible man need listen to but a single word in order to recognize the whole for egregious nonsense."

Ildefonse, absorbed in his theories, paid no heed. Herark took occasion to state that in his opinion not one, but at least two, even better, three of any class of objects was essential to understanding. "I cite the discipline of mathematics, where a series may not be determined by less than three terms."

"I willingly grant the scientist his three atoms," said Ildefonse, "though in the strictest sense, two of these are supererogatory."

Rhialto, rising from his slab, went to look into a dirt-choked aperture, to discover a passage descending by broad steps into the ground. He caused an illumination to proceed before him and descended the steps. The passage turned once, turned twice, then opened into a large chamber paved with brown stone. The walls held a number of niches, six feet long, two feet high, three feet deep; peering into one of these Rhialto discovered a skeleton of most curious structure, so fragile that the impact of Rhialto's gaze caused it to collapse into dust.

Rhialto rubbed his chin. He looked into a second niche to discover a similar skeleton. He backed away, and stood musing a moment or

two. Then he returned up the steps, the drone of Ildefonse's voice growing progressively louder: "—in the same manner to the question: Why
does the universe end here and not a mile farther? Of all questions,
Why? is the least pertinent. It begs the question: it assumes the larger
part of its own response; to wit, that a sensible response exists."
Ildefonse paused to refresh himself, and Rhialto took occasion to relate
his discoveries in the chamber below.

"It appears to be a crypt," said Rhialto. "The walls are lined with
niches, and each contains the veriest wraith of a dead corpse."

"Indeed, indeed!" muttered Hurtiancz. He lifted the brown glass
bottle and at once put it down.

"Perhaps we are mistaken in assuming this place a tavern," Rhialto
continued. "The liquid in the bottles, rather than tipple, I believe to be
embalming fluid."

Ildefonse was not so easily diverted. "I now propound the basic and
elemental verity: What is IS. Here you have heard the basic proposition of
magic. What magician asks Why? He asks How? Why leads to stultifica-
tion; each response generates at least one other question, in this fashion:

"Question: Why does Rhialto wear a black hat with gold tassels and
a scarlet plume?

"Answer: Because he hopes to improve his semblance.

"Question: Why does he want to improve his semblance?

"Answer: Because he craves the admiration and envy of his fellows.

"Question: Why does he crave admiration?

"Answer: Because, as a man, he is a social animal.

"Question: Why is Man a social animal?

"So go the questions and responses, expanding to infinity.
Therefore—"

In a passion Hurtiancz leapt to his feet. Raising the brown glass pot
above his head he dashed it to the floor. "Enough of this intolerable
inanity! I propose that such loquacity passes beyond the scope of nuisance and over the verge of turpitude."

"It is a fine point," said Herark. "Ildefonse, what have you to say on
this score?"

"I am more inclined to punish Hurtiancz for his crassness," said
Ildefonse. "But now he simulates a swinish stupidity to escape my anger."

"Absolute falsity!" roared Hurtiancz. "I simulate nothing!"

Ildefonse shrugged. "For all his deficiencies as polemicist and magician, Hurtiancz at least is candid."

Hurtiancz controlled his fury. He said, "Who could defeat your volubility? As a magician, however, I outmatch your bumbling skills as Rhialto the Marvellous exceeds your rheumy decrepitude."

Ildefonse in his turn became angry. "A test!" He flung up his hand; the massive blocks scattered in all directions; they stood on a vacant floor in the full glare of sunlight. "What of that?"

"Trivial," said Hurtiancz. "Match this!" He held up his two hands; from each finger issued a jet of vivid smoke in ten different colors.

"The pretty prank of a charlatan," declared Ildefonse. "Now watch! I utter a word: 'Roof!'" The word leaving his lips hesitated in the air, in the form of symbol, then moved out in a wide circle, to impinge upon the roof of one of the strangely styled structures still extant. The symbol disappeared; the roof glowed a vivid orange and melted to spawn a thousand symbols like the word Ildefonse had sent forth. These darted high in the sky, stopped short, disappeared. From above, like a great clap of thunder, came Ildefonse's voice: "ROOF!"

"No great matter," stated Hurtiancz. "Now—"

"Hist!" said Mune the Mage. "Cease your drunken quarrel. Look yonder!"

From the structure whose roof Ildefonse had demolished came a man.

9

The man stood in the doorway. He was impressively tall. A long white beard hung down his chest; white hair covered his ears; his eyes glittered black. He wore an elegant caftan woven in patterns of dark red, brown, black and blue. Now he stepped forward, and it could be seen that he trailed a cloud of glowing objects. Gilgad, who had returned from the plaza, instantly set up a shout: "The IOUN stones!"

The man came forward. His face showed an expression of calm inquiry. Ildefonse muttered, "It is Morreion! Of this there can be no doubt. The stature, the stance—they are unmistakable!"

"It is Morreion," Rhialto agreed. "But why is he so calm, as if each week he received visitors who took off his roof, as if 'Nothing' loomed over someone else?"

"His perceptions may have become somewhat dulled," Herark suggested. "Notice: he evinces no signal of human recognition."

Morreion came slowly forward, the IOUN stones swirling in his wake. The magicians gathered before the marble steps of the palace. Vermoulian stepped forth and raised his hand. "Hail, Morreion! We have come to take you from this intolerable isolation!"

Morreion looked from one face to the other. He made a guttural sound, then a rasping croak, as if trying organs whose use he had long forgotten.

Ildefonse now presented himself. "Morreion, my comrade! It is I, Ildefonse; do you not remember the old days at Kammerbrand? Speak then!"

"I hear," croaked Morreion. "I speak, but I do not remember."

Vermoulian indicated the marble stairs. "Step aboard, if you will; we depart this dreary world at once."

Morreion made no move. He examined the palace with a frown of vexation. "You have placed your flying hut upon the area where I dry my skeins."

Ildefonse pointed toward the black wall, which through the haze of the atmosphere showed only as a portentous shadow. "'Nothing' looms close. It is about to impinge upon this world, whereupon you will be no more; in short, you will be dead."

"I am not clear as to your meaning," said Morreion. "If you will excuse me, I must be away and about my affairs."

"A quick question before you go," spoke Gilgad. "Where does one find IOUN stones?"

Morreion looked at him without comprehension. At last he gave his attention to the stones, which swirled with a swifter motion. In comparison, those of the archveult Xexamedes were listless and dull. These danced and curveted, and sparkled with different colors. Closest to Morreion's head moved the lavender and the pale green stones, as if they thought themselves the most loved and most privileged. Somewhat more wayward were the stones glowing pink and green together; then came stones of a proud pure pink, then the royal carmine stones, then the red and blue; and finally, at the outer periphery, a number of stones glittering with intense blue lights.

As Morreion cogitated, the magicians noted a peculiar circumstance: certain of the innermost lavender stones lost their glow and became as dull as the stones of Xexamedes.

Morreion gave a slow thoughtful nod. "Curious! So much which I seem to have forgotten...I did not always live here," he said in a voice of surprise. "There was at one time another place. The memory is dim and remote."

Vermoulian said, "That place is Earth! It is where we will take you."

Morreion smilingly shook his head. "I am just about to start on an important journey."

"Is the trip absolutely necessary?" inquired Mune the Mage. "Our time is limited, and even more to the point, we do not care to be engulfed in 'Nothing'."

"I must see to my cairns," said Morreion in a mild but definite manner.

For a moment there was silence. Then Ildefonse asked, "What is the purpose of these cairns?"

Morreion used the even voice of one speaking to a child. "They indicate the most expeditious route around my world. Without the cairns it is possible to go astray."

"But remember, there is no longer need for such landmarks," said Ao of the Opals. "You will be returning to Earth with us!"

Morreion could not restrain a small laugh at the obtuse persistence of his visitors. "Who would look after my properties? How could I fare if my cairns toppled, if my looms broke, if my kilns crumbled, if my other enterprises dissolved, and all for the lack of methodical care?"

Vermoulian said blandly, "At least come aboard the palace to share our evening banquet."

"It will be my pleasure," replied Morreion. He mounted the marble steps, to gaze with pleasure around the pavilion. "Charming. I must consider something of this nature as a forecourt for my new mansion."

"There will be insufficient time," Rhialto told him.

"'Time'?" Morreion frowned as if the word were unfamiliar to him. Other of the lavender stones suddenly went pale. "Time indeed! But time is required to do a proper job! This gown for instance." He indicated his gorgeously patterned caftan. "The weaving required four years. Before that I gathered beast-fur for ten years; then for another two years I bleached and dyed and spun. My cairns were built a stone at a time, each time I wandered around the world. My wanderlust has waned somewhat, but I occasionally make the journey, to rebuild where necessary, and to note the changes of the landscape."

Rhialto pointed to the sun. "Do you recognize the nature of that object?"

Morreion frowned. "I call it 'the sun'—though why I have chosen this particular term escapes me."

"There are many such suns," said Rhialto. "Around one of them swings that ancient and remarkable world which gave you birth. Do you remember Earth?"

Morreion looked dubiously up into the sky. "I have seen none of these other suns you describe. At night my sky is quite dark; there is no other light the world over save the glow of my fires. It is a peaceful world indeed...I seem to recall more eventful times." The last of the lavender stones and certain of the green stones lost their color. Morreion's eyes became momentarily intent. He went to inspect the tame water-nymphs which sported in the central fountain. "And what might be these glossy little creatures? They are most appealing."

"They are quite fragile, and useful only as show," said Vermoulian. "Come, Morreion, my valet will help you prepare for the banquet."

"You are most gracious," said Morreion.

10

The magicians awaited their guest in the grand salon. Each had his own opinion of the circumstances. Rhialto said, "Best that we raise the palace now and so be off and away. Morreion may be agitated for a period, but when all the facts are laid before him he must surely see reason."

The cautious Perdustin demurred. "There is power in the man! At one time, his magic was a source of awe and wonder; what if in a fit of pique he wreaks a harm upon all of us?"

Gilgad endorsed Perdustin's view. "Everyone has noted Morreion's IOUN stones. Where did he acquire them? Can this world be the source?"

"Such a possibility should not automatically be dismissed," admitted Ildefonse. "Tomorrow, when the imminence of 'Nothing' is described, Morreion will surely depart without resentment."

So the matter rested. The magicians turned their discussion to other aspects of this dismal world.

Herark the Harbinger, who had skill as a cognizancer, attempted to divine the nature of the race which had left ruins across the planet, without notable success. "They have been gone too long; their influence has waned. I seem to discern creatures with thin white legs and large green eyes...I hear a whisper of their music: a jingling, a tinkle, to a rather plaintive obbligato of pipes...I sense no magic. I doubt if they recognized the IOUN stones, if in fact such exist on this planet."

"Where else could they originate?" demanded Gilgad.

"The 'shining fields' are nowhere evident," remarked Haze of Wheary Water.

Morreion entered the hall. His appearance had undergone a dramatic change. The great white beard had been shaved away; his bush of hair had been cropped to a more modish style. In the place of his gorgeous caftan he wore a garment of ivory silk with a blue sash and a pair of scarlet slippers. Morreion now stood revealed as a tall spare man, attentive and alert. Glittering black eyes dominated his face, which was taut, harsh at chin and jaw, massive of forehead, disciplined in the even lines of the mouth. The lethargy and boredom of so many aeons were nowhere evident; he moved with easy command, and behind him, darting and circling, swarmed the IOUN stones.

Morreion greeted the assembled magicians with an inclination of the head, and gave his attention to the appointments of the salon. "Magnificent and luxurious! But I will be forced to use quartz in the place of this splendid marble, and there is little silver to be found; the Sahars plundered all the surface ores. When I need metal I must tunnel deep underground."

"You have led a busy existence," declared Ildefonse. "And who were the Sahars?"

"The race whose ruins mar the landscape. A frivolous and irresponsible folk, though I admit that I find their poetic conundrums amusing."

"The Sahars still exist?"

"Indeed not! They became extinct long ages ago. But they left numerous records etched on bronze, which I have taken occasion to translate."

"A tedious job, surely!" exclaimed Zilifant. "How did you achieve so complicated a task?"

"By the process of elimination," Morreion explained. "I tested a succession of imaginary languages against the inscriptions, and in due course I found a correspondence. As you say, the task was time-consuming; still I have had much entertainment from the Sahar chronicles. I want to orchestrate their musical revelries; but this is a task for the future, perhaps after I complete the palace I now intend."

Ildefonse spoke in a grave voice. "Morreion, it becomes necessary to impress certain important matters upon you. You state that you have not studied the heavens?"

"Not extensively," admitted Morreion. "There is little to be seen save the sun, and under favorable conditions a great wall of impenetrable blackness."

"That wall of blackness," said Ildefonse, "is 'Nothing', toward which your world is inexorably drifting. Any further work here is futile."

Morreion's black eyes glittered with doubt and suspicion. "Can you prove this assertion?"

"Certainly. Indeed we came here from Earth to rescue you."

Morreion frowned. Certain of the green stones abruptly lost their color. "Why did you delay so long?"

Ao of the Opals gave a bray of nervous laughter, which he quickly stifled. Ildefonse turned him a furious glare.

"Only recently were we made aware of your plight," explained Rhialto. "Upon that instant we prevailed upon Vermoulian to bring us hither in his peregrine palace."

Vermoulian's bland face creased in displeasure. "'Prevailed' is not correct!" he stated. "I was already on my way when the others insisted on coming along. And now, if you will excuse us for a few moments, Morreion and I have certain important matters to discuss."

"Not so fast," Gilgad cried out. "I am equally anxious to learn the source of the stones."

Ildefonse said, "I will put the question in the presence of us all. Morreion, where did you acquire your IOUN stones?"

Morreion looked around at the stones. "To be candid, the facts are somewhat vague. I seem to recall a vast shining surface...But why do you ask? They have no great usefulness. So many ideas throng upon me. It seems that I had enemies at one time, and false friends. I must try to remember."

Ildefonse said, "At the moment you are among your faithful friends, the magicians of Earth. And if I am not mistaken, the noble Vermoulian is about to set before us the noblest repast in any of our memories!"

Morreion said with a sour smile, "You must think my life that of a savage. Not so! I have studied the Sahar cuisine and improved upon it! The lichen which covers the plain may be prepared in at least one hundred seventy fashions. The turf beneath is the home of succulent helminths. For all its drab monotony, this world provides a bounty. If what you say is true, I shall be sorry indeed to leave."

"The facts cannot be ignored," said Ildefonse. "The IOUN stones, so I suppose, derive from the northern part of this world?"

"I believe not."

"The southern area, then?"

"I rarely visit this section; the lichen is thin; the helminths are all gristle."

A gong-stroke sounded; Vermoulian ushered the company into the dining room, where the great table glittered with silver and crystal. The magicians seated themselves under the five chandeliers; in deference to his guest who had lived so long in solitude, Vermoulian refrained from calling forth the beautiful women of ancient eras.

Morreion ate with caution, tasting all set before him, comparing the dishes to the various guises of lichen upon which he usually subsisted. "I had almost forgotten the existence of such food," he said at last. "I am reminded, dimly, of other such feasts—so long ago, so long...Where have the years gone? Which is the dream?" As he mused, some of the pink and green stones lost their color. Morreion sighed. "There is much to be learned, much to be remembered. Certain faces here arouse flickering recollections; have I known them before?"

"You will recall all in due course," said the diabolist Shrue. "And now, if we are certain that the IOUN stones are not to be found on this planet—"

"But we are not sure!" snapped Gilgad. "We must seek, we must search; no effort is too arduous!"

"The first to be found necessarily will go to satisfy my claims," declared Rhialto. "This must be a definite understanding."

Gilgad thrust his vulpine face forward. "What nonsense is this? Your claims were satisfied by a choice from the effects of the archveult Xexamedes!"

Morreion jerked around. "The archveult Xexamedes! I know this name...How? Where? Long ago I knew an archveult Xexamedes; he was my foe, or so it seems...Ah, the ideas which roil my mind!" The pink and green stones all had lost their color. Morreion groaned and put his hands to his head. "Before you came my life was placid; you have brought me doubt and wonder."

"Doubt and wonder are the lot of all men," said Ildefonse. "Magicians are not excluded. Are you ready to leave Sahar Planet?"

Morreion sat looking into a goblet of wine. "I must collect my books. They are all I wish to take away."

11

Morreion conducted the magicians about his premises. The structures which had seemed miraculous survivals had in fact been built by Morreion, after one or another mode of the Sahar architecture. He displayed his three looms: the first for fine weaves, linens and silks; the second where he contrived patterned cloths; the third where his heavy rugs were woven. The same structure housed vats, dyes, bleaches and mordants. Another building contained the glass cauldron, as well as the kilns where Morreion produced earthenware pots, plates, lamps and tiles. His forge in the same building showed little use. "The Sahars scoured the planet clean of ores. I mine only what I consider indispensable, which is not a great deal."

Morreion took the group to his library, in which were housed many Sahar originals as well as books Morreion had written and illuminated with his own hand: translations of the Sahar classics, an encyclopedia of natural history, ruminations and speculations, a descriptive geography of the planet with appended maps. Vermoulian ordered his staff to transfer the articles to the palace.

Morreion turned a last look around the landscape he had known so long and had come to love. Then without a word he went to the palace and climbed the marble steps. In a subdued mood the magicians followed. Vermoulian went at once to the control belvedere where he performed rites of buoyancy. The palace floated up from the final planet.

Ildefonse gave an exclamation of shock. "'Nothing' is close at hand—more imminent than we had suspected!"

The black wall loomed startlingly near; the last star and its single world drifted at the very brink.

"The perspectives are by no means clear," said Ildefonse. "There is no sure way of judging but it seems that we left not an hour too soon."

"Let us wait and watch," suggested Herark. "Morreion can learn our good faith for himself."

So the palace hung in space, with the pallid light of the doomed sun playing upon the five crystal spires, projecting long shadows behind the magicians where they stood by the balustrade.

The Sahar world was first to encounter 'Nothing'. It grazed against the enigmatic nonsubstance, then urged by a component of orbital motion, a quarter of the original sphere moved out clear and free: a moundlike object with a precisely flat base, where the hitherto secret strata, zones, folds, intrusions and core were displayed to sight. The sun reached 'Nothing'; it touched, advanced. It became a half-orange on a black mirror, then sank away from reality. Darkness shrouded the palace.

In the belvedere Vermoulian indited symbols on the mandate-wheel. He struck them off, then put double fire to the speed-incense. The palace glided away, back towards the star-clouds.

Morreion turned away from the balustrade and went into the great hall, where he sat deep in thought.

Gilgad presently approached him. "Perhaps you have recalled the source of the IOUN stones?"

Morreion rose to his feet. He turned his level black eyes upon Gilgad, who stepped back a pace. The pink and green stones had long become pallid, and many of the pink as well.

Morreion's face was stern and cold. "I recall much! There was a cabal of enemies who tricked me—but all is as dim as the film of stars which hangs across far space. In some fashion, the stones are part and parcel of the matter. Why do you evince so large an interest in stones? Were you one of my former enemies? Is this the case with all of you? If so, beware! I am a mild man until I encounter antagonism."

The diabolist Shrue spoke soothingly. "We are not your enemies! Had we not lifted you from Sahar Planet, you would now be with 'Nothing'. Is that not proof?"

Morreion gave a grim nod; but he no longer seemed the mild and affable man they had first encountered.

To restore the previous amiability, Vermoulian hastened to the room of faded mirrors where he maintained his vast collection of beautiful women in the form of matrices. These could be activated into corporeality by a simple antinegative incantation; and presently from the room, one after the other, stepped those delightful confections of the past which Vermoulian had seen fit to revivify. On each occasion they came forth fresh, without recollection of previous manifestations; each appearance was new, no matter how affairs had gone before.

Among those whom Vermoulian had called forth was the graceful Mersei. She stepped into the grand salon, blinking in the bewilderment common to those evoked from the past. She stopped short in amazement, then with quick steps ran forward. "Morreion! What do you do here? They told us you had gone against the archveults, that you had been killed! By the Sacred Ray, you are sound and whole!"

Morreion looked down at the young woman in perplexity. The pink and red stones wheeled around his head. "Somewhere I have seen you; somewhere I have known you."

"I am Mersei! Do you not remember? You brought me a red rose growing in a porcelain vase. Oh, what have I done with it? I always keep it near...But where am I? Where is the rose? No matter. I am here and you are here."

Ildefonse muttered to Vermoulian, "An irresponsible act, in my judgment; why were you not more cautious?"

Vermoulian pursed his lips in vexation. "She stems from the waning of the 21st Aeon but I had not anticipated anything like this!"

"I suggest that you call her back into your room of matrices and there reduce her. Morreion seems to be undergoing a period of instability; he needs peace and quietude; best not to introduce stimulations so unpredictable."

Vermoulian strolled across the room. "Mersei, my dear; would you be good enough to step this way?"

Mersei cast him a dubious look, then beseeched Morreion: "Do you not know me? Something is very strange; I can understand nothing of this—it is like a dream. Morreion, am I dreaming?"

"Come, Mersei," said Vermoulian suavely. "I wish a word with you."

"Stop!" spoke Morreion. "Magician, stand back; this fragrant creature is something which once I loved, at a time far gone."

The girl cried in a poignant voice: "A time far gone? It was no more than yesterday! I tended the sweet red rose, I looked at the sky; they had sent you to Jangk, by the red star Kerkaju, the eye of the Polar Ape. And now you are here, and I am here—what does it mean?"

"Inadvisable, inadvisable," muttered Ildefonse. He called out: "Morreion, this way, if you will. I see a curious concatenation of galaxies. Perhaps here is the new home of the Sahars."

Morreion put his hand to the girl's shoulder. He looked into her face. "The sweet red rose blooms, and forever. We are among magicians and strange events occur." He glanced aside at Vermoulian, then back to Mersei. "At this moment, go with Vermoulian the Dream-walker, who will show you to your chamber."

"Yes, dear Morreion, but when will I see you again? You look so strange, so strained and old, and you speak so peculiarly—"

"Go now, Mersei. I must confer with Ildefonse."

Vermoulian led Mersei back towards the room of matrices. At this door she hesitated and looked back over her shoulder, but Morreion had already turned away. She followed Vermoulian into the room. The door closed behind them.

Morreion walked out on the pavilion, past the dark lime trees with their silver fruit, and leaned upon the balustrade. The sky was still dark, although ahead and below a few vagrant galaxies could now be seen.

Morreion put his hand to his head; the pink stones and certain of the red stones lost their color.

Morreion swung around towards Ildefonse and those other magicians who had silently come out on the pavilion. He stepped forward, the IOUN stones tumbling one after the other in their hurry to keep up. Some were yet red, some showed shifting glints of blue and red, some burnt a cold incandescent blue. All the others had become the color of pearl. One of these drifted in front of Morreion's eyes; he caught it, gave it a moment of frowning inspection, then tossed it into the air. Spinning and jerking, with color momentarily restored, it was quick to rejoin the others, like a child embarrassed.

"Memory comes and goes," mused Morreion. "I am unsettled, in mind and heart. Faces drift before my eyes; they fade once more; other events move into a region of clarity. The archveults, the IOUN stones—I know something of these, though much is dim and murky, so best that I hold my tongue—"

"By no means!" declared Ao of the Opals. "We are interested in your experiences."

"To be sure!" said Gilgad.

Morreion's mouth twisted in a smile that was both sardonic and harsh, and also somewhat melancholy. "Very well, I tell this story, then, as if I were telling a dream.

"It seems that I was sent to Jangk on a mission—perhaps to learn the provenance of the IOUN stones? Perhaps. I hear whispers which tell me so much; it well may be...I arrived at Jangk; I recall the landscape well. I remember a remarkable castle hollowed from an enormous pink pearl. In this castle I confronted the archveults. They feared me and stood back, and when I stated my wishes there was no demur. They would indeed take me to gather stones, and so we set out, flying through space in an equipage whose nature I cannot recall. The archveults were silent and watched me from the side of their eyes; then they became affable and I wondered at their mirth. But I felt no fear. I knew all their magic; I carried counter-spells at my fingernails, and at need could fling them off instantly. So we crossed space, with the archveults laughing and joking in what I considered an insane fashion. I ordered them to stop. They halted instantly and sat staring at me.

"We arrived at the edge of the universe, and came down upon a sad cinder of a world; a dreadful place. Here we waited in a region of burnt-out star-hulks, some still hot, some cold, some cinders like the world on which we stood—perhaps it, too, was a dead star. Occasionally we saw the corpses of dwarf stars, glistening balls of stuff so heavy that a speck outweighs an Earthly mountain. I saw such objects no more than ten miles across, containing the matter of a sun like vast Kerkaju. Inside these dead stars, the archveults told me, were to be found the IOUN stones. And how were they to be won? I asked. Must we drive a tunnel into that gleaming surface? They gave mocking calls of laughter at my ignorance; I uttered a sharp reprimand; instantly they fell silent. The spokesman was Xexamedes. From him I learned that no power known to man or magician could mar stuff so dense! We must wait.

"'Nothing' loomed across the distance. Often the derelict hulks swung close in their orbits. The archveults kept close watch; they pointed and calculated, they carped and fretted; at last one of the shining balls struck across 'Nothing', expunging half of itself. When it swung out and away the archveults took their equipage down to the flat surface. All now ventured forth, with most careful precaution; unprotected from gravity a man instantly becomes as no more than an outline upon the surface. With slide-boards immune to gravity we traversed the surface.

"What a wonderful sight! 'Nothing' had wrought a flawless polish; for fifteen miles this mirrored plain extended, marred only at the very center by a number of black pock-marks. Here the IOUN stones were to be found, in nests of black dust.

"To win the stones is no small task. The black dust, like the slide-boards, counters gravity. It is safe to step from the slide-boards to the dust, but a new precaution must be taken. While the dust negates the substance below, other celestial objects suck, so one must use an anchor to hold himself in place. The archveults drive small barbed hooks into the dust, and tie themselves down with a cord, and this I did as well. By means of a special tool the dust is probed—a tedious task! The dust is packed tightly! Nevertheless, with great energy I set to work and in due course won my first IOUN stone. I held it high in exultation, but where were the archveults? They had circled around me; they had returned to the equipage! I sought my slide-boards—in vain! By stealth they had been purloined!

"I staggered, I sagged; I raved a spell at the traitors. They held forward their newly won IOUN stones; the magic was absorbed, as water entering a sponge.

"With no further words, not even signals of triumph—for this is how lightly they regarded me—they entered their equipage and were gone. In this region contiguous with 'Nothing', my doom was certain—so they were assured."

As Morreion spoke the red stones went pale; his voice quavered with a passion he had not hitherto displayed.

"I stood alone," said Morreion hoarsely. "I could not die, with the Spell of Untiring Nourishment upon me, but I could not move a step, not an inch from the cavity of black dust, or I would instantly have been no more than a print upon the surface of the shining field.

"I stood rigid—how long I cannot say. Years? Decades? I cannot remember. This period seems a time of dull daze. I searched my mind for resources, and I grew bold with despair. I probed for IOUN stones, and I won those which now attend me. They became my friends and gave me solace.

"I embarked then upon a new task, which, had I not been mad with despair, I would never have attempted. I brought up particles of black dust, wet them with blood to make a paste; this paste I molded into a circular plate four feet in diameter.

"It was finished. I stepped aboard; I anchored myself with the barbed pins, and I floated up and away from the half-star.

"I had won free! I stood on my disk in the void! I was free, but I was alone. You cannot know what I felt until you, too, have stood in space, without knowledge of where to go. Far away I saw a single star; a rogue, a wanderer; toward this star I fared.

"How long the voyage required, again I cannot say. When I judged that I had traveled half-way, I turned the disk about and slowed my motion.

"Of this voyage I remember little. I spoke to my stones, I gave them my thoughts. I seemed to become calm from talking, for during the first hundred years of this voyage I felt a prodigious fury that seemed to overwhelm all rational thought; to inflict but a pin prick upon a single one of my adversaries I would have died by torture a hundred times! I plotted delicious vengeance, I became yeasty and exuberant upon the imagined pain I would inflict. Then at times I suffered unutterable melancholy—while others enjoyed the good things of life, the feasts, the comradeship, the caresses of their loved ones, here stood I, alone in the dark. The balance would be restored, I assured myself. My enemies would suffer as I had suffered, and more! But the passion waned, and as my stones grew to know me they assumed their beautiful colors. Each has his name; each is individual; I know each stone by its motion. The archveults consider them the brain-eggs of fire-folk who live within these stars; as to this I cannot say.

"At last I came down upon my world. I had burned away my rage. I was calm and placid, as now you know me. My old lust for revenge I saw to be futility. I turned my mind to a new existence, and over the aeons I built my buildings and my cairns; I lived my new life.

"The Sahars excited my interest. I read their books, I learned their lore…Perhaps I began to live a dream. My old life was far away; a discordant trifle to which I gave ever less importance. I am amazed that the language of Earth returned to me as readily as it has. Perhaps the stones held my knowledge in trust, and extended it as the need came. Ah, my wonderful stones, what would I be without them?

"Now I am back among men. I know how my life has gone. There are still confused areas; in due course I will remember all."

Morreion paused to consider; several of the blue and scarlet stones went quickly dim. Morreion quivered, as if touched by galvanic essence; his cropped white hair seemed to bristle. He took a slow step forward; certain of the magicians made uneasy movements.

Morreion spoke in a new voice, one less reflective and reminiscent, with a harsh grating sound somewhere at its basis. "Now I will confide in you." He turned the glitter of his black eyes upon each face in turn. "I intimated that my rage had waned with the aeons; this is true. The sobs which lacerated my throat, the gnashing which broke my teeth, the fury which caused my brain to shudder and ache: all dwindled; for I had nothing with which to feed my emotions. After bitter reflection came tragic melancholy, then at last peace, which your coming disturbed.

"A new mood has now come upon me! As the past becomes real, so I have returned along the way of the past. There is a difference. I am now a cold cautious man; perhaps I can never experience the extremes of passion which once consumed me. On the other hand, certain periods in my life are still dim." Another of the red and scarlet stones lost its vivid glow; Morreion stiffened, his voice took on a new edge. "The crimes upon my person call out for rebuttal! The archveults of Jangk must pay in the fullest and most onerous measure! Vermoulian the Dream-walker, expunge the present symbols from your mandate-wheel! Our destination now becomes the planet Jangk!"

Vermoulian looked to his colleagues to learn their opinion.

Ildefonse cleared his throat. "I suggest that our host Vermoulian first pause at Earth, to discharge those of us with urgent business. Those others will continue with Vermoulian and Morreion to Jangk; in this way the convenience of all may be served."

Morreion said in a voice ominously quiet: "No business is as urgent as mine, which already has been delayed too long." He spoke to Vermoulian: "Apply more fire to the speed-incense! Proceed directly to Jangk."

Haze of Wheary Water said diffidently, "I would be remiss if I failed to remind you that the archveults are powerful magicians; like yourself they wield IOUN stones."

Morreion made a furious motion; as his hand swept the air, it left a trail of sparks. "Magic derives from personal force! My passion alone will defeat the archveults! I glory in the forthcoming confrontation. Ah, but they will regret their deeds!"

"Forbearance has been termed the noblest of virtues," Ildefonse suggested. "The archveults have long forgotten your very existence; your vengeance will seem an unjust and unnecessary tribulation."

Morreion swung around his glittering black gaze. "I reject the concept. Vermoulian, obey!"

"We fare towards Jangk," said Vermoulian.

12

On a marble bench between a pair of silver-fruited lime trees sat Ildefonse. Rhialto stood beside him, one elegant leg raised to the bench; a posture which displayed his rose satin cape with the white lining to dramatic advantage. They drifted through a cluster of a thousand stars; great lights passed above, below, to each side; the crystal spires of the palace gave back millions of scintillations.

Rhialto had already expressed his concern at the direction of events. Now he spoke again, more emphatically. "It is all very well to point out that the man lacks facility; as he asserts, sheer force can overpower sophistication."

Ildefonse said bluffly, "Morreion's force is that of hysteria, diffuse and undirected."

"Therein lies the danger! What if by some freak his wrath focuses upon us?"

"Bah, what then?" demanded Ildefonse. "Do you doubt my ability, or your own?"

"The prudent man anticipates contingencies," said Rhialto with dignity. "Remember, a certain area of Morreion's life remains clouded."

Ildefonse tugged thoughtfully at his white beard. "The aeons have altered all of us; Morreion not the least of any."

"This is the core of my meaning," said Rhialto. "I might mention that not an hour since I essayed a small experiment. Morreion walked the third balcony, watching the stars pass by. His attention being diverted, I took occasion to project a minor spell of annoyance towards him—Houlart's Visceral Pang—but with no perceptible effect. Next I attempted the diminutive version of Lugwiler's Dismal Itch, again without success. I noted, however, his IOUN stones pulsed bright as they absorbed the magic. I tried my own Green Turmoil; the stones glowed bright and this time Morreion became aware of the attention. By happy chance Byzant the Necrope passed by. Morreion put an accusation upon him, which Byzant denied. I left them engaged in contention. The instruction is this: first, Morreion's stones guard him from hostile magic; second, he is vigilant and suspicious; third, he is not one to shrug aside an offense."

Ildefonse nodded gravely. "We must certainly take these matters into consideration. I now appreciate the scope of Xexamedes' plan: he intended harm to all. But behold in the sky yonder! Is that not the constellation Elektha, seen from obverse? We are in familiar precincts once more. Kerkaju must lie close ahead, and with it that extraordinary planet Jangk."

The two strolled to the forward part of the pavilion. "You are right!" exclaimed Rhialto. He pointed. "There is Kerkaju; I recognize its scarlet empharism!"

The planet Jangk appeared: a world with a curious dull sheen.

At Morreion's direction, Vermoulian directed the palace down to Smokedancers Bluff, at the southern shore of the Quicksilver Ocean. Guarding themselves against the poisonous air, the magicians descended the marble steps and walked out on the bluff, where an inspiring vista spread before them. Monstrous Kerkaju bulged across the green sky, every pore and flocculation distinct, its simulacrum mirrored in the Quicksilver Ocean. Directly below, at the base of the bluff, quicksilver puddled and trickled across flats of black hornblende; here the Jangk 'dragoons'—purple pansy-shaped creatures six feet in diameter—grazed on tufts of moss. Somewhat to the east the town Kaleshe descended in terraces to the shore.

Morreion, standing at the edge of the bluff, inhaled the noxious vapors which blew in from the ocean, as if they were a tonic. "My memory quickens," he called out. "I remember this scene as if it were yesterday. There have been changes, true. Yonder far peak has eroded to half its height; the bluffs on which we stand have been thrust upwards at least a hundred feet. Has it been so long? While I built my cairns and pored over my books the aeons flitted past. Not to mention the unknown period I rode through space on a disk of blood and star-stuff. Let us proceed to Kaleshe; it was formerly the haunt of the archveult Persain."

"When you encounter your enemies, what then?" asked Rhialto. "Are your spells prepared and ready?"

"What need I for spells?" grated Morreion. "Behold!" He pointed his finger; a flicker of emotion spurted forth to shatter a boulder. He clenched his fists; the constricted passion cracked as if he had crumpled stiff parchment. He strode off toward Kaleshe, the magicians trooping behind.

The Kalsh had seen the palace descend; a number had gathered at the top of the bluff. Like the archveults they were sheathed in pale blue scales. Osmium cords constricted the black plumes of the men; the feathery green plumes of the women, however, waved and swayed as they walked. All stood seven feet tall, and were slim as lizards.

Morreion halted. "Persain, stand forth!" he called.

One of the men spoke: "There is no Persain at Kaleshe."

"What? No archveult Persain?"

"None of this name. The local archveult is a certain Evorix, who departed in haste at the sight of your peregrine palace."

"Who keeps the town records?"

Another Kalsh stepped forth. "I am that functionary."

"Are you acquainted with Persain the archveult?"

"I know by repute a Persain who was swallowed by a harpy towards the end of the 21st Aeon."

Morreion uttered a groan. "Has he evaded me? What of Xexamedes?"

"He is gone from Jangk; no one knows where."

"Djorin?"

"He lives, but keeps to a pink pearl castle across the ocean."

"Aha! What of Ospro?"

"Dead."

Morreion gave another abysmal groan. "Vexel?"

"Dead."

Morreion groaned once more. Name by name he ran down the roster of his enemies. Four only survived.

When Morreion turned about his face had become haunted and haggard; he seemed not to see the magicians of Earth. All of his scarlet and blue stones had given up their color. "Four only," he muttered. "Four only to receive the charge of all my force…Not enough, not enough! So many have won free! Not enough, not enough! The balance must adjust!" He made a brusque gesture. "Come! To the castle of Djorin!"

In the palace they drifted across the ocean while the great red globe of Kerkaju kept pace above and below. Cliffs of mottled quartz and cinnabar rose ahead; on a crag jutting over the ocean stood a castle in the shape of a great pink pearl.

The peregrine palace settled upon a level area; Morreion leapt down the steps and advanced toward the castle. A circular door of solid osmium rolled back; an archveult nine feet tall, with black plumes waving three feet over his head, came forth.

Morreion called, "Send forth Djorin; I have dealings with him."

"Djorin is within! We have had a presentiment! You are the land-ape Morreion, from the far past. Be warned; we are prepared for you."

"Djorin!" called Morreion. "Come forth!"

"Djorin will not come forth," stated the archveult, "nor will Arvianid, Ishix, Herclamon, or the other archveults of Jangk who have come to combine their power against yours. If you seek vengeance, turn upon the real culprits; do not annoy us with your peevish complaints." The archveult returned within and the osmium door rolled shut.

Morreion stood stock-still. Mune the Mage came forward, and stated: "I will winkle them out, with Houlart's Blue Extractive." He hurled the spell toward the castle, to no effect. Rhialto attempted a spell of brain pullulations, but the magic was absorbed; Gilgad next brought down his Instantaneous Galvanic Thrust, which spattered harmlessly off the glossy pink surface.

"Useless," said Ildefonse. "Their IOUN stones absorb the magic."

The archveults in their turn became active. Three ports opened; three spells simultaneously issued forth, to be intercepted by Morreion's IOUN stones, which momentarily pulsed the brighter.

Morreion stepped three paces forward. He pointed his finger; force struck at the osmium door. It creaked and rattled, but held firm.

Morreion pointed his finger at the fragile pink nacre; the force slid away and was wasted.

Morreion pointed at the stone posts which supported the castle. They burst apart. The castle lurched, rolled over and down the crags. It bounced from jut to jut, smashing and shattering, and splashed into the Quicksilver Ocean, where a current caught it and carried it out to sea. Through rents in the nacre the archveults crawled forth, to clamber to the top. More followed, until their accumulated weight rolled the pearl over, throwing all on top into the quicksilver sea, where they sank as deep as their thighs. Some tried to walk and leap to the shore, others lay flat on their backs and sculled with their hands. A gust of wind caught the pink bubble and sent it rolling across the sea, tossing off archveults as a turning wheel flings away drops of water. A band of Jangk harpies put out from the shore to envelop and devour the archveults closest at hand; the others allowed themselves to drift on the current and out to sea, where they were lost to view.

Morreion turned slowly toward the magicians of Earth. His face was gray. "A fiasco," he muttered. "It is nothing."

Slowly he walked toward the palace. At the steps he stopped short. "What did they mean: 'The real culprits'?"

"A figure of speech," replied Ildefonse. "Come up on the pavilion; we will refresh ourselves with wine. At last your vengeance is complete. And now..." His voice died as Morreion climbed the steps. One of the bright blue stones lost its color. Morreion stiffened as if at a twinge of pain. He swung around to look from magician to magician. "I remember a certain face: a man with a bald head; black beardlets hung from each of his cheeks. He was a burly man...What was his name?"

"These events are far in the past," said the diabolist Shrue. "Best to put them out of mind."

Other blue stones became dull: Morreion's eyes seemed to assume the light they had lost.

"The archveults came to Earth. We conquered them. They begged for their lives. So much I recall...The chief magician demanded the secret of the IOUN stones. Ah! What was his name! He had a habit of pulling on his black beardlets...A handsome man, a great popinjay—I almost see his face—he made a proposal to the chief magician. Ah! Now it begins to come clear!" The blue stones faded one by one. Morreion's face shone with a white fire. The last of the blue stones went pallid.

Morreion spoke in a soft voice, a delicate voice, as if he savored each word. "The chief magician's name was Ildefonse. The popinjay was Rhialto. I remember each detail. Rhialto proposed that I go to learn the secret; Ildefonse vowed to protect me, as if I were his own life. I trusted them; I trusted all the magicians in the chamber: Gilgad was there, and Hurtiancz and Mune the Mage and Perdustin. All my dear friends, who joined in a solemn vow to make the archveults hostage for my safety. Now I know the culprits. The archveults dealt with me as an enemy. My friends sent me forth and never thought of me again. Ildefonse—what have you to say, before you go to wait out twenty aeons in a certain place of which I know?"

Ildefonse said bluffly, "Come now, you must not take matters so seriously. All's well that ends well; we are now happily reunited and the secret of the IOUN stones is ours!"

"For each pang I suffered, you shall suffer twenty," said Morreion. "Rhialto as well, and Gilgad, and Mune, and Herark and all the rest. Vermoulian, lift the palace. Return us the way we have come. Put double fire to the incense."

Rhialto looked at Ildefonse, who shrugged.

"Unavoidable," said Rhialto. He evoked the Spell of Temporal Stasis. Silence fell upon the scene. Each person stood like a monument.

Rhialto bound Morreion's arms to his side with swaths of tape. He strapped Morreion's ankles together, and wrapped bandages into Morreion's mouth, to prevent him uttering a sound. He found a net and, capturing the IOUN stones, drew them down about Morreion's head, in close contact with his scalp. As an afterthought he taped a blindfold over Morreion's eyes.

He could do no more. He dissolved the spell. Ildefonse was already walking across the pavilion. Morreion jerked and thrashed in disbelief. Ildefonse and Rhialto lowered him to the marble floor.

"Vermoulian," said Ildefonse, "be so good as to call forth your staff. Have them bring a trundle and convey Morreion to a dark room. He must rest for a spell."

13

Rhialto found his manse as he had left it, with the exception of the way-post, which was complete. Well satisfied, Rhialto went into one of his back rooms. Here he broke open a hole into subspace and placed therein the netful of IOUN stones which he carried. Some gleamed incandescent blue; others were mingled scarlet and blue; the rest shone deep red, pink, pink and green, pale green, and pale lavender.

Rhialto shook his head ruefully and closed the dimension down upon the stones. Returning to his work-room he located Puiras among the Minuscules and restored him to size.

"Once and for all, Puiras, I find that I no longer need your services. You may join the Minuscules, or you may take your pay and go."

Puiras gave a roar of protest. "I worked my fingers to the bone; is this all the thanks I get?"

"I do not care to argue with you; in fact, I have already engaged your replacement."

Puiras eyed the tall vague-eyed man who had wandered into the work-room. "Is this the fellow? I wish him luck. Give me my money; and none of your magic gold, which goes to sand!"

Puiras took his money and went his way. Rhialto spoke to the new servitor. "For your first task, you may clear up the wreckage of the aviary. If you find corpses, drag them to the side; I will presently dispose of them. Next, the tile of the great hall…"

AFTERWORD TO "MORREION"

I feel rather like a stage magician with a repertory of tricks; we both create illusions. Does he go to great effort to explain his techniques?

—Jack Vance 1977

THE LAST CASTLE

CHAPTER I

1

Toward the end of a stormy summer afternoon, with the sun finally breaking out under ragged black rain-clouds, Castle Janeil was overwhelmed and its population destroyed. Until almost the last moment factions among the castle clans contended as to how Destiny properly should be met. The gentlemen of most prestige and account elected to ignore the entire undignified circumstance and went about their normal pursuits, with neither more nor less punctilio than usual. A few cadets, desperate to the point of hysteria, took up weapons and prepared to resist the final assault. Still others, perhaps a quarter of the total population, waited passively, ready—almost happy—to expiate the sins of the human race. In the end, death came uniformly to all, and all extracted as much satisfaction from their dying as this essentially graceless process could afford. The proud sat turning the pages of their beautiful books, discussing the qualities of a century-old essence, or fondling a favorite Phane, and died without deigning to heed the fact. The hotheads raced up the muddy slope which, outraging all normal rationality, loomed above the parapets of Janeil. Most were buried under sliding rubble, but a few gained the ridge to gun, hack and stab, until they themselves were shot, crushed by the half-alive power-wagons, hacked or stabbed. The contrite waited in the classic posture of expiation—on their knees, heads bowed—and perished, so they

567

believed, by a process in which the Meks were symbols and human sin the reality. In the end all were dead: gentlemen, ladies, Phanes in the pavilions; Peasants in the stables. Of all those who had inhabited Janeil, only the Birds survived, creatures awkward, gauche and raucous, oblivious to pride and faith, more concerned with the wholeness of their hides than the dignity of their castle. As the Meks swarmed down over the parapets, the Birds departed their cotes and, screaming strident insults, flapped east toward Hagedorn, now the last castle of Earth.

2

Four months before, the Meks had appeared in the park before Janeil, fresh from the Sea Island massacre. Climbing to the turrets and balconies, sauntering the Sunset Promenade, from ramparts and parapets, the gentlemen and ladies of Janeil, some two thousand in all, looked down at the brown-gold warriors. Their mood was complex: amused indifference, flippant disdain, and a substratum of doubt and foreboding—all the product of three basic circumstances: their own exquisitely subtle civilization, the security provided by Janeil's walls, and the fact that they could conceive no recourse, no means for altering circumstances.

The Janeil Meks had long since departed to join the revolt; there only remained Phanes, Peasants and Birds from which to fashion what would have been the travesty of a punitive force. At the moment there seemed no need for such a force. Janeil was deemed impregnable. The walls, two hundred feet tall, were black rock-melt contained in the meshes of a silver-blue steel alloy. Solar cells provided energy for all the needs of the castle, and in the event of emergency food could be synthesized from carbon dioxide and water vapor, as well as syrup for Phanes, Peasants and Birds. Such a need was not envisaged. Janeil was self-sufficient and secure, though inconveniences might arise when machinery broke down and there were no Meks to repair it. The situation then was disturbing but hardly desperate. During the day the gentlemen so inclined brought forth energy-guns and sport-rifles and killed as many Meks as the extreme range allowed.

After dark the Meks brought forward power-wagons and earthmovers, and began to raise a dike around Janeil. The folk of the castle watched without comprehension until the dike reached a height of fifty feet and dirt began to spill down against the walls. Then the dire purpose of the Meks became apparent, and insouciance gave way to dismal fore-boding. All the gentlemen of Janeil were erudite in at least one realm of knowledge; certain were mathematical theoreticians, while others had made a profound study of the physical sciences. Some of these, with a detail of Peasants to perform the sheerly physical exertion, attempted to restore the energy-cannon to functioning condition. Unluckily, the can-non had not been maintained in good order. Various components were obviously corroded or damaged. Conceivably these components might have been replaced from the Mek shops on the second sub-level, but none of the group had any knowledge of the Mek nomenclature or warehousing system. Warrick Madency Arban* suggested that a work-force of Peasants search the warehouse, but in view of the limited men-tal capacity of the Peasants, nothing was done and the whole plan to restore the energy-cannon came to naught.

The gentlefolk of Janeil watched in fascination as the dirt piled higher and higher around them, in a circular mound like a crater. Summer neared its end, and on one stormy day dirt and rubble rose above the parapets, and began to spill over into the courts and piazzas: Janeil must soon be buried and all within suffocated. It was then that a group of impulsive young cadets, with more élan than dignity, took up weapons and charged up the slope. The Meks dumped dirt and stone upon them, but a handful gained the ridge where they fought in a kind of dreadful exaltation.

Fifteen minutes the fight raged and the earth became sodden with rain and blood. For one glorious moment the cadets swept the ridge clear and, had not most of their fellows been lost under the rubble anything might have occurred. But the Meks regrouped and thrust forward. Ten men were left, then six, then four, then one, then none. The Meks marched down the slope, swarmed over the battlements, and with somber intensity killed all within. Janeil, for seven hundred years the abode of gallant gentlemen, and gracious ladies, had become a lifeless hulk.

3

The Mek, standing as if a specimen in a museum case, was a man-like creature, native, in his original version, to a planet of Etamin. His

---

*Arban of the Madency family in the Warrick clan.

tough rusty-bronze hide glistened metallically as if oiled or waxed; the spines thrusting back from scalp and neck shone like gold, and indeed were coated with a conductive copper-chrome film. His sense organs were gathered in clusters at the site of a man's ears; his visage—it was often a shock, walking the lower corridors, to come suddenly upon a Mek—was corrugated muscle, not dissimilar to the look of an uncovered human brain. His maw, a vertical irregular cleft at the base of this 'face', was an obsolete organ by reason of the syrup sac which had been introduced under the skin of the shoulders; the digestive organs, originally used to extract nutrition from decayed swamp vegetation and coelenterates, had atrophied. The Mek typically wore no garment except possibly a work-apron or a tool-belt, and in the sunlight his rust-bronze skin made a handsome display. This was the Mek solitary, a creature intrinsically as effective as man—perhaps more by virtue of his superb brain which also functioned as a radio transceiver. Working in the mass, by the teeming thousands, he seemed less admirable, less competent: a hybrid of sub-man and cockroach.

Certain savants, notably Morninglight's D.R. Jardine and Salonson of Tuang, considered the Mek bland and phlegmatic, but the profound Claghorn of Castle Hagedorn asserted otherwise. The emotions of the Mek, said Claghorn, were different from human emotions, and only vaguely comprehensible to man. After diligent research Claghorn isolated over a dozen Mek emotions.

In spite of such research, the Mek revolt came as an utter surprise, no less to Claghorn, D.R. Jardine and Salonson than to anyone else. Why? asked everyone. How could a group so long submissive have contrived so murderous a plot?

The most reasonable conjecture was also the simplest: the Mek resented servitude and hated the Earthmen who had removed him from his natural environment. Those who argued against this theory claimed that it projected human emotions and attitudes into a non-human organism, that the Mek had every reason to feel gratitude toward the gentlemen who had liberated him from the conditions of Etamin Nine. To this, the first group would inquire, "Who projects human attitudes now?" And the retort of their opponents was often: "Since no one knows for certain, one projection is no more absurd than another."

CHAPTER II

1

Castle Hagedorn occupied the crest of a black diorite crag overlooking a wide valley to the south. Larger, more majestic than Janeil, Hagedorn was protected by walls a mile in circumference and three hundred feet tall. The parapets stood a full nine hundred feet above the valley, with towers, turrets and observation eyries rising even higher. Two sides of the crag, at east and west, dropped sheer to the valley. The north and south slopes, a trifle less steep, were terraced and planted with vines, artichokes, pears and pomegranates. An avenue rising from the valley circled the crag and passed through a portal into the central plaza. Opposite stood the great Rotunda, with at either side the tall Houses of the twenty-eight families.

*The clans of Hagedorn, their colors and associated families:

CLANS	COLORS	FAMILIES
Xanten	yellow; black piping	Haude, Quay, Idelsea, Esledune, Salonson, Roseth.
Beaudry	dark blue; white piping	Onwane, Zadig, Prine, Fer, Sesune.
Overwhele	gray, green; red rosettes	Claghorn, Abreu, Woss, Hinken, Zumbeld.
Aure	brown, black	Zadhause, Fotergil, Marune, Baudune, Godalming, Lesmanic.
Isseth	purple, dark red	Mazeth, Floy, Luder-Hepman, Uegus, Kerrithew, Bethune.

The first gentleman of the castle, elected for life, is known as 'Hagedorn'.

The clan chief, selected by the family elders, bears the name of his clan, thus: 'Xanten', 'Beaudry', 'Overwhele', 'Aure', 'Isseth'—both clans and clan chiefs.

The family elder, selected by household heads, bears the name of his family. Thus 'Idelsea', 'Zadhause', 'Bethune' and 'Claghorn' are both families and family elders.

The remaining gentlemen and ladies bear first the clan, then the family, then the personal name. Thus: Aure Zadhause Ludwick, abbreviated to A.Z. Ludwick, and Beaudry Fer Dariane, abbreviated to B.F. Dariane.

The original castle, constructed immediately after the return of men to Earth, stood on the site now occupied by the plaza. The tenth Hagedorn, assembling an enormous force of Peasants and Meks, had built the new walls, after which he demolished the old castle. The twenty-eight Houses dated from this time, five hundred years before.

Below the plaza were three service levels: the stables and garages at the bottom, next the Mek shops and Mek living quarters, then the various storerooms, warehouses and special shops: bakery, brewery, lapidary, arsenal, repository, and the like.

The current Hagedorn, twenty-sixth of the line, was a Claghorn of the Overwheles. His selection had occasioned general surprise, because O.C. Charle, as he had been before his elevation, was a gentleman of no remarkable presence. His elegance, flair, and erudition were only ordinary; he had never been notable for any significant originality of thought. His physical proportions were good; his face was square and bony, with a short straight nose, a benign brow, and narrow gray eyes. His expression, normally a trifle abstracted—his detractors used the word "vacant"—by a simple lowering of the eyelids, a downward twitch of the coarse blond eyebrows, at once became stubborn and surly, a fact of which O.C. Charle, or Hagedorn, was unaware.

The office, while exerting little or no formal authority, exerted a pervasive influence, and the style of the gentleman who was Hagedorn affected everyone. For this reason the selection of Hagedorn was a matter of no small importance, subject to hundreds of considerations, and it was the rare candidate who failed to have some old solecism or gaucherie discussed with embarrassing candor. While the candidate might never take overt umbrage, friendships were inevitably sundered, rancors augmented, reputations blasted. O.C. Charle's elevation represented a compromise between two factions among the Overwheles, to which clan the privilege of selection had fallen.

The gentlemen between whom O.C. Charle represented a compromise were both highly respected, but distinguished by basically different attitudes toward existence. The first was the talented Garr of the Zumbeld family. He exemplified the traditional virtues of Castle Hagedorn: he was a notable connoisseur of essences, and he dressed with absolute savoir, with never so much as a pleat nor a twist of the characteristic Overwhele rosette awry. He combined insouciance and flair with dignity; his repartee coruscated with brilliant allusions and turns of phrase; when aroused his wit was utterly mordant. He could quote every literary work of consequence; he performed expertly upon the nine-stringed lute, and was thus in constant demand at the Viewing of Antique Tabards. He was an antiquarian of unchallenged erudition and knew the locale of every major city of Old Earth, and could discourse for hours upon the history of the ancient times. His military expertise was unparalleled at Hagedorn, and challenged only by D.K. Magdah of Castle Delora and perhaps Brusham of Tuang. Faults? Flaws? Few could be cited: over-punctilio which might be construed as waspishness; an intrepid pertinacity which could be considered ruthlessness. O.Z. Garr could never be dismissed as insipid or indecisive, and his personal courage was beyond dispute. Two years before, a stray band of Nomads had ventured into Lucerne Valley, slaughtering Peasants, stealing cattle, and going so far as to fire an arrow into the chest of an Isseth cadet. O.Z. Garr instantly assembled a punitive company of Meks, loaded them aboard a dozen power-wagons, and set forth in pursuit of the Nomads, finally overtaking them near Drene River, by the ruins of Worster Cathedral. The Nomads were unexpectedly strong, unexpectedly crafty, and were not content to turn tail and flee. During the fighting, O.Z. Garr displayed the most exemplary demeanor, directing the attack from the seat of his power-wagon, a pair of Meks standing by with shields to ward away arrows. The conflict ended in a rout of the Nomads; they left twenty-seven lean black-cloaked corpses strewn on the field, while only twenty Meks lost their lives.

O.Z. Garr's opponent in the election was Claghorn, elder of the Claghorn family. As with O.Z. Garr, the exquisite discriminations of Hagedorn society came to Claghorn as easily as swimming to a fish. He was no less erudite than O.Z. Garr, though hardly so versatile, his principal field of study being the Meks, their physiology, linguistic modes, and social patterns. Claghorn's conversation was more profound, but less entertaining and not so trenchant as that of O.Z. Garr; he seldom employed the extravagant tropes and allusions which characterized Garr's discussions, preferring a style of speech which was unadorned. Claghorn kept no Phanes; O.Z. Garr's four matched Gossamer Dainties were marvels of delight, and at the Viewing of Antique Tabards Garr's presentations were seldom outshone. The important contrast between the two men lay in their philosophic outlook. O.Z. Garr, a traditionalist, a fervent exemplar of his society, subscribed to its tenets without reservation. He was beset by neither doubt nor guilt; he felt no desire to alter the conditions which afforded more than two thousand gentlemen and ladies lives of great richness. Claghorn, while by no means an Expiationist, was known to feel dissatisfaction with the general tenor of life at Castle Hagedorn, and argued so plausibly that many folk refused to listen to him, on the grounds that they became uncomfortable. But an indefinable malaise ran deep, and Claghorn had many influential supporters.

When the time came for ballots to be cast, neither O.Z. Garr nor Claghorn could muster sufficient support. The office finally was conferred upon a gentleman who never in his most optimistic reckonings had expected it: a gentleman of decorum and dignity but no great depth; without flippancy, but likewise without vivacity; affable but disinclined to force an issue to a disagreeable conclusion: O.C. Charle, the new Hagedorn.

Six months later, during the dark hours before dawn, the Hagedorn Meks evacuated their quarters and departed, taking with them power-wagons, tools, weapons and electrical equipment. The act had clearly been long in the planning, for simultaneously the Meks at each of the eight other castles made a similar departure.

The initial reaction at Castle Hagedorn, as elsewhere, was incredulity, then shocked anger, then—when the implications of the act were pondered—a sense of foreboding and calamity.

The new Hagedorn, the clan chiefs, and certain other notables appointed by Hagedorn met in the formal council chamber to consider the matter. They sat around a great table covered with red velvet: Hagedorn at the head; Xanten and Isseth at his left; Overwhele, Aure and Beaudry at his right; then the others, including O.Z. Garr, I.K. Linus, A.G. Bernal, a mathematical theoretician of great ability, and B.F. Wyas, an equally sagacious antiquarian who had identified the sites of many ancient cities: Palmyra, Lübeck, Eridu, Zanesville, Burton-on-Trent, and Massilia among others. Certain family elders filled out the council: Marune and Baudune of Aure; Quay, Roseth and Idelsea of Xanten; Uegus of Isseth, Claghorn of Overwhele.

All sat silent for a period of ten minutes, arranging their minds and performing the silent act of psychic accommodation known as 'intression'.

At last Hagedorn spoke. "The castle is suddenly bereft of its Meks. Needless to say, this is an inconvenient condition to be adjusted as swiftly as possible. Here, I am sure, we find ourselves of one mind."

He looked around the table. All thrust forward carved ivory tablets to signify assent—all save Claghorn, who however did not stand it on end to signify dissent.

Isseth, a stern white-haired gentleman magnificently handsome in spite of his seventy years, spoke in a grim voice. "I see no point in cogitation or delay. What we must do is clear. Admittedly the Peasants are poor material from which to recruit an armed force. Nonetheless, we must assemble them, equip them with sandals, smocks and weapons so that they do not discredit us, and put them under good leadership: O.Z. Garr or Xanten. Birds can locate the vagrants, whereupon we will track them down, order the Peasants to give them a good drubbing, and herd them home on the double."

Xanten, thirty-five years old—extraordinarily young to be a clan chief—and a notorious firebrand, shook his head. "The idea is appealing but impractical. Peasants simply could not stand up to the Meks, no matter how we trained them."

The statement was manifestly accurate. The Peasants, small andromorphs originally of Spica Ten, were not so much timid as incapable of performing a vicious act.

A dour silence held the table. O.Z. Garr finally spoke. "The dogs have stolen our power-wagons, otherwise I'd be tempted to ride out and chivy the rascals home with a whip."*

"A matter of perplexity," said Hagedorn, "is syrup. Naturally they carried away what they could. When this is exhausted—what then? Will they starve? Impossible for them to return to their original diet. What was it? Swamp mud? Eh, Claghorn, you're the expert in these matters. Can the Meks return to a diet of mud?"

"No," said Claghorn. "The organs of the adult are atrophied. If a cub were started on the diet, he'd probably survive."

"Just as I assumed." Hagedorn scowled portentously down at his clasped hands to conceal his total lack of any constructive proposal.

A gentleman in the dark blue of the Beaudrys appeared in the doorway: he poised himself, held high his right arm, and bowed so that the fingers swept the floor.

---

*This, only an approximate translation, fails to capture the pungency of the language. Several words have no contemporary equivalents. 'Skirkling', as in 'to send skirkling', denotes a frantic pell-mell flight in all directions, accompanied by a vibration or twinkling or jerking motion. To 'volith' is to toy idly with a matter, the implication being that the person involved is of such Jovian potency that all difficulties dwindle to contemptible triviality. 'Raudlebogs' are the semi-intelligent beings of Etamin Four, who were brought to Earth, trained first as gardeners, then construction laborers, then sent home in disgrace because of certain repulsive habits they refused to forgo.

The statement of O.Z. Garr, therefore, becomes something like this: "Were power-wagons at hand, I'd volith riding forth with a whip to send the raudlebogs skirkling home."

Hagedorn rose to his feet. "Come forward, B.F. Robarth; what is your news?" For this was the significance of the newcomer's genuflection.

"The news is a message broadcast from Halcyon. The Meks have attacked; they have fired the structure and are slaughtering all. The radio went dead one minute ago."

All swung around, some jumped to their feet. "Slaughter?" croaked Claghorn.

"I am certain that by now Halcyon is no more."

Claghorn sat staring with eyes unfocused. The others discussed the dire news in voices heavy with horror.

Hagedorn once more brought the council back to order. "This is clearly an extreme situation—the gravest, perhaps, of our entire history. I am frank to state that I can suggest no decisive counter-act."

Overwhele inquired, "What of the other castles? Are they secure?"

Hagedorn turned to B.F. Robarth. "Will you be good enough to make general radio contact with all other castles, and inquire as to their condition?"

Xanten said, "Others are as vulnerable as Halcyon: Sea Island and Delora, in particular, and Maraval as well."

Claghorn emerged from his reverie. "The gentlemen and ladies of these places, in my opinion, should consider taking refuge at Janeil or here, until the uprising is quelled."

Others around the table looked at him in surprise and puzzlement. O.Z. Garr inquired in the silkiest of voices: "You envision the gentlefolk of these castles scampering to refuge at the cock-a-hoop swaggering of the lower orders?"

"Indeed, should they wish to survive," responded Claghorn politely. A gentleman of late middle age, Claghorn was stocky and strong, with black-gray hair, magnificent green eyes, and a manner which suggested great internal force under stern control. "Flight by definition entails a certain diminution of dignity," he went on to say. "If O.Z. Garr can propound an elegant manner of taking to one's heels, I will be glad to learn it, and everyone else should likewise heed, because in the days to come the capability may be of comfort to all."

Hagedorn interposed before O.Z. Garr could reply. "Let us keep to the issues. I confess I cannot see to the end of all this. The Meks have demonstrated themselves to be murderers: how can we take them back into our service? But if we don't—well, to say the least, conditions will be austere until we can locate and train a new force of technicians. We must consider along these lines."

"The spaceships!" exclaimed Xanten. "We must see to them at once!"

"What's this?" inquired Beaudry, a gentleman of rock-hard face. "How do you mean, 'see to them'?"

"They must be protected from damage! What else? They are our link to the Home Worlds. The maintenance Meks probably have not deserted the hangars, since, if they propose to exterminate us, they will want to deny us the spaceships."

"Perhaps you care to march with a levy of Peasants to take the hangars under firm control?" suggested O.Z. Garr in a somewhat supercilious voice. A long history of rivalry and mutual detestation existed between himself and Xanten.

"It may be our only hope," said Xanten. "Still—how does one fight with a levy of Peasants? Better that I fly to the hangars and reconnoiter. Meanwhile, perhaps you, and others with military expertise, will take in hand the recruitment and training of a Peasant militia."

"In this regard," stated O.Z. Garr, "I await the outcome of our current deliberations. If it develops that there lies the optimum course, I naturally will apply my competences to the fullest degree. If your own capabilities are best fulfilled by spying out the activities of the Meks, I hope that you will be largehearted enough to do the same."

The two gentlemen glared at each other. A year previously their enmity had almost culminated in a duel. Xanten, a gentleman tall, clean-limbed, and nervously active, was gifted with great natural flair, but likewise evinced a disposition too easy for absolute elegance. The traditionalists considered him 'sthross', indicating a manner flawed by an almost imperceptible slackness and lack of punctilio: not the best possible choice for clan chief.

Xanten's response to O.Z. Garr was blandly polite. "I shall be glad to take this task upon myself. Since haste is of the essence I will risk the accusation of precipitousness and leave at once. Hopefully I return to report tomorrow." He rose, performed a ceremonious bow to Hagedorn, another all-inclusive salute to the council, and departed.

He crossed to Esledune House where he maintained an apartment on the thirteenth level: four rooms furnished in the style known as Fifth Dynasty, after an epoch in the history of the Altair Home Planets, from which the human race had returned to Earth. His current consort, Araminta, a lady of the Onwane family, was absent on affairs of her own, which suited Xanten well enough. After plying him with questions she would have discredited his simple explanation, preferring to suspect an assignation at his country place. Truth to tell, he had become bored with Araminta and had reason to believe that she felt similarly—or perhaps his exalted rank had provided her less opportunity to preside at glittering social functions than she had expected. They had bred no children. Araminta's daughter by a previous connection had been tallied to her. Her second child must then be tallied to Xanten, preventing him from siring another child.*

Xanten doffed his yellow council vestments and, assisted by a young Peasant buck, donned dark yellow hunting-breeches with black trim, a black jacket, black boots. He drew a cap of soft black leather over his head and slung a pouch over his shoulder, into which he loaded weapons: a coiled blade, an energy gun.

Leaving the apartment, he summoned the lift and descended to the first level armory, where normally a Mek clerk would have served him. Now Xanten, to his vast disgust, was forced to take himself behind the counter and rummage here and there. The Meks had removed most of the sporting rifles, all the pellet ejectors and heavy energy-guns: an ominous circumstance, thought Xanten. At last he found a steel sling-whip, spare power slugs for his gun, a brace of fire grenades and a high-powered monocular.

He returned to the lift and rode to the top level, ruefully considering the long climb when eventually the mechanism broke down, with no Meks at hand to make repairs. He thought of the apoplectic furies of rigid traditionalists such as Beaudry and chuckled: eventful days lay ahead!

Stopping at the top level, he crossed to the parapets and proceeded around to the radio room. Customarily three Mek specialists connected into the apparatus by wires clipped to their quills sat typing messages as they arrived; now B.F. Robarth stood before the mechanism, uncertainly twisting the dials, his mouth wry with deprecation and distaste for the job.

"Any further news?" Xanten asked.

B.F. Robarth gave him a sour grin. "The folk at the other end seem no more familiar with this cursed tangle than I. I hear occasional voices. I believe that the Meks are attacking Castle Delora."

---

*The population of Castle Hagedorn was fixed; each gentleman and each lady was permitted a single child. If by chance another were born the parent must either find someone who had not yet sired to sponsor it, or dispose of it another way. The usual procedure was to give the child into the care of the Expiationists.

Claghorn had entered the room behind Xanten. "Did I hear you correctly? Delora Castle is gone?"

"Not gone yet, Claghorn. But as good as gone. The Delora walls are little better than a picturesque crumble."

"Sickening situation!" muttered Xanten. "How can sentient creatures perform such evil? After all these centuries, how little we actually knew of them!" As he spoke he recognized the tactlessness of his remark; Claghorn had devoted much time to a study of the Meks.

"The act itself is not astounding," said Claghorn shortly. "It has occurred a thousand times in human history."

Mildly surprised that Claghorn should use human history in reference to a case involving the sub-orders, Xanten asked, "You were never aware of this vicious aspect to the Mek nature?"

"No. Never. Never indeed."

Claghorn seemed unduly sensitive, thought Xanten. Understandable, all in all. Claghorn's basic doctrine as set forth during the Hagedorn selection was by no means simple, and Xanten neither understood it nor completely endorsed what he conceived to be its goals; but it was plain that the revolt of the Meks had cut the ground out from under Claghorn's feet. Probably to the somewhat bitter satisfaction of O.Z. Garr, who must feel vindicated in his traditionalist doctrines.

Claghorn said tersely, "The life we've been leading couldn't last forever. It's a wonder it lasted as long as it did."

"Perhaps so," said Xanten in a soothing voice. "Well, no matter. All things change. Who knows? The Peasants may be planning to poison our food...I must go." He bowed to Claghorn, who returned him a crisp nod, and to B.F. Robarth, then departed the room.

He climbed the spiral staircase—almost a ladder—to the cotes, where the Birds lived in an invincible disorder, occupying themselves with gambling, quarrels, and a version of chess, with rules incomprehensible to every gentleman who had tried to understand it.

Castle Hagedorn maintained a hundred Birds, tended by a gang of long-suffering Peasants, whom the Birds held in vast disesteem. The Birds were garish garrulous creatures, pigmented red, yellow or blue, with long necks, jerking inquisitive heads and an inherent irreverence which no amount of discipline or tutelage could overcome. Spying Xanten, they emitted a chorus of rude jeers: "Somebody wants a ride! Heavy thing!" "Why don't the self-anointed two-footers grow wings for themselves?" "My friend, never trust a Bird! We'll sky you, then fling you down on your fundament!"

"Quiet!" called Xanten. "I need six fast silent Birds for an important mission. Are any capable of such a task?"

"Are any capable, he asks!" "*A ros ros ros!* When none of us have flown for a week!" "Silence? We'll give you silence, yellow and black!"

"Come then. You. You. You of the wise eye. You there. You with the cocked shoulder. You with the green pompon. To the basket."

The Birds designated, jeering, grumbling, reviling the Peasants, allowed their syrup sacs to be filled, then flapped to the wicker seat where Xanten waited. "To the space depot at Vincenne," he told them. "Fly high and silently. Enemies are abroad. We must learn what harm if any has been done to the spaceships."

"To the depot then!" Each Bird seized a length of rope tied to an overhead framework; the chair was yanked up with a jerk calculated to rattle Xanten's teeth, and off they flew, laughing, cursing each other for not supporting more of the load, but eventually all accommodating themselves to the task and flying with a coordinated flapping of the thirty-six sets of wings. To Xanten's relief, their garrulity lessened; silently they flew south, at a speed of fifty or sixty miles per hour.

The afternoon was already waning. The ancient countryside, scene to so many comings and goings, so much triumph and so much disaster, was laced with long black shadows. Looking down, Xanten reflected that though the human stock was native to this soil, and though his immediate ancestors had maintained their holdings for seven hundred years, Earth still seemed an alien world. The reason of course was by no means mysterious or rooted in paradox. After the Six-Star War, Earth had lain fallow for three thousand years, unpopulated save for a handful of anguished wretches who somehow had survived the cataclysm and who had become semi-barbaric Nomads. Then seven hundred years ago certain rich lords of Altair, motivated to some extent by political disaffection, but no less by caprice, had decided to return to Earth. Such was the origin of the nine great strongholds, the resident gentlefolk and the staffs of specialized andromorphs...Xanten flew over an area where an antiquarian had directed excavations, revealing a plaza flagged with white stone, a broken obelisk, a tumbled statue...The sight, by some trick of association, stimulated Xanten's mind to an astonishing vision, so simple and yet so grand that he looked around, in all directions, with new eyes. The vision was Earth re-populated with men, the land cultivated, Nomads driven back into the wilderness.

At the moment the image was farfetched. And Xanten, watching the soft contours of Old Earth slide below, pondered the Mek revolt which had altered his life with such startling abruptness.

Claghorn had long insisted that no human condition endured forever, with the corollary that the more complicated such a condition, the greater its susceptibility to change. In which case the seven hundred year continuity at Castle Hagedorn—as artificial, extravagant and intricate as life could be—became an astonishing circumstance in itself. Claghorn had pushed his thesis further. Since change was inevitable, he argued that the gentlefolk should soften the impact by anticipating and controlling the changes—a doctrine which had been attacked with great fervor. The traditionalists labeled all of Claghorn's ideas demonstrable fallacy, and cited the very stability of castle life as proof of its viability. Xanten had inclined first one way, then the other, emotionally involved with neither cause. If anything, the fact of O.Z. Garr's traditionalism had nudged him toward Claghorn's views, and now it seemed as if events had vindicated Claghorn. Change had come, with an impact of the maximum harshness and violence.

There were still questions to be answered, of course. Why had the Meks chosen this particular time to revolt? Conditions had not altered appreciably for five hundred years, and the Meks had never previously hinted dissatisfaction. In fact they had revealed nothing of their feelings, though no one had ever troubled to ask them—save Claghorn.

The Birds were veering east to avoid the Ballarat Mountains, to the west of which were the ruins of a great city, never satisfactorily identified. Below lay the Lucerne Valley, at one time a fertile farm land. If one looked with great concentration, the outline of the various holdings could sometimes be distinguished. Ahead, the spaceship hangars were visible, where Mek technicians maintained four spaceships jointly the property of Hagedorn, Janeil, Tuang, Morninglight and Maraval, though, for a variety of reasons, the ships were never used.

The sun was setting. Orange light twinkled and flickered on the metal walls. Xanten called instructions up to the Birds: "Circle down. Alight behind that line of trees, but fly low so that none will see."

Down on stiff wings curved the Birds, six ungainly necks stretched toward the ground. Xanten was ready for the impact; the Birds never seemed able to alight easily when they carried a gentleman. When the cargo was something in which they felt a personal concern, dandelion fluff would never have been disturbed by the jar.

Xanten expertly kept his balance, instead of tumbling and rolling in the manner preferred by the Birds. "You all have syrup," he told them. "Rest; make no noise; do not quarrel. By tomorrow's sunset, if I am not here, return to Castle Hagedorn and say that Xanten was killed."

"Never fear!" cried the Birds. "We will wait forever!" "At any rate till tomorrow's sunset!" "If danger threatens, if you are pressed—*a ros ros ros!* Call for the Birds." "*A ros!* We are ferocious when aroused!"

"I wish it were true," said Xanten. "The Birds are arrant cowards; this is well-known. Still I value the sentiment. Remember my instructions, and quiet above all! I do not wish to be set upon and stabbed because of your clamor."

The Birds made indignant sounds. "Injustice, injustice! We are quiet as the dew!"

"Good." Xanten hurriedly moved away lest they should bellow new advice or reassurances after him.

Passing through the forest, he came to an open meadow at the far edge of which, perhaps a hundred yards distant, was the rear of the first hangar. He stopped to consider. Several factors were involved. First: the maintenance Meks, with the metal structure shielding them from radio contact, might still be unaware of the revolt. Hardly likely, he decided, in view of the otherwise careful planning. Second: the Meks, in continuous communication with their fellows, acted as a collective organism. The aggregate functioned more competently than its parts, and the individual was not prone to initiative. Hence, vigilance was likely to be extreme. Third: if they expected anyone to attempt a discreet approach, they would necessarily scrutinize most closely the route which he proposed to take.

Xanten decided to wait in the shadows another ten minutes, until the setting sun shining over his shoulder should most effectively blind any who might watch.

Ten minutes passed. The hangars, burnished by the dying sunlight, bulked long, tall, completely quiet. In the intervening meadow long golden grass waved and rippled in a cool breeze...Xanten took a deep breath, hefted his pouch, arranged his weapons, and strode forth. It did not occur to him to crawl through the grass.

He reached the back of the nearest hangar without challenge. Pressing his ear to the metal he heard nothing. He walked to the corner, looked down the side: no sign of life. Xanten shrugged. Very well then; to the door.

He walked beside the hangar, the setting sun casting a long black shadow ahead of him. He came to a door opening into the hangar administrative office. Since there was nothing to be gained by trepidation, Xanten thrust the door aside and entered.

The offices were empty. The desks, where centuries before underlings had sat, calculating invoices and bills of lading, were bare, polished free of dust. The computers and information banks, black enamel, glass, white and red switches, looked as if they had been installed only the day before.

Xanten crossed to the glass pane overlooking the hangar floor, shadowed under the bulk of the ship.

He saw no Meks. But on the floor of the hangar, arranged in neat rows and heaps, were elements and assemblies of the ship's control mechanism. Service panels gaped wide into the hull to show where the devices had been detached.

Xanten stepped from the office out into the hangar. The spaceship had been disabled, put out of commission. Xanten looked along the neat rows of parts. Certain savants of various castles were expert in the theory of space-time transfer; S.X. Rosenbox of Maraval had even derived a set of equations which, if translated into machinery, eliminated the troublesome Hamus effect. But not one gentleman, even were he so oblivious to personal honor as to touch a hand to a tool, would know how to replace, connect and tune the mechanisms heaped upon the hangar floor.

The malicious work had been done—when? Impossible to say.

Xanten returned to the office, stepped back out into the twilight, and walked to the next hangar. Again no Meks; again the spaceship had been gutted of its control mechanisms. Xanten proceeded to the third hangar, where conditions were the same.

At the fourth hangar he discerned the faint sounds of activity. Stepping into the office, looking through the glass wall into the hangar, he found Meks working with their usual economy of motion, in a near-silence which was uncanny.

Xanten, already uncomfortable from skulking through the forest, became enraged by the cool destruction of his property. He strode forth into the hangar. Slapping his thigh to attract attention he called in a harsh voice, "Return the components to place! How dare you vermin act in such a manner!"

The Meks turned about their blank countenances to study him through black beaded lens-clusters at each side of their heads.

"What!" bellowed Xanten. "You hesitate?" He brought forth his steel whip, usually more of a symbolic adjunct than a punitive instrument, and slashed it against the ground. "Obey! This ridiculous revolt is at its end!"

The Meks still hesitated, and events wavered in the balance. None made a sound, though messages were passing among them, appraising the circumstances, establishing a consensus. Xanten could allow them no such leisure. He marched forward, wielding the whip, striking at the only area where the Meks felt pain: the ropy face. "To your duties," he roared. "A fine maintenance crew are you! A destruction crew is more like it!"

The Meks made the soft blowing sound which might mean anything. They fell back, and now Xanten noted one standing at the head of the companionway leading into the ship: a Mek larger than any he had seen before and one in some fashion different. This Mek was aiming a pellet gun at his head. With an unhurried flourish, Xanten whipped away a Mek who had leaped forward with a knife, and without deigning to aim, fired at and destroyed the Mek who stood on the companionway, even as the slug sang past his head.

The other Meks were nevertheless committed to an attack. All surged forward. Lounging disdainfully against the hull, Xanten shot them as they came, moving his head once to avoid a chunk of metal, again reaching to catch a throw-knife and hurl it into the face of him who had thrown it.

The Meks drew back, and Xanten guessed that they had agreed on a new tactic: either to withdraw for weapons or perhaps to confine him within the hangar. In any event no more could be accomplished here. He made play with the whip and cleared an avenue to the office. With tools, metal bars and forgings striking the glass behind him, he sauntered through the office and out into the night.

The full moon was rising: a great yellow globe casting a smoky saffron glow, like an antique lamp. Mek eyes were not well-adapted for night-seeing, and Xanten waited by the door. Presently Meks began to pour forth, and Xanten hacked at their necks as they came.

The Meks drew back inside the hangar. Wiping his blade, Xanten strode off the way he had come, looking neither right nor left. He stopped short. The night was young. Something tickled his mind: the recollection of the Mek who had fired the pellet gun. He had been larger, possibly a darker bronze, but, more significantly, he had displayed an indefinable poise, almost authority—though such a word, when used in connection with the Meks, was anomalous. On the other hand, someone must have planned the revolt, or at least originated the concept. It might be worthwhile to extend the reconnaissance, though his primary information had been secured.

Xanten turned back and crossed the landing area to the barracks and garages. Once more, frowning in discomfort, he felt the need for discretion. What times these were! when a gentleman must skulk to avoid such as the Meks! He stole up behind the garages, where a half-dozen power-wagons* lay dozing.

Xanten looked them over. All were of the same sort, a metal frame with four wheels, an earth-moving blade at the front. Nearby must be the syrup stock. Xanten presently found a bin containing a number of cannisters. He loaded a dozen on a nearby wagon, slashed the rest with his knife, so that the syrup gushed across the ground. The Meks used a somewhat different formulation; their syrup would be stocked at a different locale, presumably inside the barracks.

Xanten mounted a power-wagon, twisted the awake key, tapped the go button, and pulled a lever which set the wheels into reverse motion. The power-wagon lurched back. Xanten halted it, turned it so that it faced the barracks. He did likewise with three others, then set them all into motion, one after the other. They trundled forward; the blades cut open the metal wall of the barracks, the roof sagged. The power-wagons continued, pushing the length of the interior, crushing all in their way.

Xanten nodded in profound satisfaction and returned to the power-wagon he had reserved for his own use. Mounting to the seat, he waited. No Meks issued from the barracks. Apparently they were deserted, with the entire crew busy at the hangars. Still, hopefully, the syrup stocks had been destroyed, and many might perish by starvation.

From the direction of the hangars came a single Mek, evidently attracted by the sounds of destruction. Xanten crouched on the seat and as it passed, coiled his whip around the stocky neck. He heaved; the Mek spun to the ground.

Xanten leaped down, seized its pellet-gun. Here was another of the larger Meks, and now Xanten saw it to be without a syrup sac, a Mek in

---

*Power-wagons, like the Meks, originally swamp-creatures from Etamin Nine, were great rectangular slabs of muscle, slung into a rectangular frame and protected from sunlight, insects and rodents by a synthetic pelt. Syrup sacs communicated with their digestive apparatus, wires led to motor nodes in the rudimentary brain. The muscles were clamped to rocker arms which actuated rotors and drive-wheels. The power-wagons, economical, long-lived and docile, were principally used for heavy cartage, earth-moving, heavy-tillage, and other arduous jobs.

the original state. Astounding! How did the creature survive? Suddenly there were many new questions to be asked—hopefully a few to be answered. Standing on the creature's head, Xanten hacked away the long antenna quills which protruded from the back of the Mek's scalp. It was now insulated, alone, on its own resources—a situation to reduce the most stalwart Mek to apathy.

"Up!" ordered Xanten. "Into the back of the wagon!" He cracked the whip for emphasis.

The Mek at first seemed disposed to defy him, but after a blow or two obeyed. Xanten climbed into the seat and started the power-wagon, directed it to the north. The Birds would be unable to carry both himself and the Mek—or in any event they would cry and complain so raucously that they might as well be believed at first. They might or might not wait until the specified hour of tomorrow's sunset; as likely as not they would sleep the night in a tree, awake in a surly mood and return at once to Castle Hagedorn.

All through the night the power-wagon trundled, with Xanten on the seat and his captive huddled in the rear.

CHAPTER III

1

The gentlefolk of the castles, for all their assurance, disliked to wander the countryside by night, by reason of what some derided as superstitious fear. Others cited travelers benighted beside moldering ruins and their subsequent visions: the eldritch music they had heard, or the whimper of moon-mirkins, or the far horns of spectral huntsmen. Others had seen pale lavender and green lights, and wraiths which ran with long strides through the forest; and Hode Abbey, now a dank tumble, was notorious for the White Hag and the alarming toll she exacted.

A hundred such cases were known, and while the hardheaded scoffed, none needlessly traveled the countryside by night. Indeed, if ghosts truly haunt the scenes of tragedy and heartbreak, then the landscape of Old Earth must be home to ghosts and specters beyond all numbering—especially that region across which Xanten rolled in the power-wagon, where every rock, every meadow, every vale and swale was crusted thick with human experience.

The moon rose high; the wagon trundled north along an ancient road, the cracked concrete slabs shining pale in the moonlight. Twice Xanten saw flickering orange lights off to the side, and once, standing in the shade of a cypress tree, he thought he saw a tall, quiet shape, silently watching him pass. The captive Mek sat plotting mischief, Xanten well knew. Without its quills it must feel depersonified, bewildered, but Xanten told himself that it would not do to doze.

The road led through a town, certain structures of which still stood. Not even the Nomads took refuge in these old towns, fearing either miasma or perhaps the redolence of grief.

The moon reached the zenith. The landscape spread away in a hundred tones of silver, black and gray. Looking about, Xanten thought that for all the notable pleasures of civilized life, there was yet something to be said for the spaciousness and simplicity of Nomadland. The Mek made a stealthy movement. Xanten did not so much as turn his head. He cracked his whip in the air. The Mek became quiet.

All through the night the power-wagon rolled along the old road, with the moon sinking into the west. The eastern horizon glowed green and lemon-yellow, and presently, as the pallid moon disappeared, the sun rose over the distant line of the mountains. At this moment, off to the right, Xanten spied a drift of smoke.

He halted the wagon. Standing up on the seat, he craned his neck to spy a Nomad encampment about a quarter-mile distant. He could distinguish three or four dozen tents of various sizes and a dozen dilapidated power-wagons. On the hetman's tall tent he thought he saw a black ideogram that he recognized. If so, this would be the tribe which not long before had trespassed on the Hagedorn domain, and which O.Z. Garr had repulsed.

Xanten settled himself upon the seat, composed his garments, set the power-wagon in motion, and guided it toward the camp.

A hundred black-cloaked men, tall and lean as ferrets, watched his approach. A dozen sprang forward and whipping arrows to bows, aimed them at his heart. Xanten turned them a glance of supercilious inquiry, drove the wagon up to the hetman's tent, halted. He rose to his feet. "Hetman," he called. "Are you awake?"

The hetman parted the canvas which closed off his tent, peered out, and after a moment came forth. Like the others he wore a garment of limp black cloth, swathing head and body alike. His face thrust through a square opening: narrow blue eyes, a grotesquely long nose, a chin long, skewed and sharp.

Xanten gave him a curt nod. "Observe this." He jerked his thumb toward the Mek in the back of the wagon. The hetman flicked aside his eyes, studied the Mek a tenth-second, and returned to a scrutiny of Xanten. "His kind have revolted against the gentlemen," said Xanten. "In fact they massacre all the men of Earth. Hence we of Castle Hagedorn make this offer to the Nomads. Come to Castle Hagedorn. We will feed, clothe and arm you. We will train you to discipline and the arts of formal warfare. We will provide the most expert leadership within our power. We will then annihilate the Meks, expunge them from Earth. After the campaign, we will train you to technical skills, and you may pursue profitable and interesting careers in the service of the castles."

The hetman made no reply for a moment. Then his weathered face split into a ferocious grin. He spoke in a voice which Xanten found surprisingly well-modulated. "So your beasts have finally risen up to rend you! A pity they forebore so long! Well, it is all one to us. You are both alien folk and sooner or later your bones must bleach together."

Xanten pretended incomprehension. "If I understand you aright, you assert that in the face of alien assault, all men must fight a common battle; and then, after the victory, cooperate still to their mutual advantage. Am I correct?"

The hetman's grin never wavered. "You are not men. Only we of Earth soil and Earth water are men. You and your weird slaves are strangers together. We wish you success in your mutual slaughter."

"Well, then," declared Xanten, "I heard you aright after all. Appeals to your loyalty are ineffectual, so much is clear. What of self-interest, then? The Meks, failing to expunge the gentlefolk of the castles, will turn upon the Nomads and kill them as if they were so many ants."

"If they attack us, we will war on them," said the hetman. "Otherwise let them do as they will."

Xanten glanced thoughtfully at the sky. "We might be willing, even now, to accept a contingent of Nomads into the service of Castle Hagedorn, this to form a cadre from which a larger, more versatile, group may be formed."

From the side, another Nomad called in an offensively jeering voice, "You will sew a sac on our backs where you can pour your syrup, hey?"

Xanten replied in an even voice, "The syrup is highly nutritious and supplies all bodily needs."

"Why then do you not consume it yourself?"

Xanten disdained reply.

The hetman spoke. "If you wish to supply us weapons, we will take them, and use them against whomever threatens us. But do not expect us to defend you. If you fear for your lives, desert your castles and become Nomads."

"Fear for our lives?" exclaimed Xanten. "What nonsense! Never! Castle Hagedorn is impregnable, as is Janeil, and most of the other castles as well."

The hetman shook his head. "Any time we choose we could take Hagedorn, and kill all you popinjays in your sleep."

"What!" cried Xanten in outrage. "Are you serious?"

"Certainly. On a black night we would send a man aloft on a great kite and drop him down on the parapets. He would lower a line, haul up ladders and in fifteen minutes the castle is taken."

Xanten pulled at his chin. "Ingenious, but impractical. The Birds would detect such a kite. Or the wind would fail at a critical moment…All this is beside the point. The Meks fly no kites. They plan to make a display against Janeil and Hagedorn, then, in their frustration, go forth and hunt Nomads."

The hetman moved back a step. "What then? We have survived similar attempts by the men of Hagedorn. Cowards all. Hand to hand, with equal weapons, we would make you eat the dirt like the dogs you are."

Xanten raised his eyebrows in elegant disdain. "I fear that you forget yourself. You address a clan chief of Castle Hagedorn. Only fatigue and boredom restrain me from punishing you with this whip."

"Bah," said the hetman. He crooked a finger to one of his archers. "Spit this insolent lordling."

The archer discharged his arrow, but Xanten, who had been expecting some such act, fired his energy gun, destroying arrow, bow, and the archer's hands. He said, "I see I must teach you common respect for your betters; so it means the whip after all." Seizing the hetman by the scalp, he coiled the whip smartly once, twice, thrice around the narrow shoulders. "Let this suffice. I cannot compel you to fight, but at least I can demand decent respect." He leaped to the ground, and seizing the hetman, pitched him into the back of the wagon alongside the Mek. Then, backing the power-wagon around, he departed the camp without so much as a glance over his shoulder, the thwart of the seat protecting his back from arrows.

The hetman scrambled erect, drew his dagger. Xanten turned his head slightly. "Take care! Or I will tie you to the wagon and you shall run behind in the dust."

The hetman hesitated, made a spitting sound between his teeth, drew back. He looked down at his blade, turned it over, and sheathed it with a grunt. "Where do you take me?"

Xanten halted the wagon. "No farther. I merely wished to leave your camp with dignity, without dodging and ducking a hail of arrows. You may alight. I take it you still refuse to bring your men into the service of Castle Hagedorn?"

The hetman once more made the spitting sound between his teeth. "When the Meks have destroyed the castles, we shall destroy the Meks, and Earth will be cleared of star-things."

"You are a gang of intractable savages. Very well, alight, return to your encampment. Reflect well before you again show disrespect to a Castle Hagedorn clan chief."

"Bah," muttered the hetman. Leaping down from the wagon, he stalked back down the track toward his camp.

2

About noon Xanten came to Far Valley, at the edge of the Hagedorn lands. Nearby was a village of Expiationists: malcontents and neurasthenics in the opinion of castle gentlefolk, and a curious group by any standards. A few had held enviable rank; certain others were savants of recognized erudition; but others yet were persons of neither dignity nor reputation, subscribing to the most bizarre and extreme of philosophies. All now performed toil no different from that relegated to the Peasants, and all seemed to take a perverse satisfaction in what—by castle standards—was filth, poverty and degradation.

As might be expected, their creed was by no means homogeneous. Some might better have been described as 'nonconformists' or 'disassociationists'; another group were 'passive expiationists', and others still, a minority, argued for a dynamic program.

Between castle and village was little intercourse. Occasionally the Expiationists bartered fruit or polished wood for tools, nails, medicaments; or the gentlefolk might make up a party to watch the Expiationists at their dancing and singing. Xanten had visited the village on many such occasions and had been attracted by the artless charm and informality of the folk at their play. Now, passing near the village, Xanten turned aside to follow a lane which wound between tall blackberry hedges and out upon a little common where goats and cattle grazed. Xanten halted the wagon in the shade and saw that the syrup sac was full. He looked back at his captive. "What of you? If you need syrup, pour yourself full. But no, you have no sac. What then do you feed upon? Mud? Unsavory fare. I fear none here is rank enough for your taste. Ingest syrup or munch grass, as you will; only do not stray overfar from the wagon, for I watch with an intent eye."

The Mek, sitting hunched in a corner, gave no signal that it comprehended, nor did it move to take advantage of Xanten's offer.

Xanten went to a watering trough and, holding his hands under the trickle which issued from a lead pipe, rinsed his face, then drank a swallow or two from his cupped hand.

Turning, he found that a dozen folk of the village had approached. One he knew well, a man who might have become Godalming, or even Aure, had he not become infected with expiationism.

Xanten performed a polite salute. "A.G. Philidor: it is I, Xanten."

"Xanten, of course. But here I am A.G. Philidor no longer, merely Philidor."

Xanten bowed. "My apologies; I have neglected the full rigor of your informality."

"Spare me your wit," said Philidor. "Why do you bring us a shorn Mek? For adoption, perhaps?" This last alluded to the gentlefolk practice of bringing over-tally babies to the village.

"Now who flaunts his wit? But you have not heard the news?"

"News arrives here last of all. The Nomads are better informed."

"Prepare yourself for surprise. The Meks have revolted against the castles. Halcyon and Delora are demolished, and all killed; perhaps others by this time."

Philidor shook his head. "I am not surprised."

"Well then, are you not concerned?"

Philidor considered. "To this extent. Our own plans, never very feasible, become more farfetched than ever."

"It appears to me," said Xanten, "that you face grave and immediate danger. The Meks surely intend to wipe out every vestige of humanity. You will not escape."

Philidor shrugged. "Conceivably the danger exists…We will take counsel and decide what to do."

"I can put forward a proposal which you may find attractive," said Xanten. "Our first concern, of course, is to suppress the revolt. There are at least a dozen Expiationist communities, with an aggregate population of two or three thousand—perhaps more. I propose that we recruit and train a corps of highly disciplined troops, supplied from the Castle Hagedorn armory, led by Hagedorn's most expert military theoreticians."

Philidor stared at him incredulously. "You expect us, the Expiationists, to become your soldiers?"

"Why not?" asked Xanten ingenuously. "Your life is at stake no less than ours."

"No one dies more than once."

Xanten in his turn evinced shock. "What? Can this be a former gentleman of Hagedorn speaking? Is this the face a man of pride and courage turns to danger? Is this the lesson of history? Of course not! I need not instruct you in this; you are as knowledgeable as I."

Philidor nodded. "I know that the history of man is not his technical triumphs, his kills, his victories. It is a composite, a mosaic of a trillion pieces, the account of each man's accommodation with his conscience. This is the true history of the race."

Xanten made an airy gesture. "A.G. Philidor, you over-simplify grievously. Do you consider me obtuse? There are many kinds of history. They interact. You emphasize morality. But the ultimate basis of morality is survival. What promotes survival is good, what induces mortifaction is bad."

"Well spoken!" declared Philidor. "But let me propound a parable. May a nation of a million beings destroy a creature who otherwise will infect all with a fatal disease? Yes, you will say. Once more: ten starving beasts hunt you, that they may eat. Will you kill them to save your life? Yes, you will say again, though here you destroy more than you save. Once more: a man inhabits a hut in a lonely valley. A hundred spaceships descend from the sky and attempt to destroy him. May he destroy these ships in self-defense, even though he is one and they are a hundred thousand? Perhaps you say yes. What then if a whole world, a whole race of beings, pits itself against this single man? May he kill all? What if the attackers are as human as himself? What if he were the creature of the first instance, who otherwise will infect a world with disease? You see, there is no area where a simple touchstone avails. We have searched and found none. Hence, at the risk of sinning against Survival, we—I, at least; I can only speak for myself—have chosen a morality which at least allows me calm. I kill—nothing. I destroy—nothing."

"Bah," said Xanten contemptuously. "If a Mek platoon entered this valley and began to kill your children, you would not defend them?"

Philidor compressed his lips, turned away. Another man spoke. "Philidor has defined morality. But who is absolutely moral? Philidor, or I, or you, might desert his morality in such a case."

Philidor said, "Look about you. Is there anyone here you recognize?"

Xanten scanned the group. Nearby stood a girl of extraordinary beauty. She wore a white smock and in the dark hair curling to her shoulders she wore a red flower. Xanten nodded. "I see the maiden O.Z. Garr wished to introduce into his ménage at the castle."

"Exactly," said Philidor. "Do you recall the circumstances?"

"Very well indeed," said Xanten. "There was vigorous objection from the Council of Notables—if for no other reason than the threat to our laws of population control. O.Z. Garr attempted to sidestep the law in this fashion. 'I keep Phanes,' he said. 'At times I maintain as many as six, or even eight, and no one utters a word of protest. I will call this girl Phane and keep her among the rest.' I and others protested. There was almost a duel over this matter. O.Z. Garr was forced to relinquish the girl. She was given into my custody and I conveyed her to Far Valley."

Philidor nodded. "All this is correct. Well—we attempted to dissuade Garr. He refused to be dissuaded, and threatened us with his hunting force of perhaps thirty Meks. We stood aside. Are we moral? Are we strong or weak?"

"Sometimes it is better," said Xanten, "to ignore morality. Even though O.Z. Garr is a gentleman and you are but Expiationists... Likewise in the case of the Meks. They are destroying the castles, and all the men of Earth. If morality means supine acceptance, then morality must be abandoned!"

Philidor gave a sour chuckle. "What a remarkable situation! The Meks are here, likewise Peasants and Birds and Phanes, all altered, transported and enslaved for human pleasure. Indeed, it is this fact that occasions our guilt, for which we must expiate, and now you want us to compound this guilt!"

"It is a mistake to brood overmuch about the past," said Xanten. "Still, if you wish to preserve your option to brood, I suggest that you fight Meks now, or at the very least take refuge in the castle."

"Not I," said Philidor. "Perhaps others may choose to do so."

"You will wait to be killed?"

"No. I and no doubt others will take refuge in the remote mountains."

Xanten clambered back aboard the power-wagon. "If you change your mind, come to Castle Hagedorn."

He departed.

The road continued along the valley, wound up a hillside, crossed a ridge. Far ahead, silhouetted against the sky, stood Castle Hagedorn.

CHAPTER IV

1

Xanten reported to the council.

"The spaceships cannot be used. The Meks have rendered them inoperative. Any plan to solicit assistance from the Home Worlds is pointless."

"This is sorry news," said Hagedorn with a grimace. "Well then, so much for that."

Xanten continued. "Returning by power-wagon I encountered a tribe of Nomads. I summoned the hetman and explained to him the advantages of serving Castle Hagedorn. The Nomads, I fear, lack both grace and docility. The hetman gave so surly a response that I departed in disgust.

"At Far Valley I visited the Expiationist village and made a similar proposal, but with no great success. They are as idealistic as the Nomads are churlish. Both are of a fugitive tendency. The Expiationists spoke of taking refuge in the mountains. The Nomads presumably will retreat into the steppes."

Beaudry snorted. "How will flight help them? Perhaps they gain a few years—but eventually the Meks will find every last one of them; such is their methodicity."

"In the meantime," O.Z. Garr declared peevishly, "we might have organized them into an efficient combat corps, to the benefit of all. Well then, let them perish; we are secure."

"Secure, yes," said Hagedorn gloomily. "But what when the power fails? When the lifts break down? When air circulation cuts off so that we either stifle or freeze? What then?"

O.Z. Garr gave his head a grim shake. "We must steel ourselves to undignified expedients, with as good grace as possible. But the machinery of the castle is sound, and I expect small deterioration or failure for conceivably five or ten years. By that time anything may occur."

Claghorn, who had been leaning indolently back in his seat, spoke at last: "This essentially is a passive program. Like the defection of the Nomads and Expiationists, it looks very little beyond the immediate moment."

O.Z. Garr spoke in a voice carefully polite. "Claghorn is well aware that I yield to none in courteous candor, as well as optimism and directness: in short the reverse of passivity. But I refuse to dignify a stupid little inconvenience by extending it serious attention. How can he label this procedure passivity? Does the worthy and honorable head of the Claghorns have a proposal which more effectively maintains our status, our standards, our self-respect?"

Claghorn nodded slowly, with a faint half-smile which O.Z. Garr found odiously complacent. "There is a simple and effective method by which the Meks might be defeated."

"Well, then!" cried Hagedorn. "Why hesitate? Let us hear it!"

Claghorn looked around the red velvet-covered table, considering the faces of all: the dispassionate Xanten; Beaudry, burly, rigid, face muscles clenched in an habitual expression unpleasantly like a sneer; old Isseth, as handsome, erect and vital as the most dashing cadet; Hagedorn, troubled, glum, his inward perplexity all too evident; the elegant Garr; Overwhele, thinking savagely of the inconveniences of the future; Aure, toying with his ivory tablet, either bored, morose or defeated; the others displaying various aspects of doubt, foreboding, hauteur, dark resentment, impatience; and in the case of Floy, a quiet smile—or as Isseth later characterized it, an imbecilic smirk—intended to convey his total disassociation from the entire irksome matter.

Claghorn took stock of the faces, and shook his head. "I will not at the moment broach this plan, as I fear it is unworkable. But I must point out that under no circumstances can Castle Hagedorn be as before, even should we survive the Mek attack."

"Bah!" exclaimed Beaudry. "We lose dignity, we become ridiculous, by even so much as discussing the beasts."

Xanten stirred himself. "A distasteful subject, but remember! Halcyon is destroyed, and Delora, and who knows what others? Let us not thrust our heads in the sand! The Meks will not waft away merely because we ignore them."

"In any event," said O.Z. Garr, "Janeil is secure and we are secure. The other folk, unless they are already slaughtered, might do well to visit us during the inconvenience, if they can justify the humiliation of flight to themselves. I myself believe that the Meks will soon come to heel, anxious to return to their posts."

Hagedorn shook his head gloomily. "I find this hard to believe. But very well then, we shall adjourn."

2

The radio communication system was the first of the castle's vast array of electrical and mechanical devices to break down. The failure occurred so soon and so decisively that certain of the theoreticians, notably I.K. Harde and Uegus, postulated sabotage by the departing Meks. Others remarked that the system had never been absolutely dependable, that the Meks themselves had been forced to tinker continuously with the circuits, that the failure was simply a result of faulty engineering. I.K. Harde and Uegus inspected the unwieldy apparatus, but the cause of failure was not obvious. After a half-hour of consultation they agreed that any attempt to restore the system would necessitate complete re-design and re-engineering, with consequent construction of testing and calibration devices and the fabrication of a complete new family of components. "This is manifestly impossible," stated Uegus in his report to the council. "Even the simplest useful system would require several technician-years. There is not even one single technician to hand. We must therefore await the availability of trained and willing labor."

"In retrospect," stated Isseth, the oldest of the clan chiefs, "it is clear that in many ways we have been less than provident. No matter that the men of the Home Worlds are vulgarians! Men of shrewder calculation than our own would have maintained inter-world connection."

"Lack of shrewdness and providence were not the deterring factors," stated Claghorn. "Communication was discouraged simply because the early lords were unwilling that Earth should be overrun with Home-World parvenus. It is as simple as that."

Isseth grunted, and started to make a rejoinder, but Hagedorn said hastily, "Unluckily, as Xanten tells us, the spaceships have been rendered useless, and while certain of our number have a profound knowledge of the theoretical considerations, again who is there to perform the toil? Even were the hangars and spaceships themselves under our control."

O.Z. Garr declared, "Give me six platoons of Peasants and six power-wagons equipped with high-energy cannon, and I'll regain the hangars; no difficulties there!"

Beaudry said, "Well, here's a start, at least. I'll assist in the training of the Peasants, and though I know nothing of cannon operation, rely on me for any advice I can give."

Hagedorn looked around the group, frowned, pulled at his chin. "There are difficulties to this program. First, we have at hand only the single power-wagon in which Xanten returned from his reconnaissance. Then, what of our energy cannons? Has anyone inspected them? The Meks were entrusted with maintenance, but it is possible, even likely, that they wrought mischief here as well. O.Z. Garr, you are reckoned an expert military theoretician; what can you tell us in this regard?"

"I have made no inspection to date," stated O.Z. Garr. "Today the Display of Antique Tabards will occupy us all until the Hour of Sundown Appraisal.*" He looked at his watch. "Perhaps now is as good a time as any to adjourn, until I am able to provide detailed information in regard to the cannons."

Hagedorn nodded his heavy head. "The time indeed grows late. Your Phanes appear today?"

"Only two," replied O.Z. Garr. "The Lazule and the Eleventh Mystery. I can find nothing suitable for the Gossamer Delights nor my little Blue Fay, and the Gloriana still requires tutelage. Today B.Z. Maxelwane's Variflors should repay the most attention."

"Yes," said Hagedorn. "I have heard other remarks to this effect. Very well then, until tomorrow. Eh, Claghorn, you have something to say?"

"Yes, indeed," said Claghorn mildly. "We have all too little time at our disposal. Best that we make the most of it. I seriously doubt the efficacy of Peasant troops; to pit Peasants against Meks is like sending rabbits against wolves. What we need, rather than rabbits, are panthers."

"Ah, yes," said Hagedorn vaguely. "Yes, indeed."

"Where, then, are panthers to be found?" Claghorn looked inquiringly around the table. "Can no one suggest a source? A pity. Well then, if panthers fail to appear, I suppose rabbits must do. Let us go about the business

---

*Display of Antique Tabards; Hour of Sundown Appraisal: the literal sense of the first term was yet relevant; that of the second had become lost and the phrase was a mere formalism, connoting that hour of late afternoon when visits were exchanged, and wines, liqueurs and essences tasted: in short, a time of relaxation and small talk before the more formal convivialities of dining.

of converting rabbits into panthers, and instantly. I suggest that we postpone all fêtes and spectacles until the shape of our future is more certain."

Hagedorn raised his eyebrows, opened his mouth to speak, closed it again. He looked intently at Claghorn to ascertain whether or not he joked. Then he looked dubiously around the table.

Beaudry gave a rather brassy laugh. "It seems that erudite Claghorn cries panic."

O.Z. Garr stated: "Surely, in all dignity, we cannot allow the impertinence of our servants to cause us such eye-rolling alarm. I am embarrassed even to bring the matter forward."

"I am not embarrassed," said Claghorn, with the full-faced complacence which so exasperated O.Z. Garr. "I see no reason why you should be. Our lives are threatened, in which case a trifle of embarrassment, or anything else, becomes of secondary importance."

O.Z. Garr rose to his feet, performed a brusque salute in Claghorn's direction, of such a nature as to constitute a calculated affront. Claghorn, rising, performed a similar salute, so grave and overly complicated as to invest Garr's insult with burlesque overtones. Xanten, who detested O.Z. Garr, laughed aloud.

O.Z. Garr hesitated, then, sensing that under the circumstances taking the matter further would be regarded as poor form, strode from the chamber.

3

The Viewing of Antique Tabards, an annual pageant of Phanes wearing sumptuous garments, took place in the Great Rotunda to the north of the central plaza. Possibly half of the gentlemen, but less than a quarter of the ladies, kept Phanes. These were creatures native to the caverns of Albireo Seven's moon: a docile race, both playful and affectionate, which after several thousand years of selective breeding had become sylphs of piquant beauty. Clad in a delicate gauze which issued from pores behind their ears, along their upper arms and down their backs, they were the most inoffensive of creatures, anxious always to please, innocently vain. Most gentlemen regarded them with affection, but rumors sometimes told of ladies drenching an especially hated Phane in tincture of ammonia, which matted her pelt and destroyed her gauze forever.

A gentleman besotted by a Phane was considered a figure of fun. The Phane, though so carefully bred as to seem a delicate girl, if used sexually became crumpled and haggard, with gauzes drooping and discolored, and everyone would know that such and such a gentleman had misused his Phane. In this regard, at least, the women of the castles might exert their superiority, and did so by conducting themselves with such extravagant provocation that the Phanes in contrast seemed the most ingenuous and fragile of nature sprites. Their life span was perhaps thirty years, during the last ten of which, after they had lost their beauty, they encased themselves in mantles of gray gauze and performed menial tasks in boudoirs, kitchens, pantries, nurseries and dressing rooms.

The Viewing of Antique Tabards was an occasion more for the viewing of Phanes than the tabards, though these, woven of Phane-gauze, were of great intrinsic beauty in themselves.

The Phane owners sat in a lower tier, tense with hope and pride, exulting when one made an especially splendid display, plunging into black depths when the ritual postures were performed with other than grace and elegance. During each display, highly formal music was plucked from a lute by a gentleman from a clan different to that of the Phane owner, the owner never playing the lute to the performance of his own Phane. The display was never overtly a competition and no formal acclamation was allowed, but all watching made up their minds as to which was the most entrancing and graceful of the Phanes, and the repute of the owner was thereby exalted.

The current Viewing was delayed almost half an hour by reason of the defection of the Meks, and certain hasty improvisations had been necessary. But the gentlefolk of Castle Hagedorn were in no mood to be critical and took no heed of the occasional lapses as a dozen young Peasant bucks struggled to perform unfamiliar tasks. The Phanes were as entrancing as ever, bending, twisting, swaying to plangent chords of the lute, fluttering their fingers as if feeling for raindrops, crouching suddenly and gliding, then springing upright as straight as wands, finally bowing and skipping from the platform.

Halfway through the program a Peasant sidled awkwardly into the Rotunda, and mumbled in an urgent manner to the cadet who came to inquire his business. The cadet at once made his way to Hagedorn's polished jet booth. Hagedorn listened, nodded, spoke a few terse words and settled calmly back in his seat as if the message had been of no consequence, and the gentlefolk of the audience were reassured.

The entertainment proceeded. O.Z. Garr's delectable pair made a fine show, but it was generally felt that Lirlin, a young Phane belonging to Isseth Floy Gazuneth, for the first time at a formal showing, made the most captivating display.

The Phanes appeared for a last time, moving all together through a half-improvised minuet, then performing a final half-gay, half-regretful salute, departed the rotunda. For a few moments more the gentlemen and ladies would remain in their booths, sipping essences, discussing the display, arranging affairs and assignations. Hagedorn sat frowning, twisting his hands. Suddenly he rose to his feet. The rotunda instantly became silent.

"I dislike intruding an unhappy note at so pleasant an occasion," said Hagedorn. "But the news has just been given to me, and it is fitting that all should know. Janeil Castle is under attack. The Meks are there in great force, with hundreds of power-wagons. They have circled the castle with a dike which prevents any effective use of the Janeil energy-cannon.

"There is no immediate danger to Janeil, and it is difficult to comprehend what the Meks hope to achieve, the Janeil walls being all of two hundred feet high.

"The news, nevertheless, is somber, and it means that eventually we must expect a similar investment—though it is even more difficult to comprehend how Meks could hope to inconvenience us. Our water derives from four wells sunk deep into the earth. We have great stocks of food. Our energy is derived from the sun. If necessary, we could condense water and synthesize food from the air—at least I have been so assured by our great biochemical theoretician, X.B. Ladisname. Still—this is the news. Make of it what you will. Tomorrow the Council of Notables will meet."

CHAPTER V

1

"Well then," said Hagedorn to the council, "for once let us dispense with formality. O.Z. Garr: what of our cannon?"

O.Z. Garr, wearing the magnificent gray and green uniform of the Overwhele Dragoons, carefully placed his morion on the table, so that the panache stood erect. "Of twelve cannon, four appear to be functioning correctly. Four have been sabotaged by excision of the power-leads. Four have been sabotaged by some means undetectable to careful investigation.

I have commandeered a half-dozen Peasants who demonstrate a modicum of mechanical ability, and have instructed them in detail. They are currently engaged in splicing the leads. This is the extent of my current information in regard to the cannon."

"Moderately good news," said Hagedorn. "What of the proposed corps of armed Peasants?"

"The project is under way. A.F. Mull and I.A. Berzelius are now inspecting Peasants with a view to recruitment and training. I can make no sanguine projection as to the military effectiveness of such a corps, even if trained and led by such as A.F. Mull, I.A. Berzelius and myself. The Peasants are a mild, ineffectual race, admirably suited to the grubbing of weeds, but with no stomach whatever for fighting."

Hagedorn glanced around the council. "Are there any other suggestions?"

Beaudry spoke in a harsh, angry voice. "Had the villains but left us our power-wagons, we might have mounted the cannon aboard—the Peasants are equal to this, at least. Then we could roll to Janeil and blast the dogs from the rear."

"These Meks seem utter fiends!" declared Aure. "What conceivably do they have in mind? Why, after all these centuries, must they suddenly go mad?"

"We all ask ourselves the same questions," said Hagedorn. "Xanten, you returned from reconnaissance with a captive. Have you attempted to question him?"

"No," said Xanten. "Truth to tell, I haven't thought of him since."

"Why not attempt to question him? Perhaps he can provide a clue or two."

Xanten nodded assent. "I can try. Candidly, I expect to learn nothing."

"Claghorn, you are the Mek expert," said Beaudry. "Would you have thought the creatures capable of so intricate a plot? What do they hope to gain? Our castles?"

"They are certainly capable of precise and meticulous planning," said Claghorn. "Their ruthlessness surprises me—more, possibly, than it should. I have never known them to covet our material possessions, and they show no tendency toward what we consider the concomitants of civilization: fine discriminations of sensation and the like. I have often speculated—I won't dignify the conceit with the status of a theory—that the structural logic of a brain is of rather more consequence than we reckon with. Our own brains are remarkable for their utter lack of rational structure. Considering the haphazard manner in which our thoughts are formed, registered, indexed and recalled, any single rational act becomes a miracle. Perhaps we are incapable of rationality; perhaps all thought is a set of impulses generated by one emotion, monitored by another, ratified by a third. In contrast, the Mek brain is a marvel of what seems to be careful engineering. It is roughly cubical and consists of microscopic cells interconnected by organic fibrils, each a monofilament molecule of negligible electrical resistance. Within each cell is a film of silica, a fluid of variable conductivity and dielectric properties, a cusp of a complex mixture of metallic oxides. The brain is capable of storing great quantities of information in an orderly pattern. No fact is lost, unless it is purposely forgotten, a capacity which the Meks possess. The brain also functions as a radio transceiver, possibly as a radar transmitter and detector, though this again is speculation.

"Where the Mek brain falls short is in its lack of emotional color. One Mek is precisely like another, without any personality differentiation perceptible to us. This, clearly, is a function of their communicative system: unthinkable for a unique personality to develop under these conditions. They served us efficiently and—so we thought—loyally, because they felt nothing about their condition, neither pride in achievement, nor resentment, nor shame. Nothing whatever. They neither loved us nor hated us, nor do they now. It is hard for us to conceive this emotional vacuum, when each of us feels something about everything. We live in a welter of emotions. They are as devoid of emotion as an ice-cube. They were fed, housed, and maintained in a manner they found satisfactory. Why did they revolt? I have speculated at length, but the single reason which I can formulate seems so grotesque and unreasonable that I refuse to take it seriously. If this after all is the correct explanation..." His voice drifted away.

"Well?" demanded O.Z. Garr peremptorily. "What, then?"

"Then—it is all the same. They are committed to the destruction of the human race. My speculation alters nothing."

Hagedorn turned to Xanten. "All this should assist you in your inquiries."

"I was about to suggest that Claghorn assist me, if he is so inclined," said Xanten.

"As you like," said Claghorn, "though in my opinion the information, no matter what, is irrelevant. Our single concern should be a means to repel them and to save our lives."

"And—except the force of 'panthers' you mentioned at our previous session—you can conceive of no subtle weapon?" asked Hagedorn wistfully. "A device to set up electrical resonances in their brains, or something similar?"

"Not feasible," said Claghorn. "Certain organs in the creatures' brains function as overload switches. Though it is true that during this time they might not be able to communicate." After a moment's reflection he added thoughtfully, "Who knows? A.G. Bernal and Uegus are theoreticians with a profound knowledge of such projections. Perhaps they might construct such a device, or several, against a possible need."

Hagedorn nodded dubiously, and looked toward Uegus. "Is this possible?"

Uegus frowned. "'Construct'? I can certainly design such an instrument. But the components—where? Scattered through the storerooms helter-skelter, some functioning, others not. To achieve anything meaningful I must become no better than an apprentice, a Mek." He became incensed, and his voice hardened. "I find it hard to believe that I should be forced to point out this fact. Do you hold me and my talents then of such small worth?"

Hagedorn hastened to reassure him. "Of course not! I for one would never think of impugning your dignity."

"Never!" agreed Claghorn. "Nevertheless, during this present emergency, we will find indignities imposed upon us by events, unless now we impose them upon ourselves."

"Very well," said Uegus, a humorless smile trembling at his lips. "You shall come with me to the storeroom. I will point out the components to be brought forth and assembled, you shall perform the toil. What do you say to that?"

"I say yes, gladly, if it will be of real utility. However, I can hardly perform the labor for a dozen different theoreticians. Will any others serve beside myself?"

No one responded. Silence was absolute, as if every gentleman present held his breath.

Hagedorn started to speak, but Claghorn interrupted. "Pardon, Hagedorn, but here, finally, we are stuck upon a basic principle, and it must be settled now."

Hagedorn looked desperately around the council. "Has anyone relevant comment?"

"Claghorn must do as his innate nature compels," declared O.Z. Garr in the silkiest of voices. "I cannot dictate to him. As for myself, I can never demean my status as a gentleman of Hagedorn. This creed is as natural to me as drawing breath; if ever it is compromised I become a travesty of a gentleman, a grotesque mask of myself. This is Castle Hagedorn, and we represent the culmination of human civilization. Any compromise therefore becomes degradation; any expedient diminution of our standards becomes dishonor. I have heard the word 'emergency' used. What a deplorable sentiment! To dignify the rat-like snappings and gnashings of such as the Meks with the word 'emergency' is to my mind unworthy of a gentleman of Hagedorn!"

A murmur of approval went around the council table.

Claghorn leaned far back in his seat, chin on his chest, as if in relaxation. His clear green eyes went from face to face, then returned to O.Z. Garr whom he studied with dispassionate interest. "Obviously you direct your words to me," he said, "and I appreciate their malice. But this is a small matter." He looked away from O.Z. Garr, to stare up at the massive diamond and emerald chandelier. "More important is the fact that the council as a whole, in spite of my earnest persuasion, seems to endorse your viewpoint. I can urge, expostulate, insinuate no longer, and I will now leave Castle Hagedorn. I find the atmosphere stifling. I trust that you survive the attack of the Meks, though I doubt that you will. They are a clever, resourceful race, untroubled by qualms or preconceptions, and we have long underestimated their quality."

Claghorn rose from his seat, inserted the ivory tablet into its socket. "I bid you all farewell."

Hagedorn hastily jumped to his feet and held forth his arms imploringly. "Do not depart in anger, Claghorn! Reconsider! We need your wisdom, your expertise!"

"Assuredly you do," said Claghorn. "But even more, you need to act upon the advice I have already extended. Until then, we have no common ground, and any further interchange is futile and tiresome." He made a brief, all-inclusive salute and departed the chamber.

Hagedorn slowly resumed his seat. The others made uneasy motions, coughed, looked up at the chandelier, studied their ivory tablets. O.Z. Garr muttered something to B.F. Wyas who sat beside him, who nodded solemnly. Hagedorn spoke in a subdued voice: "We will miss the presence of Claghorn, his penetrating if unorthodox insights...We have accomplished little. Uegus, perhaps you will give thought to the projector under discussion. Xanten, you were to question the captive Mek. O.Z. Garr, you undoubtedly will see to the repair of the energy cannon...Aside from these small matters, it appears that we have evolved no general plan of action, to help either ourselves or Janeil."

Marune spoke. "What of the other castles? Are they still extant? We have had no news. I suggest that we send Birds to each castle, to learn their condition."

Hagedorn nodded. "Yes, this is a wise motion. Perhaps you will see to this, Marune?"

"I will do so."

"Good. We will now adjourn."

2

The Birds dispatched by Marune of Aure, one by one returned. Their reports were similar:

"Sea Island is deserted. Marble columns are tumbled along the beach. Pearl Dome is collapsed. Corpses float in the Water Garden."

"Maraval reeks of death. Gentlemen, Peasants, Phanes—all dead. Alas! Even the Birds have departed!"

"Delora: *a ros ros ros!* A dismal scene! No sign of life!"

"Alume is desolate. The great wooden door is smashed. The Green Flame is extinguished."

"There is nothing at Halcyon. The Peasants were driven into a pit."

"Tuang: silence."

"Morninglight: death."

CHAPTER VI

1

Three days later, Xanten constrained six Birds to a lift chair, directed them first on a wide sweep around the castle, then south to Far Valley.

The Birds aired their usual complaints, then bounded down the deck in great ungainly hops which threatened to throw Xanten immediately to the pavement. At last gaining the air, they flew up in a spiral; Castle Hagedorn became an intricate miniature far below, each House marked by its unique cluster of turrets and eyries, its own eccentric roof line, its long streaming pennon.

The Birds performed the prescribed circle, skimming the crags and pines of North Ridge; then, setting wings aslant the upstream, they coasted away toward Far Valley.

Over the pleasant Hagedorn domain flew the Birds and Xanten: over orchards, fields, vineyards, Peasant villages. They crossed Lake Maude with its pavilions and docks, the meadows beyond where the Hagedorn cattle and sheep grazed, and presently came to Far Valley, at the limit of Hagedorn lands.

Xanten indicated where he wished to alight; the Birds, who would have preferred a site closer to the village where they could have watched all that transpired, grumbled and cried out in wrath and set Xanten down so roughly that had he not been alert the shock would have pitched him head over heels.

Xanten alighted without elegance but at least remained on his feet. "Await me here!" he ordered. "Do not stray; attempt no flamboyant tricks among the lift-straps. When I return I wish to see six quiet Birds, in neat formation, lift-straps untwisted and untangled. No bickering, mind you! No loud caterwauling, to attract unfavorable comment! Let all be as I have ordered!"

The Birds sulked, stamped their feet, ducked aside their necks, made insulting comments just under the level of Xanten's hearing. Xanten, turning them a final glare of admonition, walked down the lane which led to the village.

The vines were heavy with ripe blackberries and a number of the girls of the village filled baskets. Among them was the girl O.Z. Garr had thought to preempt for his personal use. As Xanten passed, he halted and performed a courteous salute. "We have met before, if my recollection is correct."

The girl smiled, a half-rueful, half-whimsical smile. "Your recollection serves you well. We met at Hagedorn, where I was taken a captive. And later, when you conveyed me here, after dark, though I could not see your face." She extended her basket. "Are you hungry? Will you eat?"

Xanten took several berries. In the course of the conversation he learned that the girl's name was Glys Meadowsweet, that her parents were not known to her, but were presumably gentlefolk of Castle

Hagedorn who had exceeded their birth tally. Xanten examined her even more carefully than before but could see resemblance to none of the Hagedorn families. "You might derive from Castle Delora. If there is any family resemblance I can detect, it is to the Cosanzas of Delora—a family noted for the beauty of its ladies."

"You are not married?" she asked artlessly.

"No," said Xanten, and indeed he had dissolved his relationship with Araminta only the day before. "What of you?"

She shook her head. "I would never be gathering blackberries otherwise; it is work reserved for maidens…Why do you come to Far Valley?"

"For two reasons. The first to see you." Xanten heard himself say this with surprise. But it was true, he realized with another small shock of surprise. "I have never spoken with you properly and I have always wondered if you were as charming and gay as you are beautiful."

The girl shrugged and Xanten could not be sure whether she were pleased or not, compliments from gentlemen sometimes setting the stage for a sorry aftermath. "Well, no matter. I came also to speak to Claghorn."

"He is yonder," she said in a voice toneless, even cool, and pointed. "He occupies that cottage." She returned to her blackberry picking. Xanten bowed and proceeded to the cottage the girl had indicated.

Claghorn, wearing loose knee-length breeches of gray homespun, worked with an axe chopping faggots into stove-lengths. At the sight of Xanten he halted his toil, leaned on the axe and mopped his forehead. "Ah, Xanten. I am pleased to see you. How are the folk of Castle Hagedorn?"

"As before. There is little to report, even had I come to bring you news."

"Indeed, indeed?" Claghorn leaned on the axe handle, surveying Xanten with a bright green gaze.

"At our last meeting," went on Xanten, "I agreed to question the captive Mek. After doing so I am distressed that you were not at hand to assist, so that you might have resolved certain ambiguities in the responses."

"Speak on," said Claghorn. "Perhaps I shall be able to do so now."

"After the council meeting I descended immediately to the storeroom where the Mek was confined. It lacked nutriment; I gave it syrup and a pail of water, which it sipped sparingly, then evinced a desire for minced clams. I summoned kitchen help and sent them for this commodity and the Mek ingested several pints. As I have indicated, it was an unusual Mek, standing as tall as myself and lacking a syrup sac. I conveyed it to a different chamber, a storeroom for brown plush furniture, and ordered it to a seat.

"I looked at the Mek and it looked at me. The quills which I removed were growing back; probably it could at least receive from Meks elsewhere. It seemed a superior beast, showing neither obsequiousness nor respect, and answered my questions without hesitation.

"First I remarked: 'The gentlefolk of the castles are astounded by the revolt of the Meks. We had assumed that your life was satisfactory. Were we wrong?'

"'Evidently.' I am sure that this was the word signaled, though never had I suspected the Meks of dryness or wit of any sort.

"'Very well then,' I said. 'In what manner?'

"'Surely it is obvious,' he said. 'We no longer wished to toil at your behest. We wished to conduct our lives by our own traditional standards.'

"The response surprised me. I was unaware that the Meks possessed standards of any kind, much less traditional standards."

Claghorn nodded. "I have been similarly surprised by the scope of the Mek mentality."

"I reproached the Mek: 'Why kill? Why destroy our lives in order to augment your own?' As soon as I had put the question I realized that it had been unhappily phrased. The Mek, I believe, realized the same; however, in reply he signaled something very rapidly which I believe was: 'We knew we must act with decisiveness. Your own protocol made this necessary. We might have returned to Etamin Nine, but we prefer this world Earth, and will make it our own, with our own great slipways, tubs and basking ramps.'

"This seemed clear enough, but I sensed an adumbration extending yet beyond. I said, 'Comprehensible. But why kill, why destroy? You might have taken yourself to a different region. We could not have molested you.'

"'Infeasible, by your own thinking. A world is too small for two competing races. You intended to send us back to dismal Etamin Nine.'

"'Ridiculous!' I said. 'Fantasy, absurdity. Do you take me for a mooncalf?'

"'No,' the creature insisted. 'Two of Castle Hagedorn's notables were seeking the highest post. One assured us that, if elected, this would become his life's aim.'

"'A grotesque misunderstanding,' I told him. 'One man, a lunatic, can not speak for all men!'

"'No? One Mek speaks for all Meks. We think with one mind. Are not men of a like sort?'

"'Each thinks for himself. The lunatic who assured you of this tom-foolery is an evil man. But at least matters are clear. We do not propose to send you to Etamin Nine. Will you withdraw from Janeil, take your-selves to a far land and leave us in peace?'

"'No,' he said. 'Affairs have proceeded too far. We will now destroy all men. The truth of the statement is clear: one world is too small for two races.'

"'Unluckily, then, I must kill you,' I told him. 'Such acts are not to my liking, but, with opportunity, you would kill as many gentlemen as possible!' At this the creature sprang upon me, and I killed it with an easier mind than had it sat staring.

"Now, you know all. It seems that either you or O.Z. Garr stimulat-ed the cataclysm. O.Z. Garr? Unlikely. Impossible. Hence, you, Claghorn, you! have this weight upon your soul!" ·

Claghorn frowned down at the axe. "Weight, yes. Guilt, no. Ingen-uousness, yes; wickedness, no."

Xanten stood back. "Claghorn, your coolness astounds me! Before, when rancorous folk like O.Z. Garr conceived you a lunatic—"

"Peace, Xanten!" exclaimed Claghorn. "This extravagant breast-beating becomes maladroit. What have I done wrong? My fault is that I tried too much. Failure is tragic, but a phthisic face hanging over the cup of the future is worse. I meant to become Hagedorn, I would have sent the slaves home. I failed, the slaves revolted. So do not speak another word. I am bored with the subject. You can not imagine how your bulging eyes and your concave spine oppress me."

"Bored you may be," cried Xanten. "You decry my eyes, my spine— but what of the thousands dead?"

"How long would they live in any event? Lives as cheap as fish in the sea. I suggest that you put by your reproaches and devote a similar energy to saving yourself. Do you realize that a means exists? You stare at me blankly. I assure you that what I say is true, but you will never learn the means from me."

"Claghorn," said Xanten, "I flew to this spot intending to blow your arrogant head from your body—" Claghorn, no longer heeding, had returned to his wood-chopping.

"Claghorn!" cried Xanten. "Attend me!"

"Xanten, take your outcries elsewhere, if you please. Remonstrate with your Birds."

Xanten swung on his heel and marched back down the lane. The girls picking berries looked at him questioningly and moved aside. Xanten halted to look up and down the lane. Glys Meadowsweet was nowhere to be seen. In a new fury he continued. He stopped short. On a fallen tree a hundred feet from the Birds sat Glys Meadowsweet, examining a blade of grass as if it had been an astonishing artifact of the past. The Birds, for a marvel, had actually obeyed him and waited in a fair semblance of order.

Xanten looked up toward the heavens, kicked at the turf. He drew a deep breath and approached Glys Meadowsweet. He noted that she had tucked a flower into her long loose hair.

After a second or two she looked up and searched his face. "Why are you so angry?"

Xanten slapped his thigh, then seated himself beside her. "'Angry'? No. I am out of my mind with frustration. Claghorn is as obstreperous as a sharp rock. He knows how Castle Hagedorn can be saved but he will not divulge his secret."

Glys Meadowsweet laughed—an easy, merry sound, like nothing Xanten had ever heard at Castle Hagedorn. "'Secret'? When even I know it?"

"It must be a secret," said Xanten. "He will not tell me."

"Listen. If you fear the Birds will hear, I will whisper." She spoke a few words into his ear.

Perhaps the sweet breath befuddled Xanten's mind. But the explicit essence of the revelation failed to strike home into his consciousness. He made a sound of sour amusement. "No secret there. Only what the prehistoric Scythians termed bathos. Dishonor to the gentlemen! Do we dance with the Peasants? Do we serve the Birds essences and discuss with them the sheen of our Phanes?"

"'Dishonor', then?" She jumped to her feet. "Then it is also dishonor for you to talk to me, to sit here with me, to make ridiculous suggestions—"

"I made no suggestions!" protested Xanten. "I sit here in all decorum—"

"Too much decorum, too much honor!" With a display of passion which astounded Xanten, Glys Meadowsweet tore the flower from her hair and hurled it at the ground. "There. Hence!"

"No," said Xanten in sudden humility. He bent, picked up the flower, kissed it, replaced it in her hair. "I am not over-honorable. I will try my best." He put his arms on her shoulders, but she held him away.

"Tell me," she inquired with a very mature severity, "do you own any of those peculiar insect-women?"

"I? Phanes? I own no Phanes."

With this Glys Meadowsweet relaxed and allowed Xanten to embrace her, while the Birds clucked, guffawed and made vulgar scratching sounds with their wings.

CHAPTER VII

1

The summer waxed warm. On June 30 Janeil and Hagedorn celebrated the Fête of Flowers, even though the dike was rising high around Janeil. Shortly after, Xanten flew six select Birds into Castle Janeil by night, and proposed to the council that the population be evacuated by Bird-lift—as many as possible, as many who wished to leave. The council listened with stony faces and without comment passed on to a consideration of other affairs.

Xanten returned to Castle Hagedorn. Using the most careful methods, speaking only to trusted comrades, Xanten enlisted thirty or forty cadets and gentlemen to his persuasion, though inevitably he could not keep the doctrinal thesis of his program secret.

The first reaction of the traditionalists was mockery and charges of poltroonery. At Xanten's insistence, challenges were neither issued nor accepted by his hot-blooded associates.

On the evening of September 9 Castle Janeil fell. The news was brought to Castle Hagedorn by excited Birds who told the grim tale again and again in voices ever more hysterical.

Hagedorn, now gaunt and weary, automatically called a council meeting; it took note of the gloomy circumstances. "We, then, are the last castle! The Meks cannot conceivably do us harm; they can build dikes around our castle walls for twenty years and only work themselves to distraction. We are secure; but yet it is a strange and portentous thought to realize that at last, here at Castle Hagedorn, live the last gentlemen of the race!"

Xanten spoke in a voice strained with earnest conviction: "Twenty years—fifty years—what difference to the Meks? Once they surround us, once they deploy, we are trapped. Do you comprehend that now is our last opportunity to escape the great cage that Castle Hagedorn is to become?"

"'Escape', Xanten? What a word! For shame!" hooted O.Z. Garr. "Take your wretched band, escape! To steppe or swamp or tundra! Go as you like, with your poltroons, but be good enough to give over these incessant alarms!"

"Garr, I have found conviction since I became a 'poltroon'. Survival is good morality. I have this from the mouth of a noted savant."

"Bah! Such as whom?"

"A.G. Philidor, if you must be informed of every detail."

O.Z. Garr clapped his hand to his forehead. "Do you refer to Philidor, the Expiationist? He is of the most extreme stripe, an Expiationist to out-expiate all the rest! Xanten, be sensible, if you please!"

"There are years ahead for all of us," said Xanten in a wooden voice, "if we free ourselves from the castle."

"But the castle is our life!" declared Hagedorn. "In essence, Xanten, what would we be without the castle? Wild animals? Nomads?"

"We would be alive."

O.Z. Garr gave a snort of disgust and turned away to inspect a wall-hanging.

Hagedorn shook his head in doubt and perplexity. Beaudry threw his hands up into the air. "Xanten, you have the effect of unnerving us all. You come in here and inflict this dreadful sense of urgency—but why? In Castle Hagedorn we are as safe as in our mothers' arms. What do we gain by throwing aside all—honor, dignity, comfort, civilized niceties—for no other reason than to slink through the wilderness?"

"Janeil was safe," said Xanten. "Today where is Janeil? Death, mildewed cloth, sour wine. What we gain by slinking is the assurance of survival. And I plan much more than simple slinking."

"I can conceive of a hundred occasions when death is better than life!" snapped Isseth. "Must I die in dishonor and disgrace? Why may my last years not be passed in dignity?"

Into the room came B.F. Robarth. "Councilmen, the Meks approach Castle Hagedorn."

Hagedorn cast a wild look around the chamber. "Is there a consensus? What must we do?"

Xanten threw up his hands. "Everyone must do as he thinks best! I argue no more: I am done. Hagedorn, will you adjourn the council so that we may be about our affairs? I to my slinking?"

"Council is adjourned," said Hagedorn, and all went to stand on the ramparts.

Up the avenue into the castle trooped Peasants from the surrounding countryside, packets slung over their shoulders. Across the valley, at the edge of Bartholomew Forest, was a clot of power-wagons and an amorphous brown-gold mass: Meks.

Aure pointed west. "Look—there they come, up the Long Swale." He turned, peered east. "And look, there at Bambridge: Meks!"

By common consent, all swung about to scan North Ridge. O.Z. Garr pointed to a quiet line of brown-gold shapes. "There they wait, the vermin! They have penned us in! Well then, let them wait!" He swung away, rode the lift down to the plaza, and crossed swiftly to Zumbeld House, where he worked the rest of the afternoon with his Gloriana, of whom he expected great things.

2

The following day the Meks formalized the investment. Around Castle Hagedorn a great circle of Mek activity made itself apparent: sheds, warehouses, barracks. Within this periphery, just beyond the range of the energy cannon, power-wagons thrust up mounds of dirt.

During the night these mounds lengthened toward the castle, similarly the night after. At last the purpose of the mounds became clear: they were a protective cover above passages or tunnels leading toward the crag on which Castle Hagedorn rested.

The following day several of the mounds reached the base of the crag. Presently a succession of power-wagons loaded with rubble began to flow from the far end. They issued, dumped their loads, and once again entered the tunnels.

Eight of these above-ground tunnels had been established. From each trundled endless loads of dirt and rock, gnawed from the crag on which Castle Hagedorn sat. To the gentlefolk who crowded the parapets the meaning of the work at last became clear.

"They make no attempt to bury us," said Hagedorn. "They merely mine out the crag from below us!"

On the sixth day of the siege, a great segment of the hillside shuddered, slumped, and a tall pinnacle of rock reaching almost up to the base of the walls collapsed.

"If this continues," muttered Beaudry, "our time will be less than that of Janeil."

"Come then," called O.Z. Garr, suddenly active. "Let us try our energy cannon. We'll blast open their wretched tunnels, and then what will the rascals do?" He went to the nearest emplacement and shouted down for Peasants to remove the tarpaulin.

Xanten, who happened to be standing nearby, said, "Allow me to assist you." He jerked away the tarpaulin. "Shoot now, if you will."

O.Z. Garr stared at him uncomprehendingly, then leaped forward and swiveled the great projector about so that it aimed at a mound. He pulled the switch; the air crackled in front of the ringed snout, rippled, flickered with purple sparks. The target area steamed, became black, then dark red, then slumped into an incandescent crater. But the underlying earth, twenty feet in thickness, afforded too much insulation; the molten puddle became white-hot but failed to spread or deepen. The energy cannon gave a sudden chatter, as electricity short-circuited through corroded insulation. The cannon went dead. O.Z. Garr inspected the mechanism in anger and disappointment; then, with a gesture of repugnance, he turned away. The cannons were clearly of limited effectiveness.

Two hours later, on the east side of the crag, another great sheet of rock collapsed, and just before sunset a similar mass sheared from the western face, where the wall of the castle rose almost in an uninterrupted line from the cliff below.

At midnight Xanten and those of his persuasion, with their children and consorts, departed Castle Hagedorn. Six teams of Birds shuttled from the flight deck to a meadow near Far Valley, and long before dawn had transported the entire group. There were none to bid them farewell.

3

A week later another section of the east cliff fell away, taking a length of rock-melt buttress with it. At the tunnel mouths the piles of excavated rubble had become alarmingly large.

The terraced south face of the crag was the least disturbed, the most spectacular damage having occurred to east and west. Suddenly, a month after the initial assault, a great section of the terrace slumped forward, leaving an irregular crevasse which interrupted the avenue and hurled down the statues of former notables emplaced at intervals along the avenue's balustrade.

Hagedorn called a council meeting. "Circumstances," he said in a wan attempt at facetiousness, "have not bettered themselves. Our most pessimistic expectations have been exceeded: a dismal situation. I confess that I do not relish the prospect of toppling to my death among all my smashed belongings."

Aure made a desperate gesture. "A similar thought haunts me! Death—what of that? All must die! But when I think of my precious belongings I become sick. My books trampled! my fragile vases smashed! my tabards ripped! my rugs buried! my Phanes strangled! my heirloom chandeliers flung aside! These are my nightmares."

"Your possessions are no less precious than any others," said Beaudry shortly. "Still, they have no life of their own; when we are gone, who cares what happens to them?"

Marune winced. "A year ago I put down eighteen dozen flasks of prime essence; twelve dozen Green Rain; three each of Balthazar and Faidor. Think of these, if you would contemplate tragedy!"

"Had we only known!" groaned Aure. "I would have—I would have..." His voice trailed away.

O.Z. Garr stamped his foot in impatience. "Let us avoid lamentation at all costs! We had a choice, remember? Xanten beseeched us to flee; now he and his like go skulking and foraging through the north mountains with the Expiationists. We chose to remain, for better or worse, and unluckily the worse is occurring. We must accept the fact like gentlemen."

To this the council gave melancholy assent. Hagedorn brought forth a flask of priceless Rhadamanth and poured with a prodigality which previously would have been unthinkable. "Since we have no future—to our glorious past!"

That night disturbances were noted here and there around the ring of Mek investment: flames at four separate points, a faint sound of hoarse shouting. On the following day it seemed that the tempo of activity had lessened a trifle.

During the afternoon, however, a vast segment of the east cliff fell away. A moment later, as if after majestic deliberation, the tall east wall split off and toppled, leaving the backs of six great houses exposed to the open sky.

An hour after sunset a team of Birds settled to the flight-deck. Xanten jumped from the seat. He ran down the circular staircase to the ramparts and came down to the plaza by Hagedorn's palace.

Hagedorn, summoned by a kinsman, came forth to stare at Xanten in surprise. "What do you do here? We expected you to be safely north with the Expiationists!"

"The Expiationists are not safely north," said Xanten. "They have joined the rest of us. We are fighting."

Hagedorn's jaw dropped. "Fighting? The gentlemen are fighting Meks?"

"As vigorously as possible."

Hagedorn shook his head in wonder. "The Expiationists too? I understood that they had planned to flee north."

"Some have done so, including A.G. Philidor. There are factions among the Expiationists just as here. Most are not ten miles distant. The same with the Nomads. Some have taken their power-wagons and fled. The rest kill Meks with fanatic fervor. Last night you saw our work. We fired four storage warehouses, destroyed syrup tanks, killed a hundred or more Meks, as well as a dozen power-wagons. We suffered losses, which hurt us because there are few of us and many Meks. This is why I am here. We need more men. Come fight beside us!"

Hagedorn turned, motioning to the great central plaza. "I will call forth the folk from their Houses. Talk to everyone."

4

The Birds, complaining bitterly at the unprecedented toil, worked all night, transporting the gentlemen who, sobered by the imminent destruction of Castle Hagedorn, were now willing to abandon all scruples and fight for their lives. The staunch traditionalists still refused to compromise their honor, but Xanten gave them cheerful assurance: "Remain here, then, prowling the castle like so many furtive rats. Take what comfort you can in the fact that you are being protected; the future holds little else for you."

And many who heard him stalked away in disgust.

Xanten turned to Hagedorn. "What of you? Do you come or do you stay?"

Hagedorn heaved a deep sigh, almost a groan. "Castle Hagedorn is at an end. No matter what the eventuality. I come with you."

5

The situation had suddenly altered. The Meks, established in a loose ring around Castle Hagedorn, had calculated upon no resistance from the countryside and little from the castle. They had established their barracks and syrup depots with thought only for convenience and none for defense; raiding parties, consequently, were able to approach, inflict damages and withdraw before sustaining serious losses of their own. Those Meks posted along North Ridge were harassed almost continuously, and finally were driven down with many losses. The circle around Castle Hagedorn became a cusp; then two days later, after the destruction of five more syrup depots, the Meks drew back even farther. Throwing up earthworks before the two tunnels leading under the south face of the crag, they established a more or less tenable defensive position, but now instead of beleaguering, they became the beleaguered, even though power-wagons of broken rock still issued from the crag.

Within the area thus defended the Meks concentrated their remaining syrup stocks, tools, weapons, ammunition. The area outside the earthworks was floodlit after dark and guarded by Meks armed with pellet guns, making any frontal assault impractical.

For a day the raiders kept to the shelter of the surrounding orchards, appraising the new situation. Then a new tactic was attempted. Six light carriages were improvised and loaded with bladders of a light inflammable oil, with a fire grenade attached. To each of these carriages ten Birds were harnessed, and at midnight sent aloft, with a man for each carriage. Flying high, the Birds then glided down through the darkness over the Mek position, where the fire bombs were dropped. The area instantly seethed with flame. The syrup depot burned; the power-wagons, awakened by the flames, rolled frantically back and forth, crushing Meks and stores, colliding with each other, adding vastly to the terror of the fire. The Meks who survived took shelter in the tunnels. Certain of the floodlights were extinguished and, taking advantage of the confusion, the men attacked the earthworks. After a short, bitter battle, the men killed all the sentinels and took up positions commanding the mouths of the tunnels, which now contained all that remained of the Mek army. It seemed as if the Mek uprising had been put down.

CHAPTER VIII

1

The flames died. The human warriors—three hundred men from the castle, two hundred Expiationists and about three hundred Nomads—gathered about the tunnel mouth and, during the balance of the night, considered methods to deal with the immured Meks. At sunrise those men of Castle Hagedorn whose children and consorts were yet inside went to bring them forth. With them, upon their return, came a group of castle gentlemen: among them Beaudry, O.Z. Garr, Isseth, and Aure. They greeted their one-time peers, Hagedorn, Xanten, Claghorn and others, crisply, but with a certain austere detachment which recognized that loss of prestige incurred by those who fought Meks as if they were equals.

"Now what is to happen?" Beaudry inquired of Hagedorn. "The Meks are trapped but you can't bring them forth. Not impossibly they have syrup stored within for the power-wagons; they may well survive for months."

O.Z. Garr, assessing the situation from the standpoint of a military theoretician, came forward with a plan of action. "Fetch down the cannon—or have your underlings do so—and mount them on power-wagons. When the vermin are sufficiently weak, roll the cannon in and wipe out all but a labor force for the castle: we formerly worked four hundred, and this should suffice."

"Ha!" exclaimed Xanten. "It gives me great pleasure to inform you that this will never be. If any Meks survive they will repair the spaceships and instruct us in the maintenance and we will then transport them and the Peasants back to their native worlds."

"How then do you expect us to maintain our lives?" demanded Garr coldly.

"You have the syrup generator. Fit yourself with sacs and drink syrup."

Garr tilted back his head, stared coldly down his nose. "This is your voice, yours alone, and your insolent opinion. Others are to be heard from. Hagedorn—you were once a gentleman. Is this also your philosophy, that civilization should wither?"

"It need not wither," said Hagedorn, "provided that all of us—you as well as we—toil for it. There can be no more slaves. I have become convinced of this."

O.Z. Garr turned on his heel, swept back up the avenue into the castle, followed by the most traditional-minded of his comrades. A few moved aside and talked among themselves in low tones, with one or two black looks for Xanten and Hagedorn.

From the ramparts of the castle came a sudden outcry: "The Meks! They are taking the castle! They swarm up the lower passages! Attack, save us!"

The men below stared up in consternation. Even as they looked, the castle portals swung shut.

"How is this possible?" demanded Hagedorn. "I swear all entered the tunnels!"

"It is only too clear," said Xanten bitterly. "While they undermined, they drove a tunnel up to the lower levels!"

Hagedorn started forward as if he would charge up the crag alone, then halted. "We must drive them out. Unthinkable that they pillage our castle!"

"Unfortunately," said Claghorn, "the walls bar us as effectually as they did the Meks."

"We can send up a force by Bird-car! Once we consolidate, we can hunt them down, exterminate them."

Claghorn shook his head. "They can wait on the ramparts and flight-deck and shoot down the Birds as they approach. Even if we secured a foothold there would be great bloodshed: one of us killed for every one of them. And they still outnumber us three or four to one."

Hagedorn groaned. "The thought of them reveling among my possessions, strutting about in my clothes, swilling my essences—it sickens me!"

"Listen!" said Claghorn. From on high they heard the hoarse yells of men, the crackle of energy-cannon. "Some of them, at least, hold out on the ramparts!"

Xanten went to a nearby group of Birds who were for once awed and subdued by events. "Lift me up above the castle, out of range of the pellets, but where I can see what the Meks do!"

"Care, take care!" croaked one of the Birds. "Ill things occur at the castle."

"Never mind; convey me up, above the ramparts!"

The Birds lifted him, swung in a great circle around the crag and above the castle, sufficiently distant to be safe from the Mek pellet-guns. Beside those cannon which yet operated stood thirty men and women. Between the great Houses, the Rotunda and the Palace, everywhere the cannon could not be brought to bear, swarmed Meks. The plaza was littered with corpses: gentlemen, ladies and their children—all those who had elected to remain at Castle Hagedorn.

At one of the cannon stood O.Z. Garr. Spying Xanten he gave a shout of hysterical rage, swung up the cannon, fired a bolt. The Birds, screaming, tried to swerve aside, but the bolt smashed two. Birds, car, Xanten fell in a great tangle. By some miracle, the four yet alive caught their balance and a hundred feet from the ground, with a frenzied groaning effort, they slowed their fall, steadied, hovered an instant, sank to the ground. Xanten staggered free of the tangle. Men came running. "Are you safe?" called Claghorn.

"Safe, yes. Frightened as well." Xanten took a deep breath and went to sit on an outcrop of rock.

"What's happening up there?" asked Claghorn.

"All dead," said Xanten, "all but a score. Garr has gone mad. He fired on me."

"Look! Meks on the ramparts!" cried A.L. Morgan.

"There!" cried someone else. "Men! They jump!...No, they are flung!"

Some were men, some were Meks whom they had dragged with them; with awful slowness they toppled to their deaths. No more fell. Castle Hagedorn was in the hands of the Meks.

Xanten considered the complex silhouette, at once so familiar and so strange. "They can't hope to hold out. We need only destroy the sun-cells, and they can synthesize no syrup."

"Let us do it now," said Claghorn, "before they think of this and man the cannon! Birds!"

He went off to give the orders, and forty Birds, each clutching two rocks the size of a man's head, flapped up, circled the castle and presently returned to report the sun-cells destroyed.

Xanten said, "All that remains is to seal the tunnel entrances against a sudden eruption, which might catch us off guard—then patience."

"What of the Peasants in the stables—and the Phanes?" asked Hagedorn in a forlorn voice.

Xanten gave his head a slow shake. "He who was not an Expiationist before must become one now."

Claghorn muttered, "They can survive two months—no more."

But two months passed, and three months, and four months: then one morning the great portals opened and a haggard Mek stumbled forth. He signaled: "Men: we starve. We have maintained your treasures. Give us our lives or we destroy all before we die."

Claghorn responded: "These are our terms. We give you your lives. You must clean the castle, remove and bury the corpses. You must repair the spaceships and teach us all you know regarding them. We will then transport you to Etamin Nine."

2

Five years later Xanten and Glys Meadowsweet, with their two children, had reason to travel north from their home near Sande River. They took occasion to visit Castle Hagedorn, where now lived only two or three dozen folk, among them Hagedorn.

He had aged, so it seemed to Xanten. His hair was white; his face, once bluff and hearty, had become thin, almost waxen. Xanten could not determine his mood.

They stood in the shade of a walnut tree, with castle and crag looming above them. "This is now a great museum," said Hagedorn. "I am curator, and this will be the function of all the Hagedorns who come after me, for there is incalculable treasure to guard and maintain. Already the feeling of antiquity has come to the castle. The Houses are alive with ghosts. I see them often, especially on the nights of the fêtes…Ah, those were the times, were they not, Xanten?"

"Yes, indeed," said Xanten. He touched the heads of his two children. "Still, I have no wish to return to them. We are men now, on our own world, as we never were before."

Hagedorn gave a somewhat regretful assent. He looked up at the vast structure, as if now were the first occasion he had laid eyes on it. "The folk of the future—what will they think of Castle Hagedorn? Its treasures, its books, its tabards?"

"They will come, they will marvel," said Xanten. "Almost as I do today."

"There is much at which to marvel. Will you come within, Xanten? There are still flasks of noble essence laid by."

"Thank you, no," said Xanten. "There is too much to stir old memories. We will go our way, and I think immediately."

Hagedorn nodded sadly. "I understand very well. I myself am often given to reverie these days. Well then, goodbye, and journey home with pleasure."

"We will do so, Hagedorn. Thank you and goodbye."

AFTERWORD TO "THE LAST CASTLE"

Sometimes the source of a story is a mystery even to the writer himself: a seepage from his subconscious. Other times the derivation is clear and direct. In the case of "The Last Castle," both situations are equally true.

The germ of the story was contained in an article dealing with Japanese social interactions. As is well known, Japanese society is highly formalized—much more thoroughly so in the past than during the relatively egalitarian times since the last war.

During the nineteenth century, when a samurai deigned to converse with a person of lower rank, each used markedly different vocabularies, with honorifics precisely calculated to the difference in status. When the person of lower degree discussed the samurai's activities or intentions, he used a special convention. Never would he pose a simple question such as: "Will your lordship go boar-hunting tomorrow?" This would impute to his lordship a coarse and undignified fervor, a sweating, earnest, lip-licking zeal, which his lordship would have found offensively below his dignity. Instead the underling might ask: "Will your lordship tomorrow amuse himself by trifling at the hunting of a boar?"

In short, the aristocrat was conceded sensibilities of such exquisite nicety, competences of such awful grandeur, that he need only toy with all ordinary activities, in a mood of whimsy or caprice, in order to achieve dazzling successes.

So, "The Last Castle" concerns a society of somewhat similar folk, and examines their behavior when the society is subjected to great stress.

—Jack Vance 1976

BIOGRAPHICAL SKETCH
& OTHER FACTS

Jack Vance

As of this writing, I have just finished a book—*Ports of Call*—about a hundred thousand words, complete with punctuation, paragraphs, mistakes, corrections. The book has been consigned to the mail and I am done with it, a fine feeling. The book is different from anything I have done before which is not in itself a sign of excellence, but I do have modest hopes for its success.

In any case, the time has come when I must start a new book. This is not a trivial matter. Characters parade before me; some I like and admire, others I find not useful. The ones I use become very real, and many stay with me always: Cugel, Madouc, Navarth the Mad Poet, Howard Alan Treesong and Wayness Tamm, for instance. Besides the characters to be interviewed, there are a dozen concepts to be pieced together, a locale selected, perhaps a whole new way of life to be studied and evaluated; and every story has, or should have, a mood: the connective tissue which holds the story together. In this regard some writers are adroit, others don't have a clue.

In short, writing is more difficult than it seems. Nevertheless, it is an occupation which suits me very nicely, and I can't imagine doing anything else. I am not group-minded by basic preference; I like functioning to my own inclinations, although when necessary I will conform, if only to avoid being ejected from the dinner party.

I decided at a relatively early age that I would be a writer, which, along with the obvious advantages, would allow me to gratify my already well-developed streak of wanderlust. As far back as I can recall, I have been fascinated by exotic destinations: the 'far-off places with sweet-sounding names'. The romance of travel then was vastly more vivid and compelling than it is now. On the news-stands were *Argosy, Blue Book, Adventure, Golden Book*—all vehicles of romance. Where are their like now?

My first work of fiction, when I was nine, was a cowboy story written on a typewriter in my grandfather's office which, unluckily, was never finished. Next came a story which I not only finished but sent off to the *Saturday Evening Post*. It was a tale of the South Seas, complete with schooners, copra, and rascally Lascars. I don't know whether or not the *Post* accepted the story; they never returned it and I was never paid.

The glamour of travel affected me more directly, as well. When I was eleven or twelve, I resolved to float down the Danube by folboot, from Donaueschingen to the Black Sea, and began making serious plans to do so. First, I procured dozens of maps, brochures, travel guides from the German Tourist Office. I planned the trip in detail, deciding which castle to visit, at which village to halt for the night. Lovely dreams! I was not deterred by the fact that I had not a chance in the world to finance the venture. It is rather sad that in my later travels, hither and yon, never did I float down the Danube in any sort of boat whatever.

I was born in San Francisco, in that stylish and high-class district known as Pacific Heights, the third of five children. We had a large three-story house with a beautiful view over the bay. My older brothers were skilled at recognizing the passenger liners steaming in through the Golden Gate by their colour, smokestacks and other insignia. I was too young to participate but I thought it sophisticated and desirable to know. From this perspective, those years seem to quiver through a golden glow. Life was placid and full of small joys, like riding my velocipede on the sidewalk, and playing games with a little girl who lived down the street.

Somewhat belatedly, my father discovered he was not inclined to domesticity. He stood austerely aloof from his five children, so far as this was possible. He was a large handsome man: bluff, dogmatic and a bit of a bully. I remember him with awe, apprehension and dislike.

My maternal grandfather was a prominent lawyer in those days. He owned a ranch over the hills in Contra Costa County, adjacent to Little

Dutch Slough, one of the many waterways meshing the region. At this time the family moved up to the ranch, purportedly for the summer, but my father rented out our San Francisco house for a large sum to a millionaire. He then took off for Mexico and used the rent to pay child support. We never returned to the city. At the time we were baffled and angry, especially my mother, who blamed my father's sister, my terrible Aunt Nellie. No doubt my mother was right, but I think it was all for the best. I spent an idyllic childhood at the ranch. My bedroom overlooked a beautiful view of Mount Diablo and the Coast Range, running from far in the north to far south.

The ranch was a wonderful place. The kids could swim, sail, ride horses, camp along the river, go barefoot in the sand, climb trees and read books. I built a variety of fancy kites, which I flew out in the alfalfa fields. I also built several sailboats, of scrap lumber and painted canvas, which did not sail very well.

Every weekend my grandfather would arrive in his Twin-Six Packard, along with my grandmother, great-grandmother, several cronies, supplies of various kinds: an exciting time. He would arrive late Friday afternoon. We would have the yard raked and tidy; there would be an atmosphere of imminence. Presently we would see the big old car coming along the road, and the shout would go up. The car would turn into the driveway, half under the trees, discharge passengers and supplies amid happy confusion. For two days the ranch would hum with activity while my grandfather prosecuted his various projects, most often assisted by my younger brother David, who was more obliging than I.

Sunday afternoon was the climactic dinner, usually a six-rib roast beef or something similar. Then the party would climb into the Packard and depart the way it had come. My mother would heave a sigh of relief and collapse into a chair, but next week it would happen all over again. Lovely!

I grew up a country boy. I attended the two-room Iron House School and then the high school at Brentwood (not the Brentwood near Beverly Hills, but the Brentwood near the conflux of the Sacramento and San Joaquin rivers). When we originally moved up from the city, my mother brought along her books, cases and cases of them. They were a disparate lot: serious books, frivolous romances such as the works of Robert W. Chambers and others similar; also a surprising amount of fantasy and tales of the occult. Chambers himself wrote some odd books: *The Tracer of Lost Persons, The King in Yellow, The Maker of Moons*, perhaps others. There were also the books of E.R.

Burroughs: the Tarzan books and the Barsoom set. There were a few by Jules Verne; I remember particularly *The Mysterious Island*.

With five children in the family we also had hundreds of books from the Edward Stratemeyer fiction factory: *The Motor Boys, Dave Porter, Tom Swift, Bobbsey Twins, Jack Lorimer*, etcetera. I have read all of them a hundred times. We also had the Oz books, *Uncle Wiggily*, much else which I have forgotten. All of the children received books for birthday and Christmas. I remember that my devious Aunt Nellie gave me *The Greene Murder Case* by S.S. Van Dine for Christmas, when I was about twelve. Clearly someone had given it to her and she did not know what else to do with it. However, I enjoyed it.

Edward Stratemeyer also produced a remarkable set under the house name 'Roy Rockwood'. I often wonder who wrote them. The titles were *Through Space to Mars, Lost on the Moon, Voyage to the Center of the Earth*, and others. So far as I know, these were the first popular science fiction books published—not counting Wells and Verne.

In any event, these books were my earliest reading. I went on from there. I was a precocious child, and I resolved to read everything I could get my hands on, in order to encapsulate the whole of human knowledge. At the time the project seemed less impractical than it does today. I did as best I could and by the time I was ten or twelve had read what I suspect was equivalent to a college education. No question but that I was bright, but probably not very likeable, nor dripping with charm. In the first place, I was quietly arrogant, also introverted, with my own view on how the world should be run. I was not at all gregarious, and without social skills. I was considered something of a freak by my brothers and sister. The older boys never altered their opinions; they are now dead. I hasten to say that there is no macabre connection between these two facts.

There were various factors involved, but I like to think my immature behavior was for the most part attributable to my youth, only fifteen at graduation from high school. I was shy around girls. The ones I admired and tried to impress would have nothing to do with me, which caused me bafflement. My intentions were honourable enough, as I recall; I merely wanted someone beautiful to listen to my daydreams and admire the scope of my intelligence. I see now that I did everything wrong.

Fortunately, I had other interests than girls. I played tennis; I was an excellent swimmer. I began to write poetry at this time, which I considered quite good. It was at least fervent and unconventional in subject matter. At a dinner party at my Aunt Nellie's house in the city, I met Stanton Coblentz, an early science fiction writer and editor of *Wings*, a poetry magazine. I allowed him to read some of my works, but he was not at all impressed.

Meanwhile, I had discovered *Weird Tales* and *Amazing Stories*. Also the works of P.G. Wodehouse, Jeffrey Farnol and Lord Dunsany, all of whom I consider important influences in my own development. Wodehouse I consider a tremendously underrated writer.

Upon graduation from high school I took stock of myself, and saw much room for improvement. I decided to make myself over, avoiding childish eccentricities, changing myself into a person competent, skilful, adroit and a devil with the girls. It would mean lifting myself by the bootstraps, since there was no one to give me instructions. I would succeed by sheer force of will, if necessary.

First, the girls. I let my hair grow a bit longer, smeared on a teaspoon of Vaseline and combed it back in the style of Jack Teagarden and Rudolph Valentino, but to no avail. The girls still laughed when I sashayed past. I bought a motorcycle which I enjoyed tremendously, and performed a number of rash, dangerous deeds which I will not enumerate, since I am a bit doubtful concerning the statute of limitations.

My grandfather died, and an era came to an end. My mother and father were divorced, with my father still resident in Mexico, near Tepic. The family was now broke, and I could not go on to college. These were tough times: the heart of the Depression. For me, it was a time of metamorphosis. Over a span of four or five years, I developed from an impractical little intellectual into a rather reckless young man, competent at many skills and crafts, and determined to try every phase of life. During this time I roamed here and there, working at all manner of jobs: fruit-picking, farm work, three seasons at the California Cannery in Antioch, two seasons in tomatoes, one in asparagus. I became connected with Western-Knapp Engineering, which built mining equipment, mills, tanks, ore-processing plants, heavy construction, all up and down the Sierras: out of Bishop, Copperopolis, French Gulch and Camptonville. I worked on a drill rig searching for ore along Sailor Flat; on a dredge scratching the bed of the Trinity River for gold.

Returning to San Francisco, I worked for a miserable year at the Olympic Club as bell-hop and elevator operator. This was a terrible period, the nadir of my life; when I think back I wince. Ultimately I was fired, and I was glad.

Immediately I registered at the University of California at Berkeley, as a physics major. My grades were good but in the middle of my junior year I became restless and took a leave of absence. I found employment as an electrician's helper in Honolulu, at the navy yard. They put me to work at pulling degaussing cable around ships' hulls. The work was very hot and pay was bad: 56 cents an hour. I could not live on it, much less save anything, and after three months, I returned to the mainland, arriving home a month before war broke out.

I went to work at the Kaiser Shipyards as a rigger, and also started the Army Intelligence program, learning Japanese. At the shipyards I practiced calligraphy, writing Japanese characters on the iron plates of the hulls. No one ever seemed curious as to this exercise, nor questioned my intentions.

After two years it was evident that I would never learn colloquial Japanese and I was dropped from the program. I quit at the shipyards, joined the Merchant Marines and went to sea as an able seaman. My eyes were not good even then; the only way I could join was to memorize the eye chart, which I did. Bad eyes and all, I went about my duties.

I had done some desultory writing previously but while at sea I got seriously to work and produced the stories which later became known as *The Dying Earth*. After a couple of years I left the Merchant Marines and returned to Berkeley. Here I met and married Norma. I had sold two mediocre short stories, but now the business of writing became a necessity if I were to maintain any semblance of the lifestyle to which I had become accustomed. While Norma studied at the University I was attempting to produce E.E. Smith epics without much luck.

Norma and I took some lessons in ceramics and became very enthusiastic about making dinnerware, masks and other objects. We decided to open a shop to sell materials, tools, and do firing. Of course we were undercapitalized and it was hard work but we had a great time for a year or so, then had to give it up. Meanwhile, I tried first-draft writing, and sold the first two 'Magnus Ridolph' stories written on this basis. Twentieth Century Fox bought one of these wretched stories and also hired me as a scriptwriter. Before long my producer was promoted to Chief Producer and I was released. No matter; Norma and I set out for Europe where we stayed over a year. I remember finishing *Vandals of the Void* for Winston at Positano. When we returned to New York we rented an apartment from which I wrote a number of *Captain Video* scripts. Back in California, I tried to continue with *Captain Video* from an old house in the mountains near Napa, but the arrangement failed to work out.

The Santa Rosa Press Democrat sent Frank Herbert to interview me. The resulting article was headlined 'Jack Vance, Flying Saucer Expert'. In spite of this we became great friends and had many good times together. The Herberts and the Vances, seeking adventure and romance in an inexpensive location conducive to writing, planned an expedition. We took off in a Jeep Station Wagon, customized with cubbies and net slings for all manner of items and drove to Mexico. (Frank had assembled a first aid kit to do any backwoods dispensary proud.) At Lake Chapala we leased a large apartment and set up housekeeping. A red flag flying on the veranda warned. 'Writers at Work' and all respected this, the Herbert children included. It was there I started to write the novel *Clarges*, which Betty Ballantine renamed *To Live Forever*—a rotten title—the first of the type of stories I write today.

Late in the '60s, Poul Anderson and Frank Herbert began to talk about building a houseboat for use in the Sacramento-San Joaquin Delta waterways. Ever since my childhood, living near to Little Dutch Slough, this had been a dream of mine. And I suppose I pushed the most fervently, though Poul and Frank were no slouches. I put forth a plan and our partnership was established. The section of two pontoons were built in the Vance driveway, then transported to a beach near the Standard Oil refinery in Richmond. The sections were assembled and filled with white Styrofoam blocks, for flotation. The pontoons were covered over with plywood, and sealed with fibreglass. A platform was attached to the finished pontoons, which in turn were set on poles to be rolled down to the water's edge at low tide. At this point, the owners of the marina, where we would finish the houseboat, furnished a bottle of champagne for its christening; that done, we found more bottles, relaxed, listened to New Orleans jazz and waited for high tide.

We worked most weekends building a house on the platform, anxious for the day the houseboat would be moved to the delta. One night, during a bad storm, it sank to the bottom. What to do? After serious discussion we decided that two of us should put on diving gear, dive to the bottom carrying plastic sacks filled with Styrofoam blocks and air, wedge them under the platform and tie them to the outer edges of the hulls. Poul and I spent a strenuous couple of days, but the boat was finally raised to the surface. Cleaning out the muck took a bit longer.

About a year later, glistening with white and turquoise paint, all fitted out with bunks, steering mechanism, pot-bellied wood stove, even a head, the houseboat was ready for its voyage to the delta. A delay occurred when we grounded on a sand bar and were forced to wait for the tide to change; then another stop at a marina beneath the Carquinez Bridge to await daylight became necessary. Aside from this, all went smoothly on the way upriver; and once tied to a cleat on the dock of Moore's Riverboat Yacht Haven, located on the Mokelumne River, the good times were many.

Partners departed and others joined. Frank could not continue due to medical problems and a subsequent move to Seattle. One sad day even Norma and I had to find someone to take our place, due to plans for more extended travels. Our good friend Albert Hall and his two children were happy to oblige, especially since they already had become part of the group. Eventually, even Poul had no time for the upkeep and enjoyment of the houseboat. Another good friend Ali Szantho entered the partnership. All the writers had departed; new owners were enjoying it, and that's where my part of its history ends.

Since then a great deal has happened. Norma and I have traveled extensively; our son John accompanied us from the age of three-and-a-half. His fourth birthday was spent at Bondi Beach near Sydney, Australia. I recall with a great deal of nostalgia our travels together; for Norma and I, perhaps our happiest times. It was a perfect combination of work and pleasure. We would search for a pleasant locale in the country, the mountains; near a lake, a river or an ocean and rent a house, or an apartment, and go to work. I would write the first draft in longhand; Norma typed the second draft, and any others necessary, on a small portable Hermes. (Actually, we wore out two portables, the first was an Olivetti.) Prior to twenty years ago most of my stories and novels were written wholly, or partially, in foreign places.

Today Norma and I live in the Oakland hills, in a house which has been undergoing changes constantly for the past forty-three years. Our son, John, has been helping me more than half his life, and with the onset of my blindness has totally taken over all the remodeling. I see my brother David frequently; he is also an engineer and scientist of good reputation, though now retired. David's son Stephen, with his wife Marja, circumnavigated the world in a Cal 2-27 sloop. At this time Stephen and his wife are working as masters of a 93' sailing yacht, but are thinking of retiring; they want to build a large catamaran, which I do not consider feasible, since when a catamaran is flipped, that is how it remains. Still, so they claim, it floats until help arrives; while a mono-hull, once it sinks, goes directly to the bottom and remains there.

My son John and I invested in the beautiful *Hinano*, a forty-five foot ketch, with the intent of sailing the South Seas and perhaps beyond, but for various reasons, one being that John was twenty-two and had not yet entered college, never quite succeeded in bringing it off. John is unregenerate; he has his degree and still wants to own a cruising boat. Perhaps he will do so one day.

I fear not, though the spirit is willing. My vision presently is holding its own but there's not much left, cramping all kinds of enterprises. After my next book, I am uncertain what will happen. We shall see.

—Jack Vance 2000

EDITOR BIOS

TERRY DOWLING

Terry Dowling (www.terrydowling.com) is one of Australia's most acclaimed and best-known writers of science fiction, fantasy and horror, the award-winning author of *Rynosseros, Blue Tyson, Twilight Beach, Wormwood, The Man Who Lost Red, An Intimate Knowledge of the Night, Blackwater Days, Basic Black: Tales of Appropriate Fear* and editor of *Mortal Fire: Best Australian SF* and *The Essential Ellison*. He has also written a number of articles on Jack's writing, among them "Kirth Gersen: The Other Demon Prince" (which won him the 1983 William Atheling Award for Criticism) and his 28,000 word "The Art of Xenography: Jack Vance's 'General Culture' Novels" (*Science Fiction # 3*, December 1978). Terry is a close friend of the Vances and a frequent visitor to their home in the Oakland hills. Jack wrote an Introduction to *Blue Tyson*, Terry's 1992 collection of Tom Rynosseros stories, and refers to a Terence Dowling's World in *Throy*. In *Ports of Call*, he mentions a drink called a "Wild Dingo Howler, which was invented by a reckless smuggler named Terence Dowling." Terry counts these things among his most treasured possessions.

JONATHAN STRAHAN

Jonathan Strahan (www.jonathanstrahan.com.au) is an editor, anthologist and reviewer from Perth, Western Australia. He established one of Australia's leading semiprozines before moving to work for *Locus* as an editor and book reviewer. He has been Reviews Editor for *Locus* since 2002, and he has had reviews published in *Locus, Eidolon, Ticonderoga* and *Foundation.* He has won the William J Atheling Jr Award for Criticism and Review, the Ditmar Award a number of times, and is a recipient of The Peter McNamara Award. As a freelance editor, he has edited or co-edited 11 anthologies, with five more in the pipeline. He is editor of the *The Year's Best Australian Science Fiction and Fantasy, Science Fiction: Best of, Fantasy: Best of,* and *Best Short Novels* anthology series. He also edited *The Locus Awards.* He recently completed *Science Fiction: The Very Best of 2005* and *Fantasy: The Very Best of 2005* and *Best Short Novels: 2006,* and is working on a YA SF anthology for Viking Penguin and an anthology of new space opera stories to be co-edited with Gardner Dozois for HarperCollins.